RUMI'S FIELD

Books by Timothy Scott Bennett

NONE SO BLIND
All of the Above (2010)
Rumi's Field (2017)
Imbolc (Forthcoming)

RUMI'S
FIELD

TIMOTHY SCOTT BENNETT

BLUE HAG BOOKS CHAPEL HILL, NORTH CAROLINA

This is a work of fiction. All of the characters, organizations, and events portrayed in this novel are either products of the author's imagination or are used fictitiously.

RUMI'S FIELD

Copyright 2017 by Timothy Scott Bennett

Published by:
Blue Hag Books
Chapel Hill, North Carolina

timothyscottbennett.com

Cover design by Timothy Scott Bennett, Sally Erickson, and Sarah Erickson

Library of Congress Control Number:

ISBN-13: 978-1-936879-03-8

First Print Edition: January 2017

Printed in the United States of America

For Rocco. Take most precious care, my friend.

Acknowledgements

My thanks begin with Sally, who has been there beside me through the whole process, reading, editing, suggesting, challenging, cheering, and encouraging. Writing can feel like a lonely endeavor. Some days it's hard to know if I'm on the right path. How essential, for me, to have somebody who can see what I do not, and can point to where my next footstep might go.

Thanks also to my reading group, the people to whom I sent my first draft copy as it flowed out of my fingers. Simon Beer, David Bennett, Paul Chefurka, Jim Fry, Gordon Glover, Curt Hubatch, Keith Johnson, Joe Kaiser, Ann Kreilkamp, Philip Payson, Ryan Rathje, and Vincent Reynolds, just knowing y'all were there made all the difference. I might never have done it otherwise.

Thanks to Sarah Erickson, who knows about things like colors and fonts and images and marketing, and who helped me with covers and designs.

Thanks to those who read All of the Above, and then either left comments or wrote emails or posted Amazon reviews. It was a bit stunning to me, to learn that a documentary audience did not automatically mean a fiction audience. Your comments kept me going when I felt discouraged, and helped me know that there was a reason to take the time to get what was in my mind and heart onto the page, where others might share in it.

Thanks as always to the many fellow travelers whose work inspired, informed, and intrigued me. Here are a few who spring to mind right now: Douglas Adams, Richard Bach, Itzhak Bentov, Octavia Butler, Samuel R. Delany, Antoine de Saint-Exupéry, Richard Dolan, Stephen R. Donaldson, Raymond Fowler, Graham Hancock, Frank Herbert, Russell Hoban, Carl Jung, Bernardo Kastrup, John Keel, Anne Lamott, Dave McGowan, Terence McKenna, Robert Monroe, Larry Niven, Mary Oliver, Daniel Quinn, Jalāl ad-Dīn Muhammad Rūmī, Rupert Sheldrake, Starhawk, Whitley Strieber, Michael Talbot, Jacques Vallée, Paul Von Ward, Kurt Vonnegut, and

Jonathan Zap. There are, of course, others. Thanks for letting me peek over the edge and look around, folks.

Thanks, of course, to the Blue Lady, who was more gentle with me this time around, even at the expense of it taking so much longer. And thanks to that rabbit, the little bastard. You'll both be making an appearance in Book Three. I hope I do you justice. Say "hey" to Rocco for me.

Timothy Scott Bennett
Chapel Hill, North Carolina
January 2017

Out beyond ideas of wrongdoing and rightdoing,
there is a field. I'll meet you there.

When the soul lies down in that grass,
the world is too full to talk about.
Ideas, language, even the phrase each other
doesn't make any sense.
Jalāl ad-Dīn Muhammad Rūmī
(translated by Coleman Barks)

There are none so blind as those who will not see.
John Heywood

I'm just a poor wayfarin' stranger,
While travelin' through this world below.
Yet there's no sickness, no toil, nor danger,
In that bright land to which I go.
-Wayfaring Stranger, Traditional
Alas, my love, you do me wrong,
To cast me off discourteously.
For I have loved you well and long,
Delighting in your company.
-Greensleeves, Traditional English Folk Song

Author's Preface

I find it fairly easy to write a story set in what is commonly known as "the real world," the time and culture which we all now share. I just take what I know and use it as the backdrop in front of which my characters speak their lines. It's also fairly easy, I find, to write a story set in what is commonly known as "the post-apocalyptic world," because when we travel together that far down "the energy curve," we end up in a whole new place. All I need do is concoct a few basic rules – no electricity or petroleum; decimated population; fast, slow, or no zombies, etc. – and go from there. It's almost like starting from scratch, and that's as easy for me as starting from the known.

But it's much more difficult, I find, to write a story set in a time between our present world and a future dystopia; a world that's fallen a few steps down the staircase of societal collapse but which has a ways to go before it hits bottom; a world that is, in Linda Travis's words, "in free fall." And yet it's in just such a world that the story of Rumi's Field unfolds. More than three years have passed since the events that took place in All of the Above, and the world has stumbled a few steps down the stairs.

Things are all a-jumble in Rumi's Field. We're about sixteen months past the global economic event known as the "Christmas Crash," in which unfathomable amounts of money disappeared almost overnight, putting huge corporations, small businesses, and individual families out of business. Governments toppled or were overthrown. People, as the old song said, lost their jobs, wives, homes, cars, kids, and lives. Riots spread like wildfires, wildfires burned like pandemics, pandemics raged like hungry mobs, hungry mobs stormed the land like floods and droughts, and floods and droughts came and went like rich bankers and corporate personhoods, doing their damage and then absconding for someplace better, leaving devastation in their wake.

Even so, it was not the total, monolithic "collapse" that many had feared, a one-time mega-event that would instantly transform the structures and institutions of civilized society into vast heaps of bodies and dusty plains devoid of life, though both could be found easily enough if one looked for them. It was a big old world, after all, and it very much mattered where one was. Some countries fared better than others, as appears to be the case with Canada as compared to the United States. Some governments maintained their integrity and continued to function fairly well, taking actions to mitigate the worst effects of the Crash and finding ways to keep at least a portion of their societies intact, as did the Travis administration. Some corporations managed to hold together as their competitors were torn to pieces, and some even prospered in the new world order. There was enough left in place that many people could still find work-arounds and substitutions and alternatives enough to meet their needs. The mobs and wildfires and pandemics settled down after a year or so, or were brought under some measure of control. "We are down," said Linda Travis, "but we are not out." Nobody knew whether it would last, but they appreciated the chance to take a breather.

Post Crash, world governments reserved most of their fossil fuels for military and agricultural uses, and for maintaining the electrical infrastructure. While some portions of the grid were completely out, many areas still had electricity, at least part of the time. In the United States, as in many other countries, huge camps and shelters were put into operation, and great numbers of folks moved into them, or close by, in search of the food, water, warmth, and shelter they needed, not to mention the sense of safety and belonging and order they expected to get from their leaders. The rich remained in their fortresses, enclaves, castles, keeps, and holds, as far as anybody knew. The rest stuck it out in their homes, or hit the road, or formed their own communities (and even their own sovereign nations), brewing their own biodiesel, generating their own power from solar panels or stored fuels, and growing and hunting and gathering the food they needed to stay alive.

If you were lucky enough to work for the federal government in Augusta, Maine, you lived inside the Capitol City Green Zone, into which were imported the supplies which made life there feel almost normal, and around which bristled a military cordon hell-bent on maintaining order and safety for their Commander-in-Chief. If you were luckier still, the daughter of one of the secret rulers of the planet, say, you might not notice much change at all on your small, private college campus in Montreal. If your luck had run out, you might be sleeping on a cot in a gymnasium next to hundreds of others, working in the food line serving soup to nuts and watching the constant stream of news and entertainments on the Jumbotrons that looked down from where the basketball hoops once hung. If your luck had run out even further, you might be dead, murdered by a group of punks intent on stealing your blankets. Some, of course, would consider the dead the lucky ones.

It mattered where you were, how well you had planned, and how resourceful (or wealthy, or both) you were when the markets were closed for good. Whether you drank coffee, tea, or stale tap water, whether you could grow lettuce or artichokes or just weeds in dust, whether you slept on a hardwood floor, beneath an underpass, or in the comfy confines of your private island mansion's master bedroom, the range of conditions a human might encounter as the world unwound was great, and your personal situation depended as much on being at the right place at the right time as it did your own efforts to decide your fate. In that, perhaps, the world had not changed as much as most people seemed to think.

The world was a-jumble. The world was all-of-the-above. It's into this world that we now proceed.

What Has Gone Before
(or) All of the Above in Seven Minutes or Less

President Linda Travis gets a briefing from the psychopathic Agent Rice. The hidden human elite are in league with mysterious aliens and they want to bring her in. Seems most everybody in her government is part of the cabal. But Linda says fuck this shit, escapes her handlers, steals a car, and drives north through the night, hoping to find her old friend Keeley and expose the secret. In Vermont, she has an accident and goes off the road, breaking her leg. That's her meet-cute with Cole Thomas.

Linda points a gun at Cole and demands that he take her to his house. Cole is, like, overwhelmed, and complies. Linda drinks whisky and Cole reluctantly cowboys the broken bones back into place. Linda gets some sleep. Rice meanwhile, with his minions Mary and Bob, search for their escaped President via the Astral realm. Evil, but cool.

Cole's three kids come home from school. They all have a chill time together, eating burgers and dogs, reading kids' books, and answering crank calls from aliens. Eventually the kids crash and Linda tells Cole what the heck is going on. The briefing. The cabal. How she met Spud, the alien ambassador. Crazy. The woods around his house light up like a WalMart parking lot. There's little teeny people scampering amongst the trees and big red eyes at the window. Cole and Linda conk out for a bit. When they awaken, Linda's leg is healed and now she and Cole are digging each other. Linda drags Cole outside to look at the night sky. My God, it's full of UFOs!

So, Cole wants to help Linda reach her friend. But there's those kids. What to do? Cole's youngest, Grace, keeps falling asleep. The family dog, Dennis, has gone missing. Both have gone into the Astral to help protect Cole and Linda, though nobody knows about that but them. But for sure there's strange aliens following Linda. And evil Agent Rice. Seems the thing to do is draw attention away from the kids. So Cole and Linda take the kids to Grandpa Ben, kiss and hug and promise to come back, and then hightail it out of there. They come to a roadblock; the POPOs have found POTUS's stolen

Buick. And Agent Rice is right there, checking cars! Linda's hiding in the back under a blanket, so Rice passes them through, but not before finger-painting a weird symbol on Cole's windshield. Because who knows why?

They make it to Keeley's house. Meet her husband Pooch. More chillin'. More googly eyes between Cole and Linda. Keeley tells Linda how the aliens used to abduct them when they were kids, a fact Linda had been happy to forget. Damn them all to hell. Linda has a plan: get to Ottawa, where she knows an MP who can get her on Canadian TV. She'll expose the cabal. Teach those suckers a lesson. So Keeley helps Linda with a disguise, then hangs up on a weird wrong number from some guy named Obie. Linda and Cole get into Pooch's van. Keeley's Canadian husband will drive them over the border to meet his friend Elly.

Except that damned Agent Rice is at the border crossing. Pooch hits the gas and they speed into the night and rain. But then there's Rice again, standing in the middle of the road with a gun! WTF? Rice shoots. Pooch dies. Van runs over Rice and crashes into the ditch, which makes two ditch crashes for Linda Travis in less than 48 hours. No broken bones this time. Cole and Linda extricate themselves from the wreckage. There's Elly, landing in a helicopter of course. Cole and Linda hop aboard and they fly away.

Elly helps Cole and Linda catch the train to Ottawa. This gives them time to rest. And to fall more in love. Which is nice. Until another symbol like the one Rice drew on the windshield appears on the train. The bad guys are right on their heels. Grace and Dennis meet some allies in the Astral realm. This ragtag group opposes Rice's minions and slows the bad guys down a bit.

Cole and Linda make it to Ottawa. The Canadian MP, Legrand? Turns out that bastard is part of the cabal too. Rice appears yet again, pointing a gun. Cole's like "screw you" and Rice is like "take this!" and the gun is like "blam blam" and Cole's like "aarrggghhh!" and Linda's like "nooooo!!!!" Cole's dead. Rice tosses Linda into an alien lodge underneath the city. The aliens, having skipped town when Linda escaped, are no longer using it. Rice pulls the whole solitary confinement, drugs, and torture thing on the President, trying to force her cooperation. But before he succeeds, that Obie guy from the wrong number? Who turns out to be Cole's brother? He shows up in the darkness and rescues Linda. They escape in an alien ship, a wok, which Obie knows how to fly, because he used to work for Agent Rice. I know, right? Meanwhile, Mary, another of Rice's colleagues, quits her day job in disgust over Rice's evil deeds.

Obie thinks maybe Cole isn't really dead because, you know, aliens. So they go find his body in one of the cabal's front organizations, then fly way up above the Arctic circle to catch their breath. Obie and Linda get out of the wok. The wok sinks into the ice with Cole's body. Nobody saw that one coming.

Obie and Linda get rescued by some fur-clad Inuit rebels who offer them a warm mobile home to hang out in. They spend the next day talking, while Obie uses his woo to heal Linda's wounds. Obie explains about their Inuit saviors, and how shit's about to hit the fan on Planet Earth, and how the aliens are rooting for the evolution of consciousness, and that the future of humanity rests on Linda's shoulders, which is all a bit of a headtrip, especially for somebody who was just tortured.

Then Cole's living body shows up at the door, having been repaired and detailed in the aliens' chop shop. The lights are on, but nobody's home. The Inuit drag everybody out onto the ice, light a ritual bonfire, and attempt to reconnect Cole's spirit with his body. Obie and the Inuit warriors close their eyes and fly into the Astral realm, where they meet Grace and Dennis and their new friends. And a bunch of animals. Together, they fight the agents of the cabal and free Cole's spirit to find its way back home, which it does.

Meanwhile, back in the physical world, real life cabal soldiers shoot Ben and abduct Cole's two eldest (Grace having been put in the hospital with her coma) and take them to Rice in D.C. Rice then sends the soldiers up north. They find the bonfire about the time Cole gets saved and manage to kill a few Inuit before a great mythic force rises up to stop them. Monster mash.

Linda and Cole, all healed and reanimated and still in love, head back to D.C. as quickly as they can, to confront Rice and rescue the kids. Back in D.C., the children have befriended Alice, a hybrid child who's also decided to quit Rice's team and join the Light Side. They escape and meet up with Mary, who takes them to safety. Grace, in the Astral, follows them all, doing Astral stuff.

Cole, Linda, Obie, and Mary surprise Agent Rice in the alien lodge underneath the nation's capitol. Linda makes a deal with Rice: let's be friends and run this cabal together, dude. Rice agrees, cuz there's, like, a gun pointed at him? Having learned that the now-absent aliens have set their lodge to self-destruct, the group quickly evacuates the facility. At the last moment, Rice betrays them, surprising nobody and attacking Mary in order to escape in a wok. He throws a small controlled black hole at Linda. Obie grabs Rice and steps into the path of the black hole, which swallows them both. Zip. No more bad guy. But no more Obie too. Linda, Cole, and the others escape in the wok just before the lodge implodes. Whew.

Cole and Linda get Mary to a hospital, rescue Cole's two oldest, then return, along with Alice, to his home in Vermont, where Grace and Ben are both in the hospital. The news reports that underground alien lodges have imploded all around the planet, leaving huge sinkholes. Most of D.C. has collapsed. Alice goes into the Astral to help Grace reconnect with her body. Ben will be okay.

All together now in the physical, the family recuperates from their adventures, and mourns their dead. Linda meets some trusted colleagues so they can start rooting out the conspirators. Then she goes on national television to tell the truth of the alien presence on Earth. She decides not to rebuild Washington D.C., and instead moves in with Cole and his children, so they can make a life together. After a mysterious midnight call from the Fisherman, a member of a deeper layer of the hidden cabal, they go into hiding. From there, Linda reestablishes control over her government. Alice disappears, off to do some mysterious hybrid stuff with her alien dad. All is well, except that the strange symbol shows up one last time, just so they'd all know that the story isn't finished yet.

Chapter Ø One

1.1

I stop at the curb and glance up at the crosswalk signal. There are no other pedestrians in sight. The signal changes and I step out into the street. The tall, thin, red-haired man behind me lurches forward. He bumps my right elbow as he hurries past, glances back over his shoulder, and nods. My heart pounds. I know that face, though I do not remember how.

The man winks, turns his head, and resumes his hurried pace. He steps quickly up onto the opposite curb and heads to the left. His movements are fluid. Efficient. Purposeful. Like a dancer. Or a robot. I follow, keeping my distance. The man terrifies me, but I cannot lose him. He's up to something. Something important. I can feel it. It's my job to watch. The man comes to the next corner and ducks to the right. I run to keep up.

From up ahead comes a soft cry and a muttering of voices. A small crowd has formed in front of a restaurant. I watch as the tall man nears the crowd, steps around a trashcan and into the street. He disappears, vanishing like a soap bubble in the noonday heat. I begin to run. Whatever it is I am supposed to see, this is it.

I push through the ring of onlookers. On the sidewalk at my feet lies a young woman, her face marked with a bright red rash that stretches from cheek to cheek and across her nose. Her right leg is twisted at an awkward angle beneath her. Beside her head are pieces of a half-eaten cheeseburger. The top bun lies on its back like a stranded turtle, two pickle eyes staring up at the hot, searing sun. Next to the cheeseburger lies a spilled soft drink, the ice cubes melting quickly on the concrete. I take a breath to calm myself. The onlookers are strangely silent. The woman's breath is shallow. Her full, flushed face wears a calm smile. It appears as though she has simply decided to lie down for a short nap and dream of beautiful things.

The thin man reappears out of nowhere on the far side of the crowd. He stares at me with dark, curious eyes. I pull back, thinking I can take cover behind one of the others. But there is no hiding from this man.

"*She is learning once again of the ephemeral nature of human life,*" *says the man evenly. His voice is deep and clear, though his mouth does not move as he speaks. It resonates within my mind. The man's face wrinkles oddly for a moment and I realize that he is trying to smile, as if to comfort me.* "*She is only the first,*" *he says in my mind.*

I stare down at the woman. Her shoulder-length brown hair fans out on the sidewalk beneath her like an earthy halo. Her thin cotton dress, short and summery with yellow flowers, provides little protection from the heat of the concrete. A fat, balding man in a gray suit kneels beside her body and takes her hand. A teenage girl in the restaurant's green uniform bends to gather the pieces of cheeseburger in a grease-stained paper napkin. She tosses them in the trashcan with a shudder of revulsion.

I am startled to find that I can see inside the sick woman's body, and that she is filled with vibrating motes of light, sparkling and twinkling like tiny green and gold stars in the universe of her being. "*The organism will soon shut down her heart,*" *says the thin man in my mind.* "*There will be no pain.*"

I look up. The thin man is now standing next to the woman's head. It doesn't appear that anyone else can see him. The man points down at the woman with a long, pale finger. "*The others here will blame her death on the food, not understanding that the organism responsible rose to life many days ago. This will slow your human efforts to understand what is happening.*"

I study the other onlookers. There are sparkling motes in many of them, the fat man and the restaurant girl included. "*Why...?*" *I ask.*

"*It's part of a plan,*" *explains the thin man.*

I open my mouth to ask another question, but stop when the woman on the sidewalk speaks. Her voice is soft and calm. "*My love,*" *she says,* "*my love... my love...*" *She pauses for a long moment, then speaks one last word:* "*Alas.*" *I scan her again, noting the cessation of her body's electrical systems. Her mind and heart slow to a full stop. Her tender smile remains.*

I glance up at the thin man, who returns my gaze with another brief nod. "It has begun," he says. He turns, steps back through the ring of onlookers, and vanishes.

Gabrielle Legrand read the words in her journal, words written in her own hand, words that must have been written sometime during the night. They were words she had no memory of writing, words connected to a dream that she hadn't remembered until she'd read them. She tore the pages from her notebook, wadded them into a ball, and tossed them into the wastebasket next to her desk. She had no time for such nonsense. Not anymore. And she had to get to class.

1.2

The General squinted up at the television screen as the image of Linda Travis pushed a stray lock of hair from her face and stepped to a podium decorated with the Presidential Seal. She was alone in her room, and everybody knew it, but the podium would give the impression of a press conference, and add a grace note of calm normality to the event. The General smirked as he sipped his beer. Image was everything. It always would be. He checked his watch. He still had an hour before his flight. Plenty of time to enjoy this.

Dressed in blue jeans and a loose-fitting University of Maine sweatshirt, her clothes no doubt chosen to hearken back to her first campaign, the President smiled dolefully at the camera and began. "Good morning, all. Thank you for joining me. I am here today to announce my intention to seek re-election." Travis paused for a moment, giving the news a moment to sink in. The General glanced around the airport bar. There were only three other people in the room, including the bartender, but all were watching closely. This announcement had been a long time coming.

The President continued, glancing down at her notes. "This will likely come as a surprise to most of you," she said, "given the events of the past year. And surely the timing could be better." Linda stared directly into the camera. "The last thing a grieving nation needs is more self-serving blather from a politician." She stopped and took a sip from the water glass on her podium. The General lifted his mug and drained it, then knocked on the bar to get the tender's attention and motioned for a refill. The airport's air conditioning was struggling to keep up and his throat was dry.

The door behind the President clicked open and Linda turned to see the surprised face of a nurse through the thick, protective faceplate of her biocontainment suit. "Sorry," hissed the young woman, glancing at the camera in mortified horror before pulling the door quickly shut. Linda smiled grimly at the departing nurse, then turned back to her audience. The rash that stretched over the bridge of her nose from cheek to cheek glared brightly red under the overhead fluorescents.

Linda raised a hand to touch her reddened cheek, then stopped herself. She grabbed both sides of the podium and continued. "But we do not always get to choose our circumstances," she said firmly, "and the demands of this time outweigh mere political considerations. As hard as things have become, as mistaken as I have proven to be, as compromised as I now am, there is no one else as qualified and experienced as myself to lead this great nation at this time. Love me or hate me, you surely all know who I am. And you know that what I say is true."

The General raised his mug in admiration. This was masterfully done, every detail in place, and it drew its power from Linda Travis' proven ability to move people. All she had to do was tell people what to think, and most of them would just go ahead and think it. The General noted that the bartender and the other customers were all nodding their heads in agreement with the President's words. He chuckled softly. They had likely complained bitterly about Linda Travis in the past twenty-four hours, if the polls were to be believed. And yet they nodded. Such was her reputation for truth telling. Such was their longing for truth. And such was America's seeming inability to remember *anything* for more than a day or two. It was only four years ago that Linda Travis had promised to serve only one term. Would they not remember even that?

"Whether I am elected to serve another term or not, I have not yet finished this one, and I still serve the vows I took on the day of my inauguration. To that end, I have called for a new summit of political, corporate, and military leaders to discuss our next steps. We will meet tomorrow, and will continue to meet until our course is clear. Certainly this most recent aggression cannot be allowed to stand. And certainly we must bring some strong measure of relief to the American people. I will accept nothing less."

The President glanced back at the door behind her, then attended again to the camera. Her pale skin tones heightened the effect of her rash, making it look more like war paint than the "alien flu" the papers reported. And the General detected an angry glint in her eyes and a shaking of her jaw that matched that war paint. It was an interesting decision, to show such anger. He wondered how that would play on the evening news.

"We are down," the President said, her voice soft and full. "But we are not out. I am down. But I am not out. We have what we need to get through this. You have it. I have it. Your neighbors and friends and family have it. I saw that every time I walked amongst you. I see it still, even trapped in these rooms. We have what it takes. And we will make it through this." Linda Travis stopped and took a long, deep breath. She nodded firmly, allowing a brief smile of hope to flash across her countenance. "Have courage," she said. With that she pressed a button on her podium. The screen went blank for just a moment, then switched back to the studio, where commentators would no doubt comment. The bartender muted the television.

The General drained his mug and wiped his lips with a paper napkin. As far as the public would be concerned, President Linda Travis had just admitted mistakes, threatened retaliation, and was now seeking counsel from the very people she'd spent the last two years excluding. Of course she was, given what had happened at Sebago Lake. The timing was perfect.

The General stood and pulled on his windbreaker, examining himself in the mirror behind the bar. Polo shirt. Twill slacks. He was a General no longer. Just some shrunken old guy rich enough to afford plane fare. He picked up his briefcase and headed toward the door. Time to find a good novel for the flight. Then maybe he'd head to the gate. He loved to be first in line, even with so few fellow flyers. And there were sure to be protestors at the security checkpoint.

The General patted his shirt pocket to make sure his ticket was there. It was. He'd bought a return ticket, to avoid questions, but he did not plan to use it. Soon enough, flights such as his would all be cancelled, but the General had no intention of ever coming back in any event.

1.3

A light breeze cooled the sweat on the back of Claude's neck and he stood to maximize the effect. It was not even noon, but already the sun was hot on his head, and the morning's work had proven more difficult than he'd anticipated. He rolled his shoulders while stretching his neck from side to side, freeing stiff muscles. Getting old was not so bad, he thought, but getting old alone was a sonovabitch. There was too much work.

He gazed off toward the barn. Old Fritz raised his head to return the gaze. "Ya lazy old hound!" called Claude, shaking his fist in mock fury. Fritz thumped his tail on the ground, then lowered his head to the grass and continued his nap. Claude shook his head. He should have been a dog: they don't work at all. He pulled an old, gray handkerchief from his pocket and dabbed at his face, then stuffed it back in his overalls and knelt down to grab the wire cutters. He had other chores to do, and this fence was not going to mend itself.

"Daddy?"

Claude whirled as he stood, his heart pounding. Cole opened his eyes. There was his youngest, Grace, looking down at him, hands on her hips and brow wrinkled with concern. "You went away again, didn't you?" she said. It wasn't really a question.

Cole leaned forward in the recliner and rubbed at his eyes with the heels of his hands, drawing a deep, whistling breath as he did so. "What time is it?" he asked, his voice raspy. He shook his head to clear it.

Grace pulled her phone from her jeans pocket and glanced at the screen. "She's on in about five minutes." She turned to eye the television screen; it was on but muted. The end credits from some daytime drama scrolled merrily along. She turned back to her father. "You want some water?"

Cole nodded. Grace, tall and confident at eight years old, twirled to face the Family Suite's tiny kitchen, tipping her head back so that her long, chestnut hair would swirl around her as she spun. It was something she'd seen in a music video. "You want chips?" she asked as she walked away.

Cole blinked in surprise. "We have chips?" he said, a note of incredulity in his voice.

Grace glanced back over her shoulder with a grin. "Ness made 'em," she said. She reached down to scratch Dennis's head as he slept on the overstuffed sofa, then headed down the hallway. Dennis, the family's old Whippet, his muzzle now flecked with white hairs, wagged his tail but did not open his eyes.

Cole inhaled sharply. A moment ago he'd been an old man, working on a fence on a warm summer day. Now he was young and healthy again, and sitting in a leather recliner in the relatively cool, darkened family room of the Presidential Home in Augusta, Maine. These "hops" were happening more and more frequently, and they felt so vividly real, and the transitions were so abrupt, that they left him feeling like he was about to trip and fall. Sometimes it was difficult to know which "real" was the most real.

Grace came back into the room with a glass of water and a large stainless-steel bowl half-filled with homemade tortilla chips. Cole watched as she placed the water on his side table and crawled onto the recliner beside him. She placed the bowl on her lap. Cole took a chip and popped it into his mouth. Glorious. Ness, bless her heart, must have scored some more corn meal on the last shipment, and rather than settle for the usual corn bread, had produced these crispy, salty reminders of how life used to be. There was even a cup of the salsa she'd canned last fall, just chopped tomatoes and onions from the garden, mostly, nothing particularly spicy because of the pepper blight, but still wonderful. He dipped a second chip and ate it. "Where's Iain and Em?" he asked around the food in his mouth. He grabbed another chip.

"Watching in their rooms," said Grace.

"Should we...?" said Cole, motioning toward the chips.

Grace shook her head. "Ness made 'em both bowls of their own." She glanced up at her father with soft eyes of concern. "Where'd you go?"

Cole hugged his daughter gently. "The old man again," he said. "I was fixing a fence. And his old Doberman was there."

"Fritz," said Grace. She stuffed a chip into her mouth and wiped her hand on her jeans.

"Yeah. That was it." The TV screen dissolved to the presidential seal and Cole reached over to grab the remote and bring up the sound. Grace settled into her father's arms and they waited. "I feel afraid," murmured Cole. Grace took his hand and held it in her own. Cole ran his fingers through his thick, dark brown hair and exhaled deeply.

The video feed cut in. There was Linda. God, she looked so pale. And her eyes: raw, and moist with pain, gazed out over those red splotches on her cheeks like innocent prisoners peering through jail cell windows. Cole still couldn't believe they'd taken her. It'd been almost a week, but the tear in his heart was as fresh and jagged as if she'd only just now been ripped from their lives, as if those bastards had severed the connection between his heart and hers with a dull, rusted axe. Grace reached up and put a hand on his cheek and only then did he realize that he'd been grinding his teeth. He was furious. He blinked and exhaled heavily and tried to smile and hugged Grace to him as Linda Travis began to speak.

"Good morning, all. Thank you for joining me," she said. Her voice sounded small and frail through the television's speakers, but Dennis looked up at the sound of it. "I am here today to announce my intention to seek re-election." Cole took another deep breath. She'd done it. Who knew where that would lead? He sure as hell didn't.

He already knew what she would say, of course. Cole had "chatted" with her just an hour earlier. Five minutes, as usual, as if being online was bad for her health. Damnable doctors. Linda and Cole had been speaking about the possibility of a second term for months. But it was not until two weeks ago, when somebody poisoned Sebago Lake with a weaponized fungal toxin that killed over one hundred thousand Americans in and around the Federal Shelter outside of Portland, Maine, that Linda would allow herself to truly consider the possibility. And it was not until the military and the CDC arrived in force at the Presidential Home at dawn on Emily's eleventh birthday, forced Linda into a level-four biocontainment capsule, and whisked her away in an ambulance, that she could see that she had to keep fighting. Sebago Lake had been too close, a message and a threat, and her present incarceration, an obvious attempt to try to control her directly. Linda Travis would not stand for that. Not the Linda Travis that Cole knew and loved.

"But we do not always get to choose our circumstances," said Linda from the screen. Cole nodded his head in agreement. No shit. His love, his best friend, was now locked away in a state-of-the-art biocontainment facility built, supposedly for her comfort and ease, over and around her old summer cottage on Squirrel Island. Two hours away by car and boat, but it might as well be Mars. And according to her doctors, or at least that halfwit specialist Bill Bellows who showed up on the news all the time, she was suffering from "an unknown infectious agent" contracted, they said, from her direct contact with "non-terrestrial biological entities." Meaning Spud, at the very least. Now her health was failing - that red rash on her face had only manifested in the last two days - and her freedom was severely limited. Walled in, surrounded by CDC personnel on all sides, her access to the world filtered through government and military channels, she was now forced to play by "their" rules, although which "they" was responsible for all of this Cole did not know. This damned summit was part of that.

He couldn't even see her. He'd been allowed one short phone call just after she'd been taken away. She hadn't seemed herself at all in that call; it was like she'd been drugged. Since then, nothing but an occasional chat online. No one was allowed on Squirrel Island but military and CDC personnel. And direct human contact, even with medical people, was sharply limited, according to Linda.

The expression on that poor nurse's face when she stumbled into the room looked like more than just embarrassment to Cole. She seemed terrified. So maybe the press was correct in calling Linda's condition the "alien flu." But how could Linda have been infected by aliens when she hadn't seen any in years? How could the doctors and military have known about it before she had any symptoms? Had those little bastards come and taken her in the night, as they used to do when she was young? Had the military been involved? And if Linda was infected, then weren't the rest of them? Why hadn't Cole and the kids and her entire staff been rounded up and quarantined as well? It didn't add up.

No, Cole agreed, we do not get to choose our circumstances at all, do we? We live in a world where other people think they can choose for us.

"Have courage," Linda said softly, as if just to him. Cole's eyes misted over. The screen cut to black, and then to a newsroom. Cole hit the mute button, closed his eyes, and took a deep breath.

"Her hair is shorter," said Grace.

"Is it?" said Cole.

From down the hall came the muffled thunder of someone running and soon Emily and Iain burst into the family room. "Did you see?" asked Emily, coming to a stop at the foot of the recliner. Iain came up behind her, a shock of long, stringy hair falling into his face. He grabbed a chip from Grace's bowl.

"See what?" Cole raised an eyebrow.

"Her mole," said Iain.

Emily turned and punched her brother on the shoulder. "I'm telling it," she said firmly. Iain smirked but said no more. She turned back to her father. "Her mole," she repeated.

"What mole?" asked Cole.

Emily rolled her eyes. "That little beauty spot over her upper lip, Dad," she said. "Have you never noticed it?"

Cole shook his head as if irritated by a fly. "What about it?" he asked.

Emily's eyes, dark and lively and highlighted by the short, straight brown hair that enclosed her face like parentheses, grew pointed and fierce, as they always did when she was onto something. Her head moved vaguely back and forth as she replied. "It was on her left side," Emily explained. "Now it's on the right."

"Was it just reverse image?" asked Cole, confused. "You know. Because of the TV camera?"

Emily scoffed. "I'm not stupid, Dad," she said. "It moved."

1.4

Mary stopped outside Emily's door and listened. All three kids were inside and Emily was speaking with hushed excitement. Something about "finding pictures." Mary raised her hand to knock, then exhaled and turned away, forcing down the anxiety that threatened, every day, to engulf her. The kids were fine. She didn't need to worry. They were fine.

She headed along the hall through the Family Suite, checked through security, and took the stairs step-by-step down to the second floor, her hand tight on the railing. It had been months since her last fall but she would take no chances, no matter how good she felt. The dizziness could return at any moment. And this sudden change in the weather, from wet, cold rain and mushy snow to humid heat, would not help. Her limp was noticeably worse today. Reaching the next level, Mary headed toward the private offices. The last door on the right was Keeley's and Mary walked in without knocking. Keeley looked up from her desk and grinned.

"I really love you," said Mary, her heart swelling with sweet warmth for her partner. She smoothed her cotton blouse and khaki shorts and straightened her back. Being with Keeley made her want to look beautiful, and that meant overcoming her body's tendency to fold in on itself as if to ward off a blow.

"I know, sweetie," said Keeley with a grin. "You tell me all the time."

Mary walked across the room and took one of the two leather wingback guest chairs in front of Keeley's desk. Her love had triggered a flood of taste into her mouth, that same strange mixture of copper and sweet apples that had been with her since the hospital. Mary swallowed it down, grateful for the reminder. Metal and sugar was an apt metaphor for her life these days. "Did you watch?" she asked.

Keeley motioned toward her computer. "Yeah," she said, drawing in a deep breath. She reached down beside her chair to scratch the ears of her old border collie, Chapin. Mary could hear the thump of Chapin's tail against the hardwood floor. Keeley opened her mouth to speak again, but then stopped. She clasped her hands on the desk before her. "What did you think?" she asked at last.

"She looks terrified," answered Mary. "Pale. Sick." Mary's eyes filled with tears. "I couldn't see her... her field. You know? Through the TV." She scrunched her nose in disgust. "But I don't think she's in a good place."

"Ya got that right, sweetie," said Keeley. "Those bastards have her locked up tight. Not even Stan can get to her."

Mary wiped away the tears and swallowed again. "I hate whoever did this," she said. "I want to..." She motioned with her hands, making a circle with her thumbs and forefingers and shaking them sternly. At last the word came: "... strangle them."

Keeley rose and pulled over the other guest chair, then sat to meet Mary knee to knee. She took Mary's hands in her own and regarded her partner with steady eyes. "You know how strong our Linda is," she said. "And you know that what she's up to is bigger than any of those bastards who try to get in her way."

Mary answered with a single, slow nod, as if ashamed that she'd forgotten.

"So you just keep loving her, sweetie. And Cole. And the kids. Keep loving us all. And I'll keep doing everything I can to find out what's going on." Keeley reached out and caressed Mary's face with her fingers. "Okay? I'm on this. And Stan is. And we're not alone. She's the President, remember? She's got a great many friends. We'll figure this out."

Mary smiled weakly at Keeley's courage and power. Gone was her partner's plump figure and frilly hippie vibe. With her well-toned body, tanned face, ponytail, and dark jeans and t-shirt, Keeley resembled more a commando than an Earth goddess. Keeley helped Mary feel safe.

"The announcement tells us that's she's still in charge," said Keeley. Mary squeezed Keeley's hand. "I love you," she said again. Her anger had eased, leaving her face more open and relaxed.

Keeley rose, pulled Mary to her feet, and kissed her. After a minute, Mary buried her face in Keeley's neck and inhaled deeply. Her whole body was shaking, as it often did in the aftermath of stress. "Will you meet me for lunch?" she asked at last.

Keeley pulled back. "You trying to mess up my work day?" she asked. She reached out and ran a finger along the long, faint scar on Mary's forehead.

Mary beamed shyly. "Isn't that my job?"

1.5

"Look. There's pictures of her all over the place. It only takes one page of Google Images to prove it. Her mole is on the left side." Emily tossed her tablet to the foot of her bed and leaned back on her pillows. She pulled down her t-shirt to cover her stomach. The smile on her face was one of victory.

Grace stood near the air conditioning vent in the floor, enjoying how the cool air seemed to crawl up her bare legs. "So, what-" she began.

"It can't be they just reversed the image," cut in Iain, "because then the Presidential Seal would have been reversed as well." He pushed the hair out of his face, revealing the large, thin nose and prominent Adam's apple that had suddenly appeared when adolescence made claim to his body. The shock of hair fell right back into place.

Grace shot her brother an irritated squint, then faced her sister. "So what does it mean?" she asked.

Emily shrugged. "How should I know?" she said. "All I know is that it's wrong."

Grace sat on her sister's bed and picked up the tablet. She touched a thumbnail to enlarge it. And another. And another. In each, Linda Travis's mole was on her left side. Grace put down the tablet and looked at Emily. "Maybe they did it with make-up," she offered.

Iain snorted from his armchair by the window. "Oh, good one, Graceful." He stuck out his hands as if fluffing someone's hair and spoke in a feminine voice. "You're all ready for the camera Mrs. President, but that mole..." He put a hand to his cheek in mock exasperation. "It's just so, oh, I don't know... left. Could we... do you think... move it to the other side?" Iain started to laugh.

Grace closed her eyes and took a breath, then spoke again to her sister. "Or maybe it has something to do with her disease?" she asked.

Emily nodded her encouragement, recognizing her little sister's efforts to brainstorm. Grace was not one to just stop at "I don't know." In the almost three years since her "coma," she'd shown an uncanny ability to see and understand what was going on around her. Things could be figured out. Trends could be observed. Guesses could be made and evaluated. And Grace's "guesses" proved to be correct much more often than not. "I'm not sure that makes sense," answered Emily evenly. "I mean, whatever it is she's sick with does seem to be showing up on her skin. She's got that weird red blotch now. But to make a mole disappear on one side and reappear on the other? That doesn't feel like something a flu bug could do."

"Assuming it's really some alien virus or something," said Iain from across the room. Emily noted how her brother's hair glowed in the light coming in from behind him, how blonde it had become now that it was long. In the distance, through the third-story window, past the security fences and the silent streets, she could see the athletic fields, and further still, the airport, both now choked with tall grasses and weeds and a few small saplings. They hadn't seen a plane land there in over a year. The military used the new strips they'd built outside the cordon.

Grace turned and rewarded her brother with a raised eyebrow. "You don't believe what they're saying?" she asked.

Iain scrunched his nose as if smelling something foul. "I don't trust what anybody says these days, Sis," he said. He gestured outside with a sideways tilt of his head.

Emily nodded her agreement. The whole world had gone crazy in the past year and a half and nobody seemed to know what the heck to do about it. They lived in an oasis of normality compared to most people, here in the Presidential Home. There was food to eat and oil in the furnace and electricity most days. And there were soldiers all around them, keeping them safe. Out there? She shuddered to think about it. Especially now, with the early summer heat and people still shocked by Sebago Lake. It was a wonder huge crowds weren't storming the place, demanding their stepmother's head. Maybe that's why they took her away? Emily glanced over at her sister. "Did they just make up that 'alien flu' thing so they could take Linda away and keep her safe?" she asked.

Grace closed her eyes and inhaled. Emily watched closely. Sometimes, when asked a direct question, her sister could just pull the right answer out of thin air. When they first heard about the disaster in Zakryto in Siberia, Grace knew immediately that it was a sudden release of methane that had killed all ninety-seven of the village's inhabitants, even though she didn't really know what methane was. And she knew that it would happen again, which it had. Grace opened her eyes and shook her head. "They took her so they could control her," she said, her voice soft and low.

Emily took her sister's hand. "And do you know who 'they' are?" she asked.

Grace paused for a moment as if to check in with the cosmic search engine, then wrinkled her brow in frustration at the lack of hits she got. "No," she said. She glanced at her brother, then spoke to Emily. "Sorry." She reached out and grabbed the stainless steel bowl near Emily's pillow. Ness's tortilla chips were all gone. Grace ran her finger along the bottom and then stuck her greasy, salty fingertip into her mouth.

Iain cleared his throat and both girls turned to face him. "So... that mole," he said. "What does it mean?"

"Let's see if we can get her online," said Emily. She leaned over and picked up her tablet. "We'll just ask her!"

1.6

"Hep!" called Keeley. Chapin pulled his nose from the tattered denim jacket he'd found lying on the sidewalk, looked around in bewilderment, lifted a leg, then ran back to his human. Keeley gave him the hand signal to heel and Chapin fell into place at her side. She turned and started across the parking lot, three Secret Service agents in tow, an equilateral triangle of dark suits, neat hair, sunglasses, flak jackets, wireless earbuds, throat mics, and assault rifles. The noontime sun beat mercilessly on the city center, baking the concrete and pavement underfoot. Keeley, glad she'd remembered her sun hat, quickly crossed to the shadow of the Burton Cross building. She did not want Chapin to burn his feet.

An image of Mary popped into Keeley's mind and she felt a stab of guilt. Mary would be in their private rooms now, waiting and wondering, lunch ordered and on the way. But that could not be helped. Keeley was too angry right now. Too jumbled. Too confused. And Mary was so fragile these days that Keeley was loath to burden her lover with her own troubles. And then there was Mary's new "sight" that allowed her to see what she called people's "fields." Keeley was not sure she wanted to be seen that deeply. Not right now.

The agents scanned the area as Keeley rounded the corner and peered up at the State House. The city inside the cordon was a protected space, a "green zone" in which the bare-bones government staff could live and work, with the full protection of the U.S. military. As such, the people living there enjoyed greater access to fuel, energy, and consumables than did most Americans elsewhere. It felt, at times, almost "normal." And yet there were dangers, which necessitated Keeley's protective detail. It was a more dangerous world than ever, as military leaders were fond of reminding them, filled with everything from hungry folks competing for supplies to crazed lunatics wanting to strike back against the government they blamed, from enraged citizens seeking redress for their losses to international operatives (or even extraterrestrial?) hoping to destroy or expose or blackmail the American President or her people. Keeley was grateful for her security people, and felt safer in their presence.

The Maine State House loomed up before her and she started toward it. Not long after most of Washington D.C. had fallen into the sinkholes, and Linda Travis had made it clear that she did not intend to rebuild the city any time soon, Sam "Sparky" Lane, the newly-elected Governor of Maine, a rebellious independent with a penchant for shit-stirring, invited the President to move her base of operations to the Maine State House. "It's not like anybody's been using it," he quipped, a reference to his campaign message regarding his predecessor. "You can even have your own bathroom."

President Travis, drawn by her love of the Maine coast and her desire to re-invent the way her government operated, thought it was worth a try. Cole and his children, already pulled up by the roots from their home in rural Vermont, and not yet having established new roots in Montpelier, were up for the adventure. "It might be wise to live in a place with bigger skies," said Cole, motioning toward the Green Mountains that surrounded them. "If you know what I mean," he added with a wink, pointing to the stars above. Linda had accepted Governor Lane's offer the next day. Keeley had joined them three months later and taken the position of White House Chief of Staff, replacing her murdered predecessor, Steven Bickle.

Keeley wiped the sweat from her forehead with her hand. Her plan had been to hole up in her State House office for the afternoon. But she found that, now that she was out, she had no desire to go back inside. This March heat wave, coming as it did on the heels of a bitter cold and snow-packed but abnormally short winter, felt good to her today: a chance to stretch her legs, a chance to work off some calories, a chance to sweat and rant and wander off, and a chance to think.

She circled the State House on the south side, noting the girders of the unfinished addition on the east side as she passed. The steel and concrete structure, begun the month Keeley had arrived and designed to give both the Governor and the President a little more "breathing room" once the honeymoon was over, rose against the sky like monkey-bars for giants. No doubt there were unfinished buildings like this all around the globe now, their destinies thwarted by the Christmas Crash, stark reminders that even giants can be toppled when the money disappears.

Keeley crossed over State Street and down the grassy slope to the pathway that looped around Capitol Park, turning left to head north. "Off and away," she said quietly to the dog at her side. Chapin leapt away greedily, heading straight across the park grounds as if on a mission. The expanse of mown grass stirred Keeley's nostalgia, a word now on everyone's lips, with so much of the world they had known having fallen away. She had no idea how the groundskeepers kept this park as neat and tidy as they did, what with their fuel rations cut so drastically. But she understood why they did it. Such as it was, Augusta, Maine, was now the Capitol of the United States of America. If life was to somehow "go on," it had to start here.

Life was certainly going someplace, but Keeley had little faith that anybody really knew where. The traffic around the State House was sparse, and consisted mostly of military motorcycles. Foot and bike traffic was even more meager, the few denizens of this mostly empty city no doubt holed up in restaurants, taverns, or basement "cool clubs" to escape "the midday slam." Temperatures had been hitting afternoon highs above one-hundred for over three weeks now, rewriting the rules of normalcy for March in Maine and bringing out clouds of black flies far ahead of their natural schedule. Global dimming was another term on everyone's lips these days, as the interruption to the global industrial machine in the wake of the Crash made readily apparent the heat-shielding benefits of dirty skies. As the atmosphere had cleared, the true extent of climate change had been revealed. Not even the chemtrail program, which they no longer tried to hide, could keep up with the warming effects of a runaway rise in greenhouse gases.

And out beyond the military cordon? Jesus, Mary, and Ronald McDonald, what a mess. How could one even begin to wrap one's mind around it? At least half of the American population was now safely and comfortably housed in or near the government-run "camps" and "shelters," if one were willing to rewrite the definitions of "safely" and "comfortably" to include such things as the lack of healthy food, clean water, and adequate protection from both heat and cold. And the people themselves were stunned and beaten, suffering from PTSD and malnutrition, from debilitating grief and the loss of both identity and direction. They'd seen gang violence and the heads of "boomers" on spikes along city streets. They'd seen massive crop failures, runs on banks, lengthy blackouts, and epidemic diseases. They'd seen riots and suicides, famine and hoarding, terrorist attacks and lines at the gas stations and soldiers patrolling their neighborhoods. They'd seen seawater sluice down the streets of Miami, Boston, New Orleans, New York, and hundreds of smaller cities and towns. They'd seen their own neighborhoods go quiet and their towns fall empty. They'd seen the Alien Grid in their night skies. They'd seen the end of the American Dream. And they'd seen that their government was powerless to stop that end.

And yet, as bad as it had been, as bad as it still was, it was not the Zombie Apocalypse people had feared for so long. At least not yet. The Raging Hordes did not wander far from home, the mass violence played out fairly swiftly, and for every moment of horror or loss there was a moment of compassion or love. And while much of that arose from what Keeley insisted was "the basic goodness of human beings," at least part of it was due to Linda Travis's inspired leadership, no matter what her detractors might claim. In her announcement just a couple of hours ago now, Linda, *her* Linda, her *Cornfed*, had mentioned "mistakes," but Keeley didn't buy it. Linda had acted impeccably throughout, doing her best with what she had, and doing much more than any of her detractors ever managed. Over and over, she had called her people to step into their "best selves," and over and over they had responded in kind, drawing on reserves of grace and resilience many had never dreamt they had. While most Americans had now lost their jobs, their homes, their cars, and their sense of what it all meant, and while most Americans had now lost someone they loved to disease, famine, cold, heat, or violence, they had not yet, as a people, lost their humanity.

The path continued into a small grove of trees and Keeley sighed with relief. There were no leaves yet. It was anybody's guess which trees here had survived the winter and would see leaves again this spring. But the shade from the trunks and branches cut the sun's direct effects to something that felt almost pleasant. In the distance Chapin barked. Keeley turned to watch him approach. He'd apparently made his way down to the river, as his black and white coat was soaked. Chapin came to a stop in the midst of them and shook, sending three Secret Service agents into a backward scramble. Keeley laughed and Chapin barked again.

"You guys up for a beer or three?" Keeley asked her escort as they brushed at the spatters of water and mud on their expensive suits.

"Ma'am?" answered the senior agent with a raised eyebrow. The other two flashed brief, guilty smiles. Keeley smiled back. It was clear, without actually saying it out loud, that if Keeley somehow managed to lead them to a bar or tavern, they'd somehow manage to swallow something cold and wet, and it could hardly be their fault if all there was to drink had some alcohol in it. Keeley nodded decisively and turned back northward, motioning Chapin to heel. She frequented a place still open up on Child Street, tucked into the ground floor of one of the newer, so-called "sustainable," mixed-use high-rises that had come to Augusta on the heels of the President's move. The place was dark and tiny, but the home-brew was plentiful and cold and Stills, bless his heart, would no doubt have some special treat squirreled away for her. Last week it had been a full package of Oreos. Oreos! Keeley grinned at the thought of it.

Stepping out from under the trees, Keeley glanced up at the sky. The Grid was not visible during the day, of course, but she knew it was still in place, as it had been since before the Crash. She had no idea what that rat-bastard Spud was planning up there, but her gut told her that he was not to be trusted. Maybe he was on their side. Maybe not. Nobody had seen him for a couple of years now. But Keeley was not going to assume anything. If he was on *her* side, the least he could do was say so.

The senior agent ranged out ahead of her and for a moment Keeley considered having one of the three take Chapin back home. But that was a stupid idea. Having promised the agents cold beer, it would be unfair to send one of them off on an extra long walk in this heat. Besides, Chapin loved Stills almost as much as she did. And there was always a bowl of relatively fresh water on the sidewalk in front of his place. She cut across Capitol Street, crossed a parking lot in the shade of an abandoned apartment building, turned left onto Child Street, and headed toward Greensward Commons.

With two exceptions, the Commons was devoid of renters. The first exception was Stills' little pub, where they would soon quench their thirsts. The second was Augusta's last open franchise restaurant, a Burger Hut, which sold tiny cheeseburgers and "hut fries" and Cokes to those who needed a serving of nostalgia badly enough that they were willing to overlook the questionable provenance of its "don't ask, don't tell" ingredients. Burger Hut had survived the Crash by virtue of its government and military contracts. They were now one of the three major suppliers of foodstuffs to the shelters on the East Coast and across most of the South. That made them one of the major recipients of the fading productivity of the global-industrial food machine, as that machine - beset with extreme weather and changing climates; interruptions to power and fuel supplies; shortages, diseases, delays, and breakdowns – slowly and fitfully ground down to a halt. All of which meant that Burger Hut meals, though suspect in terms of healthfulness, were at least fairly consistent in taste and availability. Able to deliver, at least to some folks' minds, on its advertised promise of "good food now," the Capitol City Burger Hut was one of the busiest restaurants in town.

Which was good for Stills, as the heavy traffic meant more customers for him. Which was then good for Keeley, because she was feeling so much stress from Linda's abduction that she thought she might scream. She needed a break. A short one, at least. A couple of beers. Perhaps a shot of something stronger, depending on what Stills had in stock. Maybe she'd get one of the agents to actually say something interesting about themselves, which was always fun. Some of those guys had seen much more of the outside world than she had. And just the chance to sit in the cool dark of the pub and put her feet up for a while...

But then it was back to work. Those bastards, and she wished with all of heart she knew *which* bastards, had stolen her President right out from under her nose. She did not intend to let them get away with it. She had phone calls to make and emails to write and arms to twist and favors to call in. She had legislators to herd and the Cabinet to steer in an attempt to forge some major show of support for their President, and to hopefully force a breach in the wall of secrecy and silence that had been built around her. She'd go visit Stan at the State House and see what news he had. Together they would review and revise their tactics and strategies in their ongoing fight to regain free access to their Commander-in-Chief.

And then, home. She made a mental note to find a peace offering for Mary on her way back. Maybe some bulbs for her garden. Easy enough to dig some up from one of the dozens of abandoned plots she would pass on her way.

The thought of Mary brought heaviness to Keeley's throat and heart. Mary was her love. Her salvation. Her companion. Her hope. Mary had taken up a space in her heart where Pooch had once dwelt. And Mary needed her, and that was a precious thing.

Keeley's reverie was interrupted by the sound of a distant shout. The agents around her sprang into formation, their assault rifles at the ready. Ahead, in front of the Burger Hut, a small crowd had formed. And there on the sidewalk lay a woman.

1.7

"You following?" asked Colonel Aidan McAfee, pushing through the door. He pulled his reading glasses from his jacket pocket as he walked across the underground lab.

"I'm on it," said Paul DuPont, his eyes on his qputer display. He exhaled heavily.

The Colonel grabbed an office chair and pulled it around to face the screen. He sat next to his Chief Tech and started to read.

"It's the older one," said DuPont. "According to the login."

"The boy?"

"No. The older girl. Emily." DuPont stared at McAfee for a moment, one eyebrow raised, then turned his attention back to the chat page. Words scrolled down the screen in front of them. DuPont reached out and, with a swipe of his hand in the air, increased the magnification so that the Colonel could more easily read. The Colonel grunted his appreciation.

"Just pleasantries so far," said the Colonel.

"Yep."

"Does the Pres really call them 'kiddoes'?"

DuPont spoke without taking his eyes off the screen. "Pretty much from the beginning," he replied. "It's a casual term of affection used to dispel the Presidential aura and create a bond. Useful in such stepparent-child relationships as we have here." He turned and stared at the Colonel with a bored, blank expression, then returned to his computer.

"Right," said McAfee. He eyed his Chief Tech - a slight, cardigan-wearing, bookish type who appeared to be in his thirties - with a mixture of fearful respect and the desire to share his wisdom and experience. The Tech was a DuPont, after all, but he was also young and cocky. "You don't overuse it, do you?"

DuPont glanced at the Colonel like one might regard a screaming child. "No, Sir," he said. He looked again at his screen.

McAfee nodded toward DuPont's qputer, one of new Tech-X models that only Family members owned. "So, didn't they already chat today?"

"We anticipated a second attempt, given the televised announcement. Probably just congratulatory. We granted an exception to the rules on those grounds. And Dr. Conklin thought it would give us some useful feedback. This is the first chat with full AI, Sir," DuPont explained, glancing at the Colonel. He lifted his hands and held them in front of his face. "Look ma, no hands."

McAfee watched the screen. "Chatty little thing, isn't she?"

"The recognition software indicates that both the boy and the younger girl have also chimed in with greetings," said DuPont, pointing to the sidebar on the screen.

The Colonel grunted his understanding. "Is the Presidential response time too quick?" he asked, gesturing toward the screen. "I mean... the back and forth is faster than I'd expected. She's not taking any time to think. Shouldn't -?"

"You don't chat online, do you Sir?" asked the Chief Tech, a touch of impatience in his voice.

McAfee cleared his throat. "No, uh... I haven't really. Much."

DuPont nodded toward the screen. "This is how quickly it moves along," he said. "It's how most - " DuPont stopped for a moment and simply watched as the conversation flowed before him. "Hold on a second," he said.

"What?" asked the Colonel, trying to keep up.

"No," said DuPont, his voice almost a whisper. He glanced quickly at the Colonel before scrolling the conversation back up a bit with a wave of his hand. He read through a second time. "I... I can't believe it," he finally said.

"What?" repeated McAfee. He focused on the screen. The kids were asking her about a mole.

"Her responses!" said DuPont with exasperation, pushing his chair back and shaking his head in disbelief. "They're all over the place, Colonel. Look." He pointed at the screen. "Denial. Then confusion. Then two different explanations!" He reached over to a second screen and pulled up a headshot of the President, then opened a second window and scrolled to an image from the President's announcement earlier in the day. He studied the two faces side by side, then returned to the chatscreen. "Facial Modeling is gonna shit," he said, taking control of the interaction. He typed furiously for a moment, then pushed away his keyboard and stood. He looked down at the Colonel. "I told them it was too soon," he said, a thunderhead of frustration clouding his face. He hurried out the door.

Colonel McAfee studied the screen, reading through the chat once more. Only slowly did he realize what had just happened.

1.8

"Can you save this, Ness?" asked Mary, setting the tray of food on the stainless steel countertop. The kitchen was hot and smelled of chocolate cake.

Goodness Gracious Abernathy pulled her head out of the oven and grinned. "Did Ms. Keeley stand you up again, sweet pea?" she asked, brushing flour from her apron as she slammed the oven door. She crossed the room with arms open and wrapped Mary in her embrace. At four-feet-eleven and chicken-bones thin, it seemed as though Ness's hugs should feel like those of a child. But it was always Mary who felt comforted and engulfed. Ness's field was huge and hearty and full of good cheer. And the woman knew how to hug.

Mary buried her nose in Ness's short, gray hair. "She never... showed up," whispered Mary, her voice on the edge of tears. "I got... scared."

Ness pulled away to examine Mary's face. "Then you were right to come here, love. The kitchen's just the place for scared people. Always has been, always will be." The older woman - she called herself ancient but she looked about sixty - snatched up the tray and headed toward the refrigerator. With a quick efficiency of movement, she emptied the contents onto a lower shelf and closed the door. "It'll be here when you want it," Ness announced with a decisive nod. "You need to know that, in case the good Lord decides to take me away before your darling returns." Ness made her way to the sink, plunged her hands in the wash water, and started to scrub.

Mary let her eyes lose focus and regarded Ness's field. She saw no intimations of the older woman's imminent demise. "You're not... going to die any time soon, Ness," she said at last. "I feel confused when you say things like that."

Ness turned, saw Mary's frail, hunched form, and sighed her empathy. "I'm sorry, sweet-pea," she said, wiping at her face with wet fingers. "I think it's something my mother used to say and it got stuck in my brain. But I'm not really planning on going anywhere any time soon, s'far's I know. I'll try to remember and keep my big mouth shut."

Mary started toward the oven to see what was baking, then stopped abruptly, as if she'd hit an invisible wall. "The kids!" she cried, glancing up at the ceiling. Mary turned and ran from the kitchen, leaving Ness without another word. Ness grabbed a towel to dry her hands and followed.

Down the hallway Mary ran, through the double doors and the dining hall, into the grand foyer and toward the stairs. She took the steps two at a time, forgetting her dizziness, forgetting her last fall, forgetting the elevator that would have taken her up more safely. She rounded the landing and headed up to the third floor, no thought in her mind but that the kids were in danger. Danger!

She pushed through the door and hurried toward the private rooms, past the door to her and Keeley's apartment, past Ness's door, past Ben's old room, and into the Family Suite. She headed straight to Emily's bedroom, knowing without knowing how that all three of the children were there. Emily's door was open and Mary dashed in. Iain, Emily, and Grace, sitting side by side in front of Emily's desktop computer, looked up in surprise as she slid to a halt before them.

Mary's gut clenched with horror. There was something wrong. Something in the air around them. A darkness. A tendril. A reaching out. A grabbing. And in Emily's field, images of fire and pain and Grace screaming and Iain falling, falling. "You can't!" cried Mary. "You can not!" But the dizziness was already sweeping her away. She did not notice when Ness and Cole came running up behind her. And she did not feel a thing when her head hit the hardwood floor.

1.9

"Linda?" The voice was far away but distinct, riding above the background static like a boat on a choppy sea. The space around her was darkness.

"Yes?" answered Linda. She thought it was her father, come to wake her for school. But why did he speak with a British accent? And why was it so dark? "Daddy?" she asked.

"No doubt you will require a few moments to gather yourself, Madam," said the voice, drawing closer. "Please understand that this is normal, and that you have not been harmed."

Linda tried to raise a hand to rub her eyes but found that she could not. She felt neither numb nor strapped down. There was simply no response from her body. The sensation was vaguely familiar. Something to do with space ships. She realized that she was not a schoolgirl but the President of the United States. Her last memory was of being strapped to a hospital bed by doctors in protective suits, with bright lights overhead.

"Do you know who I am?" asked the voice after a moment.

At the question, Linda knew that she did. A bolt of fear crackled through her veins. "The Fisherman," she said, her voice dry with disuse. It had been almost three years since she'd heard his voice, but this was that man. It was not just the accent. There was a confidence in that voice that demanded her attention. It was a voice that resonated with the surety of control.

"I'm glad to finally meet you face to face, Madam President, though I'm not sure that particular phrase precisely captures the full reality of our situation here." The voice had moved from her right side to her left, as though the Fisherman was walking around her. But she heard no footsteps and felt no air movement. She couldn't even tell if she was standing or lying down.

"The connections between your mind and your body have been rerouted, Madam President," said the Fisherman. "You'll understand why soon enough. It will be much safer this way."

"It was you..."

"... who saved you, yes." interrupted the Fisherman. "And you can be happy I intervened, Madam President. You should otherwise be quite dead by now, I'm afraid, and no one the wiser." The voice had moved down near Linda's feet, telling her that she was either lying down or that she was now standing on the Fisherman's chest. She went with lying down as the correct answer.

"Where am I?" she asked. She knew that information was key right now.

"Well, that's the most exciting part of it!" replied the Fisherman. His voice trembled with laughter and surprise. "If you will permit me to restore your visuals..."

The darkness around her began to melt away, filling her eyes with a swirling brightness, yellows and reds and browns and pinks and grays that spun and floated in front of her like dancers. Slowly the images resolved themselves to something she could understand. She was lying on her back in what appeared to be a glass coffin, her head tilted to the right. Before her stretched a desolate landscape, a desiccated plain of sand and dust and rocks and boulders. And in the far distance, a mountainous mesa rose up to the sky.

The Fisherman's voice was in her ear now but Linda could not turn her head to see him. "On behalf of the Evolutionary Element of the Seven Families of the Great Consortium," he said, his voice filled with obvious delight, "let me welcome you to the planet Mars."

1.10

Ted got up and walked to the door, rattled the knob, pulled. The door would not open.

"Would you stop with that?" said Carl, rolling his eyes.

Ted sat back down and glanced at the board, then up at Carl. "It's your turn," he said.

Carl sighed his irritation and returned his attention to the game.

Chapter Ø Two

2.1

Gabrielle lay on her naked stomach on the cold, hardwood floor of her dorm room, furiously scribbling in a spiral bound notebook. She clutched the pen so tightly that her fingers were red with strain. She did not feel the cold or pain. She was not awake.

From outside came the laughter and shouts of other students as they walked across the quad, most of them likely headed back from the bars. Gabrielle gave no sign of noticing. She came to the end of the page, flipped over the notebook, and continued to write. The only light in the room came from the tiny green glow of her tablet charger. She did not need to see.

Her phone rang but Gabrielle did not move to answer it. She continued to write as her father left a message. He still wanted to talk, he said. When Gabrielle was ready. Until then, he just wanted her to know that he loved her. His voice was sad. His words contrite. But Gabrielle, unmoved, ignored him.

She flipped the page again, wrote a bit more, and then stopped. She dropped the pen on the floor next to the notebook. Rising slowly to her knees and grasping the edge of her metal desk, she pulled herself to her feet. Slowly, careful not to make a sound, she slipped back into her bed and pulled the covers to her chin. She held her strained fingers to her breast to soothe them. Eventually her face, hard and tight with anger, relaxed and softened. She began to softly snore.

The notebook and pen, still on the floor where she had left them, listened to her heavy breathing, and waited patiently, for morning, to be noticed.

2.2

Keeley stood outside the front entrance to MaineCentral Hospital and gazed up at the sky. The night, despite the haze and heat of the day, was clear, the stars crisp, the moon a mere shard. That damnable Grid still sectioned off the heavens: a cage, a fence, a prison, or a shield. Nobody really knew. Some said that the Grid, shimmering blue-white lines that sliced the night sky into diamond shapes from horizon to horizon, with a tiny, glowing wok at each intersection, had been constructed to keep humanity Earthbound, so that the insanity of human beings could not infect the Cosmos. Others claimed the Grid was actually intended to keep something out, be that evil lizard aliens, wayward asteroids, or disasters even worse. Some believed the Grid would save them from the climate catastrophe that was upon them. Others called it a message from God. Or the Devil. But at this point, most did not seem to care. The Grid had appeared in an instant on the night of November twelfth, just six weeks before the Christmas Crash. It was the Crash that had commanded the lion's share of people's attention ever since. The Grid, unchanging, impenetrable, and so far seemingly benign, no longer seemed to much matter.

Mike Portnoy, Keeley's Deputy Chief of Staff, returned with a glass of cold tea. Keeley accepted it with a mumbled thank-you. "Any word?" she asked. She took a large swallow of tea and wished for ice cubes.

Portnoy wiped the sweat from his large, bald forehead with the cuff of his sport coat. "She's resting comfortably," he said, making a joke of the nurses' repeated assurances. He smiled. His thick, heavy glasses danced and winked in the Gridlight. "Otherwise, no change," he continued. "They just want to keep her for the night. Observation. Routine. Nothing to worry about. All that crap."

Keeley drained her tea in another huge gulp, set the glass on the stainless steel ashtray post by the doors, and surveyed the area around her. Her personal Secret Service bodyguard, Agent Sanchez, stood between her and the street. Just beyond him was the security fence that now surrounded MaineCentral on all four sides, installed when the military took over hospital operations after the Crash. Beyond the fence, soldiers manned their posts. Another grid, this one made of human beings, rifles, and armored vehicles. The same questions applied: were they keeping something out, or in? All of this security was supposed to make her feel safe. That's why they called it "security." So why did she feel so afraid?

"You'll understand if I just go on worrying anyways," said Keeley. Portnoy bowed with respect. "Of course."

"You've got extra people on Cole and the kids." It was not a question.

"You know I do."

Keeley smiled grimly. "Yes. I do. Thank you, Mike."

"It's what I'm here for, Chief."

A low-flying jet screamed overhead and Keeley reached out to take her Deputy's arm. In seconds the jet had passed, leaving behind a low, rolling thunder that faded into the night. "A message from the opposition?" asked Keeley, letting go of Portnoy's arm. Her heart was pounding. She noticed that the soldiers at their posts seemed not to have given the jet so much as a glance.

Portnoy chuckled softly. "Probably. Their version of an email to Stan. The answer is undoubtedly 'no'."

Keeley glanced at her watch. It was just after midnight. "It's late. You should get some sleep."

The Deputy Chief of Staff checked his own watch and inhaled deeply. He glanced at his boss. "You'll be okay?" he asked.

"With Sanchez here?" she said with a grin, motioning toward her bodyguard. "Are you kidding me? We're drinking buddies." Sanchez glanced at Keeley at the mention of his name but did not otherwise react.

Portnoy leaned out and kissed Keeley on the cheek. "You get some sleep too," he said softly. "Promise?"

"Promise," said Keeley. She reached up and pulled off the elastic band that kept her ponytail together, freeing her long, chestnut hair to move in the breeze.

Portnoy headed back into the hospital to get his things. Keeley glanced up at the Grid, shook her head in wonderment, then followed.

The support bar of the sleeper chair pushed up into Keeley's spine. She rolled over, making another futile attempt to get some rest. It felt good for about a minute before the pressure began to hurt again. Damn! She'd never sleep this way. And she'd developed this strange, tickling sensation in her throat and chest that made her wonder whether she was coming down with something. With a muttered curse, Keeley crawled out of the tiny bed, grabbed her laptop, crept out of the room, and headed down the hall to the lounge.

What she wanted was coffee. She'd have a cup, work for a couple of hours, and then maybe stretch out on one of the lounge's sofas. But she did not expect to find any of those marvelous roasted beans in the visitor's lounge. Not these days. Not even in Augusta. Tea they could have, thanks to Linda's friendship with Senator Jackson in South Carolina. But coffee? If it was still being grown somewhere in the world, none of it was making it into the shipments that reached Augusta. Which came as a bit of a surprise, when Keeley thought about it. If the American military machine could not procure a little coffee for their Commander-in-Chief and her staff every now and then, how could they still claim to be the most powerful military force on the planet?

The lounge was empty. That made sense. There were so few people in Augusta now that the hospital probably saw little action. The television, flickering down on her from its room-dominating position near the ceiling, was thankfully muted. The camera cut rapidly between two men and one woman, all young and beautiful and vivacious, engaged in some discussion or debate. No doubt bickering and pontificating about Linda's announcement. There was nothing in Keeley that made her want to turn up the sound.

As expected, the coffeepot was empty and dry, but there was hot water and black tea. A pale substitute, in Keeley's opinion, but it would have to do. She made herself a cup and took the chair under the television to avoid the eye-catching monotony of the screen. The hot liquid soothed her throat and she exhaled a heavy cloud of exhaustion and worry. It was times like this that Keeley was glad she had developed an immunity to guilt and shame. Or perhaps she was simply too damned busy to indulge in such things. She'd done what she'd done, with good reason and the best intent. The fact that she'd been absent when Mary had fallen was nothing more than the result of those actions and intentions. There was no need for blame in any direction. There was no guarantee that, even had she been there, she'd have been able to prevent the fall. And there was no real way, in the end, to even know that Mary's fall was "bad." Painful, to be sure. Disturbing. Even frightening. But maybe it will end up being a "good" thing. Perhaps Mary will start resting more. Perhaps the doctors will find something they'd previously missed. In any event, it appeared that Mary was fine. The fall hadn't done any damage, and seemed to be nothing more than a fainting spell. For now, Keeley's love was unthreatened.

That was Keeley's darkest fear: that having found Mary, she would lose her, just as she had lost her first husband, Ken, and her second, Pooch. Just as she had lost... others. There was a delicacy about Mary that sometimes took Keeley's breath away, as if Mary had been granted a short secondment from the world of the dead to complete her work here before being whisked away again. And there were nights, in those restless, early-morning hours of fitful dozing, when it felt as though the countdown for her departure was ticking away. Agent Rice's blow to Mary's nose had pushed sharp shards of bone up into her brain, closing down some things, opening up others. She was prone to dizzy spells and balance problems. She often had a weird taste in her mouth. She needed little sleep and often found it difficult to find the words she wanted. And she had no filter whatsoever on her expression of emotions.

But the blow to Mary's brain severed something more essential, in Keeley's opinion. Somehow, it had cut her connection to her solid, flesh-and-blood-and-bones physicality, if such a thing were possible, leaving her little more than a ghost. It felt, at times, as though Keeley should be able to see right through her.

And yet it was Mary who could see right through people. The bone shards had opened up a new ability: Mary could see the human aura, the soul, what she, following the lead of Rupert Sheldrake, called, simply, "the field." And these fields were not just namby-pamby new-age rainbow light shows. Mary saw things. Real things. Thoughts, memories, desires and intentions. She saw futures and pasts and might-have-beens. She could feel right into the hearts of other human beings. She could know you completely. Like a goddess. Like a faerie. Like some advanced being from another galaxy. And sometimes what she saw scared the hell out of Keeley.

Keeley sipped at her tea. Perhaps this was what had pushed her out of her sleeper chair: Keeley was terrified by what Mary had told her. In her short time awake, before the sedatives had forced her to "rest comfortably," Mary had described what she'd seen in the kids' fields: the darkness reaching out, the pain, the fire, the falling.

Neither of them knew what those images meant. But both of them knew that something huge and horrible was now approaching them from the future.

2.3

Cole was ashamed, and he was ashamed that he was ashamed. Their lives were falling apart and here he was, hiding in his room, sobbing uncontrollably. These fits, these spells, these "hops," were taking over his life, coming at any hour of the day or night and leaving him emotionally drained and lost. But, dammit, he could not afford to be lost. Not now. Linda was being held in a maximum-security medical facility, and she was getting sicker by the day. His kids were confused and afraid. The world had gone to shit. And people were looking to him... to *him!*... for guidance and help. Cole, knocked to his knees by these soul-shattering trips across space and time, was too raw, too disoriented, and too overwhelmed with grief and pain, to offer much assistance. This was not who he knew himself to be.

This last hop still stung, like a knife stuck in his gut that he feared to remove. He'd been a lawyer. In some town out in the Wild West, it felt like. The cowboy days. He'd been sitting at his desk, reading a newspaper, when he heard a click behind him and felt something cold and hard push firmly against the back of his head. In the next instant he was floating free, looking down from above at his dead body sprawled on the floor, blood and brains spattered across his desk. And standing over him, a small, dark man with a missing eye. The man held a smoking gun. But the pain. The pain. Not his own, but the pain of that one-eyed man, the pain that had driven him to such anger and desperation. It was almost unbearable.

Cole grabbed an old cloth napkin – paper tissues no longer qualifying as an essential item - and dabbed at his face. He shuddered again, one last dry sob, then wiped his hands on his shirt and pushed himself to a sitting position on his and Linda's bed. The shame washed over him again. Christ! Lying in the dark and crying. He was of no use to anyone. The strength and calm he'd enjoyed these last few years had become a thing of the past.

The phone rang. Cole, startled, his heart pounding, called out into the darkness, a yelp of pure helplessness. When he realized what it was, he stood, walked across the room, found his phone in his jeans pocket, and answered.

"Yeah?" he said. He was the President's husband. He did not need to identify himself. Whomever had this number, and there were not many, knew exactly who he was.

There was a short pause and a single, delicate click. "Mr. Thomas?" came the voice at last. The voice had a warbled, buzzing quality. It was being electronically disguised. Cole was fairly certain it was a man.

"If you have this number then you know who this is," said Cole, his grief and shame fading as his irritation grew. "Why don't we start with who *you* are?"

The man cleared his throat. "Uh... that's one thing I can't tell you, Mr. Thomas,"

"Can I assume by the fact you have disguised your voice that I would know who you are if you hadn't?" asked Cole. He ran a hand absently over his smooth, well-muscled stomach.

There was a long pause. Cole considered just hanging up, but didn't. Linda was gone. There was too much he did not know. "I can't see it serving my purpose to answer that question one way or the other," said the man at last. The voice was so overlaid with buzzing that it took Cole a moment to register what he had said.

"I see, " said Cole. "And what purpose would that be?"

"To reunite you with your wife, Mr. Thomas."

Cole sat down at his desk and inhaled sharply.

"Are you that Fisherman guy?" asked Cole angrily. "Because if you are..."

The man on the phone waited for Cole to go quiet. "I'm afraid I have no idea who you are talking about, Mr. Thomas," he said. "What I can say is that I'm a friend, and that I might have a way for you to see the President."

Cole listened intently. There was something familiar about the voice. About the words used. Something. But Cole couldn't place it. He rubbed at his eyes and spoke again. "Okay," he said. "You've got my attention. So what's next?"

"For now, you simply say 'yes.' Then you wait. I will call you again."

Cole closed his eyes. "Okay," he muttered. "Yes."

"This will not be easy, you understand?" the man said. "And it may not work. I'll be putting myself at considerable risk."

"I understand," said Cole. "You must know that, should this succeed, we will take every measure to guarantee your safety."

"I'm counting on it," said the man. The phone clicked twice more and Cole thought the man had hung up, but then he spoke again. "I need you to know something else," he said.

"What's that?"

The man paused for a long moment, then spoke. "I think they're going to kill her, Mr. Thomas," he said at last. There was real fear in his voice. Or guilt. "I think... Cole... I think they're going to kill us all."

With that the man hung up. Cole closed his phone, tossed it on the desk, and buried his face in his hands. He knew he should think something. He knew he should feel something. But his heart and mind were both blank.

2.4

The words "have courage" lingered in Linda's mind as the virtual screen that had appeared overhead went dark and then vanished. Once again she was staring up at the yellow-pink Martian sky. She turned her head to the right, the only movement her body would make, and gazed out over the horizon. The distant mesa rose up from a flat plain, dark and shadowed. She had the feeling that she should know what it was she was looking at.

"They're very good, don't you think?" said the Fisherman.

Linda rolled her eyes toward the sound of the voice but saw no one. The Fisherman had yet to show himself. "I doubt they'll get away with it."

The Fisherman chuckled softly. "That, of course, is one of the more entertaining facets of this entire enterprise," he said, his voice that of a kindly English uncle. "The Directorate decided the technology was ready. A few remain doubtful. We'll soon enough see who was correct."

"And how will that be determined?" asked Linda.

The Fisherman's voice came close to the President's ear. "Your middle child, Emily, has already found them out!" he said, his voice filled with glee.

Linda's heart began to pound at the mention of the kids. Where were they? *How* were they? How was Cole? And how would they ever get back together again? By calling Emily *her* "middle child," the Fisherman had reached in and grabbed her heart at its most tender spot. *Her* child? Were they really her children? She'd tried. She wanted that so badly. And yet she'd been gone so much. There'd been too much to do. The needy, unraveling world had swallowed her up and spit her back out, used and exhausted and near despair. And now she'd been taken away...

Once again, the need for information asserted itself. There would be no way out of this if she did not know what "this" was. "Are they...?" she asked. She couldn't even say it.

"As of now they are fine," said the Fisherman. "Confused, to be sure, but essentially unharmed. The Families have made no move against them. There has been no need. As far as your people are concerned, you are being kept in a biocontainment facility situated near your old summer cottage on Squirrel Island. They're worried about your health. And they are angry at whomever it is they believe has locked you up. Your staff has been quite put out by the whole affair and has worked tirelessly to reestablish free and clear communication with you. The Families, of course, will prevent this."

"But you said Emily-"

"Has found them out, yes," finished the Fisherman. "Or at least she's on their trail, even if she has yet to comprehend the reality of the situation. I await her next move with unmitigated delight. She's an extraordinary child."

"Will it do any good if I threaten to kill you if you so much as harm a single hair on the kids' heads?" asked Linda.

The Fisherman chuckled warmly. "You forget that I'm the one who has rescued you, Madam President," he said.

"Well, that's your story," said Linda. "I have no way to judge its truth."

"In time..." said the Fisherman.

Linda closed her eyes. The Martian daylight was strangely stressful to her eyes. The colors were all wrong. "So, if I've got this straight, the 'reality of the situation,' as you put it, is that I was kidnapped from my home and sedated by some hidden group whom you refer to as 'The Families.' At that point, they substituted a computer-generated version of me, in order to pretend that, while I am ill, I am still in charge. And once they had that up and running, they were going to kill me. But you came in and stole me away and brought me here to Mars to keep me safe." Linda's voice had grown cold and angry as she spoke. "Does that pretty much sum things up?"

"Your brilliant précis fails to capture the full reality of your opponents, Madam President," said the Fisherman evenly, "but is otherwise correct in the essentials. Your abduction was the work of those who serve the dominant faction of The Families. You might take it as a sign of respect and admiration on the part of your adversaries, that they saw the need to contain you before they put their plans into motion. But there were many of us who were against the move. Hence my rebellious intervention. The Families have become quite divided these days, both in goals and in strategies."

Linda opened her eyes. "So you're a member of these 'Families'?" she asked.

"Born and raised, as you Americans like to say," answered the Fisherman.

Linda paused for a moment. She wanted so badly to reach up and touch her own face, but could not. "So I'm not really sick?" she asked at last.

"The 'alien flu,' as the press has been instructed to call it, is merely the ruse adopted to fend off any and all demands for a face-to-face meeting with you, Madam. Such a meeting would lie beyond their current abilities to simulate. Who, after all, can trump the priesthood of scientists and physicians purporting to care for you? And surely no one can argue with the need for complete containment of this most menacing unknown virus. Who would even *want* to risk exposing themselves to such a thing? By restricting access to your virtual counterpart to chats, emails, and the occasional phone call or videoconference, The Families exercise complete control over your continued presence in the affairs of state. You have not been abducted and murdered, Madam President. Not in the eyes of the world. Instead, you are being helped through a frightening and most unfortunate crisis. Cared for. Protected." The Fisherman stopped himself and went silent for a moment before continuing in a lighter voice. "In any event, no, you are quite well, Madam. Quite well indeed."

Linda scoffed. "Except for the fact that I'm trapped in this lobster tank on the Martian surface and am unable to move. None of which makes any sense at all." Linda inhaled deeply and stared out across the plain. The day was fading. Already there were stars rising above the distant hill. "You couldn't have just hidden me away in a cheap motel?" she asked. "I mean, really? Mars? How did we get here? What's with this coffin? Why can't I move?" As she spoke, Linda's heart had begun to pound. She realized she was furious.

The Fisherman's voice moved closer. She could almost feel his hot breath as he whispered into her ear. "Times are so urgent we have to ask our questions three at time, don't we?" he said, his tone low and full of power.

Linda froze. Those were Obie's words. Words from their long discussion in the trailer a whole lifetime ago. And the fact that the Fisherman knew those words disturbed her deeply.

2.5

"So you're telling me it's contained," said Colonel McAfee, pressing.

Paul DuPont pushed himself back from the table, shaking his head and rolling his eyes. "We don't get guarantees, Colonel," he said. "Not in this game. This is new territory we're exploring."

McAfee took off his reading glasses and rubbed his eyes. "Yeah, yeah. I got it. Nobody's ever done this before. What I want is your assessment. Your *opinion*," he said the word with obvious distaste. He put his glasses back on and peered peevishly at his Chief Tech. "Gimme you best guess, here, cowboy. Is this thing handled or isn't it?"

"I think it is, yes," said DuPont, nodding. "I drove her last chat myself. With her husband, just before he went to bed. When he asked about the mole, I grabbed the wheel from the AI and took over. Told him how Linda's skin is all blotchy from the virus, but that her old mole is still right where it has always been. Told him how bad she thought she looked when she watched herself on the video later, how poorly the camera captured the reality of her actual condition. It was a wonder Cole could tell it was her at all, she said, what with her skin changing and getting worse every day. He'll be so afraid now he won't be thinking clearly. And without him on board, his kids will just give it up."

McAfee leaned back in his chair and stretched his arms over his head. He pulled a toothpick from his shirt pocket and stuck it in his teeth. "But there are no guarantees," he said. He raised an eyebrow. "You said so yourself."

The Chief Tech shook his head. "No, Colonel. As I said..."

McAfee waved him off. "So tell me about the mole," he said.

DuPont opened a folder on his desktop and clicked on a file. "It was done on purpose," he said. The document he needed opened on the screen.

"What?" said the Colonel in disbelief.

DuPont nodded his confident assurance that he knew what he was talking about. "Yep. One of the skin guys in Facial Modeling..." he checked the screen, "... a guy named Evans. Young kid. Fresh out of college. He..." DuPont stopped to consult the document again.

"You're not gonna make me torture you for the story here, are you?" said the Colonel. He leaned back in his chair and cradled his head in his intertwined fingers.

DuPont put on a blank face and waited for the Colonel to settle into his chair. "Evans says he was *told* to move the mole. About two weeks ago, after final faces had all been signed off on. Said Stu Tollerman himself called him on the phone and ordered the change. Something about needing a quick way to ID the VLT in media coverage. To tell the Virtual from the Real."

"And Tollerman?"

"Denies it completely."

"Of course he does." McAfee sighed deeply and pulled out the toothpick. "And this Evans kid didn't realize how absurd that request was?"

DuPont smiled slightly, hoping he could generate a bit of empathy for the guilty party. This kid didn't need to be scapegoated for this. "He's young, Colonel," he said. "Got the job because of his famous uncle."

"Sid Evans? Air Force?"

DuPont nodded.

"Jesus," muttered McAfee. He poked at his teeth, digging between a couple of molars. He stared at the ceiling.

"So do we move it back?" asked the Chief Tech at last.

McAfee glanced at DuPont, his head slightly cocked in disbelief. "The mole? Hell no, cowboy. You leave that mole where it is, add the original back in, and then start blotching her up a bit more. Let's just stick with the plan, but do it correctly. You savvy? Use the rash to cover any facial distortions we might miss. And make sure the video quality is degraded the next few times we see her. Blame it on sunspots or something."

DuPont closed the document on his desktop but said nothing.

"Does the kid understand the gravity of what happened?"

"He does now, Colonel." DuPont kept his face neutral as he regarded his boss. The last thing he wanted was for the blame to blow-back on his crew when the kid was just following orders.

"He needs to be transferred," said McAfee. He tossed his wet toothpick onto the DuPont's desk and stood.

The Chief Tech opened his mouth to protest, then bit off his words. He swiped the screen and brought back the primary control interface. "Colonel?" he said.

"I'm listening," said McAfee as he walked toward the door.

"One more thing."

The Colonel stopped and turned. "Spit it out, kid," he said. "I'm way overdue for some shuteye."

"I'm sure you'd have thought of this on your own, Colonel," said DuPont, sure of no such thing, "but, well, *somebody* told Evans to do this. So don't we now have to deal with the possibility that we have a *real* mole somewhere in the operation?"

Colonel McAfee glowered at his Chief Technician with tight, squinted eyes. "I'll speak with Tollerman," he said at last. He turned, opened the door, and left.

DuPont stared after the man who believed he was the boss, wondering how such a dullard had been put in charge of such critical projects. He hoped that the good Colonel would be left behind for the Second Wave.

2.6

Grace was fairly sure that she was not sleepwalking. Iain had done that a few times and he never remembered a bit of it. But Grace felt fully awake and aware. She was just not in control of her body. But that wasn't really true. She could reach up to scratch her nose if she wanted to, and she did. If she wanted, she could turn around and go back to bed. She just didn't want to. She wanted to go to Emily's room. She wanted to do that more than anything.

Her door closed with a soft click and she hurried down the carpeted hallway, careful not to make a sound. She didn't want to make a sound any more than she wanted to turn around and go back to bed. She wanted to be really, really quiet.

She came to Emily's door, opened it, and slid inside. Emily's heavy breathing rose above the silence of the night like soft ocean waves. Grace used the sound to navigate through the dark room to the side of Emily's bed. She reached out and flicked on the bedside lamp, then placed a hand on Emily's face. "Em!" she whispered. Emily stirred. "Emily!" whispered Grace again.

Emily opened her eyes with a start. "What?" she said, so loud that Grace put a finger to her lips to shush her. Emily brought the heels of her hands up to rub her eyes, then spoke again in a hushed tone. "What?"

"Alice is back," said Grace.

Emily pushed herself up onto one elbow and looked around the room. "Where?" she said.

Grace pointed at her head. "In my dreams," she replied.

Emily frowned. "Gracie," she said, her voice tinged with frustration. "Alice is -"

"Alice spoke to me in my dream," said Grace. "We have to get Iain."

Emily shook her head in confusion. "Why?" she said.

Grace switched off the bedside lamp and headed back toward the door. She opened it, then turned back, silhouetted against the dim hallway lighting. "Because I know what we have to do," she said, her voice just loud enough to carry to her sister. Grace closed the door and headed to Iain's room.

She really, really wanted to go speak with her brother now.

2.7

Stan Walsh muttered a curse, threw off his covers, and swung his long, skinny legs over the edge of his bed. Grabbing his clothes from the floor, he made his way carefully across the darkened room, steadying himself against the dizziness of exhaustion with a hand on the wall. He found the knob and slipped quietly out of the room, hoping for a moment that the sound of the fan would cover the click of the latch before remembering that he no longer had to worry about waking his poor Loretta, gone almost two years now. Stan sighed and headed down the hallway. He needed coffee from his private stash. He needed time to think.

The first inklings of dawn peered through the front door of his modest house like curious children, throwing enough light on the steps for Stan to make his way down to the first floor. He glanced through the window at his front yard, gray and dry, and the Kennebec River beyond, noting the fading Gridlight and the regular military patrols. All seemed in order: a warm, quiet spring morning in downtown Augusta, Maine. Scratching at his large, red nose, he stepped into the kitchen to put the kettle on, then continued on to his home office. He sat at his desk and closed his eyes.

The jet that had buzzed them last night was personal, and Stan knew it. A warning. A threat. From those who now controlled Linda Travis. Stan had pressed them again on the President, demanding free access, demanding an explanation, demanding... something. But he had been shut down completely, treated like a child who asked too many questions. As if the Secretary of Homeland Security had no right to answers and information. As if he could do his job without free and direct access to his boss. As if he could not be trusted. When "national security" is the excuse used to keep even DHS out of the loop, you know things are out of whack.

Stan was a Navy man. Past sixty now, but his tall, barrel-chested body was still strong and in good shape. He believed in such things as honor, loyalty, duty, and service. He believed that good people could make a difference in the world. And he believed that he, his President, and her cabinet, were good people who had been trying to do just that. But it had been a losing game from the get-go. There was no "winning" when crops died and dollars disappeared and the gas dried up at the pump. No winning for a politician, anyways. Progressives had scoffed when Bush Senior had said that "the American way of life is not up for negotiation," but when the consequences of centuries and millennia of unsustainable living finally caught up with them, it turned out that, deep in their hearts, most of them had believed in that statement just as much as their President had. They needed somebody on whom they could pin the blame. Linda had been the most convenient target, especially since her great "revelation" on national television after the sinking of D.C. She and her "alien friends" and their inscrutable Grid. Signs and portents in the sky and all that rot, with Pastor Jeremiah Clinton in the front row, leading the shouting.

Now Linda has thrown her hat into the ring again. And she'll probably win, he thought, if for no other reason than that the American people will want her to suffer the consequences of the mess they think she created. He scoffed. As if a few well-meaning human beings could control a climate spiraling out of control, or the amount of oil left in the ground, or an economy built on delusions. As if...

But this flu she'd contracted, that was the game changer. And it had come from so far out of left field that Stan was still reeling. Linda could die from this virus, according to the medical reports. That was the long and short of it. And there were only a few people in the world who understood, as he did, that Linda was probably still the best real leader, and the best friend, that the nation could ever have. Stan shuddered at the prospect of her loss. He could not imagine someone else filling her shoes. Not now. Not when civilization itself was crumbling. America was one step away from barbarity, as far as Stan could see. One step away from every horrible dystopian future ever imagined in books and movies. One step away from utter madness. And the consensus was that this coming summer would see the first Arctic "blue ocean event" in human history. God save them all, should Linda Travis stumble and fall.

The laptop on his desk pinged and Stan waved his hand to awaken the screen. There was an email from Keeley. Stan smirked. So she couldn't sleep either. Stan opened the mail to find five short words - "Just saw this on ACN" - and a link to a video. He clicked the link and watched.

The report was short and relatively free of speculation. A new crop circle had appeared, in a field of wild grasses on a small and windswept island off the coast of New Zealand. What made it noteworthy was the fact that this was the first crop formation to be found anywhere on the globe since the Grid appeared. What made it stunning, to Stan, was that the formation was the same circle bisected by an inverted L that he'd first seen almost two and a half years ago, inscribed into the marble countertop of the President's post-revelation hideaway in Vermont. He did not know what this symbol meant. Neither did Linda or Cole, who had seen it before. Neither had any of the analysts or theorists who - in the years since she'd confronted the secret organization known as "The People" and their alien cover-up - had attempted to discern the reality behind their President's reported experiences. All he knew was that nobody understood, and Stan Walsh did not like things that could not be understood.

Stan startled. The kettle was screaming. He rose to go make his coffee.

2.8

Nighttime on Mars was breathtaking. The stars hung like fireworks frozen in glass, their color and clarity like nothing Linda had ever seen, their brightness casting an eerie glow over the surrounding terrain. Directly overhead, an even brighter object moved steadily against the background stars. Probably one of Mars's moons. Domos? Phoebus? Something like that? She could not remember.

Linda craned her neck to peer off to her left. Before leaving to "check in on things at home," the Fisherman had granted her the ability to move her head back and forth from right to left, increasing her "allowable range of motions," as he put it, "by one degree of freedom."

For reasons she did not fully comprehend, granting her complete freedom to move her body would threaten the integrity of what the Fisherman called "the container." It was not glass at all, he'd said, but energy, and he was uncertain of its stability. And as it was all that kept her from the "nasty demise" that would most certainly claim her should she find herself suddenly unprotected on the Martian surface, he trusted she would understand the necessity for her confinement. Linda hoped that, one day, should he find himself unprotected in *her* presence back on Earth, he would understand the necessity of her throwing his ass in prison. She smiled at the thought of that.

The "container" appeared to lie in the middle of a vast, flat, reddish-brown, dusty plain, with various low hills and sharp mountains poking up in the distance on either side of her. Some of the mountains were huge, and all of them stood relatively alone, rather than together in a range. One of them appeared to be a pyramid. As the tiny sun had set in a blaze of blue, the mountains had shone like bonfires, demanding her attention. Linda could not shake the feeling that she had seen those hills and mountains before.

A memory of Cole arose in her mind and Linda's heart began to ache. He'd been so happy. Using his connections as "the First Gentleman," he'd obtained a used but working iTab to give Emily for her birthday. He knew she'd be ecstatic, as her previous tablet had died months before and new ones were no longer to be had. He'd wrapped it in newspaper and hidden it in their bedroom closet, to give to his daughter the next day. But the next day was the day Linda had been taken away.

That was the hardest part now: not being able to reach out to Cole and the kids. Not knowing how they were. Knowing they must be worrying about her. Knowing they were being manipulated by those who had created her virtual doppelgänger. The confinement was bearable. She felt no physical pain. And the Fisherman had promised to soon release her from "the prison of materiality," whatever that meant. But there were untold millions of miles now between her and the people she loved. The strings of her heart had been stretched to the point of breaking.

Linda moved her head slowly from side to side, taking in the splendor of the Cosmos one more time, reaching out with her thoughts, with her love, hoping, in some dimension beyond this realm of stone and dust, that her heart was touching theirs. Then she closed her eyes. This vast Martian plain, though beautiful, was the loneliest place she'd ever seen. Perhaps, in sleep, perhaps in dreams, she could find some comfort.

2.9

"Do we need to bring anything?" asked Iain. He grabbed his watch from his desk and strapped it around his wrist.

Grace shook her head. "Not where we're going," she said. "Just don't drink anything. We don't know how long this will take."

"We don't get a pee break?" Iain smiled.

Emily stood and walked to the window to scan the wooded grounds that surrounded the Presidential Home. The Grid was fading in the pre-dawn sky. "It's getting light out," she said.

Iain checked his watch. "It's still only 6:15," he said.

"Ness'll be up," said Grace. "And she's the one who should take us."

"Will Mary be awake?" asked Iain.

"We're not actually going to see Mary," Grace said.

Iain scrunched his forehead in confusion. "And how are we going to pull that off, Gracie?" he asked.

Grace smiled slyly. "Ness has been drinking tea since she got up," she said. "And she *will* need a pee break."

Iain nodded slowly as understanding came to him. Emily pulled the curtains closed and headed for the door. She looked at her brother and sister. All three of them were dressed in sturdy jeans and t-shirts and tennis shoes, as if going on a hike. "You guys ready?" she asked as she turned the handle.

Grace closed her eyes. The image of Alice still hovered in her mind, beckoning. Alice was older now. Older than it seemed she should be. A strange, beautiful teenager. But it was undeniably Alice. And Grace knew that Alice had a plan, even if they didn't know what it was. "Ready," she said, inhaling deeply.

The three of them headed down to the kitchen.

2.10

"*That's not a word,*" *said Carl.*
"*Yes it is,*" *said Ted.*
"*Musth?*" *said Carl.* "*What the hell is a musth?*"
Ted grinned like a rogue. "*It's a word,*" *he said.*
"*What does it mean?*"
"*The rules of this game don't require me to tell you that,*" *said Ted.*
Carl scooted his metal folding chair back from the card table and stretched his arms over his head. He surveyed the bare room: four walls, a floor, a ceiling, a table, two chairs, and a Scrabble game. In one corner was a door that would not open. That was the whole of their Universe. "*They should have given us a dictionary,*" *he said in a musing tone.*
"*They who?*" *asked Ted.*
Carl lifted his shoulders. "*I don't know,*" *he said.*

Chapter Ø Three

3.1

Gabrielle's guts churned like a washing machine, cold and wet and hard. The note she'd found on her floor when she got up, the note she'd crumpled and tossed away and retrieved and stuffed into her jeans pocket, the note clearly written in her own loopy hand, the note she did not remember writing, burned at her awareness, hot and demanding and terrifying, as though it were a chunk of nuclear waste she carried, rather than a piece of paper. The food in the cafeteria was hard enough to eat on the best of days. There was no way she'd be able to stomach it now. Not with her heart pounding like this. Not with this dread pulsing through her veins. Not until she read the damned note.

She took a sip of her coffee and pulled the paper from her pocket, wondering vaguely why her fingers were so stiff and sore. The note slipped happily from her pocket. She tossed it onto the table before her with a shudder of distaste, as she might a dead bug she'd found on her plate. The paper lay there, folded and crumpled and smiling smugly, as if content to wait all day. Gabrielle stabbed a forkful of pasty pancake but then put her fork back down. With a muttered curse she picked up the paper and unfolded it.

It was the same as before, the same as it had been for over a week now: first person present tense, the scene unfolding in a lively way, the words restoring to memory a dream she hadn't remembered that she'd had. She was there, watching it happen and writing it down. She was there. And so was the tall, thin man with red hair.

Around us is a vast plain, dark and lifeless, with impossibly huge machines moving noisily in the distance, pushing, pulling, digging, loading. Smoke rises into the sky in dozens of places, wispy tendrils of black and gray. They remind me of offerings on an altar. I do not know why. His back to me, the thin man stands and gazes out over the plain. He sobs loudly, his shoulder blades hunching forward and back like the stubs of wings. When he turns to face me, I see that his face is wet with tears. His lips form a quivering O. He opens his hands in helpless despair but says nothing. Behind him the impossible machines cough and scrape.

"Will you tell me your name?" I ask. If these meetings are going to continue, I need to understand them. The thin man jerks away as if he's been slapped, then slowly returns to me. It feels like my question stuns him in some way. As if the last thing he expects from me is kindness, or even interest.

The thin man smiles momentarily in his strange, robotic way. "I have been called Zacharael," he says. His voice is soft and muffled with tears. Gentle. Open. I have no sense that he wishes to harm me.

"Why do you come to me?" I ask, casting further for answers. "Why do you show me these things?"

Zacharael looks down at the abused ground at his feet, then directly into my eyes. "I am trying to break your heart," he says. One of the machines, its huge shovel rising before it like the jaws of a tyrannosaur, turns and approaches us, moving more quickly than I would have guessed it could. Zacharael steps forward and takes my hand and we are at once hovering in the depths of space.

I should not be alive. The hard vacuum should have killed me instantly. But I feel comfortable and whole. The thin man, Zacharael, hovers beside me. The stars blaze cold and bright all around us, familiar in their configuration yet strange in their clarity. The closest star, the size of a housefly at arm's length, bathes me with its radiance. I sense that this is our own sun. Underfoot, sliding slowly beneath us like some vast whale in the black ocean of space, moves a huge rocky sphere, dirty white and pocked with holes. It tumbles unhurriedly forward like a slow-motion snowball rolling downhill. I cannot guess how big it is. There is no way to tell.

Before I can ask another question Zacharael reaches out and takes my hand again. Now we are zooming over the Earth, our bodies hori-

zontal and close to the water, as if we are Superman and Lois Lane. A vast stretch of sunlit ocean sparkles underneath. And ahead of us is a small island, rocky and green. We slow as we near the island, rising up for a better view from above. Zacharael points and I follow his finger. In the tall grasses that cover the gently rolling ground, I see a symbol of some sort. One of those crop circles, though this is not a field of wheat. The symbol is huge, a perfect circle, with a capital L running right through the center. I turn to ask Zacharael what it means, but he is gone. In his place I see a shiny black sphere the size of a grapefruit. I fall toward the ground and am gone.

Gabrielle placed the paper gently on the table before her and bowed her head, noting then the tears that dropped from her eyes. She knew that those were Zacharael's tears. Not hers. The strange, tall man had given them to her. He was trying to break her heart.

The clock on the cafeteria wall said six thirty-seven. Less than an hour and a half before her eight o'clock lecture and she had yet to do her homework. She grabbed the note and stuffed it into her backpack, then grabbed her fork and stuffed the bite of pancake into her mouth, determined not to think of Zacharael and tears and crop circles and comets tumbling through space. Determined to ignore this until it went away. Whoever this man was, whatever it was he wanted, however it was he could come to her in the night and show her these things, Gabrielle was certain of one thing: he was a friend of her father's. He had to be.

And that made him her enemy.

3.2

Cole remembered the pre-dawn light that seeped in around his window shade. He remembered getting up to use the toilet. He remembered flicking on the bathroom light. But then he was lost to himself, his life once again hijacked by another. He was a young woman, married, with a child at her breast. And she was in horrible trouble.

The herbs had worked, and Lady Guthry's eldest, James, had recovered quickly, as Agnes had known he would. But the madness of North Berwick had spread across the countryside like wildfire as James VI's persecutions continued. Agnes' healing cures had worked too well, too quickly. It was miracle and magic. It was of the Devil. The mutterings had begun almost at once. The raised eyebrows. The turning away. And then came the accusation. Witchcraft had come to Lankirk.

So quickly it had started. So slowly it had played out. Her baby crying. Her husband, attempting to fight off the constable and priests, knocked senseless and falling to his knees. The ropes and manacles. The squalor of the Tolbooth. The torture of the bridle and the turcas and the pear. The insistence on confession. The Devil's mark found on her shoulder. The trial. When it was done, Agnes had confessed to acts of evil ranging from the poisoning of the Earl's prized heifer to leading a treasonous conspiracy against her king. The madness had picked her up and carried her to her doom, a powerful wave she could neither fight nor flee. Before the wave was spent, it would carry her husband and daughter to their doom as well.

The faces of those she had known and loved were twisted with fear and fury as she was led to the stake. She could not voice her protestations. Her tongue had been cut out, so as to prevent her from spreading her evil to the watching crowd. She was lashed to a pile of dry tinder and stripped to the waist. A thick, scratchy rope was looped around her neck from behind and slowly tightened until she was dead. Agnes watched from above as they set light to the wood beneath her body, watched as her flesh was reduced to ash and bone. The pain of her body was gone by then, but the pain in the hearts of those who had tortured, strangled, and burned her body rang inside Cole as he woke again on the bathroom floor. Weeks had passed, it seemed, but it had only been minutes. The dawn had not yet come.

Cole lay panting and shivering on the cool tile, his pajamas wet with urine and sweat. His chest heaved with great silent sobs as his heart worked to expel the experience from his body. As the pain flowed, it picked up other pains, a glacier of old hurt moving inexorably to the sea. These past years with Linda had been harder than he could have imagined, even as their marriage had grown and blossomed in joy and trust and vulnerability. Their strange and trying times with the Strangers, and with the hidden forces that had been working with these so-called "aliens," had left them full of self-doubt, and unsure of reality itself. Nothing had been found in the sinkholes left behind. No woks. No alien machinery. No strange bodies. The "aliens" had vanished, leaving nothing in the real world to which Cole and Linda and the kids could bind their memories. And The People, the humans most directly involved with the aliens, had simply disappeared, melting back into the general population like ice cubes on a hot sidewalk. The accusations and ridicule had risen to a fever pitch, only to burn even hotter as the Christmas Crash unfolded and the country sank into a depression so fierce that "the great one" paled in comparison. Linda has been called names and threatened with both impeachment and assassination. Cole and his children had been ridiculed and harassed. Pastor Clinton brayed that they were all in league with "the mighty Satan himself." And Linda had been away from home so much...

The sobs at last fell to gentle heaves and Cole took a long, cooling breath. A soft knocking sounded at the outer door and Cole swiped the tears from his face with the palm of his hand. Afraid that someone had heard his cries, he pushed himself up onto his elbow and grabbed the edge of the sink to go see who it was. As he pulled himself to his feet, he slipped on the wet tile and fell backward, his arms wheeling wildly about but failing to find a hold. His head smashed down on the toilet, breaking not only the seat but crushing and splitting the bowl itself, as though his skull were a concrete block. Toilet water spilled out onto the floor, mixing with the sweat and urine. Rolling over onto his hands and knees, Cole crawled through the door to the relative safety of his carpeted bedroom. He pushed himself to his feet and stripped off his wet pajamas.

He spied himself in the large mirror over the dresser and stepped forward to examine himself, rubbing at the back of his head and neck. There was no damage. No blood. No cuts. No residual soreness. Cole realized that the fall had not hurt him at all. As if his head really were made of cement.

But that was not all. From the palms of his hands came brief eruptions of pure white light.

3.3

Their security escort took up position at the front door as Ness and the kids headed toward the main desk. The hospital was a secure facility, patrolled at all points of the exterior, including the air and the river nearby, and regularly patrolled within. There was no need for Agent Burke to accompany them to Mary's room. The nurses weren't going to release Mary this early unless her doctor okayed it, and Dr. Gholson was dealing with an emergency out beyond the cordon. They wanted some private time with their friend.

Ness, Iain, Emily, and Grace stopped at the main desk and found out that Mary was just down the hall, at the end on the right. "I gotta pee, loves," said Ness as they passed the visitor lounge. She stopped at the ladies' room door and turned. "I'll meet you there in a sec." With a wink, she ducked inside and closed the door.

With a quick exchange of glances, Cole's three children headed down the hall and then turned and passed quickly through a pair of double doors on the left. Iain pulled a folded piece of paper from his jeans pocket and placed it in the middle of the floor. Breathing deeply, hoping to look as though they knew exactly where they were going, they hurried into the stairwell and headed down the stairs. On the one hand, they *did* know exactly where they were going. But of course, in retrospect, they could never have anticipated where they would end up.

3.4

Colonel McAfee plucked a bit of lint from his uniform as he walked down the hallway. He rubbed the short bristles of dyed-black hair on his head. When the aliens went on the lam and The People dissolved, it was this haircut and this uniform, more than anything else, that had saved him from ruin. Gone was the long blonde hair. Gone was the surfer vibe and the torn blue jeans. Gone was his former name: Phelps. Now he was Colonel Aidan McAfee. Career Army. Spit and Polish. Honor and Discipline and everything that went with it. And the General, bless his heart, had somehow pulled some strings for him. McAfee had been put in charge of Operation Changeling.

And what a precious piece of cake was this gig! Long walks on rocky beaches. Beautiful views of both bay and deep ocean. Seafood up the ever-lovin' wazoo. Even with a buzz cut and military threads, McAfee could still appreciate such things. Though he longed for the sandals and shorts in this unseasonably hot weather - the Phelps persona being closer to who he knew himself to be - he found that he didn't really need them. It was rather fun, being incognito. And there was way more job security in a uniform.

And the duty? What was there to do but watch over the old girl in deep freeze and hold the reins on his techs? Changeling got every bit of funding a high-tech, top secret, extra-military program needed and deserved, and then some. The project was being personally overseen by members of The Families themselves. Colonel McAfee smiled at the thought of it. Maybe he'd get a ticket after all.

Unless this mole thing took a wrong turn. Tollerman and Evans had checked out, their stories confirmed by wholebody scans while he'd questioned them. That meant that somebody else, somebody with access and motive, had interfered with their operations. Why anyone would go to that much trouble simply to move a tiny facial blemish on the President's virtual face McAfee could not imagine. That it had alerted the President's children felt like a bad joke, and it seemed impossible that it was all connected. McAfee's security office had no idea how to proceed. So far, his people had found no track or trace of the telephone call Evans had claimed to receive, though there was a telltale hole in the qputer's mematrix from the day and time in question that could have resulted from an excision. But, Christ, who could wipe data from a qputer? McAfee had no idea. He just wished the whole affair would go away. The last thing he wanted to have to do was report it up the food chain.

He turned down a side hall, passed a pair of guards, and returned their brisk salute. He came to the elevator and pushed the button to go down to the basement lab where the President had been iced. It wasn't like the old girl hadn't asked for it. You can't expect to work against The Families for long without drawing fire. Especially not now. Word was that their timetable had been scrapped and that they were preparing for an all-out assault. The Grid must have changed everything. That and the Life's disappearance. They did not need a wild card like Linda Travis mucking things up at this point. Not when they were so close. She had to be replaced or controlled. That was where Project Changeling came in.

The elevator came to a stop and the door slid open. McAfee headed down the hallway to the left, thankful for how cool it was belowground. He had never expected to see the fruition of The Families' centuries-long project. He wasn't sure he fully understood what the fruition would *be*. And after Rice's failure and the sinking of D.C., he was not at all sure he'd be one of the chosen. But all bets were off now. Seems that Spud had forced their hand. Hence the Crash. Hence the Quietus. Hence the need to go online with Changeling, glitches and all. Maybe, just maybe, if he was smart, and if they pulled this charade off with no more mistakes, Aidan McAfee would get his ticket stamped after all.

The Colonel passed through the final checkpoint and swiped his wrist over the iDent reader to get into the viewing room. There lay the President, just as he'd left her a few days ago, her body encased in a glass container that sat on a black pedestal. The blinking lights and beeping monitors told him that all was as it should be, even though he didn't fully understand what any of them meant. Liquids still dripped into her chilled body through an IV in her arm. Soft blue lights still slowly scanned her naked body from head to toe. He did not know if she was still scheduled for destruction. That was not his concern. He just knew that she was still alive. That *was* his concern.

He yawned, noting that three hours of sleep was not enough, and promising to himself, yet again, to lay off the alcohol. He stepped to the touch-pad on the operator panel and took control of the camera. With the awkward, jerky movements of one who had only done this a few times, he flew the camera in for a close-up. After two attempts, he was able to fill the screen with her head. He adjusted the focus and whistled softly in wonder. Her mole really *was* on the left side.

3.5

"Hi, Sweet Pea," said Ness as she stepped into Mary's room. Mary rolled onto her back as Ness came to her bedside. Ness leaned over and gave Mary a hug and a kiss on the cheek. She looked around the room. "Where're the kids?" she asked.

"Hi, Ness," said Mary with a tired smile. "I haven't seen them." Her eyes felt crusty and dull. There must still be sedatives in her bloodstream. "Did you guys come to pick me up?"

"Sure did, love," said Ness, settling her tiny body into the chair at Mary's feet. "Just waiting on the A-Okay from the doc." Ness raised an eyebrow and glanced toward the door. "You sure the kids didn't come in?"

Mary frowned, an expression that highlighted the faint scar on her forehead. "I've been right here, Ness. They didn't come in." She pushed herself up onto her elbows and pulled herself around, propping her back on her pillow. She took a moment to smooth her hair, a short bob of dark brown that sometimes fell across her eyes. Something felt off. "Is Keeley here?" she asked.

Ness rose and went to the door, shaking her head. "She was here most of the night, hon," she said over her shoulder as she stepped into the hall to watch for the kids. She turned back to Mary. "She's home now getting some sleep."

"Any sign of 'em?" asked Mary. Her face had darkened to worry. The image of Iain falling appeared in her mind and then faded away to fog.

"I'm sure they're fine," said Ness, returning to her chair. "This place is locked down tighter than a Supermax. They're probably raiding the vending machines."

"There's nothing *in* the vending machines," said Mary. She reached over to grab the button that would buzz for the nurses. "I'm going to have... security... find them and bring them here," she said. These children were her responsibility.

Ness rose and walked to the door again. "They're probably right outside," she said, hopefully. The door swung inward before Ness could touch the handle. Ness took a step back. In walked the morning nurse and a soldier, a tall, blonde, black-skinned private with a piece of paper in his hand. A tag with the name "Curtis" was stitched above the left shirt pocket of his fatigues.

Private Curtis ignored Ness and walked to Mary's bedside. "Are you Mary Hayes, Ma'am?" he asked. "In charge of the President's children?"

Mary nodded. "I am."

"We have a problem," said Private Curtis. He handed her the paper.

Mary read the note, inhaled sharply, and read it again out loud. *"Dear Mary. Alice has returned and is going to help us find Linda. She came in a wok and took us away in it so don't try to find us because we are long gone. And don't worry because we're fine. Alice will take care of us and you know Alice is good. Tell Ness we're sorry we had to ditch her. We'll be back as soon as we can. Iain, Emily, and Grace."* Mary closed her eyes for a moment to take a deep breath, then looked up at the private. "You've already started a search?" she asked.

"They're the President's children," answered Curtis, his tone saying "of course." He glanced at Ness with a puffed-up expression of disdain, as if the military had already passed judgment on the woman who had allowed the children to "ditch her." He returned his attention to the President's Senior Advisor. "The perimeter has been locked down," he explained. "The CO says-"

From outside the hospital came the piercing whine of an ambulance siren. The morning nurse's pager beeped and she excused herself and hurried out the door. Private Curtis nodded respectfully to Mary and followed the nurse, stepping into the hallway to see what was going on.

There was a distant slamming of doors and a shout. Mary threw back her covers and rolled slowly to a sitting position. Feeling no dizziness, she slipped over the bed's edge to touch her feet to the ground. She stood up to grab her folded clothes from the corner table and then sat again to pull on her jeans.

"I'm sorry," said Ness, still standing near the door, shocked into immobility by the Private's glaring eyes. "I don't know-"

"Please don't take that on," said Mary as she pulled her silk blouse down over her head. She regarded Ness with understanding eyes. "It's not your fault and you know it." She reached down for her shoes and pulled them on.

"But I was supposed to be watching them."

Mary stood, walked over to Ness, and wrapped the tiny, older woman in her arms. "Our responsibility now is to find them," she said softly. "We don't have time to indulge our old wounds." With a quick kiss to Ness's cheek, she pulled away and headed toward the door.

Out in the hall, an orderly pushed a gurney through a set of double doors near the nurse's station. A small crowd of medical and emergency personnel followed along, calling out vital signs, opinions, and orders. On the gurney lay a middle-aged man in a business suit, heavyset and balding. His cheeks and forehead were flushed with pink. Through the crosstalk, Mary could just make out his soft mutterings. "My love," he said, his face calm and beatific. "Alas... alas."

3.6

The morning sun highlighted the many smaller rocks and boulders that littered the plain around her, casting dark, sharp shadows and igniting the rust-red sand and yellow dust to a dull glow. Were it not for the strange colors of both ground and sky, Linda would have thought herself lost in some desert on Earth. But this was Mars. The tiny sun and the strange moons confirmed that. Somehow, some secret group of humans on Earth had figured out a way to get here. The realization brought feelings of both helplessness and excitement. Once again, there was much more going on than she had ever imagined.

"I've no intention of leaving you here for the duration, Madam," said the Fisherman into Linda's left ear. "Not in this 'lobster tank,' as you call it."

Linda swept her head back and forth but saw no one. "You're back," she said warily, surprised and yet already tired of surprises. A night of fitful sleep had left her irritated and intolerant of games. He wanted something from her. Linda could feel it. If it were simply a matter of keeping her safe, he could have done that as easily on Earth as on Mars, couldn't he? The cost to bring her here must have been staggering. There was too much he was not telling her. "Can we get down to business now?"

The Fisherman chuckled softly. "To business," he repeated. "As if the establishment of relationship and trust were naught but distasteful appetizers to be choked down before the real meal begins." His voice moved from Linda's left ear to her right as he spoke. He was circling her. Stalking her.

"I want to know why I'm here," said the President. "I want to know how long I will be kept here. I want to go home to my family."

The Fisherman exhaled softly. Linda imagined that she could feel his breath on her neck. "And that would be our business, then?" he said. "You wish to have a plan? You want to know the end of this?"

"I want to go home," said Linda again, her voice tight and pitched with frustration and loneliness.

When he spoke again, the Fisherman's voice was at Linda's feet. "It is your longing, Madam President, which will fuel our work together. I am glad to see how powerful it is."

Linda closed her eyes and focused on her breath. In their own way, the bright, rusty landscape and yellow-pink sky were as confining as the dark, alien cell in which Agent Rice had kept her in Ottawa. The vast distances of desert on all sides and the lack of air were as effective as any walls could ever be. She was thoroughly trapped, held in control by this invisible man who calls himself the Fisherman. He had tugged on his line and reeled her in, just as he had threatened to do three years before. And now here she was, lying on the dock at his feet, gasping for air, and wishing desperately to flop back into the water of her life from which she'd been dragged.

Seeing no real choice but to accept her situation, Linda asked another question. "So what is our work together?"

The Fisherman paused for a full minute before responding. Linda opened her eyes and gazed out over the landscape. The sun had risen high enough to reveal some detail on the distant mesa that she had first noticed: a deep sunken area, and a rise in the center. She had a vague feeling of having seen this hill before, through the windows of a plane flying overhead. Perhaps she'd seen something similar from Air Force One. She'd certainly spent more than her fair share of time in the air.

The Fisherman cleared his throat and spoke into her left ear. His voice rose barely above a whisper. "The mass of humanity is destroying the planetary ecosystem, Madam. You already know this."

Linda sighed. "That seems to be the case," she agreed.

"What you may not know is that it is possible to dramatically decrease the number of humans on Earth quickly and painlessly. Such an action might allow some small portion of humanity to survive. And it may give the remaining lifeforms an opportunity to recover."

Linda inhaled sharply but did not speak.

"The choice to do so I put to you, Madam President," the Fisherman said. "It is my mission to prepare you for this task. When you are prepared, you will be returned to your home."

It seemed as though the sun itself darkened. Linda's heart pounded: furious, horrified, stunned. She remembered her friend, Obie, explaining the thinking of the Inuit group into whose care they'd fallen, and how they'd regarded her. In their opinion, he'd said, the survival or extinction of the entire human species rested on her shoulders. Linda had scoffed at the notion. How could any one person hold that much power, or shoulder such a burden? And yet here was this man, this Fisherman, with an offer of just that: a way to quickly depopulate the Earth.

Linda's voice was hoarse when she finally spoke. "Why have you put this decision on me?" she asked.

The Fisherman's playful grin was evident in his tone. "Well, that's just the thing, Madam President. You see, I can't trust my own judgment in the matter."

"And why is that?"

"Because I am not a human being," explained the Fisherman.

3.7

"We got nothing?" asked Stan, his face puffed and red under his graying shock of hair. He looked at the others assembled in his State House office: Cole Thomas, Capitol City Green Zone CO Colonel Francis Westwood, Deputy Chief of Staff Mike Portnoy, Press Secretary Stendahl Banks, and Vice President Albert Singer. Cole seemed calmer than Stan had expected, given the circumstances. There was a slack, vacant expression on the First Gentleman's face.

"We've got nothing *so far*," agreed Mike Portnoy, wiping the sweat from his thick glasses. "Nothing on the security cameras. Nothing on infrared or radar sweeps. No sightings. No UFOs. No bodies. Nobody stepping forward to claim responsibility. We've got military, police, and FBI scouring the state. Nothing. They're just... gone."

"You scanned for their chips specifically, I assume."

"Of course. Again, nothing."

"No change to the Grid?" asked Stan, turning to Westwood.

"None that we can tell, Sir," said the Colonel.

"And there are no security cameras inside the hospital?"

Westwood squirmed a bit in his chair. "Interior coverage has been down for a few weeks, I'm sorry to report." He glanced at the Vice President before returning his attention to Stan. "Awaiting repairs."

"May I ask where Ms. Benedict is?" asked Singer, cutting in. "Surely she should be here." His warm, rich, grandfatherly voice and ruddy, square face - he had the air of a wise and good-hearted football coach - conveyed the impression that everything would turn out okay in the end.

Cole turned to Singer. "Keeley's not feeling well this morning, Mr. Vice President."

"And Secretary Lowell?" drawled Singer. "Any sign of the General since yesterday?"

"Still missing, sir," said Portnoy.

Albert Singer nodded and relaxed into his chair, as if satisfied that he'd added something important to the meeting.

Stan Walsh pulled off his glasses and rubbed his eyes. "So what the hell are the kids thinking?" he said. He looked at Cole. "I mean... do they just think they can hop aboard a space ship and land at the Squirrel Island facility? And did they somehow miss the part about the President's infectious disease?"

Stendahl Banks, trim and handsome and expensively dressed, leaned forward in his chair to intercept the question. "You have to remember, Stan, that these are intelligent, resourceful children." He glanced at Cole, who sat staring at his hands. He turned back to Stan Walsh. "They've seen things few others have. They've been *inside* one of the alien ships. And they lived with the human-alien hybrid,

Alice, for some months, before she disappeared. We have no real idea of the aliens' role in all of this: in the Grid, in the President's disease and confinement, or in the kids' disappearance."

Stan smirked and shook his head. "Is that supposed to make me feel better?" he asked Banks. "Because it doesn't. Especially coming from you."

"It makes me feel better," murmured Portnoy, avoiding Stan's gaze.

Stan Walsh turned to Portnoy with one raised eyebrow. "Really, Mike? Why is that?" He snapped the notebook on his desk shut and leaned back in his chair, hands behind his head.

Portnoy cocked his head and frowned. "Not sure," he said. "It's just... well, I mean, think of the past few years. Remember how screwed up things are out there, beyond this little compound of heavily armed peacefulness. Remember it's only March and it feels like August. In North Carolina! Remember last summer, the almost ice-free Arctic, and how little ice came back this past winter, and what we're seeing in Greenland right now. Remember the riots, the plagues, the famines. We've got the four horsemen breathing down our necks, gentlemen." He looked around the room at Cole, Singer, Walsh, and Banks, who were all listening carefully. "I, for one, hope to hell these whatever-the-heck-they-are aliens *are* involved in all of this. I don't think we can solve this stuff on our own." Portnoy stopped. His face reddened, as if embarrassed by his own speechifying.

Stan shook his head. "So you think they're here to help," he said, his voice tinged with scorn. He pointed toward the sky. "Billions of tiny woks circle the planet and they just sit there while everything goes to hell down here and you think they're here to help." Stan closed his eyes and took a deep breath.

Portnoy opened his mouth to respond but then stopped.

Singer shifted in his chair to stare out the window.

Stendahl Banks shifted in his chair and cleared his throat. "I love those kids," he said, his voice low. "I think we all do. And I'm worried for their safety. But..." he gestured toward Portnoy with a vague wave of the hand, "I think I agree with Mike on this one. Whatever is going on here, if the kids are with Alice and the aliens, then I for one am going to hope that they are now playing some important role in a plan we cannot fully see or understand. I wish it wasn't so. They're... they're just kids, you know. But..." Banks stopped. Singer was pointing at Cole. Stendahl Banks turned.

There sat Cole Thomas in his armchair, his eyes closed, his face slack. His hands rested on his knees, palms up. From the center of his hands flared tiny bursts of light, like miniature fireworks or fountains of fire.

3.8

Mary's sobs wracked her curving spine and heaving chest as she struggled for breath, uncontrollable convulsions that felt like they might rip her to pieces. Here, in Keeley's arms, back in the safety of their own bedroom, she could let loose the pain that squeezed her heart. "I screwed up!" she shouted into Keeley's breast between sobs. "I screwed up. I screwed up. Oh Keeley, oh... oh... I screwed up so bad!"

Keeley kept a steady hold on Mary as best as she could, her face tightened against the sharp nausea in her gut. She knew that Mary would move through this, and that she must. All Keeley had to do was stay present with her while she did, and focus her breath to calm her own sour stomach. She kissed the top of Mary's head and held her close. "I know, hon," she whispered. "I know."

Mary raised her face to the ceiling and howled with desperate rage. She pounded the mattress beside her as she screamed, then buried her face in Keeley's breast and sobbed again. Keeley's shirt was soaked with Mary's tears.

At last, her grief largely spent, Mary rolled onto her back and inhaled noisily. She blew out a vast sigh and slowed her breathing. Keeley rolled onto her side to face her partner and put a hand on Mary's stomach. Mary opened an eye to find Keeley watching her. "I knew," she said, her voice ragged. "I saw. But I couldn't stop it."

Keeley gently massaged Mary's stomach, ran her fingers up Mary's chest and placed her hand over Mary's heart. "What couldn't you stop?" she asked.

Mary sighed deeply and grabbed a cloth handkerchief Keeley had put beside her to wipe at her eyes and nose. "I couldn't stop them leaving. I knew they would. I saw it: the... the darkness reaching out to them from the computer. I knew then that they would try to leave. But I never guessed it would happen so quickly." She folded the handkerchief and daubed her eyes. "Oh, Keeley, I'm so afraid."

Keeley's face was warm with understanding. "Because of what you saw in their fields," she said. "The images of fire and screaming and falling."

Mary closed her eyes tightly, as if that would keep the images from assaulting her again. She reached out and grabbed Keeley's hand. "I'm so afraid," she said again.

"And yet they're with Alice, they said," offered Keeley. She grabbed another handkerchief from the bedside table and wiped Mary's nose and mouth, drying the last bits of moisture that Mary had missed, then leaned over and kissed Mary's forehead.

"Oh, I know," said Mary, exhaling loudly. "And maybe Alice can keep them safe. I don't know. But the darkness I saw..." she looked at Keeley. "There's something out there, sweetie. Something... powerful. Something that will stop at nothing to get what it wants. And I'm afraid... the kids are putting themselves right in its path."

"Then we had better find them," said Keeley. "I know Stan and Mike are on it. They've probably got the entire US security machine searching for them by now."

Mary laughed quietly and shook her head. "Earlier I scolded Ness for blaming herself..." she said.

"And now you're taking on the blame."

Mary squeezed Keeley's hand. "Humans are just... crazy," she said. An image from an earlier time popped into her mind. Of herself as a kid. And the aliens. And her brother... Mary knew she had good reason to feel guilty.

"Humans in this culture, at least," said Keeley.

Keeley gathered the soaked handkerchiefs in one hand, swung her legs off the bed, and sat up. The nausea rolled around in her stomach like a caged tiger seeking escape. She inhaled sharply. Mary rolled onto her stomach and put a hand on Keeley's back. "You okay, sweetie?" she asked.

Keeley took another deep breath, turned, smiled weakly down at Mary, then rose to toss the handkerchiefs in the laundry basket in the closet. "I think it was something I ate," said Keeley. She turned back toward her love. "Hospital food, you know? I had a salad in the cafeteria. Who knows where the army's getting their produce these days?" Keeley motioned toward the bathroom with her head. "I'll be back in a minute, hon. You'll be okay?" Mary smiled and nodded. Keeley went into the bathroom.

Mary turned onto her right side, noticed the television remote on the nightstand, and grabbed it. She powered up the set, lowered the sound, and tuned to ACN, hoping for some news that would ease her heart. She caught the very end of a story on the summit Linda had called. Leaders from all around the globe would soon gather for an online conference hosted by GooglePlex. Linda would attend from her confinement on Squirrel Island. The virtual format would put them all in a similar situation. And because it would require no travel, and therefore produce no carbon, the conference would be "green" as well. There was footage from the President's press conference the day before, and old file footage of her meetings with various heads of state over the past three years. Mary wished she could see people's fields through the television screen. She desperately wanted some insight into her President's current state of being.

The anchorman switched to a new story as Keeley emerged from the bathroom. She crossed the room to lie on the bed beside her partner. Keeley's face was gray and her eyes were tight with pain. Mary pulled her in and hugged her to her side.

The new story came from Augusta. The headline on the screen said "Alien Flu Spreading?" Mary turned up the sound and Keeley turned her head to watch. A second person had died in Augusta, Maine, this one just hours ago. The television showed a photo of the heavy, balding businessman Mary had seen on the hospital gurney, a visiting contractor apparently in town to attend some meetings. And it showed what must be a passport photo of the young woman, an attorney for the Mayor's office, whom Keeley had seen die on the sidewalk in front of the Burger Hut. Two more people had just been admitted at MaineCentral, the reporter said. Though their condition was not yet known, unofficial reports said that one of them has now died as well. And there were reports of people collapsing on the streets coming in from elsewhere around the country. The reporter mentioned "speculation" that these mysterious deaths were in some way connected to President Travis's illness. "Let us hope and pray," he intoned gravely, "that such speculations are false, and that our President will not fall to this frightening new plague. This is Kenneth Wild, ACN News."

In a moment of panic, Mary attuned herself to Keeley's field. All she could see was an image of her lover sleeping peacefully. With a deep exhalation of relief, she hugged Keeley to her side once again.

"I saw that bald man at the hospital this morning," she said. She checked her watch. "Just a few hours ago."

"And I saw the young woman on the sidewalk yesterday," said Keeley.

"I know."

Keeley glanced briefly at Mary. "Did you... I mean, was there anything in his field?"

Mary shook her head. "I didn't have time," she said. "I was too panicked about the kids."

"Do you think..." Keeley motioned toward the television with a wave of her hand. "Is Linda...?"

Mary scrunched her eyes shut and inhaled sharply. "I don't know," she said after a moment. She opened her eyes and looked at Keeley. "I don't know." A wave of angry determination crossed her face and she rolled to get out of bed.

"You've gotta go, don't you?" asked Keeley.

Mary nodded, hunched over on the edge of the bed. "I'm sorry sweetie. I wish I could stay here and take care of you."

Keeley waved away the notion. "I'll be fine," she said.

Mary stood slowly, making sure there was no dizziness waiting to trip her to the floor. She slipped her feet into her shoes and headed toward the door, her limp more noticeable after her time in bed. "I have to find some way to help," she said. With her hand on the doorknob, she turned back to Keeley. "I love you," she said simply.

"I love you too, Mar," said Keeley.

"It feels like everything is falling apart," said Mary. With that, she stepped into the hallway and closed the door softly behind her.

3.9

"You said I wouldn't have to stay locked up in this container," said Linda.

"Indeed," said the Fisherman. "Perhaps we should begin your training. I have so much to show you."

"Training?"

"The Astral Realm for Dummies, as you Americans might put it," said the Fisherman, obviously amused with himself. "A primer, of sorts, to help you navigate the next step up."

"You mean-"

"Yes I do, Madam. A half-step, anyway. We'll be essentially free of the constraints of the physical, but we'll stay closely tied to that level. Things will look very much the same as they do to your flesh-and-blood eyes, even as you'll be able to move anywhere you wish, including up into the sky and through solid matter. Think of yourself as Ebenezer Scrooge and me as the Ghost. The metaphor is familiar to you."

"Yes," said Linda.

"Please know that you will be restricted to Mars and near-Mars space. You will not be able to flee the evil lizard overlord and return to Earth for help."

"Are you evil?" asked Linda.

The Fisherman sighed sadly. "It is my hope, Madam President," he said, "that by the time we finish our work together, you shall actually love me."

Linda had no idea what to say to that.

"Hang on," said the Fisherman

In an instant, Linda was hovering high above the Martian plain, clad in her favorite jeans and "Go Spartans!" sweatshirt. Before her, no more than a couple of arm-lengths away, hovered a slight, wiry man of maybe sixty-five. His feathery white hair was short and wavy and his white beard was crisply trimmed. His face was nicely tanned and his eyes, alive and fierce, sparkled from behind wire-rimmed glasses. He wore khaki slacks and a Hawaiian shirt covered with an intricate pattern of palm fronds and tropical birds. "So you're the Fisherman," said Linda, sizing up her opponent.

The Fisherman bowed at the waist. "Perhaps we should dispense with the soubriquets as well," he said. "Why don't you call me William?"

"Is that your name?" asked Linda.

"It will do," said William.

"I thought you said you weren't human."

The Fisherman smiled. "All in good time."

Linda turned to consider the space around them. They were hovering in the yellow-pink sky at what seemed to be the cruising altitude of a small plane, though it was difficult to tell, with no known reference points. She peered down to see a glinting white speck on the rust-red plain below. "Is that the lobster tank?" she asked, pointing.

The Fisherman winked. "It is."

From this height, the hill to her east took on more definition. It was clearly the Martian mesa known as "the Face," though it looked quite different from the photographs she had seen. Linda remembered reading an article or two about it decades ago. Perhaps that was why it felt so familiar. To the south and west, the various hills and mountains, many of them roughly pyramidal in shape, pushed up from the ground, a few of them reaching almost to her altitude. One mountain in particular stood out to the south, a large pyramid that was heavily weathered on the side facing her. The morning sun warmed its eastern side to a bronze glow.

"Below us is Rumi's Field," intoned William with a flourish, as though he were a ringmaster at the circus. "That is what I call it, at least." With sweeping gestures he named a number of other features: the Face, the D&M pyramid, the Tholus, the City. "These are the names given these formations and structures by those who first studied the photographs back on Earth," he explained.

Linda followed his gestures, trying to memorize names and features. She surveyed the flat plain below them, then looked at the Fisherman. "Why 'Rumi's Field,' William?" she said, knowing that her use of his name might help create a bond between them that would serve her later.

William smiled, flashing his eyebrows upward. "You remember the poem Obie recited?" he asked. "During your long conversation in the trailer on Bathurst Island?"

"Only vaguely," said Linda. "Something about right and wrong, I think. Do you mind telling me how you know so much about my conversation with Obie?"

The Fisherman waved off her question as if it were of little consequence. "You don't think we let Presidents run around unsurveilled, do you?" he said.

"I suppose not," said Linda.

William winked. "Jalāl ad-Dīn Muhammad Rūmī , known simply as Rumi to most Westerners, was a Sufi poet and mystic who lived during the 13th century. He's quite popular in both America and Britain. I can send you a packet, if you wish."

Linda remembered Obie speaking of these "packets," bundles of information that could be shared instantly in the Astral realm. "Not right now," she said. "I'll let you know if it feels important later."

"Agreed," said the Fisherman with a nod. "The poem Obie recited was this: '*Out beyond ideas of wrongdoing and rightdoing, there is a field. I'll meet you there. When the soul lies down in that grass, the world is too full to talk about. Ideas, language, even the phrase 'each other,' doesn't make any sense.'* Do you remember it now?"

"I guess," said Linda. "I remember Sina saying something about the field as well."

"Yes."

"So this," Linda pointed again to the rusty, rock-strewn plain below them, "is the field where we meet to discuss right and wrong?"

"I anticipate that right and wrong will lie at the heart of our discussion," said the Fisherman. "We will move out beyond them both."

"I see," said Linda. She noticed again the white glinting speck below her and began to drift downward, as if curiosity alone was propelling her toward the object of her attention. "I want to go look," she said to William, who had begun to follow her. Her words translated directly into action and she sped toward the container. As the plain rose up to meet her she worried that she would crash into it. She slowed immediately, as though a parachute had opened. The "lobster tank" grew slowly larger. It was coffin shaped, sitting at a slight angle on a black pedestal. And it certainly looked like glass. As she neared the container, her physical body inside became visible. She stopped, found the Fisherman right above and behind her, and frowned. "I'm naked," she said, her face tight with irritation.

"You are," said the Fisherman.

"Do you mind telling me why?" asked Linda.

William lifted an eyebrow. "Rightdoing and wrongdoing, Madam President," he said. "The work has begun."

3.10

"So there was no... violent death in this life?" asked Mary, struggling for her words. She sat on the rolling office chair facing Cole, her nose wrinkled in disgust from the strange taste in her mouth.

Cole sat across from her in one of the armchairs. He stared down at his hands in his lap, then brought his eyes back up. "No death," he agreed. "Or if there was, I didn't get to that part yet. Just me as an old man, walking through deep forest, searching for something. My hair was long and dirty and gray."

"And you don't know what you're looking for."

"If I do, I don't remember it now," said Cole.

Mary rolled back in the chair to get a better view. Cole shifted in his armchair as she gazed at his field. No matter how many times she'd done it, he still felt profoundly uneasy, afraid that some long hidden secret would pop to the surface and embarrass him. Afraid that she might discover that, deep inside, he was not the good person he thought himself to be.

Mary's eyes slid up and down and across his body for a minute or more before she spoke. "I don't see any sign of it," she said at last. "The only image I see is of you speaking on the... telephone. And I sense your worry for the kids. And your anger about Linda. But these spells you have, these "hops," don't seem to leave anything behind."

"I've wondered if these are my own past lives I've been jumping to," said Cole warily. He didn't know if the idea was silly or insightful.

"I've wondered the same thing," said Mary. "You said there were lights coming from your hands as well?"

"That's what they said: Sten and Mike and Stan and Albert. Little flares, they said. Little fireworks. Coming right out of my palms. I was off traipsing through the woods so I didn't see them. But I saw them earlier, when I hit my head."

"You hit your head?" asked Mary. She motioned to him. "May I?" she asked. Cole nodded. Mary stood and examined Cole's head closely, running her fingers across his scalp to feel for cuts or bumps.

Cole told her about falling and hitting his head on the toilet after his earlier "hop."

"I don't know what to make of all this, Cole," said Mary, taking her seat again. "It sounds like this has been... hard... on you."

"It's gotten worse the past couple of days."

"And this has been going on how long?"

Cole thought for a moment. "It started a few days before they took Linda away. I figured they were just dreams at first. Most of them of that old man with the dog."

Mary inhaled deeply and closed her eyes. Her body folded into itself as she breathed.

"Do you think this all has something to do with the Strangers coming back?" asked Cole.

Mary opened her eyes. "I don't know, Cole," she said. "Apart from that note from the kids, we haven't seen any real evidence that they *have* come back." She pointed toward the sky and the Grid. "Not that they've ever really gone away."

"But isn't that note enough? I mean... if Alice is back and they've gone to find Linda, they'll be able to bring her home, right? If... she can... you know. There's her flu to think about." Tears welled up in Cole's eyes as he spoke.

Mary reached out and touched his cheek. "You're scared," she said.

Cole's head dropped and he exhaled sharply. He wiped his face with both hands before he looked up again. "I'm more angry than anything," he said, hoping that his words were true. Anger was so much easier to bear. "But, yeah. I'm terrified."

"Your wife is ill and she's been taken away from you," said Mary.

Cole nodded.

"And your kids have run off into a dangerous world," she said.

Cole let his head hang down in helplessness.

"And you want to hope that somehow the Strangers will put everything right again."

"Yeah," Cole breathed, his voice raw.

Mary sighed wistfully. "And they might, Cole. They just might." She reached out and took Cole's hand. "But I need to tell you something."

Cole exhaled his fear.

"There's something... I saw. When I saw the kids yesterday."

"Tell me," said Cole, meeting Mary's eyes.

"I saw images, Cole. In their fields. Images of pain and fire." Mary hesitated for a moment, then continued. "An image of Grace screaming. An image of Iain falling."

Cole shook his head slowly back and forth as he listened.

"And I felt something, Cole. Something dark. Something reaching out. Something... powerful." Mary's own tears rose up as she described what she'd seen. She swallowed the weird taste and continued. "And I fear that the kids will... whatever this darkness is... the kids are headed right to it."

Cole stood and walked to the window, gazing toward the east, toward Squirrel Island and Linda and his kids and the late morning sun. Toward this "darkness." "We have to find them," he said, his back to Mary.

"Yes we do," said Mary.

Cole stood and watched the eastern sky for the longest time. Mary, knowing that he needed her to, stayed with him while he watched.

His cell phone began to ring and Cole fished it from his pocket. "Cole Thomas," he said as he put the phone to his ear.

The voice he heard had a warbled, buzzing quality to it.

3.11

"So how long do we have to wait here?" asked Iain. He checked his watch, the face of which glowed brightly in the pitch dark. "It's been almost two hours."

Grace shook her head. "I don't know," she said. "I just know that we had to come here. That I really, really wanted to."

"Just like you really wanted to look for the key in the desk drawer in the room next door?" asked Emily.

Grace nodded, though neither her brother nor sister could see it. "I don't know how I know," she said, trying to explain. "Maybe Alice told me everything in my dream and I just don't remember."

"You know we're in big trouble if this doesn't work," said Iain.

"I guess," said Grace. "I feel bad what we did to Ness."

Emily cleared her throat. "Hopefully our note will help them to not worry," she said.

"You think they'll believe the bit about Alice coming and taking us away in a wok?" asked Iain.

"I hope so," said Grace. "We need them to think we're far away. So they don't find us here." She scrunched her shoulders back and forth, trying to get more comfortable. Iain, irritated at having to be so close to his little sister, scrunched back.

"Is there some reason we need to be crammed in here?" he asked.

"I just know that I really want to be," said Grace.

"Yeah, well, I really, really, really *don't* want to be," said Iain.

"It feels like a cage," said Emily, reaching up to touch the curved surface just above them. She closed her eyes, hoping to dispel the cramped, trapped feeling inside of her.

"I wish Dennis could have come," said Grace.

"Right," said Iain with a snort. "Like they'd have let him into the hospital."

Grace sighed. "I still wish it," she said.

"How long do we sit here before we go tell everybody what a bunch of idiots we are?" asked Iain.

Grace was about to answer when the entire room began to vibrate with a low, rumbling sound. It reminded her of the subway they'd taken on their last trip to New York, before the Crash. The rumbling grew in intensity, then stopped. Iain exhaled noisily beside her. Emily reached out and squeezed Grace's knee.

The curved surface overhead began to glow, a greenish-yellow light like one of those glow-sticks they used to get at Halloween. Then, like something from the movies, a small hand pushed out of the surface directly above their faces. The hand was human in every respect, smooth and graceful, strong and well-muscled, like the hand of a warrior princess. The hand emerged to the forearm. One finger curled back on itself, beckoning.

"Alice," whispered Grace, her heart pounding.

She reached up and took the strange hand in her own.

3.12

"Were we friends?" asked Ted. He rearranged the tiles in his rack but could not find a good word.

Carl brought his eyes up from the board. He stared at Ted for a long while. "I think so," he said. "Maybe." He motioned toward Ted's rack of tiles. "You gonna go, boss, or should I go take a nap?"

Ted raised an eyebrow. "You in a hurry?" he asked.

Carl stopped and pondered that for a minute. He shrugged. "I don't know," he said at last. "I can't think of anything to be in a hurry for."

"How long we been here?" said Ted.

"A couple of days, maybe?" said Carl.

"Seems like years to me," said Ted.

"Yeah, it does," said Carl.

Ted stared down at his tiles, then shuffled them around once more. He looked up at Carl. "I don't think we were friends," he said.

Carl scratched his nose. "Does it matter?" he said.

"Not sure," said Ted. He picked up four tiles and played them on the board.

"Mork?" said Carl. "Don't you know any real words?"

Chapter Ⱦ Four

4.1

Her father had believed he was giving her the most wonderful gift. That was the great irony of it. It was her seventeenth birthday, after all, and she was headed into her senior year at Marshall Academy in Ottawa. It was time for her to "know what was really going on," wasn't it? That's what he was thinking. Time for her to step into her "true self," and "take her rightful place in this world, and the worlds to come." And Gabrielle would be so happy to finally understand, wouldn't she?

Gabrielle snapped her textbook shut, pushed it across the library table, and grabbed her notebook. "No," she wrote in a hurried hand. "I am not so happy!!!" The words were meant for her father, of course. She wanted to fling them at him like rocks. Like knives. Like plates and cups and vases. But he was not there. Gabrielle wouldn't *let* him be there. So the conversations that filled her head had nowhere to go, save, now and then, for the pages of her journal.

The guests had gone, at least. He'd waited for that. Friends from school. A few friends of her parents. That creepy Mr. Lean from the office. Mother had excused herself with a "headache" and Father had invited Gabrielle into his study to sit with him. "One last little present," he'd said with a sneaky grin. Gabrielle had expected jewelry or plane tickets or maybe even another car. What she'd gotten was a story she wished now she'd never heard.

Gabrielle noticed she was scribbling absently on her open page and her heart began to pound, afraid that once again the man known as Zacharael had taken over her body. But it was just random loops and squiggles, as if her hand were tracing her own heartbeat, or following the trail of her swirling thoughts. She closed her notebook, zipped her pen into a pouch in her backpack, grabbed her physics text, and forced herself to read. She had exams coming up covering both quantum holography and macro-wormholes. She needed to review this material.

Or maybe not. This was a Family-supported school, after all. She was studying what The Families needed her to study. But maybe she didn't have to do that anymore. Maybe it was time to quit.

That thought set her heart to hammering once again. Could she just leave? Did she dare? Did she dare *not*?

Her father hadn't told her everything, of course. Not at once. Not on that birthday night. He'd told her of The Families. How he and her mother and her sister (now her *late* sister) and she had come from illustrious bloodlines that stretched back into antiquity. How her last name was really Sinclair. How The Families were the secret overlords of the global industrial and political machines that determined the course of human history on planet Earth. And how they had a plan for humanity, a plan that would propel them through their current crop of global crises and into a grand new future. He'd told her of his decision to embed his family in what he called "the sleeping world," to take a position as an MP in the Canadian government in order to watch and listen and guide and control. He'd explained the costs to himself and her mother of leaving behind the secret enclaves of their Families in order to do their work in this "sleeping world." And he'd told her how close they now were to the fruition of their plans and preparations. Soon, they'd return to The Families. Soon, they'd be back where they belonged. And soon, very soon, they would take "the Giant Leap."

Guy Legrand had not explained what that Giant Leap was. Not on her birthday. But Gabrielle had left vaguely disturbed by the whole thing, nonetheless. There was excitement, of course, to be let in on such huge secrets. To find out she was a member of these vastly wealthy and powerful Families opened up possibilities she'd never before considered. And learning that there were people who had an actual plan to deal with the quickly unraveling world into which she'd been born was a huge relief. But there was something about her father - the wary distraction in his eyes, the grim cast of his face, maybe just the tight set of his shoulders - that made Gabrielle deeply uneasy. She knew she was not being told the whole truth. And she knew, somehow, that she would not like what she was not being told.

She'd pulled away from her father during her senior year. It was easy enough to do, as he was gone so often, out "solving the problems of the world" in his play-acting role as a Canadian Minister of Parliament. There were water salinization problems in New Brunswick and Nova Scotia to deal with, and a massive fish die-off in British Columbia. There were crop failures galore, old people dying in heat waves, and that crazy ice storm that shut down most of Ontario and Quebec just as the global economy was imploding. There was that typhus outbreak on PEI and lines that stretched on for blocks at gas pumps in most major cities. There were food riots and terrorist bombings and water shortages and the nuclear "accident" in Toronto. And there was the Grid, which had appeared in the sky in the fall of her senior year and thrown Guy Legrand into a rage. Gabrielle had heard him cursing on the phone and pounding the walls of his office more than once after the Grid appeared. He was a man obsessed, a man distracted, and he was extremely busy. And Gabrielle was glad to have him so.

It was not until the next spring that Gabrielle heard the rest of the story. As graduation approached and she began to consider colleges - she had her eye on an art school in Vancouver - she was told that she had no real choice in the matter. As a Family member, she would attend the rightfully rich and suitably private Freemantle College in Montreal, where she would study one of "the hard sciences." End of discussion.

Gabrielle was furious at the assumption that they could tell her what to do, and demanded to know why. Her father told her why: The Families would soon be leaving Earth. "We don't need artists," Guy said with scorn. "We need physicists and engineers and surgeons and geneticists." And there would be a number of other Family members also attending Freemantle, he explained. He smiled stiffly. "You could use some time with your own kind," he said.

"And why are we leaving Earth?" Gabrielle demanded, ignoring her father's obvious attempt to provoke her.

Her father's eyes hardened. "Because, my precious girl, this planet is going down the shit-hole, and the Sleepers with it." With that, he'd nodded decisively and walked out of the room.

That had been the end of it. Or the beginning. Outwardly, Gabrielle had acceded to her father's demands. She'd matriculated at Freemantle and taken up a course of studies in physics. It was the only thing her father would pay for, and she hadn't been ready to strike out on her own. And her mother, drunk more often than not in the wake of her little sister's death at the hands of a hit-and-run driver, had been no help whatsoever. College was comfortable enough. Cushy, even. Supported by Family money, life on Freemantle's campus was barely fazed by the Crash. And the other Family members she met, young people just like herself from all over the world, were nicer than she'd expected.

But over the months since she'd come to Montreal, though she hadn't been ready to strike out on her own *before*, Gabrielle had slowly and quietly begun to *get* ready. She'd come to see the tremendous mistake her father had made in embedding them in the normal, everyday human world. Having grown up in that world, Gabrielle had come to consider herself a part *of* it. This world she knew, as screwed up as it was, as damaged as it felt, was *her* world. And these "Sleepers," as her father called them, these millions and billions of people who were now slated to go "down the shit-hole"... well, some of them were her friends. And one of them, a beautiful young man named Arthur whom she'd met in Physics I, had become much more than that.

Gabrielle glanced over at the clock and blinked, surprised at how late it was. She had a class in ten minutes and her bike had a flat. She'd have to walk, and it was sizzling hot outside. She gathered her books and shoved them into her backpack, promising herself that she'd study all night if she had to. Her notebook fell back onto the table when its spiral binding caught on the backpack's fabric. It opened automatically to her page of scribbles and Gabrielle noticed that what had appeared before to be random scratchings had actually been nothing of the sort. It was messy, to be sure, but those scribbles clearly depicted a circle with an inverted capital L cutting through the middle of it. It was the crop circle she'd seen the night before in her "dream." An image of her father's friend, Zacharael, came to mind: he was sobbing loudly, with his back to her, as he gazed out over the destroyed ground. Something about that confused her. It occurred to her that perhaps this Zacharael loved the planet Earth, too.

She wondered if maybe Zacharael wasn't a friend of her father's after all.

4.2

Mary sat hunched over on the edge of Grace's bed, breathing into the wave of anxiety that had come over her as she'd entered the Family Suite. After a few moments, her calm restored, she raised her head and scanned the room. Grace's stuffed animals huddled cozily in a basket in the corner. Her books were piled on her desk. Even her clothes were put away, hung in her closet or stuffed into her hamper. *When had Grace become so neat?* Mary wondered. Grace's room usually looked like a riot zone. Had she cleaned up before leaving for the hospital, knowing that she would not return?

Closing her eyes, Mary scanned the room for vibrations, memories, and wisps of thought and feeling, trusting that this physical space could retain some echo of the girl who had been here hours earlier. She hoped that it had. If life had taught Mary anything, it was this: human beings had little idea what was really possible. Most humans, anyways. And the ones who claimed to run things were especially obtuse. The ones who claimed to know and understand. Those guys. They would scoff at the notion that such things as memories and thoughts and feelings could be picked out of the air like radio waves. That they could stick to walls and beds and clothing and toys. That they had an existence outside the human mind. But Mary knew better. These walls could talk. It was simply a matter of being able to listen. The question that remained was this: did these walls have anything to say?

Mary stood, stretched her back to stand straight, and walked slowly around the room, running her fingers along the walls and over Grace's furniture. She listened for an echo of Grace's presence. But she sensed nothing. The room did not speak to her.

Inhaling deeply, she left Grace's room and repeated the process in her brother's and sister's rooms. Again, she was gifted with no new pieces of knowing or feeling. She knew that a unit of Army investigators, following the possibility that the children had actually been abducted from the hospital by hostile human forces, had already scoured these rooms for clues, and had taken the kids' tablets and laptops, to check for any documents, messages, or emails that might help them learn what had happened. Mary wondered if that whirlwind of official, military focus, belief, and intent had blown away any lingering bits of the children's energy. She was not at all certain how this all worked.

It was the note that stuck with her, as though fastened to her mind with refrigerator magnets. *Alice has returned,* they'd written, *and is going to help us find Linda.* She pictured them all together in a hospital hallway, the kids, the hybrid child, the small, shiny alien vehicle hovering over the tile floor and stretching from wall to wall. It was possible. The woks could appear and disappear like magic. And Mary could imagine Emily insisting that they stop and write a note. But then the wording got strange. *She came in a wok and took us away,* they'd written. The tense was wrong. Those weren't the words they'd have used had they been writing the note there in the hospital hallway, with Alice and her wok waiting. Wouldn't they have written *She's here in a wok to take us away*? Something like that? And then there was the insistence that they were *long gone* and that Mary should not *try to find us.* And the fact that the note was written on the same lined stock they used for their schoolwork, rather than a piece of note paper found in the hospital, as if they'd brought paper *with* them. Mary shook her head as she stepped out of Emily's room and back into the family's common area. It just didn't feel right.

Mary could hear Cole's muffled voice coming from his bedroom. He was still on the phone. Deciding to continue her conversation with the First Gentleman later, she made her way out of the Family Suite and into what she thought of as "the last line of defense," the wing of the Presidential Home where Linda and Cole's closest senior advisors and counselors had their offices, creating a wall between the President and her family and the rest of the world. Not that "the rest of the world" could get anywhere near them at this point in time. Augusta had been emptied of everyone but essential government and military personnel, and the few private citizens needed to serve their needs. Staff had been gnawed down to the barest of bones, and offices were spread around the downtown area, some here in the Presidential Home, some in the State House, others in other nearby office buildings. Surrounding the city center was a thick and fiercely protected cordon of chain link and razor wire, bristling with weapons.

The Federal government in Augusta was not what it had been in D.C. Almost three years ago, after the failed attempt to bring Linda Travis into the vast, hidden human-alien conspiracy that purported to "really run things," the aliens, the "Strangers," as Linda's friend Obie had called them, or the "Life," as they had called themselves, had left the planet. Their underground facilities, built directly beneath the centers of government and corporate power in countries all over the world, had simply vanished, leaving many of the District of Columbia's government buildings collapsed in heaps in a vast network of sinkholes. To President Travis, the message was implicit in those toppled buildings, the White House and Capitol Building amongst them: it was time for things to change dramatically.

Linda Travis refused to simply "rebuild America," as so many insisted she do. Now more cognizant of the confluence of global environmental and economic crises humanity was facing, Linda was unwilling to spend either the time or the money it would take to return the nation's capital to its former splendor. With U.S. debt at ever more impossible levels, with the Great Recession grinding on and on, she didn't *have* the money. But it went deeper than that. The aliens, the Strangers, hadn't just pulled the foundations out from under some buildings. They'd pulled the props out from underneath a vast, secretive, corrupted government machine. Linda Travis had no more interest in rebuilding that human machine than she did the buildings it has been housed in.

So while she'd relocated her executive branch to Vermont, and then Augusta, Maine, she'd sent the judicial branch to Nebraska and the Senators and Congresspersons back to their respective homes. With her power and popularity at an all-time high, having exposed the secret human-alien cabal to the world and having told the truth about their collective situation, and with her people left stunned and afraid and yet strangely hopeful and open, Linda was able to push these changes through with little overt resistance. "It's time we get our shit together," Linda Travis said, and the people nodded and laughed. "Get down off your elitist high-horses, get your butts back home, and mix it up on the ground with the people you're supposed to be serving," she told the legislators, and the people cheered. "We've got amazing communication technologies now," Linda explained. "We don't all need to be together in the same town anymore. And if that means there will be fewer back-room deals and private, smoke-filled clubs full of rich white men deciding the fate of the world, so much the better for all of us." The people sighed with relief. Linda Travis promised to "dilute the concentrated insanity" that Washington D.C. had become. "We're not alone," she said, pointing up to the sky, "but we're on our own. We've made a mess of this planet. Let's roll up our sleeves and get to work." Many of the people who hadn't fallen in love with Linda Travis before then did so now.

Mary, feeling anxious and weakened by the morning's exertions, walked down the hall, careful to keep one hand on the railings Linda had had installed for her benefit. She glanced into Keeley's office before heading to her own. Those heady days after the fall of D.C. were no more. And truth be told, things had never been what they had seemed to be. Mary had once been a member of that secret cabal, after all. She knew that, while her President had exposed a deep layer of the conspiracy, there were deeper layers still, both human and alien, and that Linda's attempts to re-design her government would not touch those deeper layers. Mary had said as much in meeting after meeting. Having thrown in with Linda, and having taken on her new role as Senior Advisor in charge of running the President's household and minding the children, she'd told them everything she'd known. But she'd never known much beyond the workings of her own role in "The People."

And there seemed little to do about those deeper layers in any event. There were regular people to feed and house and keep warm. There were environmental catastrophes to deal with, and a climate that had spun off its axis. There was fighting at home and abroad. There were shortages, interruptions, failures, foreclosures, extinctions, riots, epidemics, and strikes. If there were deeper layers of conspiracy out there that didn't like what Linda was doing, they would have to show themselves. Otherwise, they could just hide in their plush bunkers and count their money. Linda Travis had more pressing matters to attend to.

Mary opened the door to her office and stepped inside. She had no idea why she'd come here. To cry? To think? To hide? None of those options appealed. She wanted to help but had no idea what to do. The "deeper levels" had finally shown themselves. They'd taken Linda. Perhaps they were behind whatever it was that Cole was now experiencing: his "hops." Somebody had taken the kids away. Or helped them. And then there was the matter of this "alien flu." Mary did not feel big enough, or whole enough, to counter these forces.

She might find some answers in the Astral. Back in the day she'd been one of Theodore Rice's travelers, after all. One of his "stalkers." But the thought of that terrified her. She hadn't traveled in years. Traveling in the Astral had made her feel more and more crazy, to the point where she'd quit altogether and turned her talents exclusively to communicating in the physical layer with their two "pet aliens," Spud and Mork. And that dark tendril she'd seen in Emily's field scared the daylights out of her. Mary knew that, should she step into the Astral, she would meet that darkness. She did not feel prepared for such things as that.

Mary sat at her desk. With a touch, she brought her tablet to life. A soft chime sounded and Mary touched her pad again. There, waiting to chat, was the President.

4.3

"Holy shit!" cried Iain, who hovered as a glowing orange orb in the multi-hued "sky."

"What?" said Grace.

"I'm a fireball!" He spun on his axis, laughing, then floated toward his youngest sister. "This is great!" he said.

Grace pulled back a bit at the force of her brother's enthusiasm. "You seem to be getting the hang of it," she said.

"So this is where you were before?" asked Emily. She hovered in her human form in the distance above Grace and Iain, like someone afraid to go into the water. She turned slowly to scan the area. The sky in all directions was colored like a rainbow sunset, with strange cauliflower "clouds" glowing from the inside. Below was a complex, blurred, busy landscape, stretching to a glittering horizon in every direction. Overhead, even in this bright sky, was the Grid. It looked roughly the same as it did in the night sky of the physical realm, but the luminous lines were purple now, and at each intersection twinkled a tiny star.

Grace, a ball of radiant white light, flashed her heart to her sister. "Yep," she said. "I'd forgotten. But now that I'm here again, it all comes back to me."

Iain flickered to his human form for a moment, then reverted back to a glowing ball. He blinked out and reappeared right in front of Emily. "How do you hold your form?" he asked Emily. "You know, like a human being. I try but I keep going back to being a fireball."

Emily grinned. "I don't know," she said. "I'm just me. How do you blink out and back in like that?"

Iain popped back into human form long enough to return his sister's smile. "I don't know either." He blinked out again. "I just do it!" Emily looked up. Iain had reappeared right over her head.

"You have to think it *and* feel it," explained Grace. She shifted into her human form and rose to meet her siblings. "I think," she added.

Emily pointed at Grace's jeans and t-shirt. "Those aren't the clothes you were wearing," she observed.

Grace looked down at her body, then pointed back at her siblings. "Neither are those," she said, indicating Emily's skirt and blouse and Iain's jeans and hoodie. "Our human form here is just, like, a memory, a way we think of ourselves. We're not just ghosts of our bodies or something."

Iain curled into a ball and rolled, dipping down as he spoke. "Is that the hospital down there?" he asked. "It's all blurry. Fuzzy. It's hard to make out." He formed an arm and a hand and used it to point in what felt like a downward direction.

"I think it is," said Grace, following his gesture. "People in our world call this the Astral level. That's one of its names, anyways. How things appear to us here depends on how we focus. The Astral Realm can look and feel like the world we know, with us moving around in it like we're used to doing, but like ghosts. Or it can look like colors and swirls and fuzz and waves and all sorts of stuff, where we can move around anywhere. And we might meet all sorts of strange people."

Iain formed his human head and other arm, as if he was learning to maintain his bodily form one piece at a time. He turned around to scan the sky. "Speaking of strange people, where did that hand go that pulled us out? I thought we'd be meeting Alice here."

Grace followed her brother's gaze. "I don't know," she said.

"I think we're supposed to be doing this on our own," said Emily. Just as Iain was experimenting with his human form, Emily was playing with her "fireball" form. She held out an arm, willed it into a fuzzy, glowing appendage, then back again. She beamed at Grace with a grin, her eyes wide.

"What *are* we supposed to be doing?" asked Iain. He was speaking to Grace. Having been here before, and having been the one to dream of Alice, she was obviously the one with the answers. Or should be.

Grace shook her head. "I'm not sure," she said. "I was expecting Alice to be here too. But she's not. All I remember is that we're here to find Linda. We know something's off with her because of that moving mole."

"Perhaps we should explore for a while," said Emily. "Maybe Alice will show up."

"Explore what?" asked Iain.

Emily pointed downward. "Let's go back and check on our bodies," she said. "Make sure everything's all right. And then let's go look more closely at the Grid."

Grace nodded in agreement. She had no better idea, and didn't know their next step.

"What's that?" said Iain, pointing toward a small, bright yellow light in the distance. It was approaching quickly.

Emily and Grace turned to watch it. The tiny spark twinkled and flashed as it neared, giving off a vibration of joy that all three kids could feel. The spark came right at Grace like a meteor, crashing into her and rolling her backward across the sky. Grace began to laugh with delight as the tiny spark resolved itself in her arms and licked her face.

It was Dennis.

4.4

Television commentators were now calling the new disease "Greensleeves." Keeley's heart pounded at the news. To give it a name meant that it was "a thing," something new to be dealt with, an epidemic with a cause and a vector rather than a few random, unexplainable deaths. It was real. It was growing and spreading. And Keeley, sick in bed, had to wonder whether her own illness was somehow connected.

"Alas," the woman on the sidewalk had said. *Alas* and *my love* and *alas* again. And the man on the gurney had said the same thing, according to Mary. And other victims had said the same things, if these reporters were to be believed. As if this "alien flu virus," or whatever the hell it was, played that old tune in people's heads as they died. Or as if, as they neared that fabled tunnel to the other side, what they found awaiting them there was love. Or perhaps it was a song of protestation. *Alas, my love, you do me wrong, to cast me off discourteously.* Greensleeves. Of course. And Keeley had been right there as that woman had died, and was now sick herself. And Mary and Ness and the kids had been in the hospital when that contractor had been brought in. And who knew what this disease was and how it spread? Shit!

There were cases now in cities all around the planet. Mumbai. Sydney. London. San Francisco. Chicago. Augusta had been the first, as far as anyone could tell. It had begun with the President, they now said. Linda Travis was the index case. Patient zero. Followed by the woman on the sidewalk a week later. But Keeley wasn't sure it all added up. The quick response taken by the military to sequester the President, and the even more telling fact that they'd already created a facility over and around her old summer cottage on Squirrel Island, meant that somebody knew something about this beforehand. Somebody on the inside. Though there was no mention of this in the public discourse, Keeley knew: Linda had not been showing symptoms when she'd been abducted and put into confinement. And so far, Linda was still alive.

How long between when the virus was contracted and it killed a person? What was the symptomology? Was it contracted through touch? Breath? The exchange of bodily fluids? What was its lethality? Was the President really suffering from the same thing that had killed these others? Or was it something else? If it *was* the same disease, then how long did Linda have before the situation resolved, one way or the other? Nobody could answer these questions. But the press sure did love to ask them.

Thankfully, Keeley was actually feeling a bit better. Which meant that this was probably just a matter of coincidence. She'd just happened to catch a bug at an inopportune time. One of those spring things that went around, especially with the seasons so out of whack. Or maybe a touch of food poisoning. She didn't have a rash on her face, after all. And she sure as hell wasn't hearing some old English folk song in her head. Keeley clicked off the television and took three deep breaths. Her stomach was not as sour as it had been this morning, and she had more energy. That was good. She couldn't bear to think of what it would do to Mary, for Keeley to be taken down, and even out, by this Greensleeves.

Rising from her bed, Keeley grabbed her laptop from her nightstand and sat heavily in the armchair by the window, feeling the afternoon heat pulse through the glass behind her, overpowering the air conditioning. Perhaps a bit of work. She should call Stan for an update. See where they were in their search for the kids. Make sure somebody was in regular contact with people at the Squirrel Island facility. And there were messages from the VP. She knew he'd need more handholding now than ever.

A knock sounded at the door and Keeley rose to answer it. It was Ness with a tray of food.

"You feel like eating, sweetie?" asked the older woman. Ness hurried inside, placed the tray on the end of the bed, and reached out for a hug. Keeley returned it gladly, though she wondered if maybe they shouldn't all be more careful now, given the unknown nature of this new illness. She noted how the aroma of Ness's meal made her feel suddenly ravenous, and pushed away thoughts of illness and epidemics. How could she be sick if she was hungry?

Ness released her at last and the two women stood face-to-face, arms still clasped. Ness smiled up at Keeley, who had a good eight inches on her. "I made you chicken and dumplings," she said with a flash of her eyebrows. "Though I had to use cornmeal for the dumplings."

"You're a gem," said Keeley, releasing the old woman's arms and stepping over to lift the lid on her food. Along with the chicken, Ness had prepared a salad, the greens no doubt from their private garden. One advantage of summer in March, thought Keeley with a sigh.

"Any word on the kids?" asked Ness.

Keeley shook her head. "Nothing so far," she said.

Ness placed the lid back on the chicken and lifted the tray. She placed it on the little two-seater table opposite the bed and laid it all out before taking the tray away. Ness patted the chair for Keeley to come and sit. Keeley sat, smiling. There was even a sprig of aging lilacs in a tiny vase.

"I'm worried sick about 'em," said Ness at last.

Keeley reached out and took Ness's hand. "Me too," she said.

"And I'm worried about Linda."

Keeley nodded. "We all are."

Ness pulled out the chair opposite Keeley and sat lightly on the edge. "Do you suppose it's like that Pastor Clinton says?" she asked. Her face was dark and tight, as though his name was bitter on her tongue.

"What's the ol' Pastor saying now?" said Keeley. "I don't pay him much attention."

"Oh, you know," said Ness, staring down at her lap. "Same old thing." She glanced up at Keeley. "He's batshit crazy, I realize," she said. "But I wonder if there's something to it just the same."

"What'd he say?" asked Keeley again.

Ness shook her head and waved her hand in the air, as if trying to rid herself of flies or mosquitos. "He's just... you know. Talking about retribution for our sins and all that. Like he always does. He was on ACN just a while ago. Says that this alien flu is God's retribution for our sinful ways. Says that Linda got it first because of her faithless attempts to try to save the world. Says that the world is in God's hands, and that a sinful humanity is being cast off in this Time of Burning, and that this alien flu is His way of doing that, and that the only thing to do now is get down on our knees and pray for mercy."

Keeley put down her fork and slid back in her chair. She closed her eyes and took a deep breath. "And do you believe that?" she asked. She opened her eyes. There was no judgment in her voice. No anger. No ridicule. She found, as she asked it, that she really wanted to know. Despite her disgust with such as Pastor Clinton, she couldn't deny that there was some strange power in his words. Like Ness, she wondered if there was "something to it."

"I don't think Linda is sinful," said Ness, her eyes hard. "And I don't think trying to save the planet is evil." She glanced around the room, as if checking to make sure no one else was there to hear her. "But I can't help thinking that our chickens are coming home to roost, Keeley. That we have nobody to blame now but ourselves. And if somebody's... you know... behind this thing, this flu... if somebody's stepping in to cast us off... well, I'm not sure I can blame them, whether it's God or the Devil or the aliens or whomever. You know?" Ness smiled tightly, grimly, apologetically.

Keeley regarded the older woman with open, loving eyes of understanding. The name "Greensleeves" made all the more sense now. Casting us off discourteously. Indeed. She picked up her fork, stabbed a chunk of chicken, and put it in her mouth.

4.5

Paul DuPont logged off and cleared his screen. He knew that the Colonel would show up in a moment and he had no desire to arouse suspicions at this point. He buttoned his cardigan against the cool, underground temperatures and turned to face the door.

As if on cue, Colonel McAfee turned the handle and stepped into the lab. He arrived with his usual, arrogant scowl and casual swagger. The message was clear: he considered such meetings an inconvenient interruption to his real work. DuPont had no idea what McAfee considered his real work to be. Drinking at the club, perhaps? Sleeping late? Making jewelry out of sea glass? It didn't matter. The good Colonel was as inconsequential to what happened here as the outlets on the wall. You need Colonels, of course, just like you need outlets. People function best within an organization when there's a clear understanding of hierarchy and control. But it doesn't much matter which outlet you use, and the real power comes from behind the wall. DuPont smiled at his metaphor as the Colonel approached, trusting that his nominal superior would simply assume that his Chief Tech was happy to see him.

"Everything's in order with the VLT," said DuPont, intending to steer the conversation to a quick conclusion.

"The VLT?" asked the Colonel. He ran his hand across his crew cut as if proud of his ability to grow hair.

DuPont squinted his eyes to keep them from rolling. "The Virtual Linda Travis, Colonel," he explained. "That's what we've taken to calling her down here."

"I see," said McAfee. He gazed around the lab, where at least a dozen technicians and programmers worked in cubicles. He looked down on DuPont. "The VLT. Anything to report?" he asked. He shifted his weight from foot to foot, like a man who hoped that the answer would be no.

DuPont was delighted to disappoint him. "The President just finished a chat with her Senior Advisor, Mary Hayes, Colonel," he said.

"Really?" said McAfee with uncommon interest. "And who initiated?"

"I did," said DuPont. He turned back to his screen and brought up the chat. "Ms. Hayes was added to the watch list by the folks in charge," he explained. "I have no idea how she could possibly disrupt us at this point, but with the President's children gone missing, she's likely to react in unexpected ways. I decided to check in with her, see how's she's doing, and see if I could help keep her calm." DuPont's chin jutted forward slightly as he spoke. He was brilliant. He'd managed to affect just the right mix of deference and self-justification. And his mention of "the folks in charge" was yet another decoy on the pond.

"You mean the President," said McAfee. "The President checked in with her."

DuPont's eyebrow lifted in disbelief, but he doubted the Colonel noticed. It was hard to believe this guy was once part of The People, though the Colonel did not know that his Chief Technician knew about that. "Of course," he said. He took a long, deep breath. "The language gets confusing sometimes."

"Right," said McAfee. The Colonel pulled over a chair and took a seat to peruse DuPont's monitor. "So how'd it go?"

"Most excellent," said DuPont. "The President is understandably upset that the kids are missing. Add to that the stress of her illness, the indignity of her confinement, and her upcoming Summit speech and you have one tired, frightened, angry woman. I can say almost anything at this point and it won't raise a red flag. Ms. Hayes bought the whole thing."

"So how's she doing?" asked the Colonel. "Mary, I mean. Not... you know."

DuPont allowed himself to smile openly at that. This Colonel was as thick as a brick. He gestured toward the screen. "Upset, as you'd expect," he said. "Angry. Mary Hayes is fairly compromised at this point, both physically and mentally." He explained the situation as if he had no reason to expect that McAfee might already be familiar with Mary's fateful encounter with the unpredictable Agent Rice. "She suffered a traumatic brain injury a few years ago and has never been the same. Essentially, she's a glorified nanny, and with the kids gone, she doesn't know what to do. She spent most of the chat just talking about her feelings and telling the President how much she missed her and how worried she is about Linda's health."

McAfee rubbed his stubbled chin. "Poor kid," he muttered.

"She requested voice contact but I had Linda claim a sore throat and the need to pamper her voice before her speech," said DuPont. "My tendency is to use that option more and more. It cuts down on requests for phone contact and adds to the impression of a progressing disease. I don't yet fully trust the voicing software."

"Add a sore throat? Even if it doesn't match-?"

"Doesn't matter," said DuPont, shaking her head. "They're a long way from understanding the symptomology."

McAfee sighed and slid back his chair. DuPont knew the Colonel had little interest in reading the actual chat. McAfee hadn't even bothered to put on his glasses. He preferred to have it summed up for him, a task DuPont was glad to perform, as he could then spin things any way he wished. Unlike his supposed boss, he *did* know what his real work was.

"So what's your take on the missing kids?" asked McAfee, taking a toothpick from his jacket pocket and sticking it in his mouth.

DuPont shrugged noncommittally. "Not sure," he said. "Above my pay grade. I was certainly surprised, of course. But I have no idea how this might interfere with Changeling, or whether the folks in charge had anticipated this. If the Life are back...the aliens..." DuPont let his voice trail off. He, in fact, *didn't* know what the missing kids were all about. That bothered him. He *should* know. And *if* the Life are back...

The Colonel pulled the toothpick from his teeth, examined the wet end, and stuck it back in his mouth. "Ah well..." he said. It was his way of bringing a conversation to an end. Especially when he had no idea what to say. Gotta shut that brain down before it overheats, don't you Colonel?

As if he could hear DuPont's thoughts, the Colonel stood, straightened his jacket, and headed toward the door. "We're on full alert," he said. His tone implied that DuPont should remain on duty and not pop off to the club for some nachos and beer. "My superiors fear that the kids are on their way here, and that the aliens are, indeed, involved. I don't intend to allow them access." With a brisk nod the Colonel was gone.

DuPont smirked at McAfee's back. You don't even know who your superiors are, Colonel, he thought. And you think you're going to hitch a ride in the Giant Leap? DuPont dismissed the President's chat from his screen with a wave of his hand and pulled up his unfinished report. He had some questions for *his* superiors, whom he well knew. He needed to know what was going on with the kids and the Life. After that, who knows? Maybe he would pop out for some nachos and beer.

4.6

A smiling Colonel McAfee made his way up one level to the ground floor of the President's former summer cottage. He loved his little talks with Senior Virtual Effects Supervisor Paul DuPont. What a snot-nosed little punk. DuPont clearly thought McAfee a fool, an assessment the Colonel was only too happy to bolster. It was always better to be underestimated. You never knew when other people's misperceptions might come in handy.

DuPont had no idea that Aidan McAfee had once been Sam Phelps, a high-ranking member of the unit tasked with supervising direct contact with the aliens. He'd *worked with* Mary Hayes, for Chrissake. He'd reported directly to General Lowell, who had headed The People and *then* served as Linda Travis' Secretary of Defense. Well, up until he'd gone missing. Aidan McAfee was one connected dude.

McAfee passed through the retinal scan and into his office, a nice, well-lit space that had not long before served as Linda's bedroom. He picked up his sleeping cat, Nicky, from his office chair, sat down, and placed the cat gently back on his lap. Nicky hardly seemed to notice, and settled right back to sleep. McAfee flicked on his tablet. He had reports to write. He had a full alert to oversee. And maybe it was time to give his old buddy Mary a call and see what was up. Missing kids and rogue woks could throw a wrench into the works, and Aidan McAfee didn't want a wrench in the works. He wanted The Families' Plan to succeed. He wanted a berth on one of the ships.

And most of all, he wanted the satisfaction of seeing the look on DuPont's face when he learned that McAfee would be joining them on their journey.

4.7

"So you just snuck in and whisked this whole thing away, body and pedestal and all," said Linda. She was standing next to the container that held her naked form. She'd already found out that her hands, her *astral* hands, would pass right through both the container and her body. The experience had been disturbing, and she did not wish to repeat it. Linda glanced over at the Fisherman, who stood on the opposite side of the lobster tank, watching her. The Martian light gave his bright white hair and beard a pinkish tinge.

"It was a wee bit more complicated than that, Madam, but yes, I whisked you away, as you say."

"And that's why I'm naked. Because this is how they had me... stored."

"I regret that I had no time to pop into your home for a change of clothing," said William. "Even if I had, I don't know how I would have managed to dress you." He waved toward Linda's body with a slight shrug, as though his dilemma were obvious.

Linda regarded her body now, her astral body. "So why am I wearing worn jeans and a Michigan State sweatshirt?" she asked.

William's eyes crinkled with pleasure. "Your default astral body is more habit and memory than anything, Madam President. Were we a full step up, fully in the Astral, you would find yourself to be even more fluid, with the ability to morph into what we might call energetic or vibratory states, or a variety of different and seemingly physical configurations. But, *were* we a full step up, you would also be beyond my ability to contain you here on Mars."

"And the only way you can think to have this conversation is by being in complete control of me," said Linda, her voice suddenly cold and sharp.

The Fisherman smiled weakly, closed his eyes for a moment, and took a couple of deep breaths. When he opened his eyes there was sadness in them. "It is my fervent hope that you will one day understand the necessity which compels me," he said.

Linda cocked her head to the side. "You might get caught hoping, William," she said, a playful warning that held the subtext *don't bet on it.*

The Fisherman bowed slightly and brought his hands together before his chest in *Namaste.*

Linda nodded her head in return, then turned back to her contained body and rested her hands on her hips. "You don't think they're going to notice a missing body?" she asked.

William paused for a moment. He raised a finger. "I believe I have successfully befuddled the situation," he said. He turned quickly away and looked across the plain, staring at the Face mesa for a few moments before returning his eyes to the sky.

Linda followed his gaze. Directly above were two bright spots that outshone the yellow-pink sky, one moving slowly past the other like a car in the passing lane.

"Deimos and Phobos," said the Fisherman. He glanced at Linda with a lawyer's sly expression. "Would you like to see them?"

Linda turned back to the container and stared a little longer. The body inside looked like her, and yet it didn't. Something essential was missing. It was as though she'd been laid out on a mortuary slab, not Scrooge to the Fisherman's Ghost, but Marley, dead as a doornail. Her spark, her soul, was long gone from it. This was just a shell.

It wasn't her. It never had been. Then Linda chuckled softly. Nothing had gone missing. *She* was her. She, here in the Astral, talking to this man William. *She*, this *conscious she*! *She* was herself. Apart from this body. Apart from the Earth. Apart from the whole realm of physical stuff. *She* was still here, still *her*, still alive, still thinking and feeling and wanting and doing. Death, it seemed, and as the spiritual traditions had long insisted, was not an end at all.

"Linda?"

Linda looked up at the Fisherman, both her rescuer and her captor. "Yes, William?" she said.

The Fisherman pointed to the sky. "Would you like to see the fabled moons of Barsoom?" he asked.

Linda glanced back at the form on the pedestal. This body was not her. It was just something that held her for a time, a container made of flesh and blood and bone. She, Linda Travis, was something more than that container. She could feel that now. She knew it. And that felt like a profound gift, given to her by a man who might, it seemed now, prove to be more than either rescuer or captor. She turned and nodded. "I'd like that," she said.

She felt strangely free. Even with her body confined on the Martian surface. Even with her soul confined to near-Mars space. Even with her future seemingly bound tightly to the whims and wishes of the wiry old man who stood before her, Linda felt free. She gave William a warm smile and found, despite her fears and suspicions and judgments, that she meant it.

With a deep bow, William led them up into the sky.

4.8

Speaking about it years later, Cole would explain that something finally snapped back into place. The soul wrenching "hops," the abduction of his wife, the disappearance of his kids, the unraveling of the world around him: all of these things and more piled up onto Cole until he could take no more. With an inner shift akin to a prisoner ripping off his manacles, Cole threw away his pain, his grief, and his tears. He disgorged the rotting mass of shame that lay in his guts. He coughed the worry from his lungs. He unbuckled his brittle armor of self-doubt and tossed it to the floor. He rose to his feet and noticed that his back felt strong and straight again. Whatever it was that had snapped had created a space for something new to arise.

Cole pocketed his phone, pulled on his shoes, and stepped to his door. He knew where he was headed. And may the gods damn those who might try to stop him.

Cole Thomas had found his anger.

The mysterious caller had laid out his plan in simple terms. "You must get yourself to Squirrel Island, Mr. Thomas," the disguised voice had said. "You need to be there in person, banging on the gates, raising a stink. Leave the rest to me. We'll create a media circus the likes of which they will not have anticipated."

"Why should they care?" asked Cole.

"You're the President's husband," the caller had said, his voice so heavily garbled that Cole had to strain to understand it. "Believe it or not, Linda Travis has banked a great deal of goodwill during her administration, even as things have spun out of her control. Many of her people still love her, Mr. Thomas. They'll be on your side."

The caller sounded confident in his plan, but Cole was not so sure. He'd seen cowardice and corruption enough to last him to the end of his days. He did not trust those in charge to deal openly and fairly with him. And there were vast, hidden forces on the move now. He flinched at the thought of them, circling overhead like vultures, but he knew that he'd have to face them. Cole clenched his fists. *The bastards took my wife! They involved my children!* He grabbed the handle and yanked the door open. Like it or not, he'd have to trust that the mysterious caller knew what he was talking about. He really had no choice. No other plan. His anger needed an outlet, and this was something he could do. It was better than hiding, helpless and hobbled, in the Presidential Home. And he very much wanted to bang on those bastards' gates.

The hallway was empty. Mary must have ducked out during his call. Cole was glad she was not still there, waiting for him. He didn't need her spying on his field right now. She might try to stop him. Cole walked quickly down the hall, out of the Family Suite, through the wing of offices, and into the more public areas of the Presidential Home. He knew, as was standard procedure, that he'd pick up a trio of Secret Service bodyguards on the way out. That was fine for now. All they needed to do was get him to Stan Walsh. After that, with any luck, Stan would know what to do.

I'm coming, Linda, Cole whispered in his mind, hoping that, somehow, his wife could hear him. He pictured her lying on a cold, stainless steel table in a level-four biocontainment laboratory, surrounded with high-tech machinery and grim scientists in positive pressure suits. How could they build such a thing in her old cottage? He didn't understand. He only knew what he'd been told though official channels, and that wasn't very goddamn much. No doubt Linda was as furious as he was, and terrified for her health. He trusted she was giving them hell. If the virus she had was this Greensleeves thing the media was talking about... well, Cole didn't even want to think about that. He hoped the doctors there had the sense not to tell her about the people now dying all around the planet. But Cole didn't think these people had much sense.

Cole's heart pounded with frustration at the thought of Linda having to go through this alone. That was the part that most appalled him, that they'd cut her off from the people she loved right when she most needed them. Did these doctors understand nothing of healing? Or has even the concept of healing been crushed under the hobnailed boot of the "national security state"?

He laughed at himself. Of course it had. Why did such things still astonish him, after all he'd seen? Cole descended the last staircase and crossed the main lobby. Ahead was the Secret Service checkpoint. Cole imagined ahead, into the future he would attempt to create. He imagined himself pounding on the gates, the strange sparks of light flying from his fists as he did so. He could hear himself shouting, calling, insisting, demanding. He could see himself succeeding. He took a deep breath and stepped up to the checkpoint.

Cole understood the likelihood that he'd only be able to see Linda through some plate glass window or something. There was this virus to consider, after all, and he did not know what to think of it. The fact that he and the kids had not also been quarantined gnawed at his mind. As did that mole that Emily had pointed out. Nothing seemed to fit like it should. Something was wrong. Someone was lying. Cole had thought that it was high time *somebody* figured out what and why and who. He could see, now, that that somebody was *him*.

Cole realized that he needed Linda right now as much as she needed him. He put a hand to his stomach to try and ease the pain that clawed at him, the deep terror for his children that threatened to overwhelm his ability to think and act. He needed Linda. He needed his President. He needed her power and authority, her quick mind and her fierce heart. Linda Travis could get the kids back if anyone could.

Cole acknowledged the stone-faced young woman at the desk before him with a nod. "I need an escort to Secretary Walsh's office," he said, as casually as he could manage. Stan was the first step of the mysterious caller's plan. "Start with Stan," he'd repeated before hanging up. So Cole would take that first step, knowing that it would put him on the path he had to walk, with many more steps to follow. Some of them might feel impossible. But that's what his anger was for: to empower him in the face of impossible odds.

One way or the other, Cole was going to get to Linda's side.

4.9

"I'm so glad you're feeling better," said Mary, nuzzling Keeley's neck. "I was so worried." Her knees were pulled up against Keeley's side.

Keeley buried her nose in Mary's hair and inhaled deeply. "Me too," she said, her voice a dusty whisper. She ran her hand down Mary's back, smoothing her silk shirt, hoping to help calm her.

Mary rose up on one elbow, pulled her head back, and looked Keeley in the eye. She stared for a moment but did not speak. Keeley's long, dark hair, freed from its ponytail, lay splayed out on the pillow.

"You checkin' out my field?" asked Keeley with a grin.

Mary nodded. "All I see is love," she said. "My love."

Keeley stretched up to kiss Mary, then sank into the covers. "What have you been up to?" she asked.

"I spoke with Linda," said Mary, settling back down onto the bed. "Or chatted, I should say. She's feeling even worse now. Her throat's sore and her rash is spreading down her face. She's worried about the kids, of course. And Cole. And the... speech she's supposed to give. They've yet to isolate whatever it is that's causing her illness, which is pretty depressing. She says the constant tests are exhausting."

"Have they... you know... told her about this Greensleeves thing?" Keeley pushed herself up onto one elbow and cradled her head in her hand. "I mean... Jesus..." Keeley shook her head in disbelief.

Mary exhaled heavily. "She knows. They're giving her full access to media. Or as much as they can, given the limits of where she is."

"Does she...?"

"The doctors are operating on the assumption that Linda's illness and Greensleeves are the same thing, according to Linda. The first three cases were all in Augusta, and the..." Mary stopped and took a long breath while she waited for the word to come to her, "... the symptoms are roughly the same. Well, the facial rash matches, at least. But they're hopeful about Linda's case. If it is Greensleeves, then Linda's already had it for twice as long as the first two people who died. So maybe it hits different people in different ways. Maybe Linda's immune system will... fight it off. And maybe she'll help them figure out a cure. So, yeah, she's worried but hopeful."

"They must know more than they're telling us," said Keeley. "I mean... just the fact that they brought her in before she was showing symptoms..."

Mary ran a finger along the scar on her forehead. "I know. Linda thinks they must've found something in her blood. She'd had a routine physical two days before they came to get her."

Keeley shook her head in frustration, then bent forward for another kiss, letting her loose hair brush across Mary's face. "I was worried myself," she said with a sigh.

Mary reached out and took Keeley's hand and squeezed gently. Chatting with Linda no longer stirred up her old feelings of attraction for the President, about which she'd never told another living soul. Mary was Keeley's now. And Keeley was hers. A flood of warmth moved through her body.

Keeley returned the squeeze, then twisted around and swung her legs out over the edge of the bed. "But I'm good," she said, turning to glance quickly back at Mary before looking away again. "No rash. No more stomach pain. Ready to go." Keeley stood and headed to the bathroom, where she grabbed a brush to fix her hair.

"You going back to work?" asked Mary. She slowly uncurled herself and rolled over on her side. With a loud, dramatic sigh she pushed herself into a sitting position and slid her feet to the floor.

"You're darn tootin'," called Keeley. She ran some water in the sink and splashed her face. "I got kids to find."

Mary slipped her feet into her shoes, stood, made sure there was no dizziness, and then crossed the room for a parting kiss. "Don't you wear yourself out," she said to Keeley with a stern face.

"I won't," said Keeley. "I'll wear Mike and Stan out."

"Okay." Mary grabbed her bag from the table where Keeley had eaten. The sprig of lilac sat dejected and wilting beside the remains of her meal. "You want me to get these?" she said.

Keeley poked her head around the corner to see what Mary was talking about. "The dishes? No need. I was going to go get a pot of tea anyway." She cocked her head. "Where are you headed?"

Mary shook her head. "Not sure," she said, her forehead wrinkled and her eyes intense. "I think I'm supposed to go outside now. To look around."

"Supposed by whom?" asked Keeley.

Mary raised her eyebrows. "That would be the question, wouldn't it?" she said.

4.10

Emily hovered in the sky above the hospital, adjusting her senses back and forth between the physical and the Astral, noting the differences, trying to determine the best way of seeing. The fact that they could not get back into their bodies, that they could not even get into the room where they had left them, had filled her with worry. Grace had taught them how to see the thick psychic cords that sprang from their hearts and connected them to their bodies. All of the kids' cords seemed intact. But they could not follow their cords back into their bodies, and Grace had no idea why that was. Perhaps it was the nature of their hiding place: that it kept them from being found at the cost of keeping them separated. Perhaps it had to do with the strange hand that had pulled them free of their bodies. Perhaps it was something else entirely. But the result was this: they were not sure now that they could get back home. Emily had not considered that that was even a possibility.

Determined to learn as much as she could about this realm in which they appeared to be stuck, Emily continued to test her perceptions and abilities. She'd mastered the two default forms available to them - the "fireball," as Iain called it, and the human form - and had discovered that, in fact, they could take any form they wished, though it took more energy to maintain a form different from one of the defaults. Iain, following her lead, had transformed into a huge dragon he imagined from the fantasy novel he'd been reading. He swooped and soared about them, laughing and spitting fire. But he found that it quickly drained him, and had been quiet since. Emily, more moderate by nature, and proudly so, had simply experimented with different sorts of hands.

"You ready?" asked Grace, pointing upward. "We were going to go check out the Grid." She bent down to scratch under Dennis's chin, who wagged his tail in readiness.

Emily, in human form, as were all three now, smiled weakly. "I guess," she said.

"Let's blink there," said Grace. "For practice."

Emily exhaled her uncertainty. "Okay," she said, hesitating. She was not sure she'd figured that one out yet.

"Key in on me," said Grace. "You know? Get a sense of how I vibrate. And then just follow that."

"Sounds easy enough," said Emily, her tone of voice saying just the opposite.

Grace tucked and rolled, then popped back into human form, one finger raised in remembrance. "I know!" she said. "I'll send you both a packet of my previous experiences here. Then you'll know everything I know!" Without waiting for a response, Grace rolled back into fireball form, glowed brightly, and flashed like lightening. Iain and Emily fell back as the packet of experience, memory, and data washed over and through them.

"Whoa!" said Iain. "Give us a warning next time!" He popped into fireball form and spun like a gyroscope. Emily faded and flickered but maintained her human form. Her eyes were closed.

"Sorry," said Grace.

"There's so much information," murmured Emily. She opened her eyes to speak to her little sister. "You were really afraid."

"I was," said Grace, reaching out to pat Dennis's head. "Some of the time. But I had Dennis. And others came later, to help along the way."

"I can't think through it all so quickly," said Iain, back in human form. His face was clouded with distraction.

"Just review the part about how I got around," said Grace.

"Oh," said Emily, as noticing something she hadn't seen before. "Got it." She looked at Grace and then Iain. "Ready?"

"Let's do it," said Iain.

The three of them blinked up to the Grid.

Or tried to. No matter what they did, they could not seem to get near. Every time they got close, the Grid seemed to recede into space. Yet, when they stepped back to survey the situation, nothing had changed. The Grid was right where it had always been. They tried again and again; there was no getting near it. And when they attempted to blink out beyond the Grid, they found that there was no getting through.

"We're trapped inside," muttered Emily, shaking her head in frustration.

"And we can't get back to our bodies," said Iain.

The kids drifted back down toward the city below, Dennis in tow, finding some comfort in knowing that Augusta, and their home, and their father, and Mary and Ness, were not far away, even if they couldn't reach them. Dennis began to whine, a quiet, plaintive sound that seemed to sum up all of their feelings.

Grace patted her dog and turned to face the East. She stared at that distant horizon for a full minute. Her face was slack, her gaze soft.

"What is it?" asked Emily.

Dennis sat heavily at Grace's feet and watched the East as well, his head cocked.

At last Grace turned back to her siblings. "I really, really want to head in that direction," she said, tilting her head toward where she'd been looking. "I think that's our next move."

"Couldn't Alice just tell us what the heck is going on?" asked Iain, his voice snotty with frustration.

"I don't know," said Grace. "I don't know where she is or what's going on. All I know is that I want to head in that direction." She pointed to the Eastern horizon. Dennis pricked his ears and barked, as if he really wanted to go there as well.

Emily glanced at Iain and they both raised suspicious eyebrows in unison. "Your 'wanting' is what got us into this," said Emily to Grace, her tone one of gentle warning.

"That and your fussing about one stupid mole," retorted Grace, lifting her chin.

Emily stopped, took a long breath, nodded. "Right," she said. "I'm sorry. I don't need to blame this on you. I just... well... are you sure?" She lifted her shoulder. It wasn't like she had a better idea.

Grace nodded her head, accepting Emily's apology. "I'm sure that I want to go," she said. "I don't know why I have this feeling of wanting, but I do. I'm not sure of anything else."

Dennis barked again. His vote seemed to seal the deal. With a glance down at their hometown, the three kids and their gray-muzzled Whippet set off toward the East.

4.11

Stan stood for the longest time, just staring at Cole, two tall, strong men facing off in the Secretary's hot, humid State House office. It was like a game of *Who Blinks First?*, but there was nothing confrontational about it. It was more a matter of hard drives spinning and software rendering, a matter of assessing and calculating and scenario planning. What Cole had just proposed was something neither of them would have ever considered. But that was before...

"I'm in," said Stan at last, his eyes narrowing. He scratched his large, red nose. It was clear that he didn't like Cole's proposal. It was also clear that the idea filled him with excitement. Like Cole, Stan Walsh was ready to do something.

"You can..." Cole nodded toward the closed door, "... you know... get us out without..."

Stan chuckled softly, a glint of mischief in his eye. "I can," he said. He gestured toward the door, beyond which worked his assistants and secretary. "My people will cover for me," he said. "For a while, at least."

"Will it be dangerous?" asked Cole. "Out there?"

As if on cue a siren sounded in the distance. Stan glanced out his office window, across Capitol Park and the river beyond. He turned back to Cole. "The people we need to fear most wear suits and uniforms, Cole," he said. He gestured toward the east with a wave of his hand. "I don't think regular people are our biggest problem."

Cole exhaled heavily. "When should we go?" he asked.

"I'm not heading this expedition, Mr. Thomas," said Stan firmly, reminding Cole of who he was: the President's husband. "You tell me."

Cole stepped to the window and studied the landscape. The Kennebec River might be only the first of many obstacles. Squirrel Island was less than an hour away by car, but Cole had no idea what they'd find along the way. The country had changed dramatically in the last eighteen months. It might be the zombie apocalypse out there, for all he knew. Cole sighed again and looked at Stan. "I think we go now, Stan. If you can get us out of here. Now. Before I lose my nerve."

Stan grinned more broadly. "Now it is," he said. He grabbed his keys from his pocket, unlocked a desk drawer, and pulled out a handgun. "You know how to use one of these?" he asked Cole.

Cole nodded. "I've been training," he said. He'd asked for and received rifle and handgun training from the Secret Service since coming to Augusta. The increasingly dangerous world seemed to demand that of him.

Stan reached into the pocket of the sports coat hanging on the back of his chair and pulled out a second gun, this one smaller. He held it out to Cole, grip first. Cole took it without a word, tested its heft, then held it awkwardly at his side. Stan went to a closet in the corner, pulled out a pair of backpacks and stuffed them with a few boxes of ammo from a high shelf. He grabbed a banded stack of cash, two stainless steel water bottles, and a box of high-protein energy bars. He pulled out two concealed-carry holsters and tossed one to Cole. It was as if he'd been expecting this moment. Stan was ready to bug out at a moment's notice. Cole blushed. He hadn't even thought to grab his wallet.

Stan lifted the smaller backpack and handed it to Cole. There was excitement in his eyes. "I'm ready for a meeting with my President," he said.

4.12

Paul DuPont froze the video with a wave of his hand, leaned back in his chair, and sighed with satisfaction. That'll do, pig, he thought, a line from a movie he'd loved as a kid. The higher-ups had sent a last minute change in the President's summit speech, having decided that the VLT could not give a speech now without some mention of her missing children, word of which had leaked just a few hours ago. Paul had had to bust his ass to get the speech just right, and on time.

He was the only man for the job. He'd spent more time with the VLT than anyone, and more time studying the real Linda Travis. And he'd been the lead driver on most of her communications with the outside world since Changeling had been implemented. He knew just how much sadness to put in. How much anger. How much determination. And he understood the President's manner of speaking and gesturing like no other. For all intents and purposes, he was now the sole puppeteer behind the leader of the free world. Never before had the metaphor been so apt.

With the speech ready, there was little for Paul to do but watch and wait. They'd denied all requests for contact, using the President's need to save her energy, and her ailing throat, for her upcoming speech. Paul wished they'd thought of the whole throat thing earlier. Made it a part of the Quietus, even. It would've saved him sitting through a great many excruciatingly boring conversations. The President and her husband might have some great love going on in real life, but on the phone or online they were awkward and dull. The hubby was dull, at least. Paul, driving the VLT, just went with it.

With another wave of his hand he checked his mail. He'd requested information on the missing children, and any Intel his superiors might have on alien incursions into human space. So far there had been no response. He didn't know whether no news was good news or bad news. Or whether they were just busy with Phase One of the Quietus. Or whether it was something else. Perhaps it meant that it was none of his gods-damned business. Certainly he'd been told that before.

It wasn't like he didn't understand and accept the need for compartmentalization. There was more than one player in the game now, and some of their opponents could get pretty nasty. No need for Paul to know anything he didn't need to know when there were people, or sort of people, willing to torture that knowledge back out of him. But he didn't have to like the situation. And it wasn't like *not knowing* would get him out of the torture. It was the torture that would demonstrate what he didn't know, after all. Unfortunate that it worked that way, but there it was.

But if there were aliens headed his way in woks, shouldn't he know about that? Paul certainly thought so. He was sitting on a pretty important project here. The Life could put a stop to it in an instant, if they so desired. If they even had desires, that is. Who the hell knew?

What Paul knew was that he'd be glad when Changeling software could run itself. Or when the higher-ups decided to just kill the good Ms. Travis off completely, both real and virtual. He understood the whole *need for hope* thing. And why they'd chosen to locate his VLT division here on this godforsaken rock, right beside the bozos who were keeping POTUS on ice. He just wasn't sure it was worth it. And he wasn't sure it wasn't just some Family members yanking Sleepers around for shits and giggles. Who the hell cares about the Sleepers? That was Paul's thinking. The Families were outta here soon, weren't they? Let the zombies eat each other. There would be justice in that, wouldn't there?

Paul waved off his computer, stood, and stretched. The Sim was complete. Linda Travis was ready to speak to the whole world. Now it was time for those nachos and beer.

4.13

"So this is Phobos, then," said Linda as they hovered in space near the larger and much closer of Mars' moons. They floated with their faces to the sun, with Earth hanging near their star like a tiny, pale blue jewel. Deimos had reminded Linda of a large tooth, a premolar perhaps, and it seemed to hover almost stationary over the Martian surface below. Phobos, on the other hand, was shaped like a potato, and was covered with a crisscrossing of grooves that made the moon look like it was fabricated from woven fabric, like a wicker basket. As they matched Phobos' orbit, the Martian surface rotated visibly underneath. Not that directions like "underneath" made any real sense here. With a flick of her perceptions, the great mass of Mars could just as easily appear to dominate the "sky" overhead as the "ground" below. Dominate, as in seeking to crush her.

The Fisherman turned to face the President. "It is, Madam. And it's appropriate that we begin our conversation here."

"Is it?" said Linda. "How?"

"I'll tell you inside," said the Fisherman, flashing his eyebrows. "Follow me." This Fisherman vanished.

Linda, startled, spun around, expecting to find him behind her. He was not. She floated away from Phobos, noting again the strange, unnatural lines that covered it, then flew around it's great potato shape, hoping to find him hiding on the far side. The Fisherman was not there. Linda glanced back toward the sun. Toward Earth. With a quick glance back toward Phobos to see if her captor had reappeared, she leapt toward home, speeding away from the Martian surface as quickly as she could conceive. The sense of acceleration was exhilarating and Linda put everything she had, everything she could think of, into escape. Yet when she glanced back at Mars, she found she'd barely moved. Phobos, though a bit smaller, was still right there, silhouetted against the red glow of the planet's surface.

Realizing that William's own disappearance meant that one could instantly "think" oneself from one place to the other, Linda squeezed her eyes shut and thought about home. She thought of Cole and the last time they'd made love. She thought of Grace playing in the garden and Emily reading and Iain practicing his drums. She thought of Mary and Keeley and Stan and Sten. She thought of warm baths and hot tea and Dennis's cold, wet nose. She tried to "push" herself from where she was to where she wanted to be. But when she opened her eyes, there was Mars, still looming, dominating both overhead and underfoot, depending on how she oriented her perspective in the free-fall of space. The Fisherman's container was real, and she was trapped inside of it.

"Follow me," he'd said. The arrogant bastard. How the hell did she do that? *I'll tell you inside*. Inside what? Inside Phobos? Inside a moon? He'd told her she could pass through solid matter. Jesus! She'd even passed her hand right through her own body! But inside a moon? What could there possibly be to see inside of a rock? And how would she ever find him, if that was where he'd gone?

Find *him*. That was the key. She had to key in on *him*. On his body. His face. His being. His vibration, even. It didn't matter where he'd gone. If she just followed *him*, she'd end up where he was. Linda took a relaxing breath, closed her eyes, and imagined the Fisherman in her mind's eye. His face, with its fierce eyes and gentle smile. His feathery white hair. His proper British accent. His stupid Hawaiian shirt. But he was more than these outward features, wasn't he? He was a real human being, arrogant and self-assured, and yet vulnerable, clearly wanting Linda's understanding and acceptance. Even, he'd said, her love. He claimed he wasn't human, and yet Linda sensed something in him that could feel for others. He had a plan to murder a large portion of the human population, if what he'd said was to be believed. Perhaps what he really wanted was for Linda to talk him out of it.

Linda sighed, though she understood that her sighing involved neither lungs nor throat nor moving air. This was all too much. She was exhausted and angry and aching for her family. And now she had to play hide-and-seek with a man whose motives she could barely comprehend. It was the anger that burned red-hot at the surface of her being. Linda went with it. Closing her eyes once more, concentrating on this little old man who was pissing her off, Linda willed herself to *him*.

And there he was.

She stood on what appeared to be a ledge, a balcony carved into a vast stone wall. Before her was a cavernous rectangular room, large enough to easily fit an aircraft carrier. All six sides had been roughly cut from solid rock. And on the ledge with her, standing with his hands resting atop the half-wall that served as the balcony's railing, standing with his back to her, was the Fisherman.

"I was certain that you'd find me," he said, his voice as calm and still as a prayer.

"Where are we?" Linda could think of nothing else to say.

William turned. "Inside Phobos," he said with a wink. "In what might have served as a grand hall or conclave. For those who built this." He motioned toward the vast room with a sideways tilt of his head.

"Built this?" asked Linda.

The Fisherman nodded eagerly. "Phobos is an ancient spacecraft, Madam. Battered and dead, to be sure, but unmistakably crafted by intelligence."

Linda could only shake her head. There were too many questions to choose from.

"There are many such ruined craft to be found in our solar system. Phobos and Deimos are the only ones to be found stranded in orbit around a planet." He took a step away from the railing, toward the President.

Linda frowned. "Deimos is a spacecraft, too?" she asked.

"Most certainly," said the Fisherman, "though we've not yet succeeded in exploring it. We can tell that there are artificially hollowed out areas in Deimos, but we can find no way to enter, on the physical plane or otherwise. It is blocked to us."

"But..." Linda stopped and exhaled wearily. Her anger had evaporated as soon as she'd appeared here. She missed it. She wanted to be angry. She wanted that power. But she could not maintain her anger in the face of such mystery. "Ancient, you said?"

"It would seem," said William. "The remnants of a cosmic war from the solar-system's deep past. The Gods' War, we call it, though we understand only fragments of what happened."

Linda stepped forward, placed a tentative hand on the stone railing, and peered over the edge. She appeared to be a hundred feet or so from the stone floor. On the distant wall opposite her was another balcony. In the center of all four walls, at both floor and ceiling levels, were what appeared to be enormous stone doors. It was lit as if by daylight, but she could see no source for the illumination. She turned to face the Fisherman. "So why is this an appropriate place?" she asked.

"Madam?" said William, cocking his head.

"Back outside," explained Linda. "You said that it was appropriate that we begin our conversation here."

"Ah," said William. "Right." He stroked his neat beard. "Back on Earth, at this very moment, your virtual twin is poised to address a global summit of so-called world leaders."

"I'm not following," said Linda. She motioned toward the vast, open space behind her with a wave of her arm. "What does that have to do with this?

The Fisherman looked Linda in the eye. "You stand on a balcony that oversees the grand meeting hall of a long-deceased intelligent species. What better place from which to deliver your State of the Union address?" He grinned broadly, as though he'd been waiting to deliver that line.

"My what?" asked Linda, taken off guard.

"Your assessment, if you will," said the Fisherman.

"My assessment of what, William?"

William raised an eyebrow. "Of your administration, Madam President. And of the collective human situation back on planet Earth."

"But... surely you know more than I."

The Fisherman shook his head firmly. "I don't know what you know that you know, Madam."

Linda had to run that through her mind a couple of times before she grasped his meaning. "What is it you think I know?" she asked.

William smiled gently. "You failed to save the world, Madam President. I want for you to tell me why."

4.14

"I've been thinking," said Carl.

Ted looked up from his tiles and smirked. "That would explain the sound of grinding gears," he said. He returned his attention to the game. It was his turn again.

"No, really," said Carl.

Ted sighed, sat back in his chair, and rubbed his eyes with the tips of his fingers. "You're not gonna let me get out of saying 'what?' are you?"

"Maybe we haven't always been here," said Carl. "I mean... do you think about that? That maybe we were someplace else once? Before now?"

Ted shook his head from side to side. "I'm not sure I follow you," he said at last.

Carl shrugged, a grand gesture of both uncertainty and exasperation. "I don't know," he said, his voice almost plaintive. "But... I mean. There has to be, right? Somewhere else? Notice the words we've played. Fork. Basement. Keys." Carl pointed at each word on the board as he went along. "I mean... we play these words and we both just know what they mean and agree that they're words, but there is no fork here. No basement. No keys." He pointed at Ted. "So if you and I know these words, and if we know that they describe real things, then we must have come from some other time or place where such things exist."

Ted closed his eyes to think. "So..." he said, his eyes still closed, "we haven't always been here." He opened his eyes to look at Carl. "So what?"

"So we may not be stuck here!" said Carl, as if it were obvious.

Ted got up and checked the door again. "Still locked," he said.

"Yes!" said Carl, rising to join him. He shook the handle and pulled on the door. There was enough wiggle room in both that they made sounds as he jerked on them. "But maybe it won't always be so." He folded his arms in front of his chest. The expression on his face was that of someone who had just won.

Ted rolled his eyes and returned to his chair. He bent forward to stare at his tiles, hoping to put an end to Carl's crazy ranting. Perhaps if he just quickly played a word and made it Carl's turn, Carl would forget about this nonsense.

But Ted could find no word. At least, nothing good enough to score him the points he wanted.

Carl sat heavily in the chair opposite him. "Maybe there's something we have to do," he said softly.

Ted turned his letters face down on the table. "To do what?"

"To get out of here."

Ted stared. "So you want to get out of here?" he asked.

Carl scoffed. "Don't you?"

Ted surveyed the room. "It's not so bad," he said. He returned his attention to the game, righting his rack and shuffling the order of his tiles as the put them back in place. Accepting that he didn't have what he needed to get a high score, he drew three of his tiles and put them on the board, playing off the word that Carl had just played. "Spud," he said, "another word for potato."

Carl glanced at the word, then at his own tiles, and immediately drew three of them. "Rice," he said as he played his turn. He looked at Ted. Both of them smiled.

"Looks like we've got a food theme going here, Carl," said Ted. He put down three more letters to spell the word "wok."

"Looks like," agreed Carl.

Chapter Ø Five

5.1

Another powerful wave crashes over my head and sluices down my throat, choking me with salty, metallic brine. I kick and flail to keep my head above water as all around me, huge, dark bodies twist and lung and thrash. Dolphins are dying by the dozens and the water is red with their blood. The air is filled with screams. One of the screams is my own.

A boat appears to my left and I turn to face it. Along the edge stand grim men with long, bladed poles, tight mouths, and death in their Oriental eyes. The men plunge the blades into passing dolphins, slicing away their flesh and cutting away their lives. Others lean over the gunwale with large hooks and pull the dying creatures onto the deck to finish them off. A dolphin, a slab of flesh like a huge salmon steak peeling back from its side, leaps into the air right before me. I can see the panic in its eyes. Or is that rage? The dolphin lands in the boat, knocking a man over the edge and into the sea on the boat's opposite side before coming to rest on the deck. One man crushes the dolphin's skull with an iron bar while the others help their friend back aboard. Another wave slaps me in the face and I struggle, again, to keep my head above water.

Zacharael stands on the deck as solid and unmoving as a mast as the boat tosses in the choppy bay. The Oriental men seem not to notice him. The tall, thin, red-haired man's gaunt face is covered with tears and his mouth is round with horror and helplessness. He reaches out as if to stop one of the fishermen from plunging his blade back into the water. The fisherman goes about his work, unmoved by Zacharael's ghostly touch. Zacharael steps to the gunwale, looks me directly in the eye, then raises his arms out beside him and gazes prayerfully at the sky.

In a moment, we are once again in the depths of space. The thrashing cries of dolphins have been replaced by the silence of hard vacuum. I note the huge icy rock rolling underfoot, but my attention is demanded by Zacharael. He stares at me with eyes that burn with grief and rage. One of his eyelids ticks up and down, up and down, a barely perceptible twitch, like a prison door struggling to remain closed as the inmates inside pound on it with their fists. The tears on his face glisten like ice, as if the cold of space has frozen them.

Zacharael jerks his head to the right, looking away as though I disgust him. He waves his hand dismissively and again, in an instant, we are transported. We float in the air over a high, frozen plain that ends in a cliff jutting out over the sea. A small cluster of houses straddles the cliff's edge. The plain is flat and treeless, crusted with snow and ice. Carved into the ice is another huge symbol, that same circle bisected by an inverted L.

"What are you going to do about all of this?" asks Zacharael. I open my mouth to respond. I am not sure what he is talking about. But before I can answer, he has morphed again into a shiny black sphere. As it hovers in the sky before me, the whole world seemingly spinning about us, I fall backwards, tumbling head over heels onto the sofa.

Finishing, Gabrielle placed her notebook and pen on the floor, rose from her couch, and dragged her exhausted body across her darkened room to her bed, not even stopping to take off her clothes. Walking in her sleep, it did not occur to her how unfair was Zacharael's question.

5.2

Linda stepped to the podium that the Fisherman had materialized before her, Presidential Seal, microphone, and all. She turned back and wrinkled her brow. "No teleprompter," she said, her humorous tone conveying both anger and fear.

"All they want is you, Madam President," said the Fisherman. He pointed out toward the vast, cavernous hall before them. Linda turned and gasped. There, hovering just below the balcony in the weightlessness of Phobos' orbit, standing and waiting with faces lifted and eyes expectant, was a crowd that stretched from side to side and all the way to the back.

Linda scanned the multitude. These were her people. Sprinkled amongst the nameless faces were many she knew, and some she loved: Cole and his kids, Mary and Keeley, Stan and Sten and Mike and Ness. There was Obie and Agent Rice, who'd disappeared together into the blackness of a rubix. There was Sina and Utterpok and Payok and Aamai, and countless other Inuit she'd never had time to know. There was Alice. There was Spud. There was the General. There was Pooch. There was her mother, missing and presumed dead, and Cole's first wife, Ruth, who'd died in a plane crash, and Linda's long-dead husband, Earl, who'd died in his boat. There was Cole's father, Ben, who had passed from cancer just last year. There were senators and there were congresspeople. Supreme Court justices and CEOs. Bankers and brokers and lawyers and pundits and lobbyists and reporters. There were great numbers of "average Americans." Linda knew it was all a mirage. A trick at the hands of the man who now held her captive. It didn't matter. Her heart was filled with warm love and sharp grief and bittersweet longing and stinging resentment. Pain raked her face with deep creases.

William stepped up beside her and put a hand on her shoulder. "Tell your people why you failed," he said gently.

"You're a cruel, cruel man!" spat Linda, whirling to face him.

The Fisherman nodded but did not defend himself. Linda closed her eyes and took a deep breath. "Tell them," said William again. "Tell the truth. Tell it all. Tell your people the state of their union, Madam President. They need to know."

Linda opened her eyes and turned to face the crowd. She pushed a strand of yellow-blonde hair from her forehead, opened her mouth to speak, then glanced back at the Fisherman. "I don't understand what this has to do... " she protested.

The Fisherman raised his hand to stop her. "You will," he said.

Linda shook her head in frustration and turned back to the crowd. Inhaling deeply, she leaned forward to the microphone. "I failed," she said simply, then doubled over, sobbing. Those two words had untied the knots of shame and guilt and grief that had been holding her together for months. Years. Between the sobs came huge, gasping inhales, like a swimmer coming up for air after far too long underwater. She held to the podium, her hands clutching the corners, afraid she might otherwise fall or float away. Huge tears spattered the slanted lectern top and rolled to the edge, defying the lack of gravity. The crowd watched in attentive silence.

The Fisherman leaned forward to speak into her ear. "You failed," he repeated.

Linda glanced up at him through her tears. "I couldn't do it!" she hissed. "Nobody could do it. There was no winning." She wiped her tears away with the back of her hand. "We all failed."

"You couldn't do it," said William. "Nobody could have done it."

Linda shook her head. "No," she said.

"What didn't work?" asked the Fisherman.

The President bowed her head and closed her eyes. "Nothing worked," she said. "I tried. Jesus, I tried." She glanced back at the Fisherman with one open eye. "It was all too much."

The Fisherman nodded warm understanding. "What was too much, Madam President?"

Linda wiped her nose on her sleeve, uncertain where to start. "I don't know," she said. "The climate? The population? The oil running low? I mean... Jesus, William, where do I start? There's just too much wrong with the world. Too many problems, too long ignored. Too much wrong with us. There was no way to fix it all."

"And that was your job. To fix it."

Linda exhaled heavily. "Nobody could fix it," she said.

"So you were set up, then?" asked the Fisherman. He cocked his head slightly to the side.

Anger flashed across Linda's face like afternoon thunderstorms. "Yeah," she said with a quick nod. "I was set up." She turned and looked back out over the crowd, finding there a sea of faces raptly attending her every word, hungry for answers. She turned back to the Fisherman. "But set up by whom?"

William nodded. "Indeed."

5.3

Mary, silent, her face slack in the moonlight, stared up at the sky.

"Ma'am?" said Agent Gilder. The short, dark-haired agent stepped hesitantly forward, her hand outstretched, in case Mary was feeling faint.

Mary noted her bodyguard's presence but did not respond. There was too much in this moment. The agent would have to wait. Mary squinted her eyes slightly, then opened them fully again. Something was different but she didn't know what. The Grid was still there, shining brightly against the stars. The crescent moon slid slowly across the sky, its motion made more apparent by the Gridlines. The few clouds she could see were mere wisps. But there was something about the sky that caught her attention. There was an image in her mind, of Cole's three children peering down at her from above, like kids watching an ant on the sidewalk. She did not know what this meant.

"Ma'am?" said Agent Gilder a second time. She was worried about Mary standing so long in this heat, still sweltering even after the sun had set.

Mary pulled her gaze away from the sky. "Yes?"

"Are you okay, Ma'am?"

"I'm fine," said Mary.

"Are we going someplace I need to know about?" asked Gilder.

Mary shook her head. "We're just... going," she answered. She waved her hand around, to indicate the trees looming over them, and the open field at the end of the drive. "Following." She looked at Agent Gilder. "I'm trying to feel... something."

The agent relaxed her shoulders, resting her hand on the radio at her hip. "I've heard about you," she said. "You've got a knack for seeing things most people can't see." Gilder glanced over her shoulder to make sure they were alone, then returned to Mary. "I do too," she added. "A bit."

"Really?" said Mary, giving Gilder her full attention. She was always heartened to learn that Secret Service agents were real human beings. "What do you see?"

Agent Gilder shrugged. "Not much. Just ... every now and then ... little pointers. You know? Like... signs, maybe. Or arrows. Go this way. Drive in this lane. Take this hallway. That sort of thing. I found my little brother that way, when we were kids. He was hiding. From my dad."

Mary recoiled at that, knowing exactly what it meant to hide from one's father, feeling again her shame and guilt over having left her own little brother behind, and wondering again where he'd ended up. With all the resources of The People, and then the US government, she'd never been able to find him. Danny was probably dead. Mary had a bad track record when it came to protecting kids.

"Are you searching for the President's children?" asked the young agent. There was a touch of excitement in her eyes, evident even in the moonlight.

Mary nodded. "Of course." She started ambling down the drive-way toward Parkwood Drive. The trees on either side fell away, opening up the sky. The overgrown athletic field on the other side of Capitol Street shimmered faintly in the Gridlight.

"Can I...?" said Agent Gilder, following.

Mary stopped and turned.

"Can I tell you what I sense?" asked the agent. "If I sense any-thing?"

"You must," said Mary.

Gilder studied the ground for a moment, then looked back up at Mary. "I never get to talk about this stuff. With the other agents. You know?" She shook her head in wonderment. "They just think it's stupid."

"Old habits die hard," said Mary. She started again down the drive. Agent Gilder followed, noting that Ms. Hayes seemed strong today, and was walking straight and tall. They turned onto Parkwood, keeping to the shoulder, which was easier to see. All they had to go on was Gridlight and moonlight. The streetlights of Augusta had long since gone dark.

Parkwood brought them almost immediately to Capitol Street. Mary stopped and peered in both directions. The road was empty and quiet, save for the two soldiers who sat in a Jeep in the mid-dle of the intersection. Mary glanced at their fields but saw little of note, vague images of food and sex and wanting to be in bed, then guarded suspicion towards Mary and Agent Gilder, for showing up unexpected in the night.

Agent Gilder walked over and conferred quietly with the soldiers. One was shaking his head back and forth while the other muttered short, sharp phrases. Mary joined them, noting the lack of anxiety in her gut. Searching for the missing children had called her into her power in a way she'd thought was long lost.

"Is there a problem?" she asked.

The head-shaking soldier turned to her. "No, Ma'am," he said. "Not as long as your plan is to turn around and go back to your home. We've got this town locked down tight tonight."

Mary stepped closer. "You know who I am," she said. It was more a threat than a question.

"Sure do," said the muttering soldier. "But the President's chil-dren went missing today, as I'm sure you know." Mary noted the sarcasm in his voice, and wondered if the CO had already judged her as responsible. "The party or parties responsible may still be in the area. The Colonel has upped the threat level to orange. We're under curfew."

"Then I guess we're going to need an escort," said Mary evenly.

"Ma'am?" said the head-shaking soldier.

Mary nodded as though what she was saying were obvious. "Agent Gilder and I are doing a high-level psychic search for clues as to the children's whereabouts. Of course you want this to happen, and of course you should accompany us, for just the reasons you stated."

The two soldiers looked at each other, then back at Mary. "I don't think that's going to happen, Ma'am," said the muttering soldier.

"That's too bad," said Mary, her teeth glinting in the Gridlight. "Because your careers will suffer for it."

The head-shaking soldier motioned with a head tilt to his colleague and the two took a few steps away, to converse in low tones with faces close together. The muttering soldier glanced back at Mary repeatedly as the head-shaking soldier spoke. At last, they stopped muttering, turned, and stepped closer to Mary and Agent Gilder. "We're going to have to clear this higher up," said the muttering soldier.

Mary smiled sweetly. "I think that would be a good idea, soldier," she said, amiably. "And when you get Francis on the phone, do let me speak with him, will you please?"

The muttering soldier pulled out his phone.

5.4

"I'm glad to have you back online," said Vice President Singer. He sat in the cushioned office chair behind his expansive desk, his feet crossed and resting on the desk's edge. His hands were clasped behind his neck, cradling his large head with confidence and nonchalance. The room was so well air-conditioned that there wasn't so much as a spot of perspiration under his arms.

"I'm glad to *be* back online, Al," said Keeley. "It was a rotten time to get sick." Singer's head, reflected in the night-darkened window behind him, looked to her as though it was surrounded by a halo. Keeley wondered if it was something like this that Mary saw when she spoke of people's "fields."

"Right." Singer unclasped his hands long enough to paw at a tickle in his ear. "The ship of state continues to sail, no matter the waves that smash into its prow, knocking some of us to our knees." He smiled like a salesman, obviously pleased with his metaphor. "There is more to do now than ever before."

"Of course," said Keeley, working to keep her eyes from rolling. Try as she had, she'd never grown to like Albert Singer, and had never fully understood why Linda had kept him on when so much of her government had been shaken apart. Singer was an old-school political man, not particularly bright, and he'd never seemed to fully grasp the true implications of either the acknowledged presence of alien beings in the affairs of humanity or the unstoppable unraveling of the human-built economic and industrial machine, and the environmental nightmare that that machine had caused.

But there was more. Truth be told, even though no direct connection had ever been established between Singer and The People, or between Singer and whatever hidden layers existed *behind* The People, Keeley just couldn't shake the feeling that he'd been one of *them*. It came down to a matter of trust. Keeley did not trust her Vice President.

And yet Linda seemed to. So Keeley followed her President's lead, and accepted him, even when he all-too-easily fell into the role of acting-President in Linda's absence. Keeley would have preferred a great deal more diffidence on Singer's part than he'd displayed since Linda was quarantined. There was too much relish in the man's eyes, and Keeley did not mean chopped pickles.

"So how are you holding up?" asked Keeley. "Having to fill in for the President at the times when she can't freely communicate with us?" Keeley felt it her duty to remind Singer of the temporary and supportive nature of his current role. Linda Travis, though ill and confined, was still their President, still in charge, and still able to fulfill her duties.

Singer waved off the question with an expression of humility, dropping his feet to the floor to appear as dignified as his response. "It's my honor to be of service," he said. "But I must say, this is a difficult job, one that I'm glad not to have on a full-time basis. I'm fortunate to be serving with Linda Travis. Anyone else would have plunged us straight into war right after the Crash."

Keeley raised an eyebrow. "You don't call our current actions in Congo, Turkmenistan, and the East China Sea 'wars'?" she asked.

Singer leaned forward, placing his hands calmly on his desk. "Mere policing actions," he said. "We're there by invitation only."

His eyes tightened. "I'm talking about the big one," he said.

"Of course."

Singer inhaled deeply and relaxed back into his chair. "It could have gotten way messier than it has, you know," he said. "Linda refused to escalate the situation. And she insisted that we focus simply on taking care of ourselves while we let other countries take care of *them*selves." He offered an open hand, as though acknowledging that Keeley already knew all of this. "It broke up a global political game that was otherwise destined to end badly."

Keeley nodded her reluctant agreement. "She gave up trying to control the whole world-"

"-and that gave other nations the freedom to do the same," finished Singer. "Though there were those who took a while to get it. The Chinese, in particular, had to thrash about for a while, as you know better than anybody. But now, they, too, seem to have turned their focus inward." The Vice President picked up a pencil from his desktop and started tapping the eraser on the wooden surface.

"So you don't agree with those in the party who blame Linda for America's reduced role in world affairs?" asked Keeley.

Singer scrunched his nose in disgust. "What I think, Keeley, is that under Linda's leadership, America finally became a world leader in something worth leading in: restraint, common sense, commitment to a healthy planet. The fact that she's now suffering from a possibly fatal disease could change the global political situation in horrible ways. I don't think many understand that."

Keeley pushed back in her chair. This didn't sound like Albert Singer at all. Perhaps she had misjudged him. "I think you're right, Al," she said at last. "I'm glad to hear that *you* understand."

Singer sighed wistfully and smiled. "I've learned a great deal in the last three years," he said.

Keeley returned his expression. "I guess we all have," she said softly. She glanced at her watch, then regarded the Vice President. He seemed more peaceful than he used to. Maybe what felt like ambition to Keeley was simply that he'd grown more comfortable with himself, and knew that the nation needed him to look like he was in control of the situation. She was willing to give him the benefit of the doubt. "So, time to crank it down for the day? I'm exhausted."

The Vice President sat straight in his chair and pulled closer to his desk, shaking his head. "I've got a call with Perkins in Brazil in ten minutes," he said, checking the clock on the wall. He reached for his glasses, examined the lenses for dirt, then put them on. "The Crash may have reduced State Dinners, meetings, fundraisers, and photo-ops to almost nil, but the work continues on phones and comput-ers." He nodded toward Keeley. "You?"

Keeley rose from her chair and smoothed her blouse. "I'm gonna try Stan again," she said. "He hasn't been answering his phone. Then I'm gonna get some updates on the search for the kids. And after that I'm going to watch Linda's speech."

Singer's face softened. "Ah, the kids," he said, his face grave. "You must be as worried as I am."

Keeley raised her shoulders in helplessness. "I love the little mon-sters," she said, hoping a bit of levity would distract her from the fear and anger inside of her.

Singer pulled his phone from his desk drawer. "Don't work too late," he said. "Okay? You've been sick."

"I promise," said Keeley, smiling weakly. She turned to head back to her own office.

5.5

Ness was working late in the kitchen, readying things for the next day's meals. There was nothing unusual about this at all. Ness slept very little, and spent most of her time here, cooking, cleaning, read-ing, thinking. This was her spot. Her nest. Her cave. This is where she felt the safest, surrounded by her pots and pans, by her stove and her cutting counter, by her walk-in refrigerator, by the sharp knives that sat in their block. It was cold stainless steel, most of it. Commercial grade, roomy, outfitted for cooking for the type of events and gatherings one might expect to see in the Presidential Home. But even surrounded by so much cold steel, by so many hard corners, by so many sharp edges, Ness felt safe. She did not know why, really. She just knew how she felt.

For now, there were old potatoes to peel, with rotten spots to cut out and save for the chickens, one of which would soon be com-ing full circle to the same enormous soup pot to which the potatoes were headed. Ness remembered with a smile that old song from "The Lion King," and started humming it in soft tones. The only words she could remember were the chorus, but she sang them ev-ery time the tune came around. The circle of life indeed.

Then Ness remembered the last time she'd heard that song. She'd been lying next to Grace in her bed, watching on the small television and DVD player the child had in her room, with Emily and Iain sitting in chairs next to them. It had been a year ago, maybe. Just after the draconian gas and oil restrictions had gone into effect, in order to divert those precious fuels to agricultural and military needs. Just after that long winter of old people freezing in their homes and store shelves emptying and that horrible anti-gay murder spree in Connecticut and that food riot in Pittsburgh. Just after Linda opened up the first of the huge FEMA camps that previous administrations had built, and turned them into shelters and sanctuaries for those most in need. Food had gotten scarce there in the Presidential Home for a time. She and the kids had taken to watching movies most nights. They'd needed the comfort.

Ness tossed a handful of peelings into the bucket and pulled a half dozen more potatoes from the bag she'd brought up from the root cellar that those nice soldiers had dug for her the previous summer. She still felt guilty about losing the kids at the hospital. Didn't matter what Mary said. It was how she'd been brought up. She should have known better than to let those three out of her sight. These were crazy times. And the world had become wilder and weirder than even Ness had imagined it could these past years, what with Linda outing the presence of alien beings and all. "Never let your guard down, Goody," Ness's father had told her more than once. "You never know where the next punch is coming from." Ness sighed as she picked up the peeler. At least... she *thought* it had been her father. *You never know.*

Strangely, Ness wasn't really worried about the kids. She figured she probably ought to be, but, honestly, she wasn't. Oh, she knew they were out in the big, scary world now, those three precious little souls. She knew there were strange beings, and that not all of them were nice. And she knew that those kids, seeing as how they were the President's, would make wonderful bargaining chips for somebody, should they end up in the wrong hands. But the fact that they were with Alice trumped all of that, in Ness's mind. She'd never met Alice, of course, though she'd seen many snapshots of the little hybrid, taken on their phones in the time before she left. She'd heard plenty of stories. But it was something else, really. Something beyond the pictures and stories and her mind's ability to figure things out. She knew in her gut that Alice was good. And that was all that mattered.

If Alice was one of these Gray aliens, or half-a-Gray, anyways, she had all sorts of powers and connections. The kids would be fine. All she and Mary and Cole and Keeley had to do was wait. They'd see.

Ness tried, as she often did when she was alone at night, to think back to her past, to those long years of her life before she'd shown up, like a stray, starving puppy, on Linda Travis's doorstep the very day that the President had moved to Maine. Before the President, seeing her talking to the soldiers at the cordon gate, chose to speak with her. Before Linda took that skinny old woman into her life and put her right at the heart of things, cooking the food that sustained them all - she and her husband and her kids and many of her staff. As always, Ness failed to remember much.

She'd been a housewife. She could remember that. She remembered cooking and cleaning. She vaguely remembered a baby named Roberta, but wasn't sure that it was hers. She'd lived out west somewhere. Tacoma, maybe. She remembered a tall, snow-capped mountain in the distance. She remembered she was near the ocean. She'd been married to a man named Dave, though gods-above she could not bring his face to mind. Nor did she have any idea what he'd done for a living, or how their relationship had been. She remembered she'd had a cat, a small Tabby named Bert with a little divot in his ear, who would sit purring in her lap and let her pet him. She suspected that Dave had died. That was about all. The images were dull and scattered, faded photos from magazines, chopped up like confetti and thrown into the wind. Try as she might, she could not dig up anything else.

The funny thing was, Ness didn't much care. Somehow, she'd managed to leave that all behind. Somehow, she'd made her way across the country right as it was all falling apart. She remembered walking along the Interstate and seeing the exit to Augusta. She remembered walking up the exit ramp, toward the soldiers watching warily from behind the cordon fence. She remembered she walked with her hands held high, as if at gunpoint. She remembered smiling brightly and asking for help. And she remembered how hope rose in her heart when a huge, black Humvee rumbled up the exit behind her and stopped at the gate. It was there, sitting in the back seat, that Ness first spied her new boss. Ness turned and bowed *Namaste*. Linda Travis, over the objections of the soldiers in the front seat, rolled down her window. Linda's face softened in that moment. A sad smile of camaraderie graced the President's weary face.

Ness's life changed.

The memory of that moment still brought tears to her eyes and Ness wiped at her face. Memories are worse than onions, she thought, as she picked up the last potato and began peeling. She didn't know if it was her bow, her *Namaste*, or just her old, wrinkled face, but Linda Travis had seen something good in Ness, and had reached out to her. In the time since, Ness had become a close and integral part of the President's family. Except for times like this, when stray bits of her past came back to haunt her with their fuzzy possibilities, Ness was as happy as could be.

Linda Travis saved Ness's life that day. Ness was sure of it. She'd been as skinny as a rail, there at that gate. Like she hadn't eaten in weeks. And the condition of her shoes argued that she'd walked the whole distance from Tacoma to Augusta.

Maybe she had. Ness just couldn't really remember.

5.6

Though the kids could tune to the physical level and know that night had fallen, the Astral realm did not seem to work with light. At least not the sorts of light that hit the surfaces of eyeballs and let the human brain "see." Here, seeing was not a matter of light and dark or eyeballs and brains. Here, seeing was something else entirely, something that happened at the intersection of vibration and imagination. Here, it did not matter that night had fallen. The kids stayed attuned to the Astral realm as they had first experienced it, with the sky multihued, the clouds glowing from within, and the landscape, fuzzy and jumbled, rolling slowly beneath them as they headed east. There was some comfort in that, and they needed comfort, Emily and Iain especially. This world was weird beyond their wildest expectations.

Emily pondered these matters of light and comfort as she "flew" east, following in the rear as Grace led the way. They knew they were here to find Linda. Linda, whose mole had mysteriously moved. Linda who had been abducted from their lives by men in scary space suits and a black, armored ambulance. Linda who'd become like their mother. Linda whom they loved. They had to find her. That's what Grace had told them, anyway. That's what Alice had told Grace in her dream. And they knew Linda was being kept in her old cottage on the coast, a place they'd briefly visited not long after they'd moved to Maine.

But they weren't certain how to just blink over there, and they didn't know if that was a good idea in any event. Better to approach slowly, they agreed amongst themselves. Better to see what's coming from afar. And better to give more time for help to arrive. Grace had expected somebody to meet them on this side. That somebody had yet to appear. Springing the President from a level-four biocontainment facility, if that's what they were even supposed to do, was one thing for an alien. But they were just kids. They could use some help.

Then the lights went out. It was as quick as that. Emily had just noticed a peculiar cloud ahead of them, dark like a thunderhead, and they were moving rapidly toward it. She'd just started to say something. Then the lights went out. Here in this realm where light was not really light, the three kids were thrust into pitch black.

"Hey!" said Iain and Grace, together. Emily came to a full stop. Or what she imagined was a full stop. In the darkness, there was no way to tell.

"Iain?" she said. "Grace?"

"I'm here," said Grace.

"Me too," said Iain.

Dennis barked.

"You guys okay?" asked Emily.

"Yeah," they both replied. "You?"

"I think so," said Emily. "Do you know what happened, Grace?"

"No," said Grace. "This never happened before."

Emily tried to feel herself, tried to switch from her human form to her fireball shape, tried to make herself light up from within. Nothing happened. She could make no light. She could not even tell if she was in a body any more. She felt like a tiny pinprick of thought, as if the entire Cosmos had been stripped away from all around her. All that was left was her mind and her voice.

"Em?" asked Grace.

"Yeah?" said Emily.

"Can you move? Can you even tell where you are? Or where Iain is? Or me?"

Emily shook her head, then stopped to notice that she could feel no head and no movement. The shaking was in her mind alone. "No," she said. "I don't think I can. You?"

"There's no way to know!" said Iain.

"I know," said Emily.

The three hovered in silence for a moment. But they had real no idea whether they were hovering or not.

"Anybody got any ideas?" asked Iain at last. His voice was tinged with frustration. Rightly or wrongly, he'd felt, as the big brother, that it was his job to protect his sisters. But how did you protect them from darkness and nothing?

"None," said Emily at last.

"None," agreed Grace.

"Crap!" said Iain.

The three kids hovered in silence some more.

"I guess we wait," said Grace at last.

Iain began to laugh. "Good one, Graceful!" he said.

"Shut up," said Grace.

Iain stopped laughing. They waited in silence.

"What's that?" said Emily, at last. Dennis started barking.

"It's okay, Dennis," said Grace. "We're here. Okay? Stop barking so we can listen, okay?" Dennis stopped.

The three kids hovered in silence a moment longer.

"I don't hear anything," said Grace.

"It's not a sound," said Emily, her voice was hushed, almost a whisper.

"What is it?" said Iain.

"It's... it's like I'm feeling something. In my mind. Not a body feeling, though. Not a sensation, like touch or cold or something. More an... an idea, like. An image."

"An image?" asked Grace.

"Yeah," said Emily, her tone now one of confusion. "I don't know. I just... I keep getting this picture. Like, there's somebody in my room, going through my closet and my dresser. Opening drawers and searching under the bed. Only, it's not my room. It's my head. Somebody's in my head."

"Like a mind reader?" asked Iain.

"Like a robber," said Emily.

Dennis barked again.

5.7

Colonel McAfee thought he understood exactly what it was the President had loved about this place. The view over the bay was exquisite. And at night, the distant mainland lights, fewer now but still there, sparkled and streamed across the waves in a glorious, lightshow sort of way that brought life and definition to the darkness. Sitting on the cottage's deck with a highball in one hand, Nicky sleeping on his lap, and the VLT's summit speech almost set to begin on the tablet he balanced on his knees, McAfee was in heaven. Or as close as one could get to heaven on this trodden, soiled planet.

The summit speech would be short and to the point, in part because it was easier and less time-consuming, when creating a simulation such as this, to keep it as short as was possible; in part because they wanted to emulate Lincoln's address at Gettysburg, not only because that would be a hoot but because it would resonate with the masses; and in part because they knew a short speech would get more viewings and reposts than a long speech. As the virtual POTUS stepped to the same "podium in an aquarium" they'd had her use for her re-election announcement, McAfee noted with approval the work facial modeling had done to increase the severity of her rash. The presence of a number of new, small, dark-brown markings would most certainly obfuscate the whole "molegate issue," as it had come to be called by his techs, and those new marks, along with the intensification and spread of the background redness, the exhaustion in her eyes, and that delicate touch of shakiness they'd added to her lower lip, would certainly heighten both the fear and empathy factors in the audience. The President was clearly struggling for her life now. The disease was taking its toll. It could go either way.

McAfee chuckled to himself and tossed his drink down his throat. Nicky, as if scolding him for his unkind thoughts, dug his claws into the Colonel's leg. McAfee winced but did not push the cat away. He knew that Nicky was right: he didn't have to be so nasty. As the President began to speak, McAfee increased the volume and settled back into his chaise lounge.

"*Abraham Lincoln,*" the simulated President began, "*speaking in Gettysburg, Pennsylvania, in the middle of what we Americans call 'the Civil War,' considered the United States a 'new nation, conceived in Liberty, and dedicated to the proposition that all men are created equal.'*" McAfee grinned. It'd been his idea to use Lincoln as a jumping off point. The common folk loved ol' Honest Abe. Noticing that his drink was gone, the Colonel fished a beer from the small, ice-filled Styrofoam cooler that sat beside his chair. He'd come prepared.

"We see now, of course, those of us who are paying attention, that this liberty, this equality, this new nation, fell, first and foremost, to men, just as Mr. Lincoln said. To rich men over poor. To men over women. To white-skinned peoples over peoples of color. To people living in technological-industrial societies over people living in the so-called undeveloped lands. And to human beings over every other living thing. The vast majority of souls on this planet - plants, animals, fungi, and bacteria included - would scoff at such lofty claims to liberty and equality."

It was all the Colonel could do not to break out in laughter, so delighted was he by how well this had turned out. How did the techs get that note of barely contained anger into her voice? And the weariness? This was masterful work. And the best part was how well it obliterated their tracks in the sand. McAfee knew that people were already suspicious about the "real truth" of the President's situation. He'd seen some of the wild stories online, a few of which his own people had seeded. But who could seriously believe that Linda Travis had been abducted by a hidden elite ruling group and replaced with a virtual copy when the President said such things as this? By having her continue to harp on her same, tired old themes about the "bad" people in charge, they deflected suspicion. What would *not* work was for her to suddenly change.

That was what most people did not seem to understand. Project Changeling was not about changing Linda Travis and her work in the world, to make her more like The Families wanted her to be. It was about keeping her the same. The same as she'd always been. Just for a while. To keep the proles calm and hopeful. Until the Giant Leap.

5.8

Stan and Cole stood in the hospital visitor's lounge and watched the President's speech on the television hanging from the ceiling. *"No matter what was in the heart and mind of our sixteenth president,"* she continued, *"and in the hearts and minds of those who came before him, it is difficult to argue, now, that this 'new nation' has not failed miserably. We have been brought to our knees by the laws of physics, chemistry, and biology, as some of you have long warned we would be. Forced to my knees, I, for one, am now willing to bend them."*

Cole bristled at the thought of Linda "forced to her knees." He understood why she'd chosen those words. She was trying to strike right at the heart of what she considered "the problem": our collective refusal to give up "ruling the world," even as disastrously as that project has turned out. Though not a religious person by any stretch of the imagination, Linda saw the human predicament in spiritual terms now, and knew they would have to surrender to truths larger than their rational, materialist belief systems. Once again, she was trying to lead the way. But it seemed that his wife was the only one who was willing to put her money where her mouth was.

"We are engaged now in what the late 'geologian' Thomas Berry called our 'Great Work,' the work of reconnecting to the living, real world, the work of reversing the horrible destruction we have wrought on this beautiful planet. We see now, finally, as global climate chaos exceeds our wildest imaginings, as ecosystems falter and institutions unravel, that nothing is as important to the human endeavor as a healthy, living world. But we come to this great work far too late, I think, as if we might stop a boulder from plummeting to the ground below after it has been pushed over the cliff. What hope we now have, in the physical plane at least, depends on just how much leverage we can manage whilst in free fall. It seems an impossible task. Probably because it is. No matter the claims of mystics and quantum physicists, no matter the possibility for salvation some find in the knowledge of so-called 'alien visitors,' I fear, I believe, that, before this is all over, we of massive skyscrapers and solid flesh shall hit the ground quite hard, even if we, our very molecules, are mostly empty space. I wish I could say otherwise, but I vowed when I began my term that I would always tell you the truth as I see it. We have already fallen far. The ground rushes up to meet us."

Stan put a hand on Cole's arm. "We have to go," he said quietly. He hiked his pack higher onto his back, adjusting for more comfort, then started toward the hallway. He stopped and turned back to Cole, who was watching still. He walked back to Cole, got his attention, and nodded toward the television. "We can watch the rest later, Cole. Online. Okay?" Stan smiled gently and pulled Cole toward the door. Cole glanced back toward the screen for one more look at his ailing wife, who so bravely told her people the truth. At last he sighed and turned to follow.

5.9

"So it was they who set you up?" asked the Fisherman, waving vaguely toward the watching crowd.

Linda shook her head. "It was all of us," she said. "Myself included. All of us who believed we could manage and control an entire life-filled planet. Generations of us. The whole culture, extending back centuries."

"Centuries of hoping, you might say," said William.

"And now there's no more left," said Linda.

"No more what, Madam President?"

"No more hope."

5.10

Ness watched the tiny screen on her kitchen counter with tears welling in her eyes. This was the President she'd grown to love and admire, a woman who told the whole truth. "*And yet life remains,*" Linda continued. "*Hope remains. That is also the truth. And I know about hope, believe me, as I worry for my children, now missing. As I stave off the mysterious virus that now ravages my body, and pray for others now similarly stricken. As I think of us all now living in a world of declining energy and food and water and warmth and stability. I know about hope because I know that, in the words of writer Stephen King, 'there are other worlds than these.' I've been given a peek into those other worlds. I know they exist. And I know that, while Mr. Lincoln's address may have begun in the naivety of his times, it ended in wisdom for our times. We* can *resolve that the dead shall not have died in vain. We* can *bring some measure of meaning, resolution, healing, even redemption, to the centuries of domination and destruction now lying heaped about our feet. We* can *resolve that the good and beautiful spirit of the human species shall not perish from the Earth, even as we acknowledge the distinct possibility that our bodies, our species, may fall into ashes and dust.*"

Ness grabbed her apron to daub her wet eyes. Linda's words had reached right inside and squeezed her tired old heart. The thought of her President dying was too much for her, too much to hold. So she resolved not to think about that, and focus, instead, on the hope. She was not yet ready for ashes and dust. With a shake of her head, she grabbed a knife from the block on the counter and headed for the back door, and the chicken coop just outside. There was always hope in hot soup.

5.11

"We can begin this tonight. Right now. In our shelters and in our state houses. In our neighborhoods and our corporate meeting rooms. In our own backyards, yes, and around the planet. It's 'clutch time,' ladies and gentlemen. It's time to show the Universe, and ourselves, who we really are, and what we've really got, even when all seems lost. This, at the very least, is something we can do: we can reclaim what Mr. Lincoln, in his First Inaugural Address, called 'the better angels of our nature.'

"Or in the words of writer Khaled Hosseini, 'there is a way to be good again.'

"I thank you."

Paul DuPont raised his arms over his head and clasped his hands to crack his knuckles. The tech was flawless, as he'd known it would be. But he was most proud of the copy. *Keep it going as long as you can*, they'd said. *Keep them hoping.* That was his mandate, and, in Paul's opinion, he had performed admirably. All he'd had to do was keep Linda Travis on message, no matter that it was growing ever more difficult for the good citizens of the world to believe what she said.

5.12

Crouched in the hot darkness in the back of the military ambulance, Stan opened his backpack and pulled out a small, black, rectangular device.

"What's that?" whispered Cole.

"Transmitter," muttered Stan, extending the tiny antenna. Holding it high, he pressed the single button on the transmitter's face. After a moment came the sounds of a distant explosion, a sharp crack followed by a low rumble. Stan put a hand on Cole's shoulder and pushed. "Get down," he whispered. "They'll be here soon."

It all hinged on this moment, thought Cole. Stan's hope was that the medics would just jump into the front seat and take off. If they decided to check the back first, Stan and Cole would be found out.

The medics jumped into the front seat and took off. Cole breathed silent relief. Stan squeezed Cole's shoulder in solidarity and settled in for the ride.

Cole had been amazed to learn that Stan had planned and prepared for this escape months ago. "I could read the writing on the wall," he'd said. Getting to the hospital had been easy enough. Stan was the Secretary of Homeland Security, after all. And Cole was the father of those missing children. Of course they'd want to inspect the hospital for themselves. And once there, it had been a simple matter of ducking downstairs and out to where the ambulances were parked. But getting the explosives rigged, that had been more difficult. Stan had had to invent a mission outside of the cordon and then convince his people, and the military, that he should be allowed to accompany them. It had raised a few eyebrows, and Stan had almost been discovered when he'd "gone to take a piss" in order to install the charges. But he had managed it. His stellar reputation in the military, and his close relationship with the President, had diverted any real suspicion. The explosives were set. Once detonated, military patrols would be sent to investigate. An ambulance would be sent as well. It just might work.

It did work. The burning Exxon station was coughing huge gouts of thick, black smoke, probably from the many tires in the service bays. That smoke, combined with the cover of night and the screaming of sirens, allowed Cole and Stan to slide out the back doors and into the darkness as soon as the ambulance stopped. With backpacks strapped tightly and guns at the ready, the two men stepped beyond the safety of the Capital City Green Zone and into the wilds of post-collapse America.

5.13

"I didn't understand," said Linda.

The Fisherman nodded slightly. "What didn't you understand, Madam?"

Linda exhaled with great weariness and gestured toward the audience. "I didn't understand that they were trying to kill themselves. That they were actually trying to collapse the whole system."

"They being...?"

"Everybody!" said Linda, turning away from the imaginary crowd. She took a step toward William, her hands low and outspread in a gesture of exasperation. She could scarcely believe what she was saying. "The Senators and Congresspeople. The CEOs. The bankers. All the usual suspects. But it wasn't just them, William. It was environmentalists, too. Greenies. Designers. Inventors. Progressives. Butchers and bakers and candlestick makers, for Chrissake." Linda looked at the floor and shook her head. "It was all carbon offsets and solar roads and cars that run on water and vertical farming and clean coal and tree planting and dumping tons of iron filings into the sea. And the geoengineering ideas! Building giant sunshades in space? Jesus!" Linda raised her eyes to the Fisherman. "Nobody got it, William."

"Got what, Madam?"

"I think you can call me Linda now," said the President.

The Fisherman smiled and bowed. "Got what, Linda?"

Linda opened her mouth to speak but stopped when the Fisherman raised his hand. "Tell *them*," he said, pointing toward the audience.

Linda stepped again to the lectern and sighed again. Her forehead was creased, and glistened with beads of perspiration. "You never understood about death!" she said, her voice rising, an angry accusation. The people in the audience continued to watch in respectful attention.

"You never grokked that none of your so-called solutions could work inside of a system that insisted on endless material growth." Linda's voice was sure and commanding now. She was being given an opportunity to say what was really in her heart. To tell the truth she'd held inside. The truth she'd felt she *couldn't* tell. The words tumbled out. "And the growth you could never face into was that of your own numbers. As if all there was to do was figure out how to grow more food and make cars that ran on sparrow farts and then, by God... then you could just keep growing and growing and growing. Eight billion. Ten. Twelve! I mean, why the hell not? If all the humans on Earth can fit shoulder-to-shoulder into the state of Texas, then we've got lots of room, right? Jesus! How stupid can you be? You built an entire global system designed to defy human death at all costs. And not just death! You thought you could defy pain! And discomfort! Develop more pharmaceuticals. Saturate your bodies with chemicals and your minds with distractions. Figure out solutions to every last goddamned discomfort and inconvenience your fat, couch-coddled asses could feel. And all it took was killing off everything else!"

Linda stopped, closed her eyes, and inhaled deeply. She turned and glanced shyly at the Fisherman, as if afraid she might be punished for breaking the rules. She hung her head. "I'm just so tired, William," she said softly.

William took a step closer. "They couldn't understand," he said.

Linda shook her head, then looked up at the Fisherman. "All they did was fight me," she said. Her voice was tinged with a moan of sadness. "The corporations. My own government. The people. They fought me at every turn. I could see that we needed to question our deepest assumptions. That we needed to change everything. That we needed to shut down the global industrial machine and find some real way to walk more lightly on the Earth. That we needed to allow our numbers to diminish. But they just couldn't go there. They couldn't face it. They couldn't face that the life they knew had to die." Linda's face was plaintive with quiet apology. "And I just couldn't fight them any longer."

"And yet you said that they were trying to kill themselves."

Linda's eyes widened. "That's just it, William. They tried to defy death at every turn, but they were also *craving* death. That's the only way I can explain it. I mean… look at our collective actions over the past few decades. We kept going even when the consequences of our actions became undeniable. It looks to me like the people, unconsciously, at least, actually *wanted* to crash the system. As if that's the only way they could break free. Like an addict who tries to hit bottom. So that they'd either die and get free of the pain or find, at the bottom, some other way out of it."

"They're tired too," said William.

Linda nodded in agreement. "Well… yeah. But they couldn't admit it out loud. They knew they could never break free of the cultural mandates to cheat death and seek comfort and grow, grow, grow. To always trade today for tomorrow. They knew they were addicts. And they knew, even before I came out and said so, that there were others out there. The aliens. The Strangers. The gods. Whomever. So they were, like, acting out. Taking the deepest, darkest path they could find, hoping for an intervention." Linda scoffed. "My coming in and saying, 'No, I think we can come together and consciously create a new society'… I think it was just a distraction, William. Just more blather, even if I seemed to actually understand the problems we faced. They didn't believe me. They, too, as you said, were exhausted with trying. They just wanted release. Death."

The Fisherman waved a hand and materialized a glass of water on Linda's podium. With no reaction to the act of manifesting itself,

Linda picked up the glass and drank.

"It's interesting, Linda, how you use the past tense," said the Fisherman.

Linda frowned.

"When speaking of your people," he said, waving toward the audience. "'They knew they were addicts', you said. 'They were exhausted,' you said."

Linda closed her eyes and took a moment to do a gut check. Her head nodded slightly and she opened her eyes. "I think part of me considers them already dead," she said, pointing to the vast audience in the great, cavernous hall of Phobos, her face shifting from thoughtfulness to surprise as her words settled into her consciousness. A tear quivered on the edge of her eyelid. "I mean... I just don't see..." Her voice fell away to a whisper and she exhaled slowly and deeply. She shook her head. "I guess I'm done with them, William," she said. "Done trying to lead them. Trying to persuade and convince. I'm done."

The Fisherman tilted his head. "Yet back on Earth you've just announced your bid for re-election," he said with a smile.

5.14

Mary could hear her escorts' boots clunking sullenly on the pavement. The muttering soldier and the head-shaking soldier were clearly not happy to be walking. Especially with the explosion they'd all heard a few moments before, somewhere off to the East, out past the cordon. But they'd been ordered to assist the President's "senior advisor," and said "senior advisor" had insisted that they walk, and that they keep to their mission, explosion or no explosion. Mary smiled to herself. They were so easy to read. And they obviously considered her a whacko. That was fine by her. Rather than try to get involved, they had resigned themselves to just standing back and watching the show. Which left Mary alone to work.

She was following that image of the kids in the sky. There was a feeling of movement to the image. A feeling of beginnings and endings. As if the image were a rainbow. As if she could find the end of that rainbow if only she walked far enough, and in the right direction. As if the pot of gold at rainbow's end might be the children themselves. So far the image had brought them down Capitol Street to the State House, through Capitol Park and up Gage Road to the

Memorial Bridge, in the center of which they now stood. Before them, across the Kennebec, was one of only a handful of buildings with interior lights still shining: the hospital.

Mary stopped. It didn't make any sense, that the feeling had brought her here, to the one place they knew the children were not. Shaking her head in confusion, she turned to scan the sky. She must have lost the trail...

"Ma'am?" said Agent Gilder, who stood to one side. The soldiers were a few yards away, leaning on the bridge's railing.

"Yes?" said Mary.

Gilder nodded across the river. "Go on. You're right." She indicated the hospital with a wave of her hand. Her eyes shone in the Gridlight. "Don't doubt yourself."

Mary turned and regarded the hospital again. In the distance beyond she could see the flickering flames of a burning building. The result of that explosion. Probably a gas tank. Or maybe the Burners. But she didn't see any signs of the kids. "Do you see...?" she asked Agent Gilder.

"I just know this is right," said Gilder. She pointed to the exit ahead. "We take Stone Street. Then double back to the hospital."

"But..."

Gilder shook her head emphatically. "Doesn't matter, Ma'am," she said. "It's where we go next. Your initial impulse was correct."

Grabbing Gilder's hand, Mary led the four of them across the bridge.

5.15

Keeley flicked out the light. Mary had told her she'd be late and not to wait up. For once, Keeley was inclined to obey. She was exhausted. Except for Linda's speech, the night had been a complete bust. No response from Stan. No leads on the kids. And her sour stomach had returned. Linda's strong, hopeful words had filled her heart with determination, but determination alone was not enough. Not tonight. She needed help. And she needed sleep. Come morning, her plan was to hit the ground running. Find Stan. Figure out just how they were going to get in to see Linda. Step up the search for the kids. Get to work on the re-election campaign. The ship of state was chugging along, just as ol' Albert Singer had said. It was time for Keeley to find her sea legs.

Keeley pulled her sleep mask over her eyes and rolled onto her side. The mask almost completely covered the slight reddening of her skin that, in her exhaustion, Keeley had failed to notice.

5.16

The hospital had few patients. There was the poor man who'd been badly burned in an explosion at a service station outside the cordon, and there were two still-living victims of the strange new alien flu, Greensleeves, both tucked away in the previously unused fourth-floor infectious disease ward, and both expected to expire as rapidly as the previous six. Other than that, the place was empty, which made their search go more quickly than Mary had expected it would. The emptiness created a "psychic silence" that helped cast the image Mary was following into sharper relief. Agent Gilder had been right: if it was a rainbow they followed, the pot of gold was somewhere here in the hospital, despite the military's failure to find it.

Mary led them with flashlights through a dark hallway in the hospital's unused wing. Back when the city was mostly emptied, many buildings, such as the hospital, had been "downsized," with sections locked up or partitioned off. In MaineCentral's case, the unused wing had simply had its breakers flipped and the double-doors closed. It was easy enough to enter.

Mary walked slowly, face slack, eyes open but softly focused. Agent Gilder followed right behind her, searching for signs. The two privates hung well back, just wanting the nonsense to be over so they could return to their post. What doors they had tried had all been locked. So far, Mary had not needed to go in.

It was Gilder who found the door. It had a feeling to it, a sign, a beckoning, and the agent knew it as soon as she saw it. "Here," she said simply as they turned the corner. She walked to the door and pulled on the handle. The door was locked.

Mary, sensing that Gilder was correct, went searching for a key in the abandoned nurse's station across from the door. Finding none, she pointed her flashlight up at the soldiers' faces. "We need to get in here, gentlemen," she said. "Can one of you please go find somebody who can unlock this door?" The two soldiers looked at each other and shrugged. Acting in accord with some pecking order unknown to Mary, the head-shaking soldier turned and started down the hall, shaking his head.

It took only a few minutes before he returned with a nurse, a stout, gray-haired woman with a deeply creased face. In her hand was a large ring of keys. She drew one as she approached the door, peering suspiciously at Mary. "That's the old MRI room," she said, her voice crabbed and peevish. "There's new equipment upstairs." She stopped and inspected Mary from top to bottom, as if expecting Mary to give up her silliness and tell her never mind.

"We need to go in," said Mary with a hopeful smile. The nurse rolled her eyes and unlocked the door. The door swung open easily, revealing another ring of keys on the floor just inside.

Gilder gasped as she scanned the room with her flashlight. There, lying side by side on the patient table inside the old MRI scanner, were Cole and Linda's three children.

5.17

Ness stood in the back yard near the chicken coop. She stood in the Gridlight and the moonlight, her arms at her sides, the "chicken knife" on the ground where she had dropped it. Some part of Ness, the part of her that had survived the death of her husband and her subsequent descent into depression and madness, the part of her that cooked the meals and loved the children and remembered very little of her life before, stood for a long, long time, seeing nothing, thinking nothing, feeling nothing. She stood while the bright light flashed overhead. She stood as the light washed like a scanner across her wrinkled face. She stood as the large, metallic, bowl-shaped craft landed just beyond the chicken wire.

The other part of Ness, the part of her that had compelled this body to walk across the continent, the part of her that extended across time and distance to another life and another body, the part of her that watched and waited, the part of her that was Other-than-Ness, knew exactly who she was, and what was happening, and understood the compelling needs that shaped this moment. She watched the strange craft as its illuminated surface faded to a dull, reddish glow.

A small, grayish, four-fingered hand reached out from behind her and touched her forehead. The Other-than-Ness looked up to see the hand pulling back, then sighed softly as the hand's owner stepped out in front of her, revealing his slight, thin, carmine-robed body, his large, shiny black, almond-shaped eyes, and his huge, bald head. Other-than-Ness used Ness's body to form a welcoming smile.

"YOU ARE WELL," the tiny being said in her mind.

"I AM," said Other-than-Ness.

"AND YOU CONTINUE TO LEARN," said the being.

"I DO," said Other-than-Ness. "I DO NOT SEE HOW THEY CAN BEAR IT MUCH LONGER."

"THE TIME APPROACHES," said the being.

Other-than-Ness sighed. "AS IT ALWAYS HAS," she said.

The tiny being cocked his hooded head. "YOU ARE IMPATIENT?" he asked.

"WE ARE," said Other-than-Ness.

"WE?" The tiny being pulsed a wave of feigned confusion toward the other.

"THERE ARE MANY OTHERS LIKE ME," said the Other-than-Ness. "AS YOU WELL KNOW."

"AH," said the being. "THE OTHERS."

"AND WE AWAIT OUR TIME."

The red-robed being gazed up at the Grid for a few moments, then back at the old woman's body standing before him. "THE TIME APPROACHES," he repeated. "THE CHOICES WILL BE MADE. UNTIL THEN, THE CHILDREN MUST BE PROTECTED." He stared steadily into Ness's eyes, seeing the Other-than-Ness inside. "DO YOU UNDERSTAND?"

"I WILL DO AS YOU HAVE DIRECTED," said the Other-than-Ness.

"I MUST GO, DAUGHTER," he said.

"WE WILL MEET AGAIN," said the Other-than-Ness.

The tiny being held out a finger and touched Ness's forehead once again, then turned and started toward the craft, walking through the chicken wire as if it were a strands of smoke, disappearing completely before he was half-way to his ship. The Other-than-Ness was alone once again. She had a duty to perform, but she also had plans of her own. It was time to take steps to achieve both ends. The Other-than-Ness took a step backwards in Ness's mind and watched as the strange craft rose into the air and flashed away.

After a time, Ness blinked her eyes and continued toward the coop to grab a night-befuddled bird for her soup pot.

5.18

Grace was the first to spot them: two tiny lights in the pitch black, distant motes in an otherwise starless sky. Initially, they were right on the edge of visibility, faint blurs in the blind spot. Eventually they grew strong enough to focus on.

"Do you guys see those lights?" asked Grace.

Emily and Iain swept their awareness outward and eventually spotted them. "I do," said Emily. Iain grunted his agreement. Dennis growled. They watched for a time.

"They seem to be getting bigger," said Grace.

"Or closer," said Iain.

The three waited and watched a while longer. The lights were definitely increasing in size and intensity. When they were large and bright enough, they revealed their pale green coloring, and began to take on a football shape.

"Eyes," said Emily, finally.

"Yes," said Grace.

Dennis barked once. A warning.

The eyes came steadily closer. As they neared, the kids could begin to see, or maybe just imagine, to whom they might belong: a small black cat. The cat approached to what seemed a distance of perhaps ten feet, then stopped. In the blinking, changing glow from its eyes they could infer that it was washing its face with a paw.

"I supposed you want to get out of here," said the cat. The cat did not speak in English, but the kids knew what it had said.

"We sure do," said Iain.

"Yes," agreed Emily and Grace.

"Follow me," the cat said. It turned and began to walk away. With its eyes pointed the other direction, the kids could barely see it, just a faint fuzzy halo. They hurried to follow. Without the light from its eyes, they were lost here. Without the light from its eyes, there *was* no other direction.

5.19

"Go," muttered Ted.

"Hold your horses," said Carl.

Ted, annoyed, pushed back his chair and crossed his legs. He cradled his chin in the palm of his hand and closed his eyes.

Carl leaned out and played some tiles.

At the sound of Carl fumbling through the bag of tiles, Ted opened his eyes and looked at the board. "You motherscrubber," he said, shaking his head in disbelief.

"What?" said Carl.

"You took my place!" Ted stood and loomed over the board. "And for what? 'Bob'? You can't use people's names."

"It means 'a short, jerky motion'," said Carl.

"You're a short, jerky moron!" said Ted. He stepped forward and hit the table with his knee, sending the board sliding to the edge of the table and scattering the tiles, many of which fell to the floor.

"Hey!" said Carl.

"It was an accident!" said Ted.

"Screw you!" said Carl as he made his way around the table. He charged Ted and punched him in the stomach. Ted fell backwards, landing on his ass with an 'oomph!'

Carl stood, glaring down at Ted, breathing heavily.

Ted, rubbing his stomach, looked up at Carl and began to laugh.

"What's so funny?" asked Carl.

Ted laughed until there were tears in his eyes.

Carl continued to glare.

Eventually Ted's laughter ran out and he sat up. "That felt good," he said.

"What?" said Carl.

"Feeling," said Ted.

"Feeling?" said Carl.

"Feeling... something... anything," said Ted. He pulled himself onto his knees, then his feet. His eyes sparkled as he took a step toward Carl. "Let's do that again," he said.

Chapter ⏀ Six

6.1

Gabrielle had to admit that, whoever he was, Zacharael's method made some sense. Without the notes from her midnight episodes of automatic writing, she would never recall her "dreams" in such detail. She'd awakened with bitter anger in her mouth, a head full of hazy images, and a vague sense of uncleanliness that did not wash away in the shower. It was only when she read her notebook that she fully understood where these feelings had come from. That was dolphin blood she felt on her skin. And it was Zacharael's question that had so affronted her. What was *she* going to do about all of this? Screw you, dream lover. I'm not gonna do shit.

Still, the sticky feeling of blood lingered. Gabrielle could feel her skin crawling under her shirt as she walked through the humid morning air to her eight o'clock class. She could hear the screams of dolphins echoing in her mind. She could see the ball of rock and ice hurtling through space, and the strange symbol in the snow. The dreams were invading her daytime now, and she was not at all happy about that.

A short, slight man in a black windbreaker stepped out from behind a tree just before her. Gabrielle started from her thoughts and came to a quick halt. It was her father, Jay Sinclair, whom the world knew as Canadian MP Guy Legrand. His Tom Cruise face was tanned and his dark hair tousled by the breeze.

"Gabby?" said Sinclair. His eyebrows were angled into a look of hopeful contrition.

"Don't call me that," spat Gabrielle, turning to walk the other direction

Sinclair hurried after her. "Gabby! Wait!" he shouted to her back. He reached out and touched her elbow. "Gabrielle," he said quietly.

Gabrielle stopped, sighed loudly, then continued on more slowly. Sinclair stepped up to walk beside her. Gabrielle stared into the distance, refusing to acknowledge her father.

"It's all moving quickly now," said Sinclair. "The Life forced the issue and The Families are stepping up to the challenge. The Directorate has agreed that it's now or never. We're calling it the 'One-Two Punch.' And the Quietus has been triggered."

Gabrielle glanced at her father with a snort of derision. "You guys and your code names and shit," she said, shaking her head. "A bunch of little boys..."

Sinclair grabbed his daughter's arm and brought them both to a halt. She was a bit taller than he, and her pale skin and red-blonde bob contrasted with his dark brown hair and tanned face. "These 'little boys' are going to save our lives," he said. His face was stern and tight.

"What a wonderful choice you've given me, father," said Gabrielle. "Stay here and die in an environmental apocalypse or cram myself into a tin can with a bunch of cowboys and blast off into the deadly vacuum of space. I wish you had thought of this before I was conceived. You could have pulled out of dear Mummy and saved us both a great deal of anguish."

"Gabby," said Sinclair, his voice a sad whisper. "I wish..."

Gabrielle jerked her arm free. "That's all you have, isn't it? Wishes and fantasies."

"We have plans," said Sinclair.

"So do I," said Gabrielle. She gestured toward the sky with a quick jerk of her head. "I'm not going. I've been there. It doesn't feel like a fun place to die."

"You're not going to-"

Gabrielle shook her head to cut him off. "You just don't get it," she said.

Sinclair closed his eyes and took a deep breath, his standard technique for keeping his cool with his children. He opened his eyes. "Get what?" he asked.

"My work is here," said Gabrielle.

Sinclair laughed, a clipped, barking sound that burst out before he could control it. "Your work?" he said with a smirk. "What the hell does that mean? And what do you mean you've 'been there'?"

Gabrielle stared at her father for a long time, breathing slowly. She glanced over his shoulder, then back to his eyes. "I'm late for class," she said. She stepped around her father and headed across the square. Sinclair stood and watched her for a long time, but did not follow.

Gabrielle, her heart pounding, ascended the steps of the Banker Building as quickly as she could. She slipped through the door and exhaled her relief when it closed behind her. Her hands were shaking and there were tears welling in her eyes. Up until a moment ago, she had not realized that she even had a "work" to do. Now she knew that she did, and the realization touched her deeply. Gabrielle had something she had to do. Something... real. That was something that all of their money had never been able to buy her.

She headed down the hallway to the left. At the end, silhouetted against the daylight from the huge windows that overlooked the quad, stood a tall, thin, red-haired man. With an odd, fluid movement, the man pushed through the double doors to the stairwell and disappeared.

6.2

"So why didn't your sensors find them before?" asked Mary, gesturing toward the President's children, who lay as if in comas in the MRI. She felt strong and whole in the moment. Indignation and righteousness fueled her spirit and eased her body.

"The room is one big Faraday cage, Ma'am," said Colonel Westwood with a raised eyebrow. "Designed that way. Because of the scanner. It blinded us to what was inside." He glanced back toward the children. "It blocked their iDents."

"It blinded you to the fact that the President's children were right under your noses the whole time, Francis," said Mary, her face a stern mask. "Did you not know this could happen?"

The Colonel stared down at his shoes. "It hadn't... occurred to us, Ma'am," he said.

Mary smiled peevishly, like a schoolmarm. "It's a good thing you let us paranormal whack-jobs have a crack at it then," she said. "Perhaps you should add a new item to your search protocols: 'When searching for someone important, watch out for Faraday cages.'"

Westwood glared but did not respond.

"Can I trust you to inform the children's parents right away?" asked Mary.

The Colonel nodded once, glad for the implicit dismissal. "Ma'am," he said, a word that signaled both contempt and embarrassment. Mary dismissed him with a wave of the hand and the Colonel turned crisply and stepped into the hallway. Mary crossed the room to the children.

There were armed guards stationed on either side of the MRI. Standing next to the kids were a resident and a nurse, fiddling with leads and listening through a stethoscope. So far, the children had checked out fine. No physical harm. No obvious trauma or disease. They were just... asleep. The doctors could not explain it.

Mary could explain it. She knew exactly where they were, and glanced up toward the ceiling. The kids had somehow freed themselves from their bodies and journeyed to the Astral realm. Those eyes she'd imagined peering down from the sky? Those had been real. The kids had gone with Alice, all right, but they'd left their bodies behind. And they'd found the perfect place to hide them. Well, thought Mary with a chuckle, almost perfect.

She already regretted giving the Colonel such grief. He didn't deserve it, and it would not help the situation, for her to make enemies. Wondering at that, Mary closed her eyes for a moment to study her own field, something she had only recently learned she could do. What she saw there was neither pretty nor surprising: it was her own guilt over having failed to protect the kids, and the residual guilt from her long-past failure to save her little brother from their abusive father. Those old feelings had had her lash out like she did. Both of those failures clung to her like spider webs, laden still with bits of shame and regret, despite her efforts to clear them. None of that could be pinned on the Colonel. He had not earned her blame. The fact of the matter was, this hiding place had almost thwarted *her* as well. Had it not been for Agent Gilder, she would likely have turned back. She made a mental note to go apologize to the Colonel as soon as was possible.

Mary reached out and pushed a lock of hair from Iain's face. He'd grown so gangly in the last year, and his face, so calm now, had matured. And the girls... there was something about their sleeping forms that made them all look older and wiser than their tender years should allow. Mary scoffed, allowing a slight smile to soften her face. What was she thinking? These were not normal children. They *were* older and wiser. They'd been places few children go, and seen things most people have never seen. That had changed them. It was a mistake to think of them as just children. And now they were off again, their spirits traveling in a realm most modern adults still had trouble believing even existed.

A distant alarm bell rang and Mary shuddered, a mixture of excitement and dread. She'd traveled in those realms herself, once upon a time. She knew the magic and wonder those kids could encounter. And the dangers. She trusted that Alice and her kin would do everything they could to assure the kids' safety. But she'd looked into their fields, Mary had. She'd seen those terrible images. She'd felt the dead menace of that black tendril. And past experience had taught her that such images were not to be underestimated. She stepped closer to the children and bowed her head, praying that Alice, Spud, and whoever else was behind this were on guard against such things. And praying that they were a match for whatever forces lay behind that blackness.

The resident cleared her throat and Mary looked up. "We're all finished here," she said.

Mary nodded. "So we can move them now?" she asked.

"As soon as Dr. Gholson gives the go-ahead," the resident said, walking toward the door.

Mary turned back to watch the children. She was glad. The room, the Faraday cage, would not only thwart military sensing technology, it would probably prevent the kids from reconstituting in their bodies. They could be out there right now, trying to return, and not be able to. Dr. Gholson had *better* give his approval, she thought. She'd attempted to explain the urgency of the situation to him when he'd first arrived. He couldn't seem to grasp "all this paranormal mumbo jumbo."

Mary muttered a short curse. She would be so glad when such blind nonsense had passed from the Earth.

6.3

Keeley grabbed her keys, patted Chapin on the head, and started toward the door. Her heart was beating wildly, and had been since the moment she'd seen herself in the bathroom mirror. Stretching across her face, from cheek to cheek and over her nose, was the faint pink outline of a rash. Shit.

Keeley yanked the door shut and started down the hall, her mind racing. There was a new plague in the land. Both protocol and common sense dictated that she should call both the military command center and the hospital and then remain locked in her room until trained medical personnel could quarantine her and transfer her to the infectious disease ward.

But the thought of calling for help made her feel weak and ashamed. Images of Keeley's mother came to mind, her smirking disbelief, her refusal to listen, her insistence that Keeley go to school no matter what. Keeley shoved the images aside and kept walking. This was no big deal, really. She wasn't sick. She was just being a baby. It was just a food reaction. She was just being silly. And she would not bother anybody with her silliness. Keeley would walk, just as she always did. Mary hadn't returned in the night, but had left a message that she was at the hospital. Keeley would pop in to see her. She'd have the docs check her out while she was there. No big deal. Really.

She took the back stairs down to ground level and ducked through the kitchen to the back yard with a quick, gotta-run greeting to Ness that gave the old woman no opportunity to look closely at Keeley's face. Already the day was hot. She hurried across the lawn and ducked into the woods, hoping to avoid both the military and the Secret Service. In her time in Augusta, Keeley had created a mostly-off-road jogging trail that took her through backyards, across streams, along driveways, and up the power line cut that took her over the ridge and toward her office in the State House. She hated running with agents in tow and more than once had snuck out this way. While she didn't feel up to jogging this morning, she also didn't want to be with people right now. She was perfectly capable of getting to the hospital on her own.

The trail brought her eventually back to Capitol Street. As soon as she stepped out onto the shoulder, Keeley realized that she was hungry. She immediately thought of the Burger Hut up on Child Street and headed quickly in that direction. Her ponytail bounced against the back of her neck as she walked. She could feel the dampness from her exertions. But she didn't slow down.

Keeley hated fast food. Always had. She'd been mostly vegan during her hippie days with Pooch and, though she could hardly be picky in this time of severely diminished food choices, she still maintained what standards she could. But there was something about one of those breakfast sandwich things with the egg and cheese and sausage that sounded like exactly what she needed this morning. Maybe even two of them. They'd hit the spot. The fact that she was hungry was a good sign, as far as Keeley was concerned.

She picked up her pace in the morning heat, knowing that patrolling soldiers could spot her at any time. Greensward Commons was just a couple of blocks away. She'd shadow the buildings and stay off the roads as much as was possible. That would be cooler. She pictured a large glass of ice-cold orange juice to go with her food. Or whatever fake orange drink they were selling as juice. Didn't matter. She was ravenous.

Sausage biscuits, here I come.

6.4

The Fisherman waved his hand and the vast audience hall was once again empty of people. Gone as well were the podium and the glass of water. All that remained was Linda and William, standing face-to-face on a high balcony overlooking a huge, empty room carved from the solid rock of Phobos. "I found their weight oppressive," explained the Fisherman with a slight shrug. "And we no longer need them."

He turned and walked toward a tall doorway at the back of the balcony. Linda followed. "I'm surprised by how quickly you got to the heart of things, Madam," said William, glancing back at her and offering a quick smile.

"I'm in a hurry to get home, Teach," said Linda. Her joke came with an edge of frustration.

"Understood," said the Fisherman, as he turned left and headed down a long, curving hallway.

Linda came to a stop. Something didn't make sense to her. The hall, perhaps fifteen feet wide and at least that tall, seemed to be as brightly lit as the meeting room had been. "I don't see a light source here, William," she said, puzzled.

"It's a matter of perception, Madam," explained the Fisherman, stopping and turning. "There *is* no light here. Not in the physical realm. We've never been able to determine if there *are* any light sources here. But we can shift our modes of perceiving," he said. "As I have been doing for the both of us."

"And you're controlling the gravity as well, I assume," said Linda. "Because we're walking like there's gravity here, but I'm guessing that there isn't really."

William flashed his eyebrows. "You are correct," he said. "Our powers of both perception and creation are greatly enhanced in this level of consciousness. I'm adjusting your default vibratory state to the near-physical wherever appropriate, so as to keep distractions to a minimum. But you are free to experiment with your perceptions if you wish." William smiled. "Within limits," he added. He turned and started back down the curving corridor.

Linda followed, thinking about how dark it must really be inside Phobos. At once the hallway was as black as any cave she'd ever been down. She could feel the long eons of time through which this ruined ship has orbited Mars, dark and dead. The place felt positively spooky, as if haunted by its builders. She shifted her perception again, imagining how the hallway had looked before. The light came back. Or the seeing.

"So why do we no longer need them?" she asked, referring back to what William had said in the great hall, hoping to dispel the gloomy mood the blackness had conferred on her. "The people?"

"Because you are done with them," said William. "You said so." They came to a small alcove carved into the rock wall on their right, one of those arched recesses like Linda had seen in cathedrals and museums, but large enough to fit three or four people. The Fisherman stepped in and turned back toward the hallway, acting as if he'd just entered an elevator. He flashed his eyebrows and winked. Linda stepped in and stood beside him.

"So what's this?" she asked.

"The lift," said William.

Linda bobbed her head cheerfully, as though speaking to a crazy person. "I see. And how do we work it?" she asked, gesturing to indicate that she saw no buttons.

The Fisherman stepped back into the hallway. "We already did," he said with another wink. He turned left and started walking, heading right back the way they had come, as far as Linda could see.

She shook her head, but decided to not get distracted by what seemed to be William's deliberate attempts to confuse her. "So what do you mean I 'got to the heart of it'?"

The Fisherman stopped. "You got to the deep wisdom of your people," he said, as if it were obvious.

"Really?" said Linda, raising an eyebrow. "And what deep wisdom is that?"

"The wisdom that drives them to annihilate themselves as quickly as is possible, Madam."

Linda frowned. "*Are* we annihilating ourselves as quickly as is possible?" she asked.

"The aliens certainly thing so," said William, returning her raised eyebrow with one of his own. With that, the Fisherman turned and started down the hallway once again.

Linda followed, expecting that any moment they'd come upon the entrance to the balcony that they had passed through shortly before. But there was no such entrance. Instead, the hallway began to spiral downward and to the right. The incline gradually increased to the point where Linda wished she had a railing on which to grab. She slowed her pace.

"Oh," said the Fisherman, noticing her hesitancy. "My mistake." He waved his hand and at once both of them were hovering a few inches above the floor. "This next piece is easier without gravity."

"You do love to be in control of things," said Linda.

The Fisherman stopped and turned to stab Linda with a sharp look. "It makes it all so much easier," he said. "I thought you were in a hurry."

Linda sighed. "Yes. I am. You're right."

"You're not the only one feeling urgency right now, you know," said William.

Linda noticed that there was deep sadness in the Fisherman's eyes. "What is *your* urgency, William?" she asked, her voice now softer.

The Fisherman turned and started floating down the hallway. "It's not time for that," he said, shaking his head. Linda followed.

The downward spiral got steeper and tighter. In a few moments they neared the end of the corridor. The tunnel appeared to terminate in solid rock, but the Fisherman continued to move forward and disappeared into the wall as if it were made of smoke.

Linda stopped, then shook her head again in wonder and followed, certain that beyond this wall she would find herself on the floor of the conclave hall in which she'd given her speech. Instead, she found herself in a cramped tubular hallway that quickly led her to a very different room, this one wide and circular, with a low ceiling and a smooth, polished walkway or ramp that spiraled down to the center like a funnel. The Fisherman was floating in the room's center, out over the spiral. He flashed his eyebrows good-naturedly. Linda joined him. Directly underneath them was a gaping, round hole that opened to the vacuum of space.

"Is that from some battle or something?" asked Linda. "You said there'd been a great war."

The Fisherman shook his head. "Look at the spiral itself."

Linda did. It appeared to be smooth, blue-gray stone. But as she stared, she began to notice details underneath the surface. She let herself sink down to the spiral walkway, which created a series of concentric "benches." Up close, the stone looked more like crystal or frosted glass. Under the surface, lying head to toe, were what appeared to be frozen human bodies.

"Not human," said the Fisherman, as though he could read her thoughts. "Were you seeing them from the side, you'd find they have greatly elongated skulls. But you can certainly make out other differences from here. Their torsos are unusually long, and their legs correspondingly short. And they have webbing between both fingers and toes. And internally…"

"You've dissected them?" asked Linda, looking up at the Fisherman.

"Of course," he said.

Linda exhaled sharply in frustration. She glanced around the room and back to the Fisherman. "What is this place?"

"It was how the Fortunate buried their dead at sea," he explained. "In their view, this was simply the doorway for a return trip home."

"The Fortunate?" asked Linda.

"It's the name given them by the Life," explained the Fisherman. "In their eyes, these people were the fortunate ones. It is almost impossible to know whether the Gray aliens are being ironic."

Linda considered the body beneath her. "They don't look very fortunate to me," she said.

"There are worse things than death, Madam President."

6.5

Vice President Albert Singer answered his ringing phone. "Singer," he said.

"Confrère," said the voice on the phone.

Singer smiled. "It is good to hear your voice, Julien," he said. The older man's continental manner and Parisian accent reminded him of home.

"Bien sûr," said Julien. "Of course. You have seen?"

Singer nodded, as if his gesture could be transmitted through a telephone. "The new symbol? Yes." He reached out to touch his laptop. "It's up on-"

"Bathurst," said Julien. "Up near Greenland, no?"

"Isn't that...?"

"Oui, Albert," said Julien, his accent molding the Vice President's name into *al-bare*. "She was there. Three years ago."

The Vice President rubbed his nose. "Thought so," he said. He swiveled in his chair to move away from the glare of the morning sun. "So what does-?"

Julien cut him off. "It does not matter. Let the Angel paint his pretty pictures in the snow. It will help no one. The Directorate is meeting now. They will almost certainly decide to initiate the countdown. They know we must move very soon. Before we become trapped."

"I see," said Singer.

"I am sure you do," said Julien. "And I am sorry."

"For what?"

"I know that you are having fun... playing President," chuckled Julien. "I am sorry that it must so quickly come to an end."

6.6

Stan had awakened Cole as the first brush of coming dawn had washed across the eastern sky. There was already hot water, which Stan had heated on a tiny pocket stove with a single fuel tablet. They'd washed down nutrition bars with tea, secured their backpacks, and stepped out of the abandoned ranch house in which they'd spent the night. Venus had been twinkling still in the predawn sky, hung like an ornament in one of the fading diamonds of the Grid.

As they walked they discussed the matter of Cole's strange hops and the weird light in his hands, and spoke of the kids and Linda's mysterious mole, which the three youngsters were no doubt now investigating. They reminisced about Alice, whom they'd both known from three years ago, and pondered the unknown tactics and goals of her alien father and his people, the Life. Cole shared his hope that, in making it to Squirrel Island, not only would he be able to speak face-to-face with his wife, he would find his children and bring them back home. They noted smoke in the air any number of times as they made their way, though whether it came from the burning service station or something else they could not say. They stuck to the wooded areas, and couldn't see the smoke for the trees.

Now the mid-morning sun glinted through the branches as they made their way along Belfast Avenue, keeping roughly fifty yards from the road itself. Stan had brought along an atlas with a full set of Maine topographical maps, and had plotted their route before they'd left his office. They would travel cross-country, using secondary roads as their guides, making their way first east and then due south. That would give them the best chance of reaching Boothbay Harbor without encountering a patrol. The military presence out here was sparse, but neither of them wanted to take any chances.

The locals might be another matter entirely. Stan knew that while most had fled to the shelters, many had remained in their homes, or had set out on their own journeys to parts unknown. Though summers had grown longer, hotter and dryer, winters had grown correspondingly shorter, colder, and wetter, at least in New England. After the Christmas Crash, there'd been a large population shift to the Southern states, as if, given the choice, people preferred to die in the heat rather than the cold. Maine, never highly populated, now probably ranked lowest in density of all fifty states.

But low was not zero. There were still people here. People living post-crash lives outside of what little governmental assistance and control remained. People that had proven themselves capable, in the past eighteen months, of both great compassion *and* great depravity. Things had settled down a bit this past winter, but with this hot, early spring, and with basic resources growing ever more scarce, there was no telling what trouble was brewing in the land. Both Cole and Stan kept their holstered weapons strapped for quick and easy reach.

Cole stopped and went silent. Stan stopped and turned to face him. "You hear something?" His voice was quiet and wary.

"Up ahead," Cole nodded.

Stan turned to peer through the trees, his eyes following the wooded slope down which they were making their way. He could just make out a house on the distant slope opposite them, one of the many single-family dwellings that dotted this road. He stood and listened for a while, then turned back to Cole. "What did you hear?"

Cole shrugged. "Hard to say, Stan," he replied. "A hammer, maybe. Somebody pounding. Just a couple-three knocks. Not a woodpecker."

"Hmm," said Stan. His hand was resting naturally on the handle of his gun. "Could be anything." He listened for another moment, then raised an eyebrow. "Firing range, maybe? Back in town?"

Cole shook his head and gestured toward the distant house. "I'm pretty sure it came from that way."

Stan relaxed his hand. "Okay, then. Probably nothing to worry about, even if there're people there. Most reports have the majority of indies just keeping to themselves. We'll skirt wide in any case."

Cole shook his head in disbelief. "I never thought I'd be this afraid of my fellow Americans," he said.

Stan smiled. "I understand, Cole. Lots of unknowns out here. Lots of scary stories. But like I said before, the indies, though unpredictable, are not our biggest problem."

Cole reached up to reposition his shoulder strap and check his weapon. "If you say so, my friend," he said. "Ready?"

Stan patted his own holster. "Ready as I'll ever be," he said.

The two men continued their hike down the ridge.

6.7

Iain didn't understand how pitch-blackness could get smaller and tighter, but it did. As time had gone by, and Iain would not swear that time was going *anywhere*, the sense of nothingness had gradually shifted. Slowly, he'd begun to imagine that he had a body again, though it was more a mental impression than something he could move or feel. But with the return of an awareness of body came a cramped sensation; he felt like he had to hunch over more and more as he moved on. It was as if that strange cat was leading them down a hallway that was getting ever smaller, like the one Alice had encountered in Wonderland. The fact that it was another Alice who had started them on this journey did not escape Iain's notice.

Which made that cat more than a little Cheshire, when he thought about it. But it wasn't a grin, this time. It was those eyes, those faint, greenish, almond-shaped cat's-eyes that stood out like beacons in this lost, dark place. Those eyes were the only things to hold onto, and Iain clung to them as tightly as he could. His sisters, somewhere "behind him," if it made any sense at all to even use that term, were depending on him right now. He was the big brother, after all. It was his *job* to protect them, if he could.

"You guys doing okay?" asked Iain into the blackness.

"Right here," said Emily.

"Me too," said Grace.

Dennis barked once.

Iain sighed, though he had no lungs with which to exhale air, and no air to exhale. He had his mind, and somehow they could speak to one another, and there were those eyes. Beyond that, there was nothing; the whole of the universe had simply ceased to be.

And then it shifted. A door opened and the universe flooded back into awareness and there were Emily and Grace and Dennis standing beside him in a row, four weary, wary travelers on a grand adventure. Before them, seated on a red velvet cushion on a small, golden throne, sat a cat... the cat... their cat... licking its left paw. Surrounding them were golden walls hung with thick, colorful tapestries depicting scenes of battle. Against each wall was an ornate settee. In every corner stood a solid gold pole six feet tall with a large, burning taper in a crystal holder at the top of each.

The cat, sleek and black save for a single white star on its chest, looked up from its licking and languidly blinked its eyes. "Oh," it said in a bored voice, "the dog is just an old, stuffed toy." The cat went back to its licking.

"Excuse me, but this 'old toy' has fought beside foxes and polar bears," said Grace, stepping forward. Her tone was protective and indignant.

The cat waved her away with a flick of his paw. "I did not say it was useless," said the cat, glancing apathetically at Dennis before returning its attention to Grace. "I am merely stating that its presence here is far less impressive than its noisome barking in the Murk had suggested."

Emily stepped up to join her sister and put her hands on her hips. "Well... that's what you think," she said, her voice flustered and shaky, "you... you... cat."

The cat stared at Emily for a long moment, slowly blinking. "Having a moment, are we?" it said at last. "Feeling better?"

Emily opened her mouth to respond but then thought better of it.

Iain decided it was time to step in and get whatever information he could. "We thank you for your help," he said, trying on a formal, diplomatic voice. "Can you tell us what that blackness was that you found us in?"

The cat shifted its weight and began to lick its right paw. "Going to forego the social niceties altogether, I see," it muttered. It kept on licking.

Grace knelt down, picked up her dog, and held him to her chest as she rose. "My name's Grace," she said, as cheerfully as she could. "This is Dennis. What's your name?"

The cat looked up and scrunched its nose. "Well, aren't you the quick learner?" it said.

"I am," said Grace. "And you're right. You helped us and now we're guests in your home. I'd like to hear your story."

The cat stopped licking, put his paws together on the cushion, and stretched his neck to his full sitting height, looking for all the world like an old Egyptian statue. "My story?" he asked. "You do not need my story, child. You need only my name. Once you hear my name, you will know my story."

"Okay," said Grace. "Tell us your name."

The cat raised its nose slightly higher. "I am Mihos," it said, a touch of drama in its voice.

The kids looked at each with quizzical faces. Iain shook his head. Emily frowned. "I'm sorry," said Grace. "But we don't-"

"Son of Bast?" said Mihos. "Maahes? Prince of war? Protector of the innocent?"

The three kids just stood and stared.

"Damn," spat Mihos.

6.8

Ness stormed down the hallway and slammed her fist on the nurse's station countertop. "You will not separate them!" she demanded, her voice cold and her eyes on fire.

The nurse, a tiny woman of Oriental descent, looked up at Ness with a practiced smile. "Ma'am?" she said.

"The President's children," said Ness, shaking her head no, no, no. "They must be kept together. You cannot put them in separate rooms."

"But Doctor Gho-"

"The doctors do not understand!" said Ness angrily, pushing the sign-in clipboard toward the nurse. It landed on the nurse's keyboard, knocked over an empty coffee cup, and clattered to the floor.

The nurse stood and reached down to thumb an intercom button. "I need security at Station 6," she said evenly, as if this happened all the time. She bent to pick up the clipboard, set it gently back on the counter, then looked up at Ness. "Ma'am," she said again with another smile, this one obviously insincere. "I must ask you to back away and wait for the soldiers."

Ness raised an eyebrow. "Soldiers?" she spat. "You think soldiers are going to understand what is happening here?" She reached out to slap the clipboard again but was stopped by a hand on her elbow. Ness whirled to find Mary standing behind her.

"Ness?" said Mary gently, rubbing the sleep from her tired, red eyes. She'd been napping in the visitor lounge, having been awake most of the night.

"I just got here," explained Ness, her eyes darting back and forth as if for a moment she'd forgotten where she was and how she'd gotten there. She gestured down the hallway toward where the kids had been moved. "Did you approve this?"

Mary shook her head in confusion. "Approve what, Ness dear?"

Ness motioned angrily down the hallway. "The kids. You've got them in separate rooms.

At that moment two soldiers arrived, their hands on their weapons. "Ma'am?" the shorter one asked the nurse.

Mary held up a hand to stop them. "Hold on a sec," she said. She turned back to Ness. "Is there a problem, Ness?" she asked.

"They must be kept together," said Ness, gesturing angrily at the nurse with a nod of her head. "These bozos don't understand what's going on."

Mary breathed slowly and deeply, her face a warm smile. "And what *is* going on, my friend?" she said, her expression was open and gentle.

Ness matched Mary's deep breathing and closed her eyes to think. After a moment her head began to shake slowly back and forth. "I don't know, Mary," she said, her voice now calmer. "I just... they have to be together." She opened her eyes. "All three of them. I have to sit with them. I have to pro-" Ness stopped, as if the word she'd almost spoken had come as a surprise to her.

Mary nodded. "You have to protect them," she said, finishing Ness's sentence. "From the alien flu. And from the people who took their mother."

Ness sighed deeply and nodded sadly.

"Even though the staff has isolated the kids' rooms from the rest of the hospital. And even though there are guards stationed at each of their doorways."

Ness glanced at the soldiers, then back to Mary. "Yes," she said. "They need to be together. So I can... protect them."

Mary reached out and put a hand to Ness's cheek, then turned to the nurse. "I'll need to see Dr. Gholson immediately," she said.

"But he's gone-"

"Then get him on the phone, please," cut in Mary. "Now. We must get these children moved as quickly as is possible."

The nurse opened her mouth to protest, then nodded curtly and picked up the phone.

Mary turned to Ness. "I should have thought of this myself, Ness," she said. "I apologize."

She turned to the soldiers. "I need you to make whatever arrangements are necessary," she said. "The children are to be roomed together immediately. And Ms. Abernathy will act as the White House liaison in all security matters pertaining to the President's children as of right now. She's going to need a cot set up for sleeping, and will need all of her meals delivered to the room." The soldiers, used to taking orders, nodded once and turned to do as Mary said.

Mary turned back to Ness. "Is there anything else you need?" she asked. She reached out and took Ness's hand. The older woman, having had her requests now met, was clearly terrified. There were tears hovering in her eyes and her skin had paled.

Ness shook her head. "I don't... I don't know what came over me," she said. She turned to the nurse. "I'm so sorry," she whispered. The nurse, looking up from her phone call, nodded her acceptance.

Mary squeezed Ness's hand. "I don't know either," she said. "But whatever it is, it shall not be trifled with. Your field has grown to such intensity that I can barely stand to open up to it, Ness. There's something inside of you that... well, whatever happens next, I think we may all soon find out just why it was you came here."

The tears spilled from Ness's eyes at that and she dropped Mary's hands and turned away to head back down the hallway. Mary watched as the older woman made her way back to those three dear children. Ness was right. Something *had* come over her. Something new, perhaps. Or just hidden deep inside. Something very different from the old woman she appeared to be.

A sense of relief flooded through Mary, offsetting the disturbing news of Cole's disappearance that had come to her an hour earlier. Now she was not alone in her need to care for the kids. And she would not be alone as this played out. Wherever this present moment would take them, whatever that dark tendril intended, Ness, it seemed, was burning now with a bright light to counter that darkness.

With a sigh of thanksgiving, Mary turned back toward the lounge, wondering if there might be hot water for tea. What she saw instead, when she turned, down near the double doors at the front entrance, was Keeley, just as she collapsed to the floor.

6.9

"I'm not really done with them, you know," said Linda as she hovered in the room's center. The opening to deep space called to her, an offering of escape or adventure. Or just an end, as it had served for these "Fortunates" who'd used this room for burials.

"I do understand that, Madam President," said William, who sat on the top spiral near the room's curved outer wall. "You have loved ones back home whom you wish to rejoin. And, like it or not, you are still the leader of your people. This cannot be simply dismissed."

"No."

"And yet there was truth to your words when you spoke them. When you said 'I am done with them.' I could feel that truth. So could you. What is that truth? What *are* you done with?"

Linda closed her eyes to think, a habit from physicality that accompanied the dimming of sensory perceptions she could now automatically effect in order to decrease distractions. After a few moments she opened back up. "I am done trying to control things that are much larger and more powerful than I," she said with a slight nod of acceptance.

The Fisherman smiled. "And what are those 'larger' things of which you speak, Madam? Do you know?"

Linda glanced around the room and gave a brief, sad chuckle. "Are you kidding me?" she said. "Where do I start? Ancient aliens? *Current* aliens? The climate going all out of whack? The fact that we can now barely feed ourselves? I mean... Jesus, William, what was I thinking?"

The Fisherman gave a gentle nod of understanding. "You were thinking, were you not, that even in the face of all of these things, you could somehow help your people get through them with more grace and less pain than they would otherwise?" He raised his eyebrows. "Am I right?"

Linda exhaled loudly. "Yeah," she said. "Something like that."

"But there was another 'larger' thing that you hadn't counted on," he said.

"Yes," Linda agreed. "There was."

"The death wish, of which we spoke earlier."

Linda exhaled loudly.

"The quest for self-annihilation, which I just a few moments ago called 'a deep wisdom.'"

The President drifted over to where the Fisherman sat and came to rest on the spiral just below him. "If we kill ourselves off, then maybe we won't kill off everything else," she said, her voice low and tentative. She glanced at him quickly, checking his reaction. She wasn't sure the idea made any sense.

"Perhaps," said William, gazing out over the room. "Perhaps that is a part of it, and perhaps there is wisdom in it. Individual humans *are* capable of that sort of self-sacrifice for someone they love, it would seem. But I rather doubt, given the level of disconnection between civilized humans and what they call 'nature,' that 'saving the beloved,' or whatever we might term it, is really the deepest motivation. As I said, perhaps that is a part of it."

Linda sat with that for a moment. The alien body, stiff and frozen in the spiral arm right beneath her, stared up with a neutral expression, the lifeless face of a mannequin. The animating force had abandoned it completely, and in so doing had left behind the concerns of life. No horror. No pain. No grief. No regret. Not even peaceful acceptance or relief. Nothing. She looked up at the Fisherman. "So what's the larger part of it?" she asked.

William turned and caught Linda's eye. "Do you remember what I said the Fortunate thought of this room?" he asked.

"Something about a doorway home?" said Linda.

The Fisherman flashed his eyebrows with delight. "That is how the Life have explained it," he said. "As far as we can make out, the Fortunate were creatures of the higher levels. Their primary existence did not play out in the physical bands. This ship," he continued, gesturing to the walls around him, "and these bodies, are just discarded shells, Madam President. They're just the trash left behind from a trip to the physical, if you will. Diving suits used to explore the deep oceans of materiality. They do not represent death. Just transition."

Linda raised an eyebrow. "And you think we humans are up to something similar?" she asked.

"Some are," said the Fisherman evenly, "though few hold the thought consciously, and fewer still would admit it. But, yes, I think some large portion of the dominant mainstream global culture is running toward the brick wall as fast as it can, in order to either die and relieve their misery, or to somehow break through to the other side. They seek not the death of spirit, the death of consciousness. They seek the death of physicality. They wish to shed the confines of materialism and follow their parents home."

Linda frowned. "Their parents?"

"Of course," said William. "Have I not said? The Fortunate are our distant ancestors, Madam. We are their children."

6.10

The motorcycle sat parked in the driveway, glinting in the late-morning sun, pointed toward the road as if ready for a quick getaway. Was it providence? Bait? Or simple confidence on the part of the owner? They could not tell. Stan motioned to Cole to stay behind the brick wall and then slipped through the open gate before ducking back into the trees. He stood motionless for a full minute, watching, listening. There were no sounds from the house. No barking dogs. No ruffling curtains revealing a watcher. Save for the shiny red Harley parked in the drive, the place looked and felt dead.

The house before this one, a mile or so back now, had not felt dead. Cole had, indeed, picked out from the background of forest sounds the intermittent rapping of a hammer on wood. They'd given the place a wide berth as they passed, pausing only long enough to catch a distant glimpse of a single older man in his back yard repairing what appeared to be a bird feeder. The sight had given them some relief. If the world was still safe enough for lone old men to hammer on bird feeders, then it was safe enough for Stan and Cole, and much safer than their worst imaginings.

Still, it would not serve them to let down their guard, and they both knew it. Stan went through the gate with his weapon drawn. One old man did not a scientific study make.

After a second minute had passed, Stan glanced back at Cole and nodded. Their plan was for Cole to take a position just inside the gate with his gun drawn while Stan, experienced with motorcycles, would attempt to start the Harley. If there was fuel in it, and if Stan could get it started, he'd hightail it out of there, stopping only long enough for Cole to jump on behind him. If it all went as they planned, their trip down to Boothbay would go much more quickly than their feet could achieve. Given the day's heat, the idea of getting quickly to the coast teased them both with the hope of cool ocean breezes.

Cole drew his pistol, scooted through the gate in a hunkered crouch, and took a position with his back to the brick wall. Stan turned and started toward the motorcycle.

He got within a few feet of it when an upstairs window flew open, revealing a scoped rifle held by small hands. From the back of the house came the sound of a slamming door and in seconds an angry, fearsome mixed-breed dog with more than a little Rottweiler in it came charging around the corner. On the dog's heels came three men with pistols out and aimed right toward him. The oldest was middle-aged, balding and heavy. The other two were just teenagers, thin and wiry. All three were dressed in a similar uniform, a mix of blue denim, Carhartt work clothes, and stray pieces of military gear.

"Bullet! Hold!" shouted the older man as the dog zeroed in on Stan. Stan stood still with arms raised as the dog skidded to a stop right in front of him, nailing him with his fierce eyes since his teeth had been forbidden. The older man stepped up and put a hand on the dog's head. The younger two fanned out on either side of him.

The older man squinted at Stan. "You need to drop that," he said, nodding toward Stan's gun. Stan dropped his weapon to the gravel, then turned to Cole. Cole, afraid and indignant and thinking that Stan's look was a plea for him to step in, raised his pistol and began to walk toward them. "Now listen," he said, "you have no idea-"

From the window upstairs came two gunshots in rapid succession. The first hit Cole squarely in the chest, then fell to the ground at his feet without doing any harm. The second Cole snatched from the air with his bare hand.

"Hold!" shouted the older man again, aiming his voice high and toward the hidden shooter. The firing stopped.

Stan glanced up to see the gun withdraw into the upstairs window, then returned his attention to Cole. The President's husband was standing with both hands held at shoulder level, his gun in one and a slug in the other.

"Cole?" said Stan, blinking. "Are you...?"

Cole dropped the hot slug to the ground, where it came to rest near the other one. He dropped the gun. Immediately, showers of sparkling light sprang forth from his palms. He looked at Stan in disbelief, then lifted his hands and studied the bright light pouring forth. After a few moments he glanced again at Stan. "I'm ... fine," he said, his brow wrinkled in confusion.

Stan turned back to the armed men. All three stood staring at Cole with expressions of surprise. Their weapons dangled at their sides. Even the dog had relaxed back onto its haunches.

The back door slammed once more. Around the corner ran an even younger child, a girl of only twelve or thirteen, dressed like the others in denim and olive green. "Daddy!" she said as she joined the three men.

The older man, obviously her father, put an arm on her shoulder and drew her to him. "It's okay, girl," he said gently. "You did good."

"But-" protested the girl, glancing shyly at Cole. She looked up at her father and then back to Cole. "His hands!" she said.

The older man nodded, his face serious, his voice low, as if reciting scripture. "That's right," he said to his daughter, motioning vaguely toward Cole. "He's the Magic Man. The Wayfaring Stranger. He cannot be harmed, even by the weapons of old." The man looked over to Cole and removed his hat. Cole pulled his eyes away from his sparkling hands and looked at the man.

"Welcome, Stranger," the man said. He studied Cole intently, as if the President's husband was a long-lost friend he barely remembered. "Welcome back."

6.11

Ness stood in the hospital hallway, waiting as the nurses moved the kids into a larger room where they could be together. But while Ness waited, Other-than-Ness had work to do. Closing herself off from the distracting sensory input of Ness's body, Other-than-Ness cast outward with her mind, seeking the others of her kind and touching them with her thoughts. "LET US BEGIN," she said to them, the words acting as a call, a trigger, and a beacon.

Other-than-Ness scanned the planet's vast field of consciousness some humans called the noosphere. She tuned out the human channels of mental activity so that she could more easily connect with her people. She listened for a moment. Her message had been received. Already, there was movement in the field. Satisfied, Other-than-Ness stepped back, leaving Ness to her waiting.

6.12

"Will you tell us what's going on?" asked Grace of Mihos. The cat had slunk down off his perch and now sat nose to nose with Dennis. Dennis trembled. It was all the poor old Whippet could do to hold his ground and not run away.

Mihos glanced up at Grace with a blank face, then returned his attention to the dog. "You speak as if 'what's going on' can be told in short and simple words," he said. He swiped a paw at Dennis just to watch the dog flinch, then sat back on his haunches and began to lick the paw, as if it had been dirtied. "You monkeys have always been in such a hurry."

"I apologize," said Grace. "But our stepmother is in trouble. We were on our way to try to help her."

"Until you were swallowed by the Murk," said the cat with a snort. "Some help."

"Can you tell us about this 'Murk'?" asked Emily.

Mihos sighed deeply. "You guys really should have sprung for a guidebook before setting out on your little vacation," he said with a shake of the head. "You couldn't be more lost, could you?"

Emily gestured around the room. "Could you start by telling us where we are?"

Mihos raised his shoulders. "You're in my home," he said, as though it were obvious.

"And where-"

"My home. You know? Astral plane and all that rot. Third star on the right and straight on 'til you smell catnip. The great scratching pole in the sky." Mihos stared up at Emily, his eyes slack with boredom.

"But where-"

"You do understand that the idea of 'location' doesn't mean the same thing here as it does back on good ol' Terra Firma, don't you?"

Emily opened her mouth to respond, then thought better of it and just nodded.

"Good," said Mihos. "Now we're getting somewhere. Time. Space. Distance. Location. Matter. Even the notion that you are in a body right now. Throw 'em all out and start fresh. In this time, we are in my home. In another time, you were lost in the Murk. I found you there and pulled you out of it with my special cat-lasso." Mihos raised a paw over his head and circled it like a cowboy. "That's a joke. You know that, right? Batman?"

Emily nodded again and Grace knelt down to scratch Dennis's ears. Iain, arms crossed, stood back and observed. His eyes were narrow with judgment.

"So how did you find us?" asked Grace. "And why did you help us?"

Mihos chuckled sadly. "Gods only know," he said. "The Great Ones said to help you and I did. Finding you was easy enough. The Murk's a nasty one but he's also pretty stupid. He doesn't even think to cover his trail. And we cats are good in the dark."

"So-"

"The Great Ones say your mission is important," said Mihos, interrupting Emily.

Grace nodded her agreement. "We need to find Linda Travis and set her free," she said.

"Whatever," said Mihos. "You can be selling Girl Scout cookies as far as I'm concerned. Doesn't matter. The Great Ones say jump, I ask 'how high?' Know what I mean?"

"Who are these Great Ones?" asked Iain, stepping forward.

Mihos glanced up at the boy, then back at Grace. "Your brother?" he asked, raising an eyebrow.

"Yes," said Grace.

"He seems a bit of a dolt," said Mihos. "Is he?"

Grace shook her head. "He's a good guy," she said. "He's smart and-"

"Yeah, yeah. He ain't heavy and all that." The cat looked up at Iain and blinked. "The Great Ones, young man, are obviously none of your damned monkey business."

"But-"

"If you have to ask, then you can't afford it," said Mihos with a sniff.

Iain shook his head and slunk back a step, his face clenched and dark.

"So this Murk is a being of some sort?" asked Emily. "And he's a bad guy?"

"Oh I love that," said Mihos, laughing loudly. He nodded once, with finality. "Yes. The Murk is the Bad Guy. You three are the Good Guys. I'm the funny but complicated magical animal mentor that comes in to help you on your way while providing comic relief. All we need now is a quest and we've got ourselves a show, kids. Who's gonna play me?"

"So you're going to help us?" asked Grace, focusing on the part that applied.

Mihos returned to licking his paws. "The Great Ones seem to think your 'Linda Travis' person will play some role in the unfolding train wreck you monkeys seem to have created. As we cats like to keep one paw in the physical, so to speak, and as we consider the planet you call 'Earth' our ancestral home, we have some stake in the matter. We'd rather you not blow the whole stinking place to bits, ya know what I mean?" He looked up at Grace. "So, yes, little girl, I'm going to help. Mihos, son of Bast, Prince of War and Protector of the Innocent, is going to help. That okay with you, Princess?"

"Is there some reason you have to be so sarcastic?" said Emily.

Mihos cuffed Dennis on the nose, turned and raised his tail to stick his bottom in the poor dog's face, then walked slowly and confidently to a sofa near the wall. With a lazy leap he settled onto a cushion. "Would you believe me if I told you that I'm filled with shame and terribly insecure?" he said, as he kneaded the upholstery with his claws.

"Are you?" asked Grace.

"No," said Mihos, closing his eyes with a loud sigh. "I just hate monkeys."

"Why do you hate monkeys?" asked Emily.

Mihos opened one eye. "You should see the one that feeds me," he said.

6.13

McAfee dumped a can of scavenged, long out-of-date chicken-and-rice Kitty Dinner on top of the dried out lumps of tuna-and-egg that clung like barnacles to the bottom of Nicky's bowl. He tossed the container into the trash. Nicky sniffed at the brown, gelatinous hockey-puck-shaped mass, then turned and walked out of the kitchen.

"Fine," said the Colonel. "Go hungry for all I care. That's all there is."

Nicky collapsed into a heap on a warmest, sunniest part of the sunroom floor and closed his eyes.

McAfee pulled a bottle of vodka from the freezer and poured some into a tumbler, then added a splosh of military-issue orange drink from the refrigerator. He stirred it with his finger, picked up the tumbler and the paperback novel sitting splayed on the counter, and followed the cat out into the sunroom. The sun was sharp on the bay today and the bounce of light filled the room with wavy brightness. The Colonel lowered his sunglasses, sat heavily in his lounge chair, placed his drink on the floor beside him, and opened the book, grateful for the fact that Stephen King was still churning them out, even if the books themselves were little better in quality than the dime novels of old.

He lifted his glass and took a deep swallow of his drink, then placed the glass back on the floor and closed his eyes, reveling in the bit of sea breeze that wafted in now and again from the open window. The bright, sunny room had engulfed him in its sauna-like warmth and he saw no reason not to accede to its invitation. Why should he? He could always use a nap. And it wasn't like he was needed for anything. DuPont was all over the VLT's Summit participation. Osterman, the Colonel's aide, was overseeing the vaccination program, to be implemented as soon as possible now that the Quietus was on the move. The real Linda Travis needed no more attention than a turkey in a freezer. The ship did not require that the Captain stand always at the wheel.

The Colonel picked at his shorts. The thought of the President lying so naked and open on her slab in the basement always got him a bit hard. It didn't matter that she was the President, or that she was married, or that she was probably going the way of the dodo more quickly than he'd anticipated. She was a babe, pure and simple. What he really wanted to do, if he was honest, was head to the basement, thaw the President, and screw her brains out. And wouldn't some time in her cold basement room be a relief from the day's heat! Like taking a dip in a nice, refreshing pool. The ol' girl was a PILF, for sure. McAfee smiled at the acronym. Yeah. That was it. Linda Travis: *President I'd Like to-*

A small bird smashed into the window right in front of him, causing him to jerk and distracting him from his reverie. A cloud of tiny brown and white feathers drifted to the ground. Nicky glanced up at the hard thump on the glass, then lowered his head and closed his eyes. "There's some chow for ya, Nick," said McAfee. "If you're hankering for fresh meat."

Lacking a flexible middle finger, the cat did not respond.

McAfee lifted his glass and finished his drink, then laid back in his chair and closed his eyes again, the paperback now lying open on his stomach. There was something about the weight of a book on his belly that he found calming. Probably some leftover from his youth. The Colonel took a long, deep breath. That was not a territory he was willing to enter: his youth. With an effort of will, he set such thoughts aside and focused again on that vision of Linda Travis lying naked on her slab. With a soft, moaning exhale, Colonel McAfee followed his cat into sleep.

6.14

Ness sighed sadly. Keeley had been quarantined immediately and poor Mary had stationed herself as close to her sweetheart's room as she could, not to be budged, and not to be persuaded to go home and get some rest. Ness was not surprised to learn that this alien flu thingy was spreading, or that it had reached right into the President's staff. There was no telling how this bug was spread, how long it took to appear as a disease, or at what point it became infectious. Augusta seemed to be one of a dozen or so places around the globe where Greensleeves was now appearing in ever increasing numbers, with the President as what they called "the index case." Ness didn't know what that meant, exactly. Maybe the aliens had infected Linda. Or maybe it was those hidden elites she'd heard stories about. Maybe it was a terrorist thing, like the poisoning of Sebago Lake. Ness did not know.

What she did know was that she had no fear of contracting this flu herself, and no fear, now that she was on guard, that the children would either. In fact, it felt like, in some odd but real way, her primary job here was to make sure they were not infected, especially now that both their parents had gone missing. She had no idea how she might achieve that, of course. What she knew about diseases and epidemics you could fit in a shot glass, as... somebody from her past... she couldn't remember who... used to say. But even so, she had a clear sense that this task was on her.

Not that that was the only reason she was here. Truth be told, she felt a bit silly insisting on acting as some sort of guardian, what with armed soldiers right outside the door twenty-four-seven. If there was some danger of terrorists breaking in and stealing them away, Ness couldn't believe she'd be anything but in the way. What, she'd stab them with her keys? She'd just be another target, most likely. Or they'd use her as a shield, like in the movies. But silly or not, Ness knew without a doubt that her job was to stay with these kids. The image that kept coming to her was of a bright purple ball of light surrounding all four of them. And she felt - and she could really feel it, a tingling of her scalp, as if her gray hairs were actually standing up, no matter how often she reached up to find that they were still neatly arranged - she felt like this bright ball of light actually came out of her head. Like a fountain, maybe. Or a balloon.

She wished she could extend this ball of light to surround Keeley as well. But Ness sensed that it was too late for that. Mary had told her about Keeley's facial rash. The same rash now on President Linda's face. The same rash that appeared on the faces of those people now showing up sick or dead at hospitals all around the world, if the news was to be believed. Ness breathed a short prayer for her friends: for Keeley now struck with illness and Mary now struck with fear. She didn't know to whom she prayed. She simply knew that there was something, someone, somewhere, who was listening.

A cloud passed overhead and the room dimmed a bit. Ness looked up at the children, now situated side by side on three gurneys, as close together as could be, with space only for a nurse to squeeze in between them when necessary. Their faces were so calm. So full of peace. So vulnerable. Mary said they were off traveling in the Astral plane. Ness believed it. She knew such a place was real, though she'd never been there herself. Ness said another prayer, for these three young souls on their adventure. Then she leaned back in her chair and closed her eyes. The bright purple ball was right where she'd left it. Remembering how her Daddy - it must have been her Daddy - had always said that maintenance was love, Ness exhaled with focus and intention and added her energy to the ball.

This was her work now. Now she was really cookin'.

6.15

Vice President Albert Singer hung up his phone and immediately began to dial another number. He leaned back into his ergonomically designed mesh chair and scratched his nose while the phone rang.

"Yes?" came a voice on the other end.

"You know who this is," said Singer. He was not asking a question.

"Yes, sir," said the voice.

"You've received the updated timetable?"

"I have."

"You're prepared at your end."

"I am, sir," said the voice without hesitation.

"You understand what that means."

"I do," said the voice.

"You can expect your orders very soon now," said Singer.

"I will, sir," said the voice.

Singer thumbed the off button and returned his phone gently to his desktop. He pictured the young man he'd just spoken to sitting at his desk. He could imagine the excitement now rushing through his veins. Singer smiled. Soon enough, they'd be popping corks of celebration.

Just a few nasty details to take care of first.

6.16

Carl sat studying the board, his elbow on his knee and his chin in his palm. "I can't figure out where these last six letters went," he muttered.

Ted, searching under the table on his hands and knees for any lost tiles, raised his head to respond, stopping himself with a jerk before he hit the table and sent the tiles flying once again. "What are the letters?" he asked.

"M, D, O, R, N, and A," said Carl.

"Random," said Ted. "You spelled 'random.' Your fifth turn. You got twenty points for it. Double letter on the R and a double word."

Carl studied the board and saw where the word had been placed. "How do you remember shit like that?" he asked.

Ted scooted backwards out from under the table and lifted his head above the playing surface. "I keep most of my brain in another universe," he said. Grabbing the table's edge, he pulled himself to his feet and plopped into the chair opposite Carl. He watched as Carl put the last letters in place.

"Is that all of 'em?" asked Carl.

"I didn't see any more." Ted surveyed the room with theatrical exaggeration. "Not many places to lose one in here," he added.

Carl sighed with relief. "Good. The board's back the way it's supposed to be."

"You always were a rule-bound, detail-obsessed pain in the ass," said Ted.

"Was I?" asked Carl, looking up.

"Yes."

"So we did know each other?" said Carl.

Ted crossed his arms. "It would seem."

Carl returned to the board. It was his turn.

"I've been thinking about what you said," said Ted.

Carl lifted an eyebrow. "What'd I say?"

"You said there must be another place from here. That this is not the whole of existence, here in this room. And that that meant we could get out of here. And you said that maybe there's something we have to do to get out."

"Ah," said Carl, nodding. "I remember."

Ted leaned forward and looked Carl in the eye. "So, I've been thinking, is all," he said with a shrug.

Carl returned his attention to his tiles.

"Because I just felt a strong sense of irritation with you," Ted went on. "And then I called you a pain in the ass." Carl looked up again and Ted offered a slight, embarrassed smile. "And we had that fight and knocked over the board." He inhaled and exhaled slowly. "So, yeah. We knew each other. And so maybe that's why we're here. Because we knew each other in that other place. And maybe we weren't friends. And maybe there's something we're supposed to be doing here besides playing this stupid game of Scrabble. And maybe it has something to do with the feelings that keep coming up in me."

Carl grinned. "Those are the most words you've put together at one time since we got here," he said.

Ted looked down at his lap. "So…" he said at last, glancing up for a moment before returning his attention to his clasped hands, "what do you think of my ideas?"

Carl cocked his head and thought for a moment. "I think you're onto something," he said.

Ted smiled slightly.

"Do you have any idea what you're supposed to do with these feelings you keep having?" asked Carl.

Ted's eyes welled up with tears at Carl's question and he wiped at them with the back of his hand. "I think I'm supposed to tell you about them," he said with a wet, heavy voice.

Chapter Ø Seven

7.1

Gabrielle's professor had begun his class with a reminder that there were still a few students who had not yet participated in Freemantle College's mandatory vaccination program, which had begun last week. Nobody questioned why it was that Freemantle students were receiving this vaccine, or how there was a vaccine at all for a disease that had only just appeared. Some people there knew exactly where the school's wealth and resources came from. The rest at least understood that there were shadowy powers involved. And none of them were inclined to look a gift horse in the mouth, as the saying went. Not when said horse's saddlebags came stuffed with boxes of vaccine which would spare them from what appeared to be a fatal new pandemic. The word had come down, the program had been implemented, and most everyone there knew better than to think too deeply about something they clearly had no need to know. Especially now. The professor's warning was implicit. Montreal local news had just the night before reported the city's first fatal case of Greensleeves. It was time.

They spent the rest of their two hours together watching the live coverage of the Earth Summit. Gabrielle was not sure exactly how that fit in with a torsion-physics lesson plan, but she wasn't going to complain. High-level mathematics made her head spin. She was glad for the break.

Class over, she grabbed the iron railing and made her way down the steps. The handrail, baking in the noonday sun, was hot to the touch, but Gabrielle found that she wanted and needed both the stability and the slight discomfort the hot metal afforded her. Something about her encounter with her father had left her almost giddy with anxiety. Perhaps it was the notion that she had some work to do here on Earth. Perhaps it was the glimpse, real or imagined, of the tall man from her dreams. Or perhaps it was simply the fact that she'd told her father 'no.' Gabrielle could not be sure. What she *could* know was that her knees felt a bit weak and wobbly and her heart was still pounding. And her head felt fuzzy, as if her thoughts themselves, like the hot metal railing, were shimmering in the blasted heat.

The Summit broadcast had been exasperating: old, rich, white men jockeying for power and position, with the occasional voice of sanity and reason thrown in just to highlight the nuttiness of it all. None of those participating knew what was really going on, it seemed, or understood who was actually in charge. The American President, Linda Travis, was certainly one of those voices of sanity, save for the fact that she thought that she still mattered. She was no "sleeper," as Gabrielle's father might call her, that was for sure. Yet she was getting sicker by the day. The video feed from her hospital room showed a raw-eyed, exhausted, and sad looking woman, the fact of which had forced the matter of this Greensleeves epidemic onto the Summit agenda. Gabrielle felt sorry for the President. Whatever the whole truth of this "alien flu," it seemed certain to Gabrielle that Linda Travis was losing her fight against it. One less voice of sanity, which was the last thing the world needed. The rest of them would just go on arguing about carbon taxes and high-tech alternative energies and how to jump-start the global economy until the whole planet went up in a flash.

Maybe her father was right. Maybe Gabrielle should just get the hell out of here.

But what, then, of her dear Arthur? Gabrielle kicked at a stone in the path as she made her way across the quad. She shook her head in anger. This was all just so unfair. The Families ruin the planet and then take off, leaving the rest of the world to suffer the consequences? Gabrielle laughed at her own indignation. Like there was anything new to *that* story. The scenario had been playing out for millennia. She was just one of the most recent victims.

Gabrielle had decided to head over to Arthur's room when she was hit from behind and knocked to her knees. She gave a tiny yelp as a tall human body thumped to the ground beside her, its head smacking wetly on the paved walkway like a watermelon. Scrambling to her hands and knees, Gabrielle pulled away from the body and twisted around to land on her bottom. It was the man from her dreams: Zacharael. He appeared to be dead.

Gabrielle scanned the quad. Two young men, soccer players on their way home from practice, it looked like, were running toward her. Gabrielle, suddenly terrified, pushed herself to her feet and started to run away, ignoring the cries of "hey!" and "wait up!" that followed her. She rounded the corner of the MedLab and headed down toward the creek, hoping to get lost in the maze of trails and trees that buffered this side of the campus. She imagined phone calls and police and paramedics and ambulance sirens behind her as she crossed the short footbridge over the shallow creek that separated the campus from the forested park beyond.

The trees rose up to surround her, engulf her, protect her. Gabrielle slowed her pace. She had no idea what had just happened, but she couldn't get involved. That she knew. She didn't recognize the young men who'd been running to help, and so assumed that they couldn't identify her. With any luck, nobody that *did* know her had witnessed the event.

The cooler air of the park felt good on Gabrielle's skin and she stopped for a moment to catch her breath. She looked back toward the campus. There was no one following her, and already there was the sound of a distant siren. That was good. Let those whose job it was deal with that mess.

Gabrielle pulled off her backpack and let it hang in one hand while continuing to walk. On the far side of the park was a strip of shops, with a coffee shop she frequented when doing homework. That sounded good. A big glass of iced tea, and witnesses that would say she'd been there working on her tablet at the time of the incident.

Wiping the sweat from her face, Gabrielle hefted the backpack over one shoulder and headed across the park. Her breathing was heavy with heat and hurry and adrenaline. What the hell had just happened? And what would come next? Up until a few moments ago, Zacharael had been little more than a strange dream. Now he was not only real... but dead? Gabrielle felt a pang of grief in her gut at the thought. Zacharael had been intimately entwined with her sense, her hope, her excitement, her notion that there was something she was supposed to do. Zacharael was the "supposed to." And now he was gone.

"Gabrielle."

Gabrielle spun around. A voice. Speaking her name. Right in her ear. Uttered from just inches behind her. But there was no one there. She was alone in the woods. She turned again toward the coffee shop when the voice spoke again.

"I apologize for frightening you back there," the voice said in her head.

It was Zacharael.

7.2

Cole accepted the glass of iced tea with a wink. The girl, Dizzy they called her, though it seemed her given name was Dorothy, smiled shyly in return and went back to sit next to her father, Vince. Cole looked down at his tea. Dizzy had hung a wedge of lemon on the rim. How these folks had gotten their hands on a lemon was just one of the many mysteries here.

Cole was seated in an armchair near the fireplace. Across from him, tightly wedged on the sofa, sat the whole family, Vince and Dizzy in the middle, with the boys, Sam and Pauly, surrounding them like bookends or guard dogs. Stan remained standing near the door. The expression on the faces of Vince and his children was a mixture of awed respect and meek wariness, as though they feared judgment from their king. The look on Stan's face was one of intense interest.

"I'm sorry to hear of your wife," said Cole, sipping his tea. The cool liquid provided some welcome relief in this hot, stuffy home, reminding Cole once again that, while they still had working air conditioning in the Presidential Zone, the rest of his fellow Americans were not so lucky.

Vince nodded his thanks. "It's been hard, Stranger," he said, reaching out to take Dizzy's hand. "Hardest on the kids, you know?" He glanced at his sons, then looked down at his lap for a moment before returning his gaze to Cole. "I'm not... you know... the most patient and loving man in the world. I... I try." Vince smiled grimly, as if hoping that Cole would see how much he tried.

"I'm sure you do your best," Cole said. He took another sip of the tea. The taste was strange. Woody, with a bitter tang. Yet the lemon and the dab of honey were wonderful. "So why did you folks stay here?" he asked at last. "Why didn't you go to the shelters?"

Vince closed his eyes and inhaled deeply, his head shaking slightly from side to side. "With all due respect, Sir," he said at last, opening his eyes, "why didn't *you* go to the shelters?"

"I take your point," said Cole. "This is your home. Of course you want to stay here."

"Them shelters ain't nothing but trouble," muttered Sam. His eyes had grown dark.

Vince nodded his agreement. "We heard stories," he explained to Cole. "Early on, you know? We just hunkered down here when the troops came through. Got a cabin up on the ridge. Holed up there for a few days, while the soldiers went door to door to *encourage* people to leave." He smiled at the word "encourage," then sighed and shook his head. "The patrols since have been easy enough to dodge. Less and less of 'em now."

"There has been a great deal of trouble in the shelters," said Stan from his position near the door. "Some of it got pretty scary for a while. But people seem to have settled down now."

Vince glanced up at Stan, then returned his attention to Cole. "They're only going to *stay* settled down as long as you folks can feed 'em," he said. "We'll take our chances here. And besides, some of us had to keep the Watch."

"Keep the watch," repeated Cole. "You mean for this Wayfaring Stranger."

"We mean for *you*, Sir," said Vince, his eyes piercing.

"But... you know who I am..." said Cole, shaking his head.

"We had a television," Vince said, smiling to cover his irritation. "You and the Mrs. even made the cover of People magazine, you know."

"But..."

"So?" said Vince. "I mean... sure, it comes as a surprise to us too. But there you have it. No reason the President's husband can't also be the Stranger, is there? In fact, it all kind of just fits together right, you know?"

"*'He will not know himself until the Time Has Come'*," said Dizzy, her face rapt with the recitation of scripture.

"That's right!" said Vince, laughing and patting his daughter's hand. He turned back to Cole. "I say again, sir, 'welcome back.'"

Stan stepped closer. "So this whole story-"

"Ain't no story," said Pauly seriously.

"This whole... idea, then," said Stan. "This Wayfaring Stranger? Where's it come from? What's it mean?"

Vince scooted forward to the edge of the sofa and looked Cole in the eye. "This is Church teaching, Sir," he said. "This is the heart of it: *'The Wayfaring Stranger,' also known as 'The Wandering One,' the 'Magic Man,' and 'The Hand of God,' will rise amongst us in the darkest of times to lead us all back Home. You shall know him by the light of his hands and the righteousness of his Quest. Be awake and aware, for we know not when he shall arrive. Give him what succor and aid you might, and do not stand in his way, for he is powerful beyond measure, and his work is God's work.'*" A few tears had welled in Vince's eyes as he spoke and he let them roll down his cheeks. "Do you understand?" he asked of Cole.

Cole's face was tight, his forehead wrinkled. "This church..." he began, trying to make sense of it all.

"The Church of the Strangers," said Vince, pointing toward the sky. "We ain't no Burners."

"The Church of..."

"And you are the Wayfaring Stranger, Mr. Thomas." Vince closed his eyes and started to sing, his voice low and full. "*I'm just a poor wayfaring stranger, while traveling through this world below. Yet there's no sickness, no toil, nor danger, in that bright land to which I go.*" He stopped and opened his eyes, a look of embarrassment on his face. Beside him, Sam grinned.

"And you know this," said Stan, pointing toward Cole, "because of the light we all saw coming from Cole's hands?"

Cole examined his hands, turning them over to view both sides. There was no light now, no fireworks. And there were no signs left behind that the light had ever been there. His hands looked and felt as they always had. He looked over at Vince. "I don't know what that's all about," he said, shaking his head in confusion.

"You grabbed a bullet from the air, Sir," said Sam. "And you took one to the chest that just fell to the ground like you was made of steel. You should be dead now." He turned to his father with a headshake of amazement. "He really doesn't know!" he said. "Just like Pastor Tom said."

"Know what?" said Cole, staring at the floor, afraid to hear the answer.

Vince cleared his throat and sighed. "Stranger?" he said gently. "Mr. Thomas? I gather that this is all a bit of a shock to you, but the Time Has Come and you have work to do. And it seems the Good Lord has given it to me to tell you..." Cole looked up and Vince leaned forward to close the distance between them. "I'm not quite sure how to put it, but... you ain't from around here, Sir."

7.3

"You're taking a big chance here, Sweetie," said Keeley with a tired smile. "Didn't you hear? I'm toxic." She reached up and aimed the remote to mute the television news. Her hair, dull and damp, splayed out on her pillow under her head like a splash of brown paint.

Mary stood, hunched and small, behind the yellow taped line the nurses had put on the floor. She breathed heavily through the mask they'd made her wear. With her gown, her cap, her gloves, and her booties, Mary felt like a space traveler, stepping foot onto the surface of a hostile planet. The notion that the air of this room, or the surfaces of its many objects, was somehow infected with a deadly virus which nobody understood, cast the whole scene in a surreal light. That was her partner there on that bed. It was just a bed. Those were just sheets, and all around them was just air. And yet nothing was as it had been. An invisible presence haunted the room like an angry ghost. Mary wiped the hair from her forehead and tried to smile in return. "They didn't... want me to come in," she said. The long, faint scar on her forehead seemed to shimmer under the overhead fluorescents.

"But of course you talked them into it," said Keeley.

Mary nodded, hugging her hands to her sides in hopes of stopping their trembling. "I merely pointed out that I was taking no more chance than they were. Those... who are caring for you. And that I am responsible for my own risks."

"You probably scare the hell out of them, Babe. What with your psychic gifts and all."

Mary closed her eyes for a moment and took a long breath, trying to ward off the dizziness that seemed to be crouching right behind her, ready to spring. "Yeah," she said at last. "I guess."

"So," said Keeley, turning her face to profile. "How do I look?" The red on her cheeks and nose resembled bad stage make-up.

"You look good," said Mary automatically. "You-" She stopped and shook her head and exhaled deeply. "No," she said at last. "You... your face. The rash. It's come so quickly. It... it frightens me."

"You slept through the bedside manners class, didn't you doctor?" said Keeley.

"Oh, Sweetie," said Mary, her eyes filling with tears. She shivered in the coolness of the hospital's central air conditioning.

Keeley shook her head. "I expect nothing else from you, Mar," said Keeley. "Having somebody tell me the truth is like a breath of fresh air around here."

Mary let the tears flow without words of explanation.

"You've come to look at my field, haven't you?" said Keeley. There were tears in her own eyes now. Shame and grief and fear had all risen to her face.

Mary nodded again. "I have," she said.

"Now *I'm* the one who's frightened," said Keeley.

"Oh..." was all Mary could say in response, a soft, breathy, moan.

Keeley held up a hand, pulling at the IV in her arm. "I need to know," she said softly.

Mary closed her eyes and took three long breaths. Then she opened her eyes slightly and peered at Keeley, cocking her head to the left like she always did when she opened her newfound power of sight to the spiritual landscape of another, as if tilting her brain might throw her thinking mind offline enough to let the non-rational get through.

Beneath the upper and more dominant emotional layers of shame and grief and fear, beneath the rapidly shifting series of images that hovered around her like floating television screens, Mary could see the new presence she'd come to observe. The virus. The pandemic. The alien flu. It flickered in her field like glitter tossed across a shaft of sunlight. And yet it was as much dark as light, as if each particle of glitter had both a silver side and a black one.

Mary willed her awareness of Keeley's field to shift, and brought her focus directly on the being they now called Greensleeves. Images of high-tech labs came to her then, of masked men and gloved hands, of dark, rich rooms and hushed conversations. The virus, if that's what this was, did not feel evil to Mary. No more evil than a tiger that kills to eat or a fire that burns. Neither did the men feel evil, really. And yet there was darkness here. Intention. Secret plans. A disregard for the greater good. Even a stain of scorn. But look as she might, these shadier whiffs remained elusive. They would not resolve into anything that Mary could see clearly.

And then the images shifted and Mary, with a start, pulled herself out of her trance to speak to Keeley. "You ate fast food," she said with surprise and confusion. She pushed the hair from her face.

Keeley blushed, causing her rash to fade momentarily away. "I..." she said, a slight squeak of protest that stopped as soon as it had begun. There was no arguing with Mary's statement.

Mary closed her eyes again. "That's the key," she said after a moment. "Or *a* key..." She opened her eyes. "Did you feel a craving?"

Keeley smiled weakly. "I don't know what came over me," she said. "I was on my way here to see you and..." She stopped. Mary understood.

"That's how it works," said Mary with a single nod of certainty. "This flu. There's the... virus itself, but there's a secondary trigger in the food. Probably the GMO corn syrup." Mary, now shaking with excitement, turned to leave.

"Mary?" said Keeley.

Mary turned and rolled her eyes. "Oh, Sweetie," she said. "I'm sorry. I just... I need to tell the doctors right away. They need to know this. I'll be right back. Okay?"

"You go, girl," said Keeley.

Mary turned and left the room.

7.4

The Fisherman raised his eyebrows playfully, then disappeared. Linda sat and breathed deeply. She knew that he intended for her to follow him again. And she would, soon enough. But she felt a distinct relief at his absence, and preferred to simply enjoy that for a moment first. She was becoming more than a little annoyed at how long this was taking. William's "I hope you understand one day" and "I want you to love me" were losing their endearing quality. They felt more and more like bait, with Linda the fish on the Fisherman's hook. He'd told her, years ago, that he would reel her in. Now he was doing just that, it seemed. And Linda did not like the feel of the lure in her mouth.

The frozen "Fortunate One" underneath her stared up blankly. For a moment, Linda envied him. He was at rest, at least. She was exhausted. It was not a body thing, this exhaustion. She wasn't *in* a body. It was her mind that was tired beyond words. Her soul. Her spirit. She shook her head in wonderment. The constant pressures of the weight of the world had brought her to the point where she was now wishing for her own eternal rest, though her present experience indicated that there was no such thing. And William was heaping on even more, trying to pawn off on her the decision to oversee the depopulation of the planet. Wouldn't *that* look good on her resume?

It felt nuts. One morning she's abducted from her home and drugged into unconsciousness, and she wakes up trapped in a lobster tank on the planet Mars. It's not the sort of thing one imagines as a kid when the teacher asks what you want to do when you grow up.

Linda closed her eyes and bowed her head. Right now, on another planet, there were three kids... not *her* kids, exactly, but they *felt* like hers... living in a world where even the question of what you want to do when you grow up no longer made much sense. Grow up? Who could think that far out with the climate spiraling so quickly out of control? Yeats had been right. The center had not held. Things were now falling apart. Anarchy, as she and her people all now knew from rough, painful experience, was anything but "mere." And the kids' innocence had long since been drowned. How could it be that the President of the United States, the so-called "leader of the free world," could be so powerless in the face of it all? Yeah. She'd been set up all right.

How long had she been gone? Was Cole holding things together? And was her staff even looking for her? Or had this computer simulation fooled them all? The only way for her to get answers, it seemed, was through William. But could she trust anything he might tell her? Linda sighed heavily. This was the source of her deepest exhaustion, she thought: it was impossible to trust anything anymore. There was no steady ground. All there was was tripping and falling and falling further. All there was was staying on the hook and seeing what boat the Fisherman hauled her into.

And why the hell not? Jesus! *Let* this Fisherman take charge. With the whole world falling apart, with all hope lost, who was she, President or not, to think she knew which way to lead? William was right. She had failed. So perhaps it was time to let go of leading and just follow for a while. There were good forces and bad, Obie had told her. Maybe the good guys were responsible for Linda's present situation. Maybe she was actually being helped here. Maybe there would be answers at the end, and meaningful actions she might take. So what if she didn't like the feel of the hook in her mouth? Maybe it would stop hurting if she would just quit tugging on the damned line.

Something suddenly softened in Linda as a piece of acceptance slipped into place. She was who she was, and she was doing her best. That would have to suffice. With a quiet sigh, she reached out to pat the bench on which she sat, as if she could somehow comfort the frozen figure beneath the surface. These people were a teaching tool. That's why William had brought her here: to use these Fortunate as an example. Discarded shells, he'd called them. Fortunate to be done with their physical bodies. Fortunate to have gone back to their true home. The thought of that brought an illusory tear to Linda's immaterial eye. Jesus. She was sitting in what people called the Astral realm! Was it really true, that her own body was just a shell? Was this *her* true home? How much evidence did she need?

William wanted her to accept the non-material reality of the human spirit, no doubt thinking that to do so would make depopulating the Earth an easier task. But it just didn't feel that simple. Immortal sparks of spirit or not, the kids, Cole's kids, now maybe even *her* kids, were walking in physical bodies on a dying world right now. *That* was real too. And Linda was not convinced that the physical realm should be dismissed out of hand. It may be that William suspected the same thing. Perhaps that's why he did not trust himself.

What Linda trusted, right now, was her heart. There was no "figuring things out." There was no "knowing what to do." But there was her heart, and her heart felt honest and true to her. She could trust it, even when all else failed. Her heart told her that William, despite his membership in a secret layer of society that Linda did not trust, was trying to do good. Her heart told her that there was no way out but to go through, to stay on his line and let him reel her in. Her heart reminded her that there was good in the world, and that she could trust her sense of the good, and go toward it. William's expression before he'd left was not the mocking, teasing grin of an arrogant, controlling monster. It was the playful request of a colleague who was truly asking for her help. It was an invitation, perhaps from the Universe itself, to take the next step on her journey.

Obie had told her that her fate was much larger than to lead her people for a term or two. It was to help lead the whole of humanity to the stars. She ached to be on that path. Perhaps she was. Perhaps, even now when it seemed that all was lost, all was not lost.

Linda smiled tenderly at the dead alien, then stood and rose into the air of the tiny, circular room. It was time to go find William and see what he had in mind next. She had no choice but to trust her heart. But she would remember that her heart, this blood-pumping, truth-knowing, reality-sensing organ, was not just a thing of spirit, but a thing of muscle and blood as well, beating slowly but surely in a body encased in a force field of some sort on the surface of Mars. She closed her eyes, conjured an image of that strange, older man in the Hawaiian shirt, and stepped forward to meet him again.

7.5

"So, kiddos," said Mihos, "unless you want to stay here all day and bat balls of yarn across the floor, we should talk about destination and means of conveyance, you know what I mean?"

Emily stepped closer to the settee upon which Mihos lay. "Our destination we have already told you," she said. "We want to find Linda Travis and speak with her."

"Oh, right," said Mihos, bringing a paw to his face in mock forgetfulness. "The President Monkey. The Great Ones' designated hitter. And you kids' ersatz mother, if I am not mistaken. I'd forgotten." He winked at Emily. "And you know how to find her?" he asked.

"Grace tells us it's a matter of focusing on Linda's... on our *stepmother's*... pattern," said Emily with a defiant flick of her chin, trying to clarify the relationship that Mihos had just tried to disparage. "From what we know, she's been taken to a hospital of some sort on Squirrel Island, where her old cottage was. It's on the Maine-"

"Uh, uh, uh!" said Mihos, sticking his paw out like a stop sign. "We're not *in* Maine, girlfriend. Save the Google map for another time." The cat put his paw down and turned to Grace. "So you're the expert here, are you?"

Grace nodded and knelt beside her dog. "Dennis and I have been here before," she said. "We-"

"So you know all about getting around here, then."

"I-"

"So what'll it be? You guys wanna walk the mock physical? Or should we fly amongst the stars? Take a bus? A train? A spaceship? Or maybe some horses? We could even go underground." Mihos had closed his eyes while he spoke, as if he could barely stay awake, so bored was he.

"Can't we just 'blink' there?" asked Grace.

Mihos opened his eyes and raised a brow. "And lose all of that precious travel time together? Are you kidding me? Why, I have stories to tell, and wisecracks to make. You've not even asked of my long and illustrious past!"

"But we feel like we need to hurry," said Iain, stepping forward to join the conversation.

Mihos looked crossly at the boy, then brought his paws in front of him and patted the claws together like a patient teacher. "Ah..." he said slowly. "You wish to hurry."

Emily cleared her throat. "What Iain means is-"

Mihos raised a paw and Emily stopped. The cat closed his eyes and sighed in exasperation. He took three long breaths, then opened his eyes and looked directly at Iain. "The Murk is still out there, boy. You do understand this, right?"

Iain nodded his head.

"The Murk. It has been instructed to imprison you. Probably to kill you. It will not be particularly delighted with my interference, and it no doubt knows exactly where you are headed." He looked from Iain to Emily to Grace and back again, like a commander sizing them up for a mission. "On my own, I could likely get past the Murk to your President Monkey. The Murk is, as I said, rather stupid. But I will not *be* on my own, will I? I've got to drag you three lost little tourists past his defenses, a lovely little assignment for which I must deeply thank the Great Ones when next we meet. And you guys are so green you still think the physical is the most real." Mihos shook his head from side to side.

"We will do our best," said Grace with earnest.

Mihos looked at her. "I've no doubt of that," said the cat. "And that's what worries me. Believe it or not, I've already grown fond of the three of you in our short time together, even if, as I cat, I shall never show it." He smirked. "In the end, it may be your earnest striving that gets the best of you, as it always is with monkeys." He glanced at Iain. "The Murk will be a more difficult challenge than any of you have ever faced." He turned to Emily. "And it will take not only wits, but speed, and courage, and the willingness to take orders, if you wish to defeat him." He turned to stare down at Dennis for a long moment, before coming back to Grace. "And I fear that not all of you shall make it." Mihos jerked his head to the left and began licking his haunch.

To Emily, it looked like the cat was hiding a tear. But Grace was not watching the cat. Her gaze was on her little dog, who trembled still at her side. For the first time, Emily wished that their dog had not followed them.

"I've got it!" said Mihos cheerily, looking up at the three of them. "We'll go by flying carpet!"

7.6

Paul DuPont sat straight in his chair, eyes closed, feet flat on the floor, hands on his knees with the palms facing upwards. He inhaled slowly and deeply, and exhaled in the same manner. Even on his busiest days, he found time for his practice.

Strike that. He didn't find time. He made it. "Finding the time" was something the Sleepers did. Or tried to do. The Sheeple. The Useless Eaters. People so dumbed down, so disempowered, that they couldn't even take control of how their days went. He remembered a snippet from an old science-fiction movie: "They're already dead." Yes. It soothed him, to think of them that way. It made their imminent demise so much easier to think about.

With a slight wince, Paul brought his focus back to his breathing and managed to hold it there until the chime sounded. With a measured inhale he opened his eyes and reached out to tap his virtual keyboard, bringing his screen back to life. There was the computer-generated Linda Travis, *his* Linda Travis, still attending to the Summit.

Khalid bin Whatever-the-Hell was still droning on, that fat bastard. Paul had known he would, which had meant the VLT would have little to do but sit and listen and blink and move her head occasionally, which had meant that the software could handle her, which had meant that Paul could get in some sit-time. The afternoon was shaping up to be just one speech after another, with each nation moving its first pawn and grabbing what ground they could. No matter the lofty verbiage that had issued forth from press rooms all around the globe in the days and hours preceding this Summit, there was no way this spectacle was ever going to be anything but yet another round of bullshit politicking, chatroom deal-making, prime-time grandstanding, and down-and-dirty tit for tat.

Maybe Reagan had been right. Maybe these bastards might have come together in some useful way to fight off an alien menace. But they weren't fighting the alien menace, were they? Not these yokels. They still regarded those pesky ETs as "out of the picture now," as the real President Travis had once put it, even though the evidence to the contrary shined down on their stupid heads every damned night. No, the enemy here was not the aliens. The enemy here was themselves. All seven billion of them, still burning down and digging up and knocking down and eating up every last thing in sight in an effort to prolong their desperate lives as they circled the drainpipe of history. The enemy here was their acculturated minds, their beliefs, their values, their assumptions, their habits, and their expectations. Pogo had gotten it exactly right, and they all knew it, and still it didn't matter.

The Families had been correct, to choose as they had all those decades ago. Centuries, even, if the records were accurate. Time to pull down the tents and close up the circus. Fire the clowns. Put the suffering animals out of their misery. Send the rubes home. They'd be grateful, if only they could understand.

Not long now. Singer had confirmed it. The first trigger had been pulled and the others would follow in perfect order. One of those triggers would spell the end of the President. No need now for the original when the copy was performing so smoothly. And Paul intended to be right there when the plunger was pushed. It made sense, in a hostage-and-captor sort of way. They'd warned him about it ahead of time, this potential sympathetic bond between an abductor and his hostage. It even had a name: Lima Syndrome. In diving so deeply into the mind and heart of Linda Travis, DuPont had grown, in his own way, to respect her. Maybe even love her a bit, as a predator sometimes comes to love its prey. He owed it to her, to be at her side as they put her down. And what a story that might one day make, on whatever distant soil he found himself.

The sound of silence intruded on his reverie and Paul glanced up at his screens. The fat guy from Bahrain had finished and the various attendees, each hooked in via their latest devices (all good enough, but no match for The Families' HereNow technology), shuffled their papers and cleared their throats and examined their watches. It was an interesting thing to observe, this virtual Summit. There was no applause when the speakers finished. Maybe it just felt too creepy - disbursed as they were around the globe, each in their own little office or conference room, each with an aide or two nearby - to slap the flesh of their hands together and make a noise that signaled appreciation or agreement. That was an activity for ancient monkey bodies, it seemed, something for families and groups and tribes to do *together*, and just did not feel right when people were so alone and apart. Perhaps they should add an applause track.

Paul smiled, thinking there would be a useful metaphor in there, if he could find it. But the thought got sidetracked by the Ambassador from the great nation of Nunavut. "I'd like to hear a response from President Travis regarding the accusations just made by Bahrain," said the short, hawk-nosed Inuit woman in Iqaluit, looking directly into her webcam.

Paul DuPont rolled his shoulders and put fingers to keyboard, crafting the words which would, in mere seconds, issue from the virtual mouth of the virtual President of the United States as she sat in her virtual chair behind her virtual Great Seal and her virtual microphone in a virtual biocontainment facility in Maine.

It was show time.

7.7

Ness pushed the rubbery carrot sticks to the side of her plate, disgusted with the quality of the lunch they had brought for her. Supplies were tight, yes. She understood that. But there'd been no reason to boil her broccoli to mush, had there? And did they truly not know that they could refreshen limp lettuce by soaking and then refrigerating it in a moist cloth bag? She shook her head with a scoffing sigh, wishing she could pop back to the Presidential Home and grab her own food, knowing that she could not. Whatever came, she knew she had to stay right where she was, and damn the inconvenience.

The kids lay peacefully on their gurneys. The nurses had tried, an hour or so ago, to change out their IVs, but Ness had not allowed it. Not yet. Not until they could assure her that the solutions they were using didn't have any genetically modified corn products in them. Not after what Mary just saw in Keeley's field. "You go find me some organic stuff and then we'll talk," she'd told the head nurse, a younger woman with strangely pointed ears. The head nurse glanced briefly at Ness, barely catching her eye, then turned and left. A tiny smile flickered across Ness's face. She was speaking for the President herself now. Mary had made sure of that, and everybody knew it. *Might as well just do as I say*, she thought.

Ness scooted her chair back and stood, stepping over to the window. Outside, the hot spring sun beat down on the cracked and faded parking lot, empty but for a couple of military Jeeps. Beyond the lot and past the fencing lay the Kennebec River, partially hidden by a thin line of leafless trees and looking sick and stagnant in the afternoon haze. In the distance stood the State House and beyond that, she knew, up near the Interstate, was the Presidential Home. Ness replayed the short journey she'd taken with the kids from there to here, just the morning before. The Jeep. The agents and soldiers. The short ride in the warm morning air. The kids had been so anxious to get going. But truth be told, so had she.

The clock ticked on the wall and Ness scratched at her scalp, mussing her short gray hair. She sat heavily in the armchair by the window and took a deep breath. Truth be told for real, that whole morning was a blur in her mind, and not all of it made sense. She remembered a dream about a strange cat with huge green eyes. She remembered quickly drinking a whole pot of tea. She remembered hurrying to see Mary when she knew damned well that Mary had not been released yet, and likely wouldn't be for hours. And she remembered... she remembered... and she could feel it now, still, in her heart... that there was a part of her that wanted... actually *wanted*... these poor dear children to do what they did. At some level, unacknowledged at the time by her conscious mind, she had... oh dear... let them.

Shaking her head as if dispelling cobwebs, Ness reached out and took Grace's hand. The girl's flesh was warm to the touch, pulsing with life, but Grace herself was nowhere to be found inside of it. So different from the hand that had held hers as they'd walked from the Jeep to the hospital doors. Ness squeezed lightly and let go, then rose and smoothed her dress and hair. That little pointy-eared nurse, or some nurse, or a whole gaggle of doctors, residents, nurses, and soldiers, would soon enough be barging back into the room, messing and fussing and ordering and testing, trying to get to the bottom of things, trying to control something that, Ness intuitively knew, was beyond them all.

None of the medical people knew what needed to be done, really. But Ness knew. And it was time to get started. She would need some supplies, and would not be able to get them herself, like last time. But that wouldn't be a problem. That nice young private down the hallway - Eddie Burns, his name was - would be more than glad to bring her what she needed. She'd brought cookies to his post more than once, after all. He would remember that. And he always smiled and called her "ma'am."

For now, she'd work with what she had. There was tubing in that cabinet drawer. A stethoscope. And she'd seen wire hangers in the closet. Ness couldn't be sure, because this was something beyond thinking and understanding, but it felt like even those rubbery carrot sticks on her plate might come in handy. The way they lay there in a pile, the way they formed a crooked triangle, filled her with a sense of déjà vu. *Like last time*, she thought again, having no idea what the heck she meant by that. There had been no last time. Not that she knew about. Unless maybe it had something to do with her life back in Tacoma, with a man named Dave whose face she could not recall.

Ness grabbed the carrots and bent to place them in her purse, then went to the door to yoo-hoo Eddie Burns.

7.8

"So it's still a no-go, then," said the man with the bushy silver eyebrows, looking from screen to screen. "Does that sum it up?"

The others assembled in this virtual conference space nodded or grumbled their reluctant agreement. "The qputers would not lie to us," said the bald man with the red glasses. "Until Modeling ups our estimates of success, we'd be fools to fully implement."

The first man raised a bushy silver eyebrow. "Haven't we already established that?" he asked, with only a hint of self-mockery. "We were so sure our systems were ready..."

A couple of the Directors laughed nervously.

Jay Sinclair, known to the world as Canadian MP Guy Legrand, did not laugh or nod or raise an eyebrow. He did not want to be noticed, as if to give himself away would ruin everything. Though the others didn't know it, he'd just been granted a reprieve, some extra time in which to convince his beloved Gabrielle to join him and her mother for their next great step. He was giddy with relief.

"We can expect a successful test-firing soon, though, yes?" said the man with the blue bow tie. "The Quietus. Your scientists said..." he glanced nervously from screen to screen. "My wife's family..."

The man with the bushy silver eyebrows raised a hand to calm the other man. "We gather in The City as we agreed, Damon. Starting immediately. Most of our people should be there already, and most have either been vaccinated or are genetically immune. But there's no need to risk exposure, and certainly no need for any of us to watch. The schedule of triggers will proceed as planned."

The man with the blue bow tie nodded grimly, his mouth scrunched tight, as if to keep himself from confessing without his lawyer present.

"Still no word from the Insider?" asked the woman with the very long fingernails.

The bald man with the red glasses shook his head. "He indicated that communication would likely become impossible," he said. "That was back before the Grid went up. We'll continue to trust that he's still in position."

"We put a great deal of faith in somebody we've never met face-to-face," muttered the man with a missing finger.

"We believe our faith to be well-placed," said the bald man with the red glasses.

"And the American problem?" asked the man with the bushy silver eyebrows, his eyes glancing up to a screen near the top.

The wiry, white-haired man dressed in a Hawaiian shirt covered with palm fronds and tropical birds glanced into his camera for a moment before looking away. "She's quite handled," he said, the corners of his mouth rising almost imperceptibly.

7.9

Linda found William standing next to the container that held her naked form. He smiled warmly when she appeared. "You see the similarity?" he asked, nodding toward her body.

"You mean with the...?" responded Linda, gesturing vaguely toward the sky, and the Fortunate she'd just left behind. She started to say more, but the Fisherman raised a hand and, in another instant, the two of them blinked to a point in space above Rumi's Field. Below, staring up at them, was the famous "face" that Linda had seen before. The lighting was such that it appeared almost exactly as it had in the iconic photos most people knew best.

The President glanced at William with an eyebrow raised. "You will, of course, be explaining to me how this face was constructed by ancient aliens."

"Half right, Madam President," he replied. "While this mesa was clearly shaped and utilized by non-terrestrial intelligences in our deep past, the fact that it looks like a human face in certain lighting conditions seems more a matter of chance than anything, since this facility was highly damaged in the Gods' War." William raised a shoulder. "That, at least, is the general consensus. But it's entirely possible that these ruins were designed to appear as they do, and to do just what they did, which was draw further attention to the many other so-called anomalies to be found here. The Life were never particularly clear on the matter, and the original builders have long-since moved on."

Linda blinked in confusion. "Many other anomalies?" she asked.

William's eyes flashed with excitement. "Scads, Madam, though it only makes sense to call them 'anomalies' when you are certain you know what's 'normal.' You'll find them here, on Mars. On the moon. On the surfaces of most of the rocky planets in this solar system, as well as a multitude of asteroids, moons and moonlets. Towers. Tunnels. Bridges. Facilities. Cities. And then there are the many artifacts floating about in space, from abandoned space stations and unexploded ordnance to derelict ships of all kinds and sizes, like our old friends Phobos and Deimos orbiting above." The Fisherman turned slowly before her, his arms spread wide as he indicated the depths of space all around them. "This was quite the happening place at one time," he said, his voice tinged with awe. He looked at Linda and winked. "As you Americans used to say," he added.

As if on cue, Phobos appeared on the distant horizon. Linda stared at it for a moment, then turned back to the Fisherman. "And when did this all occur?" she asked.

William waved a dismissive hand. "Oh, eons ago, my dear," he said. "Millions and tens of millions of years, some of it, though some of it more recent. And not really the point of this at all." The Fisherman moved a bit closer to the President. "I mean to say, Madam, that little of that history directly impacts on our present dilemma, I should think. Ancient aliens. Cosmic wars. Artifacts. All true. And all long past. But the ancients, including our distant forebears, the

Fortunate, left behind a genetically manipulated race of confused, traumatized primates with more cleverness than common sense - us - and we've rather cocked things up here since being left to our own devices." The Fisherman stopped and sighed deeply, running an astral hand through his astral hair. He glanced shyly at Linda, then turned to watch Phobos' slow approach. "As you have already concluded," he added in a low voice.

Linda raised an eyebrow. "You and I both know that we haven't exactly been 'left to our own devices,' William," she said. "Not unless what I went through three years ago was all some grand theatrical con job. And not unless that Grid in the Earth's sky is you guys."

William smiled tightly and bowed. "Point taken," he agreed. "The Solar System was not entirely abandoned by non-terrestrial intelligences eons ago. In fact," he pointed down toward the Martian surface, "we could find living alien beings at work on Mars even today, were we to look for them. I was referring more to the builders of these ancient structures we find scattered about."

"Because the aliens that are still here today *don't* leave us to our own devices, do they William?"

The Fisherman wrinkled his nose. "We shall have to tease the truth of that apart as we go, Madam. But yes... those still present do have some impact on our present situation."

"So why show me all this ancient alien stuff then?" asked Linda.

The Fisherman rubbed his hands together. "A bit of context, Madam. To inform our little chinwag. It was the Fortunate who left the Life here, after all, those whom people call the Grays or the Watchers. Like us humans, the Life are another created race that has been here in the solar system, and on Earth, since time immemorial, though there are good reasons to believe that the gray aliens were not abandoned, but chose to stay. Whether as caretakers or inheritors or masters or slaves no one is quite sure. Probably all of the above, as far as they're concerned. It has been difficult to trust what they say."

Linda stopped and watched as Phobos passed silently and quickly directly overhead, a curiously lined potato, an ancient space vessel. She looked at William with a furrowed brow. "How could it -?"

William lifted his shoulders. "Time is more malleable in this band," he explained. "I sped things up so we'd get that little fly-by. Dramatic, yes?"

Linda watched as Phobos hurried away, glanced down at the "face," then back at William. "Time is still flowing back on Earth, William," she said firmly. "My husband and my... his... children need me. Can we get on with it?"

The Fisherman bowed. "Of course." In an instant, they were both in deep space. The sun was no more than a distant spotlight. What Linda assumed was the gas giant Saturn, her rings glowing brightly, filled the sky overhead. William grabbed Linda's hand and flew her closer in, pulling her around and over and down below a smaller sphere, if such words as "around" and "over" and "below" made any sense here, as unhinged from reference points as they were.

To Linda's eye, the sphere looked at first like the Earth's moon. But as she neared, she could see that it wasn't nearly as pockmarked with craters, and that the blue-gray surface was lined with veins of green. It reminded Linda of a melon of some sort, save for the speckling of lights clustered near the equator on the shadowed side.

"Enceladus," said William as they came to a stop. "One of the inner large moons of Saturn, and the quickest way I know to make my next point."

Linda spun slowly around, taking it all in. "It's beautiful," she said.

William followed her gaze. "I quite agree."

"So we *can* leave the confines of Mars, then."

William winked. "When you are with me, Madam President, we can go anywhere we wish."

Linda scrunched her nose. "And your 'next point'?"

"Ah," said the Fisherman. "Well. It's like this. You are burdened, I fear, with a particular mandate handed to you by the homeless wanderer you called Obie. No doubt you remember, back to those thrilling days of yesteryear, as the two of you sat in that beat up little mobile home on Bathurst Island? Your hair was different then."

Linda *did* remember. Obie, Cole's brother, had rescued her from the tortures of Agent Theodore Rice and the confines of one of the aliens' underground lodges. He'd whisked her away to safety in the far North. There they'd spent a day in deep conversation and welcome healing, a much needed respite from the long days of running, and a chance to grieve what had seemed, at the time, like the death of her new love, Cole. She had nothing but wonderful memories of that day and place, and would not let the Fisherman's attempt to belittle them take the good feelings away. "You presume too much, William," she said, her voice steady and strong.

William closed his eyes and breathed slowly before looking at her again. "You understand that we heard every word?"

"Yes, William. And still you presume too much."

"Perhaps," said the Fisherman with a nod.

Linda nodded back, making a note of the moment. Despite his power and seemingly endless access to information, there were still things this Fisherman did not understand. Like people from all walks of life and all corners of the world, he had his own set of limiting stories and beliefs and assumptions. Perhaps one of them would trip him up at some point, giving Linda an advantage she did not now see.

"In any event, Madam President, you came out of the long conversation with a mandate. Do you remember it?"

"You know I do, William. I've made no secret of it in the years since. As President of the United States of America, it has been my job, my duty, my calling, ever since those "thrilling days" you seem to want to mock, to help lead my people *through* the unraveling of our present social systems and *toward* our place amongst the stars. I used words very close to that in my State of the Union speech a few months after my return. I'm sure you know all of this."

The Fisherman smiled. "Of course. And we've already established your failings with regard to the first goal, have we not? The American People, most of them at the very least, had little interest in, or capacity for, taking the real steps required to create what you might have termed, with a bit of humor, a 'kinder, gentler collapse,' did they? And you know now that there was never any hope that you would be able to somehow thwart the vast forces responsible for the unraveling of the global industrial culture."

"I'll agree for the present," said Linda.

"And so now - and it pains me to do so, Madam President - I find myself in the unenviable position of having to point out your failure with regard to the second goal."

"And how is that, William?" asked Linda.

The Fisherman gestured toward the Saturnian moon. "No doubt you noted those lights on the surface of Enceladus as we circled about?"

Linda nodded. "I did."

"That's the Herschel Colony, Madam President. Named after the man who first discovered Enceladus in the 18th century and built almost sixty years ago. By us."

Linda shook her head in confusion. "But... that would have been in the Sixties, William. We hadn't even reached the moon yet."

William smiled and patted his hands together, a gesture that felt, to Linda, both impatient and scornful. "Please understand, Madam President: When I say *us*, I don't mean *you*." The Fisherman drifted slowly upward, as if rising behind his desk to peer down at a stubborn student. "There's no need for you to 'lead your people to the stars' or some such nonsense, you see. The human race now has colonies in over a dozen locations in this solar system, and is establishing new colonies in nearby star systems as we speak." He stopped, then moved in more closely and continued in a quiet voice. "We've been at it for many decades now, Madam. You're really much too late to the game to be of any help at this point. The human species has already taken its rightful place amongst the stars."

7.10

Mary rode the elevator to the second floor. She'd found Ness and explained what she'd seen in Keeley's field, headed down to the ground floor, and stepped outside to make a call on her cell. It took her a few tries, but eventually she'd reached Keeley's doctor. She conveyed what she'd learned about the alien flu's possible trigger, but the notion seemed beyond him. Frustrated, she ended the call, vowing to speak with her own doctors as soon as she could. She headed back inside. It was time to get back to her sweetie and see what else she might learn.

The elevator doors slid open and she stepped out into the brightly lit hallway. With no more than a brief nod to the nurse sitting at the corner station, she turned to the right. Consumed by Keeley's situation, she scarcely registered that the nurse was someone she hadn't seen before. Mary's heart was skittering with fear. Her right hand shook uncontrollably.

Mindful of her movements, wary of a dizzy spell hitting her in this time of stress, she reached out to run her left hand lightly along the railing as she walked, her head down to watch her step. She inhaled deeply, then pushed a smile onto her face. Keeley was right: Mary was so accustomed to just spilling her feelings out, to letting Keeley be the strong one, that she hadn't stopped to wonder how what she said might affect her partner. She was determined to put Keeley's feelings first this time. Keeley needed that from her.

Looking up, Mary was puzzled to find Keeley's door already open. She came to the entryway and started in, expecting to find a doctor or nurse speaking with her partner. She found only an empty room and an empty bed. The covers were still disheveled. The machines were all still on. Mary stepped inside and scanned the room, confused, incredulous. She checked the drawer of the tiny bedside table, expecting Keeley's things, finding nothing but a pharmaceutical pamphlet. She looked in the closet and bathroom. Keeley's things were gone from there as well. Her heart pounding fiercely, Mary turned and headed out the door.

Forgetting her shaking hand and ignoring any fear of dizziness, Mary marched down the hallway to the nurses' station. "Where's Keeley Benedict?" she called out ahead of her as she approached the counter. She came to a stop and put her hands on the edge of the station and dropped her head to take a couple of breaths. She looked up at the nurse sitting there staring back up at her. "Where's Keeley?" she asked again. Her voice was shaking and there were tears at the edges of her eyes.

The nurse smiled sweetly. He was a handsome young man, unusually thin with bright green eyes and beautiful blonde hair. "Greetings, Ms. Hayes," he said.

Mary frowned. She'd never seen this man. How did he know her name? "I need to know where Keeley is," she said again. "Keeley Benedict. She was in A213. She's the President's Chief of Staff." As she spoke, the two other nurses working at the station turned to watch her. A tiny, black-haired woman with unusually wide eyes gave her a smile. A dark young man with a bald head put a hand to the Bluetooth headset on his ear and mumbled something Mary could not hear, then went back to his computer. Mary's heart began to pound more quickly. She'd never seen *any* of these nurses before. All she could think to do was ask her question again. "Where's Keeley?" The question triggered the release of a tear, which started to crawl down her cheek.

The green-eyed man brought his hands together in front of his chest. "She's been transferred to the facility at Squirrel Island, Ms. Hayes," he said. He cocked his head slightly and watched her intently, his gaze following Mary's tear as it slid down her face. Another nurse, this one an extremely tall young woman with a strikingly beautiful, vaguely feline face, stepped into the nurses' station from the hallway behind them.

Mary took a step back and reached out to grab the counter before she could fall. "She... " Mary said. "They took her? But she was just... " She shook her head as if dislodging mosquitos, then looked around from nurse to nurse. "I can't... I mean... she was just..." She closed her eyes and blew out a hot cloud of frustration, then glanced at the green-eyed nurse. "Is Doctor Gholson in yet?" she asked. She needed to speak with someone she knew. Somebody who would know what was going on. Somebody she could trust. She'd just spoken to the doctor on the phone. "He said he was on his way."

The green-eyed nurse's face went blank for a moment before he responded, as if he was downloading information. "No, Ms. Hayes," he said at last. "Dr. Gholson will not be in today." Two more nurses approached from the left and stood at Mary's side. They were both short and thin. They appeared to be identical twins, save that the one on the right had eyes the color of Dijon mustard.

The tiny, wide-eyed woman stood and approached the counter. "They will take good care of your partner while you are away," she said. Her eyes were huge and dark and intense, like black holes that could swallow a person whole.

Mary stepped away again, backing slowly across the hallway until her shoulders met the block wall behind her. She looked at the nurses, one after the other. Their fields were naught but faint blue hazes. Her hands trembled. Her knees felt weak and wobbly. Her heart beat against the cage of her ribs like a sledgehammer. Inhaling deeply in an attempt to calm herself, Mary turned and headed for the elevator without another word.

Mary paced the first floor hallway near the hospital's back door. She stared at her phone, unsure what to do next. She'd wanted to go back inside, assert her authority, tell them who she was and who she worked for, and make them listen to her. But she knew now that that wouldn't work. Not anymore. There was no one here to back her up. The President was in confinement. Keeley had been whisked away. Cole had gone missing. As had Stan Walsh, curiously enough. As had the General, some days ago.

She'd tried calling Mike Portnoy, Keeley's Deputy, but apparently he'd just left the state on some emergency. Neither had she been able to get in touch with the VP, Albert Singer. Nor had she been allowed to speak with Colonel Westwood, the Commander in Charge of all military operations within the Capitol City Green Zone. Even Gilder and Sanchez, her usual Secret Service escorts, had been replaced that morning by a strange little man named Boots whom Mary had never seen before. And there was not a soldier in the entire hospital that would respond to her requests and demands. Mary could claim all the authority she wished, but if the guys with the guns paid her no mind, and there was nobody around to back her up, then her claims were just so much talk, the distracted ramblings of the President's glorified, whack-job nanny, distraught and panicked that her carpet-munching lover had the alien flu. Dismissed.

But that wasn't the worst of it. As Mary had stepped back from the nurses' station, realization had bloomed in her mind. These young people had a force about them. A power. A pulsating psychic wall that would thwart, Mary knew, any attempt she might make to see and read their fields. Mary had encountered such walls before. She knew who these nurses were. And she knew that these nurses could read *her* field. Mary turned and walked out the hospital door as quickly as she could. There was too much happening that she did not understand. She needed time to think.

Outdoors, in the late afternoon heat, Mary bent forward and steadied herself, propping her hands on her knees, drawing deep breaths to calm her pounding heart and shaking shoulders. The situation on the ground had changed right under her feet. Those were hybrids back there. Tubies. Neomorphs. She was sure of it, even though these looked more perfectly human than any she'd ever before seen.

She'd thought that the Tubies, save for Alice, who had stayed behind for a time, had all gone missing with their creators three years ago. Yet here they were, taking over the hospital for reasons she could not comprehend, and obviously aligned with strong forces whose goals and intentions Mary could not yet divine. They'd taken Keeley away. Hidden her out of reach behind a wall that Mary could not breach. They'd taken the hospital, where her friend, Ness, and the President's three precious children, were all being guarded. They'd replaced part or all of the MaineCentral medical staff, and at least a part of the local military command, and who knew what else?

Mary pushed herself back to a standing position, wiped the sweat from her forehead, and scanned the sky. There was only one thing left to do. She hated the thought of it, but saw no other way. Never again would she leave a child behind. And never would she cease her efforts to be reunited with Keeley. Mary inhaled deeply and started across the parking lot. She realized that she had made a decision, one she'd been trying to avoid since first discovering Linda's kids in the MRI. Since the forces lining up against her could not be opposed here, on the ground, Mary would have to fight them in another realm.

She would, indeed, and as the tiny, wide-eyed woman had said, be going away. Mary wondered just how it was that this Tubie nurse could have known that.

7.11

Cole had never ridden on a Harley, as far as he could remember. He had no idea what model this was, or how old it might be. But it was clean and seemed to be well-maintained, and had saddlebags in which they could pack their meager belongings, including the food that Vince had given them. It wasn't much, that extra food, but it didn't need to be. A couple of last fall's apples. Some jerky. Water. A small bottle of what Vince called "fortifier," which Cole assumed was some nasty tasting form of alcohol. They were only an hour's drive or so from Boothbay. A straight shot south on 27. They'd be there before nightfall. And there would be more help, and more food, when they arrived. As long as Cole didn't have one of his damned "hops" while riding on the back of a motorcycle going sixty miles an hour, they'd be okay.

"I've put the word out, Stranger," said Vince to Cole, handing him the key to the Harley. Sam and Pauly stood slightly behind him on either side, looking down toward the ground. Dizzy had disappeared into the house. "The electrical grid's a bit flighty here these days, but many of the Church folk have generators and ham radios, and the cell system is still pretty robust. Helps to be so near the coast, where a few of the rich folk still hang out." He glanced at Stan, then back to Cole. "Things're better here than most places, I expect."

Cole passed the key on to Stan and reached out to shake Vince's hot, sweaty hand. "Thanks, Vince," he said, smiling gently. "We'll get this bike back to you just as soon as we can. Your President will appreciate how you've helped us."

Vince held Cole's eye. "Wish it had a full tank, Sir," he said. "We didn't know you were coming. Here... I mean." He looked down at the ground, as if was disrespectful to stare at their savior.

"So your Church is active in these parts, I take it," said Stan, inserting the key into the ignition and pulling his sunglasses out of his shirt pocket. He gestured toward the leather bag hanging on the side of the Harley where his pistol was stored. "Can your people help us out with... you know... thieves and such? Or am I going to need that gun?"

"Highwaymen, Mr. Walsh? Brigands? There are some, but we Church folk try to maintain some sense of law and order in this county. The Burners are getting more active around here, but they don't bother the rest of us."

"Burners?" asked Cole.

"Pastor Clinton's Church," explained Vince. "Bunch of morons, if you ask me, burning things down like that. No doubt you've heard the good Pastor on the TV."

Cole nodded. "Just a bit," he said.

"So there's not much danger on the road?" asked Stan, cutting in.

Vince shrugged. "Nowhere near as much as you might expect," he said. "In any case, yeah, we'll be helping with that too. There's a couple of young men down Wiscasset way already out patrolling the road between here and there. We're lining up a couple more. We'll clear the road for you, don't you worry."

Stan bowed his head in appreciation. "My thanks to you all," he said. He wiped the heat and humidity from his face and neck with a handkerchief he kept in his pocket.

"And there's somebody to meet us in Boothbay Harbor, you say?" asked Cole.

"Ken Swathers," said Vince. "Pauly just raised him on the radio. He'll meet you at the Thieving Seagull Cafe on McFarland point, like I showed you on the map. Got a place down on Pig Cove. Put you about as close as you can get to Squirrel Island without being in a boat. Nice guy, too. You'll like him."

Cole glanced up at the late afternoon sun, then at the Harley, before returning his attention to Vince. "You folks need to get going, I know," said Vince.

Cole sighed heavily. "I sure wish I knew as much about what's going on as you seem to, Vince," he said. "I mean... I appreciate the help and all. I'd just prefer to know what it is you're helping me to *do*."

Vince chuckled softly. "Maybe that would just get in your way, Stranger. Knowing, I mean. Seems like sometimes we get where we're headed more quickly when we follow our guts rather than our heads, if you know what I mean."

"You said I'm not from around here," said Cole, finally asking the question foremost in his mind. "Do you mean...?"

Vince glanced up at the sky, then back to Cole, raising his eyebrows in amusement. "Is it really so hard to believe, Sir?" he asked. "After all you've seen?"

Cole frowned, thinking back over all the strange things he *had* seen. "It's just that..." Cole shrugged, looking Vince straight on. "I'm just me, you know? I'm not some..."

Vince laughed again. *"'He'll find his way in the end, as he always has,'"* he quoted. "That's what the book says, Stranger. It's just as it has to be. You *are* the Wayfaring Stranger, after all." Vince looked back down at the ground underfoot, clearly embarrassed to have spoken so boldly. The back door slammed and they all looked up to see Dizzy running around the corner to the front yard, their dog, Bullet, now as friendly as could be, loping happily behind her.

"Stranger!" called Dizzy as she ran. In her hand she carried a piece of paper, rolled up like a scroll. She came to a stop in front of Cole and held out the paper, glancing for only a moment at the man before her. "This is for you, Sir," she said, catching her breath.

Cole took the scrolled sheet, tied with a length of red ribbon. "What is it?"

"It's from a coloring book I got last summer at Church School," she said. "It's your picture."

Curious, Cole slipped the ribbon off the end of the scroll and unfurled it. It was a page from a comic book, sure enough, one obviously photocopied many times, and bound at home by hand. At the top was the legend, "The Wayfaring Stranger Loves Animals." And underneath, a crude line drawing suitable for coloring, depicting a man who, when you already knew the connection, looked just like Cole, and who was kneeling next to, and scratching the neck of, a dog that looked just like Bullet.

7.12

"It's a beautiful day here in Augusta, Maine, boys and girls," intoned Mihos in his best radio voice as he steered the flying carpet high over the city. "Drive time temperatures in the upper-nineties and falling slowly, promising an evening low of eighty-five. Better get those sweaters out! And just look at that sunset. If you dip down into the physical, you'll get a good glimpse of that wonderful purple glow that hangs above the western horizon, courtesy of the uranium oxide left in the atmosphere from the nuking of Beijing. Whoever said apocalypse couldn't be beautiful, am I right?" Mihos stood near the leading edge of the carpet, his face to the wind, his anus waving back and forth in front of Dennis's muzzle as the dog sat in Grace's lap. He turned, smiled, and flashed his eyebrows. "You guys seen enough?" he asked.

"I have," said Emily. It was she who had requested that they go back to the beginning, a strategy she remembered from one of her favorite old movies. She held tightly to the edge of the carpet, a rectangle maybe four feet by six, just large enough to hold them all, shoulder to shoulder in sitting position, but far too closely packed for Emily's taste. The design was not classic Persian, as she had anticipated, but looked instead like a screen shot of a Pac Man game. Both the size and the design were jokes on Mihos' part, no doubt. But Emily was not yet sure what to think of the Son of Bast.

Emily glanced up at the Grid, the network of purples lines and bright stars that caged them in from horizon to horizon. "Can you get us through the Grid?" she asked.

Mihos spoke without turning around. "Not me, Nancy Drew," he said. He sat and flicked his tail back and forth. "I can get through, but there's no way I'll risk trying to break the Seal with you three. They tuned it for monkeys, you know." He turned and winked at Emily. "On purpose. You know what I mean?"

"I think-" started Emily.

"Besides," continued Mihos, turning back to face forward. "There's no need. The President Monkey ain't out there, am I right? She's down here."

"I think Emily was wondering if we could get around-" said Iain.

"- the Murk," finished Mihos. "Yes. I got that." He turned to survey all three of the kids. "I think you'll find that the Murk is, by nature, a sphere, extending out from this Squirrel Island place on all sides. Even were we to somehow slip up through the Watchers' Seal and then back down through it to our destination, we'd still have to deal with His Murkiness. The only way in is through."

"How big a sphere?" asked Emily.

"Now don't get all geometric on me, Emmy," said Mihos. "He's probably more of a blob. Most Murks are. Like a... a... oh, what's that creature you guys always refer to when talking about blobs?"

"An amoeba?" said Grace.

Mihos pointed at Grace with his paw. "Right. An amoeba. Only big. And dark. And ornery. And designed to resist the very thing we are going to attempt to do."

"Which is...?" asked Iain.

Mihos rolled his eyes. "Uh... go through it? Hello? Did you miss the first episode?" The cat closed his eyes and started licking his front paws, back and forth.

Iain frowned, annoyed. "Any reason you keep licking your paws, Mihos?" he asked, his voice confrontational.

Mihos opened one eye to scrutinize the boy. "Yes. It calms me. Sorta in the same way stuffing my face with mutant corn and fake sugar and deadly pesticides might calm me were I a monkey, only not quite so self-defeating." He closed his eye.

Iain pulled his feet around as if he meant to stand up and push the cat off the rug, but Grace reached out and put a hand on his arm to stop him. She spoke to the cat. "So what's our plan, then, Mihos?" she asked. "How do we get to Linda?"

Mihos stared for a long moment at Iain, then slowly turned his attention to Grace. "I've drawn us a map," he said at last. "We've got our carpet. We've got the sun at our backs and the wind in our hair. We've got life, sister. Seems to me it's time to make like Michael Jackson and beat it."

"We've got a map?" asked Emily.

Mihos sighed. "You're sitting on it," he said, shaking his head.

Emily studied the pattern on the carpet. A Pac Man screen shot, yes, but also what maybe looked like a route through a maze. And there, woven into the fibers under where Iain's tennis shoe had been, a small icon that looked, a bit, like a magic carpet with people sitting on it, with one of the "ghosts" in hot pursuit.

Mihos shrugged. "My first rug," he explained. "Got the scale all wrong. And there wasn't room to draw all of us. But it'll work." He looked at Grace. "I think we'll get there," he said, almost as if he was trying to comfort the girl.

Dennis, sitting still in Grace's lap, reached up and licked Mihos' nose. Mihos, shivering in disgust, turned back to the front and began to wash his face with his paws.

7.13

"So we're dead then?" asked Ted.

"I think so," said Carl.

"Heaven is a Scrabble game?"

"Whatever this is seems to be a Scrabble game," answered Carl. "For us." He stared at his tiles, then glanced up at his opponent. "Maybe this is more like Purgatory."

Ted leaned back in his chair, folded his arms over his chest, and scrunched his eyes tight. After a long exhale he opened his eyes. "So this is about purging," he said.

Carl shrugged.

"The life review. The lessons learned. Sin and redemption. All that bullshit."

Carl turned his attention back to his tiles. "You okay with it, if that's the case?"

Ted wrinkled his nose, shook his head. "I don't know. I guess. Are you?" He looked at Carl. "I mean... maybe you killed me."

"Maybe you had it coming," said Carl.

Ted picked at his teeth with his tongue. "Maybe. Or maybe you're a real bastard. Maybe that's why I feel so angry with you sometimes. Maybe I'm supposed to kill you now."

"Maybe it's somebody else you're angry with," ventured Carl

"You trying to get me to talk about Mummy and Daddy, Doctor?" asked Ted in a snotty tone.

"You brought 'em up, Bro," said Carl. "Not me." Carl picked up some tiles and laid them out on the board, then looked up at Ted. "Twenty-two points," he said.

Ted looked down at the word. "Singer," he said. "Too bad you missed the double word." He pointed toward a pink square on the other side of the board. "Would've fit there just as easily," he said with a smirk.

Carl nodded. "I guess you're right," he said. "Your turn."

Ted looked down at his tiles.

Chapter Ø Eight

8.1

A light sprinkle fell on the park, dampening the trees and bringing a note of coolness to the warm evening. Eventually a few drops slipped from the leaves and fell to the ground. One of them spattered onto Gabrielle's forehead. Another hit her chin. And another her eyelid. This third drop caused her eyes to fly open. With a gasp, Gabrielle awakened.

She sat up. Night had come. Judging from the line of tiny solar patio lights she could see through the foliage, Gabrielle was in a small gully ten yards or so off the path she'd been following. She was alone.

"Not alone," said Zacharael in her head.

Not alone. Yes. Not at all alone. Not for a very long time. Years. Seconds. Ages. Minutes. Decades. Eons. Judging by the darkness, the storefront lights in the distance through the trees, and the traffic she could hear on the road, it appeared that a few hours had passed without her conscious awareness. But she had not blacked out. In those hours, Gabrielle had lived the life of the entire planet.

She would have expected to be traumatized. Distraught. Doubled over in sobbing sorrow. She was not. Grief she had felt in full. She remembered that. And rage. And blame. And shame. Joy she had felt as well. Awe. Gratitude. Peace. Communion. Zacharael had not spared her feelings. As he had told her, he was trying to break her heart. But curiously, now, with her heart broken wide open, she was not filled with grief at all. She was filled, instead, with relief. Purpose. Even power. She had lived through the decimation of the life of the Earth and she was still standing. Still here. Still able to draw a breath. Still able... to choose.

How deftly he had drawn her along, this being from who-knows-where. Contrasting the countless millennia of burgeoning, exploding, branching lifeforms as they peopled the planet with the tight, cramped, spiteful activities of her own species as it had tried, and failed, to rule the Earth, he mixed beauty and horror like a master filmmaker, adding an epic, heart-wrenching score to bitter scenes of destruction and despair. From the ruins of oil refineries to the putrid bogs of animal waste, from the crumbling tundras and bursting methane pockets to the burning forests and the cramped cages of desperate chimpanzees and factory chickens, Zacharael escorted her on a grand tour of suffering and loss, continuing the work he had begun on their nighttime journeys, but taking it to a whole new level. No longer was Gabrielle an observer. This time, Gabrielle *was* the water, the soil, the tree, and the chimpanzee. This time, the pain was *hers*.

It seemed they visited every corner of her dying world. And always the message was the same. Muttering from the slag heaps, whispering from the irradiated soil, moaning from the smoking mountain-sides, crying out from the stagnant waters, came the voices of those still living. *We're not dead yet*, they said to Gabrielle, over and over, in the languages of life. *We remain. We remain.*

Yes. It was that which was inside of her now. They remain. And Gabrielle remains. And where life remains, hope remains. And now, in some way she did not quite understand, they had all become one. She. The planet. Zacharael. All one. Not yet dead. And yearning. Longing. Wanting. Because that's what life does on the physical plane. Zacharael had taught her the most simple thing: he had taught her to care. Gabrielle was in love with the living world.

She rolled to her side and pulled herself up to one elbow. The light rain had stopped, as if, having done its work, it could move on. She pushed herself to her knees, then got to her feet. She gazed down where she had lain. There, illuminated dimly by the lights of the busy commercial strip just up the hill, was Zacharael's body, looking just as it had when she left it back on the campus sidewalk.

She felt a pulse of sadness move through her. Zacharael had shown her *his* life as well. His being. His people. How they'd been with the Earth for so long. With humanity. Guiding and helping as they could. Their interactions with humans across the span of history were mostly forgotten now, remembered only as the intercessions of angels and the visits of messengers. But Zacharael remembered. He had dedicated his almost immortal life to the severance of attachments and the act of letting go. At a time when his people had all but withdrawn from the Earth, hesitant to interfere any further and unwilling to cross the Interdict, Zacharael continued on with his attempts to correct the mistakes made in the ancient past. He was motivated by his deep love both for the life of the planet as a whole and for the human species in particular. Gabrielle knelt down to touch Zacharael's leg, but as she did so he began to fade away. In a moment, the body had disappeared like a wisp of fog. It was gone.

"Zacharael?" asked Gabrielle, her voice hoarse and meek. There was no response from the presence in her head. He was gone from her mind as well. Glancing up toward the road, Gabrielle picked her way through the shadowed undergrowth to the park's trodden, lamp-lit path. There lay her backpack along the edge. Surprised that no one had taken it, Gabrielle hoisted it to her shoulder and headed up the hill.

8.2

Ness surveyed the pile of supplies she'd hidden in the closet. Private Burns hadn't been able to find a laser pointer yet, but maybe that was okay. She didn't know what the pointer was *for* anyways. And she had the feeling her cell phone would work in a pinch. It was all magic, as far as Ness was concerned. Something coming to her from the Great Beyond. 'Twasn't up to her to think it through. She was like Noah. "Just tell me how many damned cubits, Lord!" she muttered to herself, smiling at the thought. That Bill Cosby had been so funny.

A quiet knock sounded and the door opened. Light from the hallway spilled into the darkened room. "Will you need anything before sleep, Ms. Abernathy?" asked the night nurse, a tall, thin, young man with unusually large, almond-shaped eyes as black as space. His scrubs sported a name patch that read, simply, "Jack." Something about him reminded her of Keeley.

Ness closed the closet door with nary a glance back, hoping this Jack had not seen what was inside. It was essential that she keep this quiet, though she was uncertain exactly whom it was she had to keep this quiet *from*. The strange new nurses that had apparently taken over the entire hospital didn't seem harmful to Ness. But she could not be sure.

"I'm good for the night now," answered Ness, hoping to dismiss this "Jack" for the rest of the evening. She needed to be left alone for a long enough time to... No. She shouldn't even think about it. She offered a warm smile. "I'll buzz you if I need anything." She headed over to her cot and pulled back the covers, showing Nurse Jack just how ready for bed she was.

Jack nodded once, glanced at the sleeping children, then stepped back and pulled the door quietly shut. Ness could hear a hushed conversation between the nurse and the guard just outside her door, but could not make out what they said. After a few moments, the conversation ended. She heard footsteps receding - Jack - and the squeaking sounds of someone sitting heavily in a metal folding chair - the guard.

Ness exhaled slowly and fully, then crept back to the closet door. She would have to work in the dark, her project lit only by the tiny lights on the machines and monitors, the light coming in under the door, and the distant lights from the cordon fence that filtered in through the window shade. She knew the children were being monitored back at the nurses' station, not only by the various instruments hooked up to them but by a video feed, the camera for which she could see mounted on the ceiling. She was fairly certain the camera could not see her cot. And she was fairly sure that there was no audio. She was glad of that. If she was quiet enough to not attract the attention of the guard outside her door, and if she could hide in the dark and avoid the camera as much as was possible, she just might pull this off without interruption.

Should interruption come, Ness would just have to hope that her authority as the President's advisor would be enough to prevent interference. It's not like she was hurting the children, after all. But she didn't want to take that chance. Best to just hurry her old carcass along and get this darned thing finished. Then it would be able to protect *itself*. After that, well... they'd see what's next, wouldn't they?

Pulling her purse from the closet, Ness reached in and found the small bunch of carrots she'd stashed there. She collected the rubbery sticks, set down her purse, and turned and walked back to the kids. Emily was in the middle, lying on her back with her hands on her stomach. Ness leaned over and placed the carrots on Emily's chest, just over her heart. She arranged the carrots in a triangle pattern, like a tiny, orange split rail fence. Then she stood and took a step back, glancing quickly at the video camera, hoping, if anybody was watching, that all they could see was a silly old woman giving a child a hug in a darkened room.

The carrots rightly sparkled with energy now. She'd been right to save them. This was magic, after all. And they were Life. And it always took a bit of life to make your magic work. That's just the way the universe was built.

With a quiet moan of satisfaction, Ness headed back to the closet for more of her supplies.

8.3

Cole shook his head and pulled at his eyelids, trying to force them to stay open. He couldn't believe how tired he was. The grandfather clock in the hallway, keeping time by virtue of the fact that it ran on gravity, which civilized peoples had not yet managed to screw up, said that it was just after eight. It felt much later than that. The heavy plate of food, the two shots of "fortifier" - these church folk did not mess around when it came to "strong drink" - and the warm, humid air, had gone right to his head. He was ready to call it a night. But the room full of people around him would have none of that.

Their trip to Boothbay Harbor had gone off without a hitch, as if it had been no more than a simple Sunday-afternoon motorcycle jaunt in a pre-Crash world. Though they encountered the smoking remains of a recent house fire, neither brigands nor highwaymen barred their way, and the only other vehicle they saw in operation was a diesel Volkswagen Jetta sitting at a street corner just before the bridge over Montsweag Bay, in what now passed for downtown Wiscasset. The two men in the Jetta - whom they suspected at the time to be the two that Vince had told them would be patrolling, and whom they knew now were called Simon and Keith - waved as Cole and Stan passed, then pulled out and followed the motorcycle at a respectful distance.

From there it was a short drive south to Boothbay Harbor and The Thieving Seagull, which appeared to be a long-established, and still operating, restaurant and pub at the end of McFarland Point

Drive, right on the water. It was a local landmark, impossible to miss, and from the deck you could just make out Squirrel Island in the distance, which is why it had been chosen. Stan and Cole pulled into a parking space. Keith and Simon pulled into the space beside them. As they were shaking hands, out of the front door strode Ken Swathers. Vince was right: they liked him right away.

The last leg of their journey was made in Ken's old Dodge Caravan. Ken drove. Cole sat in front passenger seat. Stan sat in the middle seat and Simon and Keith piled into the back, leaving their Jetta at the pub. It was another couple of miles to Southport, where Ken lived with his wife, Celia. Vince's Harley would be returned to him, so Cole and Stan were not to worry about that. When Stan made mention of the amount of fuel they'd expended to cart himself and Cole sixty miles or so, Ken just laughed. "This is the Wayfaring Stranger," he said with a snort, pointing at Cole, but looking at Stan. "Him we spend gas on." Simon and Keith laughed in the back seat.

Since arriving in Southport, it had been a long succession of hugs and hellos and *let me show you this-or-that* and *you need to meet so-and-so*. The whole congregation had shown up for the potluck supper, it seemed to Cole, filling his head with more names and faces than he'd ever be able to remember: Gordon, Curt, Sally, Joe, Ann, and a couple of dozen more. It didn't seem to matter whether he could remember their names or not. To them he was the Wayfaring Stranger, some sort of savior, and it was their honor and privilege to help him in any manner they might, and they were just glad to have met him.

Ken and Celia were kind and gracious hosts, though Celia seemed distant and worried. The congregants brought venison and chicken, potatoes and onions and salad greens. There were zucchini fritters with real butter and baked beans with real maple syrup. One woman, Ellen, brought Greek yogurt with dried blueberries. A man named Ryan brought corn bread hot out of his brick oven. One person, an older fellow whose name Cole couldn't recall, brought a whole case of six unopened Mylar bags full of Cape Cod Salt & Vinegar potato chips, a treat he'd been saving because, as he put it, "Where else would the Wayfaring Stranger come but to Boothbay Harbor?" The food was better, and more plentiful, than either Cole or Stan would ever have expected. And the people were happier. Save, it seemed, for Celia.

"We're not really a church, you know," an old woman named Annabelle told Cole after the meal. She'd grabbed him by the elbow and ushered him to the back porch as the others had gone about cleaning up. Five-feet-two at best, with short, iron-grey hair and a Roman nose, there was more than a little of Ness about her. But where Ness was all sweetness and comfort, Annabelle was quiet and firm, with no time for nonsense. She got right to her point. "We organized as a church to give us some cover with the State and Federals," she said. She glanced over her shoulder, back into the kitchen, to make sure they were alone. "And to keep the Pastor Clinton crowd off our backs. You understand?"

Cole shook his head. "I'm not..."

"Churches are about God and Jesus," said Annabelle. "We're not. Or not all of us, at any rate. But after all the craziness, and with the good Pastor on television every night rousing the rabble, it feels much safer to pretend that we are. You heard what happened in Oakland, right?"

Cole shook his head. "No, I don't think-"

"They executed a coven of Wiccans in a public park, Mr. Thomas." She pierced him with her gaze. "The Clinton folk. Just last week. They killed eight people. Then burned down three blocks of the city. 'God-fearing Christians,' this was. We're not that."

"So what are you?" asked Cole. He nodded toward the others in the house. "You just seem like regular people to me," he added. "Like I was, before I met Linda."

Annabelle reached out to take Cole's hand. "We're the ones who've been paying attention, Stranger. The ones who've long known that society as we knew it would soon unravel. The ones who could see that there was much more going on than any of us were being told. The ones who knew to prepare and make ready." She stepped closer to Cole and gazed up into his eyes. "We were the ones who were laughed at and dismissed. UFO buffs, they called us. Conspiracy theorists. Doomers. Contactees. Abductees." She pointed to the stars above. "Most of us have met the Strangers, Sir," she said, her voice hushed. "Many have been taken by them, taken into what appear to be their ships, or their homes, though that doesn't happen these days, as far as we can tell. Not since the Grid appeared." Annabelle took a moment to stare up at the Grid she had just mentioned, then turned back to Cole. "When an artist, musician, and blogger named Derrick Lasko published *The Book of the Stranger*, which he said was given to him in a vision on the very day the Grid went up, those of us who saw his posting knew. It was as if something inside of us was switched on. Something put there by the Strangers. We knew then that we'd been taken into their confidence for some vital purpose. Made ready. Instructed. We remembered being shown a small black cube. And we remembered being told…" Annabelle stopped to wipe a tear from her eye like she might flick off a mosquito. She let go of Cole's hand and turned to take hold of the porch railing, gazing out over the Grid-lit yard.

"You remembered being told…" coaxed Cole in a gentle voice.

Annabelle raised her shoulders slightly and cocked her head. "We were told about your coming," she said evenly. She turned back to Cole and gestured toward the house with her hand. "Most of us. By the Strangers themselves. Not about you, specifically. But about the Wayfaring Stranger, one of *their* kind, come to Earth as one of *us*, to give us aid in a very grim time. Believe me, we were just as surprised as you, to learn that the Wayfaring Stranger was the President's husband. But of course, in retrospect, it all makes perfect sense."

Cole smiled and shook his head. "And that's what I don't get," he said. "I mean. Because of some flashes of lights that came out of my hands? I mean… really? If I were this Wayfaring Stranger guy, wouldn't I know about it? Wouldn't I remember if I was an alien from another planet? Wouldn't I be having nightmares or… or memories or something? And strange…" Cole stopped. His face had grown dark with confusion.

"You have been, haven't you," said Annabelle. "Having nightmares? Memories? Glimpses into past lives? *The Book of the Stranger* says that you've been here before, many times. Learning the ways of human beings. Adding your consciousness to the human spirit. And now there's a power emanating from your hands, Stranger. Vince saw it, and we believe him. And you snatched one bullet from the air, and survived the impact of another."

"And the coloring book…"

Annabelle nodded. "Drawn by Derrick Lasko himself," she said.

Cole looked down at the porch's worn planking and sighed heavily, then rubbed his eyes. He remembered being a kid, building tunnels in the haylofts on the family farm. He remembered growing up, going to school, holding hands with his first girlfriend, getting that horrible sunburn that itched so much they'd had to sedate him. He remembered his Mother singing in the kitchen and his father's love of maps. It was all so... human.

"Let me show you something," said Annabelle, pulling open the back door and disappearing into the noisy house. In a moment she was back with a book in her hand. "This is *The Book of the Stranger*," she said, holding out the thin, trade-sized paperback. "An original copy from the first print run supervised by Derrick himself, just before he was murdered." She handed the book to Cole. "Look at the title page." She reached back inside the door and turned on the porch light.

Cole took the book in hand and turned to get the best light. The cover was lurid, a black and white star-field with a classic "flying saucer" graphic zipping through space. It reminded Cole of fifties UFO movies and comic books. Flipping to the title page, he found another line drawing, this one more finely rendered than the coloring book image, but undoubtedly by the same artist. It showed the Wayfaring Stranger apparently walking on water, a shoreline in the distance, with squiggles of what looked like light or energy emanating from his entire body.

"The resemblance is uncanny, wouldn't you say?" said Annabelle, peering over his shoulder.

Cole nodded. It was.

"Lasko was murdered?" asked Cole as he stared at the image.

Annabelle sighed heavily. "Last October. He was living in Brooklyn and they were moving people into the Shelters before winter hit. Tried to stop some kids from stealing his blankets. They attacked him. Nearly took his head off.

"Jesus!" muttered Cole.

Annabelle pointed at the image of Cole. "It's a wonder none of us made the connection," she said, looking from the drawing to Cole and back again. "I mean... it's not like your face wasn't known to us."

Cole leafed quickly through the rest of the book. Seeing no more illustrations, he closed it and handed it back to Annabelle. "So Lasko was in Brooklyn. Is the Church of the Stranger centered there? Is it all over the country?"

Annabelle clutched the book to her breast. "There are church members all over the world now, Stranger," she said. "But in the past couple of years, a large percentage have moved to New England, with the largest concentration right here in Maine. Partly because many other areas of the country were more quickly unraveling, from the drought and fires and violence. Partly because Derrick said in *The Book* that the Wayfaring Stranger would most likely appear somewhere in the Northeast United States. And partly because you and President Travis came to Augusta." She reached back in and turned off the porch light so they could better see the Grid.

One of the dishwashers, Philip, came to the door and started to say something, but Annabelle shook her head and closed the door on him. She stepped closer to Cole, took his elbow, and walked him down the steps to the back yard so that they could see more of the sky. "When Linda Travis broke the silence," she said, looking upward, "we paid attention. We were experiencers and researchers and writers, doctors and PhDs and scientists and contractors and housewives, seekers and thinkers and knowers. We knew that her revelations were the most important news in the world. We knew that everything would change. And we knew our time was coming." She glanced at Cole, then stared again at the stars, beckoning from beyond the Grid. "*The Book of the Stranger* served to bring us together," she said. She reached out and grabbed Cole's hand again. "And here we are." She turned to face him. "And now here *you* are. And we're so happy to have you."

Cole frowned, remembering Ken's wife at the dinner table. "So what's up with Celia?" he asked. "She does not seem happy."

"Ah..." said Annabelle. "It's Celia's sister, Beth. She woke up this morning with a rash across her face."

"Oh, my," murmured Cole.

Annabelle nodded. "Yes," she said. "Greensleeves got here before you did."

Cole sighed, closing his eyes, trying to assemble the pieces that did not seem to fit. He glanced down at his hands, remembering the flames that he'd seen spouting from them, then turned to the house at the sounds of laughter. Somebody was tuning a violin. He pointed at the book in Annabelle's arms. "Does that book say what I'm supposed to do?" he asked.

Annabelle looked away, only for a moment, but long enough for Cole to notice. She did not want to answer this. The porch light came on and Ken stepped out, his face a question. Annabelle held up a single finger and Ken nodded and went back inside. She looked up at Cole. "They want us back inside now," she said. "It's time for some music. And then they'd like you to say a few words."

Cole opened his mouth to protest but Annabelle held up a hand to stop him. "But we can't do any of that until I tell you what I brought you out here to tell you."

Cole froze at the grim tone of her words. "And what is that?" he said at last.

"*The Book*," she said. "It says only one thing about what you are here to do." Annabelle cleared her throat. "*He comes to stop his greatest love from destroying the human race*," she recited. She held Cole's gaze. "We think that refers to Linda Travis, Stranger."

8.4

"Just watch," said the Fisherman. Linda looked where he pointed as they hovered in space a few hundred feet above the Herschel Colony. Below was a complex of buildings - domes and spheres and one enormous cube - all connected with covered tramways and glass-domed tunnels. The complex was roughly triangular, each corner marked with a huge tetrahedron constructed, it seemed, from stainless steel. William was pointing at a wide, flat expanse of what appeared to be stone or concrete. Up through it, as if passing through smoke or fog, rose a small, silvery disc perhaps twenty-five feet across.

The disc cleared the concrete pad by fifty feet, tilted approximately thirty degrees, glowed brightly, and jumped away into space. Not toward the Earth or Sun, but away from them both. Off into the depths beyond. In a moment it was lost from view.

"Probably a supply run," said William, turning to Linda. "The extra-Solar colonies are not yet self-sufficient in many things."

Linda shook her head in frustration. "This is all too much, William," she said. "I know you're having fun showing off your secrets, and I have so many questions, but I need to get home. Please. Tell me what I need to know. And tell me how this all relates to your thinking that you can talk me into pulling the plug on the human race. Give me the Reader's Digest Condensed version, okay? I'm tired of this."

The Fisherman raised an eyebrow, as if Linda had just committed a major breach of protocol or politeness. Linda didn't care. As charming as William could be with his accent and his stories, she'd reached her limit. Enough was enough. She had a family to get back to. She had a country to run.

"Ah," said the Fisherman at last, struggling for a response. "I see." He cleared his throat. "My apologies. I see your point." The Fisherman turned to stare down at the Herschel Colony once again. Then, his back to Linda, he spoke again. "Excuse me," he said. The Fisherman vanished and was gone.

So was the Herschel Colony. Linda was no longer hanging in deep space over Saturn's moon. She was standing in a rectangular room seemingly cut out of the bedrock. It was unfurnished, save for a series of metal boxes or cubicles that lined one wall. Linda's heart began to pound. She whirled around, scanning the space. She knew those cubicles. There had been one just like it in the cell in which Agent Rice had confined her, in the alien Lodge under Ottawa. It had held a dormant Gray. One of the Life.

Linda put a hand to her hammering heart and inhaled deeply. She did not know where she was, but she could feel the oppressive weight of this room, the solid, smoothly cut rock on all sides, the mass of stone overhead.

Once again, she'd been imprisoned underground.

8.5

The situation was getting weird and The Families were expecting Aidan McAfee to take care of it. That, at least, was the message delivered earlier in the evening by that slimy mouth-breather, Albert Singer. McAfee closed his paperback and pushed back his covers, exposing naked skin to the wet, warm night air. He exhaled sharply through his nose, a soft, scoffing surge of exhausted incredulity and bemused exasperation.

Apparently the Augusta folks were having a wee bit of a problem keeping track of people. First, the President's kids disappear. Then the First Hubby goes AWOL, with Secretary Stan at his side, no less. Good ol' Keeley gets herself a raging case of the alien flu, taking her out of the game, and reportedly to Squirrel Island, though if she was on the island then nobody had told *him*. And then Mary vanishes. McAfee had heard of rats fleeing a sinking ship, but this was too much.

But was it really a problem, let alone *his* problem? The Colonel was not convinced. The lost kids were a bit of a scare, sure. He understood that. But the authorities were now in possession of the bodies, were they not? Cole Thomas and Stan Walsh were both tagged, so they were easy enough to track. Granted, it was a bit disconcerting to learn how easily they'd slipped through the Cordon, but Stan was the Secretary for Homeland Security, for Chrissake. If anybody could get through, he could. And while Mary had removed her own alien implants years ago - a ballsy act for which her old pal Colonel Phelps had awarded her bonus points in the you-go-girl category - surely, given her position in the U.S. government, she carried iDents in her bloodstream? So what was the problem? Enquiring Colonels wanted to know.

The problem, it seemed, was not so much that they'd gone missing, but where they had gone missing *to*. Stan and Cole were now right across the water, no doubt intending to storm the castle gates in an attempt to rescue their damsel in distress. Though the kids' bodies were accounted for, their consciousnesses were off traveling. And if the note they'd left could be believed, they were on their merry little astral way to Squirrel Island with the help of the Life themselves! And Mary wasn't showing up on anybody's scans, military or Family. For all McAfee knew, Mary was headed this way as well, in some misguided, superheroine mission to get to the bottom of this flu thing, save her lover, find the kids she lost, and free her President.

If she was, that would mean that the President's entire inner circle, or most of it, was converging on his doorstep. Cole. Cole's kids. Mary. Stan Walsh. Maybe even Keeley. Gettin' all up in his shit, as the youngsters might say. Crowding his space and causing problems. All of which meant that Stephen King would have to wait a bit, while McAfee dealt.

The Colonel sighed. Okay. He could deal. That's why he made the big bucks, right? McAfee put the paperback on his nightstand and rolled onto his side, accidentally kicking his cat in the head. Or maybe not accidentally. Nicky slinked onto the floor and walked out of the room.

Ah well. At least Linda Travis was still tightly wrapped. And Squirrel Island was now a heavily fortified position. So what was there to worry about, really? They had standard high-security military fencing in place, plus eControl fields, plus a Level 3 Toroidal Shield Wall. They had more itchy-fingered soldiers with weapons at the ready than anybody in their right minds should be shaking a stick at. And they even had, if what Technician DuPont said was true, defensive fields in the next two levels up. A Mirror Pool, maybe.

Or a Murk. That was a shit-load of defensive force for guarding one middle-aged woman's drugged, naked body. Nobody was getting in, and the PILF wasn't getting out. McAfee was sure of that. He'd gone down to check on her before climbing into bed. He'd stared at her for a really long time.

The one thing that nagged at him was the possibility that the Life were involved. Back down in the muck and mire, ye damnable bugs? The kids' note spoke of Alice and a wok. They knew now that the kids had lied, as they obviously hadn't been taken away in a wok at all, bodily at least. Still, the mention of Alice bothered him. If Alice was back on the scene, then very likely the great Spud himself was lurking not far behind. McAfee understood that The Families, or at least the Directorate, considered Spud an inconsequential player at this point, seeing as how he had betrayed the Plan and all, and given his long absence from human affairs. McAfee was not so sure. Those were miniature woks at the intersection points of the Grid. Millions of them. The Life hadn't really gone away, so much as just taken a step back. Like you do before you hit somebody. And he suspected that Spud had other irons in the fire here, beyond The Families and their precious little Plan.

McAfee winced. It was dangerous, to think that way. No telling what the new generation of nanoplants could pick up. And he was certain to be on The Family's watch-list. The Colonel took a calming breath and coaxed a smiled. It was the worry, that's all. They'd expect worry. It was his *job* to worry. Keeping the POTUS on ice was a career-maker. He knew it and they knew it and he knew they knew it and they knew he knew they knew it. And he was up for the job. He really was. He could handle whatever came his way. Happily and efficiently. All in the service of The Families and their Plan. All with the hope that, when the time comes, he would be chosen.

McAfee pulled the top sheet back up to his neck, not so much for warmth but for a sense of protection. He felt so exposed, here inside so many layers of defense. There were eyes everywhere, it seemed. And some of those eyes were large and black and slanted. Spud had pulled the rug out from under them before. Not only had he withdrawn the assistance of his people, he'd put another obstacle in their way. Who knew what else he had up his sleeve? And who knew, really, whether it was possible to stop the little bastard, if he decided to stir up more shit?

McAfee didn't. And the thought of that kept him from sleep. So he rose, pulled on his robe, and stepped out onto the back deck. The night was clear and pocked with bright stars, and the Gridlight cast a bluish glow on the surface of the bay. Most of the island's defenses were invisible to his eye, but he knew they were there, extending above and beyond the tall steel fence, and reaching far past the range of the arsenal of weapons he could see glinting in the Gridlight. From his post on the shoreline, one of the soldiers looked up and spotted the Colonel watching from the cottage deck.

The soldier saluted.

McAfee returned the salute.

Nicky, the Colonel's cat, stole silently onto the deck and slipped over the edge, disappearing into the shadows and the trees.

8.6

It surprised Mary, lying alone in her bed, how easily the protocols came back to her. The strict procedures, ingrained into her during her training, were still right there when she needed them, a full operator's manual she could open with her mind's eye. Even so, the process was difficult. Excessive emotionality had always been a source of distraction for those attempting to step away from the body and travel up to another level. Emotions, in fact, were a large part of what the Protocols were designed to counter. But Mary was all emotion these days, with her feelings always at the surface. And after her experience at the hospital, she felt like a wreck. Setting aside her feelings felt impossible.

But necessity and urgency helped Mary to focus. They'd stolen away her Keeley, and would not explain why. Just as they had taken the President away from her. And the kids had gone off on their own. Mary could not afford to be stopped by her feelings. Not now. The people she loved needed her. So she slowed down her pounding heart. She stopped her frantic thoughts. She breathed. She cleared. She chanted. She breathed some more. And she went through the steps she'd gone through so many times before, though it had been years now. Years. But even then, even after repeated attempts, Mary failed to step away from her body. She squeezed her fists, digging her nails into her palms. There was too much at stake for her to fail.

Then Mary remembered that she had another path she could take. She rose from her bed, headed downstairs, made her way through the kitchen, and walked out into Ness's garden behind the Presidential Home. She looked up to the night sky and asked for help. From whom she was not certain. Not at first. God? Jesus? Allah? Satan? She didn't see the Universe in those terms. The ancestors? The spirits? The many beings she'd encountered in her years as a traveler? None of these. Or all of them. She asked for help from all of the above. And then, finally, she asked for help from Spud. So many long hours they'd spent together down in the Rock. Communing mind to mind. Teaching. Learning. Sharing. There must be something still between them. Some bond she could call on. Some help he could give. Mary asked.

Whether it was Spud that helped her just then Mary would never know. She saw a flash of bright white light through a crack in the garage door and went over to investigate. She opened the smaller side door and stepped through. Inside, pulsing dimly in the dark, two-stall garage, hovering in the space where a car used to sit, was a small wok, perhaps seven feet across. There was an opening in the side.

Mary recalled the last time she'd stood this close to an alien craft, and those harried moments down in the Rock with Linda and Cole and Alice. And with Agent Rice. She'd been helping carry Bob's unconscious body into a wok before the facility imploded. So that her colleague might be saved. But in that last moment, Rice had lashed out with a blow to Mary's nose that had put her in intensive care, near death and in need of multiple surgeries. That blow had damaged her brain and altered some fundamental qualities of her being. She had never fully healed.

Mary glanced around the garage. There was no Agent Rice here now, as far as she could see. She could sense no danger. No evil. No risk. And she could feel the essential goodness of the wok itself, though she could read no field, no thoughts, no intentions.

Mary stepped forward and put a hand on the wok's sleek surface and whispered a prayer of thanksgiving. Then she climbed through the open doorway and lay on her back on the wok's soft deck as the opening melted shut behind her. She waited there in the blackness and breathed deeply. She felt around the confines of the interior, but found no operator's helmet. That did not matter. Mary hated flying these things, and she did not intend to go that way in any event. Flying was not what this wok was for, and both of them, Mary and the wok, knew it. This wok was for hiding. For protection. For alignment. To provide her a safe space from which she could travel. This wok was the help she'd prayed for.

Mary followed the protocols once again. Still they did not work. She wiggled around, cleared her mind, and then reached toward the wok's ceiling to stretch her shoulders. She gasped. There in the darkness was a tiny, clawed, leathery hand reaching back down toward her. The hand grabbed hers and jerked her upwards. She was away.

Had Mary been standing in the garage at that point, she'd have seen the wok sink through the floor, as though the concrete were quicksand or mud. In a moment the wok was gone, taking Mary's body with it.

But Mary was not standing in the garage. Mary was in the next level up from the physical realm, hovering in the sky that was not really a sky.

8.7

Mihos had taught the kids how to tune their awareness to what he called the *mock physical*. "It'll look like home-sweet-home to your monkey eyes, but otherwise we're still a level up," he had said. "That'll make it easier for you." It had. They flew now through the skies over Maine; three kids, one old dog, and one condescending cat huddled together on a Pac Man rug. The rural countryside beneath them glowed with purple Gridlight. The Kennebec River glinted and sparkled as it led them South to the sea.

"So," said the cat as they flew, "what brings you kids here, anyways?" He sat at the rug's leading edge and scanned the landscape ahead of them. "I mean... you're kids, you know? What's with the whole rescue-the-stepmother-from-the-Forces-of-Evil thing? Don't you have a Dad to do that kind of stuff? Or the cops? And if you needed to get to Squirrel Island, why didn't you all just pile into the family Buick and drive down to visit her?"

"Emily noticed the mole," said Iain.

"And Alice spoke to me in a dream," added Grace.

"And then the hand pulled us up through the MRI machine," explained Emily.

Mihos turned to face the three, his eyes rolling upward in a look of bemused incredulity. "I seem to have missed a few episodes," he said dryly. "Care to give me the two-minute synopsis?"

The kids told Mihos the rest of their story.

"So you think the President Monkey you saw on TV wasn't really the President Monkey?" asked the cat when they were finished.

Emily stared at Mihos. "Something is wrong," she said evenly. "We don't know what."

Mihos nodded. "You think maybe they cloned her?" he asked. "Or maybe that was a robot you saw. Evil Robot Stepmom, perhaps. Or maybe she's turned to the Dark Side and she had her mole moved as a sign of her new devotion to the Emperor?"

"Is everything a joke to you?" asked Iain, angry.

Mihos glanced at the boy, then looked away. "I just..." he said. He sighed, then looked at Iain again. "Sorry. You're right. You're step-mom's missing. And she's sick. Of course you're worried about her. And you want to help."

"And even those Great Ones you talk about seem to be on our side," said Iain, chin out and brow furrowed.

Mihos flinched but did not respond, then turned and scanned the horizon toward which they were headed. "We're catching a bit of luck," he called back to the kids. "I figured we'd have encountered the Murk by now, but I don't see a sign of him."

"Do you think he's gone away?" asked Grace, glad for the change of subject.

Mihos turned and smiled at the girl. "Wouldn't that be nice?" he said, turning forward again. Grace could not tell whether he was being sarcastic or genuine.

"Well do you?" said Iain, his voice rising.

The cat's tail began to flick up and down, but he did not turn around. "No," said Mihos at last. "I don't know. Maybe." His tail settled back down onto the rug. He turned and looked at Iain. "I'd like to think we're catching a break here. But my fear is that he's just pulled back to consolidate his defenses." Mihos turned back to scan the sky. "In which case... when we finally *do* meet him, he may be tougher to fool." The cat's voice was soft and sad.

Emily cleared her throat. "Does it make sense, Mihos," she asked, "to just fly right to him like this?" She gestured in the direction they were heading. "I mean. Can we sneak-"

"I'm sorry, Emily," said Mihos, raising a paw. "But again... no. The Murk isn't watching out for us. He doesn't have eyes. He's not even really a 'he' at all. Sneaking up on him would be like sneaking up on a trip wire. He only notices us when we break through his outer membrane. Until then, just like a trip wire, we could stand right next to him and he wouldn't react to us."

"But once inside?" asked Emily.

"He'll react. And he'll probably know immediately that it's you again, and he may be rather annoyed at having to deal with you guys a second time. I have no idea whether he's been programmed as a simple general defensive shield, or whether he's been informed you are coming. Did you tell anybody in the physical that you were headed this way?"

The kids glanced back and forth at each other. "We did leave a note," said Grace at last.

Mihos snorted and shook his head, but did not look back. "Good thinking," he muttered.

Emily nodded toward the sky ahead of him. "So will we be able to see the Murk before we get to him?" she asked. "Last time we-" Emily stopped talking.

All around them was blackness. There was nothing else.

8.8

They'd sung *Wayfaring Stranger* more than once, undoubtedly for his benefit, though Cole did not really understand how the lyrics applied to him. Didn't matter. The mandolin player, a young woman named Marionette who had an eye-patch and a scar that ran from her forehead and across her nose to her cheek, played such sweet, soulful, soaring solo lines that Cole felt transported back to simpler times. The band - a mandolin, two guitars, a stand-up bass, an old man on harmonica and a very young boy on a kid's drum kit - played a wide variety of songs, from traditional string-band pieces to rock songs so classic that Cole had tears in his eyes. He thought about joining in. They tried to coax him, even. But all Cole knew by heart were the songs from *Ziggy Stardust*, and he was pretty sure that if he tried to sing one of them he'd start sobbing.

So Cole watched and clapped and kept his tears mostly to himself. There was more food. More fortifier. And at one point Marionette put down her mandolin, grabbed Cole by the hand, and pulled him up to join in the dancing. Stunned and honored and moved and embarrassed, Cole let go of his inhibitions and allowed his body to take over. It'd been years since he'd danced. Not since before Ruth had died. But it felt great, and soon Cole didn't give a damn what he looked like. After a while he noticed that Stan was up dancing as well and he laughed and laughed, to see them both cutting loose. This was not at all what they'd expected to find when they snuck through the Cordon and into the post-collapse world.

Then the music stopped and Annabelle stood up. The room fell quiet and she spoke.

"We never thought it would go this way," she said, "and yet," she winked, "we knew it would, didn't we? The Wayfaring Stranger is amongst us, and we all, I think, know what that means."

"Party time!" called a man named Robert from the back of the room. Others laughed.

Annabelle smiled. "Yes. We get to celebrate. As we have been doing. As we will do again." She peered out over the crowd. "But we have some work to do now, don't we?" she asked.

Many nodded.

"And it could get dark," she said, "for it's darkness we shall oppose." Some of her words sounded, to Cole, like they must be lifted straight from *The Book of the Stranger.* He'd have to read the whole book one of these days.

"So we shall hope that the Stranger's Light can lead us," said Annabelle. With that, she held out a hand toward Cole. Those few folks standing between the two stepped to the side and Cole, as if caught in a dream, stepped forward to take both of the old woman's hands in his own. He was hot and sweaty from dancing and wished he had a towel to wipe his face, but Annabelle did not seem to notice. She studied his palms for a moment, then looked up at him and lifted an eyebrow. "Do you have a plan for tomorrow?" she asked.

Cole shook his head. Partly to deny having a plan and partly to clear his thoughts. It was so late, and he was exhausted. "There were phone calls," he said tentatively, trying to find some words that might meet the huge expectations Annabelle seemed to have for him. "A man with a disguised voice. He... he told me to come here. To raise a stink. 'A media circus,' he said. I haven't really thought it out... beyond that..." Cole shrugged.

Annabelle nodded. "Your mystery caller thinks you can force their hand," she said evenly. "What do you think?"

"I think..." Cole exhaled loudly. "I don't know. Maybe. It depends on who we're dealing with here... who's in charge." He looked down to the floor for support. "I'm just... we're all just regular people, you know?"

"Indeed," agreed Annabelle. "And yet you have other resources to draw upon now." She squeezed his hands in hers, to give him a hint of what she meant.

Cole let go and held up his hands. "The lights?" he said. He shook his head in a vigorous 'no.' "But I can't control them!" he explained, waving his hands wildly to prove his point.

His point was not made. From both of his waving palms, fireworks of green and gold burst forth. Cole clenched his fists and the fireworks stopped. He opened his palms and held them facing upwards before him, then studied them with intention and focus. The fireworks sprang back to life, softer this time. Like tiny faerie ballerinas dancing in his hands, the lights sparkled and spun. Cole watched them closely, as one might regard a dragonfly alighting on one's finger. He looked up at the rapt faces of his audience and smiled.

"*The Wayfaring Stranger will bring the Light*," quoted Annabelle. Her voice was hushed and reverent, but the room was so quiet that everyone could hear her.

8.9

Tears streamed down Linda's cheeks. She gulped for air. With measured slowness, she surveyed her underground cell, making sure that William hadn't suddenly reappeared. There was an arched opening in the wall opposite the cubicles, but the doorway was empty, and revealed only a bare hallway beyond.

She could feel her lingering trauma buzzing inside like a nest of hornets, angry at having been disturbed. She flashed back to her incarceration in the Ottawa Lodge: waking up on the cold stone floor, her body bruised and bloody, her scalp screaming with pain from the lacerations left from Rice's sadistic haircut. Rice had held her for days in a room like this, naked and cold and distraught at the death of her new partner, Cole. He had laughed at her pain. Though Obie's gentle ministrations had healed her body and eased her soul, and even though Cole had been restored to her, the nauseating memory of that time had ingrained itself into every bit of her flesh. With a hesitant, shaky hand, Linda reached up to touch her hair. It felt normal, long and clean and neatly ponytailed. She lowered her hand to her heart and took another calming breath.

Slowly, Linda lowered herself to the floor and sat cross-legged on the waxy stone, facing the doorway. Her stomach churned and her head ached. She sensed that there was no real light here, and that if she adjusted her perceptions, she would be engulfed by blackness. But she would do no such thing. She would not even close her eyes. To add darkness to this imprisonment would overwhelm her. Linda had no intention of letting that happen. She would not be undone by this. She looked up at the ceiling and cursed William for turning out to be no better than that damnable Rice.

But already she could see that the Fisherman was no Agent Rice. William hadn't left her in the dark. He hadn't stripped her naked and beat her. He did not seem to hold her in contempt. For all his maddening presumptions, William was neither cruel nor violent. If her sense of him was accurate, the Fisherman was, she had to admit, trying to be a good and honorable person.

A wave of calm passed through her at the thought. Linda rolled onto her knees and pushed herself to her feet. Unlike Theodore Rice, William was not going to use torture to get what he wanted. She could be thankful for that. But he did need something from her, and he'd obviously left her here to puzzle and ponder what that might be. Her request that he stop dawdling and tell her what she needed to know had stopped him in his tracks. He'd looked lost. Embarrassed, even. And then he'd disappeared without a word of explanation.

Linda turned and stepped across the room to the alien cubicles. There were seventeen of them, three-sided boxes with open tops, made from what looked like burnished nickel. They were roughly eighteen inches wide and two feet tall, just large enough to contain a small gray alien. But there were no aliens here, and no sign of such creatures. Just bare, clean metal boxes and a polished stone room. And a doorway. Linda turned and approached the arched opening in the opposite wall.

William had "tuned" her to the "near-physical," he had said, so that gravity and light and her body all worked in ways that her habituated mind could most easily comprehend. It was certainly effective. Her body, and the room, felt solid and real. The air was comfortably warm. Were it not for the line of metal boxes, she might have thought she was in a storage vault on Earth. But she knew those cubicles. And there was no discernable light source. And the feeling of pressure convinced her that she was deep underground.

Linda had had enough of being left alone in underground rooms.

She put a hand on the side of the doorway and leaned forward to inspect the hall. The corridor stretched off in the distance in either direction. It was no wider than a shopping cart but was twice as tall as she, and Linda wondered what sorts of people it had been built for. If this room housed the small aliens like Spud, as the cubicles seemed to indicate, were there also tall, spindly aliens here that needed such headroom?

The hallway was empty. No Agent Rice, no William, and no aliens, tiny *or* spindly. So Linda stepped forward and studied both directions. To the right, the corridor seemed to go on forever. To the left, she could see what appeared in the distance to be a stainless steel door with a circle on it. She turned left.

It was a door. And the circle was a handle, a ship's wheel like you would find on a submarine hatch. An entrance, perhaps, to an airlock of some sort. Linda stepped to the door and reached out, thinking that, in this near-physical state, she would have to turn it. She found, to her surprise, that her fingers passed right through the metal wheel. She raised an eyebrow, then moved forward and stuck out her hand. Her arm passed freely through the door, just as it had on Phobos. Glancing back down the hallway to the underground room, trusting that in whatever plane of existence she currently inhabited she would need no oxygen, Linda stepped through the door.

Beyond was another corridor, the rock more roughly hewn than in the one she had left behind. Linda continued on, noting other airlock doors on either side of the passage. She turned a corner. Fifty feet ahead the hallway ended in a stairway leading upwards. She came to the foot of the stairs and looked up. It seemed to go on forever. Feeling like she had no choice, Linda started her ascent, taking care not to trip on the tiny steps.

At the top, which came sooner than she'd expected, was a landing and another airlock door. This one she stepped through without hesitation. Before her was a scene out of the American Old West, a desert landscape, with distant mountains silhouetted against the sky.

It was too dark to make out much detail on the landscape, but the sky was bursting with stars. And right overhead was her old friend, Phobos. Linda was back on the surface of Mars, alone in the desert, in a body but not really, and free, apparently, to explore wherever she wished.

8.10

Ness put her phone on the table and rotated it slightly until it was just right. She glanced up at the surveillance camera, then pushed the button to wake up her phone. The tiny screen came to life. The brightness would likely show up on the monitor in the nurses' station. No doubt they would come check on her soon. It did not matter. She was finished. Her structure was built. It fairly sang with life and energy. The magic worked, and she was inside of it, and so were the kids. If she was right, then nothing could disturb them now.

8.11

Mary hovered in the Astral plane, scanning the Cosmos. She could sense Linda's presence at Squirrel Island but could find no trace of Keeley's vibration at all, there or anywhere. She scanned for the children, and would have sworn she'd sensed their vibrational patterns, when all three suddenly disappeared. No amount of subsequent scanning would reveal their presence.

Without their patterns to key in on, she could not blink directly to them. Or to Keeley. Now she would have to go searching.

And she would have done just that, had not a second wok appeared right in front of her.

"Damn," she muttered.

8.12

"Damn," said Mihos in the blackness.

8.13

Cole trudged through the new-fallen snow, his boots now and again breaking through the icy crust underneath, causing him to lurch forward. Were it not for his staff, he'd have fallen already. At his age, that could be disastrous. Old bones were brittle, they said. He preferred not putting them to the test.

The others scolded him for walking alone, especially at night. But Cole was tired of being escorted everywhere he went. Tired of needing help. Tired of the constant closeness of human bodies. He needed time alone. Time to think. Time to slowly get back in touch with his feelings. Change was the constant background of their lives now, to the point that change itself had become routine. It was all he could do to keep up. And maybe he wasn't really even managing that. Who would tell him?

The quarter-moon shone down on him as he walked, having risen once again in the wrong part of the sky. Same old moon, though. Same bluish light on the snow. Same glints and sparkles in the air. So cold. So dry. So hushed that even the distant howls of the dog pack were muffled and soft, as if those poor old beasts were still chasing rabbits in their dreams as they slept in front of their masters' fires. Cole stopped to take a breath and held his staff out before him, turning it slightly so that the old Moody Blues CD, wedged into the top, would catch the moonlight and reflect it back to the stars. An old habit. A silly game. To think he could reach them this way. To think he even wanted to.

Grace's cabin was just ahead. She insisted on being called Rowan these days, and of course he would comply, but to Cole she was always Grace. Cole had a can in his pocket with which he intended to surprise his youngest. The salvage crew had brought it back this morning. The label was gone, but he was pretty sure it was milk. Maybe that condensed stuff. Maybe even the sweetened stuff. Something about the shape of the can, maybe. Or perhaps he just had the ability to suss out the contents of cans now. Who knew, these days, when all of the rules were changing? He hoped it hadn't spoiled, whatever it was. Grace... Rowan... could use a treat tonight.

Cole sighed and his eyes misted. He blinked to clear them. Goddamn, he missed Linda. And it was times like this, when one of them passed, that he missed her the most. He had never been too good with grief. Not on his own. But if Linda had been there... Cole shook his head. She wasn't there. She was gone. Gone so long he could barely remember her face. Janie was fine. Janie was great. Janie had saved him when nobody else could have. And still he missed Linda.

Cole patted his jeans with his gloved hand to assure himself that the can was still in his pocket. If it fell out into the snow, he might never find it. Satisfied, he thrust out his staff and took another step. It would not help his case, to be found outside by himself on such a night. If he got to Grace's, they could make up a story about how she'd helped him. And Cole would wink and Grace... Rowan... would wink back, and all would be right with the world. No one else need know otherwise.

Rowan's lamp (there, he remembered her name...) was burning. Up late reading, probably. Cole was glad of that. He turned down the path to her cabin, brushing the snow from low-hanging pine branches as he passed, an old game, an old habit. One branch dumped a load of fresh snow on his face and Cole sputtered, reaching up to wipe the cold, wet stuff from his mustache and beard. He came to Rowan's porch, stomped his feet, and knocked on the door. With no response from his daughter, he worked the latch with his gloved hand and pushed the door open far enough to announce himself.

"Rowan?" he said, but his voice was tentative and confused. There was no lamp burning after all. The room was cool, and dark as a cave. Grace... Rowan... was not there.

Cole opened his eyes, pushed back the covers, and stood. He stepped to the window and gazed out over the Grid-lit waters of Boothbay Harbor. He'd gone on another hop, this time to some weird alternative future in which he was still himself. But it was not real. There was no snow, and he was not old, and Linda was not dead. She was being held captive on Squirrel Island. He could see that island now, a dark mass rising from the waters, barely visible in the night.

In the morning, he would go see his wife.

8.14

"I'm gonna pass," said Carl, lifting his wooden rack and dumping his Scrabble tiles back into the bag. He shook the bag a few times to mix the tiles, then started choosing new ones to put on his rack.

"You can't do that!" Ted blurted, wide-eyed.

Carl cocked his head and smiled. "Of course I can," he said. He pointed toward the box on the floor. "It's in the rules."

"But you can't get new tiles!" said Ted.

"I can if I give up my turn, Ted. That's how the game works." He gestured at the board. "It's your go."

"But you have to play with..." said Ted, sputtering out before he could finish his sentence. He glanced down at the box, then back at Carl.

"That sounds more like a philosophical statement on the nature of reality than a Scrabble rule, Ted," said Carl. "You care to elaborate?"

Ted shook his head. "Shut up."

"I mean," continued Carl, "maybe you felt trapped in your life, Ted. Stuck. Limited. Didn't know how to get out. How to start fresh. How to change. You had to play with the cards you'd been dealt. That's how it felt to you. You ever think of that?"

"You're an asshole," said Ted.

"Maybe. Or you could think of me as an angel here to help you. You think maybe you have a difficult time accepting help?"

"Go screw yourself."

"I'm just saying, Ted. Cuz I've noticed that you're pretty resistant to feedback. And that's not going to serve you, if what we're up to here is to process things from our previous lives. I don't see you doing that on your own, do you?"

Ted looked up from his tiles and glared at Carl. "You really are a dick, aren't you?"

Carl grinned. "So what if you're stuck with me until you do what you came here to do?" he said. "What if we're both stuck here?" Carl began to chuckle. "You've got me 'til the end of time, Ted. What fun, eh?"

Ted focused on his tiles. Carl leaned back in his chair and crossed his arms over his stomach. After a long while, Ted picked up his rack and dumped his tiles into the bag. Then he lifted the board, bent it into a V shape, and poured the tiles already played into the bag as well. He looked at Carl, chin out, one eyebrow raised, a mischievous glint in his eye. "New game," he said, setting the empty board back onto the table.

Chapter ⱷ Nine

9.1

Gabrielle stuffed a change of clothes into her backpack, grabbed her wallet and keys and phone, checked her red-blonde bob in the mirror, and headed out her dorm room door. The pre-dawn light was enough to see by as she made her way down the hallway and stairs and out the side door. In the warm, moist morning air, she slipped her backpack over one shoulder, glanced around to make sure she was alone, then headed quickly along the concrete pathway. The bus stop was only two blocks away.

There had been no night visitation from Zacharael. No strange and awful dream. No mysterious writing in her notebook. And he was no longer in her head. She could feel his absence, as if a portion of her memory had been wiped. She'd seen his body fade to nothing. Was he dead now? Gone forever? Or did he still watch her from afar? Gabrielle exhaled loudly in frustration. There was no way to know. If Zacharael wasn't finished with her, she'd just have to wait until he made himself known.

In the meantime, Gabrielle had something to do. She didn't know what it was, exactly, but she knew that it would come down to a single moment. She could see it in her mind's eye, like a drop of time embedded in amber. She was standing in a hallway. Underground, it felt like. Concrete and white tile and overhead fluorescent lighting. In front of her stood the American President, Linda Travis. In the President's hand was a small brown object. And Gabrielle was reaching out to grab it.

She laughed at herself as she walked. Was it crazy, to think such a moment might come to pass? The US President was deathly ill, and locked down in some military hospital in Maine. Who the hell was Gabrielle, to think she could get in to see her? Perhaps if she'd taken her rightful place in The Families. But on her own? A rebellious child? And now sneaking away?

Screw it. She didn't have to know how the moment would happen. She only had to know that it would, or that, in some weird way she could only feel, the moment already *had* happened. Nothing could stop it. Nothing could stop *her*. Nothing.

Gabrielle stepped into the bus stop shelter and stood near the back, to keep her chances of being spotted to a minimum. She had no idea whether her father had spies following her, but he might, and she wanted to get away unnoticed.

As the bus approached, Gabrielle saw the stack of newspapers in the rack in the corner. She stepped over to look down at the headlines as the bus pulled in to the stop. She lifted a paper from the rack and unfolded it. Above the fold was a story about how Greensleeves had come to Montreal. Below the fold, a story and photo: a new crop circle, depicting that same strange symbol she'd seen before, had appeared on an overgrown golf course on the Maine coast, close to some placed called Boothbay Harbor.

Slipping the paper into her backpack, Gabrielle boarded the bus.

9.2

Keeley woke up in her hospital bed, disoriented and confused. It was a different bed. In a different room. She wondered why they'd moved her.

She turned her head to look out the window. Was it lighter out, or darker? Was it dawn or dusk? And what day was it? She couldn't tell. Her sense of time had slipped from the nail on the wall and fallen to a heap on the floor. She slept. She woke up. She slept some more. She woke again. Mostly she slept, and was glad of that. Her sleep felt so peaceful, so right, so transcendent, that she would happily sleep until the Day of Judgment, she felt so good.

She remembered eating a sausage biscuit. She'd been so hungry! But that could have been days ago. Or just hours. Mary hadn't come back. She knew that much. Mary had left for a moment and not come back. She smiled, thinking of her partner. My love. Alas. My love.

She drifted into blissful sleep. She woke again. She looked out the window. It seemed brighter than before. Mary might come back at any moment! Keeley closed her eyes. Her heart was filled with glad excitement. She wanted to tell Mary how good she felt. Mary would be so happy! But when Keeley opened her eyes she was still alone.

The nurses were different. Young. Strange and beautiful. Coldly professional. They hardly spoke at all. But Keeley loved them so much. Even though they wouldn't tell her anything.

The television told her all sorts of things. Things Keeley didn't want to know. Like how quickly Greensleeves was spreading, and the growing number of deaths from the disease. It told her about the grounding of flights and the closing of cities. It told her about a riot in a FEMA shelter near New Orleans, which broke out after three cases appeared there overnight.

The TV told her that the high today would be over one hundred degrees in most of Maine. It told her how the Global Environmental Summit was going, and how the President was holding up. It re-played Linda's impassioned response to the ambassador from Nuna-vut. It showed dramatic footage from the collapsing ice shelf in Ant-arctica. It reported on failing crop yields in Europe and China. It told of the assassination of the President of Mozambique. It played a snippet from the latest tirade from Pastor Clinton. It reported on a new crop circle that had appeared on the Maine coast.

The television wanted Keeley to be afraid. Or angry. But Keeley only felt calm and peaceful joy. The only thing she wanted was Mary, but the television would not tell her where Mary was, or when she would come back. Keeley smiled. Mary would be so happy, when she returned.

Keeley wondered why she was in this bed. Why did she sleep all the time? Why did she feel so full of joy? Linda had this same flu, didn't she? But the President was still up and awake and addressing the summit from her biocontainment room on Squirrel Island. You could see her on TV, speaking and participating. And that young woman lying on the sidewalk in front of the Burger Hut: she hadn't been bedridden for days, had she?

The TV said that people with the alien flu felt pretty good, and then they collapsed and died. So why was *she* confined to a bed? Keeley didn't understand. She wasn't strapped down. She was just so tired.

It didn't matter. She felt so *good* here!

Keeley glanced again at the window. It was definitely lighter out. Which meant it was morning. Which meant that a whole night, at least, had passed without Mary returning. But Keeley didn't know what that meant. Keeley wanted to call Stan and see if he knew where Mary was.

But that would have to wait.

She felt so sleepy right now. And sleeping felt so good.

My love.

Alas.

9.3

McAfee gasped. Corporal Osterman's insistent knocking had pulled him up and out of the deep well of drug-induced unconsciousness that passed for sleep these days. "What?!" he shouted at the door. When the Corporal told him "what," he rolled quickly out of bed and got dressed. Somebody... somebody from The Families... had just wokked in for a surprise inspection. Great.

"Good morning, Sir," said the Colonel as he entered the conference room they'd built inside the President's old garage. He feigned a chipper gladness he did not feel. If he was being monitored, and he was, then he was surely being closely watched right now. He trusted that "the show" would suffice. And why not? If people could hide their true thoughts and feelings from themselves, then surely they could hide them from an implant and a qputer? Having been tagged by the Life years ago, Aidan McAfee was an old hand at this game. He smiled warmly and stuck out his hand.

The man standing before him was older, wiry, and slightly stooped, with a full head of feathery white hair and a neatly trimmed white beard. He was dressed in khakis and a colorful Hawaiian shirt. "Colonel," said the man with a nod. "You may call me William." He took McAfee's hand and shook it. His skin was warm and soft. His voice was confident and richly British.

"To what do we owe this honor?" asked McAfee, as if he truly meant it.

William flashed his eyebrows. "I should rather think it more a pain in the bottom than an honor, wouldn't you, Colonel?" he said with a slight twitching of the corners of his mouth.

McAfee smiled in return, the sort of smile that came embedded in a pained and knowing face. "It *is* early," he agreed. He wouldn't go any further than that. Obsequiousness would stand out as much as resistance or resentment.

"Quite," said William.

McAfee glanced around the room but saw only his own people. "Did you come alone?" he asked. "And will you need accommodations, Sir?"

William shook his head. "Regrettably I must soon be off. I piloted the AB12 myself, you see, and have pressing business elsewhere. I do thank the Life for not absconding with the ships we built ourselves when they pulled out of the game." He flashed his eyebrows again. "Makes a trip like this all the less painful."

"Are you expecting a painful visit, then?" asked the Colonel, suddenly worried.

"Not at all, my good man," said William, raising his hands and showing his palms. "Simply making small talk by referencing the trials of commercial air flights, as your comedians are so fond of doing." He grinned.

McAfee relaxed. "So how can I help you?"

"Yes," said William, clapping his hands. "Brilliant. To it, then." He looked around the room at McAfee's staff, then returned his attention to the Colonel. "I need to see President Travis," he said.

McAfee opened his mouth and William raised a hand. "I am aware of exactly what I shall find," he said. "I merely wish to view her body. To confirm for myself, and others, that her condition is unchanged."

The Colonel almost sputtered an objection, then caught himself and smiled again. "Of course," he said warmly. "I just..."

"Your facility computers have scanned me, Colonel. I am exactly who I have presented myself to be, and I have every right to make this request."

"Of course," said McAfee again. He scratched vaguely at his temple. "I'm just... has there been a problem?" he asked. "My reports-"

"-are professional and clear and greatly appreciated," said William, finishing the Colonel's sentence for him. "And, I must say, I am comforted by your hesitancy. The Quietus has been triggered and Changeling has been implemented. It is important, in this time of great moment, to be wary of subterfuge, is it not? I understand your position, and take no offense at your question."

Colonel Aidan McAfee knew a coded threat when he heard one. Another moment of hesitancy on his part and this William surely *would* take offense, and in ways that the Colonel would no doubt find inconvenient. McAfee smiled tightly, turned, and spoke to his aide. "Corporal Osterman, arrange a viewing for us immediately," he commanded.

"I will be going down alone," said William, his voice reasonable and assured.

McAfee turned, forced one last smile to his face, and nodded. "By all means," he said.

William raised his eyebrows in apparent delight, then strode out of the room.

Apparently William knew exactly where he was headed.

9.4

Ness was surprised that the nurses had not checked in on the kids since she'd powered up her creation. She'd expected a confrontation, but nothing of the sort happened. The check-ins, adjustments, treatments, and caregiving had been regular and frequent during the previous day. She'd thought the same would continue throughout the night, though perhaps not quite so often. But nothing?

Now it was fully light out and Ness could hear the sounds outside her door as the hospital staff made ready for the day. Surely the door would open any moment. Surely. Ness looked across at the children. Had she planned more thoroughly, she'd have slid her own cot in next to their gurneys before building the construct. But she hadn't thought that far ahead, and it was only after she turned on her phone and brought the construct to life that she realized her error. After a while, after standing there in the darkness until her feet hurt, she'd just crawled into bed next to Grace. It was sweet, really, to hold the girl. And there was room for the both of them, yes there was. Ness had managed, finally, to get some sleep.

A soft knock sounded and the door opened, just as Ness knew it must. In stepped a nurse, a dark young man with a shaved head. She'd seen him briefly the day before. "You are doing well in here," said the young man. Ness couldn't tell if he was asking a question or not. He surveyed the room, looking at Ness, at the kids, and at her construct, a weird, wild, wiry half-dome made from curtain rods, automobile antennas, cutlery and cooking utensils, coat hangers, and a couple of rolls of aluminum foil, held together, seemingly, with rubber bands, paper clips, clothespins, and surgical tape. Resting on the blanket at Emily's feet was Ness's cell phone, connected to the outer structure with a single wire. On Emily's stomach was a pile of carrots resting on a sheet of foil, also connected with a wire. The construct seemed to almost buzz with energy. The nurse's gaze landed back on Ness and he studied her for a moment.

"I know what you are," said Ness in a low defensive voice, having no idea what she meant by that.

"And we know you," said the nurse. He gestured widely with both hands, to indicate the construct. "Do not be afraid of us," he said. "We are here for you."

He turned and left, closing the door behind him.

Ness frowned and shook her head as though she were bothered by a bee. She did not understand what had just happened.

9.5

"I didn't expect the Spanish Inquisition," muttered Mihos in the blackness.

Cole's three children turned their attention to their cat guide. His eyes glowed as they had before, but so small and weak were they in the immensity of the Murk that they might as well have been single photons traveling through the depths of spacetime. Still, they were something, some tie to the world they knew, and the kids were glad to be able to perceive them, no matter their intensity.

"Is this different than you expected?" asked Grace. There was no speaking here, really. No sound. No breath. No voice. There was thinking, and there was the perception of others thinking. And there were the cat's eyes. And that was all. But even then, there was worry in Grace's voice. The complete absence of light and body and feeling, of reference points and up and down and in and out, of each other and of herself, and of her ability to know how Dennis was doing, was driving her quickly toward the idea of tears. Even time had lost its meaning here. Had it been hours or moments? She could not tell.

Mihos' eyes went black and then glowed again. A blink. "I haven't actually made it a habit of hanging out inside of Murks, yo," he said. "I just know what I've been told."

"I think we're being pushed," said Emily, her tone hushed.

Mihos blinked again. "Pushed?" he said. "Pushed by whom?"

"I don't know," said Emily. "When we were here before, I felt like there was somebody in my head. Not a feeling, really. An idea. And now I have the idea that we're being pushed. Kinda like animals. Rounded up. Herded."

"Hmm," said Mihos, closing his eyes for a moment. He spoke without reopening them. "I don't feel it," he said. "Are you sure?"

"So much for the map," said Iain, his frustration clear in his voice.

Mihos cleared his throat in this place of no throats, and no clearing of them. "Excuse me, monkey-boy?" he said.

"We can't see," explained Iain. "And there's no rug underneath us. Not here."

"You forget," said Mihos. "I made the map. It's all inside of me."

"Then why aren't we following it?" said Iain.

"My dear fellow," said Mihos. "We have been, since the moment we were engulfed in the Murk." He blinked. "I, for one, am moving forward. Since you all are still with me, I can only assume that you are moving with me. Perhaps that's what you are feeling, Emily."

"I don't know," answered Emily in the blackness. "Maybe..."

"You said this Murk was like a trip wire," offered Grace.

Mihos blinked. Every now and then a small portion of his eyes were occluded by blackness. Eventually it became obvious that he was licking his paws, though how he could do such a thing in this place of no bodies Grace did not understand. After a while he stopped and answered. "Yes?" he said.

"So," interjected Emily, "I was expecting something else. Something more... I don't know. Explosions. Monsters attacking. A big mean man chasing us, like that skeleton guy that chased Grace when she was here before. Something. You said the Murk would not be happy with us. That it might try to kill us. But it's just more blackness."

"Ah. Yes. And here, without your guidebook, you three look to me as the expert."

"Well, that and the fact that you act like one."

Mihos closed his eyes, leaving them with no reference points at all.

"I just mean..." added Iain, worrying that he'd pushed too far.

"Shush," said Mihos, still not opening his eyes. The three kids, and presumably Dennis, waited for what felt like a whole minute. Then Mihos spoke again. "I apologize for that," he said softly. "Perhaps I know less than I thought I did."

"So you don't-" said Emily.

"-wish to discuss this any further," said Mihos, cutting her off. He opened his eyes. "Grace," he said, "I was basing my metaphor on my previous, but quite limited, experience with Murks. My rescue of you three was only my second time inside one of these black beasts. My first experience was many centuries ago, in monkey years, and in a very different lifeline. Murks are rare, you see. They are created beings, and few venture to use them. So while I have an idea of how to pass through this one, and even made a map based on my best guesses, I am less certain of myself than I might have... ahem... seemed." Mihos stopped, then spoke again to Iain. "You satisfied, boy?" he asked.

"I-" started Iain.

"But I do know this, Emily," he continued, cutting Iain off. "Monsters? Mean men? Explosions? I don't think that Murks work that way. Ultimately, I can think of few ends, few situations, few deaths that would be worse than being trapped forever in this disembodied dark. Were it not for my cat's eyes, I fear you would all soon be mad."

The four of them fell silent at Mihos' words, none of them able to argue his point. Whatever this was, it felt horrible, and madness *did* feel right around the corner. The eyes of the Son of Bast were the only things keeping them sane.

They waited in silence. Time passed. Or it didn't.

"Here door," said a voice in the blackness.

Mihos blinked his eyes. Nobody said a thing. This voice was new. Hesitant, yes, but steady and very close. It was an older voice. Wiser. Heavier with authority. A voice that seemed to know the way to proceed.

"Who's that?" demanded Iain at last, feeling both protective and helpless.

After a moment, the voice spoke again. "Dennis," said Dennis.

9.6

Cole stepped quietly onto the deck, hoping he wouldn't wake anyone. He needed time alone. He scanned the sky, the water, and the distant islands floating in the morning fog. He thought about his children, gone off with Alice in an alien craft, and maybe headed to Squirrel Island as well. Perhaps already there. A frown crossed his face like the shadow of a crow. He hadn't really been there for the kids. Not with these gut-wrenching "hops." Not with the rage and panic that had consumed him since they took Linda. He put a hand to his nervous stomach. The kids are strong. He knew that. They'd lived through times that had hardened them all. But he still worried. They were his children. They were all that was left of their mother, Ruth. Worry was in the blood.

But perhaps today he could make up for his negligence. He imagined Alice and his kids, landing on Squirrel Island in the distance. He was headed there to help them find her. He studied the tiny white blob he could see through the trees, wondering if it was the cottage. Wondering what sort of prison were they all trying to break in *to*? Who would they find there? The military, surely. The doctors. But more than that? Those shadowy figures that ran things from behind the scenes? Cole did not know *who* had stolen his best friend away. He intended to find out, and take care of his children in the bargain.

He'd gone on a hop during the night. It felt like he'd taken a trip to the future. Linda had not been there, in that time and place. He was with some other woman. Cole shook his head. He could not conceive of the sequence of events that could ever result in such an end.

But perhaps that's what Annabelle had been pointing to. He was supposed to *stop his greatest love from destroying the human race*. That's what she'd told him. Cole's teeth ground together as he stared out over the water. What a head-trip to put on him. What a curse, and damn her for speaking it. Already he could feel the words eating away at his soul.

The morning sun was rising behind Squirrel Island, sparkling on the waves, making it difficult for Cole to see. He imagined Linda in her room in the facility they'd built for her. What are you up to out there, sweetheart? Who has you captive, and what are they telling you? Annabelle's warning about her destroying the human race was absurd. Linda had done nothing but work *for* the human race. There wasn't any part of her that could cause such great destruction. Nothing.

A knock sounded on his bedroom door and Cole stepped back into his room, sliding the deck door closed before answering. "Yes?" he called out.

"It's Ken," came the reply. "Are you awake?"

"I am," said Cole, walking over to open the door.

Ken smiled. "Morning, Stranger," he said. "We've got a crew ready to roll and people setting up at Pig Cove. We can head out as soon as you're ready. Breakfast?"

Cole nodded. The mission terrified him. Breakfast would be good.

9.7

The underground facility in which William had left Linda had turned out to be fairly close to the "lobster tank" that held her body. Linda gazed out over the Martian plain William called "Rumi's Field." She could see the container gleaming in the distance. But she had no need to examine it again. She'd already done that. And the Fisherman was gone now. She wanted to use this time to explore on her own.

But, Jesus, how far could she go? She looked up to the sky, half expecting to find William hovering directly overhead. You tie me down with gravity? And then leave me alone in an underground prison? Really? Her fists clenched and relaxed and clenched again. She felt chained to the ground. There'd be no flying. No blinking. No zipping about the galaxy. It'd take her hours, or days, just to reach the nearest mountain.

She peered again at her naked body, tiny and vulnerable in the vast expanse. The whole set up was so surreal she could hardly believe it. It occurred to her that perhaps belief was the problem. Maybe she wasn't stuck. Maybe what held her fast was the heaviness of belief. The easiest way to control her - and William was certainly trying to do that - would be with words. All he had to do was just *tell* her something and darned if she didn't accept it. And if she was convinced that something wasn't possible, then she wouldn't even think to test it, would she?

The truth was that she didn't really know what the rules were now. How could she, when William kept changing them? She had assumed, down in that underground corridor, that because she felt bound by gravity, because she did not sink through the floor, because she could feel the cold hard stone underfoot, that she would have to turn the ship's wheel to open that door. But she'd been able to pass right through it like it was nothing.

So what else could she do?

William had told her that she was confined to Mars. And her previous attempt to escape back home had seemed to confirm that: she'd been stopped by an invisible barrier. But that was then. The Fisherman was obviously trying to teach her something with his series of examples and object lessons. And he was no doubt testing her. He needed her to act in the world in a way he could not. He wanted her to oversee the depopulation of the planet. So he was trying to forge her into the instrument of his will. Make her strong and smart and resolute. Or something.

Linda scanned the sky. Maybe she had more power here than she'd been led to believe. She imagined herself leaping upward from the Martian surface, reaching the barrier, and bursting through it. She imagined the barrier breaking apart like shards of glass. And she saw herself journey instantly back to her home. Linda glanced one last time at the lobster tank, noting how her body and her spirit were in similar situations. A tiny smile crept onto her face. Nothing here is by accident, is it William? You've got it all planned out. This moment is a test, and you're waiting to see how I do.

With love and longing swelling in her heart, Linda put all of her focus and attention on Cole's vibratory pattern. In an instant, she was at his side, back on Earth. If there'd been a barrier, she'd passed right through it. If it had been a test, she had passed it.

9.8

Mary screwed the top back onto the peanut butter jar and placed it in its spot in the cupboard, label facing outward. Then she pulled it back down and loosened the lid just a bit before replacing it. Danny would be up soon, and he'd want something to eat, and he wouldn't be able to open the jar if she screwed it down tight like Daddy demanded. She'd be back home long before the old man returned. She could retighten the lid then.

It didn't matter. It never did. Her father would find his reasons, no matter what she did. Mary grabbed some coins from the sock she used as a hiding place and stuffed them into her pocket. Enough to buy a Coke, at least. And D'Neal would give her one of those egg sandwich things. He always did when she promised to meet him after he got off work. That would be nice. The peanut butter never lasted very long.

Her chores were already done, so she'd have lots of time for D'Neal. She was glad of that. The pieces all seemed to fit together, just like she'd planned. She had one day a week that didn't feel just totally batshit crazy. She wanted to enjoy it.

Mary checked her watch, grabbed her tattered sci-fi paperback, and headed out the door, down the dingy hallway, through the sparsely furnished living room, and out the front door. To sunshine. To sanity. To freedom. She felt bad, leaving Danny alone. But he had his cartoons and his comic books and his Matchbox cars. Their father was off on his weekly. Danny would be okay. Maybe D'Neal would give her two of those sandwiches. She could bring one back for her brother. He'd like that.

Mary glanced back at their tiny shitbox house, sitting on a street packed full of shitbox houses. Ticky tacky, like the song said. But hers was different. In her house there lived a madman.

The morning was cool and still, but already she could feel the warmth of the day rising in the air. Danny would have to wait. Her father would have to wait. This was Saturday: Mary's self-proclaimed "day off." She was going to make the best of it.

Mary hurried along the sidewalk, heading into town.

9.9

Linda stared at her husband and shook her head. What was Cole doing, standing on the shore, looking out over the water? And who were all of those people beside him? With her body still on the surface of Mars, Linda felt the frustration of the ghost: able to move about in the physical realm and see what was going on, and yet utterly unable to have an effect there, or to make herself heard.

Cole was extremely worried about the kids. She could feel the emotions emanating from him like heat from a wood stove. So Linda attempted to blink again, this time focusing on Grace's pattern, with whom she felt the strongest connection. But she could not find Grace anywhere. Neither could she find Emily or Iain. In a panic to learn what was going on, Linda tried to focus on Mary's pattern, then Keeley's, only to fail each time. Finally she keyed in on Ness and, finding her old friend, jumped instantly to Augusta. She was horrified by what she found: Ness, sitting and watching over the bodies of the children, bodies which were still healthy and alive, but bodies from which their essential selves were gone missing! What the hell was going on?

She blinked back to Cole. His attention was out on the water, so Linda followed his gaze. He was staring at Squirrel Island. Of course. As far as he knew, that was where she was being held, sick with the alien flu. He must be trying to get to her. She blinked again, focusing on her felt memory of her old getaway. In an instant, she was standing on her cottage's front porch.

Linda hadn't been here since she and Cole and the kids had spent a single night, not long after moving to Maine. One visit was all she'd been able to spare from the pressing demands of her job, and, sadly, she'd been glad of it. The cottage was where her old friend, Fred, had been brutally murdered by Agent Rice. The place had felt haunted. She hadn't wanted to come back.

Linda glanced back toward the mainland, noting the tall military fencing at her property line. She turned to face her front door. There would be answers inside. She stepped through the door and walked from room to room, inspecting each in turn, searching for clues. Apart from some uniforms and personal articles in the upstairs bedroom, three bottles of liquor in the fridge, and a filthy cat bowl by the sliding glass door - not to mention the fact that her dining room had been turned into an office, with a soldier there now, typing happily away - her cabin looked much as it had the last time she'd visited.

She shook her head. This was not what she'd expected. Then she remembered the hidden elite's propensity for burying their secrets underground. She looked down at the floor. That's where her answers would be: beneath the cabin.

But how to get there in her present state? However it was that William had "tuned" her astral body, it made her a strangely limited ghost back here on Earth. While she could pass through doors and walls, she seemed unable to simply drop through floors. She glanced at the typing soldier. There was definitely something going on here. There had to be a way to find out what. She passed the soldier like the ghost she was and stepped into the kitchen, then through to the hallway. There, around the corner and past the bath: a new entranceway that opened to the back yard. She followed the hallway and stepped outside.

Not far from the door was a new concrete staircase that took her down to a basement she'd never had. At the bottom was a metal door with a red stencil: a stylized Earth inside a red oval. She passed through the heavy steel door, walked down another set of steps, and took a short hallway that ended at a set of double doors.

Here. This was it. She stepped into a brightly lit hallway: concrete floors and white tile walls and ceilings. She started forward. The corridor turned and turned and turned again, wrapping around itself in a large rectangle, with gray metal doors on either side, most of them closed, and most of them leading to office spaces, some of which were occupied by soldiers of various rank. It was uncannily like the facility she and Obie had explored in Ottawa, where they'd found Cole's dead body in the wreckage of an airplane. Linda breathed deeply, marveling at the size of the place. They had to have built this since her last visit. Easy enough to keep the secret when she never asked to go there.

Linda found another stairway and descended another level. This one was divided into larger rooms filled with computer stations and cubicles. It must be early morning here, she thought. There were only a few people present, drinking coffee and peering blearily into their computer screens. Linda stood behind one of them and watched him work. On his screen was a close-up of her face. She looked haggard and sick, her skin blotched and stained with that red rash. The man was using his finger to add tiny purple spots just underneath her eyes.

She returned to the staircase and descended another story. This third level was dimly lit and seemed to be uninhabited. There were no doors on the outer walls of the rectangular corridor. And there were only two doors on the inner walls, one directly opposite the other. She passed through the first to find a medical laboratory, complete with a surgical suite. She passed through the second to find an empty room, the wall opposite the door made of glass. A viewing room. Beyond the glass, she saw her own body, lying naked and still on a pedestal.

Slowly, stunned with disbelief, Linda passed through the glass wall and approached her inert form. Save for the clear glass box, which was missing here, she was looking at an exact replica of the body she'd seen on the surface of Mars. She looked down at her sleeping face, healthy and unblemished. She had no idea how this could be. She reached out to touch her unconscious self. Her hand was trembling with rage. "You bastard!" she spat, as if William could hear her.

A voice behind her cleared its throat. "Perhaps," it said.

Linda whirled to find the Fisherman, standing in the corner. "Good morning, Madam," he said cheerily.

"You can see me?" said Linda, confused.

"Time you and I got back to work," he answered, ignoring her question. In an instant, they were standing face to face in the desert Martian plain called Rumi's Field.

9.10

"You can talk?" cried Grace into the darkness. "Since when can you talk?"

"Dunno," said Dennis. "Never... tried. Before. Didn't think..."

Mihos closed his eyes, extinguishing the only light they had, drawing attention back to himself. "Yes," he said after a long pause. He opened his eyes again. "Talking dogs are always good for a laugh. No doubt your little pooch can ride a unicycle here as well. But we were talking about-"

"You said something about a door?" asked Iain, cutting Mihos off.

Mihos did not say anything.

"Door," agreed Dennis. "Here."

They waited in black silence for Dennis to continue, but that seemed to be all he had to say. "We don't know how to find you here," said Grace at last. "The only way we know directions at all is with Mihos's eyes. We can't-"

"Oh for crying out loud," said Mihos in a huff. The kids watched as Mihos seemed to move. It was impossible to tell if he actually did. After a moment the cat spoke again. "Okay, monkeys. I've got my paws on yer mutt. So where's this door, Scooby Doo?"

The three children waited. There was a muffled sound, then nothing, then Mihos again. "That's not a... Oh... wait. Got it." A small round hole appeared in the Murk, brightly lit from beyond, momentarily overloading their visual senses. The kids watched as Dennis nosed his way through, pushing up what looked like a plastic flap that covered the hole. Mihos followed him through, calling back to the kids over his shoulder as he did so. "Looks like Astro here found the way," he said. The kids followed them through the door.

In the light outside the Murk the five of them gathered, standing on the shoulder of a secondary road. Filling the sky on one side was the towering black wall, the Murk. On the other side, the Maine countryside stretched out for as far as they could see.

Mihos surveyed the scene, then shook his head and coughed. He turned to Dennis. "You found a doggy door that took us back outside?" he said. "What? You gotta pee?"

9.11

"It appears you are all doing a brilliant job here," said William cheerily as he stopped at the underground facility's security checkpoint. The sharp-eyed young lieutenant manning the station glanced up at his approach, then stood as the older man arrived to sign out on the clipboard. "I commend you all on your work," continued the Fisherman. "You seem to have the situation well under control."

"Thank you sir," said the lieutenant. "Shall I call Colonel McAfee?"

"Posh," said the Fisherman with a wave of the hand. "No need. I'm late and he has more important work, I presume. I'll just be off." William dotted the i's firmly and put down the pen, then pushed his way through the turnstile and scanner and headed toward the elevator. The lieutenant lifted an eyebrow as the older man passed but said nothing more.

A quick ride up one level brought William to the island's surface. He stepped out into the cottage's old garage, now serving as the facility's entrance lobby. He checked through another security station and hiked the short trail up to the landing pad, hidden away beyond the trees behind the cottage. The AB12's door slid open at his approach. The plankway descended. Not nearly as fluid and seamless as a Life-grown wok, to be sure, but it would do. Eventually their engineers would learn to think more gracefully inside the new paradigm.

William stepped onto the craft and slipped into the support field. The plankway and door retracted and the light gathered. In a moment, with only the slightest hum to give it away, the craft rose into the sky. Then it was gone.

9.12

Cole stood at the end of a long pier that stretched out over the rocks and mud. When Vince had told him that Ken Swathers had a place down near Pig Cove, Cole had envisioned a tiny cabin near the water. But this place was huge, well built, and richly furnished, just as Ken's other house in Southport had been. He'd assumed that Ken and his wife must be quite well-to-do, but that came from forgetting the sort of world he now lived in. "Not many people left out here, Stranger," said Ken with a smile when Cole commented on the place. "We kinda get our choice of places now. Not that we'd want to try to heat this monstrosity in the winter." It was obvious, when Ken explained it. Cole wondered if maybe he'd been a little too sheltered from the real world back inside the cordon. He felt like the Stranger indeed.

The morning sun warmed his face as he stared due East over the water. Squirrel Island was approximately half a mile away, backlit and shadowed. After taking office, and thinking that the Squirrel would serve as Linda's Presidential retreat, most of the south end of the island had been bought up by the government, with houses torn down and roads blocked off. The cottage itself was barely visible from where Cole stood, but Cole could make out that distinctive chimney topper he'd noted on his previous visit: it stood as tall and strong as a queen on a chess board. That's where Linda was.

Something rose from amongst the trees, extremely bright, a tiny sun. In a flash, it streaked away, leaving naught but a visual blur. Cole blinked his eyes to recalibrate his vision. Whatever it was, it was gone.

He shook his head and turned to make his way back up the catwalk and along the path through the woods. Stan and Ken and the others would be gathered at the house, waiting to take him down to Cape Harbor. The boat was ready. They even had a reporter from the Portland paper with them, another connection through their so-called "church." The plan was for Cole and a crew of six to loop around Squirrel Island as far to the east as they could, make their way to the north side, and then approach the island from the same direction as the old ferry. That would bring them to the island's north end and allow them to approach the cottage - and whatever military/medical establishment that now surrounded it - on foot, or in a vehicle, if they could find one. Cole was glad of the plan. Arriving on foot felt vastly preferable to arriving on their doorstep in a wobbly boat.

It was going to be another scorcher. Already Cole could feel the heat, even walking through the trees. He spotted a young maple beginning to bud and felt a bit of hope rise in his heart. This winter-summer one-two punch was causing untold damage to the state's trees and forests. Perhaps some would survive.

Up ahead, Stan and Ken stood at the tailgate of a pickup, laughing and talking. With him were the two young road wardens, Keith and Simon, a plump, balding older man whom Cole assumed was the reporter, and the young mandolin player, Marionette. His crew, it seemed. Ready to help him. Ready to help the Wayfaring Stranger, at least. He still had no idea if the two were one and the same.

9.13

Paul DuPont sat at his workstation. On one screen was an image of the Virtual Linda Travis. The day's Summit proceedings had not yet begun, so she was on hold, her eyes blank and lifeless as Paul waited for the live feeds to begin. On another screen was a news feed. Paul scrolled down through the headlines, noting in particular the stories about Greensleeves and the dreaded "alien flu." All in all, there was less panic in the streets than he would have predicted by this point. Perhaps the VLT was providing the bit of hope they'd predicted. And perhaps the virus's designers had been right, to create the Quietus as they had, giving the Sleepers such an easy, peaceful way out. They were probably ready to go, most of them, and good riddance. Much less destruction to property that way.

Not that that mattered. The Families were leaving soon, and the new owners wouldn't want it.

9.14

They sat together on the surface of Mars, the President of the United States and the mysterious Family member known as the Fisherman. They sat in two finely-crafted leather armchairs, deep reddish-brown in hue, with brass claw-and-ball feet digging into the dusty desert surface. They sat with no protection from the cold, the heat, the grit, the radiation, or the lack of breathable air. They sat as mirages, ghosts, images, reflections, habits of spirit, with bodies resting elsewhere while their essential selves could travel the Cosmos. They sat facing each other, seeming opponents and enemies, one holding the other captive, both determined to get what they needed. On William's face was a look of patient interest. On Linda's face was a thunderstorm of rage.

"You cannot do this, William!" she said again, her voice tight with fury. She leaned forward in her chair, hoping to force her words into him. "You want me to love you? Well this is *not* the way to do it. Tell me what's going on with Cole and the kids. Tell me what in the bloody hell my body is doing lying in some underground lab beneath my cottage. I've had it, William. You lied to me. You're keeping me prisoner. I want it to stop. I want to go home." Linda slumped back in her chair.

"Yes," said William evenly.

Linda glared.

William waited.

"Yes what?" said the President at last.

William nodded slightly. "Yes it's time to more clearly tell you what's going on," he said. "Yes I need to do so as efficiently as I can." He looked up and scanned the Martian sky, as if searching for their home planet. He returned his gaze to Linda. "Things are moving quickly back on Earth."

Linda stood and looked down at the Fisherman. "So let me go home and deal with them, William," she said, her eyes pleading. "The kids..." She glanced at the sky in the direction the Fisherman had just looked. "They need me."

William raised an eyebrow. "Then we'd better hurry," he said. "Shall we begin?"

Linda's eyes flashed with anger. "I want to go now," she said, her voice a low growl.

William gestured for her to sit. Linda shook her head in frustration, then sat lightly on the edge of her armchair, leaning forward, poised to stand again as though she might make a run for it. Or attack him. The Fisherman watched Linda with interest, his face open and curious. He seemed neither afraid nor perturbed by her anger. After a moment Linda turned her gaze to the ground.

William took a long, resonant breath and spoke again. "You Americans have the phrase 'half-cocked,'" he said evenly. "As do the British. I'm sure you know it."

Linda did not respond.

"To go off 'half-cocked' is to act prematurely and without a plan, and ultimately, to fail due to that lack of preparation."

Linda glanced up at William but did not speak.

"I'm sure you remember what happened the last time you went off half-cocked, Madam. People near and dear to us lost their lives, did they not? And others simply vanished."

Linda looked down at her lap. "And your Plan got messed up," she muttered.

"Indeed," said the Fisherman. "And while we have yet to determine whether that will ultimately prove to have been for good or ill, we in The Families have a strong tendency to stick to the path we've chosen."

Linda looked back up at William.

"So you need to understand, Madam: you are not yet ready to be released. You are being prepared, so that you, as our agent, will function properly. There will be no sneaking away from Mary Hayes this time around, I'm afraid, no matter how much you might wish for it. Do you understand?"

"But the children..." said Linda. Her voice trailed off, as though she knew there was nothing more to say in the face of the Fisherman's resolve.

"There's nothing you can do for them there that is not already being done," said William. "Your work is here. Complete that work and then you may go home."

"So how did I get to Earth, then?" demanded Linda, changing the topic in search of sense of control. "You said I couldn't but I did. And how did you know I'd be there?"

The Fisherman relaxed back in his chair. "I've been working with human beings for a very long time, Madam," he said. "And I know where this is going. I needed to see what you're capable of figuring out on your own, and I needed you to see for yourself what's at stake now."

9.15

"Cats use eyes," explained Dennis. "Dogs nose."

"For the love of all that's holy and good," muttered Mihos. He sat off to the side as the kids crowded around their old dog, laughing and petting him and asking questions. None of them seemed to hear the cat's words. Mihos licked his paws.

"So do you have a different plan we should follow?" asked Grace of her dog. Dennis was leaning against her leg and she was scratching his rear, which caused his right leg to jerk uncontrollably, scattering the gravel underfoot. Dennis seemed to suffer no loss of dignity in the exchange.

Dennis looked up to Grace as though she were a goddess. "Follow smells," he said.

Mihos cleared his throat loudly and the kids turned to regard him. "If we follow Old Yeller's plan," he asked dryly, "are we not destined to end up either at a fire hydrant or another dog's butt?"

"Don't be silly," scolded Emily. "Dennis knows what we're trying to accomplish."

"Oh," said Mihos, returning his attention to his rear paws. "Right. I forgot. Whippet. Whippet good. Got it."

Iain leaned down to add to the petting. "So how do we follow the smells?" he asked.

Dennis closed his eyes in bliss, speaking softly and slowly, as the ecstasy allowed. "Murk," he said. "Inside. I could smell. Fresh air. Ocean. I smell."

"You do at that," offered Mihos, but nobody paid him any mind.

"So that means..." said Emily, trying to draw Dennis out.

"Murk... has... holes..." said Dennis through the bliss.

"And you can find your way through them?" asked Iain.

Dennis opened one eye a tiny bit. "Follow smell," he said again. "Follow ocean. Smell gets through."

The three kids turned to Mihos, wondering what this cat, who lived in this realm, thought of Dennis's plan. Mihos assumed a regal, Egyptian pose, his chin out, his face serene. He studied the wall of Murk towering over them, then returned his attention to the kids. "There must have been something wrong with my map," he said at last. "So... yeah. Sure. Let's give the dog a bone and see what he can do. I'm smart enough to use every tool at my disposal." Mihos closed his eyes and licked his paws some more. Didn't matter that the stupid dog came up with the plan, now, did it? They still turned to Mihos to lead the way.

The cat sighed, then stepped a bit closer to Dennis. "C'mon, Bandit. Jonny and Hadji are ready! Let's go find this President Linda monkey! Okay? Find her? Find her!!? There's a good boy." He turned to the kids. "My eyes. His nose. Shouldn't be a problem."

Dennis reached out and licked Mihos on the face again, then started off. The rest of them followed. Even Mihos.

9.16

The President sat back in her chair and crossed her arms in front of her chest. "Start by telling me what has happened to the children."

William looked down at his hands and took a long breath. "Their bodies, as you saw, are quite well," he said, examining his fingernails. "But their conscious selves have chosen to leave their bodies and go off in search of their mother." He looked up at Linda. "You," he said.

Linda raised an eyebrow.

"As I told you earlier, they'd begun to unravel the ruse of your virtual doppelganger and were anxious to explore that mystery. Some other players in the game unexpectedly stepped in and helped them on their way. The children are, as far as I know, now exploring the Astral realm in an attempt to make contact with you, while their bodies are being guarded back in Augusta. Just as you're here, speaking with me, while your body lies safely on the surface of Mars."

"Right. So there's that, too. I mean… what the hell, William? How can my body be on Mars *and* underneath my cottage at the same time?

The Fisherman nodded. "It was important that we do our work without alarming your opponents, Madam. That required that I leave behind a copy."

"You're saying that was a fake I saw?"

"Yes."

Linda sat for a moment and breathed, her head wandering back and forth in disbelief, her eyes tight with anger. She didn't know what to trust anymore. And there were more important matters. "But they can't do that, can they?" asked Linda after a few moments.

"Who can't do what, Madam?"

"The children can't make contact with me, William. Like you said. Because I'm here with you, kept under lock and key."

The Fisherman shook his head. "So it would seem," he said.

"That's all you have to say?" asked Linda. Her words were sharp and fierce.

"Believe it or not, Madam," said William, "I am not in control of everyone and everything." He reached up and smoothed his ruffled white hair.

Linda opened her mouth to reply but then bit it off. She took a couple of long, even breaths to calm her furious heart, all the while staring into the Fisherman's eyes. "Can you promise me that they'll be safe?" she asked at last.

William shook his head. "I believe their bodies to be in safe hands at this time," he said evenly. "But as for their conscious selves, I cannot say what adventures they may find, or how it will turn out for them. I trust that those who have stepped in to help them are not of evil intent, and are interested, ultimately, in the same thing I am interested in. Beyond that, I cannot say, nor will I release you such that you can go off and try to save them from their choices. As I have said, the needs of this time are great. They outweigh the needs of yourself or your children. Whether you agree with me or not, I believe that, when we are finished here, you will at least understand why I say this." The Fisherman's eyes softened as the corners of his mouth twitched up, a wistful smile that conveyed a deep hopefulness on his part, that he might be understood.

"You're playing word games, William," said Linda. "Who was it that stepped in to help them?"

The Fisherman closed his eyes and inhaled deeply, as though fighting a natural inclination to withhold information. After a moment, he nodded slightly and looked at Linda. "I believe you know her as Alice," he said with a meager smile.

Linda's eyes widened at that bit of news. She had no idea what to make of it, or what it meant. Linda knew Alice to be a good soul. She'd live with the little hybrid long enough to feel that in her gut. But Alice had left them three years ago and was off elsewhere in the universe, as far as Linda knew. If she was back, then who else was back? Spud? Alice's mother, Bob? And could Alice be trusted to keep the kids from harm? She was just a little girl.

Linda sat for a long time just staring at William, one eyebrow raised slightly as though she could hardly believe what she was hearing. At last she exhaled loudly. "We'd best get to it then," she said quietly.

William nodded again. "Indeed," he said.

9.17

The board Ted placed on the table was no longer a Scrabble board. This one was old, multi-colored, with cartoon drawings of animals and strange creatures and numbered paths connecting various places. "Uncle Wiggily," said Ted in a low, awed voice.

Carl bent forward to examine it, then looked up at the other. "You know this game, Ted?"

Ted nodded. "Played it as a kid. Had a great aunt with an old wooden box full of toys. This game was in there." Ted picked up the bag that had held Scrabble tiles and pulled out a deck of small, tattered cards and half a dozen painted wooden markers. "Looks like it's all here," he said.

"Wibble Wobble Duck Pond, Ted?" said Carl, reading from the board. "Aren't we a bit old for this?" Carl smiled.

Ted ignored Carl's question and just stared at the board, his eyes darting from place to place and character to character and all around. Without taking his eyes off the board he placed the deck of cards on the table, then chose the red marker and placed it gently on a picture of a rabbit standing in front of a cottage.

"Uncle Wiggily's Bungalow," read Carl.

"That's where we start," said Ted, glancing up to meet Carl's gaze. A tiny flash of smile flickering across his face.

Carl chose the blue marker and placed it next to Ted's. "You go first, Ted," he said. His tone was kind and gentle.

Ted leaned forward and picked up the top card.

Chapter Ø Ten

10.1

Gabrielle was jostled awake by the lurching of the bus as its brakes started to hiss. Peering through the front windshield, she saw a border crossing sign: Beecher Falls Station. Stretching into the distance on either side of the station, following the lay of the land, was a line of tall, razor-wired fencing. They were about to enter the United States.

Though the border guards looked big and dark and mean, Gabrielle had no reason to expect trouble. She'd shown her passport to the bus driver before they'd left Montreal, and had been passed through without question. Since the Crash, buses like this were used primarily for troop transport and official or corporate business travel, and she stood out like a sore thumb amidst the uniformed soldiers and well-dressed movers and shakers who sat all around her, she in her college attire and scarves and backpack. But it wasn't illegal for her to be on this bus. It was still open to the public. There was even an older couple three rows ahead of her, obviously on holiday. She was fine.

Images flashed in Gabrielle's mind as the bus slowed. Oncoming headlights. An overturned white van. Zacharael's dead body splayed out in the middle of the road. Gabrielle understood that these were after-images from the long vision Zacharael had given her while he'd been in her head. Their sharing of minds. But the flashes faded quickly, and Gabrielle was glad to be rid of them. She had to get her belongings back into her backpack.

They slowed behind a row of three vehicles, two of them military. One of the border patrolmen waved their bus into another lane closer to the station. The driver steered them awkwardly to the right and came to a stop. Directly outside the bus door stood a newly installed sign with bold black letters on a yellow background, apologizing for delays in processing due to the threat of the alien flu, Greensleeves.

Gabrielle closed her eyes and breathed slowly and deeply. Another image flashed in her mind, this one of the same white van, but this time from overhead. Sitting behind the wheel, she knew, as though she could see right through the van's roof, was a large, bearded Frenchman. Beside him, in the passenger seat, sat the American President's husband. Another flash, this of a small black cube hurtling through the air. Then the flashes were gone.

Gabrielle opened her eyes. The bus driver opened his door and stepped down off the bus to confer with a border patrolman. Then he stepped back onto the bus. Gabrielle could feel the heat from the parking lot push in behind him, overpowering the air conditioning. "They're ready for you in Customs," the driver told them. He stepped back down to open the luggage bays.

The driver had explained how customs would work a half-hour out from the border crossing. Passengers would step off the bus, bring all of their personal belongings with them, grab any luggage they had stored underneath, then make their way into the Customs office. There they would present their documentation, answer a few questions, and submit their bags and belongings to be scanned. Next they would step into the scanners themselves, including a secondary scanner, newly installed, which would screen for the presence of infectious diseases.

After passing through the scanners, they could use the facilities before re-boarding. The driver had told them they should consume any food they'd brought along with them before going through customs, as it would otherwise be confiscated. The entire process would take approximately thirty minutes, even with the extra screening for Greensleeves, since there were so few civilian passengers these days. The customs procedure for the soldiers was separate and much more streamlined.

Gabrielle stood and waited for the rows in front of her to clear. She grabbed her backpack and her water bottle and headed down the aisle. At the top of the steps she caught the eye of the first of two border patrolmen, a thin, wiry young man with a shaved head and large nose who was sweating profusely in the heat. Smiling, she stepped off the bus, glanced up at the hot sun, and followed the others to the Customs office. She flashed for a moment on a vision of a tall, red-haired man striding quickly and purposefully toward her, and she whirled to face the Canadian station across the way, a shudder rippling through her body. It was striking to her, how much that man in the vision looked like Zacharael. And yet they were not the same person.

A soldier opened the door for her as she approached the station. She thanked him and entered the building. It was fairly new, all hard counters and plastic cubicles and overhead fluorescent lighting and, thankfully, air-conditioned. Adjusting her backpack on her shoulder, she took her place in line behind the other travelers, passport in hand. She waited, closing her eyes to rest them. They felt cracked and dry from the early departure and the long ride.

Just when it was her turn to approach the first checkpoint, the wiry young man from outside stepped around the corner and approached her, his hand outstretched to take her passport. "Please step this way, Miss," he said, his tone even and firm. Gabrielle followed.

"I told you," said Gabrielle, her eyes steely with defiance, "I'm meeting my father in Augusta." She wriggled a bit in the hard plastic chair they'd pointed her to, but could not get comfortable. She looked down at her hands in her lap. It hadn't occurred to her that she'd be questioned about her plans. It should have, but it hadn't. So she'd had to concoct a cover story in the time it had taken her to walk back to the office in which she now sat.

"And your father is...?" asked the hawk-faced Customs Officer sitting behind the desk. His tag said "Devons." He had the air of retired military, his graying hair as short and as bristly as his personality.

"Guy Legrand. He's a respected MP in Ottawa. He's down in-"

"In Augusta, Maine, right now, waiting for you. Yes. You said. And why is he in Augusta, Miss? There are no scheduled meetings or gatherings there, and certainly he has no business with the President at this time."

"My father's a relative. And I... I met her once too. The President? She's my cousin or something. And he wanted to stop by and leave a gift for her. Some maple syrup. A gift. On his way back home from a meeting in New York." Gabrielle's heart was pounding. She had no idea if she was even making sense.

The Customs Officer confirmed that she was not. "So, then, you're traveling by bus from Montreal to Augusta to meet your father, who's on his way back to Montreal? I'm afraid that doesn't make much sense, Miss. This is not a safe world for a young lady to go joyriding in, even for a play date with Daddy."

Gabrielle opened her mouth to respond, then flashed on the moment again: the moment in the hallway with the President, the moment from the future that had already happened, the moment Zacharael had seared into her consciousness. It didn't matter that her heart was pounding. It didn't matter what she said. That moment would happen, no matter what. She took a breath and spoke. "So why did you pick me out of the line?" she asked.

Officer Devons, raised an eyebrow. "Excuse me?" he said, his eyes blinking.

"I was just another passenger on that bus. I'd already been passed through with my documents in Montreal. So why are you picking on me? Is it because I'm young, Officer Devons? Because I'm pretty?" Gabrielle smiled coyly and held his gaze.

Devons inhaled slowly, one eyebrow raised, as if Gabrielle's suggestion was beyond his comprehension. "It's because, Miss," he said slowly, "when you passed through our exterior scanners, your iDent chip alerted our computers." He leaned forward in his chair to read his laptop screen. "'F 12,' it says." He looked at Gabrielle. "That makes you my business. Do you understand?" Devons' voice had grown hard and cold as he spoke.

"And what does 'F 12' mean, Officer?" asked Gabrielle.

"It means we hold you here until we receive further instructions."

Gabrielle sat back and sighed. The iDent chip. So that was it. Family members who were embedded in the common world had been required to get one. Having a chip was supposed to make it easier for them to fit in and move around without anybody asking questions. Not that they got the same chips the Sleepers got. Those chips, commonly known as iDents, carried not only identification information, but allowed for tracking, surveillance, and even some measure of control. Family members' chips carried identification information only. Unlike the Sleepers, members of The Families were not to be tracked, listened to, or controlled in any way.

It had never occurred to Gabrielle that she should worry about her chip. But apparently, after their last conversation, and her disappearance from Freemantle, her father had tagged her identity, so the scanners would watch for her. And find her. And catch her. The bastard.

So what would those "further instructions" be? What would Devons do once he received them? And what could Gabrielle do then? Her heart pounded in her chest as she considered the possibility of being taken into custody and remanded to the care of her loving parents. She thought about acting angry and entitled and petulant, like the spoiled daughter of a high-ranking official who was simply not at all used to such horrible treatment at the hands of mere functionaries. She almost demanded that she be released immediately. But again, the image, the moment, came to her mind unbidden, and she calmed back down.

"Perhaps it's not working," offered Gabrielle, helpfully.

Devons leaned back in his chair, raising an eyebrow. "Your iDent?" he asked. "Perhaps." He glanced toward the door, then back at Gabrielle. "In any event we'll know soon enough. Your passport checked out, but we've got a call into Peoria. And we're seeing if we can get eyes on your father in Augusta. Until then, I'm afraid you're going to have to-"

Customs Officer Devons stopped speaking when a soft knock sounded at his door. Another officer entered, stepped around to stand next to Devons, handed him a sheet of paper, and whispered into his ear. Devons read the note, then looked at Gabrielle. His face went pale. He placed the paper on his desk and closed his laptop. "I'm sorry to have kept you waiting, Ma'am," he said, offering his hand to shake hers. "Please. Enjoy the rest of your trip."

Acting on instinct rather than propriety, Gabrielle ignored Devons' offered hand and instead leaned forward to grab the piece of paper from his desk. She glanced at it quickly, then folded it and shoved it into her jacket pocket. She stood and, without a word, walked out of the office.

Her heart pounded wildly against her ribs as she picked up her pack at the checkpoint and made her way back to the waiting bus. But it wasn't fear this time. It was glee. Power. Purpose. Resolve. The vision Zacharael had shown her, the moment with the President, was real. It pulled her toward it. Ever forward. And it appeared that it could not be stopped.

There was only one question in her mind now. It was that piece of paper. It said "Sinclair. Untouchable. AB Dispatched." "Sinclair" she knew. That was her real name. "Untouchable" must have to do with her being a Family member. So whomever they'd contacted in "Peoria" had known who she really was. And it seemed that The Families, or her father, didn't want the bozos at the customs office handling her. Maybe being part of The Families wasn't all bad after all. Gabrielle stepped back onto the bus and took her seat.

The question that remained was this: what was an "AB"? And what did it mean that it had been "Dispatched"?

10.2

William considered Linda closely as the dust twisted and blew around them. The sky had turned to daylight, a pinkish, washed-out white that made the distant mountains difficult to discern. He planted his elbows on his thighs, clasped his hands, and rested his chin on his thumbs. He took a deep breath. "It is difficult to know where to begin," he said at last, sighing heavily.

Linda nodded. "Maybe if you just start talking, it'll get the ball rolling."

"Maybe" said the Fisherman. He wrinkled his nose. "Let's see… " He closed his eyes for a moment to think, then looked at Linda. "It seems like I have a number of things to tell you," he continued. "I need to explain who The Families are and what they - we - are up to." He counted off on his fingers. "I need to explain what I can of the aliens and their interests and intentions. And I need to explain the quandary we and they now find ourselves in." He stopped and smiled slightly.

Leaning forward, Linda matched the Fisherman's pose, elbows on her knees. "It's good to have an outline," she said evenly. "But haven't we already touched upon your so-called 'quandary'?"

"Madam?" said William.

"Well, you've said it. The Earth's planetary ecosystem, and the human species, is now circling the drain, right? In part because I failed to save the world, as you've so kindly pointed out."

William raised a hand as if to interrupt or explain.

"And you Family guys," continued Linda, "or the aliens, or whomever the hell, have devised a way to quickly wipe out vast swaths of the human population, which you think might be enough to stave off a full-scale planetary extinction event. And *your* task is to convince me to pull the switch." She sat back in her chair and brushed at her sleeves. "Does that about sum it up, chief?"

The Fisherman pushed back into his chair and crossed his legs. "You are mistaken in two respects, Madam," he said, shaking his head. "First, this is not about me convincing you to 'pull the switch,' as you say. As I said before, there is a choice to be made in the matter, and that choice has been given to you to make. But one cannot make a real choice unless one has been freed of one's own limiting stories and assumptions. It is the creation of that freedom which I am here to facilitate. Convincing you would take away your freedom, not increase it."

Linda pulled her feet up underneath her bottom and rubbed at her eyes. "Okay," she said after a moment. "And the second mistake?"

William flashed his eyebrows. "Is thinking that you can rationally determine which choice will achieve the result you wish to see. The fact is, none of us, neither my colleagues nor the aliens with whom we've aligned, know, or can know, how Earth's future will or should play out. This is why the choice has been given to you, as the representative for your species. We are not qualified to speak for humanity."

"Surely you must know more than I, William."

"All we know is that, on its current trajectory, the future holds a high probability for the end of human life on the physical Earth, and the extinction of the vast majority of other living species. We also see an alternative path, one which might avert a significant portion of the devastation, and which could achieve for humanity as a whole the cosmic belonging they have long sought. And we see the possibility that, should you fail to deal with the situation on your own, there may be other interested parties who will take action in your stead. Beyond that, I do not know how you should choose. I know only that the choice is yours, and that the choice requires a freedom of thought and feeling which you do not yet possess."

With a slight shake of his shoulders, the Fisherman relaxed back into his chair and put his hands on his lap. He stared at her, his gaze fierce and piercing, his chin slightly lifted. It felt to Linda like William harbored some measure of guilt or defensiveness about what he'd been tasked to achieve with her, and was pleading his case. She realized that she bore some of the responsibility for that, and made a mental note to drop the chiding tone. The fact was, she still knew too little, to judge fairly whether the Fisherman's actions were warranted or not. She could, for now, give him the benefit of the doubt, and leave her anger and judgment for some future time. Perhaps that would even speed things up.

A wave of openness passed through her. She could feel her whole being soften. She allowed a warm smile to bloom on her face and nodded gently. There was nothing to do, it seemed, but to proceed.

"So tell me about The Families," she said.

10.3

From the water, Squirrel Island looked at first glance like a peaceful vacation spot, though that notion was soon challenged. The island rose up from rocky beaches and ledges, and was covered with browning pines and hardwoods still mostly leafless in the scorching spring heat. There were a few huge vacation homes dotting the shoreline, one of which had been burned to the ground, with only the brick chimney still standing. There was an old chapel, its steeple standing proudly in the morning sun, defying the forces of change that threatened to render it meaningless. And there was the Presidential compound, now sprawling across the island's southern end, surrounded by high prison fencing and dotted with squat block buildings, new roads, watch towers, radio towers, armored vehicles, and communications dishes.

Cole and his crew headed due east out of Cape Harbor on a fairly new fishing boat called *The Pokey Joker*. It was owned and skippered by a young man called Doobie who looked, to Cole, far too young to be operating a boat of this size. Accompanying Cole were Stan and four members of the Church of the Stranger: the local businessman Ken Swathers, the eager young helpers Simon and Keith, and the scarred and eye-patched young mandolin player, Marionette. Sitting in the stern, sick to his stomach, was a heavyset man named Steve Waymax, another church member and a reporter for the *Portland Rough Times*, who'd come up to chronicle the day's events.

There was little conversation as they sped eastward, keeping Squirrel Island on their port side as they pushed through the water. They steered northward when they reached Fisherman Island, hugging the shoreline in hopes of cutting down their profile. The synchronicity was not lost on Cole, who wondered if that mysterious phone caller from three years ago was still around, and what he might be up to. Reaching the north end of Fisherman Island, they crossed some choppy open water to the southern tip of a finger of mainland and a quiet spot called Card Cove. Crossing the mouth of another bay brought them to Spruce Point, and then into Boothbay Harbor, with the town of Boothbay Harbor visible on the north end.

All the while, Cole stood on the port side, both hands on the railing, scanning the jellyfish-laden waters and keeping a stern, watchful eye on Squirrel Island. For all he knew, there were eyes on him as well, binoculars and cameras and even satellites. Cole did not flinch from their gaze. The garbled voice on his phone replayed over and over in his mind. The whole point here was exposure. Cole *wanted* them to know he was coming.

But it was deeper than that. Cole felt deeply protective of Linda, who had become much more important to him than he'd ever expected. He did not want to lose her. And he was not going to be held hostage by his own fears. If he did not do whatever he could to protect his wife, life would not be worth living. They were going to have to put a bullet between his eyes to stop him. And that would not play well on the evening news.

Cole shook his head. He knew what he was up against. He knew that, whatever happened, "they" could make it look however they wanted it to look. And he knew that he and his ragtag band of do-gooders were going up against the powers of the secret state. Who was he kidding?

And yet he'd caught a bullet in mid-air. And there was fire in his hands. And there was help from unexpected quarters. Stan. Ken. These Church members. Even a young lady with an eyepatch. Cole inhaled deeply and exhaled loudly, trying to calm his anxious soul. They had Linda. That was the thing to focus on. They had Linda. He wanted her back. It felt crazy to his rational mind, what he was doing, but it also felt right and true.

The Pokey Joker pulled into a small marina in Boothbay Harbor just long enough to get more fuel, then put back out into the bay, this time heading south, straight for Squirrel Island. Cole moved around to the bow and faced into the breeze. Stan came and stood next to him. Together, they watched as the boat sped toward their destination.

10.4

The Colonel picked up the phone. "You got this?" It was the General. McAfee hadn't heard from him since he'd gone to ground, but he knew that voice anywhere.

"We've got eyes all over him," replied McAfee. "They'll turn him away at the pier. Should be a no-brainer, Sir."

"No-brainer is an appropriate euphemism for soldiers, Colonel. Make sure you're instructions are clear and complete." The General had never been one to mince words or make small talk.

"Yes, Sir," said McAfee. "Can I ask where-"

"You may not ask, Colonel. You may hang up now and discharge your duties."

"No need to worry, Sir," said McAfee.

"I'm not the one who needs to worry here, Colonel." The General fell silent but did not hang up.

McAfee waited, then cleared his throat and spoke. "Will it be soon, Sir?" he asked.

"Everything will be soon, Colonel," said the General. "And if I may... a piece of advice."

"Yessir?" said McAfee.

"Get your rain gear out," said the General. He hung up.

McAfee clicked off his phone and placed it on the counter. He'd have to speak with Osterman right away. Nicky jumped up and sniffed at the phone, then looked at his human. McAfee reached out and scratched the cat under the chin. "The General says we might have some rain, Nicky my boy," he said in a mock-serious tone, his face an overdrawn frown. "Do you have your galoshes?"

Nicky, embarrassed for the Colonel, closed his eyes and just enjoyed the scratching.

10.5

Mihos sat still, eyes closed, overwhelmed with sensation. Emily called back to him to keep up. The cat opened his eyes and did his best to follow. This wasn't like before. In fact, this wasn't like any place Mihos had ever visited. He'd seen some crazy shit in his nine lives, but he'd never been anywhere like this. Is this what dogs experience all the time? That would explain why they were so nuts. This level was insane.

Visually, it was a mess. No color to speak of, save for a faint, pastel tendril now and then. Otherwise, black and white and gray all over. But it was the corners and edges that really got to him. All pinched and squeezed. And everything was covered with patterns: shapes and squiggles and lines and grids, all just... buzzing. And the thing was, Mihos couldn't exert any control over it. In other layers and modes, he could switch things around at will: what he perceived, how he perceived it, things like that. Here, once they'd all followed Dennis into Doggyworld, they were stuck. It was like the tribe of Wolf had its own little amusement park here in the Astral, and once you bought a ticket, you were on the ride until it came to a full and complete stop. Please keep your paws inside the car at all times.

They were back inside the Murk now. Going through seemed to be the only way to get to where they were headed, so they'd formed a new plan with Dennis leading the way, and then plunged back in. And to be fair, which Mihos hated to do, Dennis seemed to be better at leading than he had been. The first time Mihos had saved the kids, they were right inside the Murk's leading edge and the Great Ones had been guiding him. His natural cat abilities allowed him to see just enough that he could make his way back out.

But that second time, on the flying carpet, well, perhaps he'd been a bit... arrogant. Or if not arrogant, then hopeful, maybe. He did okay at first, but this Murk was far more befuddling than he'd anticipated, and soon he was just as lost and blind as the kids. Whomever had built this damned thing, or summoned it, or whatever the hell you did to put a Murk in place, had built themselves a whopper. The Taj Mahal of Murks, right here in Small Town, USA.

Dennis must have slowed because Mihos had caught up with Emily. They were well inside the Murk now. Mihos knew that much. But they were not in the black. Dennis had been right. The Murk was full of holes, tiny, meandering tunnels winding their way like blood vessels through the big black beast. As long as they stayed in the holes, they could still see, as weird as seeing was here inside the canine perceptual field. Dennis led the way, his nose to the ground, the black and white, pinched and squeezed, rippling buzzing Maine countryside sliding past as they walked. The faint tendrils of color were scents, and Dennis was following them.

Mihos fell into line behind Emily, taking the rearguard position in case something bad tried to sneak up from behind. Exactly what he would do should something bad actually *appear* he was not at all clear about.

Mihos felt a stab of fear. He hoped that his metaphor was merely words, and that these little tunnels were not actually veins, taking them into the Murk's black heart.

10.6

The nurse drew the needle from Keeley's arm and swabbed her skin before applying a bandage. Keeley roused a bit, opened her eyes, yawned. Apparently she was still alive. That surprised her. She'd thought the alien flu would have killed her by now.

She smiled up at the nurse: a tall, thin man, his head shaven, his eyes fierce and golden. Beside him stood another nurse, a tiny woman with large, strangely-wide dark eyes. They both wore surgical masks and latex gloves. Keeley wanted to reach out and grasp them both and hold them tightly, such love she felt for them. But her arms were so weak, and it felt so grand to simply lie there and bask in her warm love and dozy contentment. She smiled as brightly as she could and hoped that that would convey her deep feelings.

The tall nurse turned and looked at the tiny nurse for a moment, then they both looked down at Keeley and lifted the corners of their mouths. "We are here for you," the man said, his voice even and gentle and strangely inflected. Keeley sighed and closed her eyes. That was a stupid thing for a nurse to say, she chuckled to herself, before falling back into restful slumber. Of course they were here for her. They were nurses.

But where was Mary?

10.7

Mary sat in a plastic booth in the back corner, drinking her orange soda as slowly as she could, reading her paperback, and watching D'Neal work the counter. He was so beautiful. His face just shone. And he made it a point to speak with every customer he had, laughing and joking and winking. The old ladies loved him. Maybe Mary loved him too. She could never be sure. The word 'love' had never really made any sense to her.

Daddy would be furious to learn that his daughter was seeing a black boy. But maybe that was the point. Or part of the point. Mostly the point was that D'Neal was kind to her. He thought she was smart. And pretty. And that felt like magic to Mary. When she looked in the mirror all she could see was how blotchy her skin was, and the tiny gap between her front teeth. That was when she didn't have bruises. When she had bruises, she did not go near the mirror at all.

D'Neal finished with a customer and glanced up to find Mary staring back at him. He winked and grinned. He'd told her he would save some of the throwaways for them. They'd stop by and give one to Danny, then head down to the fairgrounds and hang out for a while. There was a car show today or something. Lots of people. They could get lost in lots of people. Mary could feel safe with lots of people.

Another customer came in and Mary sent D'Neal back to work with an Imperial flourish of her hand and a giggle. Then she sipped at her drink and went back to her book. It was a tattered old thing she'd found out behind the school, a crazy story about aliens and the President of the United States, but Mary loved that sort of thing. Anything to take her away from the world she lived in.

Mary read, waiting for D'Neal's shift to end. She failed to notice, across the room, the tiny old man in the hooded robe sitting in the far corner booth. Every now and then he'd glance at Mary. Mostly his attention was on his food: little round hash brown things that he popped into his tiny slit of a mouth with strange, gray fingers.

10.8

"You and I first spoke almost three years ago," said the Fisherman. "Do you remember?"

"Of course." Linda sat leaning to one side, resting her elbow on the chair's padded arm. The winds had stopped and the dust had settled, leaving the Martian morning sky clear and crystalline.

William looked down and picked at his fingers. "At the time, you no doubt formed an opinion of me, I would venture. One of your enemies, no doubt. A member of the hidden elite, the wealthy, secretive rulers of the world. A 'one-percenter,' as some call us. A member of the Illuminati or some other secret cult. A reptilian overlord or Bilderberger or Satanist, even." He glanced up at Linda. "Am I right?"

Linda sighed and nodded. "Sure," she said. "I guess. I mean, as soon as I figured out who you were- when I first woke up in that lobster tank - I felt wary of you. Afraid. Angry." She gazed off in the distance for a few moments, then returned her attention to the Fisherman. "I went through an awful time with Agent Rice and the People, William. And I think of you and your 'Family' as the hidden group behind that organization. So it makes sense for me to be suspicious of you."

William smiled. "Of course," he said. "And your suspicions come not without reason. So let me shine my torch into this matter of 'secret rulers' and see if I can make some sense of it."

"Okay."

The Fisherman shifted in his chair and took a deep breath. "We can begin by looking at our modern global society and noting that leadership, governance, and control manifest as a number of layers. There's the public layer, comprised of those whom we have traditionally thought of as being in charge, and who largely operate out in the open. There's a more hidden layer, which operates behind the scenes to pursue more selfish goals of worldly wealth and power. And then there's what I call the secret layer, which is even further removed from the public eye, and which pursues a variety of what we might call more ideological or conspiratorial goals."

"Okay," said Linda. "And The Families are members of this secret layer?"

"We'll get to The Families soon, Madam."

"Got it."

The Fisherman shifted in his chair. "So, if we grant the existence of these layers, we can then observe that, over time, the hidden and secret layers of leadership and governance have grown in power and control at the expense of the public layer. This might be considered common knowledge these days." He looked pointedly at Linda. "Even you, as a powerful participant in the public layer, would surely agree that the old stories of selfless public servants working toward a better world for all no longer describe the reality of the situation."

Linda nodded slowly. "I guess I would say that, sure."

"Of course," said the Fisherman. "The hidden and secret layers of control have increased in size and dominance along an exponential curve, alongside such things as crime, poverty, oppression, war, and environmental destruction, all with roots reaching far back into antiquity, and all reaching a fever pitch in our present time. The hidden layer is focused on competition and winning. The secret layer is focused on breaking away from the mainstream culture and creating something else. Both can be seen as rational responses to increased population pressure and its attendant effects."

"Right," said Linda. "That makes sense. We used to live in what felt like a lush, roomy, resource-rich world, so we could think in terms of making a better future for everyone. We could do that out in the open. But now, it feels like we're living in a damaged, crowded, resource-scarce world, so we feel like we have to compete to get what we want and need. And that competition gets more and more fierce, more underhanded and illegal, and needs to go on behind the scenes."

'Yes," said William, nodding.

"But aren't those layers just two sides of the same group of people, William? I mean, I've known a great many politicians and business leaders in my day, and while they pretend to be selfless public servants operating out in the open when the cameras are pointed at them, they go right back to their greedy, power-grabbing ways when they're out of sight."

The Fisherman flashed his eyebrows. "I would say that you're spot on, Madam," he said. "A great many people operate in two or even all three of these layers at the same time."

Linda sighed heavily, her forehead deeply furrowed. She closed her eyes to think and breathe. "This hiding... " she said after a few moments, "it feels... I don't know... like contempt." She opened her eyes. "You know what I mean, William?"

The Fisherman nodded. "Indeed, Madam. By focusing on competition, members of the hidden layer created winners, and therefore losers. By breaking away into exclusive groups, members of the secret layer created insiders, and thus outsiders. And we all know about losers and outsiders, do we not? They're lesser beings in some way, readily identifiable as such, be it by income level, education level, skin color, ethnicity, intelligence, nationality, language, sexual preference, or the like. As population pressure, resource-scarcity, and the game of winning at the expense of others all increased, so did prejudice, contempt, and disgust."

Linda unfolded her legs and pushed herself to the edge of her chair. "So tell me, William," she said, her eyes wide and hard. "Where do The Families fit into all of this?"

10.9

"Looks like they're waiting for us," said Stan, standing next to Cole in the bow of *The Pokey Joker*. He gestured with his head toward the small pier at the Squirrel Island Ferry Landing. Standing on the dock were two soldiers, clad in black combat gear and carrying large weapons in their hands. In the gravel lot beside the ferry landing sat a military Humvee.

Cole exhaled loudly, trying to ease the pounding of his heart. "I guess we had to expect that, didn't we?"

"I did," said Stan, patting his waist. Cole glanced down as Stan pulled his shirt aside enough to reveal a pistol tucked into his belt.

"We said no guns," said Cole, looking at Stan with eyebrows raised.

"Yes we did," Stan answered. "And it's a good rule for these guys." He motioned vaguely back toward the rest of the crew. "But for me, I'm keeping my options as open as I can."

Cole looked again at the soldiers on the dock, then back at Stan. "You're not-"

Stan shook his head. "I'm not an imbecile, Cole," said Stan with a sly grin. "And I'm not about to start a firefight with guys like this. Like I said, I just want my options open."

Cole nodded. "Okay," he said. He turned to watch as the boat neared the dock. As if oblivious to the soldiers, young Doobie pulled right up like he owned the place and gunned his loud engine before shutting it off. The soldiers in their fearsome garb and mirrored helmets stepped forward, looking wildly out of place in this picturesque tourist spot. They must be dying in this heat, thought Cole.

"By order of the commander of this facility," said the shorter of the two, "we ask that you turn your boat around and head back to where you came from." His voice was muffled by his helmet, like Darth Vader's.

Cole glanced at Stan, who stepped around to the side of the boat to get closer to the soldiers. "Do you recognize me, privates?" he asked, emphasizing their low rank.

Neither of them replied.

"My name is Stan Walsh. I serve as Secretary of Homeland Security, at the pleasure of our President, Linda Travis." He gazed at one, then the other. "Perhaps you've heard of me."

The shorter soldier glanced at his taller partner, then stared back at Stan. "Nevertheless, we are instructed to turn you away. You may not disembark at this facility."

"I thought Squirrel Island was a tourist destination," called out Ken from the cabin door, his brow tightly clenched. "I have friends here!"

"I have to pee!" said Marionette with a laugh. Her raucous tone and her eye-patch gave her a piratical air. She plopped down on a pile of netting as if to say that she wasn't going anywhere anytime soon.

The soldiers slowly scanned the faces of those on the boat, as if they were memorizing them. Cole had little doubt that this entire encounter was being watched and recorded by unseen cameras and mics. He stepped closer to Stan and spoke to the soldiers in a quiet tone. "I would like to see my wife, the President of the United States," he said. His voice quavered with fear, but he'd said it. Steve Waymax, the Portland reporter, scribbled in his notebook as he watched from inside the boat's cabin.

The shorter soldier regarded Cole for a long moment, then turned to the others. "My instructions are to ask you three times to leave peacefully. This is the third time. If you do not comply, you will all be taken into custody and transported to the Federal Penitentiary in Newton, Georgia, pending trial. Your boat will be confiscated." He stepped to the edge of the dock and brandished his rifle. "Do you understand me?" he asked.

Stan turned and motioned to Doobie, who immediately started the boat's diesel engines. The Secretary of Homeland Security turned and scowled at the soldiers. "You will be hearing from me," he said, his voice as hard and cold as carbon steel. The boat began to back away from the dock.

Cole, fingers clenched on the handrail, seethed with frustration as the boat pulled away. Before they got too far away, he called out, loud enough for the soldiers to hear him. "I want to see my wife!"

10.10

Paul DuPont stared at his monitor as the boat pulled away. "Bye-bye, First Gentleman," he muttered, smirking. "Better get your asses to shelter, you bunch of nut-balls." DuPont had just received a secret communiqué from higher up, informing him that a storm had been ordered. He could not have been happier

He glanced at the screen with the Summit feed, glad that it was yet another day of political pontificating, with no major responses expected from the VLT. Satisfied, he clicked a tab and scanned the global radar. A couple of hundred miles out from the mid-Atlantic coast he could see a series of nested curved lines, regularly spaced.

This was the trace left behind from a major pulse. Already he could see the beginnings of the hurricane. It looked like it might become a big one.

DuPont sighed his relief. Finally. A couple of days to build the storm and steer it here. Maybe three. And then, whammo! No more President. No more whining husband. No more crazies. And no more of this godforsaken island. DuPont could return to The City, which is where he should have been all along, as far as he was concerned. Hopefully, the Directors would be ready to punch out of here. That would be all the better. DuPont was so sick of this planet he could scream.

He opened another screen and typed in a message to the central hangar facility at *Urbem Orsus*, requisitioning an AB to be delivered as soon as was possible. He knew how crazy things could get once the go-ahead was given. And he'd learned long ago to trust nobody but himself. After all, Uncle William had made an appearance this very morning, apparently, and hadn't even checked in with him. Not that he was really an uncle, but still. DuPont had known the old man since he was a kid. At this important time, it seems he could have stopped by to confirm that all was well.

But DuPont knew better than to think like that. He would watch out for himself, as he always had. That meant having an AB, a wok, coded to his pattern and sitting ready on the flight line. Hopefully one of those new twenty-fives with the integrated control that felt almost as alive as the ones the Life had given them.

Paul DuPont would not be left behind.

10.11

"So you guys have never heard of Mihos, then, I take it," said Mihos, making conversation as they wound their way through the Murk's holes and the doggy Maine countryside. "I mean, you never asked." The cat cleared his throat.

Emily turned and raised an eyebrow. "You mean that stuff you said back in your house?" she asked. "Like, something about a being the 'lord of war' and stuff?"

Mihos stiffened and slowed to a stop. "'Prince of War,' thank you very much. 'Son of Bast' and 'Protector of the Innocent.'"

Emily stopped to speak with Mihos. "Okay. Yeah. You told us all of that back at your place, but we've been rather busy since then."

"Ooh, nice attempted save, chickie-baby," said Mihos. "But we had all that time together on the flying carpet."

Emily raised an eyebrow. "I, for one, was focused on not falling off."

Mihos sighed. "Fair enough. But we have time now." He started walking again and Emily stepped in line behind him. Grace and Iain were a dozen yards ahead, keeping up with Dennis. "And you're the smart one, right? I'd rather just talk to you anyways."

"Well... I don't know about that..." said Emily.

"Yes you do, Ems. Don't play humble. It doesn't look good on you."

Emily blushed. "So, what does that mean? 'Son of Bast' and all that? Who's Bast?"

Mihos held his nose up and stepped along, rather jauntily. "Bast? Only an Egyptian war god. Mihos is usually depicted as a lion-headed man, and his cult was centered in Leontopolis. He carried a knife and was often referred to as the 'Lord of the Massacre.' He-"

"I'm confused," broke in Emily. "You're an Egyptian war god with the head of a lion? And why are you talking about yourself in the third person?"

Mihos stopped and hung his head for a moment. Then he turned to look at Emily. "Okay. I'm not really *that* Mihos, okay? I mean, we cats live a long time, right? And we live double lives in two realms at once. So we're *like* gods, right? And I *am* pretty fierce." Mihos regarded Emily for a moment, then flicked his gaze down to the strange, buzzing ground. He hunched his shoulders up and exhaled loudly.

Emily cocked her head and smiled. "You've been wanting to tell me this for a while, haven't you?" she asked.

Mihos closed his eyes and licked his paws for a moment. Then he opened one eye and scrunched his nose. "I just don't want you to have the wrong idea is all," he said. He turned and started walking again. "C'mon, girlfriend," he said. "We don't want to lose the others."

Emily followed. "Is your name really Mihos?" she asked.

Mihos glanced over his shoulder for a second, then turned back. "I just really like Mihos, okay? I mean, who wouldn't? Fierce. Protective. Smart." He stopped and turned. "A cat could have worse role models, you know what I mean?"

"Makes sense to me," said Emily. "I think it's sweet, that you want to be like Mihos. And I'm also glad that you told me... what you told me."

Mihos nodded. "I just thought... you know, it could get sticky again." He looked around at their weird, wild surroundings. "And I already messed up once. I didn't want you thinking I was this, you know... god, you know?" He raised an eyebrow, then turned to walk again.

"I think I'd rather have a friend than a god," said Emily.

Mihos' shoulders stiffened but he kept on walking, acting as though he hadn't heard. Emily followed. Slowly, they caught back up with the others.

"So what's your real name?" she asked, before they got too close.

Mihos glanced quickly back, then away again. "Nicky," he said, his voice so low Emily could hardly make him out. "But I think I'd rather stick with Mihos, if you don't mind."

"Nice to meet the real you," said Emily. "Whatever your name is."

"Back atcha, toots," said Mihos.

10.12

"I would consider The Families to be a specific, and perhaps extreme, example of a group which operates in the secret layer of leadership and control," said the Fisherman, pushing himself forward to the edge of his armchair.

"And those are the groups who are trying to break away somehow," said Linda. "The conspirators, right? The secret societies and cabals and elite clubs and such."

The Fisherman nodded. "Exactly right, Madam. That portion of the wealthy and powerful who are interested in things beyond mere wealth and power."

"Which is easy enough to do, once you've got wealth and power."

William smiled. "Touché," he said. "Yes. Their influence today in global affairs is significant. And I would say that the creation of the modern tendency to scoff at 'conspiracy theories' has been their greatest single achievement, as it allows them to hide in plain sight while they pursue their goals."

"And what are their goals?" asked Linda.

The Fisherman thought for a moment. "To my mind, the defining characteristic of the secret groups is their interest in spiritual matters. These societies are often described, or describe themselves, in religious, philosophical, or spiritual terms. The Bavarian Illuminati, the Brethren of the Free Spirit, the Knights Templar, the Rosicrucians, the Freemasons, the Moriah Conquering Wind, the Knights of Malta, Ordo Templi Orientis, the Hermetic Order of the Golden Dawn, the Black Pope, Al Qaeda, the Priory of Sion, the Church of Scientology, Opus Dei, the Chinese Triads, the Ku Klux Klan, the Thule Society, and Skull and Bones: whether for good or ill, secret conspiracies often describe themselves in religious or spiritual terms, and use symbol, myth, secret knowledge, and ritual as a means of more strongly binding themselves together. Even some of the groups which appear from the outside to be purely secular - the Bilderbergs, the CFR, the Bohemian Club, the Trilaterals, groups like that - have a philosophical or spiritual worldview or vision at their core."

"And those descriptions point to what you called their 'ideological goals'?"

"I think so, yes," said William. "They are attempting to bring meaning and purpose to their lives and their world, in opposition to what they regard as the insanity and meaninglessness of the global industrial culture's pervasive materialist worldview."

"Okay," said Linda with a sigh. "And they need to hide because... "

William smiled. "They need to hide because they've committed the cardinal human sin of exclusivity."

"Not because they're responsible for centuries of human misery and the destruction of the planetary ecosystem?" asked Linda, her eyes widening.

The Fisherman smiled tightly. "I haven't yet-"

"C'mon, William," said Linda, cutting him off. "I mean... we're talking about the wealthy elite here, right? The people who own, like, every government and every world leader and every corporation and every media outlet worth owning. They start wars, order assassinations, sponsor terrorism." Linda ticked the items off on her fingers as she spoke. "These are the people who think GMOs and weather modification and mind control are good ideas, William! The people who vacuumed up the wealth of an entire planet and stuffed it into their pockets. All at the expense of most of their fellow human beings. *And* the global ecosystem. And these are the people who abducted me, and who were going to-" She stopped and inhaled deeply. Her shoulders shuddered, as if trying to shrug off the memory of monsters. She leaned forward and looked the Fisherman in the eye. "We're talking about *you*, aren't we, William? You and your Families? People are not very happy with you people," she said, cocking her head to the side. "Did you know that?"

William sat for a moment, holding her gaze. His hands slid along his legs, smoothing his slacks. "We've made quite a mess of things on Earth, haven't we Madam?" he said at last. "And you care very deeply for your people, and for the planet."

Linda stared at him, giving him nothing.

The Fisherman cleared his throat and continued. "As I said, we can regard both the hidden and secret layers as understandable if regrettable responses to population pressure and resource depletion. I would point out that it's the mainstream culture's impulse to dominate and control that is ultimately responsible for the situation. While leaders and groups working in all three levels have played a role in the destruction, the public layer alone would have been sufficient to bring humanity to its present predicament, given its fierce dedication to one of the most planet-despoiling forces ever known: a healthy, growing economy. I grant you that the hidden and secret layers have made things more painful. But I think *some* of the secret groups are truly trying to break away from the destructive impulses of the dominant global culture, and that they are despised for just the reason I first mentioned."

Linda nodded. "Because they're exclusive."

"Indeed, Madam," agreed the Fisherman. "People working in the public and hidden layers like to maintain the fantasy that wealth and power are available to all who work hard to attain them. But the secret societies maintain no such illusion. They are playing a different game altogether, and it's not a game to which most people are invited. They proceed from an overt philosophical or spiritual worldview, with long term plans and goals, and often with a decidedly uncommon view of the human endeavor, the future of Earth, and the nature of reality itself. And they pursue goals and enact plans which effect everyone, whether they've been consulted or not."

Linda stood up and reached her arms overhead to stretch her shoulders. The sun had moved enough to shift the shadows on the distant Face mesa. A pinpoint of light glinted back from the peak she thought of as the 'nose,' as if one of the aliens William had mentioned was signaling her with a shard of mirror. Unable to divine any meaning from the scene, she took a couple of deep breaths, dropped her arms, and retook her seat. "So you want me to believe that The Families are the good guys in all of this, William?" she asked, raising an eyebrow.

"Heavens no, Madam," said William with a laugh. He stopped and took off his glasses to rub his eyes, then continued. He looked pointedly at the President. "I think you'll find that The Families have been as deeply complicit in the misery and destruction as anyone." The Fisherman stopped and drew a long breath. He smiled tightly. "What did that old wizard say in *Star Wars*? Something about *scum and villainy*?" He wrinkled his nose. "No, we have our fair share of psychopaths, Madam, and their long term efforts to accumulate wealth and power have created a great deal of suffering. I will not deny it. We have committed many sins. But no matter our sins, there has always been a core, or a distinct subset, or an aspect of our group that has been trying with good intentions to walk an honorable spiritual path."

"And this is the group you represent," prompted Linda. "The group that stole me out from under the watchful eyes of those who abducted me and brought me here."

"Indeed, Madam," he agreed. "No matter how twisted and cruel many of our fellow Family members have become in these end-of-days, I like to think that we in the Evolutionary Element have managed to stand apart from the insanity as much as has been possible, and that our goals, if not all of our methods, have been to the good."

"And yet you've still allowed the insanity to proceed, William," said Linda, cocking her head to one side. "Why is that?"

The Fisherman flashed his eyebrows. "Well that's the question, isn't it?"

10.13

"Five hops forward, five hops back, Teddy my boy," said Carl with a grin. "Looks like your ass is stuck on that alligator."

"Shut up," said Ted.

Carl glanced up from the board. "So you said you played this as a kid?"

Ted stopped and closed his eyes for a moment. "It was my Aunt Peg," he said with a wistful tone. "Funny, how I remember that now." He looked at Carl. "Like, wasn't it just yesterday we were talking about how we couldn't remember anything?"

Carl shrugged. "Yesterday or a year ago. I can't tell."

Ted put his card back on the deck. "She was this tall, thin woman, Aunt Peg. Always wore these expensive dresses. Glasses. Gray hair. All very neat and proper. We'd play for hours and hours."

"Was she a favorite of yours?" asked Carl.

"I guess," said Ted. "I was there a lot, when I was little. My mother... she would start drinking. And my father was gone a lot, which was the good news. So I'd end up with my aunts. They were good to me. They talked to me. They gave me treats."

"So there was more than one aunt," said Carl.

Ted's eyes widened. "It's like I don't remember anything and then you ask and then I remember. Yeah! There were a couple more aunts. Henny. Nora. They were my haven. They just let me be me, you know?"

Carl took a card, read it, looked at Ted. "So your father was bad news?"

Ted scrunched his eyes and nose for a moment, then shook his head and pointed at Carl's card. "What's it say?" he asked.

"You dodging-?"

"It's your turn," said Ted, pointing again at Carl's card.

Carl read his card. "It says I'm to head straight to the five and dime."

"And from there to number thirty five. Lucky you."

Carl moved his marker, then looked at Ted. "So, your father?"

Ted leaned over and picked up a card. "I don't want to talk about my father," he said, reading his card.

Chapter Ø Eleven

11.1

They'd picked up a State Police escort at the U.S. border. When Gabrielle asked about it, a blonde, young businessman sitting in front of her explained that it was standard procedure these days, as there had been so many problems along this line. There weren't always soldiers on this bus, he said, running a hand through his curly blonde hair. And there were some rather "wild and lawless people" in this part of the country. He pointed out the shotgun now resting ready-to-use in the metal tube next to the driver's seat. "It's a different world," he said, shaking his head in wistful remembrance.

Gabrielle smiled politely and stared out the window, noting the distant columns of smoke she'd been seeing since entering the U.S. "Pastor Clinton's goddamn Burners," a soldier behind her muttered. A different world indeed.

Gabrielle watched as the police cruiser put on its blinker and the bus driver followed suit. They were coming into another small town - Winthrop, the sign said - and the driver announced that they'd be taking a brief stop, long enough to grab something at the restaurant and use the facilities. The bus slowed behind the cruiser and they both turned into the large gravel parking lot of a place called 'Snoot's Safe Spot.' Gabrielle hoped that Snoot was right.

She'd heard on the news, of course, about how unstable things had gotten here. As bad as things had been in Canada since the global economic crash, they'd been worse in the U.S. Sickness, hunger, riots, looting: both countries had seen their share. But somehow things had gone easier in Canada. Or at least that's how it had been reported in the news. Gabrielle had to admit that her own life circumstances were so insulated, both at home and at Freemantle, that she really had little idea about the reality of the situation. And now, with Greensleeves raging across the continent, who knew what she'd encounter?

What she *had* noticed, riding through the New England countryside in a bus full of soldiers and government types, was how empty everything seemed. Boarded up or burned down houses and businesses, abandoned cars, empty streets, apocalyptic graffiti; she felt like she was in one of those post-plague movies on Netflix, where ninety-nine percent of the population had died. She knew that wasn't the case. She knew that many people had ended up in the many shelters the government had built. And she figured that those who remained in their homes were likely pretty shy now, remaining out of sight when a bus went by. But it sure looked like a movie. It felt creepy.

The bus pulled up alongside the cruiser. Winthrop looked a little livelier than the other towns they'd passed through. Across Main Street from Snoot's was an open grocery store with real shoppers in it. And there were people walking on the sidewalks. Even a child on a bicycle. It was probably the proximity to Augusta that explained the difference. A bit of law and order near the nation's capital. Most likely policed by local forces intent on holding onto their lives for as long as they could. Good for them.

Gabrielle stood with the others and hiked her backpack up over one shoulder. She stepped off the bus to see a few of the soldiers and a couple of the government types lighting up cigarettes. How they could smoke in this heat she didn't understand. She smiled at the driver, who stood near the door, then noticed the State trooper from the cruiser standing near the door to Snoot's. So who were the two military types wearing black uniforms and black helmets with mirrored visors, standing in the middle of the parking lot, surveying the scene? Were these guys the reason Winthrop still seemed to have some life in it? Gabrielle shuddered. The two black-clad soldiers both appeared to be watching her. With their mirrored faceplates, she could not quite tell.

Ducking her head, she hurried into Snoot's, glancing back over her shoulder as she passed through the door. The two strange soldiers were now headed her way. Something told Gabrielle to get moving. A flash of memory, a part of Zacharael's legacy to her, showed two similarly-uniformed soldiers rising up out from what looked like a flying saucer and shooting people in fur parkas with weird laser beam weapons. She had no interest in meeting a similar fate.

Her heart pounding, Gabrielle quickly surveyed Snoot's little pub, then headed straight toward a dark hallway in the back where the restrooms were. The young, blonde businessman who'd spoken to her on the bus turned on his barstool as she approached.

"Something wrong?" he asked.

Gabrielle grabbed the sleeve of his sports coat and jerked him off his stool, pulling him along with her to the back hallway. She turned to him with fierce eyes. "I need your help," she said, gesturing back toward the door with her head. The blonde guy turned to see the two black-clad soldiers enter the pub. With their faces covered by visors, they looked like a pair of evil robots.

Gabrielle grabbed the blonde man's shoulders from behind and whispered into his ear. "Stop them for me," she whispered. "Please?" Before he could respond, she fled past the bathroom doors and ducked through the exit at the end of the little hall. The sign on the door said "No Entry."

She passed quickly through the sparsely stocked storeroom and pushed through a metal door at the back. Outside, in the rear lot, she found a flying saucer much like the one she'd seen in that snippet of Zacharael's memory. It hovered inches above the hot gravel. There seemed to be nobody in it or near it. Looking both ways, Gabrielle ran quickly across the lot to the tree line, passing the strange craft on the left so that it would block her from view from the side lot where the bus was parked. Once in the trees, she just kept going, pushing her way through a rusted wire fence and down a short, steep slope to an abandoned railway.

Glancing toward the sky and finding nothing, Gabrielle began to run.

11.2

Ness did not see the two nurses when they opened the door and looked in on her. She was lost to that world. Dancing, whirling, spinning, singing, Ness moved around the room, just inside the bounds of her construct, her arms flailing about like a wild conductor leading an orchestra that hovered around her, above and below. Her voice, thin yet strong, sang out a nameless tune from another world. There were words to her song, sometimes rough and muttery and sometimes low and drone-like, but what they might mean she had no idea. She did not know she was singing. She did not even know she was dancing. The consciousness of Ness had sunk into formless bliss.

Ness did not see the large, purple sphere that had formed around herself and the three lost children. It flowed like syrup and pulsed like a heartbeat, and tiny flickers of energy skittered across its surface like fairies, buzzing faintly in the quiet room and filling the air with the scent of power. The sphere responded to Ness's presence and movement, mirroring her body with purple opacity and sparkling motes. It looked, from the outside, as if the sphere were alive, a friend of Ness's, a thick cover of living light that clung to the construct like flesh on bone.

Ness did not see the faces of the children as the purple light danced and changed above them. She did not see the sky outside of their hospital room window, how the clouds were building up, dark and active. She did not hear the military jet as it roared over Augusta, on its way to who knows where. And she did not see the two nurses, when they looked at each other and did the thing they so rarely did, which was smile. She did not see them duck back out and softly close the door.

And yet the Other-than-Ness saw all of this, for Ness's eyes still worked, even with her soul gone to bliss, and the Other could use them. The Other saw the smiling nurses and the pulsing sphere and the passing fighter. The Other regarded the young bodies lying safely in their gurneys. And the Other was pleased with how well it was all working out.

11.3

"So am I correct in assuming that The Families is composed of actual families?"

The Fisherman nodded. "Indeed you are, Madam," he replied. "The Families' most fundamental motive is to protect and serve the interests of their own bloodlines. And those bloodlines, and that interest in protecting them, go back many, many centuries. As a general rule, The Families have no particular loyalty to any nation, flag,

280 | TIMOTHY SCOTT BENNETT

or company. They simply use such things when it suits their purposes. Family members have worked in every level, from government and corporate roles in the public and hidden layers to leadership roles in most of the so-called 'secret societies' I named earlier."

"These are like the old rich we've known about for a long time, right? The Rockefellers and DuPonts and Vanderbilts and Rothschilds and such."

"Certainly," agreed the Fisherman. "Though your examples are skewed to the European and American. The Families come from all over the globe, and some play very far under the radar. Not all members have a famous moniker. One's bloodline and allegiance is not determined solely by the last name on a birth certificate."

"So 'protecting the bloodlines' isn't as strict as the phrase might imply, then," said Linda.

William nodded. "Not as strict," he repeated. "The old interest in bloodlines has lessened as we've figured out who and what it is we're dealing with. But there is inertia in the system. And protecting one's own family is a very ancient bit of genetic programming. While the definition of a Family member has relaxed somewhat, and while The Families' plans now includes some with little or no blood relation, the name still suits us. Family members are still at the center of it."

Linda shifted in her chair. "And The Families became a separate, secret group long ago."

"Indeed," agreed William. "Though there have been analysts who have divined our existence, it's really only the members of The Families who understand what we are up to. And since The Families, like many other secret societies, have a great many different layers, or levels, or degrees, then it's only those in the innermost circles who have the whole picture."

"And... what... ? You guys in the inner circle keep a mummified demon's horn in a glass case in a Swiss vault or something?"

William grinned. "We do indeed," he said. "Next to the Virgin Mary's training bra and Kennedy's still-living brain. We'll show them to you for the right price. For an extra pound we'll reveal the true identity of Jack the Ripper and give you the present whereabouts of both Waldo *and* Carmen Sandiego."

"Ah," said Linda. "Such a deal."

"Right," said the Fisherman with a smile.

"So that leaves us with this, William," said Linda. "You said that things changed once you figured out who it is you're dealing with. I assume you mean the aliens. And I assume you have much more to say about them. So, exactly whom *are* we dealing with?"

"Ah..." said William.

11.4

Paul DuPont hit 'play' and sat back in his chair. The Directorate had ordered an expanded Linda Travis presence in the media, both to stir the pot at the summit and to moderate growing fears regarding the Quietus. DuPont had already prepared some appropriate text, so it had taken only a moment to edit her statement and load her performance. It was once again show time for the VLT.

Which was damned disturbing, when DuPont thought about it. The orders could only mean more delays with the Plan. Otherwise, it'd be 'off the bitch!' and 'adios muchachos.' Delays were one thing. The Plan had been in place for decades now, after all, and the Grid had thrown everything off kilter. But there was a Category 6 brewing off to the southeast now, and DuPont would really rather be elsewhere when it hit.

Once again, Paul DuPont had to face the fact that he didn't understand what Project Changeling was even *for*. Not really. Like, the Plan was to gather everybody in, punch through the Grid, and leave this hellhole behind, but not before cleaning it up a bit for the next renters. So why hadn't they just taken Travis out in an 'accident'? Why make her the hopey-changey poster girl for the Quietus? And why go to the expense and trouble of creating and operating this grand charade, this virtual Linda Travis? Was it just showing off? Was it revenge? Was it all according to some esoteric system, some occult ritual timetable, like the old-timers still followed? DuPont wasn't into the occult stuff, but he understood showing off, and he knew revenge. It was cool as hell, driving the VLT and pulling the wool over the eyes of Sheeple who were too stupid to save themselves. But, really, enough was enough, wasn't it? Sure. They wanted to keep their options open. Fine. Keep the old girl on ice. But c'mon...

DuPont sighed and shook his head. He hated it when he fell into a rant like this. Not that anybody would ever know. It wasn't like he was chipped or something. But because it clouded his clarity and threw him off his game. In the end, he had to just trust the Directorate. As frustrated as *he* was, they had to be far more so. They would pull this all off as soon as they could. In the meantime, they needed him and his team where they were. For whatever reasons. Fine. They'd all been immunized, and they lived in an underground bunker. They'd be fine. And they'd do their part for the greater good, whether they wanted to or not. That's how it worked. You served the Plan before all else.

The screen flickered to life and Paul reached out to turn up the volume. The chairwoman had granted the U.S. President the floor.

11.5

Cole and Stan and their crew had pushed together a couple of tables on the Thieving Seagull's expansive deck and ordered three pitchers of Macy's home brew. The wind was picking up, bringing a bit of relief from the midday heat. The beer helped soothe their parched throats and ruffled feathers. The power had gone out again, but the home brew was still pretty cold.

"I don't know, Stan," said Cole quietly, shaking his head. "I'm not sure it's time yet for covert ops."

"I know," said Stan with a heavy sigh. "I'm just really pissed."

"You have any luck on the phone?" asked Marionette. She took a long swig of her beer and placed her glass heavily on the table. She looked around the deck. They were the only ones there.

"Bastards just kept me on hold," answered Stan, shaking his head. "I left this number, but I don't expect them to do me the courtesy of returning my call."

"But you're the-"

"They cut me out of the loop when they took the President into custody," interrupted Stan. "Since then, I can't get the goddamned Postmaster to return my calls."

"Custody..." mused Ken. "Right." He looked at Stan. "You're right. It's a sham. She's probably not even-"

"The flu ain't a sham, Ken," said Cole. "You're wife's sister..."

Ken stopped and exhaled and shook his head in wonder. "The whole thing stinks." He gestured southward over his shoulder, in the direction of his house. "You hear about the crop circle that appeared in the field across from my place?" he asked. "Celia saw it yesterday late afternoon when she went to the isolation ward to visit Beth."

Stan glanced at Cole and raised an eyebrow. "You think it's *them*, screwing around with us again?" he asked. He pointed toward the sky.

Cole raised his shoulders. "Wouldn't surprise me," he said.

"Anybody seen that Steve fella?" asked Simon, looking around the deck. He and Keith were already on their second beers.

Cole pointed toward the doors leading back into the pub. "On the phone," he said. "Filing his story."

Andrew, who ran the Thieving Seagull with his wife Macy, came out onto the deck with a small portable radio in his hands. "You need to hear this," he said, placing the device on the table in front of Cole. Everybody quieted to listen.

"... for two whole days now and I'm beginning to think I'm at a poker game."

"It's the President!" said Marionette.

"Shhhh!!" said Cole sharply.

"I mean, listen to yourselves. 'I'll do this if you do that.' 'I'll give you what you want when you give me what I want.' 'You go first and then we'll follow.' It's maddening. And I'm sitting here in this hospital cell thinking 'really?' Really? Is this the best we've got? Cuz we have people that need food and water, folks. We've got nuclear plants spewing radiation into the atmosphere. We've got diseases moving across the land. We've got rogue militaries and insane leaders battling for land and resources. We've got summer coming. As hot as it is right now, it's going to get hotter. And what I want to know is: what are you going to do to help matters, regardless of what anybody else does?"

There was a break in Linda's speech as she cleared her throat. *"The doctor's tell me I may make it through this. Who knows? Maybe I've reached the bottom and am on my way back up. But I gotta say, if I pull through this, I may just renounce my candidacy and let somebody else do this job. Cuz I'm tired of it. I'm tired of feeling like I'm working alone. I'm tired of the politics. And I'm tired of people who just don't seem to want to understand the situation we're in."*

The radio fell silent for a moment, then a reporter broke in to say that the American President had stopped speaking and had slumped in her chair, apparently feeling dizzy from her exertion. Cole listened intently as the announcer described how two nurses had come into her room and were helping her to her bed. The live feed from Squirrel Island was terminated. All they could do now was speculate.

Cole clicked off the radio and gazed out across the harbor, peering at the island in the distance. Something rose to prominence in his heart, a blob of relief and anger and fear. Linda was doing better? That news allowed him to feel just how much raw emotion he'd been holding inside. A few tears welled up in his eyes and he wiped them away, then turned and looked at the others gathered there together: his crew. "So," he said gravely, "what do we try next?"

11.6

On the third floor of MaineCentral Hospital was the isolation ward. At the end of the central hallway of the isolation ward was a negative-pressure room. Around the room pulsed a nullspace field.

Inside the room was a hospital bed. In the bed, with an IV in her left arm, lay a sleeping Keeley Benedict, President Travis's Chief-of-Staff. Through Keeley's veins and tissues moved the disease known as the "alien flu" or "Greensleeves."

Hanging from the ceiling of Keeley's room was a television, its sound turned down low. Standing in the room's corner near the door were two nurses, watching Keeley in silence. One nurse was the tall, thin man with a shaved head and fierce, golden eyes. The other nurse was the tiny woman with dark, wide eyes. Neither nurse wore any sort of protective gear.

"... still no word on the American President's condition at this time. Summit Chairman Ban Mogul-Stoward expresses his hopes and prayers for the President's quick recovery and vows that Summit attendees will continue their deliberations in her absence..." said the television, gravely.

"THE DISEASE VECTOR CANNOT HARM US," said the golden-eyed man. He made no sound. His mind spoke to hers.

"IT WAS CREATED FOR HUMANS," answered the wide-eyed woman.

"... are beginning to worry that it's the alien flu talking and not their President..." said the television, incredulously.

"WE WERE CAUGHT BY SURPRISE," explained the wide-eyed woman.

"THE TRUTH WAS KEPT FROM US BY BOTH OF OUR PARENTS," said the golden-eyed man.

"... Coming up next: the earliest Atlantic hurricane ever? Stay tuned for details about the storm now brewing off the Mid-Atlantic coast..." said the television, worriedly.

"AS WE HAVE WITHHELD OUR TRUTH FROM THEM," said the wide-eyed woman.

"AND AS WE HAVE KEPT THE TRUTH FROM MS HAYES," agreed the golden-eyed man. He raised an eyebrow.

"... you'll love the new MexiCali Pop-Ums," said the television, confidently.

"THE RUSE WAS NOT OUR IDEA," said the wide-eyed woman.

"YET THE GOAL IS ONE WITH WHICH WE ALIGN," said the golden-eyed man.

"... Sandbox brand cat litter: now with blue spice crystals..." said the television, slightly embarrassed.

"NOW WE WAIT," said the golden-eyed man.

"UNTIL WE ARE FULLY IN POSITION," agreed the wide-eyed woman.

"... Side-effects can include nausea, fatigue, and headaches. So ask your doctor about..." said the television, assertively.

"THE SUBSTITUTION HAS PROCEEDED WITHOUT NO-TICE," asked the wide-eyed woman.

"BY NIGHTFALL WE SHALL HAVE THE CITY," said the golden-eyed man.

"... Tonight on ACN's Manic Monday, the season finale of *None So Blind*..." said the television, excitedly.

The nurses stood and watched and contemplated their new situation. Keeley moaned and fluttered her eyelids for a moment. "My love," she whispered, her words so soft that even the nurses had to strain to hear them. She slipped into a deeper sleep and went still. Her face softened into a slight smile. The nurses looked at each other and then exited the nullified room.

"... We go now to P.J. Numan in Atlantic Beach, North Carolina... P.J.?..." said the television.

As always, the television had the last word.

11.7

Mihos looked up at the sound of Grace calling out "whoopsy!" to see the girl disappear before his eyes. It looked like she'd been sucked into a vacuum cleaner hose, a phenomenon the cat was familiar with in his other life. One second, she was reaching out toward what might have been a tree branch, the next second she was gone.

"Grace!" yelled Iain, stepping into the spot she'd just occupied.

Dennis turned and barked. "No!" he said. Iain stepped back.

"What happened?" asked Emily in a panic.

Dennis shook his head. "Make chain," he said sharply.

Iain and Emily exchanged glances. Iain shook his head in confusion. "I don't know-"

"Chain," said Dennis. "Cat. Me. You. Emily." He pointed his muzzle toward each of them in turn.

Mihos, comprehending the dog's plan, stepped forward. "Got it," he said to Dennis. He looked at the others. "Grace must've touched the edge of the Murk and gotten drawn in," he explained. "If we hurry, we may be able to pull her back out." He stepped in front of Dennis. The dog grabbed Mihos' tail firmly but gently with his teeth. "Iain, you hold onto Dennis's tail. Emily, take Iain's hand. Then hold your ground. Underdog and I are going in." Without waiting for a response, Mihos turned and stepped into the space where Grace had last been seen.

There. Behind that branch. That was what the edge of the Murk looked like here when one got close: a shifting patch of brightness not unlike the static one might see on a television screen. Mihos reached up with his nose to touch the bright patch. He was immediately pulled into the blackness.

"Grace?" said Mihos. "Dennis?"

"Here," said Dennis. From somewhere. There was no *in front of* here. No *behind*. And certainly no sensation of the dog's teeth on Mihos' tail.

"I'm here," came the sound of Grace's voice. It was fainter than the dog's voice. Did that mean she was further away? It must.

Mihos opened his eyes wide and willed them to be as bright as was possible. "Grace? Can you see my eyes?"

"Yes!" said Grace, in this place where no mouth said anything, where no breath made a sound.

"Do you remember how you followed my eyes before?" asked Mihos.

"No," answered Grace. "I don't know how-"

"But you did it, Grace," said Mihos.

"Did it," repeated Dennis.

"So just do it again," said the cat.

"Okay," said Grace. Was her voice louder now? Maybe. Mihos couldn't tell.

"Do you know how to get us back out of here, Dennis?" asked Mihos.

"Wag tail," said Dennis.

"What?" said Mihos. "How can I wag my tail? I can't even feel my tail!"

"Me," said Dennis.

"Am I closer?" said Grace.

"You sound closer," answered Mihos. "Dennis? You can feel your tail here?"

"No," said Dennis. "Can wag though."

"Your eyes are close now," said Grace. Her voice was stronger.

"Can you reach out and grab my paw?" asked Mihos.

"I don't have any hands!" said Grace.

"Understood, girl. And I don't have a paw. But if Dennis can wag a tail he doesn't have, surely you can reach out a hand you don't have and grab a paw that I don't have, right?"

Grace was silent for a long moment. Then she spoke, her voice closer than ever. "Okay," she said. "I got it."

"You got it?" asked Mihos. "I don't feel-"

"I thought we were imagining," said Grace. Her voice sounded afraid.

"Right," said Mihos. "I forgot. Okay. I got your hand." Mihos inhaled sharply. "Okay. Dennis? You ready?"

"Ready," said Dennis.

"Start wagging!" said Mihos.

"Wagging," said Dennis.

The three of them waited together in silence for a moment, then slammed their eyes shut against the brightness that assaulted them as they popped back into Doggyworld. There were the five of them, all in a row, connected together with hands and feet and paws and jaws and tails. "It worked!" exclaimed Iain. "We pulled 'em out!" He started laughing. Emily called out with surprise and gladness. Dennis gently released Mihos' tail from his teeth and stepped forward to lick Grace's face.

Mihos sat on his haunches and started licking his tail. "Dog spit," he muttered. "Criminy."

11.8

"Cotton candy?" said Mary, one eyebrow raised. "Why you spending money on that?"

D'Neal winked and dug into his pocket, pulling out a couple of one-dollar bills. "I paid myself a day early," he said.

Mary glanced around them as they walked between the rows of old cars. "You what?" she said.

D'Neal shrugged. "I'll pay it back tomorrow," he said. "When I get my check. They won't know it was-"

Mary turned and grabbed D'Neal's biceps with both hands. "I can't..." she said, her face dark with anger. "I mean... D'Neal. You can't do that."

D'Neal looked down at his feet. "I was just-"

Mary reached out and put a hand to his chin, lifting his face up so she could meet him eye to eye. "I don't need candy," she said softly. "I don't need you to buy me anything. Okay?"

D'Neal wiped a tear from his eye. "What do you need then?" he asked. His voice was filled with water.

Mary caressed the side of his face. "I need you to be really, really good, D'Neal. Okay? That's all I need."

D'Neal exhaled heavily. "I wanted-"

"I know, sweetie," said Mary. "I know. But you can't. Not like this."

D'Neal looked at Mary and smiled. "You just called me 'sweetie,'" he said, his eyes flickering shyly away.

"I know," said Mary, returning his smile. "Is that okay?"

D'Neal gazed around the fairgrounds, then stuffed a piece of the cottony sugar into his mouth. Mary did the same. "Yeah," he said at last, looking her in the eye.

"So no more of that," said Mary, gesturing toward the bills in his pocket.

"No more," agreed D'Neal. He took another piece of cotton and ate it, then took Mary's hand and pulled her along with him. "A Corvair!" he said, turning to flash Mary a grin. "My Dad talks about having had one of these as a kid." They stopped beside a small, powder blue sedan. "I can't wait to tell him," said D'Neal.

Mary squeezed his hand, sharing his excitement. She was about to ask the owner if they could sit in it when she saw her father, standing by the phone booths across the lot.

He was staring right at her.

11.9

Linda and the Fisherman sat in their armchairs, facing off on the Martian plain William had dubbed "Rumi's Field." The sky overhead was washed out pink with traces of yellow, giving them both a bruised and battered cast. The sun interrogated them from directly overhead.

"So," said William, inhaling deeply. "The aliens. But first I need to flesh out The Families a bit more."

"Okay," said Linda, shrugging her shoulders as if resigned to the Fisherman's need to explain.

William closed his eyes for a moment to think, then spoke with eyes closed. "Let me begin by restating that the history of The Families stretches back into antiquity."

"Got it," said Linda, hoping to hurry him along.

"During this long history," William continued, "The Families' defining interest has been a spiritual one." He opened his eyes. "In broad strokes, we've been exploring a mystical worldview rooted in large part in the beliefs and cosmology of such groups as the Gnostics and the ancient Egyptians. Our focus is on the evolution, enlightenment, and exaltation of human consciousness and spirit, the primacy of knowledge, intellect, and visionary experience over dogma and teaching, and the ongoing human journey to realms and potentials far above and beyond that which is believed possible in the dominant materialist paradigm."

Linda smiled tightly. "That sounds like copy from a brochure, William," she said.

The Fisherman chuckled. "I suppose it does," he says.

Linda clasped her hands in her lap. "From what I remember, William, the Gnostics and ancient Egyptians are generally considered heretics and pagans by most folks. Certainly Pastor Clinton would paint you all as Satanists."

William flashed his eyebrows. "You move us forward nicely, Madam," he said. "Yes. Precisely. We are tagged with all sorts of loaded labels, 'Satanist' being perhaps the most provocative. Gnostics. Pagans. Free thinkers. Intellectuals. Occultists. Esotericists. Humanists. All of which are assumed to be bad and wrong. Evil, even. Which leaves us in the rather surreal position of being reviled for believing that humans can be good, and can reach perfection by their own efforts, or for believing that intellectual achievement is a worthwhile endeavor. Were it not so sad, it would be humorous."

"Trying to get to heaven without God, William?" said Linda with a smile. "How very arrogant of you."

William smiled sadly in return. "Right. Not only do we cut the priesthood out as middleman, we negate the need for submission and obeisance to all the usual pretenders to the Godhood. Of course we must be reviled." He leaned forward and lowered his voice, as if even here he could not say such things out loud. "Let me tell you something, Madam. Some Gnostics considered Yahweh Himself to be part of what they called the Demiurge, a sort of malevolent and false god. For them, the Devil's greatest trick was not in convincing the world that he does not exist. The Devil's *greatest* trick was convincing the world that he is God."

"Wow," said Linda. "You guys really *are* heretics."

The Fisherman sighed. "Indeed," he said. "And so *of course* we've been labeled, dismissed, and reviled. The Abrahamic religions, especially their more fundamental factions, are united in the belief that humans are sinful creatures who must remain subservient to, and dependent upon, their God. We have begged to differ, and have argued, instead, that this belief system has kept human beings small and disempowered."

"And then you went and formed your own club... "

"Aye. And people hate to be left out, and hate those who would exclude them, as I have said."

Linda sat forward in her chair and smiled. "So how would *you* describe The Families, William?" she asked.

The Fisherman thought for a moment. "In the past decade or so, some analysts, looking from the outside at the various levels we've been discussing, began to use the term "breakaway civilization" to describe the totality of behind-the-scenes elite activity proceeding unobserved by most people living in the public layer." He returned Linda's smile with one of his own. "I think the term works nicely for us, and would say that it's The Families who have articulated, implemented, and funded the overarching plan for that process of breaking away."

"The word 'breakaway' feels relatively free of derision, William. No wonder you like it."

"I think you're right, Madam. While acknowledging the separation, the word does not carry the baggage inherent in so many other descriptors. And the people who use this term to describe us seem to understand that, when considering the vast amounts of insanity that exist in this time, breaking away makes a great deal of sense."

11.10

They had decided, in the end, to just do it again. Crew up. Pilot *The Pokey Joker* out to Squirrel Island. Try to dock at the landing. Confront the scary soldiers in their intimidating uniforms. Oppose the system behind them that would steal their President and lock her away. "What are they gonna do, shoot the President's husband?" asked Marionette, finishing her beer and wiping her mouth with the back of her hand. None of them could imagine that "the powers that be" would really do such a thing.

"But mightn't they throw us in prison, like they said?" asked Steve Waymax, his face drawn with worry.

No one responded, as if afraid that to name their real fears might make them come true. Cole shrugged helplessly, apologetically. There was nothing else to be done.

The second trip out was much the same as the first, though the wind was steadily increasing and the seas were choppy. The early afternoon sunlight, now filtered through the leading edge of a swirl of clouds moving up from the south, shone down on them from above, giving everything a hazy look.

And the crew was more nervous. Cole stood again at the bow, watching the island, struggling to maintain his defiant anger as his fears churned in his gut. Stan stood next to him, silent and solid. But even Stan had admitted that he did not know what to expect. Doobie, who'd put on a t-shirt so as not to feel so exposed when they faced the inevitable soldiers, seemed as carefree as ever, but the rest of them were pensive and sober. Steve, the reporter, tried to stand outside of it all, the fabled "impartial observer" who could report on the affair without being affected by any of it, but it was clear from the look in his eyes that he was terrified. Cole hoped that Steve's presence, and the fabled "power of the press" that came with him, would stand in their favor.

The black-clad soldiers, six of them now, stood in a line on the dock, an unwelcoming party bristling with weapons and riot gear. As *The Pokey Joker* neared the landing, maybe fifty yards out, one of the soldiers leveled his weapon and fired. The bullet took out a masthead light, which exploded in a tiny shower of plastic and glass. "Hey!" shouted Cole in surprise. Doobie veered to the left and cut the engine. The boat fell silent.

From behind the ferry landing rose a helicopter, small, black, and unmarked. It leapt up and outward more quickly than any helicopter Cole had ever seen and rushed *The Pokey Joker*, hovering and buzzing overhead like an angry dragonfly. Cutting through the noise and the wash came a sharp, emotionless voice advising them to leave the area immediately or be boarded and arrested. As if to add an exclamation point to the demand, a second helicopter joined the first, and a small Coast Guard Interceptor raced around the point and into the cove.

Cole motioned to Doobie and the young captain restarted his engines and punched the accelerator, keeping them in a tight turn that would take them away from the landing. For a few moments it looked as if they were on a crash course with the Interceptor, but as they closed in the Coast Guard boat veered to the right to circle around behind them. It followed nearby, a mirror-windowed escort itching for a fight. Doobie whisked his crew away as quickly as he could, with the Coast Guard turning away only when they were halfway back to Boothbay Harbor. The Interceptor sounded one harsh, blaring siren, then sped back toward Squirrel Island.

The helicopters dogged them the whole way, one buzzing the small seaside town while the other hovered over *The Pokey Joker*, flattening the umbrellas on the Thieving Seagull's deck as Doobie pulled his boat up to the dock. Then they were off, back toward the Squirrel, moving so quickly that it was difficult to keep an eye on them. Cole, his face red with helpless anger, watched as they receded in the distance. It was difficult to tell for sure, but it appeared as though one of the copters changed shape as it neared Squirrel Island. It looked almost as if it had become a sphere.

Cole raised his right hand and shook his fist in frustration. From between his fingers shot bright sparks of hot, white light.

11.11

Jay Sinclair rubbed his eyes with the heels of his hands, a habit he'd fallen into recently, even though it left his eyes dry and sore. There was something about the tickling sensation that helped to ground him. He looked up at the young man standing in front of his desk, a messenger sent from Security.

"You can't find one silly girl with a backpack?" asked Sinclair, his voice tired.

The officer's eyes narrowed. "No sir," he replied. "As you know-"

Sinclair cut him off with a wave of his hand. "I know what I know, officer," he said sharply. "What I care about is what *you* know."

The officer stiffened. "The target is on foot, Sir. Or was. Somewhere near Augusta, Maine. We assume she-"

"I asked what you *know*," said Sinclair, cutting the messenger off. He picked up a pencil and tapped it on his desktop, noting the brass "Guy Legrand" desk plate and thinking, for the thousandth time, how good it will feel to dump that stupid little sign into the trashcan. He looked up at the officer. "Do you know anything?"

The officer looked at the floor and took a quick breath. "We do not know where she is now, or where she is headed."

Sinclair leaned back in his chair. "You've interrogated this Arthur fellow?"

The officer looked up at Sinclair. "He claims to have no knowledge of the target's -," he stopped and looked squarely at Sinclair, "-at your daughter's whereabouts, Sir. Standard interrogation techniques confirm the truthfulness of his claim."

Sinclair smiled slightly at the officer's euphemism. He hoped for the boy's sake it had only taken the drugs. "You're running IR scans on the area to isolate possibles?"

"Of course, Sir," said the officer.

Sinclair pulled at his tired eyes with his fingertips. He would have to go to Maine himself. He was about to request a wok when his phone began to vibrate in his pocket. Glancing at the officer, he pulled out his phone and looked at the screen.

The new text message said, simply, *Urbem Orsus.*

Sinclair closed his eyes and exhaled a silent curse. *Dammit, Gabrielle!* He made a mental note of the hour and slipped his phone back into his pocket.

Their time was almost up. The loading had begun.

11.12

Despite what Mihos had told the kids early on, it seemed that location did, indeed, matter here. Having been free his entire life to blink about the Astral, he found it both a surprise and a bother to be stuck in Doggyworld, where apparently they had to go walkies all the way across central Maine. It was taking forever, and Mihos was sick of the constant wariness and the crazy visual effects.

"You got any idea how much further, Muttley?" Mihos called to Dennis.

The old Whippet, still leading by a nose, turned and wrinkled his muzzle. "Smell bigger," he said with one eyebrow raised. Then he turned back and kept walking.

"Oh. Smell bigger. Well, that's a relief," muttered the cat. He inhaled heavily. "I need a rest, yo," he said, just loud enough for the kids to hear him. He sat back on his haunches and started to lick his front paws. Emily was the only one to turn around at his words. She cocked her head and gestured him back into motion with her hand, then turned to follow her brother. Mihos sat right where he was and ignored them.

He could handle the indignity of being led by a dog. Like, really, why would he envy somebody so intimately involved with the world of odors, stenches, and stinks? And then there was Dennis's obsequious need to please monkeys. Did he have no shame? And besides, when things got crazy with Grace, was it not Mihos, Son of Bast, who went first into the Murk? Mihos, whose bright eyes Grace could use to find her way back? Mihos, who was the first to understand Lassie's barking when lil Timmy fell down the well, and who could explain Dennis's plan to the rest of them so that they could act as swiftly as they had? Yes, it *was* Mihos, wasn't it? And Mihos knew that, when things got scary, it was *his* brain and *his* eyes that were going to make the difference.

It was just that... well, the kids were like, "Oh, Dennis, you saved her!" and "Oh, Dennis, you're leading the way!" and "Oh, Dennis, we couldn't be doing this without you!" Mihos rubbed his paw across his eyes and forehead. Sure. Right. They'd thanked him too. Told him how great it was. But it just didn't have that same... whatever. Mihos didn't have the word for it. Warmth, maybe? Feeling? Like, they said it, but it just didn't feel the same. They were different with Pluto. Like... they loved that damned dog.

Criminy, thought Mihos. Maybe he *couldn't* handle the indignity after all. And maybe he wanted to be loved as well. And maybe... and this felt like the hardest part of it... maybe it had something to do with *him*. Mihos closed his eyes and sighed. Monkeys had always confused him. And he wasn't sure he understood what 'love' really meant. If it meant that Mihos, Son of Bast, Protector of the Innocent and Lord of the Massacre, had to become some sniveling, face-licking, stick-retrieving, butt-wagging, ball-licking sycophant, than these monkeys could keep their whole "love" thing. He wanted no part of it.

Mihos opened his eyes and looked up. Nobody had stopped for him, and they were now far ahead. Mihos pulled himself back to all four feet and started plodding forward. Things were so much easier in the physical world, where love had never been part of the equation, where life consisted of simple calculations based on food and water and warmth. Mihos had learned, over his many lives, to keep his expectations low. But these darned kids were changing that.

11.13

Linda scanned the desert plain on which they sat. The distant sun was lowering in the sky. Another day was passing. She looked at William and raised an eyebrow.

William shifted in his chair and continued. "Human history is packed with the exploits of men and women," said the Fisherman, sounding like the narrator of a British documentary series. "Warriors and kings. Inventors and industrialists. Politicians and generals and celebrities of every description. What is more striking, I think, is that human history is *also* packed with the exploits of the gods and spirits. High gods and low. Angels and demons. Pantheons and elementals and fairy folk of all sorts. There is no argument today that spiritual belief systems have profoundly shaped the course of history. But the question of whether gods and spirits are actually *real* has become a source of great conflict. In these materialist times, many people regard such beings as little more than delusions. And yet across the expanse of human history the gods and spirits were a known reality that intersected in important ways with the human experience." William stopped and smiled tightly, as if proud of his summary.

"Go on, William," said Linda.

The Fisherman drew a long breath. "The Families have long concerned themselves with this question of gods and spirits," he continued. "The experience of spiritual beings is open and available, of course, to anyone who is ready, willing, and able to meet them. For many, that access comes through individual visions and callings, participation inside an established religious framework, shamanic journeywork, the fairy traditions, the encounters made under the influence of various psychoactive substances, things of that sort. The rich and powerful pursued all of these paths, and more, and rose to positions of influence and control wherever they could. But some of them were also inclined to create more private institutions, traditions, and texts that could contain their accumulation of knowledge and ritual, and carry them forward through time."

"Of course they were," said Linda with a smirk.

The Fisherman flashed his eyebrows. "Let's face it, Madam, in the dominant global culture, it's the rich and powerful who have had the time and resources for such pursuits, not being shackled to the daily task of mere survival. They've felt, perhaps, with their accumulated wealth and influence, that their stakes were higher, requiring more from the gods and spirits in terms of guidance, omens, knowledge, and the like. And, as winners in the great game of competition, they were deserving of the gods' attention. The rich and powerful did not think of themselves as fallen, sinful creatures worthy only of subservience and worship. They wanted to meet the gods as colleagues, and join them as equals, and share in their immortality."

"Okay," said Linda, pulling her legs up to tuck her feet under her bottom. "I think I get that. Rich folk had the free time to pursue their interests, they were motivated to acquire knowledge and power, to hold onto it when they got it, and to keep it for as long as they could. So they tried to meet the gods, feeling somewhat godlike themselves. That all makes sense."

William smiled. "Good," he said. "Now... some have searched for the gods through Gnosticism, Hermeticism, Alchemy, Theosophy, or one of the other groups and societies I spoke of before. Some have worked within the more mystical or heretical wings of the various majority religions. Others have taken paths that are generally regarded as 'Satanic,' and therefore evil, by those majority religions. Always the goal has been the direct experience of the gods and spirits.

"And all through the centuries, Family members have encountered, experienced, and worked with various manifestations of god or spirit. Everything from the All and the One, or what some Gnostics call the Pleroma, to such things as the various monotheistic deities, the Aeons and Archons and Demiurge, the Angels and Demons and ol' Lucifer himself. Whether regarded as flesh and blood entities or spoken of, as Jung did, in more psychological and metaphorical terms, the various entities were considered to be real and active in the human world, and were accessible to direct experience for at least some portion of the human population. No matter the language used to describe them, no matter the forms and rituals used to access them, no matter the philosophical systems through which they were viewed, the gods and spirits, were always regarded as worthy of our concern."

"But something must have changed," said Linda. "Because you're speaking in the past tense."

"You are correct, Madam. Our conceptions changed. For so very long, we regarded ourselves, and the Earth, as the obvious center of absolutely everything of any import. The gods either lived here on Earth with us or flitted about in the heavens just overhead. Always their focus was on human affairs. The assumptions of the dominant materialist, Earth-centric, Abrahamic paradigm dominated our thinking.

"But slowly, over the centuries, we learned to reconceive the cosmos in more modern scientific terms. Inspired by our own technological advancements, we began to imagine traveling between the stars. This in turn allowed us to consider the possibility that there might be others like us out there who also wished to explore the cosmos. The human experience of gods and spirits began to look to us, more and more, like interactions with visiting extra-terrestrial species."

The Fisherman looked at Linda with one raised eyebrow. "Imagine our surprise, Madam, to learn that our gods were, in fact, just alien beings from other planets. And imagine our subsequent surprise, to learn that this new story of aliens was no more accurate than the previous stories had been."

11.14

Nicky padded across the deck and down the steps. He treasured the heat of the paving stones on his paws as he walked along the back of the house. And the smell of the sea was strong in the wind, evoking thoughts of fresh fish and other wonderful morsels. He could feel that rain was coming, and he wished it were not, but for now, sun and wind and smells and warmth.

The path divided and he took the fork to the left, away from the house and up the hill. The paving stones came to an end and the path turned to grass, and then dirt, as it wound its way into and upwards through a stand of trees and tall shrubs. At the top of this hill lay a wide, open expanse of wonderful blacktopped concrete that soaked up the sun like nobody's business. Usually the pad would be far too hot for comfort, this time of day. Usually he would not venture up here until dusk. But with the clouds coming and going, and with the wind, Nicky hoped it would be just right. He could get an early start on his favorite time of day, that long, juicy, sleepy time when he was warm underneath but the air around him was cooling. It'd had been so hot lately that the experience had not been what it used to be. He hoped today might be different. Cats could hope, as long as they didn't let anyone know.

The trail took him exactly where he knew it would and he squinted his eyes against the bright sky. He looked up to see a huge, hazy cloud just beginning to occlude the sun. He sighed with pleasure. This might be perfect. He started across the grass toward the concrete pad.

But then the pad darkened as the leading edge of a circle of shade moved rapidly across the open expanse. Nicky looked up again to see one of those large metal circles he'd seen before. This one moved quickly and silently to a spot directly over the concrete and then settled toward the ground. Three shining limbs poured out from the bottom to touch the pad. The slender legs reminded him of a grasshopper or cricket, but this metal circle was much too large for him to chase and catch. Nicky waited and watched, but no door materialized and no people emerged, as was usually the case. The big metal circle thing just sat there, silent, unmoving, unthreatening.

Perhaps the circle had had the same idea that Nicky had had. He couldn't tell. But it did not appear that anything was going to happen that he had to worry about. And it did not appear that the metal thing was going to leave soon. So Nicky inched slowly forward, keeping one eye out for the giant metal insect and the other eye out for the juicy little spot of warm concrete and sun that had his name on it. The metal circle did not cover the whole expanse of concrete, after all. There was room for the both of them.

With one last glance at the metal thing, Nicky plopped himself down onto the concrete, pulled his paws and tail in just right, and closed his eyes. In a way, it was nice to have some company for a change. There were no other cats on the island now, and Nicky often wished for another warm body to have nearby. His man human was warm, yes. But it just wasn't the same.

Whatever this metal thing was, maybe they could hang out for a while.

11.15

They were on their fourth or fifth round of Macy's home brews when an old, black diesel Mercedes pulled into the Thieving Seagull's parking lot and came to a quick stop near the sidewalk. Cole got up and stepped to the deck railing to see who it was. Car doors opened on both sides. From the driver's side came a large, burly, bearded man Cole didn't know. The man nodded hello and then opened the rear door and started digging through something in the back seat. Stepping out on the passenger side was Cole's friend, Stendahl Banks, former ACN anchorman and now Linda's Communications Director.

Cole smiled as he caught Sten's eye. "What the hell?" he called.

Sten walked up the sidewalk and along the side of the restaurant to the back deck. Cole fingered the latch and opened the door in the railing and Sten stepped through to give him a hard, long hug. "I came as quickly as I could," he said, releasing Cole and stepping back to look him in the eye.

"What are you doing here?" asked Cole. "I mean-"

"You don't think I read the papers, Cole?" said Sten with a smile. "Especially after you and Stan go missing without a word?" Cole glanced back at the crew, all sitting around a large, wooden octagonal table in the corner. Sten gestured vaguely toward Steve Waymax, the guy from the Portland papers. "The *Rough Times* is all online, Cole," said Sten. "Saw Mr. Waymax's piece after your first little adventure and we headed right down." He checked his watch, then looked at Cole. "Made pretty good time, too."

The bearded man, whose name was Eddie, now with video camera and sound gear in hand, stepped onto the deck behind Stendahl Banks. At the same time, Stan, Ken, and the rest of them, came over to join Cole. Introductions were made and hands were shaken and chairs were added and more beer was ordered and they settled in together on the deck of the Thieving Seagull as the afternoon sun dipped lower in the sky and the clouds and wind continued to gather.

"So how'd you guys get past the cordon?" asked Stan.

"How did *you guys* get past the cordon?" retorted Sten with a grin.

"A classic diversionary strategy," said Stan with a theatrical shrug.

"Called in a couple of favors," said Sten with a wink.

Both of them finished their beers and set their glasses on the table with an audible clunk. "Listen," said Sten, looking at the sky and out across the water before returning his gaze to Cole. "There've been some developments since you left. I need to tell you about them. And your kids..."

"What about my kids?" interrupted Cole, leaning forward.

"They found them," said Sten.

"What? Where?" demanded Cole.

Sten raised a hand. "Mary found them, Cole. Found their sleeping bodies, anyways. Hiding inside an old MRI machine in the basement of the hospital. Right under our noses."

"What do you mean their sleeping bodies?" said Cole. "Are they awake? Are they okay?"

Sten nodded. "They're okay. Their bodies are. Intact and healthy and unharmed. And Ness is with them, acting as their guardian. She won't leave their sides. But the kids are in comas, Cole. And Mary insists that their souls, their spirits, are off traveling in the Astral realm, just like she used to do." The Communications Director, having delivered his most important bit of news, sat back and exhaled.

"Jesus." Cole exhaled loudly and tried to slow his breathing. "They must've worked it out," he said absently, to no one in particular. "They must've... they had a plan. They left a note. And Alice..." Cole stopped, rubbed his eyes, looked around him, then at Sten.

Sten nodded again. "It would seem, my friend. They went there on purpose, hid there on purpose. They must've worked something out with the Life."

"They're off to find... they're *here*..." said Cole, gazing out toward Squirrel Island. "To find Linda. But not in their bodies. Not in this... plane..." A slight smile twitched across his face. "They saw that damned mole and knew something was off and hatched a plan." He looked at Stan and shook his head in wonder.

"Mole?" asked Stendahl.

Cole told them all about the mole. None of them knew what to make of the tale. Cole looked at Sten. "You said there were other developments?"

"Yes," said Sten. "Keeley was hit with a case of Greensleeves, it seems. She was in MaineCentral, but then last we heard *she'd* been transported out to the facility on Squirrel Island." He gestured out into the bay. "So she's there now as well." He drained his beer. "Oh, and Mary has disappeared. Found out about that just before I left. Gone without a trace. Probably on her way here too, looking for Keeley."

Stan shook his head in disbelief. "Poor Keeley. And Mary's gone? Christ! Are there *any* of our people left in Augusta?"

Sten turned to look at Stan. "Well, that's a topic in and unto itself, Stan. But..." he glanced worriedly at the sky, "as sweet as it is to hang out on the deck and drink beers with y'all, I'm not sure you - we - should stay here."

"And why is that, Sten?" asked Stan.

Sten gestured out toward the open ocean. "In the first place, the weather people say that that's a whopper of a storm brewing, and it's headed this way. And my people on the fringe are convinced that this is not a natural storm."

Cole blinked. "They can-?"

"Indeed they can," said Sten. "The hidden elite have never really gone away, as we all know. And they can both create and steer massive storms now, if what I hear is correct."

"They're throwing a storm at us?" asked Doobie. The young captain's head lolled forward with the weight of alcohol. "Those bastards!"

Sten smiled and looked at Cole. "In the second place, everybody knows you're here now, I'm pretty sure. Not just the forces on the island, but the rest of the military, the Secret Service, and every last one of the folks who used to be in The People, or in one of the even more hidden groups that worked with them."

Ken leaned forward, his face a frown. "But haven't they always known?" he said. He looked from Cole to Stan. "I mean, you guys are chipped, right?"

Cole rolled his eyes upward in disbelief. "Jesus, Ken, yeah, you're right. Linda and I were the first ones to get the new iDents. And I assume Stan..." Stan nodded in confirmation. Cole exhaled loudly. "So... they must have known where we've been the whole time, right?"

Stan shook his head in wonder. "Must've," he said. "I didn't even think about that damned chip. First one I ever had."

"I didn't think of it either," said Cole.

The people gathered together on the deck fell into silence as they pondered the implications. At last Cole spoke to Stan. "So why didn't they send a copter and bring us back right away, Stan? Even before we met Vince and his kids? The Secret Service is charged to protect me at all times. So why... ?" Cole shook his head. None of it made any sense.

Sten looked around the company. "So here's what I think," he said, his voice low and conspiratorial. "Before Eddie and I left, it had gotten, well... weird... back in Augusta. I mean, things changed a great deal after Linda was... taken. But then the kids up and ran away. And then the General disappeared and you two left. And Keeley got sick. And Ness holed herself up in the kids' hospital room. And then Mary Hayes disappeared. And all of a sudden there were new faces around. New soldiers at the cordon. New Secret Service agents. New doctors and nurses. Pretty much everybody we knew had disappeared. And the whole town got strangely quiet."

Cole's guts clenched at the mention of his kids. He already felt awful for having abandoned them yet again. And now he learns... Christ, they weren't even in their bodies! Damn! Cole closed his eyes and tried to calm his pounding heart.

"So I'm thinking." continued Sten, "that huge forces are at work behind the scenes, Cole. Not just the folks that went to ground when Linda called them out three years ago, but even deeper layers of elite control. So all those new faces? Maybe they work for the hidden powers. Maybe they're responsible for the disappearances. Maybe even Keeley's illness. And maybe they've begun their last battle against us. To take complete control of everything. For whatever reasons that motivate them. They've long had some master plan, Cole. Rice alluded to it often. Maybe kidnapping Linda was just their opening move."

"But weren't you one of them?" asked Marionette, motioning toward him, her face dark with suspicion.

Sten turned to face the young woman. "I had some peripheral involvement," he admitted. "I was paid to follow orders and not ask questions, and was given information only on a 'need to know' basis. My need was never great, apparently, as I never really knew who 'they' were, apart from a few players." Sten's face had gone red and his eyes had a pleading look to them, as if he wished for no further questions, and wanted to be believed. "I've worked closely with the President since then, young lady..."

"Marionette," said Marionette.

"Marionette. I've worked with Linda ever since. Giving her what information and insight I could to help her better do her job. I was...

ashamed, if you'll believe that? And Linda Travis gave me another chance."

Marionette smiled slightly and nodded. Acceptance. For now.

"So they're just letting us do this?" asked Cole. "Even helping us?" He looked at Stan, then the rest of his crew, then Stendahl Banks. "Why? So we can dig our own graves?"

Sten ran a hand along his forehead. "I don't know why they're doing what they're doing, Cole. I've never met anybody who could truthfully say they understood the real motives of the hidden elite. But I fear that they do not mean well for the human race."

Doobie slammed his beer mug on the table, sloshing some of its contents onto the weathered wood and causing Cole and Sten to push back to escape getting wet. His head was tilted and his legs were splayed out and he looked like he'd exchanged most of his blood for Macy's home brew. "What I want to know," he drawled, mushing his words, "is who the *hell* is gonna pay for my boat light?"

11.16

"And so we can add a new layer to our scheme, Madam," said William with a flourish. He counted them off on his fingers. "There's the public layer, the hidden layer, the secret layer, and now the alien layer."

"You don't think the word 'alien' is too loaded?" asked Linda. "Seems like 'alien' means 'extra-terrestrial.' And you just said that *that* story is wrong as well."

"I'm not sure it matters, Madam. It's the word that just comes to the tongue, and I do not wish to spend thought or energy battling that impulse. Let's simply define 'alien' as 'other,' which is its oldest meaning, and trust that the language will sort itself out as we continue. Perhaps we shall discover a better word as we proceed."

Linda nodded. "Okay. You're driving."

The Fisherman flashed his eyebrows. "Brilliant. Now. Yes. Over the course of centuries, it slowly became clear that those who had presented to us as gods, spirits, demons, fairies, and angels were in fact visitors from elsewhere in the universe. On the one hand: how exciting. Whoever could they be, and what did they want? But on the other hand: how frightful."

Linda shook her head slightly in confusion. "Why frightful, William?"

"Three reasons, Madam. First, because whoever they were, they were obviously quite powerful."

"And you in The Families were used to being in control by that point."

"Right," said William with a nod. "Though our control had not yet consolidated into one governing body, as it has now."

"And you were familiar with the gods and spirits, because they'd been around for a long time, and didn't seem to pose a threat to your power on Earth."

"Which brings us to reason two," said William, raising his fingers. "Because if the gods were actually physical beings from elsewhere in the universe, then *they* might be like *us*. Did these beings wish to interfere in our affairs? Would they invade us? Control us? Enslave us? Wipe us out? Were they hostile or peaceful? We did not know."

"You mapped your own motivations onto them," said Linda, nodding.

"Indeed we did. Which leads us to reason three, because it eventually became clear that they were *not* like us. Which left us quite perplexed. These aliens were not acting at all as we had first expected they would. Their motives were almost impossible to divine. Their behavior was too absurd."

Linda shifted in her chair and stretched her legs out. "How was their behavior unexpected, William?" she asked. "I think I know what you mean, but it would help to hear your take on it."

The Fisherman shook his head as if in disbelief. "Well, there were so many of them, first off," he said. "So many types of spacecraft. So many kinds of beings. So many shapes and sizes. Some were indistinguishable from human beings. Some were strange but at least humanoid. Some were quite outlandish in appearance. And they kept doing the same things over and over. Were they scientists? Well, how many soil or semen samples did they need? Were they explorers or anthropologists? Why intrude so dramatically and then remain so elusive? Were they secretive because they meant to wage war against us? Then why not get to it and let the battle begin? And why wait years and decades and even centuries while we amassed an ever more powerful arsenal of weapons and technology to use against them? They were inscrutable. You see what I mean."

Linda nodded. "Sure," she said.

"These are the questions that drove the public UFO enquiry throughout most of the twentieth century and into the twenty-first," said the Fisherman.

"But The Families took their investigation underground."

"We did," replied William. "When we got more clear whom it was we were dealing with, we could look back in time and see that we'd been interacting with non-human intelligences for a very long time. There are stories in The Families that go back many centuries. Sightings. Exchanges of information. Meetings. It proceeded along in fits and starts for a long time. They were so... elusive, you see. And we were busily gearing up to conquer the world."

"But at some point things must have ramped up, William. I mean... for you to have built the Herschel Colony back in the sixties..."

"Indeed," said William with a nod. "Our current trajectory began late in the 19th century, about the time of the so-called 'mystery airship' flap. Meetings with a number of intelligent species. Treaties. Deals. Crashed and gifted ships and devices. Back engineering. Technology transfers. The world you know, the space program you've seen, NASA, the whole thing, it's all been a front, a way to control the story while working behind the scenes to further our plans. As a general rule, we are decades to centuries ahead of the mainstream human culture, technologically. We have been for a long time. With the help of the aliens, we've built and flown our own conscious ships, we've explored the Solar System, and we've begun, as I've shown you, to move our species beyond the confines of the planet Earth."

"Well that's all very nice for you then," said Linda.

William smiled indulgently at Linda's tone. "I'm afraid it hasn't been nearly as neat and simple as my little recap implies, Madam," he said. "As one Family member once put it, partnering with aliens has proven to be as befuddling and dangerous as staging a Broadway musical with a cast of tigers." William smoothed his neat beard. "Some are so strange that it's unsettling to be in their presence. Their motives, ranging from helpful and supportive to decidedly antagonistic, seem fluid and even bizarre. And it often feels like they are all in on some massive joke, with us as the laughing-stock."

William closed his eyes and took a long breath, then returned his attention to Linda. "Still, there has been a core, long-term experience, with a few species, and one in particular, that we've grown to trust. Or had trusted, until the Life retreated in response to your rather careless and ill-informed actions some years back. But we know now, or have an inkling at the very least, I should say, of what is out there awaiting us, of what the stakes are, and how we might proceed, given the situation we have found ourselves in."

"And that is...?"

"The Cosmic Community, Madam. The chance for humans to take their place in the commonwealth of intelligent beings, out amongst the stars, just as you've been saying. And the opportunity to step beyond the confines of the materialist paradigm, and into a reality most people can barely imagine. It's the grandest spiritual quest ever, and we're taking it."

"Sounds like the copy for another brochure," said Linda.

The Fisherman scoffed. "Sounds to me like something worth achieving at any price."

"And 'Cosmic Community' sounds an awful lot like extra-terrestrials to me," she said.

"Some are, if by that you mean physical beings visiting Earth in technological devices from elsewhere in this manifest cosmos. But the reality, it turns out, is so much more than that. The Cosmic Community includes beings from levels and realms outside of either time or physicality, and beings from seemingly physical realities so different from our own that even our laws of physics are not the same."

"And why is it that The Families got to know all about this but the rest of us didn't?" asked Linda.

"We were invited to the party," said William, raising one eyebrow. "And we accepted the invitation."

"Ah," said Linda, nodding. "No doubt because you already had tuxedos." She wrinkled her brow. "But it does not seem fair to me, William, that only a few of us humans get to attend this grand party."

William leaned forward and opened his mouth to respond but Linda cut him off with a raised hand. "I mean, c'mon, William. Think about it. You and your people are decades ahead of us, you say. You've got alien technology that has allowed you to start colonies on Saturn, for crying out loud. You' got... I don't know... anti-gravity and... and... free energy. All sorts of shit. Undreamt of power. And look what you've done with it."

Linda stood and waved her hand over her head to indicate the totality of her exasperation. "Look what you've done," she repeated. "All that power, and all you and your people could think to do with it is go off on your own and leave the rest of us behind as the planet burns up?" Linda fell heavily into her armchair. "Why, William?" she asked, her voice now soft and gentle. "Why have you allowed things to get so bad that genocide could begin to sound like a good idea? Why did you not bring us all along with you?"

William nodded, his eyes downcast, his thoughts elsewhere. He took a long breath, then another, and another. Linda watched as he sat with her question. It felt like maybe she'd touched something deep inside that he had not known was there. But it also felt, or at least Linda had the suspicion, that even this was all for show, part of a grand manipulation so far beyond her understanding, so alien, that she could not wrap her mind around it.

At last William looked up. "The aliens insisted," he said sadly.

"Jesus," Linda spat. "Okay." She pushed back into her chair and hugged her knees to her chest. "Tell me about that."

11.17

"That's the third damn time I've gone down the rabbit hole!" said Ted. He sat back in his chair and crossed his arms.

Carl looked up and smiled. "You quittin' boss?"

Ted leaned forward, resting his elbows on his knees and his chin in his hands. "No, I ain't quittin'," he said.

Carl picked a card, read it, and moved ahead six space. "You okay?" he asked.

Ted sighed. "You asked about my father," he said.

"Yeah, I did."

"It made me remember," he said. "Your asking. I didn't want to remember." Ted looked at Carl and wrinkled his nose. "But I do."

"He beat you or something?"

Ted shook his head. "Never laid a hand on me. Was a pretty good guy, actually. But he disappeared."

Carl nodded. "Left your mother when you were young?"

"Nope," said Ted. "Stayed with her until they both died of old age. He just left... inside. He... he went into hiding."

"So he wasn't available emotionally, then," said Carl.

Ted rolled his eyes. "Listen to yourself, Bro," he said. "You sound like some TV shrink. Leading questions. The correct jargon. All interested and shit. Could you just shut up and let me talk and try to get it?"

Carl closed his eyes and breathed slowly. He nodded slightly, then opened his eyes. "You're right, Ted. I keep doing that. Pretending I'm here to help you. Which allows me to ignore the question of whether I have anything that I need to deal with."

"*Right*," said Ted. "*Like you're Mr. Healed or something.*"

"*Sorry,*" said Carl. "*You wanna tell me more?*"

Ted stared down at his feet and thought for a while. "*It was those aliens,*" he said at last. He looked up at Carl. "*Damned little green critters that came and took my Dad away in their ship. And he was a physicist, and he ended up working in some underground military facility and shit. He was gone a lot. And when he was home, he was always distracted. Always reading. Or just sitting and staring into space, or up at the sky. Couldn't or wouldn't talk about any of it with my mom. Said he'd get us all thrown in jail if he said anything. He smoked a pack a day. Drank every night. It all just shut him down.*"

"*That sounds hard,*" said Carl.

Ted looked Carl in the eye and nodded. "*Yeah. It was hard.*" He motioned toward the Uncle Wiggily board. "*I don't remember ever playing a game with him. Or joking around. Or just hanging out. He worked. He slept. He stared into space. Sometimes he'd sit with us for the evening and watch the television with my Mom and me. I think that was the best time.*" Ted stopped. His face was dark and his eyes were small and tight.

"*He disappeared,*" said Carl.

Ted inhaled deeply. "*Yep,*" he said. "*And then the little green monsters grabbed my mother and me and we started to disappear too.*"

Chapter Ø Twelve

12.1

What caught Gabrielle's attention first was the smoke. She initially thought that the fire must be up on the Interstate. An accident, perhaps. A burning vehicle. But as she approached I-95 from the west, the smoke receded further in the distance, drawing her eastward under the overpass. Dusk was approaching, and Gabrielle was looking for a safe place to hide away for the night. She didn't know if the smoke meant safety or danger. She wanted to at least scope it out from a distance.

When she'd fled Winthrop, Gabrielle had stayed mostly in wooded areas, her route shaped by a body of water that pushed her due south. Eventually she'd come to a road that looked so desolate and quiet that it felt safe to follow. That had brought her into the tiny town of Bowdoin, where she'd found a state road map in an abandoned service station. She learned from the map that she'd been following the shoreline of a small lake called Annabessacook. And she found that knowing where she was gave her great relief. Her route, chosen in a moment of panic and desperation, had set her up to make her way down to Squirrel Island while avoiding Augusta.

Avoiding Augusta, with its government and its military presence and its cordon, felt like a smart thing to do. She'd seen that flying saucer once, glinting in the afternoon sun. That must be what they meant by the "AB" that had been "dispatched" to pick her up. It was far away when she saw it, back in the direction from which she'd come, but the way it moved, slowly passing just above the treetops as it tracked methodically back and forth, made it clear that it was searching for her. She was thankful that her chip did not allow them to follow her, but she had to be careful in any event.

Squirrel Island was her destination. That was where the President was being treated. That was where the moment would happen. So that was where she had to go. And it didn't look that far away, really. Twenty miles? Twenty-five? Surely she could walk that far, if she didn't run into trouble.

But not today. It was getting dark and Gabrielle's feet hurt and she needed to find some clean water. And there was that smoke ahead, a dark gray column rising against the fading sky. Which probably meant people. Which meant food and water and shelter. The question was: did it mean food and water and shelter for *her*.

What caught Gabrielle's attention next was the music. It sifted into her awareness slowly, like the coming twilight. There was a deep insistent booming beat that seemed to travel through the earth underfoot, with snippets of guitars and horns and voices flitting about in the breeze, first loud, then soft, then a bit louder. It was joyful music, thought Gabrielle with a smile. Funky, it seemed, when she got close enough to make out the actual songs. Some classic rock. A couple of country tunes. And with the recorded music she heard snatches of extra voices, as people sang along. Gabrielle imagined a block social, a dance party, a joyous celebration erupting under the warm night sky of a small Maine town. She quickened her step, her heart beating with hope.

Eventually she could see the flames, or the reflections of flames at the very least, as they danced across the side of what looked like a long, white barn. The sign on the roadside said she was at the edge of Bowdoin*ham*, Maine. Keeping to the edge of the woods, Gabrielle walked closer, her heart pounding with the funky beat, her mind wary. She scanned the small houses across the road, but found nothing and no one to fear. She crossed a yard behind a burned out trailer, then stepped out onto the rough, open, corrugated surface of an old field. She could see the barn clearly now, and a huge bonfire in the driveway between it and an old farmhouse. The wind was starting to come up, catching the flames.

And then a young man grabbed her from behind and put her in a chokehold. His thin, steely arm was black with soot and grime and tattoos and he reeked of old sweat and bad breath as he pushed Gabrielle toward the fire, causing her to lurch forward to keep from falling. She tried to call out but her throat was clenched tight, so she grabbed his arm with both hands and tried to pull it away.

"Just chill out, girl," said the man as he pushed her across the field. "We'll be there in a second." He eased up on Gabrielle's neck and she sucked in a deep breath of cool air. She tried to turn her head, tried to speak, but he tightened his chokehold again and grabbed her hair with his free hand, keeping her gaze on the fire. "You don't take direction too good, do you?" he said, panting from the exertion of holding her and walking.

When they stepped onto the farmhouse yard, he called out a name. Jeff, it sounded like, though it was difficult to tell with the music blaring. Gabrielle could see two or three others standing near the fire, and a few more sitting in lawn chairs further back from the flames, and half a dozen children chasing each other around. One man, must have been Jeff, turned at the sound of her captor's voice and started walking toward them.

"Found this young thing watching from Mike's place," said the man who held her when Jeff got close enough to hear.

"I said we ain't doin' people yet, Scotty," said Jeff, his brow furrowed in frustration. "Let her go."

"But what if-"

"I said 'let her go'," said Jeff. Scotty sighed with frustration and released his hold. Gabrielle fell to her knees in the tall, brown grass.

"This 'young thing,' as you call her, is a person," said Jeff as he bent and offered Gabrielle a hand. Gabrielle, regaining her breath amidst her sobs, took his hand and stood, then stepped to Jeff's side, away from Scotty.

Scotty, a short, thin young man with a shaved head and missing front tooth, glanced shyly at Gabrielle, then down at his feet. "I'm very sorry, Ma'am," he said. He looked again at Jeff, shrugged a reluctant apology, and walked toward the barn, disappearing into the gloom.

Jeff turned to Gabrielle and smiled. "He's young and stupid," he said, nodding toward the barn, "and he doesn't really get what we're doing here. Not yet." He offered Gabrielle his hand and she took it and he led her back toward the fire.

"What *are* you doing here?" asked Gabrielle. Her voice was shaky and dry and faint and Gabrielle could barely hear herself over the music.

"Satisfying God's demand," said Jeff, leaning over to speak right into her ear. His voice was warm and calm with quiet confidence.

The music quieted a bit as they approached the fire. Somebody had noticed that they had a guest. Close up, Gabrielle could make out what was burning: furniture, mostly, but also what looked like siding boards and picket fencing and the trunks of a couple of small trees. On one side of the burning mound was a smoldering pile of clothes. Next to the clothes was a wooden rocking horse, almost unrecognizable. And above that was what appeared to be the charred corpse of a cat or small dog, sizzling in the flames. "We built this sacrificial flame to honor and appease the Lord our God in this time of great tribulation," said Jeff, loud enough for said Lord to hear him from above. As they stood there a young girl in a flowered dress and bare feet ran up to the fire and tossed a headless chicken onto the fire. An older boy came up behind her, a hatchet in one hand and the chicken head in the other. He tossed the head on the fire and took the girl's hand and together they ran back toward the house.

"But why are you burning a chicken?" asked Gabrielle, shaking her head. "Was it sick? Aren't people hungry?"

Jeff regarded Gabrielle with a gentle smile. "The Lord is coming with fire this time," he said. "Those of us who have been left behind are given the task of helping." From the far side of the fire came a shout to "watch out!" and Gabrielle stepped back in time to see Scotty and an older man toss a futon frame on top of the pile. The impact sent a fountain of sparks into the twilit sky.

As soon as the fire settled back down, a pair of young boys approached, carrying a dead goat between them. They tossed the goat as high as they could, but it landed on a slope that couldn't hold it and rolled back down to the base of the fire and away from the flames. As quickly as they could, the boys dragged it back from the heat, got a better hold on the animal, and ran forward to toss it again. This time it stayed lodged in the flames. Its fur ignited almost immediately. The boys, satisfied, wiped their hands on their shorts and ran away.

Gabrielle looked more closely at the people sitting in lawn chairs. This group was mostly women, with a few older kids mixed in, and they appeared to be sorting things. Clothes. Toys. Kitchen utensils and appliances. Lamps. Some of them sang along with the verses as they sorted, more joined in on the choruses. Anything that was obviously wood and paper got tossed closer to the fire, where a one-armed man picked it up and tossed it onto the mound. But other things got put into boxes and bags. "The metal, glass, and plastics go into separate piles, awaiting further instructions," explained Jeff when he noticed where Gabrielle was staring.

Gabrielle turned, her face clearly puzzled. "But why are you doing this?" she asked.

Jeff sighed. "I told you. We burn now for God, in reparation for our sins and to further His holy judgment. Pastor Clinton has declared it: everything must go. Every board in our house and barn. Every stitch of clothing. Every toy. Every book. Every bit of wood or paper. Every bookmark and playing card. Every morsel of food. And into this great flame, we offer what flesh we can, our livestock, our working animals, our dogs and cats and other pets, in remembrance of days long past, and to prove our faith, just as God Himself is burning the flesh of the unworthy with the Great Plague called Greensleeves. When our house is gone we will move on, meeting with others who are doing the same as us, burning every house we see, every barn, every store, every building. Burning our entire town, and the next one, and the next after that, burning the food that sustains us, the homes that shelter us, burning even the clothes we wear to hide our shame. There will be no more hiding when we are finished. No more humans taking their lives into their own hands. There will be only us, God's naked servants, dependent on His grace for all that we need, or dying gladly, if such is His will. Everything must go." Jeff smiled again, a gentle expression one might use to greet an old friend. He watched as two men tossed a dresser onto the pile, then looked again at Gabrielle.

"So tell me..." he said. He stopped, cocked his head, clearly waiting for Gabrielle to tell him her name.

"Gabrielle."

"So tell me, Gabrielle." He gazed at the fire with pride and excitement, then turned his attention back to her. "Do you know the God of the Burning? And will you join us in our work?"

12.2

When word finally came to Colonel Aidan McAfee, it came in an email from Paul DuPont. It pissed the Colonel off no end, but he would never allow himself to really feel that anger, let alone express it. Not with that chip in his arm. Not with cameras and microphones built into every corner of the facility. But the anger was justified. It was *he* who was in charge here, after all. Not that snot-nosed tech, Family member or not.

McAfee sighed. *Urbem Orsus*. The City of Beginnings. The Loading. The Launch. The One-Two Punch. The Great Journey. Plans within plans within plans. And if he wanted to be included in those plans, he'd have to keep his nose to the grindstone. A smile and a song and all that. That's how he'd catch his ride, if there's to be any hope of catching one. Prove his usefulness to the powers-that-be. Hope that he already had. After all, he and his troops had all been immunized against the alien flu. Obviously The Families had need of them. Surely they would not kill off their own work force?

He put down his tablet and scratched behind Nicky's ears. The cat had sauntered back in as the twilight darkened to night, sniffed at his food bowl, then leapt up onto McAfee's lap in a rare moment of tolerance. The Colonel, in an equally rare moment of fondness, let him stay, even when Nicky sunk his claws into McAfee's leg. There was just something about a warm cat on the lap that was nice.

"Well, Nick," said the Colonel with all the cheeriness he could muster. "Looks like it's time for the old girl to meet her maker." The cat turned his head and looked at his human eye to eye. "By which I mean to say, buddy, that I've got to get up now and go kill the President of these United States."

McAfee wiggled a bit in his recliner. Nicky sunk his claws in deeper. The Colonel grabbed the cat around the middle, lifted him unceremoniously, and dumped him quickly onto the floor. Nicky sat back on his haunches and started licking his front paws. His tail slapped repeatedly against the floor.

The Colonel sighed, pushed the recliner forward, and pulled himself to his feet. He reached down to grab his glass and drank the last gulp of his highball, then headed to the kitchen to put the glass in the sink. He grabbed his jacket from the back of a chair and started pulling it on as he headed toward the door. He glanced back at the cat, who now stared at him from the living room carpet. "I wonder if I'll end up in any history books," he said to the cat.

The cat just stared and slapped his tail. McAfee shook his head and headed out the door.

12.3

A sharp blade of anxiety sliced through Mihos like a phantom knife. He stopped and caught his breath. Looking around, he could not see that anything had changed. They were still in Doggyworld, still following a tunnel through the Murk, still surrounded by the crazy black and white visuals, still apparently walking through what the dense ones in the physical layer fondly referred to as "rural Maine."

Iain, just ahead of him now, stopped and raised an eyebrow. "You okay, Mihos?" he asked. He seemed genuinely concerned, which just added embarrassment to the cat's anxiety.

Mihos coughed. "Just a hairball," he said. "Still, I think we should try to hurry."

Iain nodded. "You got some reason for that? Or is this just your cat radar or something?" He gestured toward the dog at the head of the line. "I mean... Dennis is working pretty hard, it seems. Maybe we should just trust-"

"Maybe you could trust both of us," interrupted Mihos, raising his chin. "It's not like I'm a newbie here, you know. Not like you."

Iain opened his mouth to respond, then stopped. He looked at Emily and Grace, who had stopped now as well, then back at the cat. "You're right, Mihos. My apologies." He turned to Dennis and the girls. "Mihos says we need to go faster," he said.

Dennis nodded once. "Go faster," said the dog. He turned and put his nose to the air and started off again, now at a quicker pace. The kids fell back into line, increasing their speed.

Mihos, his heart still anxious, followed along, glad to be moving again. Whatever it was he was sensing, they might as well find out what it was and get it over with.

12.4

Dinner at the Thieving Seagull had turned out to be a bit of a re-play of the welcoming party the Church of the Stranger had thrown at Ken's house when Cole and Stan had first arrived. Annabelle had come, bringing a half dozen others with her in her old Nissan pickup. There was fresh seafood, more beer, a bottle of "fortifier," and a large helping of hugs, handshakes, and laughter. Outside, the wind bellowed and howled, gusting fiercely at times. Inside, the human beings huddled together, hearts and minds and bodies. Ken would not be joining them, Annabelle had explained. His sister-in-law, Beth, had died a couple of hours earlier. Now his wife, Celia, was sick. Those assembled closed their eyes for a few moments of silence.

Cole could hardly believe it had only been a day since they'd all first met. He was glad to see that Stendahl Banks and his camera-man, Eddie, were welcomed and included as graciously as he and Stan had been. Cole understood Marionette's suspicions, but he'd worked with Sten for years now, and knew him to be a good man. In fact, Cole had figured something out: Sten was the mysterious caller who'd started Cole on his journey. He'd given himself away earlier, on the deck, when expressing his fears about their enemies, and how "they do not mean well for the human race. The tone of Sten's voice had reminded Cole of that call. The more he thought about it, the more obvious it had become. He smiled. Sten was a good man indeed.

It was Doobie, now sobered up, who'd first come up with their next plan: sneak out to the island in the cover of night and the grow-ing storm, land a small crew in a tiny cove he knew about on the north side of the ferry landing, see how close they could get on foot, and see what they could see. It was just the sort of dangerous, crazy, covert operation that Cole had most wanted to avoid, and he said so, but the idea had already caught on with the younger folks in the room. Doobie argued that he knew that island like the back of his own hand. Marionette protested that surely they couldn't have patrols all along the shoreline. Simon, Keith, Gordon, Joe, Ann... they all expressed their willingness to give it a try. "We can do this, Stranger," said Marionette, her voice grave and low. "It's why we're here."

"Then I'm going along," said Cole, shaking his head.

Annabelle rose to her feet and the conversation came to a halt. She turned slowly, her gaze moving from face to face, stopping at last at Cole. She smiled. "I think we need to let these young people do this, Stranger," she said to Cole. "I think you need to let us help you."

"But-," Cole began, only to be stopped when Annabelle raised her hand.

"I understand, Stranger," said the old woman. She looked around the room. "I think we all do. This is a risky venture." She gestured through the window out toward the bay, and Squirrel Island in the distant night. "The people who abducted your wife are far more powerful and dangerous than just the U.S. military."

Stendahl raised his hand like a schoolboy, and only spoke when Annabelle nodded to him. "I think at the very least Eddie and I need to go, to get some video and..." Sten's words faltered when Annabelle started shaking her head.

"I understand that the whole 'media circus' angle is a big part of your plan," she said. "But it's dark, and this is dangerous. Let that part wait for the light of day. Tonight, let's do a bit of stealthy recon and see what we can learn from that."

Stan stood in the back, shaking his head. "This is stupid," he said, his voice a low growl. "You got a storm coming and you're sending out a bunch of green kids?" He looked at the folks gathered in the dining room. "You're not trained commandos." He turned to Doobie. "You're not some seasoned naval captain." He looked at Annabelle. "Hell, Annabelle, I *am* a seasoned naval captain and even I wouldn't venture out on a night like this. Not against an enemy like the one we're facing. Not even for a bit of recon." He glanced at Cole and sighed, shaking his head.

Annabelle smiled gently at Stan, then turned to Cole. "Stranger," she said, "there's a piece you do not have." She looked around at the young people in favor of the mission, then back to Cole. "In **The Book of the Stranger**, it says this: *Venture into the darkness and the storm, and know that the Stranger's light will be with you. Be as his arms, his feet, his very eyes, as he faces his worst fear and confronts his horrible foe. Spend yourself in the Stranger's service, and know that your sacrifice will have meaning.*" The old woman stopped and exhaled softly.

Cole rubbed his eyes. "Jesus, Annabelle," he said at last, his voice heavy and tired. "We're gonna risks these young people's lives because of a few Bible verses?" He shook his head.

"We're all we're ever going to have, Stranger," said Annabelle softly, looking him in the eye. "We'll either be enough, or we won't be, but we're all we have. And the time is here, as we knew it would be, and we will never be more ready than we are now." She looked at the quiet, expectant faces around here. "Marionette?" she said when she caught the eye of the young woman. Her voice had risen both in volume and pitch, as if it was time to change the mood to one of action.

"Ma'am?" answered Marionette, stepping forward.

"Doobie will be in charge of all boat-related matters. You will lead the reconnaissance mission. Can I trust you not to do anything stupid?"

Marionette lifted her chin. "I don't know," she said, "can you?"

Annabelle grinned. "Good point. Yes. I can. And I will And I will also trust you to know when it's time to abort the mission and get your mouthy, one-eyed little ass back here as well." She turned to Cole. "This is what we've been waiting for, Stranger. A chance to help you. Please allow us to do our best."

Stan sighed but otherwise held his tongue.

Cole looked at Annabelle and nodded almost imperceptibly. He glanced at Sten, who winked and grinned at what they both now knew: you did not stand in the way of this tiny old Church lady and her magic **Book**. "Okay," said Cole, turning back to Annabelle. "Okay."

In the end, it was decided that Eddie should join the Church members and get as much night-vision video as he could. Depending on how things went, some of that video might be used to help stir public interest, and it would allow those who were not going to see, upon the mission's return, at least some of what those in Marionette's group would experience in person.

They packed what they needed and boarded *The Pokey Joker* for the third time out. Just five of them this time: Doobie, Marionette, Gordon, Ann, and Eddie. They hoped that a smaller group would be an asset, and both Gordon and Ann had served in the military, Gordon as a medic and Ann as a communications specialist.

The sky was completely overcast now, though brighter than they'd expected, with the Gridlight illuminating the cloud layer from above, giving enough glint to the waves that they could distinguish, just barely, where they were. The wind was stronger than ever, and gusty, and the seas were choppy, but no worse than Doobie had seen fishing in the winter, their captain assured them. In fact he was glad for the wind and waves, he said, as it would help cover the rumble of *The Pokey Joker's* diesel engines.

They calculated that the mission should take no longer than 90 minutes total. Those staying behind hugged those who were leaving, voicing stern warnings and strong wishes for these brave young people to be careful, and to come back safe and whole. Then Doobie started his engines and they were gone in the night.

Cole stood on the dock, watching. He glanced down at his hands, wondering how the hell he was supposed to make his "Stranger's light" be "with them" out on the boat. Had he just sent these young people to some huge disaster? Capture? Injury? Death? Had he sent anybody to anything, or had they simply chosen? Cole was too tired to sort it out, and decided that he didn't need to. They were all at risk. The whole world was at risk now. And greater forces than he were deciding the outcomes. Cole had his children to worry over. And Linda, sick and imprisoned on an island just a mile or two out across the water, held by the military, and by those who wanted to control things from behind the scenes. Annabelle was right: Cole had better learn to accept help.

But then something occurred to Cole that hit him smack in the gut. Based on what Annabelle had told him just yesterday, and based on the quotes she'd just recited from *The Book of the Stranger*, it was Linda that he was supposed to stop from destroying the human race. In the minds of these Church people, Linda Travis was "his horrible foe."

12.5

Linda gazed out across the landscape. The Martian night had come, the yellow-pink sky slipping into star-studded blackness much more quickly than it ever could on Earth. The President tweaked her seeing slightly and gasped at the beauty of it all. The constellations pulsed with life, and the vast plain before her glowed with possibilities far beyond both rightdoing and wrongdoing.

Across from Linda sat an empty armchair. William had disappeared again, this time without so much as a word of farewell. Linda sighed. That strange little man could stand to learn some manners.

As soon as he'd gone, Linda had attempted to blink back to Earth. She couldn't do it. She'd focused on Cole. On the kids. On Ness and Mary. Nothing had worked. She couldn't blink anywhere, whether back to Earth or to some other point here on Rumi's Field. William had left her tuned to the near-physical. She was confined to the desolate surface of Mars.

Something glinted in the far distance. Linda squinted her eyes. Glass, it looked like. It must be her "lobster tank," the container William had used to transport her body to Mars and keep it from harm. William had told her it was nearby.

Linda rose from her chair and searched the night sky. Somewhere out there was Earth. On it were all the people she cared about. She felt like she could collapse in a sobbing heap and never get back up. But she knew that that would not get her back home. And she knew that, with William gone, she might be able to learn something she couldn't otherwise.

It did not appear that the Fisherman was going to blink back anytime soon. And if he did, so what? To be frank, Linda didn't really give a rat's ass if she inconvenienced him or not. So she decided to go take a look at her body and make sure that all was well. Perhaps there'd be some clues there that she'd missed before. She'd have to hoof it, but that'd be fine. Give her a chance to think. And she hadn't been getting her morning walks in anyways.

She set out. The near-physical tuning felt surreal. Gravity held her in place. Her tennis shoes left tracks in the dust and gravel. Stones skittered away when she kicked them. Gusts of the thin Martian atmosphere dislodged wisps of her hair. She seemed to be breathing in and out. None of this should have been possible.

Not for the first time, she wondered if she was really on Mars at all. Maybe she was still on Earth. Maybe this was all an elaborate dream or vision. Maybe that *was* her real body underneath her cottage. But the evidence of the sky told her where she was. The sun had been so small. And there was Phobos again.

Linda Travis walked toward the container that held her body. She felt no soreness, no fatigue, no imbalance. She was strong and able. She could easily make it, if William did not return to stop her. It might take all day, but who cared? What else should she do? Sit in that stupid chair and wait?

12.6

The tall, bald nurse stepped out the double front doors of the MaineCentral Hospital and looked to the west. The short, dark nurse took her place beside him. The thin, pale private left his barracks and faced to the south. The thickly muscled sergeant stopped his Jeep and looked to the east. The short, old woman stepped into the hospital hallway and faced the west. The beautiful blonde woman in business attire stood at her eleventh-floor window and looked out to the north. The short, curly-haired assistant walked down the ramp and looked to the east. The strangely exotic blonde man put down his phone and faced toward the west. The older woman with large, black eyes stepped onto the front porch of her home and looked to the south. The Other-than-Ness stood amidst the bodies of the comatose children and looked to the north. All over Augusta, the men and women who now occupied the city, mostly young, mostly strikingly beautiful or foreign in appearance, stopped what they were doing and faced the city center and met mind-to-mind. An invisible beam pierced the city from the sky above.

"IT IS WELL HERE," said the short, curly-haired assistant.

"IT IS WELL HERE," said the short, dark nurse.

"OUR CHARGES ARE SAFE," said the thickly muscled sergeant.

"AND OUR HOME IS QUIET," said the exotic blonde man.

"THE PLAYERS ARE IN MOTION," said the large-eyed older woman.

"AND THE TRANSITION TIME NEARS," said the tall, bald nurse.

"A NEW WORLD AWAITS THEM," said the beautiful blond woman.

"AS IT ALSO AWAITS US," said the thin, pale private.

"THE CITY NOW RESTS," they all said together.

"IN PREPARATION FOR THE NEW DAYS AHEAD," they said as they stood alone.

"THOSE IN OUR CARE," said the Other-than-Ness, "WHO SLEEP NOW IN BEDS OR REST IN THE LOVING ARMS OF OUR MACHINE SISTER, DESERVE OUR PROTECTION, AS THEY MEET THE FATES GIVEN THEM, AND MAKE WHAT CHOICES THEY MUST. WE ARE HONORED TO SERVE."

"WE ARE HONORED TO SERVE," said the others in unison.

"FOR WE SHALL SOON SERVE OURSELVES," said the short, old woman.

"WE SHALL SOON SERVE OURSELVES," said the others together.

As the night covered the streets, homes, and businesses of the city like a warm blanket, the men and women who now inhabited Augusta turned as one and went back to their work.

In her hospital room, the Other-than-Ness receded into the background. Ness, standing between the gurneys, had some trouble remembering what it was she'd been up to.

12.7

Doobie stubbed out his cigarette and peered through the windshield. The glass was spattered by the choppy seas, but if he was not mistaken, that was Squirrel Island ahead of them, a black mass rising from the undulating, faintly-blue surface of the harbor. Above it blinked a steady white light, no doubt attached to a tower. Doobie was running no lights at all.

"How much longer?" asked Marionette, standing beside him. She held onto the handhold as the boat lurched to the left.

"Ten minutes, maybe," said Doobie. "Need to go slowly or I'll miss the cove."

Marionette exhaled sharply. Her single eye sparkled fiercely in the boat's dashboard lights.

"You nervous?" asked Doobie.

"Of course," said Marionette. "You?"

Doobie nodded. "Yep. *The Pokey Joker's* my livelihood. I'd prefer to not smash her into the rocks."

"I'd prefer to not smash *me* into the rocks," said Marionette, smiling shyly.

"That too," said Doobie with a wink.

Eddie, who'd been scanning the seas ahead through his night-vision camcorder, rose and joined them, careful to keep one hand on the railing. "We seem to have a bogey," he said to Marionette.

Marionette turned to Eddie. "A boat?" she asked.

"Uh, uh," said Eddie, shaking his head. "Look." He flipped out the viewscreen and held the camera in position. "Up above the tower and to the right. You see it?"

Marionette watched the screen for a bit. "That tiny speck?" she asked at last.

Eddie nodded. "It appeared just a minute ago."

Marionette leaned forward to peer out the front windshield. She couldn't see anything but the tower light. She pushed open the cabin door and stepped out onto the starboard deck and moved to the fore. Eddie followed, holding his camera against his chest to protect it from the spray. Marionette watched the sky ahead for a moment, then turned to Eddie and spoke into his ear. "I don't see anything!" she said, shouting above the wind and waves and diesel engines.

Eddie pulled out his camera, used it to scan the area ahead, then showed it to her again. The speck, now larger, still hung in the sky over the island. Marionette handed the camera back and scanned the sky again. There was something there now. Maybe.

Then the faint speck flared in the night sky, bursting forth in brilliance so powerful that both of them raised an arm to shield their eyes. The speck grew larger and larger, taking on a football shape and lighting the island underneath it like a stadium. It came to a stop near the tower, hovered for a moment, then settled slowly downward, its motion that of a falling leaf. It sank amongst the trees, then winked out, leaving the island again in darkness, and leaving the crew of *The Pokey Joker* blinking away their temporary blindness.

"Looks like they've got company," said Marionette.

"Yeah," agreed Eddie.

"Which will make things either easier or more difficult for us," she added.

Eddie shook his head. He had no idea what to think of this.

In the faint light, the two of them made their way back into the cabin.

12.8

This time it was Dennis who called out. They'd been hurrying along at Mihos' urging, almost trotting, the cat convinced that something bad would happen if they did not get there soon. Then Dennis disappeared. A single, sharp bark of surprise and he was gone. Into the blackness of the Murk.

None of them knew what to do. For a while, they just waited, as Dennis had twice now proven his ability to find his way back out. But when he didn't reappear, Grace grew ever more afraid for him, and finally Mihos proposed that they do what they had done before, and form a human-feline chain with which to pull him back out.

"I'll go in first," said Mihos to the kids. "Give him my eyes to cue in on. Grace, you take my legs. Then Emily. Then Iain, as the anchor." The cat looked at the boy with something approaching respect. Iain nodded.

Mihos stepped forward to where they'd last seen Dennis. He stuck his nose out. At last he touched the edge of the Murk, and it pulled him right in.

But it didn't just pull Mihos in, as he'd expected. It pulled them all in.

"Damn!" spat Mihos, when they figured out what had happened.

"Dennis?" called Grace.

There was no response from the dog.

"Dennis?"

"Dennis?"

No Dennis.

Grace called out for Dennis again, but her voice was now faint. "Grace? Where are you going?" shouted Mihos, assuming that a fainter voice meant she was moving away.

There was no response from Grace.

"Grace?" called Iain. "Grace!"

"Grace?" called Emily.

No Grace.

"Damn!" spat Mihos again.

"Damn!" agreed Iain.

Emily, Iain, and Mihos sat, or stood, or hovered together in the blackness of no experience, not sure of anything beyond the voices in their own minds. Sometimes they called out. For a long time they listened. Mihos was puzzled. He imagined himself turning slowly in all directions, shining his eyes like a lighthouse for their lost companions, a beacon to which they might return. He could not be certain that he was turning. But none of it seemed to make any difference.

At last Emily spoke up. "You remember that first time we were in here?" she asked. "How it felt like we were being pushed?"

Iain said that he remembered.

"I'm feeling it again," said Emily. "It's almost like we're being... herded."

12.9

"Oh... great," said Colonel McAfee, rolling his eyes. His aide, Osterman, turned and headed down the hallway, having delivered his news: the Family member who'd visited earlier, the one named only "William," had again appeared unannounced at their door.

McAfee turned and put a smile on his face just in time to see the elevator slide open and the man himself step into the hallway, bringing a wave of warm salt air down with him. William flashed his badge at the security station, crossed the hallway and stepped into the Colonel's cramped office.

"Mr. ... William," said McAfee with a confident nod, rising from his chair and thrusting out his hand as the other approached.

"Good to see you again, Colonel," said William, flashing his eyebrows with excitement. "I expect you thought you'd seen the last of me." He took McAfee's hand in both of his and shook it warmly, something the Colonel had only ever seen politicians do.

McAfee smiled more brightly. "Big doings today, Sir," he said. "Seems things are again moving forward."

William cocked his head and studied the Colonel's face. "Indeed," he said at last. "'Big doings,' as you say. I trust you've not yet...?" He gestured toward the floor. Two soldiers and a doctor in scrubs stepped quickly past the office doorway.

McAfee followed William's gesture. Two levels below them was the room in which Linda Travis lay. He looked at William. "No, Sir," he said. "The Directorate said 8 P.M." He looked at his watch. "It's four minutes until."

"You are no doubt on your way there," said William.

McAfee knew an order when he heard one. "Yes, Sir," he said. "No fuss. No drama. The doctor is there and ready. And Mr. DuPont insisted that he be present as well. One push on the hypo and the job will be finished. You and I can make it a foursome."

William wrinkled his brow. "Yes," he said slowly. "Though your colloquialism... a golfing term, if I am not mistaken... casts it in a rather less serious light than I would have preferred."

McAfee froze, inhaled slowly, nodded gravely. Shit, he thought. "My apologies, Sir," he said. "No disrespect intended. Just a careless word in a stressful time." He smiled slightly, as if to try, subtly, to encourage William's agreement.

"Quite," said William. He gestured toward the door. "Shall we, then?" he said.

The Colonel nodded. "Indeed."

12.10

Keeley lay in her hospital bed, watching the television. Her eyes were open, at any rate, and had been for a number of minutes. Little of what she saw was actually getting through to her awareness.

She'd heard a voice. Or thought she had. Her sleep - so peaceful, so full, so happy - had been jostled awake by the voice. Two words, the voice had said. Spoken with a British accent. "Urban horses," they sounded like. She did not know what they meant.

The television muttered on and on, repeating the same stories it had been telling all day, as if hoping somebody would notice, as if the television itself were uncomfortable with silence. Keeley closed her eyes and settled back into the joyful calm of her illness. Mary had yet to return. Alas. My love. Keeley hadn't seen the nurses since nightfall. She had no idea what time it was. Or what day. She was so sleepy. And sleep felt so full of joy. But the joy had a stain in it now. A sting. A single discordant note.

Two words, the voice has spoken. Something horrible would come of them.

Keeley closed her eyes tightly against the memory and wandered her way back to sleep, slipping into the peace of Greensleeves.

Alas.

12.11

Doobie had found the cove, and the small private dock he'd expected to find. But the combination of chopping waves and gusting winds and the boat's great mass had done a number on the dock as he pulled up beside it, twisting it almost beyond usability. But only almost. Marionette, Eddie, Gordon, and Ann had managed to pull and crawl and stumble their way to shore, and had made it to the old inn that had claimed this cove as its private bit of ocean.

The inn was clearly abandoned, so Marionette broke a sidelight pane with the heavy bolt-cutter they'd brought along. She unlocked the front door and they stepped inside. Protected from the wind, they breathed a collective sigh of relief.

Marionette led them upstairs. From the inn's third story dormers, they took turns looking out over the island through Eddie's night-vision camera. Mostly what they saw was trees. But here and there, along the island's old roadways, they saw lengths of fencing, as if the entire island was now encircled with ten-feet-high chain link and coils of razor wire.

"I don't see any patrols," said Marionette, scanning with the camcorder.

"They probably don't have much need for them here," said Ann. "It's an island, after all. And they no doubt have electronic surveillance up the wazoo."

Marionette reached out and grabbed Ann's hand in the darkness. "I've got some things I'd like to stuff up their wazoos," she said, her voice almost a whisper.

"What next?" asked Gordon, sounding excited and ready to move. "We've got the bolt-cutters. If there's no patrols, maybe we can get a closer look."

"I don't like the sound of that," said Eddie.

"You don't think the Wayfaring Stranger is with us right now?" said Gordon, his tone defensive.

"I don't know about any of that," said Eddie. "I just know that when I see razor wire and hear about electronic surveillance, *my* thinking is: do not enter."

"Which is exactly what they want us to think," said Gordon.

"I think we should just go get a closer look at the fence," said Marionette. She turned to Eddie in the faint Gridlight. "Just a look. To see what we're dealing with." Eddie sighed but said nothing. Gordon and Ann agreed with the plan. The four of them headed down the stairs and out into the night.

The wind was warm and gusty. The coming storm would foul the military's surveillance systems a bit, according to Ann. Eddie was grateful for that. They headed up the inn's driveway to the main road and turned right, the direction that would take them in toward the center of the island, and directly to the fence. For a few moments, the clouds overhead broke apart, revealing the ever-present Grid and bathing them in brighter blue-white light.

"You think that ship thing we saw from the boat was one of theirs?" said Eddie, pointing up at the Grid.

"Or one of ours," replied Gordon. "Hard to know these days."

Marionette shivered. The thought of strange little beings wandering around in the dark creeped her out. She'd never met one. She didn't *want* to meet one, regardless of what Annabelle might have to say about the matter. "C'mon," she said, "let's check out the fence while the lights are on."

It was just a tall chain-link fence. Just razor wire. No patrols. No cameras. No snarling Pit Bulls. If they wanted to, they could cut their way through it with ease. If that was what the Stranger wanted, they would.

But that would have to wait. They'd done their job. The clouds had moved back in, darker than ever, and the wind was starting to howl, knocking dead branches to the ground in the woods around them. Best to get back to Doobie and his boat and get back home. No telling how long he could stay moored there, with that dock so messed up.

"Just let me make one cut," said Gordon, pulling the cutters from his pack. "So we know it can be done. If that's what we decide to do later." Eddie shook his head but Marionette nodded hers. The four of them stepped closer to the fence and Gordon kneeled to make his cut.

Then an invisible hand picked them all up and threw them across the road.

12.12

Linda was struck again by the beauty of the Martian terrain. There was much more going on here than just desert and desolation. The colors, as viewed through her astral sight, were quite striking. And the edges of things, how they looked in the starlight: stark, and yet lively. Cheery, even.

She felt no sense of struggle or fatigue, only a weariness of soul. It was a constant struggle in her heart, to surrender to her situation, and to William. He had so much to say. Like Agent Rice, he wanted something from her, and was willing to hold her captive to get it. But he was also like her friend Obie: he wanted her to know and understand him. He wanted her to feel the predicament they both faced. He wanted her, in the end, to make a choice, one that he felt unqualified to make himself. And he was convinced that she could not make the choice until he had said his piece. Linda put her hand out and ran it along a large boulder as she passed it by. Perhaps he was right.

William wanted Linda to understand why The Families had done what they'd done, and why they felt the need to take such drastic action as to kill off a large portion of the human population. Linda recoiled at the notion. But, truth be told, she was fascinated by it as well. And she was fascinated with the Fisherman. Her distrust of the hidden elite did not square with her experience of William himself. There were things he'd said that made sense. There was a sanity to his story she found difficult to argue against. But still there was a queasiness in her gut she could not deny. She wondered if she was simply being charmed by a psychopath.

Linda started down the shallow slope of a sandy dune and glanced up at the night sky. Out there. Whatever it was that could justify the actions of William and his people, it was "out there." Ancient ruins. Colonies on Saturn. Space ships flitting around the galaxy. Human beings were already reaching for the stars. The human experiment *was* continuing. So why did it need to end on Earth?

Walking up the far side of what had now revealed itself to be a shallow crater, Linda turned to look back in the direction from which she had come. In the distance, dozens of tiny lights flew toward her like a swarm of bees. Soon they were speeding overhead, huge glowing woks, each flaring brightly for a moment as it passed, as if in greeting. Then they were gone.

She continued to the rim of the crater and searched the sky. The woks were gone, but the Cosmos remained. All of it was waiting on her, it seemed: to learn, to understand, and to choose, just as Sinaaq had said she must. She gazed out across the plain. There was the lobster tank, glinting in the starlight, so close now that she could make out the contours of her body. All looked well. Linda walked on. She would be there soon.

12.13

"You keep cats in your facility, Colonel?" asked William as they walked down the hall. A small black cat with a white star on its chest had just turned the corner and was headed toward them.

McAfee moved forward quickly. "Nicky!" he said angrily. "What are you doing down here?" He bent and lifted the cat and handed it off to his aide, Osterman, who trailed behind them. "You bad kitty!" he said, smacking his hands together as if washing them of responsibility. He turned back to William. "Again," he said, "my apologies. That cat has twice snuck down here on the freight elevator." He looked at Osterman sternly. "Get it out of here," he ordered, as though the whole sad affair was the aide's fault. He again returned his attention to the member of The Families.

"Just a moment," said William. He stepped over to Osterman and bent to look the cat in the eye. He cocked his head and stared for a moment before speaking. "You've been busy, haven't you little one?" he said in a playful voice. He looked up at Osterman. "Be gentle with this one," he said to the soldier.

McAfee nodded toward his aide. "You heard the man," he said. Osterman saluted and left with the cat.

William turned on the Colonel. "I'm beginning to wonder how you folks have managed as well as you have here," said William. He was smiling. The corners of his mouth were raised and there were sparkles in his eyes. But McAfee knew that he had just been threatened again.

"We have done an excellent job of carrying out The Families' orders precisely and efficiently, Sir," said McAfee, holding William's gaze. He knew that any hesitancy or groveling on his part would only confirm that he deserved to be punished. Screw that. If he was going down, he would go down fighting. "You may have noticed that we are now operating under threat of a major storm. I dare say a stray cat is not going to mess up the Plan." He stood his ground, his chest heaving with both terror and pride.

William flashed his eyebrows and smiled again. "Yes," he said. "I just flew through that storm." He gestured toward the door and started walking, taking McAfee gently by the elbow and guiding him along. "It's a doozy, as you Americans like to say. Quite the spectacle. The weather people should be proud of their work."

They reached the door and stopped. McAfee slid his card and waited for the lock to click. He pushed the door open and he and William stepped into the viewing area. There, behind the glass, stood Paul DuPont, the lead Changeling Tech, and a doctor in scrubs, lab coat, and mask. Between them, lying naked on her stainless steel gurney, was Linda Travis, the President of the United States.

DuPont came out to meet them. He nodded at William, who nodded in return.

"You got your assistant driving the VLT?" asked McAfee.

DuPont tried to not role his eyes. He failed. "The Summit's not in session at this late hour, Colonel," he explained, as if to a child. "No real need for the VLT. That's why the Directorate specified 8 P.M. So I could be here."

"Right," said McAfee, turning to William as though DuPont had just confirmed the Colonel's brilliance. He gestured toward the second room. "Shall we?" William stepped in and stood near the President's head. DuPont and McAfee followed. The doctor pulled the door closed, then grabbed a hypodermic from a tray on a stand. He took his place near the IV and glanced at the clock. It was now a few minutes past eight.

McAfee glanced at William. William looked at DuPont, then the doctor, then back to McAfee. "I believe it's your call, Colonel," he said.

"Right," said McAfee again. He nodded to the doctor. "Go ahead, Tom," he said. The doctor, with a sigh, slid the hypodermic into the IV tube and then pushed the plunger, emptying the yellow liquid into the line.

He pulled the hypo back out and placed it carefully on the tray. The four of them stood and watched over the President's naked body. Her heart monitor beat steadily. After about thirty seconds, her monitor began to beat wildly and Linda Travis convulsed, her chest rising violently and then falling gently, as though she'd just been shocked with electricity. Then she was still. The monitor now showed a flat line.

William reached down and straightened a lock of Linda's hair that had fallen out of place from her convulsion. DuPont looked down at his feet. The doctor stared straight ahead, as if seeing nothing. Colonel McAfee exhaled loudly and rubbed at his nose.

"I guess that's that," said McAfee at last.

"Indeed," said William.

12.14

Linda made her way across a flat expanse of deep, dusty grit. She still hadn't figured out the workings of this strange level, where she seemed to be both body and not-body, real and not real. The footprints made no sense at all to her, and yet there they were, stretching back toward the horizon in the direction from which she'd come. She sighed. That was the least of her worries. She reached the far side of the thick dust and stepped onto a slightly rippled plain of glossy, bare rock. She kept moving. The lobster tank was not far now.

Linda stopped and gave a sharp yelp. For a moment - she was sure of it! - her body had moved, a lurching upward of her head and chest. She shook her head and squinted her eyes, hoping to improve her vision in this strange place. It must have been some vagary of light or shadow or atmosphere, some trick of the eye. Her body looked as it had before: still and restful, lying on its pedestal.

Linda started moving again. She'd be there in a minute now.

12.15

Mihos was alone in the Murk. What had happened to Grace had happened to them all. Voices had grown fainter, then disappeared altogether, as if Emily and Iain had simply walked away, or as if *he* had. But none of them had just "walked away." They were, indeed, being pushed. Herded. And Mihos was appalled. You simply did not herd cats.

He'd never been so far inside of a Murk. Had no real idea how they worked. All he knew, really, is what he'd heard: most people never came back out of one. The Murk was the most powerful roach motel in existence.

"Damn!" he muttered again.

How he could know he was being pushed he had no idea, since he had no sensation of body, orientation, distance, location, visuals, or movement. But he knew. There was something here. Someone. And he or she was pushing him. Mihos imagined a faint drumbeat in the distance, growing ever louder, and glowing red walls and ceiling, as if he was trapped in the caves of hell. But he didn't really hear drums, did he? Or see red light? That was just imagination, wasn't it? That was too many old movies.

Worse than being herded was the feeling that, if he let himself, Mihos might start sobbing at any moment. Which was not okay for a cat, even if there was nobody there to see him. The tears were welling up in eyes he could not feel, rising on a moan of grief he could not utter. For once, he was glad to be disconnected from his own body.

And the urgency was gone. The urgency that had had him push them all faster and faster. The urgency that had resulted in Dennis getting pulled into the Murk. The urgency that had left them all lost here in the black. *That* urgency was gone. And the lack of urgency, and the thoughts of grief and tears, told Mihos that whatever it was he'd been hurrying *to* had now come to pass. They were too late. Too late. Here in this damnable blackness where time did not even exist, they were too, too late.

Let them push. Let them herd him. Let them try to shove him into a river of lava. Let them beat their cursed drums. Maybe he deserved it. He was too late anyways. He was too far gone. Not even the Great Ones could save him now.

12.16

Mary came in through the kitchen, crossed through to the front hall, and peeked in on her father. There he sat, slouched in his recliner, snoring, just as she and D'Neal had observed through the living room windows. As quietly as she could, she made her way up the stairs, avoiding every squeaking step, memorized out of dire need and past experience. She looked in on Danny's sleeping form, then started down the hall to her room. She just needed her wallet and some clothes. If she could get those, she could go. Leave. Run away. She and D'Neal would go together. They weren't sure where. They just knew that her father would likely kill them both if he caught them.

Maybe they should have faced him at the fairgrounds. There in the open, in the light of day, surrounded by people. Mary could have grabbed D'Neal's hand and they could have walked over to her father, proudly, chins raised, and told him exactly how things were, and how they were going to go from now on. But that was just a silly fantasy. Her father would have remained calm, there in public. But he would bide his time. He'd *enjoy* biding his time. And then, one day, he would lash out. It was etched into stone. It could not be avoided.

But it might be avoided if Mary ran away. She just needed her wallet. And her father was dead drunk in his recliner, as usual. I can do this, she chanted. I can.

The light went on downstairs. It raced up the stairway and down the hallway to slap the back of her head. Mary froze. She listened. Then she ducked into her room, grabbed her wallet, forgot about clothes or anything else, and headed toward her window. Just like times before, when things got really bad. Once, she'd sprained her ankle, falling to the ground, but other times she'd managed to climb down the porch columns, using the pair of flag holders as footholds.

But there wasn't time. Her father was now racing up the stairs, calling out her name in that high, wild voice he used when he was at his angriest. Her door slammed open and the light flicked on and he leapt across the room to grab Mary's arm before she could slip out the window. He dragged her back inside, clenching her upper arm so hard she started to cry, slapping her head with his other hand. "You're screwing a nigger?" he screamed, over and over. "A nigger, girl? A nigger?" He lifted her with one arm and threw her onto the bed and brought his other hand down onto her stomach like a sledgehammer. Mary screamed for breath, pulled herself into the fetal position, scrunched her eyes shut, screamed and screamed and screamed again.

She heard a moan and opened her eyes to see Danny, standing in the doorway, watching, tears wetting his face. Her father slapped her again on the face. Again. Again. Then he put his hand.... down there. He started to push. His other hand was on her throat now, pinning her to the bed. Mary called out for God to save her, please save her, please please please save her! Her voice made no sound.

"You like that, nigger lover?" her father said, his voice now low and menacing and full of heat. "You like that? You like that? You like that like you like that nigger?"

And then the room filled with bright white light, trapping the whole scene in the horror of that moment, like a bug trapped in amber.

12.17

Marionette sat up in the darkness. She'd landed in a ditch on the edge of the tree line. The wind was howling. Tree branches lashed back and forth right behind her. Clouds stampeded overhead, allowing bits of Gridlight to sift down to the ground.

Something moved to her left. It was Eddie, scrambling in the dark, searching for his camera. He found it, held it to his stomach, and pushed himself to his feet. Beyond him was Ann. She was kneeling over a body that lay motionless on the ground. Gordon. "He's still alive!" shouted Ann, turning back to face them.

Marionette rolled onto her knees, then stood. She stepped forward and pulled on Eddie's sleeve to draw him in. "We've got to get him out of here!" she shouted into his ear. Eddie nodded. He handed the camera to Marionette and knelt at Gordon's side.

Marionette surveyed the situation. Something had thrown them across the road, but she saw no sign of what it might have been. She felt unharmed, but stunned. Eddie seemed no worse for wear. Ann as well. But Gordon had a gash on his forehead. Must've hit a rock or a tree branch or something when he fell. His face was covered with blood, but he was still breathing.

Eddie worked one hand under Gordon's neck and the other under his knees. He hugged the unconscious man to his stomach, then pushed himself to his feet. Ann grabbed Gordon's legs. Slowly, they picked their way up the ditch to the main road. It was a short walk back to the driveway, and the inn, and *The Pokey Joker*, but Marionette had no idea how they'd get Gordon out to the boat, with the dock in the shape it was.

That would wait. For now, they just had to get moving. Eddie yelled into the wailing wind, a battle cry of defiance and power that was quickly snatched away by the storm. They started down the road, moving as swiftly as they could. Ann took her share of the weight. Together they could do this.

Marionette stepped ahead to act as scout, afraid of what they might encounter. Ground troops? Little gray men? Something even worse? She wished she'd brought that damned revolver she kept in her pack. She wished she'd listened to her gut instead of Stan Walsh.

But then a light began to glow underfoot, as if their path was lined by those little solar lights people sometimes used. Marionette looked immediately to the sky, expecting to see a helicopter, or maybe a flying saucer, about to scoop them all up. But there was no saucer, no copter. There were just clouds, lit dimly from above by the Grid, churning slowly across the sky.

Marionette looked back down at her feet. The path light was still there, a bit stronger now, like a strip of fog lit from within and hugging the ground like a runner rug. It led them down the driveway toward the inn. She glanced behind her. Eddie and Ann were moving more quickly than ever, as if the light gave them some new measure of power and hope.

Shivering, scanning the area for little Gray beings and finding none, Marionette led her friends down the well-lit path.

12.18

"I assume you gentlemen will be evacuating soon?" asked William.

DuPont nodded. "I've got a 12-footer on the pad. Need to collect my family. Then straight to *Urbem Orsus,* as per the Directorate's instructions," he said.

William looked at McAfee expectantly. McAfee stood still and smiled. He had no idea what his situation was, whether he was being invited or left behind. And he was afraid to ask directly. Best to just play it out and see what was offered him. He nodded toward Linda Travis's dead body on the gurney. "I want to oversee disposal, first, Sir," he said. He glanced at DuPont, wrinkled his nose, and then returned his attention to William. "Then I think I'll stay here and ride out the storm with my troops." He inhaled sharply. He'd just created an opening, hoping that William would clap a hand on his shoulder and say, "Nonsense, man, you're coming with me!" But he knew that 'riding out the storm' could mean far more than just this one little hurricane. He smiled at William, who simply returned the smile with a slight nod. "We should be okay here," added McAfee. "Underground and all."

"Indeed," said William. "Brilliant."

McAfee made for the door to the viewing area. "I guess you two will be off, then," he said. DuPont followed close behind, but William hung back.

"If I might," said William, standing next to the President's body, "I'd like to stay a few moments longer." He glanced down at Linda's body, then back to the Colonel. "To say goodbye." McAfee nodded respectfully and ushered DuPont out the door and into the hallway, leaving William alone.

The Fisherman placed the palm of his hand on Linda's forehead and sighed deeply, then turned and walked to a corner cabinet. Reaching into his jacket pocket, he pulled out a small, brown glass vial. He opened the cabinet door and, rising on tiptoe, placed the vial on the top shelf, near the back, behind a number of other glass bottles of various sizes.

He closed the cabinet door, then stepped once more to the gurney's side to observe the cooling corpse. There were plain white sheets folded and stacked on a stainless steel cart in the corner. William walked over, lifted the top sheet from the stack, and returned to the gurney. He laid the sheet gently on Linda's feet, then slowly unfolded it, pulling it along as he went until she was covered up to her neck. With a slight nod to the President, he headed toward the door. He crossed the viewing room and stepped into the hallway, closing doors softly behind him as he went.

The hallway was empty. No sounds intruded from the storm blowing overhead. With an almost imperceptible smile, William headed toward the elevator, to make his way back to the surface.

12.19

Cole stood on the Thieving Seagull's deck, facing out to the harbor, watching for the return of *The Pokey Joker*. He was worried about the crew, *his* crew, and had tried to offer what help and encouragement he could from the mainland. He tried closing his eyes, tried seeing where they were and what they were up to, tried doing something weird or magical or psychic. But he really had no idea how the hell to go about such things. In the end, he just pictured some lights for them, glowing underfoot as they made their way around the island. He felt silly, but it was all he could think of, and he hated feeling so helpless.

The wind had slackened off, as often happened as a hurricane approached. Bands of rain and wind, outer arms of the huge spiral storm, rotated slowly overhead. Cole was thankful for the reprieve. There had only been a sprinkle of rain so far, which meant that the eye was still far out to sea, but from the way the wind had been gusting not long ago, it felt like it was going to be a big one. How they would pull off a "media circus" in such a situation he did not know.

He hoped that Linda's captors were prepared for this storm. Her old family getaway was a fairly rickety affair, and was surrounded by trees large enough to smash it to pieces should they be pushed over by the wind. From the photos he'd seen on the news, they'd built an additional entrance on the back wall of the garage, and it was in there that the biocontainment unit was no doubt located. Perhaps they also constructed a whole new structure inside the old shell. They'd have had to, wouldn't they, to make it airtight and safe? That would at least put Linda in a stronger building. But who would think to build for hurricanes on coastal Maine?

Cole sighed. Maybe they'd added some rooms underground. The military loved to do shit like that. Maybe Linda would weather this storm in some warm, underground bunker. Maybe she had good doctors and nurses, even if their bosses were members of some secret cabal. Maybe she *was* getting better now. He could hope.

Something flashed brightly in the distance, lighting the churning surface of the harbor and casting the tree line of Squirrel Island in sharp relief. Cole watched as a bright ball of light, glowing orange and yellow, rose above the island, hovered for a moment, then sped away so quickly that all he could see was the afterimage it left on his retinas.

He knew what it was. He just didn't know who was using it. He shook his head, hoping to dispel his feelings of helplessness and dread, and replace them with a more useful anger. The people involved here were not just military and medical professionals caring for their President. This had the frightening stink of hidden powers, and that Fisherman guy, all over it. And probably the so-called "aliens."

Stendahl Banks came out through the sliding glass door and walked over to stand next to Cole. Cole glanced at the President's Communications Director and smiled. "Just saw a wok take off, Sten," he said.

Sten sighed. "That doesn't surprise me," he said.

"You think there's aliens out there?"

Sten peered into the darkness for a moment. "Maybe," he said.

"You said you wanted a media circus," said Cole. He turned to face Sten.

Stendahl raised an eyebrow. "I'm... excuse me, Cole?" he said. "When did I-"

"Back in Augusta, my friend. On the phone." Cole grinned. "And thank you for that. I probably wouldn't be here otherwise. 'Banging on the gates,' as you said I should." He gestured vaguely toward Squirrel Island. "It feels good. You know? To be doing something."

Sten nodded. "It does," he agreed. "But whomever it was that called, my friend, it wasn't me."

"But I thought..." Cole frowned. He'd felt so sure. But Sten did not seem to be lying. And when Cole thought about it, what reason would Sten have for being so secretive in the first place? It would have been much easier to just come speak with Cole and tell him his plan. "So it wasn't you?" he asked.

"This is the first I've heard of it," said Sten, shaking his head. "You want to tell me about it?"

Cole told Stendahl everything he could remember about the mysterious phone calls. The former anchorman listened intently and asked good questions, as though he were conducting an interview for television.

"You're sure it wasn't you?" asked Cole after he finished his tale.

Sten laughed. "Yeah, I'm pretty sure," he said.

Cole turned and gazed out over the water, thinking of Linda, and the kids, out on their own mission. He was glad to be doing his part. But he sure wished he could know what the heck was going on. He shook his head. "So if it wasn't you, then who was it?"

Sten exhaled loudly. "I haven't a clue, Cole," he said.

12.20

Linda leaned against the lobster tank and stared down at her body. It looked the same as it had before, though Linda didn't remember that stray lock of hair on her forehead. Her face was peaceful and composed and her color, such as it was, was good. All seemed well.

Linda pushed herself back and walked slowly around the container, observing her body from every angle. William had said that this was how he'd found her on Squirrel Island. There was something distinctly disrespectful about the way they had left her naked and exposed. As if they wished to demean her. As if they had *had* to demean her in order to do what they were doing. She could scarcely believe that there were people capable of such things.

She moved slowly around, examining the container itself, and the pedestal upon which it sat. The construction looked cheap and flimsy to her, like what one might see with an inexpensive fish tank. Surely not the thick glass, rubber seals, and stainless steel she had expected. And where were the mechanisms that would keep her body a constant temperature on the Martian surface? And recycle her air? And shield her from radiation? She saw no pumps, no tanks, no tubes or hoses. Just a thin glass box on a black metal stand. Perhaps all the mechanisms were hidden underneath?

"Rarely do we get a chance to see ourselves as others see us," said William. Linda whirled to find the Fisherman standing behind her, feathery white hair and Hawaiian shirt and all. He flashed his eyebrows.

"You scared me!" said Linda.

William nodded. "Shall we continue?" he asked. He raised a hand, and they blinked away.

12.21

Doobie docked *The Pokey Joker* as quickly as he could and tied her off. Cole, Stan, Stendahl, and Simon were waiting there to help. Ann explained what had happened and the four men lifted Gordon and carried him up to the Seagull. Gordon, having regained some level of consciousness on the ride back, moaned with pain. They lay him on the deck next to the back wall near the kitchen. Andrew left to get the nearest doctor.

"The rest of you okay?" asked Cole, kneeling at Gordon's side, looking up to Marionette.

"All good," Marionette nodded. "A bit stunned. Scared. But all good."

"I'm glad," answered Cole. He motioned toward Gordon. "What happened?"

"Some sort of force field or something," said Ann, standing behind Cole. "Knocked us on our asses."

"You got onto the island?" asked Cole.

"A little ways," said Marionette. "They've got the whole interior surrounded by fencing and razor wire. We didn't encounter any soldiers but..." she gestured toward Gordon, "he tried to cut through the fence."

"I got some of it on vid," said Eddie, patting the camcorder slung around his neck. "But then I had to help carry."

"If it wasn't for that light, I don't think we'd have made it," said Ann.

"What light?" asked Cole.

"Strange light," answered Marionette. "Lighting up our path. Went all the way along the road and driveway, past the old inn, and out along that old dock. Which was good, because that dock was really messed up. Twisted all out of shape, with deck boards missing and the whole thing leaning. And the waves were pushing it up and down. We'd never have been able to make it to the boat if we couldn't see where we were going."

"Strange light," agreed Ann.

"Yeah," said Eddie.

12.22

"It is strange, isn't it?" said Carl. "I mean, until you said 'aliens,' I didn't even remember that there was such a thing. And then I did. I knew just who you meant."

Ted nodded. "It's like we're walking through our memories, or our past lives, or whatever, and it's pitch black, and all we can see is what we shine our flashlights on."

Carl sighed. "You suppose that's what it's like? The life review thing. When we die?"

Ted raised an eyebrow. "I thought that's what this is," he said. "Right."

Ted chose a card, read it, moved ahead three spaces. No more rabbit hole. "Your turn, dude," he said.

"So you guys had aliens that came to your house when you were a kid?" asked Carl.

Ted looked off to the right and stared at the wall. "Yeah. I think they started coming to my Dad when he was a kid. I remember somebody saying that. One of my aunts, maybe, though I think we mostly avoided that whole topic." He looked Carl in the eye. "I think that's one of the reasons my Dad was away so much. He was with them."

"And then they came and took you and your mother?"

Ted closed his eyes. "It was really weird, Bro. I mean, with my Mom, they just did their usual bullshit. Poke and prod and extract some eggs and all that. But with me... it was like they were only interested in my brain. I remember this one time I was lying on some metal table with them all huddled around my head, and I swear they took the top of my skull off and were poking my brain with, like, little probes and shit. They showed me this little black cube thing, and the little gray guy motions like they're going to stick that thing into my head." He looked at Carl. "And then the next morning I woke up and looked in the mirror but my head was fine. No stitches and no blood and no cuts. Just my regular head with my hair on it. Really strange."

"Did you ever, like, talk to your Dad?"

"Oh!" said Ted. "I did! I asked my Dad about it. I told him there was a little cube in my brain and asked if we could go to the doctor and have them take it out! Man, you should've seen him. Face turned as gray as all get out. Eyes got all wide. And he just..." Ted shook his head quickly, in short tight movements, and hunched his shoulders. "He did this little shaky thing, like 'get away from me I can't talk about that' or something. And he grabbed his keys and got in the car and went to his office."

Carl picked up a card, moved his piece. Ted did the same, smacking his playing piece on the board as he counted out his move. "Damn!" he said. Carl started laughing. Ted was once again stuck in the rabbit hole.

Chapter Ø Thirteen

13.1

Gabrielle wanted to stay. These people were creepy as hell, but they didn't feel dangerous. They were no danger to her, anyway. Not with that Jeff guy around. And Gabrielle didn't really feel like walking alone at night through this unknown landscape. But then Scotty and another man threw two human bodies onto the fire: a middle aged woman and a young boy, maybe four years old.

"God's cleansing agent," said Jeff, gesturing toward the bodies.

Gabrielle stepped further from the flames. She understood that what Jeff was calling a "cleansing agent" was the alien flu, Greensleeves. And while the sight of burning humans was disturbing enough, she had no intention of breathing in the smoke from their virus-infected bodies. Maybe these folks wanted to catch the alien flu. Let God sort 'em out and all that. But not Gabrielle.

So when Jeff went into the house to help with a sofa, and the rest of them looked otherwise occupied, Gabrielle backed slowly away from the fire and into the cool, dark night. When she reached the edge of the field, she turned and fled, running as quietly as she could over the soft, uneven ground.

Crossing the ditch to the road, she turned left, heading east toward Bowdoinham, continuing on the way she'd been going before Scotty had grabbed her. Her way was lit by faint Gridlight filtering down through the heavy swirl of clouds. After a few minutes, she stopped to look back at the farm. All she could see was a faint flickering on the farmhouse siding. The fire itself was hidden by the barn. Nobody was following her. Gabrielle breathed a sigh of relief.

She was forced to walk on the pavement now. Dying pines and leaning birch trees crowded the road, reaching out in the wind like shuddering ghosts, making the ditches impassible. Bowdoinham felt as ghostly as the trees. A smattering of houses. A couple of stores. A burned out church. But no lights. No people out in the night. No sounds. And no signs warning of Greensleeves. The town must have died after the Christmas Crash.

She did see two more bright spots on the horizon, both of which looked like the bonfire from which she'd come. Maybe this God of the Burning thing was bigger than she'd imagined. But both of these fires were far away. Nothing for her to worry about. Unless the wind took hold of them and they spread. It had been so hot and dry.

What Gabrielle *was* worried about was a place to sleep, and a source of fresh water, and some food if she could find it. She hadn't eaten since the bus, and she only had one small water bottle in her pack.

She scanned the sky but saw only the dark blanket of clouds. She hadn't seen the flying saucer in hours. With no chip for them to track, they'd have to wait until she passed through another scanner before knowing where she'd gone. Gabrielle had no intention of doing any such thing.

She left the tiny town, crossed a set of train tracks and a rusted steel bridge, and followed the road as it curved to the south, taking her past a tiny airstrip. To her right, back in the direction from which she'd come, came a bright flare that lit the clouds from underneath, revealing a huge column of smoke. Gabrielle assumed that Jeff and his friends had set fire to their barn or house. Or maybe a gust had done that for them. "God's Wind," they would probably call it.

She stopped. Up ahead, on the right, was a faint glow, like a single cat's eye, greenish-white, coming from a small white building set in the darkness of the tree line. She started moving slowly toward it, her tennis shoes silent on the pavement, watching for movement, listening through the gusting wind. Slowly the glow revealed itself: another one of those symbols, the circle with the upside down L through it. A flash of remembered images scrolled through her mind, of previous symbols, of Zacharael. She knew this mark came from him. And she knew she did not have to be afraid.

Gabrielle walked toward the glowing symbol, down a short drive and across a small parking lot. The symbol had been painted on the door of a small mobile home that had served as a hair styling salon. An old, faded "going out of business" sign hung lopsidedly in the window. It didn't look like anybody had been here in a long time.

She took the metal steps up to the tiny landing and pushed on the door. It swung in easily and Gabrielle stepped back, fearful that some animal might come rushing out. None did, so she stepped into the pitch-black parlor.

Directly across from the door was a sofa. Gabrielle set her pack on the floor and felt around on the sofa in the darkness to make sure it was clear and safe. Satisfied, she turned and closed the door, shutting out the noise of the wind. She crossed again to the sofa and sat down. The symbol on the door assured her she was safe. Somehow, Zacharael was still with her, watching out for her, helping her as much as he could. Gabrielle lay back on the sofa, pulled her jacket tight around her neck, curled up her knees, and closed her eyes. Sleep came almost immediately.

13.2

"You can't just dive back in," Linda said, her voice sharp with irritation. "You were gone for hours without explanation. And while you were gone, I took a closer look at my body in that damned container. I have some questions."

William held her gaze but said nothing. Linda closed her eyes. She was too tired to be angry. Not from the long walk she'd just taken, but from the never-ending game William seemed determined to play. "Well?" she said at last, opening her eyes.

The Fisherman looked down at his hands and sighed heavily, then looked up at Linda. "I apologize, Madam," he said, his voice low. "I do realize that I have likely burned through your supply of forbearance. I can only plead, as I have already done, the great need that has shaped my actions." He glanced at the sky, as if searching for the distant Earth, then looked again at Linda. "Things are moving rapidly back on Earth. The urgency is extreme. The clock is ticking, as you Americans say."

Linda nodded slowly. "So you're not going to take time to explain your absence," she said. It was not a question.

"I'm going to ask you to trust that all your questions will be answered if we but proceed as I have planned."

Linda shook her head in disbelief. "I hate this," she said. She pulled her feet up onto her chair and shifted to get comfortable.

The Fisherman nodded. "It is right and natural to hate being controlled," he said. "And yet, as I have explained, the situation warrants it." He nodded slowly, as if in respect. "If, when we are finished, you still believe my actions to be uncalled for, I shall submit to your due process of choice, in order to sort the matter out and make what amends I might. Agreed?"

Linda scoffed. "You know I'm going to hold you to that, right?" she asked.

William cocked his head playfully. "I would expect nothing less, Mrs. President," he said, acknowledging her power and position.

She looked at the Fisherman, her face a frown. "I guess you should proceed, then," she said.

"Right," said William, straightening in his chair. He looked away for a moment in thought, then began. "So... one way to approach the reality of the aliens is through the philosophical," he said. "Which is to say, we start with the nature of reality and work our way backwards." He wiggled in his chair with obvious delight. "Are you aware, Madam, that during your lifetime, the foundational paradigm on which you stand - that is, the basic understanding of the nature of reality itself - has shifted dramatically?"

Linda raised a shoulder a bit.

"Didn't get that particular memo, then?" asked the Fisherman. "Didn't read about it in *Time* or *Newsweek* or *The Wall Street Journal*? Didn't hear about it in a Presidential Daily Briefing?"

Linda sighed and shook her head. "No, William," she said. "Should I have?"

"In a wiser world, Madam, you'd have felt the Earth move. But the ground has been shaking for well over a century now, and few have fully understood what the trembling underfoot really means. Even folks like yourself who have actually touched the evidence have mostly failed to make the leap from the old paradigm to the new, so wide has the chasm grown between the two. Such is how it usually goes when a scientific and philosophical revolution occurs. It takes a while to unfold."

Linda nodded thoughtfully. "Okay," she said. "So we've all missed something hugely important. Keep going."

The Fisherman cleared his throat. "But that's just it, Madam. Just because you didn't get that memo doesn't mean no one did. And those of us who did get it, especially we rich Satanists in our tuxedos, took it quite seriously. Remember that what I'm telling you is greatly condensed. Suffice it to say that new data, insight, and analysis from such disparate fields as physics and quantum mechanics, psychology, spirituality, philosophy, parapsychology, neurology, ufology, *et cetera*, have rendered untenable the realist or materialist paradigm, paving the way for a rising idealist paradigm to take its place. On the way out is the notion that reality consists of such things as 'matter' and 'energy' that are 'out there,' existing independent of our consciousness. On the way in is the notion that mind, or consciousness, is primary, and that all of reality is contained *within* consciousness, not the other way around. At this point, at least in my estimation, it's all over but the shouting, of which there has been a great deal already."

Linda squinted her eyes slightly. "Wow," she said, blinking repeatedly. "That's quite a mouthful." She closed her eyes for a few moments to think, then opened them again. "So it's a 'thoughts create reality' sort of thing, then?" she said. "It reminds me of some of what Obie said."

"Indeed," agreed William. "Though not in that oft-disparaged 'the Universe is my shopping mall' way that people associate with the New Agers. This new formulation of the old idealist philosophy does not automatically grant superpowers to every fellow on the street."

"Which is the part of 'thoughts create reality' that people laugh at."

"Exactly, Madam. And to the extent that some people have promoted this misunderstanding of the evidence, the laughter has served as a healthy correction, I think. But to the extent that this laughter serves as an outright dismissal, it misses the mark. It's easy to laugh at an extreme distortion or obvious mistake. It's much more difficult to look closely at the more nuanced reality behind the many mistakes and distortions, and give that more subtle truth a fair consideration."

"So saying that 'mind is primary' does not mean that I get to be in control of reality," said Linda. She closed her eyes and focused on Cole back on Earth, attempting once again to blink back home. She failed. With a shake of her head, she looked the Fisherman in the eye. "Obviously," she said with a smirk.

"Right. There are other levels of mind at work in the universe beyond those of any particular conscious individual, as you just experienced when I stopped you from blinking back to Earth. There's the collective human consciousness. There are levels of both personal and collective unconscious. And there are the levels of what Huxley called 'Mind at Large.' All of these combine to create what one philosopher calls 'consensus meta-reality,' a sort of group mind or shared dream, in which we have some power to navigate and create, but over which we cannot, as single individuals in most circumstances, exert absolute control. If you're in the physical, and if you step out in front of a consensus meta-reality bus, even though it arises from consciousness alone, it will still crush you, regardless of the number of affirmations you chant in its face." The Fisherman flashed his eyebrows in a playful way.

The President closed her eyes for a moment, taking some time to let the Fisherman's words sink in. "And yet here we sit, William," she said at last. She looked at the Fisherman and swept her arm in a circle, indicating the landscape surrounding them. "On the surface of Mars, and yet not really in bodies. Here, but not material. And were you to lengthen my leash a bit, as you seem willing to do whenever it suits you, I would be able to flit about the Solar System by the power of thought alone. I could even..." she stopped and examined the sleeve of her sweatshirt. It changed color in front of her eyes, flipping from blue to pink in an instant. She looked back to William. "I could even change my appearance at will," she said, a bit of amazement in her voice.

William smiled and nodded. "Indeed you could, Madam," he said. "Which is what I meant earlier when I said that you had already 'touched the evidence.' You have already transcended the boundaries of the physical. But I dare say that, even now, you still tend to consider your physical body - the one over there in what you call the 'lobster tank' - as your real self and your real home. You might be able to leave your body for a short time, become a little spark of energy or entangled particles, say, that can explore the greater ocean of time and space, but you can only do so as long as you're tethered to your body and brain, which is the real source, the true ground of reality. Am I right?"

Linda nodded. "It's a pretty hard shift to make, William. Even sitting here, it's like... the mental habits of physicality are still really strong."

"And made all the stronger because your experience has been created and shaped by sources of mind much larger than your own individual ego. A consensus meta-reality is a powerful illusion, Madam. Which is why a revolution of paradigms can take so long, and why they often play out as a bitter and protracted war of words and ideas. And it's why the primary assumption of materialism in the human consensus meta-reality can be forgiven: because that meta-reality *does* have a certain existence apart from our individual minds. It *feels* like it's 'out there' and 'material.'"

Linda stretched her legs out and massaged her thighs. She leaned forward in her chair. "So how does all of this help us understand who and what the aliens are, William?" she said, her brow wrinkled in confusion.

The Fisherman's eyes flashed with excitement. "Here's where it gets good, Madam! Once we accept that what *we* call 'reality' is merely a limited consensus meta-reality created by our group of conscious entities found in this portion of reality we call 'Earth,' 'The Solar System,' or even 'The Universe,' we can *then* posit that there may be other groups of conscious entities existing independent of, and parallel to, our group, who have created their own consensus meta-realities."

"Hold on," said Linda, raising a hand. "I'm getting lost in the jargon."

William stopped. "Okay. Why don't you see if you can say it back to me in your own words."

Linda widened her eyes playfully and inhaled. "Jesus, William," she said. "Okay. Gimme a minute." She closed her eyes to think, then opened them and looked up toward the sky. "You're saying that if what we humans think of as reality is only the reality we've created in our little corner of... uh... reality, then there might be other species who have created *their* own version of reality somewhere else."

"Nicely done, Madam. And we can then posit that it is possible to bump into, visit, or tune into these other groups and their consensus meta-realities. In which case, we can begin to see that our experiences with so-called 'aliens' need not mean they are all just 'Spam in a can' physical beings from other planets in our reality that found a way to traverse galactic distances. We can begin to see, in fact, that we're actually bumping into complete other realities, not just other creatures inside of *our* reality. And that these other realities may differ from our own even down to the level of their fundamental laws of physics." William looked at Linda and raised an eyebrow, to add emphasis to what he'd just said.

"So now we're going to throw the laws of physics out with everything else," said Linda, shaking her head.

William smiled. "Do your so-called *laws* help explain how you have come to be a disembodied spirit sitting in an armchair on the surface of Mars?"

Linda's face darkened and she glanced down at her hands. "I..." she said. She looked up at the Fisherman. "I don't think so," she conceded.

"Then perhaps it's time to suspend your unwavering belief in them, hmmm?"

Linda sat silent for a moment. "So..." she said at last, "how does it help us to think about the aliens in this way?"

"It helps us in three ways, Madam," said William. "First, it helps us to understand why communicating with these alien consciousnesses has been such a confusing and challenging endeavor: we're trying to converse across realities. Second, it helps us to identify and let go of our own preconceived notions and expectations, not only about who aliens are and how they should behave, but about the nature of reality itself. Third, it helps us begin to grasp more fully what is being offered here."

"And what *is* being offered here?" asked Linda.

William smiled. "It's an invitation to an even larger party than we've so far attended, Madam," he said. "One where *our* consensus meta-reality gets combined with the consensus meta-realities of other groups of conscious entities, where reality itself gets redefined ever more fully, ever more grandly." He flashed his eyebrows again. "Imagine yourself off your leash, Madam, and free from any tethers holding you tightly to your body, your brain, your planet, and every notion you have that limits the possible. Imagine where you might go, who you might be, what you might do. Visit the stars and galaxies, Madam. Visit other planets, meet other peoples, see things you've never imagined, and explore powers and possibilities far beyond the reach of your physical body. That's the party to which we've been invited, Madam."

Linda closed her eyes again. As William spoke, she'd found her thoughts stretching back to Earth, to the warm, cozy bed she shared with Cole, his gentle touch, his goofy laugh; to his three young children, so smart, so inquisitive, and so full of life; to her home, her friends, her constituents, her colleagues; to the way the morning sun used to rise over Boothbay Harbor and warm her face as she sat on her cabin deck; to the taste of lobster rolls and coleslaw and those kettle chips she just couldn't get enough of; to the way Dennis would sit on her lap and stare into her eyes in a way no dog ever had. Her heart broke open at the thought of these things. She was filled with grief. Longing. Love. Anger. She opened her eyes and looked at William and smiled. "I can hear that you really want that, William," she said, her voice heavy. "And I know you want me to want it too. I do. But right now..." she reached up to wipe away the tears that arose in response to her own words. "Right now, all I really want is to go home."

William closed his eyes, inhaled deeply, exhaled, breathed again. He looked at Linda and smiled gently. "I understand," he said.

13.3

Cole sat on the edge of the bed and pulled off his shoes. They'd gone back to Ken's house for the night, after taking Gordon to the local health center and saying their goodbyes to Annabelle and the others. Ken was not home, as Celia had been taken to the makeshift viral isolation ward they'd created for Greensleeves patients. Cole sighed sadly. He and Ken were now in the same situation. But at least Ken could be at his wife's side.

It seemed that Gordon would probably be fine. He had some sort of radiation burns on his hands, but the wound to his head was not serious. Ann stayed to watch him through the night.

The rest of them stayed up late and talked about what had happened. Watched Eddie's tape. Discussed tactics with Stan and Sten. Listened to the weather report on Ken's radio. The storm was still raging offshore, to the south and east of them, moving slowly, building in intensity. Already it was a Category 2, which was unheard of this far north, this early in the spring. Forecasts had the center of the storm hitting the southern Maine coast in about twenty-four hours. The expectation was that it would be a Cat 4 or above by then.

Cole stood, walked to the window, gazed out over the water. The cloud cover was so dense that little Gridlight got through, but there was enough to get a sense of motion as the surface of the water chopped and churned. He thought about light. About the lights he imagined and the lights Marionette and the others followed as they made their way back to the boat. It was hard to believe that the two things were connected, but it seemed that they must be. As many strange and crazy things as he'd seen since Linda Travis had come zooming over that hill in her borrowed Oldsmobile, he still found it difficult to find himself in the middle of it. He was now a major player on a magical stage he didn't really understand, a mythic hero called the Wayfaring Stranger, with a purpose and a destiny, and a whole church full of believers by his side.

He lifted his right hand, examined his fingers and the palm, then squeezed his hand into a fist and willed a light to appear. The light flared up: soft, white sparkling flames that squeezed out from between his fingers, as if he held a nugget of star stuff in his fist. He turned his hand slowly, examining the light from all sides. He willed it brighter and watched it get brighter, taller and watched it get taller, redder and watched it turn redder. He willed it to get hot and it got hot. He opened his fist and let the light roll over and under and around his fingers. He let it rest on the back of his hand. He let it spin in his palm like a fairy dancer. As he watched, a slight smile came to his face, and the light danced in his eyes. He didn't know how this light would help them. But he did know that it was real, and that it hinted at possibilities he might not otherwise consider.

Cole extinguished the light with a flip of the mind and walked back to his bed. He crawled under the covers and closed his eyes to sleep.

13.4

Linda crossed her arms as she looked around the flat, rock-strewn plain upon which they sat. In the far distance rose the huge mountain she'd seen before, its sides roughly flattened like the sides of a pyramid. She turned to William. "So what's next?"

The Fisherman twisted in his chair to get comfortable. "The UFO and alien experience was instrumental to us in unraveling the old paradigm," he said. "Eventually some of the more clever UFO researchers in the public realm came to understand what we had already ascertained: that the aliens' primary goal was to free people to think, feel, and experience beyond the confines of materiality."

"And they did this how, William?" asked Linda.

"With signs, miracles, and wonders, Madam," said the Fisherman, flashing his eyebrows.

"Ah," said Linda. "You mean like having ships that fly in ways that ours could not?"

"Oh, much more miraculous than that, Madam President, as you well know," said William. "Such ships can be explained as pushing against the limits of materialist technology alone, with nary a threat to the underlying paradigm. No, I'm speaking of things like walking through walls and floating through windows, appearing and disappearing in an instant, shapeshifting, telepathic communication, time travel, and consorting with our own dead. Things that put the lie to the dominant culture's deeply held beliefs regarding the laws of time and space and matter, and the limits of what is possible."

"Okay," said Linda. "So... did you just say 'our dead'?"

The Fisherman opened his mouth to speak, then stopped and frowned. After a moment he continued. "I was going to embark on a long-winded explanation of the many and varied types of aliens with whom we have knowledge, Madam. But I wish to honor your sense of urgency as best as I can, and I am not convinced that that time would be well spent. You can probably guess, given what we've talked about so far, that the reality of 'aliens' is far stranger than some simple story of physical creatures crossing the galaxy to visit us. They come from a variety of reality types or bands, from our own or other meta-realities. And depending on their integration into the Cosmic Community, they have full or partial access to the grand meta-meta reality as well."

"And some of them actually *are* physical beings from our own galaxy?" asked Linda.

"Some are, indeed, Madam. Some even consider the Earth their home. Some of the 'fairy folk' fall into the category. As does one group of Gray aliens, the Life, which is the group to which our mutual friend Spud belongs. This group was bioengineered by a race of non-material aliens many millions of years ago, and were left behind after the solar-system-wide war that also left these ruins we see about us." The Fisherman gestured at the various distant peaks that surrounded Rumi's Field.

"So who was that man we saw back when we crossed the border into Canada? When Pooch got killed? Cole remembers him better than I. We've always assumed he was an alien."

William nodded. "That was Zacharael, Madam. One of those whom we call the Elders, or Angels, who arose as a species in a non-material band. They've been keenly interested in Earth for a very long time, and take on an idealized human form when they visit the planet, as they have no habitual form of their own. Zacharael had a funny habit of assuming an appearance very close to that of our gone-but-not-forgiven friend Theodore Rice. But he hasn't been seen by anyone in our network since just before the Grid went up, so apparently the Angels are heeding the Life's Interdict."

"Yeah," said Linda, her eyelids fluttering in confusion. "I could never figure out what he was up to."

"Probably no need to worry about him at this point, Madam," said William. "Both Zacharael and Rice are long gone."

"We can hope," said Linda.

William inhaled deeply. "Indeed. Now, back to your question. As I indicated before, these many beings don't just show up as ETs in UFOs, even now. You can meet them in a book store, a DMT trip, a near death experience, a dream, a ghostly, demonic, or angelic encounter, as a monster in the woods, or even as the Blessed Virgin Mary. And they live in, or pass through, the various bands through which human beings traverse after death, as our dead transition between physical lives, or graduate to other levels. Some groups, Spud's included, work closely with the human dead, and it is not unusual for someone to encounter their own deceased friends or relatives in a UFO experience."

"Okay," said Linda. "I think I'm getting the larger picture."

"It should be easier for you than most," said William, "given your own history. I know that Obie told you of your lifelong involvement with some of these groups of aliens, Madam. But I find it curious that you've not done any work since then to recover your memories of these encounters. I would have thought you'd be motivated to better understand what had happened to you."

Linda sighed, shook her head back and forth, and closed her eyes to think. "It was too... painful, William," she said at last. "And they had gone away. And there was so much to do. And Cole and I and the kids were just trying to be normal and happy." She looked at William and raised her shoulders. That was all the explanation she had.

William smiled gently. "Perhaps, when all of this is finished, you and I shall find the time to uncover those things that have been hidden from memory. Such work might be healing for you."

"Perhaps," said Linda.

13.5

Iain was angry. He did not like feeling helpless, and there was no greater helplessness than to be lost in the Murk. How long had it been now? He had no idea. No light. No sound. Just that weird pushing-pulling. He'd called out to his sisters, to Dennis, to Mihos, but none of them had replied.

How was he supposed to protect people he couldn't find?

Protecting felt like what he was supposed to do, really. He wasn't as smart as Emily. He knew that. And he wasn't cute like Grace. And he did not have her ability to know things. But he was smart. In his own way. And he did know some things. He knew that his little sisters were precious. He knew that they needed him.

But the Murk had taken them away. Separated them from each other. Just like it had separated them from the world. And their own bodies. It was like they'd all been stuffed into boxes and put on a shelf in a dark warehouse, left there to go on thinking and wondering and wanting and worrying forever. Maybe this was what people meant when they spoke of "Hell."

But there was that pushing and pulling. Which meant movement. Which meant that maybe... maybe... there'd be an end to this. Iain allowed himself the faintest thought of hope. If there were an end, then in that moment, maybe there'd be something he could do.

Iain imagined the others in the same situation as himself, thinking similar thoughts, worrying similar worries. He hoped that Grace wasn't too frightened. He hoped Emily was thinking of some way out. He hoped that Dennis's nose might lead him to freedom. And he hoped that Mihos might know something that could help. But hope was all he had, really, and it did not seem to be a potent force here. Hoping felt like trying to turn a light on from across the room, using a ten-foot length of cooked spaghetti to flip the switch.

He laughed at the image. Maybe when they got back he'd draw a cartoon. He liked to draw, and was getting pretty good at it. He'd even started to wonder if maybe he'd be an artist when he grew up.

If he grew up.

13.6

"Okay," said Linda. "So. There are all sorts of aliens out there, living in a bunch of different realities. You've referred to it as a big party. This Cosmic Community thing." The President ran her fingers through her hair. "So why all this interest in Earth, William? I mean... what makes Earth such a destination spot for these guys?"

"Well, some of them live there, as I have said," answered the Fisherman with a brief smile. "Under the oceans. Underground. In some remote corners of the planet."

"So those underground lodges I was in... " said Linda. A memory of her time spent trapped in the blackness scraped across her mind like a rusty chain.

"Those belonged to the terrestrial Grays I mentioned earlier, Madam. The Life had been on Earth since the God's War that destroyed so much of the Solar System. They left, *en masse*, just before your prime-time exposé."

"But it sounds like those guys are just the tip of the iceberg in terms of all the alien species The Families know about," said Linda.

"Yes," said William. "Alien peoples have visited Earth for many reasons over the millennia. Some have been traders. Others have come looking for resources. In recent decades, many have come as tourists or observers. It is known throughout the Cosmic Community that the Earth/Human system is at a major choice point, and this is of great interest to most member groups, especially since so many of them have already been down the same path humans have taken. Some... " William leaned forward and lowered his voice a bit, "... some have even chosen to live out entire lives in human bodies."

Linda's face went dark at the thought of that.

William flashed his eyebrows. "Yes, Madam," he continued. "The distinctions between 'alien' and 'human' begin to break down rather rapidly when we think of a 'person' as an individual concentration of self-reflexive mind that can manifest in many forms, in many places, in many levels. Your husband is untangling this particular thread as we speak, and doing a fine job of it, if I may say so."

Linda sat forward in her chair. "What?" she said. "You know what Cole's up to down there? I saw him on the coast. I couldn't understand-"

The Fisherman raised his hand. "He is well, Madam, as are your children, and he's fighting the good fight, as are we all. To say more would create far too much distraction for our work here."

Linda sighed deeply, wiped away a tear. "He's just..." she said, shaking her head. "I just miss him, William. You know? He needs me. We're a team."

William nodded. "I do know, Madam. Let us continue, so that you can get back to him."

Linda held her questions and said nothing more.

"So. Tourism. Curiosity. A bit of resource exploitation here and there, by some of the more material-bound ETs, since they're in the neighborhood. Technology transfer. As you saw with the Herschel Colony, we in the so-called Breakaway Civilization have been benefitting from the transfer of alien technologies for a long time now. That's one thing Spud's people were very much involved in. The transfer has come in fits and starts, always with limitations and strict agreements, and they've shared only a small portion of what they actually have, but they've given us the ability to make a starting move, not only in the physical bands, but beyond."

"So far, William, these all sound like things *we* might do," said Linda.

"Indeed, Madam. But aliens have been up to other things as well, and these activities point to goals and intentions which might seem more, well... alien." William stopped to smile at his own wordplay. "They have, for instance, allowed for huge numbers of sightings over the years, and yet have not performed that oft-wished-for act of landing on the White House lawn and asking to be taken to our leader. They've made repeated warnings about our collective human activities on the Earth. And they've behaved in ways both charming and cold, loving and indifferent, helpful, absurd, and obstructionist, interacting with humans without their consent and against their will, and causing pain and trauma on the one hand, and emotional and spiritual development on the other."

Linda closed her eyes for a moment to think. She breathed deeply and let the implications come together in her mind. She opened her eyes. "Right," she said. "We focus so much on you bad guys and your cover-up that we forget that the aliens must be complicit in the secrecy. So on the one hand, they keep flitting about in the sky, letting us see them, exposing themselves, teasing us. But on the other hand they could come out in the open and end the mystery at any time. And they don't."

William raised an eyebrow, smiled slightly, as though Linda had just scored a big point. "Quite," he said.

"So what's the goal of all that, William? Why do they do that?"

William's eyes grew larger with excitement. "Because that, Madam, is how one sends an invitation."

13.7

Mary lay on her bed, her hands raised over her face to ward off her father's blows. Her father stood bent over the bed, his right fist raised, as if deliberating whether to hit her one last time. His other hand reached downward, to touch her where he should not touch. But he did not strike her, and Mary did not scream. They were frozen in a moment that would not end, bathed in a bright white light.

She'd seen them come in, four little beings all in a row. Floating through the window she'd meant for her escape. Floating to a stop right beside her father. Behind them came another being, this one slightly taller, robed in red, hood thrown back to reveal his huge, bald head. This fifth being slid up to her father's side and touched his forehead with a short, dark wand. The wand was tipped in silver fire and almost impossible to see directly.

Her father stood straighter in response, removing his hand from her shorts, lowering his raised fist. In a moment he was standing at attention, staring blankly into the space before his eyes, head slightly lowered like a scolded little boy, as if there could be such a thing as shame or sorrow or penitence in one such as he. The fifth being raised a hand and drew it down in front of her father's face and his eyes closed. It was how one closed the eyes of the dead.

The four-in-a-row took positions in front of and behind her father and they began to move as one, her father and the beings together, floating up and back out the window, sliding up a hazy beam of blue, sparkling light that angled into the sky. In a moment they were gone.

Mary could see Danny, standing still in the doorway, his face wide with horror. The fifth being waved his long-fingered hand at him. Danny's eyes fell closed and his face softened. The being turned to Mary and used the wand to direct her hands down from their defensive pose and back to her side. He regarded Mary with his huge, insectoid black eyes, then cocked his head slightly. Something about the gesture moved Mary deeply. She knew, in that instant, that this being, whatever he was, was a person. She remembered that she'd seen him many, many times before. And she realized that she loved him. The being reached out and used the power in his hands to bathe Mary with gentle waves of relaxation and peace.

Mary closed her eyes and rested. She realized that something about this felt strangely familiar, as if she'd lived through this very moment before.

13.8

"In a nutshell, Madam, the aliens' first and primary concern is the evolution of consciousness. That's what the Cosmic Community is up to. That's what the member groups are up to. That's what the Cosmos is up to. That's what the whole of reality is up to. Methods and tactics will vary wildly depending on whom we are talking about, but if you are looking for the underlying meaning, goal, purpose, or intention of these alien peoples, it's the evolution of consciousness, seeking always the expansion, exploration, increase, and fulfillment of all conscious potentials, seeking always to add to the consensus meta-meta reality of the Cosmic Community, seeking always more growth, more love, more maturity, more wisdom, more life, more experience, more playfulness, more creativity, more diversity, more novelty, more awareness, more wholeness, more understanding, more acceptance, more peace, more joy, and more ecstasy."

Linda shifted in her chair and smiled. "That sounds nice," she said.

William nodded. "Naturally, the Cosmic Community keeps tabs on the rise and progression of any and all self-aware species, especially when a species begins to take steps that would bring it into contact with other members. Increased self-awareness adds a multiplier effect to consciousness, increasing the rates of change, expansion, and evolution. When a group or species crosses over into what is deemed 'self-awareness,' it attracts the attention of others in the multiverse."

"Kinda like that old idea about how they pick up our TV shows out there," said Linda, nodding her understanding.

"A bit," said William with a smile. "Save that human self-awareness was picked up by the Cosmic Community many millennia ago. In any event, your mention of TV shows is a notable synchronicity. I assume, Madam, that you watched the *Star Trek* shows as a child?"

Linda nodded. "Sure," she said.

"Good. And do you remember that the officers and crew, as members of the United Federation of Planets, as they explored the galaxy, operated under a mandate that prohibited them from interfering with the internal development of alien planets? It kept them from taking actions in planetary affairs that would shut off possible choices for the indigenous populations. And it kept the crew from making their existence known to native peoples before they were sufficiently advanced, such that a clash of cultures would not do the natives irreparable harm. Do you remember?"

"It was called the Prime Directive, wasn't it William?"

"Yes it was, Madam. And the starship crew's most solemn oath was to follow this Prime Directive?"

"I guess I knew that," said Linda. "What's your point?"

The Fisherman nodded. "My point is this, Madam: the producers of this program were strongly... encouraged, shall we say... to include this notion of the Prime Directive as part of the show's premise. Rather a large source of funding was put at stake, you see, to which the producers very much wished to have access. Fortunately, the Prime Directive was in alignment with the values of the show's creative team, it being a bit of progressive wisdom garnered from human history."

"So The Families were funding television programs?"

William flashed his eyebrows. "It wasn't *us* doing the encouraging, Madam," he said. "It was those whom we've termed 'aliens.'"

Linda stopped and thought for a moment. "So you're saying..."

"I'm saying that, from the beginning, it was made precisely clear to us that our very future as a member of the Cosmic Community hinged on the necessity of choice for all involved." The Fisherman wiggled in his chair to get more comfortable. "Like the crew of the Enterprise, neither we nor the aliens were to act in ways that would interfere with the evolution or maturation of human consciousness, or would cut off humanity's ability to make its own choices."

"Because without it being a choice, it's not really an invitation, is it William?" said Linda.

"Exactly, Madam!" he said, nodding enthusiastically. "And so here they are, these various alien groups, watching as humans rise to sentience and grow in understanding and mastery and technology. Watching. Waiting. And offering us little nudges along the way, giving us opportunities to make choices, revealing themselves in ways that could always be dismissed. They were inviting us, across the centuries, across the millennia, to consider that there was someone else in the Cosmos, someone we might strive to meet. They *had* to show themselves, for how can one make a choice if one does not know that a choice is available? But always they were confined by the dictates of the Prime Directive. And always, they were challenged by the astounding difficulty of communicating across realities so different from each other that sometimes the humans and the aliens could not even see each other.

"Still they watch, as we quickly gain the power of coal, oil, and agriculture, as we increase in numbers and technology and military might. They see one horrible war. Another one. Another. Suddenly we have huge arsenals, powerful explosives, vast armies, and finally nuclear weapons. Along with all of this growth and power comes overpopulation. Resource limitations. Environmental damage. And all at once a newly sentient species becomes both finally ready to begin exploring the Cosmos and, *at the same time*, poised to destroy itself. And still the Prime Directive holds." William leaned forward in his chair. "I think it's a testament to their commitment, Madam, that they did not give up on us." He sat back and exhaled. "They held their invitation out, just waiting for us to grab it. When some of us understood what they were up to, we joined them in that work. The invitation is still there, for anyone to take." The Fisherman closed his eyes and breathed deeply.

Linda sat and thought for a while, her chin cupped in the palm of her hand, her elbow on her knee, her eyes closed. At last she spoke. "It's just, I don't know... weird, William. You know?" The Fisherman opened his eyes and nodded. "I mean... really?" Linda continued. "Your explanation for why the aliens have acted the way they've acted comes from a television show?"

William smiled. "It's been staring us in the face for a long time now," he agreed. "More than one UFO analyst has mentioned it as a possible explanation for the aliens' strange and unexpected behavior. But very few were able to take it seriously."

Linda sat forward in her chair to meet the Fisherman face to face. "I think I know why people did not take the idea seriously," she said.

"That would not surprise me," said the Fisherman with a smile.

"It's easy, really," said Linda. "Obie said it. We project all over the aliens. We imagine them to be like ourselves in every way. And we totally suck at following the Prime Directive, even if we pay lip service to the idea. We 'civilized peoples,' as you call us, are masters at conquering, controlling, and interfering, William. So of course we can't take seriously the notion that the aliens would follow such dictates. That would make them better than us."

The Fisherman smiled broadly. "I could not have said it better myself, Madam," he said.

13.9

Dennis sniffed. Thought he sniffed. All he could do. Try to see. To smell. To move. Fail and try again. He was moving. Moving. Something. Pulling him. Somewhere.

Had sad thoughts. Missed his people. His Grace. His Emily. His Iain. Even cat. Though cat was pretending. Dennis knew cats. All cats pretend. Want to be more than they are. This made no sense. Not to Dennis. Keeps them apart from people. Which was stupid. People had such wonderful fingers.

Dennis was moving. Just knew. Saw pictures in his head. Fire. Bright fire. Loud noise. Sharp teeth. Heat. Something pulling him to fire. Could not stop it. Could not smell a way out. Tried again anyway. Nothing else to do.

13.10

"So here's the thing," said Linda. She'd risen from her chair and was leaning against its back, stretching her arms and shoulders as if she were truly physical. "You're not giving *me* a choice here at all."

William started to respond but Linda cut him off. "I mean, c'mon, William! You talk all high and mighty about how important choice is, but you shackle me to this near-physical state, strand me in this Martian desert, and refuse my request to return to Earth? Does that not seem a bit, well, contradictory to you?"

The Fisherman nodded. "I understand how it would look so to you. The contradiction, I think, is caused by a common cultural mistake. May I untangle that for you?"

"I'd rather be untangled from this whole situation," said Linda.

"Perhaps you could entertain the possibility that you are learning to untangle yourself, Madam. 'Teach a woman to fish,' and all that." He smiled slightly.

Linda gestured for him to proceed with a backward flip of her hand.

The Fisherman sat forward. "The distinction I would make is this: you say you want freedom of choice, but what you really want is freedom from circumstance. The problem is, while we always have complete freedom of choice, we never have complete freedom from circumstance. Not in the physical bands. This, Madam, is the realm where circumstance most comes into play, and it's the reason so many beings, from so many realities, regularly dip into this or other physical bands or levels, if they do not already live in one. Circumstances, you see, are simply limitations, but they are one of the most valuable commodities in the whole of Mind-at-Large, as they provide experiences unlike any other."

"Too much, William," said Linda, her voice filled with irritation. "Slow down."

"Right," said the Fisherman. "So. Take this armchair to which I have so impolitely shackled you, to use your metaphor. That is your current circumstance, and right now you have little control over it. You can get up and move around, but because of the way I have tuned your vibrations, you cannot blink back to Earth, and to get far away from me you would be forced to travel by foot over vast distances. But, even so, within the boundaries of your circumstances, you continue to have choice. You can be angry. You can shout and call me names. You can ask questions and seek further understanding. You can close your eyes and breathe to calm yourself. You can make requests. You can cry and plead. You can try to see the world through my eyes. No matter your situation, there are always realms in which you have complete freedom to choose." He stopped and raised an eyebrow. "Theoretically," he added.

Linda sat on the arm of the chair and frowned. "Why theoretically?"

William cocked his head. "Well, what would you do, were I to free you from your shackles?"

Linda sighed heavily. "I don't know, William," she said. "Slap you? Get the hell out of here and go home? Get my husband and my kids together and get everybody safe? Come looking for you in the physical universe with the full force of my military and throw your ass in jail?" She jerked her chin forward. "Maybe see how you like being locked up for a change."

William closed his eyes and breathed for a moment, then looked at Linda. "Again," he said, "you move the conversation along nicely."

Linda opened her mouth to reply, then stopped. She sighed deeply and rubbed her eyes with the palm of her hand, then glanced warily at the Fisherman. "Because I just demonstrated what you're talking about," she said, her voice low.

"Indeed you did, Madam. You went right into your ingrained reactions, which keep you in shackles just as surely as my control of your movements does. When you are in reaction, you give up your freedom to choose."

Linda twisted around and stared off across the Martian plain, and up toward the sky. The strange astral night was glorious, lit with bright and colorful stars, bisected by the same Milky Way she knew from Earth, but even brighter and more beautiful here. "Okay," she said, turning to William. "I get it. You may have to keep telling me, but I get it."

"Tell me what it is you get, Madam," said the Fisherman, his eyes intense with interest.

Linda raised a shoulder, as if to say it was no big thing. "I get it," she said again. "You're not talking about freedom of choice like I get to control the Universe and everybody in it. You're talking about the choice I have to respond in the moment, no matter the circumstances." She patted the arms of her chair. "Like you keeping me trapped here on Mars," she continued.

William sat back in his chair, his eyelids fluttering as though he'd been hit. "I hope you understand that I take no particular joy in being your captor," he said. "But sometimes the point must be felt, as you are feeling one now. If I have ignored your wish to be free from circumstances, Madam, it was to give you a new freedom of choice you have never before had. You cannot exercise a free choice until such time as the choice has been made clear for you. And the choice I am putting before you is like none other; it requires this extremity of circumstances to make plain. I understand that you do not like it. I ask *you* to understand that it was not I who put you into this role as choice-maker." William stopped and took a calming breath.

Linda rose and stepped around to again take a seat in her chair. "So who was it that gave me this marvelous opportunity?" she asked.

William glanced toward the sky, then back to the President. "All of the above, Madam," he said. "All of the above."

13.11

The Other-than-Ness stood on the concrete walkway in front of the hospital and looked out over the crowd of faces. She'd risen from her sleeping spot next to Grace, stepped right through the bubble of purple energy and the physical construct that held it in place, and walked quickly and easily down the hallway and out into the night. The nurses at the station had nodded to her as she passed, then fell in behind.

Ness, the woman whose body this was, knew nothing of any of this. The Other-than-Ness had taken complete control.

In front of her, crowded together under the dim light of the Interdict and the few streetlights that still burned, their hair and clothing flapping in the gathering storm, were a few hundred souls, nurses and doctors and soldiers and government functionaries all, and much more than that. They were mostly young, mostly hale and strong, and all highly intelligent. They regarded her with expectation and respect. Other-than-Ness stood in front of them, turning her head slowly to meet them all with her gaze, giving them a moment to recognize who she was. Then she looked to the sky and raised both hands as if in offering or supplication.

The clouds parted, making a small hole, and through that hole in the storm a light descended. A ship. A wok. The lights glowed white then yellow then orange then red as the ship descended, bathing the sea of upturned faces in a beautiful play of color and shadow. The gathered souls parted just as the clouds had done, making a space for the ship to land in their midst. The ship settled quietly to the pavement and faded to dull metal. A triangle of blue light began to sparkle on the ship's side. The beings around it grew still and expectant as a door melted open.

Out walked a being, small and large-headed, robed in red, his huge black eyes glistening in the faint light. He strode forward as the gathered souls parted to create a path for him. Stepping up onto the concrete walkway, he stopped in front of Other-than-Ness. He bowed, then turned to look out over the gathering before returning his gaze to the old woman. But the robed little man did not see an old woman. He saw his daughter, Alice, a hybrid being born of both Human and Alive One, as were all of these gathered souls.

"YOUR PROJECT PROCEEDS AS PLANNED," he said to Alice.

Alice nodded. "IT DOES, FATHER," she said. "I AM GRATEFUL FOR THE OPPORTUNITY." She motioned toward the others with her head. "WE ARE ALL GRATEFUL."

The robed little being, named Spud by the humans who knew him, nodded back. "YOUR GRATITUDE IS NOTED," he said. "YOU SERVE THE GREAT GOAL. THERE CAN BE NO FAILURE."

"SO IT GOES IN THE MIND OF GOD," said Alice, repeating an old wisdom of her people.

"SO GOES THE ONE," answered Spud. He gestured toward the hospital with a flick of his long, spindly fingers. "THE YOUNG

ONES ARE WELL?" he asked.

"YOU KNOW THEY ARE," said Alice.

Spud bowed again. "YES," he said. "STILL, I... WORRY," he said, struggling to find the right word. He looked up at Alice. "THEY ARE LOST TO US NOW IN THE BLACK, AS WE KNEW THEY WOULD BE. WE HAVE RISKED MUCH. LET IT BE THAT THE RISK SHALL BE WORTH IT."

Alice reached up to brush a tear from the old woman's cheek. She smiled, a gesture so slight that no one but her father would have even noticed it. "IT HELPS ME," she said, "TO HEAR OF YOUR WORRY. I HAVE MY OWN. THEY ARE MY FRIENDS."

Spud nodded, then turned again to gaze out over the gathered hybrids that watched them. "DO YOU ENTER WILLINGLY INTO THIS PROJECT, MY CHILDREN? ARE YOU READY TO GIVE WHAT AID YOU MAY?"

"WE DO," said the gathered ones in unison. "WE ARE."

Spud turned back to Alice. "THE TIME APPROACHES, DAUGHTER. MAY YOUR EFFORTS SUFFICE."

"MAY THE ONE BE SERVED," said Alice.

Spud bowed. Alice returned his bow. They held each other's gaze for a long moment, then Spud turned and walked back to his ship. Soon he was gone. The gathered souls, and the clouds above, filled in the open spaces they had created for him. The mass of hybrids turned to Alice. Alice stepped into the crowd and began to speak of their next steps.

13.12

"So let me take a moment and make sure I'm following you," said Linda.

The Fisherman bowed his head. "By all means."

Linda pulled her knees up and tucked in her feet. "This whole conversation is meant to free me up to make a decision... a choice... about whether to use whatever virus or poison you guys have concocted to take out most of the humans on Earth. Is that fair?"

"It serves as a rough summary."

"So everything you've done and said has been to that end, then. Showing me the Fortunate. That whole thing about the death wish. Just having this discussion out of our bodies like this. It's all supposed to free me up about death."

"Indeed."

"So why are we spending so much time talking about The Families and the aliens?" asked Linda, her head cocked to the side.

William clasped his hands together. "We learn new ways to think about things by hearing how others think about them, wouldn't you say?" He flashed his eyebrows. "I'm merely explaining to you how we, and the aliens, think about this matter."

Linda frowned for a moment, then looked at William. "And by 'we' you mean your small group of good guys. This Evolutionary Element. Right?"

"I am," said the Fisherman. "When the aliens reached out more directly, we in the Element were ready to meet them on their terms, and chose to align with their goals. The Families' ancient Plan was revised to meet the coming challenges, and to ensure the continuity of the species should humans on Earth choose to follow their destructive path to its likely end."

"And you're planning to explain all of that in more detail?" asked Linda.

"I am," said the Fisherman.

"Okay," she responded with a tired sigh. "Let's keep going."

The Fisherman nodded. "Yes. Right. So, we've established the aliens' primary focus on the evolution of consciousness, and that they are bound by the constraints of the Prime Directive. Does that serve as a concise summary?"

"Sure," said Linda.

"Then let me turn to a quote," he said. "One that will take us where we next need to go. It comes from Elizabeth Kübler-Ross, of whom I'm sure you've heard. She said *'The most beautiful people we have known are those who have known defeat, known suffering, known struggle, known loss, and have found their way out of the depths. These persons have an appreciation, a sensitivity, and an understanding of life that fills them with compassion, gentleness, and a deep loving concern. Beautiful people do not just happen.'*" He stopped for a moment, then spoke again. "Do you know it?" William raised his eyebrows in anticipation.

Linda shook her head. "I don't think so," she said.

"Then I am pleased to bring it to your attention," said William. "She's speaking directly to the issue of the evolution of consciousness, and pointing to a key factor in how consciousness evolves: it notices the consequences of its actions and learns from them. The aliens, with their focus on the evolution of consciousness, look for this ability to learn, and make their assessments about other species accordingly. I take it you are familiar with the notion of triage?"

Linda nodded. "Sure," she said. "When you're in an emergency situation and your ability to respond is limited, you first help those whom you deem most likely to benefit from your efforts."

"Nicely defined," said William. "It contains all the elements I wish to speak about. Thank you." The Fisherman twisted in his armchair to get more comfortable. "Now, imagine yourself lying upon a battlefield somewhere. It's dark, so you can't see anything, but you can feel some blood seeping through your clothing. Something hit you in the darkness but you don't know what it was. You must've been shot, you think, but, all in all, you don't feel too bad. Not like the others around you, screaming and gurgling and moaning in pain. The medics come. One kneels down and examines you with the use of a flashlight. He curses, and says "Hang on, okay? You're going to be okay." But the expression on his face says otherwise, and he gets up and goes on to check another person, and another, until he finally calls in a stretcher team. But the stretcher is not for you. The medic moves on and you're left there in the dark. What do you do?"

Linda exhaled sharply. "I think I start yelling for help," she said.

William nodded. "Of course," he said. "Because you feel pretty good, right? Sure, there's some blood, but you don't feel guts hanging out or anything, do you?"

Linda nodded. "No guts, William," she said.

"No guts, no screaming, no moaning, no gurgling, not much pain. 'Just a flesh wound,' as the joke goes."

"Right," said Linda.

"And yet the medic took one look at you, cursed, gave you an obviously false pep talk, and walked away."

"What does *he* know?" said Linda.

"Right," agreed William. "What does he know?" He looked at Linda and winked.

Linda smiled. "The Parable of the Medic and the Dying Soldier, William?" she said.

William returned her smile. "Quite," he said. "With the human species playing the part of the dying soldier, and the aliens playing the role of medic. And as we quickly see, it is almost impossible for the dying soldier to see what the medic sees, and to trust the medic's assessment regarding which of the wounded he should, in your words, 'deem most likely to benefit from his efforts.'"

"Okay," said Linda. "Got it."

William flashed his eyebrows and continued. "In the case of aliens and humans, the assessment is even trickier, as the wounds *they* are concerned with are not so much physical as they are psychological, emotional, cultural, and spiritual. When the medic tells you that you're not going to make it because both of your legs have been blown off, you might argue with him, if you're feeling no pain. But if you have a light, you can also look and easily determine whether he's right or not."

"Okay."

"But what if the medic tells you that you're not going to make it because you have unprocessed anger? Or a head full of childish and unfounded assumptions? Or a highly reactive ego-structure that makes it almost impossible for you to look at your own behavior? Were you to ask the medics, Madam, they would tell you that what *they* encounter on the battlefield of human existence is a people largely mired in a matrix of beliefs, expectations, values, reactions, and assumptions which keep them from reaching the wisdom, maturity, clarity, and understanding they would need not only to survive their present predicament, but to reach for and find their place amongst the stars."

"There aren't any missing legs they can shine their lights on," said Linda.

"Indeed. And people like to think they know themselves pretty well. So it's 'Hey, I'm fine' and 'Why don't *I* get a stretcher?' and 'You have no idea what you're doing.' But the aliens *do* have an idea, Madam. They know us intimately. They've known us since before our own history began. There is no one else better qualified to perform triage on the battlefield on this dying planet, Madam. That we do not trust their assessments is simply part of the equation."

"Okay, William," said Linda. She took a moment to let it all in, eyes closed. Then she looked at the Fisherman. "Continue, please," she said.

"So let's test your own reactivity, Madam. I say that the aliens have been here for a long time, inviting us to see, accept, and feel the non-material reality that our best scholarship has already revealed, inviting us to reach out and grab our membership in the larger consensus meta-meta reality, inviting us to join them all in their work of furthering the evolution of consciousness, that 'stuff' from which everything is derived."

"Okay," said Linda. "No reactions so far."

"They've been here all along," William continued, "acting mostly within the dictates of the Prime Directive, and always with the great difficulty that arises when attempting to communicate across radically differing realities. They've acted as teachers, guides, helpers, goads, and tricksters, inviting us into self-determination, into gnosis, into the realization of our full human potential.

"And all the while, Madam, despite their love, despite their caring, despite the great work to which they are committed in this grandest reality, these beings have, by and large, had the good sense, and the grace, to not stand in our way as we've made our choices. They've allowed us, as a culture, as a people, to venture out on our own great vision quest, to see and test the limits of our understanding, knowledge, and power, to learn more fully who we are, and to find our own vision, our own meaning and purpose, as it is given to us by the Formless One who holds us all.

"They've allowed us to drive the beautiful Earth deep into the caves of terror, destruction, pain, disconnection, and delusion, watching us in horror, fascination, and great hope, to see where such an experiment might take us. They've allowed it all, Madam, because they've known, from the beginning, that they were looking for what Kübler-Ross has called 'beautiful people.'"

The Fisherman stopped and pushed forward in his chair. "The beautiful people, Madam. The ones they deem most likely to benefit from their efforts. The ones who accepted the visions their quest has given them. The ones who have noticed and learned from their experiences, and from the consequences of their actions, and from the consequences of this collective death march we call 'the global industrial economy.' People who hit bottom and then pulled themselves up out of the depths. People who did not 'just happen,' Madam. Because this is a time of emergence and emergency, and their resources are limited by the Prime Directive. Because triage is the necessity of our time."

He stopped and took a long breath. "Those humans who have taken this journey are a relative few, I'm afraid," he said, wincing. "Believe me when I say that I am very sorry that this is the case." He sat back and said no more.

Linda sat and stared down at the shoes of the Fisherman for a very long time. Then she looked up. "I swore to serve *all* of my people, William," she said. "Not just the beautiful ones."

The Fisherman nodded. "And so you shall, Madam. It just won't look like you expect it to look."

13.13

Emily was being pulled, not pushed. It felt different, and the difference was important. Before, when she'd felt pushed, she could imagine somebody pushing her. People or little creatures or monsters or something. But now the images were not of monsters. It was more like falling down a well. Or maybe a black hole. More like circling a drain. More like sliding down a hill. There wasn't anybody pulling her.

Maybe being pushed was better. There was no getting out of black hole, was there? And if it was people, or somebody, pushing her, well, she could maybe talk to people, couldn't she? Or fight them. Or run. Seemed like getting away from *somebody* pushing was more possible than getting away from *something* pulling. Seemed like.

None of which mattered at all, because Emily was just a little tangle of thoughts. She had no body to do anything with. There was nobody to help. So there was nothing to do but wait and see what happened, if anything ever did. Emily detested waiting.

Emily imagined closing her eyes, imagined sleeping. She was sick to death of thinking the same thoughts over and over. The endless looping chatter. Her own mental Murk. She wanted sleep now, more than anything. Unconsciousness. Relief from the waiting and the not knowing. She wanted to go as black inside as it was outside.

But she didn't go to sleep.

Because one of her thoughts was this: maybe her going to sleep was how the Murk would finally win.

13.14

"I have one last thing I'd like to discuss before I pop off for a bit, if that is suitable to you," said the Fisherman.

Linda smiled. "You keep ducking out to check the basketball scores, William?" she said.

"Cricket, Madam," he said. "Cricket."

"Right," said Linda. "So very British."

William smiled. "Quite. So. Here's the thing, Madam President: I'm guessing that the idea that most sticks in your craw, so to speak, is the whole notion of elitism, the idea that *anybody* is qualified to triage the human species, that not all of you shall receive an invitation, and that many will be left behind. Am I right?"

Linda nodded. "You are, William."

"Of course," said the Fisherman. "If we had the time, I might unpack an extended analysis of the extreme amounts of shame, judgment, and reactivity to be found in the dominant global culture, and how those factors conspire to enforce conformity, hinder personal growth and maturity, and promote mediocrity. The culture's long shared history of greed, corruption, abuse, trauma, war, and destruction - and perhaps even their ancient abandonment by their alien creators - has left its members, as a people, convinced of their fundamentally flawed nature, and aching for belonging to something larger than themselves."

"And all of that would help explain my silly reaction to The Families' elitist ways, and the idea that the aliens are looking for 'beautiful people?'"

"I believe it would widen your viewpoint, yes," said William. "The thing is, I'm not certain that such an analysis would be helpful right now. What I do know, Madam, is that we in the Evolutionary Element have done our best to align with the actions and thought-patterns of the aliens themselves, and that their modern relationship with The Families was a matter of *them* coming to *us*."

Linda leaned back in her chair, her head shaking almost imperceptibly from side to side. She inhaled deeply and sighed. "I don't know, William. It just... rankles. You know?"

William nodded his understanding. "Perhaps it would help to think of the Earth as a training ground, a school for the evolution of human consciousness, as the force known as Seth has explained it. Seth would argue that the training here is karmic. Ethical. Spiritual. It's about learning to create responsibly, and usually takes repeated embodiments in the material bands for an individual knot of consciousness to 'graduate,' so to speak, to the more non-material or other-material bands. The consequences of circumstance must be real in order to be felt. Otherwise, we'd just be passing students up a level without first completing their lessons, something which school systems eventually learn creates more problems than it solves."

Linda shrugged. "I don't know. Maybe."

"Or we could liken the situation on Earth to the ancient tribal practice known as the vision quest. When the tribe sends a group of young folk out into the wilderness to seek their visions - the visions they require in order to find and take their places as initiated adult members of the tribe - you can be sure that there is a desire for them to all return safe and sound. And yet they do not all return, Madam. Some of them do not make it. And the tribe accepts the necessity for this, you see. As Ms. Kübler-Ross observed, we need the experience of defeat and suffering in order that we might grow in maturity and consciousness. We need the risk and the consequences to be real."

Linda sighed again but did not speak.

William sat forward in his chair. "Or I might observe that evolution *always* proceeds by choosing some small segment of a population and guiding it forward through time, while the unchosen majority sinks into the depths of history. It chooses those - whether we are talking about individuals, populations, species, or ecosystems - who are ready, willing and able, who are fit, who are suited, who have the characteristics necessary for survival in a changing environment. In all of these cases, whether we're talking about a school, a vision quest, or a species evolving on Earth, it seems to me to be a fundamental aspect of human experience on the physical plain that individuals are different from each in a multitude of ways. Some of those differences confer advantages in certain circumstances, and those differences are selected for, by teachers and tests, by medics on the battlefield, by the rigors of a vision quest, or by what we call, collectively, the forces of natural selection."

Linda raised a hand for the Fisherman to stop. William relaxed back and watched, his expression calm and focused. The President closed her eyes and took a series of long, deep breaths. Her eyelids fluttered rapidly, as though she were compiling and organizing both the Fisherman's words and her own jumbled thoughts. There was a war raging inside her soul. On one side stood William's fervent explanations and reasoned justifications. On the other side stood Linda's own heart: her love, her grief, her fear. There was something so... cold... in the Fisherman's words. As if he had no first hand experience of the countless millions of souls he and his Families and their alien friends were so casually consigning to the dustbin of history. As if his "breakaway civilization" had journeyed so far out to the extreme edges of the human experience that they'd lost all touch with the people from whom they had come.

She'd just spent the last three years with her people, meeting with them on-the-ground and face-to-face as they tried, together, to respond to the great challenges they had been forced to confront. Were her people lost and confused? Dumbed down and anguished? Reactive and childish and filled with rage? Certainly. A great many of them were all of that, and worse. But to Linda that was only part of the story. She'd seen such good intentions in her people. Such longing. Such love. Such striving. As angry as she felt with them at times, as disgusted, as hopeless, she knew that, underneath their insanity and woundedness, the vast majority of them were, at the very least, trying as hard as they could to be good. Did that count for nothing?

And how could The Families or the aliens claim to really, truly know exactly who it was who was fit to be selected, or was worthy of being saved? It didn't feel possible to Linda. She'd been surprised too many times, as people whom she had written off as insane or stupid or greedy had turned out to be wiser and smarter and more generous than she would ever have guessed. If it had been William who had encountered the scrawny, dirty old woman at the cordon gate, he'd have left her in the dust to meet her no-doubt imminent demise. But that old woman had turned out to be her dear, sweet Ness, a woman with more wisdom, more common sense, and more fierce loyalty than almost anyone else she knew. It was Ness who now stood guard over the bodies of the children! And she would have been selected against as unfit?

Linda exhaled loudly. Shit. It was all so confusing. Maybe there was something to what William said. Maybe the aliens knew humans better than they knew themselves. But if this was evolution, then she didn't like evolution. Especially now, when William was asking *her* to be a force of natural selection.

She opened her eyes to find William still watching her. She cleared her throat and spoke, her eyes cast downward to the dusty ground between them. "I don't know, William," she said. "I mean... I hear your words, and they kind of make sense, but they just... they leave me cold, William. You know? They don't feel right to me. They feel like they're... I don't know... too bound up with the world. With the physical world. With people in bodies. And I'm not sure that makes sense any more." She looked up at the Fisherman, expecting more argument and explanation. Instead she found him grinning and nodding with warm appreciation. "Brava, Madam," he said gently. He pushed himself to the edge of his chair, reached out, and took her hand in his own. "Brava," he said again.

Linda shook her head in confusion. "Brava what, William?" she asked.

The Fisherman squeezed her hand. "Upon my return," he said. Then he was gone.

13.15

Mary opened her eyes at the sound of animals scampering and saw that her father now stood facing the corner of her room, like a child being punished. The beings must returned him just moments before, floating him through the window on their beam of light and setting him gently into place. The fifth being, the robed one, touched his forehead with that small wand. His head fell forward, chin to chest, his shoulders slumped, and his arms hung limply at his sides. He was switched off. Mary smiled. Her life would be so much easier if she knew how to work his switch the way they did.

It was Danny's turn next. He stood in the doorway where they had left him, and they didn't even bother to open his eyes as they floated him away. Danny's breathing was slow and easy, for which Mary was thankful. Perhaps he was not as terrified as she sometimes felt. Danny was gone in a moment.

The robed being looked down at Mary as she lay on the bed, paralyzed. Mary eyed him in return. The moment felt so familiar that she could swear she'd been here before, not just in their presence, but in this exact instant. But then the being did something that shattered that: he nodded once, and spoke in her mind a single word. *Amends*, he said. Then he turned and followed Danny, and the other four, out through the window. This had never happened before.

Mary closed her eyes so as not to have to stare at her scolded father. Amends? What the heck did that mean? She knew the word. Her father talked about amends sometimes when he was attending meetings for his drinking. But as far as she could tell from his example, making amends meant making excuses, and she didn't think that's what this being was talking about. Amends were like fixing things, right? Mending them? What was Mary supposed to fix? And how was she supposed to fix it when she was stuck in their damned paralyzing fog?

13.16

How the entire island could be without electricity McAfee did not understand. The storm wasn't all that strong yet, and the undersea cables had all been beefed up and hardened off when they'd built the facility. But there was nothing coming through the grid, and their backup generators would not start. Techs could not explain it. The gennies appeared to be in perfect condition, and were fully fueled. They just wouldn't start.

Which left Linda Travis's dead body still on its slab in the bottom level, with no furnace in which to incinerate it, and no refrigeration to keep it fresh. McAfee wondered when it would start to stink. And he wondered where he might find an undertaker to come and take care of the body for him. One they could dispose of afterwards.

He took a big swallow of his highball and dug his fingers into the fur on Nicky's back. The cat was unusually needy tonight, it seemed. Distracted. Quiet. As if he didn't like having the power out any more than the Colonel did. He sat in McAfee's lap and hardly moved. No purring. No claws digging into his leg. None of his patented "death gazes." Just a nice little kitty needing some lovin' from his daddy. McAfee sighed deeply and finished his drink. He needed to get another one, but did not want to disturb the cat. Maybe he should call Osterman? Oh, wait. No phones either.

DuPont had gone. McAfee had watched the little bastard zoom away in his wok. William was long gone, no doubt soaking in a hot tub in some fancy hotel in *Urbem Orsus* with a couple of young birds. Or whatever. Who knew what the hell those guys were into, really? McAfee sure didn't. Maybe William was a necrophiliac or something. Like, what the heck was that whole "saying goodbye to the President" thing about, anyways? What? Did those two have a fling or something? McAfee shook his head. What a world.

So it was all up to him now. Him and his soldiers and his techs. Hopefully they'll get the gennies going soon and he can take care of that unfinished business down in the morgue. And he was running out of ice. And he couldn't even microwave some popcorn, now that he thought about it. He shook his head. Maybe he should just go to bed and get some sleep. Assuming they had power in the morning, these kids were going to need a clear-headed commander. Storm's-a-comin', y'all. There will be hatches to batten down and shit.

McAfee scratched behind Nicky's ears, pushed back on the recliner, and closed his eyes. Maybe he'd just sleep here.

13.17

Linda had risen from her chair and was standing with her back to it, looking out over Rumi's Field toward the distant starlit pyramids. A bright ball of light had descended from the sky, circled the pyramid near its apex, and was settling to the ground near the pyramid's base. But it was far too dark to see anything else, no matter how hard Linda tried to tune her vision. Still bound to the near-physical, there was no way she could walk that far to check it out.

Behind her William cleared his throat. Linda whirled to find him once again sitting in his armchair. "Let's see if we can tied some threads together, shall we?" he said with a smile.

Linda, tired of fighting, tired of being angry, just nodded and took her seat. "That would be nice," she said evenly. "You did say that things were getting urgent back home."

William flashed his eyebrows. "I bought us a bit more time, Madam," he said. "Pulled a plug, you might say."

"Okay," said Linda, motioning toward him. "Let's use it wisely, shall we?"

William nodded. "Indeed," he said. "So. Humanity finds itself standing on a precipice. Just as you are about to leap out into the universe and the greater Cosmic Community, you find yourselves sliding down the unraveling slope of unsustainable behavior, perhaps to fall into the black hole of extinction. The aliens watch you on your grand vision quest. It appears that many of you will die in the trial, but the aliens are there, as elders, as medics, to offer aide and guidance to those who might benefit." He leaned forward a bit and lowered his voice. "To you this all seems a bit cold. The aliens with their triage do not seem particularly interested in your opinions. And evolution's seemingly mindless, uncaring culling appears to be immune to your consultations." The Fisherman smiled warmly. "Does that about sum it up?"

Linda raised a shoulder. "Sure," she said.

"The thing is, Madam, and as you so deftly pointed to before I left, all of this talk of triage and evolution is conceptually bound to the physical realm of limitations and circumstances. Which is to say that, if and when we step more fully into an acceptance of the fundamental non-material nature of reality, in which all-that-is arises from mind and consciousness, then the discussion expands enormously, does it not? While the physical bands are as real as any other, and while they do operate under what can seem like cold and uncaring laws and limitations, those bands can be viewed as simply special cases, which exist inside of a much larger reality. In that larger reality, nothing is ever lost."

The President shook her head from side to side. "You're going to have to tease that all apart from me," she said.

William stopped a moment and looked at his watch, his face pulled into a frown. Then he looked at Linda. "It will take some time to flesh out, Madam, but I can give you two quick reasons why neither I, nor the aliens, nor the universe itself, deserve to be thought of as uncaring or elitist."

"Okay."

"The first is as I just said. Evolution beyond the physical *is* for all, because All is One. Nothing is lost. Every part of the human experience is captured, contained, and cherished inside the great Mind-at-Large. Every scrap of consciousness enters into the sacred process of the evolution of consciousness.

"The second is this: because self-reflective awareness is particularly prized and tended in the larger meta-meta-reality, our alien cousins have extended their invitations across the board, meeting with members of the 'breakaway civilization' one day and showing up in the bedroom of some average Joe the next, to offer a glimpse of something beyond the confines of his or her paradigm. They have gone to great lengths to present new choices to everyone they could reach, Madam, including some Earth's *other* self-aware species. Many humans have taken steps to enter the new worldview the aliens have offered, and are as important to the evolution of consciousness as the Plan that The Families are enacting in the physical bands."

Linda closed her eyes. "I need to think for a bit," she said, sighing. "Before you go on."

William smiled. "That works perfectly for me, Madam, as I must now pop off once again to check on those cricket scores."

Before Linda could open her mouth to respond, William had disappeared.

13.18

"So I'm not sure if they put an actual black cube in my brain or just the idea of a black cube. I mean, later, when I was working with them like my Dad, it was clear they could do all sorts of..." Ted stopped, frowned, cocked his head. "Oh," he said, looking at Carl. "You were there too. You worked for me. We called ourselves The People." Ted smiled, fluttering his eyelids. "Hey, Carl," he said with a wave.

"Hey, Agent Rice," said Carl, also smiling. "Nice to see you again."

Ted laughed. "Wow," he said, shaking his head. "This is so weird!"

"It is that, Ted," said Carl.

"Anyways," said Ted, "well, you know. If they wanted to put an actual black cube into a kid's brain and leave no blood or wounds, they could, right? But I don't know if they did. To me, anyways. Either way, the effect was the same. I had a black cube in my head."

"And that changed you somehow," said Carl. "As a kid."

Ted nodded. "I remember one night, this one being, little guy with a fetish for long red robes, came in and rushed to my bedside and grabbed my head with both hands and drew my face up to his and stared into my eyes. And it was like... I don't... either he was using that black box to communicate with me, or to hook me up, or whatever, but my mind was filled with, like, the whole of space. Stars, galaxies, nebulae, all sparkling and swirling in my mind. And I was out there zipping around from one to the next, and this being was watching me to see how I'd act, what I'd do. And what I saw was reflected in his big black eyes, like a mirror. It was weird."

"That was Spud," said Carl.

"Spud!" said Ted with another laugh. "Right! Spud! It was that little bastard. Self-styled King O' the Grays and all-around meddling sonovabitch. Man, he used to drive me nuts..." Ted breathed a long, wistful sigh. "Man, oh, man."

Carl glanced down at the Uncle Wiggily board. "You gonna take your turn?" he asked.

Ted regarded the board. He was back on square 13, sent there via the Rabbit Hole. He leaned forward and drew a card and moved a few spaces. He looked up at Carl. "You think that little creep is involved with this place?" he asked, gesturing to indicate the room they were sitting in.

Carl shrugged. "Dunno, Ted," he said. "You remember how we got here?"

Ted frowned in thought. "A rubix?" he said, remembering only vaguely.

Carl nodded. "You threw it, trying to take the President out of the game," he said.

Ted grinned. "Those were the days, weren't they Carl?"

Chapter ∅ Fourteen

14.1

Because Gabrielle was busily dreaming of that moment, dreaming it again and again, she and the President face to face in a dark corridor, because she was dreaming of those strange symbols showing up around the planet, of people traveling toward them and gathering around them, flying driving walking running to get to them in time, because she was off and away, seeing and hearing and acting in the realms beyond, she did not feel the quiet whoosh of air as the black ball came into the trailer and hovered right over her face. She did not hear the squeaking of the metal steps just outside the door. And she did not see the light in the sky that popped like a flashbulb before fading away. Because she did not feel or hear or see these things, she was destined to be caught by surprise by what she would encounter, upon waking.

14.2

Linda studied William with fierce intensity. The Fisherman had returned to his chair as unexpectedly as he'd departed. "I don't suppose you're going to tell me what you do when you take off like that, are you?"

The Fisherman flashed his eyebrows. "Suffice it to say that I have interests back on Earth which require frequent monitoring. And then there are *your* interests, which I monitor as well."

"Making sure your ruse is still working?" asked Linda.

"Yes, Madam, that is a part of it. So far, all is quite well."

"And my family?" asked Linda.

"Madam?"

"You said you're monitoring my interests as well, William. My primary interest is Cole and the children, which I believe I have mentioned. My husband is down on the coast of Maine untangling something to do with aliens, you said. And the children's bodies are lying in hospital beds in Augusta while their conscious selves are trying to find *me*. You've assured me that they're all okay, William, but I think we can agree that this strains belief, given what we know of the situation. So I want some reassurance here. I want you tell me how 'quite well' they all still are, so that I can quit worrying so much."

The words were even, but as she spoke, an undertone of deadly menace moved into her voice like a cold fog. *I will hunt you down and kill you if anyone in my family comes to harm*, the undertone seemed to be saying. William nodded and leaned forward. "I assure you that I am unaware that any harm has befallen any of them, Madam."

Linda's eyes narrowed. "Such careful wording, William. Does it surprise you to hear that I do not feel reassured?"

William sat back. "I suppose it does not," he said, his face dark with confusion. "I suppose were it me..." He looked at her. "I can only beg the necessity of circumstance," he said. "As I continue to try to explain..." He inhaled deeply.

Linda shook her head and waved him away with her hand. "Just get on with it," she said.

14.3

It felt to Grace like she was slipping. Falling. She wasn't sure how she could tell that, as she didn't really seem to be feeling anything. But that's what she thought, here where thought was all she had. She was so worried about Dennis. He was getting old, and hadn't seemed himself as of late, back in the real world. He seemed smart and strong here, and he could talk now, which was new, but still she worried. He needed his people. He needed her. And, well, Grace needed him. They'd been through so much together.

The worst thing about the Murk was this: the fear that this would go on forever. Thought, forever, with no body, no feeling, no change. Thoughts, over and over, looping and spinning, chattering, bickering, doubting, analyzing. Thoughts and thoughts and more thoughts, with nothing to break them up. She'd tried to sleep but found it impossible. Apparently she needed a body for that. It was just thoughts and then more thoughts, with thoughts of sleep and of trying to sleep and of failing to sleep mixed in.

Grace called out for help. Or tried to call out. It was difficult to tell if she was actually doing anything, without a voice to speak and ears to hear. She thought out, at least. To that woman, Evlyn, who'd helped her before. To that Elder she'd met. To that Inuit woman. To Utterpok, the old shaman, whom she'd loved. She thought out to Dennis and Emily and Iain and Mihos. She thought out to her father, and to Linda. She thought out to her dead mother, Ruth. She put as much energy and force and passion behind her thoughts as she could, and imagined them blasting out in all directions, cutting through the Murk and spreading out across the Cosmos, to catch the ears of those who loved her. But no one had come. No one had responded. And so she had no idea whether her thoughts had really gone anywhere.

As scary as that skeleton had been, as frustrating as that house of glass had felt, as powerful as that red-haired man had seemed, this Murk was worse. She wished they'd never set foot back inside of it, despite Dennis's confidence. Mihos was right: they'd come to the Astral without so much as a map or guide. They had no business being here.

And yet it was Alice who had drawn them here, was it not? Alice, who had come in Grace's dreams and caused her to want so badly to do this. And that strange, gray, clawed hand that had pulled them from their bodies: that was one of Alice's people. It had to have been. Grace was sure of this if nothing else: Alice was good. She would not lead them into danger without good reason or great need.

If she could have sighed, Grace would have sighed. If she could have shed tears, Grace would have sobbed and moaned in fear and worry and grief and pain and loneliness. If she'd had lungs to scream with, she'd have howled in fury. But she didn't have any of these things. She had only her thoughts, and they wouldn't stop, and they wouldn't go away, and they wouldn't leave her alone.

And she kept on sliding. Falling. Falling. Falling.

14.4

William sighed deeply and continued. "Right," he said. He shifted in his chair. "So as I said, the aliens stepped up their presence on Earth in the last decade of the 19th century. Some in The Families took note of their presence, and began to look for ways to meet them. It was not until much later that we understood why they had come: already the first signs of major Earth changes were appearing, and the aliens had grown concerned."

"By 'Earth changes' you mean climate, right?"

"Yes. That and the many other effects of rapid population growth and industrial activity."

"And you found a way to meet with them."

"We found a way to meet with one group of them, yes. A small circle of Family members met in the library of an old German castle one evening. This was the spring of 1897; the same day the first oil well was drilled in Oklahoma, or so the story goes. Anyway, those present, using ancient rituals of meditation and concentration, succeeded in calling one of the aliens into the room." William scrunched his nose and leaned forward to look Linda in the eye. "He was tiny. Slight of build. With a large head and huge, black eyes. He was the Life's first ambassador to Earth. And eventually we learned that his favorite human food was french fries." William smiled slightly. "We called him Spud."

Linda sat back and shook her head. "Jesus," she whispered. She inhaled deeply and blew out a heavy sigh. "So, what happened?"

The Fisherman flashed his eyebrows. "That's the thing, Madam!" he said. "Nobody really knows!"

"What do you mean?"

"I mean nobody knows, Madam. Those who were there remember bright lights outside the library windows. They stood and went to look, then heard behind them a high-pitched cough. Whirling about, they found Spud, standing next to the blazing fireplace, ripping pages out of a book and tossing them into the flames. Some of them swore he disappeared again almost immediately. Others were sure they'd engaged with him in a long dialogue, although what they'd discussed no one could say. One man, my grandfather, was certain he'd been taken on Spud's craft and flown about the solar system. All they could agree on for certain was that, when they regained their wits, Spud was gone, the fire had gone cold, and the sky was beginning to brighten with the dawn."

Linda shivered. "That sounds like Spud to me," she said.

"Indeed. It was only when those present underwent hypnosis that they were able to recall bits and pieces. There *had* been a long discussion that night, though none of them could remember what they talked about. My grandfather *had* been given a ride in Spud's wok, but he could not remember what it was he'd been shown. And two weeks later, one of the castle's groundskeepers discovered a tiny version of the aliens' craft in an unused shed. It was the first of many such gifts."

"And that's how it all began?"

"That's how it went for a long time, Madam. Strange meetings, only partially remembered. Sightings around the planet. Reports of face-to-face encounters from time to time. And every now and again, a bit of physical evidence left behind, including the odd ship or device. We eventually met openly with three different alien species, but the Life were always the most accessible. Finally, in 1913, the first of us were brought to one of the Life's lodges, the one underneath Buckingham Palace. We learned that there were many such facilities around the planet, and that some had been constructed centuries before. It was there that our scientists began to work directly with alien representatives, and took their first baby steps toward understanding the source of the aliens' vast technological supremacy."

"All of which meant lots more wealth and power for you guys," said Linda with a smirk.

"Yes it did. And that's what most members of The Families cared about. But to a man, those who'd been there in that castle library had been strangely touched, and cared only for the spiritual and philosophical implications of Spud's manifestation. Those folks formed the core of what became the Evolutionary Element."

"And it was the promise of alien technology and wealth and power that fueled the secrecy?"

"From our side, certainly. At first. But things changed, as they always do. The First World War came. Then the Second. And the aliens responded. All of a sudden they were everywhere. Sightings began pouring in. To my grandfather, it seemed as though we'd angered them; they were swarming, like a nest of hornets. But I think we frightened them terribly. Hiroshima, you see. Nagasaki. Not only our power to destroy, but our willingness. In their eyes, the human species was going mad, and was on a course for self-destruction. I think they felt like they had to do something."

"There were all those UFOs hovering over nuclear missile silos, right?"

"Sometimes they shut them down, Madam. Once they even stole the missiles away! You can imagine how disturbing that was to some people."

"And so you had another reason for secrecy."

"When the aliens stepped it up in the late 40s, The Families quickly wrested control of the situation. We created a culture of ridicule and denial to minimize public layer interest, and used incentives and threats to keep those who had a need to know under our control. Most were only too happy to comply. This gave us the time we needed to figure out our own next steps, and to develop our Plan."

"And the aliens could have exploded your cover-up at any moment, and they didn't."

William pointed a finger at Linda. "As we have said, Madam. Yes. The Prime Directive, you see. They chose to honor that guiding principle, and yet act in such a way as to keep their commitment to the evolution of consciousness."

"They couldn't just land on the White House lawn, because that would have been too disruptive to our culture." She cocked her head. "It would have taken away our freedom, in your words."

"Indeed," said the Fisherman. "But they *could* show up at the periphery of our cultural vision and irritate us, an anomalous speck in the eye we could neither dislodge nor clearly see. Something to push us out of our comfortable worldview."

"The strange lights in the sky," added Linda, nodding. "The impossible flight paths. The reports of little green men."

"Little green men who float through windows," said William with a smile.

"Coming into our bedrooms because they wanted to wake us up?"

"Exactly right," said the Fisherman. "To give us a choice: whether to remain asleep inside of our comfy materialist paradigm, or to go outside and look up at the skies and wonder if maybe there was more going on than we had supposed."

"But weren't they also breaking their Prime Directive, William? I mean... they were still working with you behind the scenes, were they not? Somebody helped you build those structures on Enceladus, right?"

William nodded. "In their minds, working with us was not in violation of their rules. By reaching out to them as we had, we'd proven ourselves ready and able to meet them on their own terms, at least in some small ways. We had already reached the point where open contact was allowable."

"It was those tuxedos."

The Fisherman grinned. " We were well versed in matters both spiritual and scientific, and were already dedicated to the evolution of human consciousness. We understood how old paradigms unraveled and new ones arose. And because of our wealth and power, we could manage the need for secrecy and align with the Prime Directive. This put us in the middle of things from the beginning."

"And behind the scenes, you were working on this Plan you keep mentioning," said Linda.

"Yes," said William. "It was apparent to some of us that the human race was turning the sharp inflection point on the exponential growth curve, and that we were facing the eventual unraveling of the entire global social system. We saw, with the aliens' help, the possibility of escaping that fate, and so updated our centuries-old Plan. Our aim had long been one of steering the course of human history. But we'd only ever seen that project in terms of how it unfolded on Earth. Now our goal was to leave our planet of origin and seed the stars with human life. The ultimate in 'breaking away,' you might say."

"So The Families could see the current mess coming as far back as the late-40s?"

"We could, Madam. It's preposterous to think that we were simply stupid and could not see the obvious, as so many of your people love to believe. We had access to much better information than you, and we always had it first. We just didn't respond to it the way you wanted us to."

"When the going gets rough, the rich get going. Does that about sum it up?"

"For many in The Families, it was indeed a matter of saving their bloodlines. But we in the Element were keen to join the Cosmic Community, and to help keep the human experiment going in the physical bands, should it end entirely on Earth."

Linda stopped and looked down at her lap, shaking her head slightly from side to side as though the pieces wouldn't quite fall into place. Her face was dark and lined. "So the aliens helped you with that. Helped you build your own woks, for instance. Propulsion systems. Weapons. Space stations. All of that." She looked up at the Fisherman. "So what did *they* get?"

"They demanded that their secrecy be maintained. And they demanded the right to continue to interact with individual humans on Earth however they saw fit."

"Demanded?" asked Linda.

William sighed. "Spud is one tough gannet, as my mother used to say."

"And ya'll were happy to go along with the secrecy, since it served your interests too."

"Of course. We had no idea, at the time the deal was struck, that one of their projects would include the creation of human-alien hybrids. Imagine what people would have done, had they suspected that the creatures coming into their bedrooms at night were there with our permission."

Linda leaned forward in her chair and pierced the Fisherman with her eyes. "Because it's been pretty painful for some of them, hasn't it William?" she asked. Her voice quivered as she spoke, and her hands shook. They both knew that Linda herself had had her own terrifying experiences.

"Aye," answered William, looking down. He exhaled heavily. "Aye."

Linda sat back in her chair and pulled up her legs. It looked as though the Fisherman felt bad about what had happened, but whether his feelings were frank or feigned she could not be sure. He was a member of this "breakaway civilization." No longer a member of the human community. One foot already out the proverbial door. So how much empathy could he really have? She watched him for a moment as he sat there, looking down at his hands, pulling at his fingers. He looked more frail to her than he had at first. More in need. More uncertain. "I wonder," she said, "if sometimes you and your people look back on those agreements you made and think that it was *then* that you sold your souls to the Devil?" He seemed to want her understanding. This was all she had.

The Fisherman looked up and smiled weakly. "Did I not say, Madam, that they offered us an opportunity that was worth grabbing at any cost?"

14.5

It was all exactly the same, and yet it wasn't. The ride up the beam. That weird door that muddled her memory. The table. The strange screen. The pinball machines and boxes of yarn. The ribbons. The poking and prodding. All the same. And yet, in her mind, that single word rang like a bell: amends. These beings did nothing by chance or lack of design. Amends meant something.

She was in her bed now, flat on her back, unable to move. Were they making amends, these aliens? The four identical beings stood in a line, back to front, facing the window, ready to leave at any moment. The fifth being, the robed one, the tallest of them, stood at her bedside, gazing down at her. Was he making amends? It was hard to see how, unless they'd done something to fix her father's horrible ways. But they'd never done that before, and they'd had plenty of opportunities.

The robed one cocked his head again, and his face crinkled slightly. It looked like he was trying to smile. Almost. The being shrugged, then turned to the others, and nodded once. They all began to slide toward the window.

WAIT! cried Mary, though she made no actual sound. Her mouth would not move. Her voice would not work. All she had were her thoughts. WAIT! she shouted again. They were leaving. If they wanted to make amends, they could start with her. TAKE ME WITH YOU! Mary strained to move her head, to follow them as they moved out of her field of vision. But all she could do was roll her eyes. WAIT, YOU BASTARDS! she yelled, hoping maybe that would get their attention.

The four-in-a-line glanced back at her with mouths agape, then turned and floated up to the window. The first one passed through. Then the second. STOP! shouted Mary as loudly as she could think. She pushed against the invisible restraints, the ropes, the straps, the heavy, immovable weight. The veins in her neck pulsed and bulged as she pushed and struggled, trying to sit up, to twist around, to push her hand into the air. STOP!

All of a sudden her head whipped to the side and she saw the last of the four pass through the glass. The robed one rose in the air toward the window and Mary lifted her head and shouted again, this time with voice and mouth and air and sound. "Take me with you!" she shouted. "Take me! Take me with you!"

The robed being stopped, turned, settled back down to the floor, and regarded Mary. It was like being observed by a praying mantis, that wild, shivery feeling you get when you know that the Other knows that you are there. When you feel their eyes on you. When you find that your mind is in theirs. "Wait!" said Mary again, this time softer, and punctuated with sobs. "Wait... please..." she said. She pushed again and was able to roll onto her side, to bring her hand to her face to wipe away the tears. "Please," she said, turning her face up to see the robed being looking at back at her. "Please. My father is going to kill me. Please take me with you."

The being looked out the window, up toward his waiting ship. He looked back at Mary. Then he nodded once.

Mary's restraints lifted and she pushed herself up to a sitting position.

14.6

"The Element didn't agree with The Families' decision to take me out, so you rescued me and brought me to Mars." She gestured toward him like it was his turn. "Why did you do that?"

William nodded. "The relationship between The Families and the aliens has always been two-pronged, Madam. On the one hand were the scientists and engineers, the security forces and the politicians. For them the aliens were a source of information and technology. On the other hand was the Element, most of whom now are descendants of the legendary First Circle, that original group that met in Germany. For us, the aliens were a source of understanding and wisdom. We found and trained gifted individuals who could communicate with Spud and his colleagues mind-to-mind, and who began to learn their techniques for transcending the physical. The Life only answer the questions they wish to answer, which are not many. When they do answer, it is often in riddles. So we know much less about them than we would like to. But it was we in the Element who've been able to learn what little we *do* know, about their history, their motives, and their projects."

"Agent Rice and his group were with the Element?" asked Linda.

William shook his head. "Rice trained with us early in his career, Madam. As did Roberta Reese. As did Mary, who now works for you. But as so often happens, other factions within The Families put our efforts to a different use than we had intended. The People were not aligned with the Evolutionary Element. They reported directly to the Directorate, the central governing board for The Families as a whole. Rice and his people were tasked with safeguarding the Plan, monitoring Astral-level activity, and maintaining secrecy, which they achieved by telling lies, like that fairy story they sold you about the Life. While they used our techniques for Astral-level travel and manipulation, they used them in the service of wealth, power, and control. Perhaps it was his attempt to serve two masters that drove Mr. Rice insane."

Linda sat for a moment and breathed, resisting the lure of painful memories. "So you guys are a breakaway group inside of a break-away group," she said at last. She wanted to stay on task. The Fisher-man had not yet answered her question.

"You don't know the half of it, Madam. In some very real ways, we in the Element are different enough from the dominant human society and paradigm that we constitute a different consensus meta-reality. We are almost as alien as the aliens."

"You seem like a normal human elite overlord to me, William," said Linda, smiling at her joke.

William flashed his eyebrows. "Born and raised in captivity amongst you, Madam. I learned your language well."

"Embedded, were you?" asked Linda.

The Fisherman nodded. "My father, perhaps to get distance from my grandfather's rather forceful personality, left our family's estate in York and moved to London, where he got into broadcasting. Had a fairly distinguished career as a news presenter, at a time when The Families' interest in shaping the content of mass media was growing by leaps and bounds. I was raised in the comfortable, established middle class lifestyle that fit my father's position, though we all un-derstood who our real people were."

"I see," said Linda. "So, again. Why did you save me?"

William nodded and sighed. "About the time of your first elec-tion, the Life received information which, in their minds, changed everything. They've been acting on that information since. They in-sisted that you be 'brought in' very soon after your inauguration. They aided your escape from the People. They dismantled their vast system of underground facilities and withdrew themselves from the Earth. Then they installed the Grid - what they call the Interdict."

"And is the Grid keeping us in, or other people out, or something else entirely?" asked Linda.

"Yes," said William with a wry smile. "But let me continue. Because all of their actions were leading somewhere. Unbeknownst to everyone but themselves, you see, they had been working on another program: they had carefully crafted a new being, someone who might create new openings for choice-making in the rapidly unraveling situation on Earth. When the new information arrived, the decision was made to awaken this new being, to shake things up such that new choices might be made. We in the Element aligned with this as best we could."

Linda frowned. "So... this new information was what, exactly?" she asked.

William smiled. "The Life said very little about this before they departed," answered the Fisherman. 'The Fathers are returning,' is how Spud explained it. We take that to mean the Fortunate, whom you met earlier."

"Okay," said Linda, nodding. "Whatever that means. So who's this new being? One of those hybrids? Some sort of super-alien with fantastical powers that can save us right before the end credits roll?"

The Fisherman flashed his eyebrows in surprise. "Why, you are, Madam," he said, as though it were obvious. "Linda Travis. The Choicemaker."

14.7

He stood before the Conclave.

You are returning with freedom and clarity? asked the Architect.

The choice is mine to continue the work, he answered.

And your commitment to the First Law holds steady? asked the Builder.

And the One Goal, Builder, he responded.

You know the promise of pain you face? asked the Artist.

And the possibility for failure? added the Scientist.

There can be no failure where there is choice, Scientist. And pain is often the companion of learning, he said. *Who can know this better than I?*

The Artist nodded in agreement. *Still, it must be spoken*, she said.

Yes it must, he said.

This will likely be your last time, said the Mathematician. *For good or ill, the time is now here.*

May you leave with our thanks and blessings, said the Mother.

I will take them with me to my new life, he said. With that, he bowed deeply. When he stood back up, the Conclave was gone. He turned and walked into the light.

14.8

Linda, unable to contain herself, had stood, and was pacing back and forth behind her armchair. "So you saved me because I'm some alien-bred savior?" she asked, her hands on her hips. She stopped and grabbed the chair back with both hands. "Really? That's your plan?"

"Have I not made that plain from the beginning, Madam President?" said William, using her title to remind her who she was.

She shook her head in disgust and started pacing again. "But how...?" she said, raising her hands in supplication. She stopped and peered at the distant pyramid, then turned to face the Fisherman. "How did they...?" Linda exhaled loudly and shook her head.

"We don't have time to explore exactly how it was that you were 'crafted,'" said William. "Some of it you already heard from your brother-in-law. The rest will have to wait for a better time."

Linda blinked in disbelief. "In my staff meetings, we call that 'tossing a bomb and running,'" she said.

The Fisherman nodded. "Fair enough," he said. "As I said earlier, I look forward to a time when we might have that discussion. For now, suffice it to say that, in the eyes of some, you are now one of the most important forces at work in the Earth/Human matrix. And different enough to warrant my declaring you a separate layer of leadership unto yourself. I imagine you feel some resistance to such statements. I understand why you might, and regret any pain this might cause you."

"And yet necessity compels you," said Linda, a bit of scorn in her voice.

"Assuredly," said William, nodding slowly.

14.9

Nicky pushed through his cat door and stepped out into the dark and stormy night. His man human was snoring away in his soft, warm bed, but Nicky couldn't sleep, his dreams filled with fears of darkness and fire and falling. He ducked quickly to the left, crossed the paving stones, and took his secret path to the freight elevator, the one that hugged the cottage's foundation. His heart filled with excitement when he rounded the corner. There were soldier humans carrying boxes and shoving them hurriedly into the back of a truck, their work lit by flashlights. And there was a door left open! In a flash, Nicky slipped past the soldier humans and through the open door, disappearing into the darkness. He found a stairway leading downward, lit by tiny lights on the wall rather than the regular overhead fixtures he was used to. As quickly as he could, Nicky raced down the stairs.

At the bottom was another door, this one shut. Seeing no way to open it, and seeing nowhere else to go, Nicky hunkered down in the darkest corner and waited. Soon enough, another soldier human opened the door and came through, carrying another box. Nicky darted through the door before it could close, into the empty corridor beyond. There were more of the tiny, dim lights, spaced at long intervals along the hallway. Slowing, Nicky began exploring.

This was where he'd been before when his man human caught him earlier in the day. He could tell by the smell. Chemicals in the air, like a hospital, but something dead now as well. It was cold down here, so different from the warmth above. He moved along the dark hallways, peeking through the open doors, sniffing under the closed ones, pushing against the latter to see if any would open at his touch. At last he came to the source of the smells: a room with windows to the hallway. The door was closed, but the windows had a small ledge, so he jumped up to get a better view. The room on the other side of the glass was empty and dark, but there was another set of windows on the opposite wall, and in the room beyond that was a strange bed, with a woman human body lying on it, and another of those tiny lights overhead. Nicky knew that this body was important to his man human, though he wasn't sure how or why. He remembered seeing her when she was first brought in on a helicopter. All wrapped up in a bundle then, but he knew it was her. She was the whole reason they'd come to live here on this island, his man human and himself.

She was also the source of the dead smell.

14.10

Mihos was falling. He was sure of it now. First he'd thought he was being pushed by somebody. Then pulled. Then pushed again. Now he was falling. What made it worse was this: he was beginning to suspect that he could actually see what it was he was falling toward. It was difficult to be sure. It might have been just another mental game, a bit of random imagery, occasioned by his fears, perhaps, or left over from some other life. But maybe not. It was faint, to be sure. Dim, like stars could be dim in the physical bands, where you could only see them when you weren't looking at them. But it was still there, every time he looked. And it might be less faint now than it was before.

What it was he was seeing he could not yet tell. If he was falling toward something, then he was tens of miles above it. A spot of light. Maybe yellow. Maybe orange. Maybe round. A blur. A round blur of orange, right there at the edge of his ability to see. Far below him, and he falling toward it.

Maybe it was the ground. Maybe he *was* in the sky, falling like he'd jumped from an airplane. Or a flying carpet. He just couldn't tell.

Wherever it was he was falling to, Mihos hoped very much that he would land on his feet.

14.11

Linda sat for a long time, just looking at the Fisherman and thinking. William waited, then leaned forward and spoke. "Every bit of consciousness on the planet Earth will be cherished, Madam," he said, "no matter where the future takes it."

Linda shook her head. "I, uh..." she said, blinking repeatedly. "Could you say that again?"

The Fisherman nodded. "You were thinking that people will be lost. Left behind. Left out. You serve them all. I understand that. I'm telling you that no one will be lost. Every bit of the human experiment as it has played out on the planet Earth exists already in the Mind of God, adding to it, serving the evolution of consciousness. Evolution *is* for all, because All is One."

"Okay..." said Linda, warily. "Keep going. What's your point here?"

"I want you to think more expansively about human beings, Madam. In the eyes of the Cosmic Community, the human species as it exists in the physical band of reality represents a marvelously self-reflexive training ground for the evolution of consciousness. The particular suite of senses, abilities, potentials, and experiences contained within the human species is exceedingly novel, and the consensus meta-reality we have created amongst ourselves is thus greatly cherished amongst other sentient groups."

"And that's why the aliens are so interested in helping us?"

"They've acted as both goad and guide to human beings for millennia," said William. "Many individuals have already joined the larger consensus meta-meta reality, like bubbles rising from the boiling cauldron of human experience."

"But now they're only helping The Families get off planet."

"Their focus is two-fold, as I have explained. They work to aid some small portion of us to carry on the human experiment elsewhere in the physical universe. And they continue to offer their invitation to everyone on Earth. Their hope is that the human species as a whole will soon join the Cosmic Community, consciously, openly, and freely.

"But only a 'small portion' of people get a ticket on your magical spaceships."

"Only a small portion will leave this planet in their current physical bodies, yes. To start colonies elsewhere, as I showed you, so that human bodies can continue to exist on the physical plain."

"And the rest of us poor slobs?" asked Linda.

The Fisherman smiled. "Many will leave physicality behind altogether, as your friend Pooch did. Some will reincarnate in human bodies in the new colonies. Some will live subsequent lives on other planets in the same general meta-reality. Some will remain stuck in highly individualized realities of their own creation. Some will choose to forfeit their individuality and dissolve back into Mind-at-Large. And we must remember that we cannot yet predict the final outcome on Earth, Madam. Perhaps some will survive the bottleneck, and some may live subsequent lives on a future Earth we cannot yet see."

"But nothing gets left behind, you say," said Linda with a frown. "It all works out eventually..."

William nodded. "All of reality is on the sacred journey: the evolution and expansion of consciousness. The process simply proceeds at different paces for different bits of that larger Whole. Some graduate and move ahead quickly. Others plod along more slowly. Others get stuck in loops for a time. Others go backward. Some start over. But all of us are moving somewhere, as Mind-at-Large itself is in motion, and contains the whole of reality. So while the alien medics offer a hand to some few of us, inviting us to consciously take our rightful place in the consensus meta-meta-reality and the Cosmic Community, inviting us to join them in the *conscious* advancement of consciousness from our physical realm, it remains true that every other bit of mind is a necessary part of that sacred process. Self-reflective awareness is a great and rare thing in the Cosmos, something to be noticed and cherished and put to use for the evolution of consciousness. But it is not the only thing that is cherished. It's all cherished. Does that help?"

"It doesn't sound much like a 'continuation of the human experiment,' William," said Linda. "I mean, space colonies on other planets and moons? That sounds like a pretty different experience."

William nodded his agreement. "It will certainly be different, Madam. Yet the human body will continue, and with it its shared meta-reality, its vast collective unconscious." He leaned forward in his chair. "This is a time of triage, remember. The limitations of circumstance are more demanding than ever. It is thought that a different experiment is better than no experiment at all."

"Okay," said Linda. "So The Families are jumping into their lifeboats before the whole planet sinks. The aliens helped build those boats, but they're also throwing out life preservers for the rest of us. Does that about sum it up?"

"Quite colorfully, Madam," said William. "Behind the scenes, unbeknownst to most humans on Earth, we in the so-called 'breakaway civilization' put the vast resources of the global industrial machine to the task of designing and building the various ships, transport containers, terraforming equipment, and off-world habitats needed to achieve this end. This explains where so much of what has been referred to as the 'missing wealth' or 'black budget' actually ended up. It also explains why the global economy remained intact as long as it did, which was much longer than many outside observers predicted it would. We kept it going on artificial life support for as long as possible while we finished building our first colonies and our fleet. And the continued burning of fossil fuels, along with the additional particulates from the chemtrail project, kept global dimming in place while we worked, putting off the inevitable greenhouse spiraling we are beginning to see now. We thought of the process as analogous to an unborn bird using up all of the resources in its shell before hatching, or a caterpillar gorging itself on sustenance before transforming into a moth and flying away."

"All the while laughing at the rest of us as you vacuumed up the Earth's wealth to save your own skins," said Linda, her nose wrinkled in disgust.

At this the Fisherman pushed himself forward to the edge of his chair and reached out again to take Linda's hand. "I truly wish it had been otherwise, Madam," he said, his voice soft and gentle. He let go of the President's hand and sat back. "The Families, alas, have been blinded by their own cultural assumptions. After centuries of winning, after having broken away from the dominant global culture, most of them have lost all sense of kinship with the rest of the human population, and have acted out a great deal of contempt and disgust toward the 'unwashed masses' and 'useless eaters.'"

Linda was shaking her head. "I mean... Hello? Why did you guys decide to cut and run? If you'd taken all of the wealth and power and resources you've spent to get away, could you not have stopped the destruction of the planet and retooled society to be more sustainable?"

The Fisherman looked down at his lap. "This may be The Families greatest failing, Madam," he said, his voice quiet and sad. He looked up at Linda. "Our greatest sin, some might say. And one for which I believe we shall pay." He sighed heavily. "Could we have saved the Earth from the terrible challenges it is now facing? Maybe we could have. I don't know. But you yourself experienced how difficult it is to counter the driving impulses of a global culture bent on control, domination, and unending growth. We in The Families were 'done with them' long before you were, you see. Perhaps we suffer from an utter lack of faith in human beings."

"Maybe we both do," said Linda.

William shook his head in uncertainty. "I think most of our attention was on the aliens, Madam. The technology. The possibilities. We were tired of Earth. Bored, even. And some of us were horrified by the world wars. We *wanted* to leave. We *wanted* to go to the stars. And as the population grew and the climate worsened and the seas filled with trash, the news only confirmed that we'd made the right choice. Even we in the Element were guilty of this. Even if we'd had the power to steer the Directorate, which we did not, our minds were on where we were headed, not what, and whom, we were leaving behind. It was... " William stopped and sighed deeply. "It was a lapse, Madam.

The Fisherman slapped his hands on his knees, then rose to stretch his legs and shoulders. He stood with arms raised, turning slowly, surveying the great plain that surrounded them, then dropped his arms and turned back to the President. "But here's the thing, Madam. As difficult as it may be for you to believe, a few of us through the decades, and including the aliens themselves - have actually been rooting for the masses of humanity all along."

"How do you see that, William?"

The Fisherman sat on the edge of his chair, his voice pitched with excitement. "Have you not noticed the great lengths we've gone to, Madam? To create as much absurdity as we could? It's as though The Families, while trying to break away from the masses, have also been unconsciously attempting to wake them up! Public statements about our goals and intentions. Nonsensical explanations, obviously false denials, and enigmatic documents about our true interest in UFOs. The release of paradigm-challenging data about our paranormal pursuits. Hints and bits of evidence for what really happened on the moon. We've allowed public layer leaders to act like complete morons in the face of obvious environmental concerns. We've promoted idiotic and clearly fabricated explanations for the 9/11 events, the Boston Marathon bombing, and the Miami nuke. We've done everything we could to say 'Hey! You over there! There's more going on than what the mainstream culture is telling you!' And all while being constrained by the Prime Directive and the necessity of choice.

"And the aliens, Madam! They've continued to reveal themselves in absurd and provocative ways. Mass sightings over major cities, Madam. Face-to-face encounters in the private lives of tens of thousands of individuals. Ever more intricate crop circles. Some aliens even incarnated into human lives, in order to help lead people to a greater understanding of reality. They've done their best to deliver their invitation to as many people as was possible, while honoring the necessity for freedom of choice. Not just to the rich and powerful, but across the board. And you know what? People from all walks of life, all the layers of society, all around the globe, all throughout history, have accepted their invitations and done their work. And many have already moved on ahead of us, joining the great consensus meta-meta-reality that is being offered to us as a species." William inhaled sharply, pushed himself back in his chair, exhaled. His face was tight with defensive lines, yet his eyes were wide open, almost expectant.

"And you could not have just told us all the truth?" said Linda.

"'We want disclosure,'" said William in a mocking tone. "''Tell us what's real!' 'We deserve to know the truth!'" The Fisherman frowned, then sat forward in his chair and lowered his voice. "Really, Madam. It does not work that way. We will have to save ourselves. Of what use to the evolution of consciousness are beings who can only know the truth of things when it's given to them by experts and authorities and parents? Beings who are unable or unwilling to do their own spiritual work so that they can seek and find the truth themselves? Most of the UFO community was so offended to be left out by the 'cover-up,' and so affronted by what the aliens had to teach, that they could never actually see the possibilities before them, let alone take actions to explore those possibilities. Well 'boo-hoo,' to quote our friend Agent Rice. Somebody has been left behind since the first tetrapod hauled his inquisitive little self up out of the sea and onto the mud flats. Don't like it? Grow the hell up!" The Fisherman sighed deeply and sat back, his face dark and his brow creased.

"You're really angry, aren't you William?" said Linda.

William nodded. "It appears that I am, Madam," he said.

14.12

MaineCentral Hospital was abuzz with conversation and activity, but an outside onlooker, a human being, would have noticed mostly silence and stillness. The new doctors and nurses, the hybrids - the Tubies, as Mary had called them, though that was not what they called themselves - went about their business with an economy of motion and clarity of focus and intention that did not in the least resemble the madhouse one might expect from the medical shows one saw on television. Able to communicate mind-to-mind, there was little need for the shouting and argument and orders and joking conversation that might have otherwise filled the air. There were, at times, soft sighs and clicks of the tongue, and there was even a brief chuckle now and then. But mostly the doctors and nurses were quiet. The hospital was filled only with the sounds of televisions turned down low, and the happy, eager chirpings of machines that go ping.

There was a meeting taking place at the nurse's station around the corner from the guarded door to Keeley's room. Present were five nurses and two doctors. They stood facing each other in a circle and said many things, though the conversation took little time, and did not necessarily follow in this order.

"... APPEARS TO BE DERIVED FROM INFLUENZA A H7N7..."

"... INFECTION RATE STILL UNKNOWN..."

"... POSSIBLY RELATED TO GLOBAL EMP DETECTED 3/22..."

"... CONTINUE WITH REST AND FLUIDS INSIDE PRO-TECTED CHAMBER..."

"... NEURAMINIDASE INHIBITORS SO FAR INEFFEC-TIVE..."

"... QUESTION THE NECESSITY OF ISOLATION FROM HER PARTNER..."

"... NO DOUBT OF FAMILY ORIGIN..."

"... EUPHORIC SYMPTOMS PUZZLING..."

"... FATALITY RATE CURRENTLY 98.2 PERCENT..."

"... LASTED LONGER THAN ANY OTHER REPORTED CASE..."

"... MARY HAYES PROJECT PROCEEDING AS WAS PRE-DICTED..."

"... NOW WE WAIT..."

At once, and without any obvious word, sign, or gesture, the meeting's attendees joined hands and closed their eyes and reached out with their minds to the rest of their people, sharing their conversation with the larger community. After a few moments, they turned and walked away, returning to their previous duties. What needed to be shared had been shared. What needed to be decided had been decided. What needed to be communicated had been communicated.

Now they waited.

14.13

"So you feel like you've been doing your best to help, don't you William?" Linda's voice was gentle and kind.

The Fisherman nodded. "I do, Madam. And in some very difficult circumstances. As have the aliens who have stuck with us this long." William rubbed his eyes with the palms of his hands, then looked down at his lap. "I don't feel like... " He stopped and sighed heavily, then looked at Linda. "I would like for you to see that."

Linda nodded. "I'll do my best to remember it. And you think the aliens are also doing their best?"

"I believe that the Life are, yes."

"But they fled after I exposed them," Linda pointed out.

"They've done no such thing, Madam, as any glance at the Earth's night sky will confirm."

"But they've stepped back, at least," said Linda. "What changed?"

"It is difficult to know for certain," said William. "We've had virtually no direct contact with the Life since their hasty departure. We know they were extremely unhappy with Agent Rice and his group. We know that exposing them changed the situation dramatically. And we know they had successfully activated the next stage of their project, which is you." His face softened as he spoke. "But in my opinion, they left because they realized that they didn't know what to do next, and that they were no longer needed."

"Really," said Linda, raising an eyebrow.

"Think of it, Madam," said the Fisherman. "If we regard the aliens as an elder or parent species, then we see that, just like we do, they find childrearing to be a particularly difficult job. How best to parent? How best to be an elder? What to allow? When to intervene? And how best to help an adolescent self-aware species mature into its adult form? These are not simple questions, Madam. Not for anyone. And the Life have made plenty of mistakes in the past, so they know self-doubt."

"But to just give up... "

"There comes a time, Madam, when the parent must push the adolescent out into the wilderness for his vision quest. Think of the aliens' departure as their last hug and kiss before they left us on our own. And think of the Grid as the line behind which the parents and elders now wait, to see if their beloved children will return from their quest. They have given us a gift, Madam: They are allowing us to take our next steps on our own. And the Grid itself serves as our one-last-challenge - the tiger in the forest, so to speak - against which we must test ourselves before we step into our new vision."

"The Grid is some sort of test?"

William winked. "All in good time," he said.

Linda sighed. "So why do we need to be tested, William? Tested to the point of the destruction of an entire planet and most of humanity?"

William smiled. "Because that is how beautiful, mature, adult human consciousness is created, Madam, just as beautiful, mature, adult butterflies are created when they push their way out of their cocoons and unfurl their wings, as that famous environmental parable shows."

Linda frowned and shook her head from side to side. "I just don't know," she said.

"You still wonder whether we should have simply told the truth all along," said William with a sigh.

"Yes."

"I would counter that the Prime Directive exists for a reason, Madam. Modern humans seem to understand this when they consider their own history. They've seen first-hand the destruction and loss that occurs when vastly different cultures clash. But they think, like any teenager convinced of their own invincibility, that this would not apply to *them* should *they* encounter a more powerful species.

"The aliens understand this far better than we. They have seen it play out countless times. Revealing themselves, and sharing their advanced technologies, would be the equivalent of taking young Bobby's hand and walking him out into the wilderness for his vision quest, taking care of him, protecting him, doing everything for him, even sneaking him candy bars because Bobby just hates to go hungry, the poor dear. You end up with arrested development, Madam. But the Cosmic Community sees far too much potential for humanity than to allow them to remain as adolescents."

William stopped, took a deep breath, and continued. "In the greater consensus meta-meta reality to which we've been invited, the powers to create, to manifest thought and feeling into shared realities, are greatly increased, and work much more quickly than they do in the physical bands. The Cosmic Community will not give humans access to such tools until they are mature enough - emotionally, psychologically, and spiritually - to handle them wisely."

"But I told the whole world about the aliens on ACN. So didn't I already spoil things?"

"Had that happened a hundred years ago, it would have made a huge difference. As it was, with wholesale environmental collapse so imminent, it made little impact. In these extreme evolutionary times, those who matter already knew, and those who did not already know had ceased to matter."

"Spoken with all the coldness of heart we've come to expect from you people," spat Linda.

The Fisherman scoffed. "Would you call us evil, Madam? As I have said, you would not be the first. But does it not strike you as odd that those who insist upon the freedom of choice and the evolution of human consciousness by one's own efforts are branded 'evil,' while those who insist on dependence upon, and salvation through, experts, leaders, angels, aliens, and gods are branded 'good'? The fact remains: no matter the circumstances - and yes we of the Element, and the aliens, have allowed some extreme circumstances to arise - freedom of choice is always right there for anyone to grasp and use." William stopped again, exhaled sharply, closed his eyes and rubbed at the lids.

He opened his eyes and smiled gently. "We seem to have reached that field of which Rumi spoke, Madam." He glanced around the Martian plain that surrounded them. "Language fails us. Nothing makes any sense."

Linda nodded. "It would seem," she said.

14.14

Mary rose to her feet. Her father stood in the corner, head hung low, his back to the room. Danny stood in the hallway where they'd placed him upon his return, staring in through the door with wide, unblinking eyes. The line of four beings had all passed through the window and were riding the blue beam up into the sky like an escalator to the stars. The robed being stood near the window, watching it all, like a conductor, a judge, a god. Everything was exactly as it was, as it should be, as it had been. Everything was the same, save for that word in her head.

She took a step toward the window. The robed being watched her carefully. Mary knew that if she stepped up onto the sill and stuck her head out, she could simply put her feet down into the blue light and it would carry her away. And she knew, though how she could know this she did not know, that the blue beam would carry her to a strange and wonderful life. There was no choice, really: stay here to be beaten to death by her father, or join these mysterious creatures in their bright, pulsing ship. She peered through the window to see the four beings melt into the huge, bowl-shaped light. She looked at the robed being still standing inside her room. Then she started forward on legs that were no longer bound by their damnable paralyzing fog.

She took a step, and another. Soon she was right next to the robed being. She could have reached out and touched the side of his face. But those eyes: so huge, so utterly black, like stairways down into dark, dank basements, and what would rush up the stairs to attack her if she got too close?

The robed being stared into Mary's eyes. Mary stared back. She glanced at the open window, then back at the being, and then to the window again. It was time to take another step.

The robed being cocked his head. A slight movement. Almost a twitch. And yet she could tell it was purposeful. She looked in the direction his head had moved. There was Danny in the doorway, eyes like half-dollars, shiny and filled with amazement. Mary looked at the robed being. He gestured again toward Danny with a slight nod of his head. Mary turned to look again at her little brother.

Then she turned back to the robed being and smiled. "I want my brother to come with me," she said.

The little robed being did his best to smile back.

14.15

"You don't feel evil to me, William. Neither did Spud, when I met him. But aren't some aliens pretty awful, just like some Family members are?" Linda had pulled her feet up under her bottom and was leaning her elbow on the arm of her chair. "I mean... people have had some pretty traumatic experiences with them, right? The abductions. The implants. The cattle mutilations. And I ran into a lot of people these past few years who told me about evil lizard aliens who were going to invade Earth and enslave us."

"Are there alien species with goals and methods humans would consider 'bad' or 'evil'?" asked William. "A few might fit that description, and we've had to deal with them from time to time. But now, with the Life's Interdict in place, none of them are a factor in Earth-Human affairs."

"Because the Grid keeps bad aliens out?" asked Linda.

"Among other things," said William.

"I guess that's a good thing."

"Well, that's the more important question, is it not? What is good? Who is good? And how do we know? I find that easy distinctions tend to fall apart here on Rumi's Field, so let me turn again to metaphor and story, if I may," said William.

"By all means," said Linda with a wave of her hand.

"There's a wonderful movie. American. Came out about thirty years ago. *Jacob's Ladder*, it was called. Do you know it?"

Linda shook her head.

"Pity. It's a marvelous thriller. In it, there's a character who sees visions of Hell. Another character relates how the theologian Meister Eckhart also saw visions of Hell. Eckhart explained that what burns away in Hell is your attachment to your present life. Your ego. Your personality. Your memories. The burning is painful, but it's not a punishment. Your soul is being freed. If you're afraid of dying, if you're not ready to let go of your Earthly life, then the burning will seem like demons, tearing you apart. But if you have made your peace with dying, you'll see angels instead of demons. Angels who are freeing you from the cares of Earth."

William stopped and smiled. "I was never able to find any clear source material linking this to Eckhart himself, but the notion resonates, does it not? We all experience in our lives how good and bad can shift back and forth, depending on the context. 'Out beyond ideas of wrongdoing and rightdoing... "

Linda held up her hand and closed her eyes. William fell silent. "The Earth is going through a great dying right now, William," said the President at last. She looked at the Fisherman, her face lined with sadness. "Not just humans but... God, William, the oceans and dolphins and... and have you see the forests burning in the north?"

The Fisherman nodded.

Linda sighed deeply. "And they're so scared, William. My people. They're so scared. Holding on for dear life. You should see them in the shelters we built. So scared. Not just for themselves and their children, but because they *know*. They don't know that they know, but they know! They're scared for everything. For the end of everything."

"And so they see demons everywhere, punishing them," said William softly. "The aliens. The elite. The whites. The blacks. The government. The atheists. The Jews. The next-door neighbors. Even themselves."

"They saw *me* as a devil, William! You should've heard the things they said!"

"I did, Madam," said William.

"Right," said Linda with a frown. She took a couple of deep breaths. "So the aliens are angels, then?"

William smiled. "They would scoff at the idea, but they *are* offering to free us from the old worldview in which we've become mired. Those of us who are ready."

"But it's all so coldly Darwinian, William. You know? All this talk of competition and winners and losers. Haven't scientists found all sorts of new evidence for cooperation and symbiosis and things like that? Does it have to be so harsh?"

The Fisherman nodded. "They did indeed, Madam. Nature turns out to be nowhere near so 'red in tooth and claw' as civilized humans like to think. However, all that really does is change the unit of selection. Instead of nature selecting for individuals who win the competition, it selects for symbiotic clusterings, or cooperative communities, or entire ecosystems. Whether it's dominance or cooperation, things are still getting selected for and against by changing circumstances. Notice that, no matter how cooperative and symbiotic life on Earth might be, it is estimated that 99.9% of all species that have ever lived are now extinct. Cooperation does not stop the cold process of selection in the long term, Madam, no matter how nice that might sound."

"I think what strikes me as cold, William, is the blame I hear in your words. You go on and on about the freedom to choose, yet I'm not sure all these people really have that freedom. The ones that have ceased to matter, William. That's who I'm talking about."

William closed his eyes and took a couple of long breaths. He opened his eyes. "You are correct to point out my coldness, Madam. I thank you. The old Family training still trips me up from time to time."

Linda nodded, her eyes angry. "Yeah. It's like what Spud said to me in that dream I had. After... everything happened. He acted the same way. Tossed out that old quote about repeating the past if we don't learn from it. And that 'there are none so blind as those who *will* not see' quote. As if it was a simple matter of will. It really pissed me off."

The Fisherman nodded. "Again," he said, "we find ourselves in Rumi's Field. Is the choice to break free from the confines of culture and paradigm a matter of ability or will? Are Kübler-Ross's 'beautiful people' born or made? If they're made, were they able to 'find their way out of the depths' because of something they were born with? Or is it always a bit of both?"

"It's tempting to call it a matter of will, when you see so much blaming in the world," said Linda.

"Yes," said William. "But in truth, I find that I agree with the statement that people are at all times 'doing the best they can with what they have.' If I tend to hold people as totally responsible for their choices, that allows me to feel angry with them, which is easier than feeling helpless or sad at the realization of how unable most people are these days."

"And yet people are making choices all the time, William," said Linda. "Even with the Grid in the sky, there were still people who judged me as crazy for saying that there were aliens visiting the Earth."

William started to laugh heartily. "So it goes in Rumi's Field, Madam. We begin to argue for the other's point of view!"

Linda joined in the laughter.

"So it's always both, Madam," said William, still grinning. "Both and more and all of the above. Choice and circumstance, ability and will, doing our best and ignoring what we already know, choosing openness and healing and freedom, choosing to stay in the unlocked prison cells of story and belief, each of us walking our individual path through the Mind of God. We get to do that, Madam! We get to choose to choose, *and* to choose not to choose! That's what makes the Prime Directive so important, Madam. And that's why we in the Element, and the aliens themselves, have tried always to open up more choices rather than shut them down. And that's why I have spent these past days with you: to open up for you a choice you would not otherwise have."

The Fisherman sat forward in his chair. His voice grew lower. "But here's the thing, Madam: in the end, this matter of choice, whether it be ability or will or both, ceases to matter in the physical realm. It does not matter to evolution. And it does not matter to the medics doing triage. In this time of the Great Unraveling, whether we blame the One True God, the many gods, the aliens, or the cold, hard laws of nature, there will be selections made. Whether you make good grades because of inborn talents or hard work or smart choices, your final numbers are what will win you that valedictory speech.

Whether you do not see, cannot see, or choose to ignore the traffic light ahead of you, if you run that stop light and pull out in front of cross-traffic, you will be hit by a car. Such is life in this physical band. If we need to blame someone, Madam, we can blame the creator of this cold, hard, sharp-edge reality."

"Who created this place, William?" asked Linda. "God?"

"Why no, Madam," said William, blinking his eyes in surprise. "We did."

Linda sat forward to match the Fisherman's posture and tone. "So is that why you want me to kill off the human race?"

14.16

Cole sat on the edge of his bed, elbows on his knees, face buried in his hands. His dream, his "hop," had been so strange that he could hardly hold it in his mind, and yet it felt important that he try to do so. He'd been standing before some sort of council or tribunal or something. Half a dozen beings, all those little Gray type of aliens they called the Life. And he was one of them! He wasn't in his body; he was in one of theirs! And they were talking about something. About Cole going somewhere. Going back for the last time. To someplace he might fail.

And then he was a baby. A human baby. The baby Cole, with his mother and father and his older brother, Carl. And he was standing in a thing... a playpen or something... and his mother was ironing and the television was playing some soap opera and Cole, baby Cole, a year or two old, knew, in that moment, that he was alone here, and that he had to hide who he really was. And so he did.

Then Cole woke up, with the feelings of that small gray body still clinging to him, a head full of words he did not know, and images he had never seen, and thoughts he could not comprehend. Thankfully, they receded quickly into the dark closet full of half-remembered dreams. He was glad of that. He'd remembered enough. More than he wanted to, important or not.

He lifted his face and looked out the window. The wind was battering the panes and there were fat drops of rain in it now, splatting on the glass like bugs on a windshield. There was enough pre-dawn light to show the choppy surface of the bay and the churning mass of clouds overhead. It was going to be a hell of a storm. Cole could feel it. Its ferocity felt like disgust and contempt.

The day would bring the full force of this storm. That much he could predict. Beyond that, he had no idea what to expect. Linda was still out there on that island. He and Stan and Sten and these Church of the Stranger folks were still all here, trying to figure out how to get to her. They had a boat. People. A couple of hand guns. Determination. Grit. The folly of youth. The experience of age. And they had the strange light that came from Cole's hands.

What they would do with all of that Cole did not know. Was that him in that dream? Him in some other life? Some other reality? Was the church right, that he wasn't human at all, but one of *them*? One of these Life things? Had he really been here many times before, on some mission that had lasted for centuries, maybe? And... Jesus... was his mission really to stop his own wife from doing something awful? The thought of that filled him with cold fear. He had no idea anymore who or what he could trust. He was on his own. That was truly terrifying.

14. 17

William closed his eyes and sat still and silent for a very long time. When he reopened his eyes, he smiled gently. "I was going to just push away from your question, Madam. Defend myself. Tell you that you are wrong, that it's not *me* who's responsible for this, that you shouldn't judge *me*. But it occurs to me that your question just takes us where we now need to go. You are right: It is time to finally get back to our central question, having put so much of the foundation in place." The Fisherman glanced up into the sky, toward the approaching Martian dawn. "Many pieces are falling into place back on Earth. Our time together must soon come to an end."

"I'll believe that when I see it, William," said Linda.

"Right," said William. "So the way I put it to you was carefully thought out beforehand and precisely worded. Do you remember what I said?"

"You said you had a way to kill off humanity so that the planet could recover, and that you were putting the decision on me," said Linda.

The Fisherman smiled. "Not quite, Madam," he said. "What I said was that it's possible to dramatically decrease the number of humans on the Earth quickly and painlessly, an action which might allow some small portion of humanity to survive on Earth, and which might give the remaining life on Earth a chance to recover. The choice to do so I put to you. And I said that my mission was to prepare you to make that choice, and that when you were prepared you would be returned home. Do you remember now?"

"I guess."

"Do you see the difference?"

"You only want to kill off ninety-five percent instead of everybody?" said Linda.

"I would say that the percentages remain unknown, Madam. Surely a large segment, but the method is unlikely to cause the death of everyone. Human extinction on Earth would remain a distinct possibility, but would result from other forces coming into play. Do you notice anything else?"

"I notice that I don't get out of here until you say I'm ready, William. That doesn't exactly feel like a free choice to me."

William smiled. "Yet surely you can see that a choice remains. Not liking the choice that circumstances have put to you is not the same as not having a choice."

"And you are the circumstances," said Linda.

"Indeed," said William. "Anything else?"

"Stop with the guessing games, Mr. Circumstances. Just make your damn point."

The Fisherman nodded. "I notice two things, Madam. First, that you want to insist that I am killing people, and, second, that the 'quickly and painlessly' part seems not to register with you. In other words, Madam, you seem angry. Appalled, even. And I find that a bit odd."

Linda started to laugh. "Only you would think that odd, William," she said. "Where I come from, mass murderers tend to raise an eyebrow or two."

William stopped and thought for a moment, then nodded. "During your predecessor's term, there was an Ebola outbreak. I know you remember it, as you were serving as Governor of Michigan at the time and there was a case in Flint."

"I remember," said Linda.

"So tell me," said William, "why is it that the best and brightest of you, the environmentally aware, the ones who could most clearly see the need for human population reduction, were so universally appalled when Ebola came to town? I mean, here you are, population far above the Earth's carrying capacity, knowing that something like Ebola could easily arise to correct that overshoot, as has happened so often in the history of life on Earth, and you were appalled? Angry, even? As if what you could think about in purely abstract terms became unthinkable when it manifested in your actual lives. Is that not fascinating to you, Madam?"

"Wouldn't it have been even more odd and fascinating, William, had people just calmly accepted an Ebola pandemic as the right thing to allow to happen for the rest of the life on the planet?"

William nodded, closed his eyes. "Of course," he said. "Of course. I know that. So maybe 'odd' and 'fascinating' are not the right words." He inhaled deeply. Exhaled loudly. He opened his eyes. "I don't know the right word."

Linda smiled gently. "Perhaps you just feel really lonely, William. Maybe you think or feel or know or can see things that very few others do. Maybe you're just tired of being alone with that."

William bowed his head and sighed. "Maybe," he said.

"It may also be, William," said Linda cautiously, "that you and your people are particularly insulated from such things. I mean, you can jump on a spaceship and skip town if the virus gets near, not unlike the kings and queens of old England. Perhaps you would find it less fascinating were you and your loved ones actually at risk of being swept up in a pandemic, whether it benefits the Earth or not."

William nodded heavily. "You may be right, Madam."

Linda let him think for a moment, then spoke. "So were you guys involved in the Ebola thing?"

William looked up and shook his head. "Usually we get wind of such things early on. But we in the Element were caught by surprise with that one. It had been... encouraged, shall we say... by a group called Nature's Way, a rather deeply hidden organization of whom I'd never even heard. When it became clear that normal public responses were not adequate to the task, The Families put their resources behind the containment efforts, finally bringing the outbreak to a halt by the end of the next year."

Linda nodded. "By which time eighty-thousand people had died."

"Indeed," agreed the Fisherman. "A rather inconsequential number in terms of the total human population, and in terms of other diseases which routinely take more lives than that every year, and yet the number felt huge and frightening to most people."

Linda frowned. "So, I don't get that, William. Why stop *that* global pandemic, only to come to me a few years later with a plan to achieve the same thing that Ebola would have? It doesn't make sense."

William smiled grimly. "Because, Madam, it was not yet time, and Ebola was far too nasty a tool for the job.

14.18

Colonel McAfee sat up with a start. Must've been lightning, he thought, as he watched the raindrops smash against the sliding glass door. There was a touch of dawn in the sky, for which he was thankful. He hated storms when it was dark. He wanted to be able to see what was coming.

Staying up on the surface might be a bad idea, however, this time around. This storm might be strong enough to wash this little island cabin right into the sea. Much better to hunker down in the lower levels with the bulk of his forces, leaving only a skeleton crew to maintain security. Who'd come calling in this mess, anyways? Surely not the First Gentleman and his merry men, who'd been sent packing with their tails between their legs three times now. Nobody in his or her right mind would be out on the water today.

Ah well. There was no way he was going to sleep any longer. The Colonel rose and went into the bathroom, flicking on the light before remembering that the power was out. Deciding not to flush - who knew what the water pressure situation was? - he headed out to the kitchen, wanting coffee. But that was a nonstarter as well, with no way to grind the beans. He grabbed a canned cola from the cool but warming fridge and went to get dressed.

He'd find his aide. That Sparks fellow. Danny, was it? Get a report and all that. See if anybody needed anything. These guys were a crack team. Chosen by the General. They knew far more about operations here, and this island compound, than McAfee ever had. He was sure they would be on top of things.

14.19

"So you're hoping for a kinder, gentler genocide, then, are you?" asked Linda.

"Would you prefer the zombie apocalypse, Madam?" replied the Fisherman.

"Are those my only two choices?"

"What if they are?" asked William.

"I would find that unacceptable," said Linda.

"Spoken like a true 'ruler of the Earth,' Madam," said William.

"Says the man who wishes to kill off the bulk of humanity," said Linda.

"Says the man who has spent a great deal of time doing triage with the medics," said William.

Linda opened her mouth to retort, then stopped herself. She closed her eyes and breathed.

The Fisherman pushed forward and rested his elbows on his knees. "Let's see if we can tease apart this 'killing off' of humanity, Madam."

Linda opened her eyes. "That would probably be more useful than bickering," she said with a nod.

William glanced at the brightening sky for a moment, then returned his gaze to the President. "I can think of a number of different ways in which we might view the action I am proposing," he said. "The first is the one we've been discussing so far: we're talking about mass murder and genocide. This would, of course, be the default, culturally-approved way of viewing such an act. I certainly take no offense at your reactions, as I understand where they come from. But again, reaction is less than the free choice I wish for you to make."

"The truth is," William continued, "there are ways in which your anger and abhorrence are right on the mark, Madam. Those in the various layers of control and governance have instigated or allowed all sorts of horror over the years, including mass murders and genocides. They did it in the service of wealth and power, and with ever-increasing levels of contempt and disgust. In fact, even now, were some faction of The Families to unleash a pandemic designed to reduce the human population, they would do so with relish, Madam. Really, for those who have been paying attention, the real surprise is that some hidden elite group has not *already* created a pandemic to wipe out humanity."

"And the real *real* surprise is that some group *has* done that, but you Element guys stopped them," said Linda.

"Exactly, Madam," said William. "The group that deployed the latest Ebola virus was not the first to have tried such a thing. I believe there have been a dozen serious attempts made over the years. The Element has successfully put a stop to them all. And always for the same reason: if this were to be done, there was no need for it to be horribly painful. No one needs to be punished, as far as we can see. Evolution does not make its selections based on contempt and disgust. Neither do medics."

"I see," said Linda. "I guess that's something. So what's the next way to look at it?"

"Ah," said William. "The next *two* ways relate to the discussion we had early on, in which you identified what feels like an addict's desire to seek release by hitting bottom. The force at work is the wish for self-annihilation, and it allows us to consider the actions I am proposing as either a 'right to die' issue or a matter of 'mercy killing.'"

"You really believe there is such a thing as a death wish?" asked Linda.

"I see it as a strong force in play, Madam. Think about it. Humans have doused the soil, the rivers, the forests, the oceans, their food, and themselves with known poisons, toxins, and radioactive particles. They've poured billions of tons of greenhouse gases into the atmosphere, even though the warnings about doing so have been sounded for decades. They've destroyed or damaged the planetary systems that maintain such things as ground temperature, oxygen levels, and precipitation, all of which are now spiraling into chaos. They've grown their population to levels that can only be sustained by the continued functioning of precarious financial, agricultural, political, and energy systems. They have, with the exception of yourself and a few others, put into positions of leadership people who do not understand what they are doing, and who are committed to the ramping up of all of these activities." The Fisherman raised an eyebrow. "Do these not sound like the outer expressions of an inner death wish to you?"

"It does sound pretty crazy," said Linda with a sigh.

"As the poet David Whyte said, 'Sometimes we have to make a complete and absolute disaster of our lives in such an epic, unavoidable way so that it can suddenly become absolutely clear to us what we have been doing all along.'"

Linda shook her head in quiet incredulity.

"Some in the Cosmic Community believe the death wish to be built into the fabric of reality, given how often it shows up in the development of self-aware species. Perhaps it's the necessary balance to creativity. Perhaps it's simply an expression of the force of entropy as it opposes the forces of organization. In any event, there is plenty of reason to regard it as a defining motivator in the Earth-human matrix. You saw the evidence for yourself. I called this wish for death a great wisdom."

"Yeah," said Linda. "It just doesn't sound like wisdom to me."

"It's odd, isn't it?" said William. "Your habitual reactivity wants to hold me as an elite, evil killer, yet to my mind I'm actually holding more respect for your people than you are."

"And how is that, William?"

"By believing them, Madam. By respecting their choices. By trusting that they can figure out what they need."

"You think they're consciously choosing this?"

William shook his head. "Not at all, Madam. This is all playing out in the unconscious. How could it be otherwise? The cultural conditioning with regard to death is so strong and so conflicted that any such impulses must be swept under the psychic rug. Notions of societal suicide are virtually unthinkable for most people. So they don't think about it. But that doesn't mean that their actions don't reveal their unconscious wishes."

"But I don't feel like I'm wishing for death, William."

"Most people would say the same. And that is true as well. As I said, humans are filled with opposing forces. Just the same, the vast majority of humans on Earth are craving the death of something, would you not agree?"

Linda thought for a moment. "I think so," she answered. "I mean... I've met a lot of people, William. And yeah, most of them just seemed ready for it to end. Their own life situation. The whole system. The crazy culture. The government. They seemed afraid. Miserable. Stuck in bad jobs and worse relationships. Appalled at how bad things had gotten."

"If you examine the statistics, Madam - crime, divorce, substance abuse, interpersonal abuse, mental illness, physical illness, violence, consumption, you name it - you see the evidence for a culture in complete collapse. People have lost their meaning, their purpose, their tribe, their belonging, and their healing arts. They are grief-stricken at those losses. And they carry the weight of generations of unmetabolized grief and pain. It is, as Jacob Marley said to Ebenezer Scrooge, 'a ponderous chain.'"

"But I don't think people know this, William. Not even about themselves."

"People still have bits of joy, meaning, and intimacy in their lives, to be sure. One can find a comfortable corner even in a prison cell. But I think they know, deep in their hearts, that what they have is a scant shadow of what is possible for human beings. And they sense that the only way to end their misery is to hit bottom so hard that they are either thrust into some new life, or cast into the peacefulness of death. They long to hit the reset button, Madam. It is this which I term their 'wisdom.'"

"So, if humans are already enacting this unconscious death wish, why do we need to step in and kill them all?"

"You already know my answer, Madam. They have been enacting their death wish for a very long time now. That it has manifested as an act of killing off their very bodies, rather than just their culture and paradigm, is unfortunate, but perhaps unavoidable. What *is* avoidable is the 'collateral damage' associated with that suicide, which is the death of the vast majority of other living things."

Linda thought for a few moments. "So you said there are two ways to look at this," she said. "Related to this death wish."

William nodded. "Certainly. If you have a patient who is terminally ill, and that patient decides to end his or her own life, it becomes a matter of 'the right to die' or 'death with dignity.' Many states have seen fit to honor the wisdom of such patients, though many others still debate this. The aliens, of course, would regard this as a Prime Directive matter."

"Of course," said Linda with a brief smile.

"If, on the other hand, this same patient lapsed into a coma before expressing his or her wish to die, and this patient was experiencing a great deal of pain and suffering, then it becomes a matter of whether to allow or perform what some call a 'mercy killing,' or the more clinical 'euthanasia.' This might require that we make an assumption regarding whether the patient would *want* to die were they conscious and able to say so."

"So *does* the human race have some sort of an illness, William?"

"Some have seen it that way, Madam. A cultural illness, perhaps. Or a spiritual one. One Native American writer wrote of the 'Wetiko disease,' borrowing imagery and metaphor from the old Algonquin tales of the Wendigo, a gluttonous half-human-half-beast who fed on human flesh. Others have diagnosed modern humans in terms of psychosis, psychopathy, narcissism, sociopathy, and addiction."

"And some of the fundamentalists think we're all possessed by demons."

The Fisherman nodded. "Indeed. So people seem to have a deep knowing that they are 'infected' with something, which may explain their fascination with viral and zombie apocalypse stories."

"They know, William. That's how it always felt to me. Which was what I found so frustrating, trying to get them to act on what they know."

"They don't know at the top layers of their consciousness," said the Fisherman nodding. "But they know. They know they feel miserable much of the time. They know they are unhealthy. They know they are eating poison. They know that 'things' don't make them happy. They know they have a great deal of guilt and shame hiding in their hearts. They know that their leaders are liars and murderers and greedy, power-hungry psychopaths. They know that growth and destruction cannot continue indefinitely. They know that they have no idea how to heal their pain. They know that there is more to reality than the dead, random materialism they've been told to believe in. They know this because each and every one of them, apart from some few misfortunates, perhaps, was born into the world with the potential to become a sensitive, connected, and sane human animal. Had they been born into a different culture. Had they not been raised and schooled and acculturated and poisoned in the way they were. They know." William opened his mouth to continued, then stopped and sighed. He sank back in his chair and looked at the President. Linda nodded slightly. Together they sat with the truth of the human predicament.

At last Linda broke the silence. "So what are you arguing for here, William? Is it a mercy killing you're proposing?"

"I don't feel like I'm arguing for anything, Madam, so much as offering some alternatives for how you might think about the choice you have been given to make."

Linda shook her head, still unable to wrap her head around it. "Okay," she said. "Okay." She pulled her knees up and tucked her feet into the chair cushion. "So. Next?"

William flashed his eyebrows. "You remember the film *The Exorcist*," he prompted.

Linda nodded. "I saw it as a kid."

"At the end, the young priest, the hero, manages to free the possessed girl by taking the demon into himself. What does he do then? He jumps out the window and falls to his death."

"Self annihilation as a means to free oneself," said Linda. "Die and take the demon with you."

"Exactly right, Madam. Self-annihilation *and* self-sacrifice, which brings us to our fourth possible way of thinking about my proposal: that of protecting the beloved. Do you remember when we spoke of this before?"

Linda closed her eyes and thought for a few moments. "If I remember correctly," she said, opening her eyes, "you didn't think that 'saving the Earth's creatures' was a very good explanation for the death wish. Is that right?"

William nodded. "I did say that, yes. I don't think that this is a primary motivation for most people. The question is: can it be a primary motivation for *you*?"

Linda frowned. "You mean, if it meant saving the rest of the life on the planet, would I go ahead and flip the switch that took out humanity?"

"Or just a very large portion of humanity, Madam. Quickly and painlessly. It may or may not mean the end of human life on Earth."

Linda sighed deeply.

The Fisherman continued. "While your people cannot make a decision to die for the beloved life of Earth, mostly because they do not consciously know that it *is* beloved, can *you*, as their chosen representative, make that decision for them?"

Linda shook her head and closed her eyes. "Jesus," she whispered. A pair of tears slid slowly down her cheeks and she wiped them away. She looked at William. "I don't know if I can," she said.

William waited for a few moments, then continued. "This notion of 'sacrifice for the beloved' might be similar to how sometimes a fetus is aborted in order to save the life of the mother. The fetus, so far as we know, is not the one choosing to make the sacrifice. The choice is made by an outside party, who makes an assessment of the situation, weighing the needs of the various parties involved. In our case, the metaphor yields another way to access the question before us: do we 'abort' humanity in order to save the life of the 'mother,' the community of life?"

Linda looked at William and just shook her head, as if this was all too big for her to even think about.

"And yet we could turn it all around, Madam," said William. "These metaphors focus on the killing and the killer: on the murderer, on the genocidal maniac, on the doctors taking the patient off life-support, or administering the lethal drug, or making the decision to abort the fetus. We focus on these things because I have focused on the choice you must make and the actions you might take. Yet if the people of the dominant global culture are miserable and seek an end, could we not put it on *them*? Could we not view this as a case of 'suicide by cop,' where one cannot perform the wished-for release for oneself, and so creates the conditions by which one is killed by another?"

"Suicide by Linda Travis?" said Linda, her face twisted with a bleak smile. She inhaled deeply and closed her eyes.

"I find the notion worthy of consideration, Madam, regardless of how difficult it might be to take it seriously," said William. "We might also posit that the dominant global culture has been trying to commit suicide by climate change, or suicide by pandemic, or suicide by global agricultural meltdown, or suicide by nuclear poisoning, or suicide by global financial catastrophe. Surely in the realm of actions taken, if nothing else, it looks to me like an attempt to create an end, a death, without consciously acknowledging that one is doing so."

"So I'm the cop, shooting the crazed guy with the gun before he hurts other people. Isn't the whole 'suicide by cop' story just a justification, so the cop doesn't have to feel guilty?" Linda exhaled loudly. "I mean, how do we know it was suicide the guy was seeking?"

The Fisherman nodded. "Indeed," he said. "How *do* we know?" His smiled, his eyes alive with light.

"When you do that it's because you think I already know the answer," said Linda.

"Do you forget the speech you made to your people assembled in the great meeting room on Phobos?"

Linda shrugged. "Yeah," she said. "I remember."

"I'll leave it to you to know what you know, then, Madam. For now, I have one last way in which we might view the actions I am proposing."

"Okay," said Linda. "Shoot."

William flashed his eyebrows. "Well, Madam, it's simply this: if there is no death, then you will not be killing anyone!"

14.20

Ness slept, curled next to Grace in her hospital bed. Outside, the sky was brightening, though the sun would not be shining today. Vast, gray clouds scudded across the firmament as if fleeing the forthcoming storm, and the wind rapped on the window pans, demanding entry. Ness slept, dreaming of a forgotten life, of a house full of children, and a husband, and of friends she had known. Though she could not allow such dreams to filter into memory, Alice allowed them to unfold in sleep. Ness had lost so much. At least she should have her dreams.

The three children lay as they had since Saturday. This would be the third day. They were not sleeping. They were not dead. They were simply absent, and their bodies carried on, awaiting their return. In the meantime, they were as safe as they could be. Ness's construct held, even as she slept, and her purple shield, and surrounding that was an even larger bubble of consciousness, one woven by the created beings that had gathered, finally, in Augusta. There were more forces at play in this moment than just this storm. They must be allowed to play out, without interruption. Choices had to be made.

Alice, hiding in this shell of Ness, knew that she was one of these forces. She knew that she, too, would have a choice to make. She was fairly certain that that choice would come today.

14.21

Albert Singer stood in his office doorway, surveying the scene. It looked just as he wished it to look, as if he'd been raptured away while working at his desk, or beamed up by the aliens. Though he knew that it would never matter, the politician in him insisted that he take pains to preserve his image. He would not go down in history as a spy or turncoat, his reputation forever tarnished by betrayal and treason. Not if he had anything to say about it. And he did.

Singer turned and walked down the hallway, noting the first intimations of dawn. Outside the State House sat a twelve-footer, waiting for him. With a glance over his shoulder to assure himself that he was not being watched, he climbed into the tiny wok. Not wishing to draw attention to himself, he piloted the wok slowly upward, avoiding the bright white flash that accompanied faster speeds. With no feelings of regret or remorse, and a rising excitement regarding his future, Albert Singer headed toward the East.

14.22

"You remember the story *The Little Prince*, of course. It's one of your daughters' favorites."

Linda nodded.

"So you remember that when the Little Prince had learned all he could learn about love and roses on Earth, it came time for him to go home. The flock of geese that had brought him to Earth had long since flown away. But on his journeys he had met a poisonous snake who had offered to release him from his body, his Earthly shell, so that he might return to his asteroid. The pilot was appalled, of course, but the Little Prince was ready. He snuck away in the night and made his date with the snake. The pilot woke to find the Little Prince gone. Searching, all he found was a dead body. The Little Prince himself was back home. While the Pilot was sad to see him go, he knew that the Little Prince was not dead. He knew. He could hear the dear boy's laughter amongst the stars."

The Fisherman stopped and looked at Linda closely for a moment. "This is what the Fortunate knew that most of you have forgotten, Madam. It's probably why the Life *call them* the Fortunate. And while it made perfect sense that human beings - a small, localized population of self-reflective motes of consciousness - would create a consensus meta-reality in which most of you forgot this - how else to explore the depths of circumstance and limitation that you have explored? - it is time to bring the experiment to an end, and to re-member. It's time to know that death does not automatically represent the annihilation of consciousness, but can be regarded as little more than the tossing away of a costume or vehicle."

William sat forward in his chair. "These are not parlor tricks, Madam. You sit now in a non-material body separate from your physical body. Your consciousness has floated in the depths of space and passed through solid stone. And you witnessed the death and resurrection of your husband. It's time you just accept the reality of it. Were people to know and understand what it is that lies beyond death, there would be mass suicide. There would be no need for you to make this choice at all."

Linda sighed and held up a hand, palm out. "Can you just... let me think for a bit, please?" she said.

The Fisherman nodded.

Linda closed her eyes and breathed deeply for a very long time. As she thought, the Martian dawn came, lighting her face. She opened her eyes. "So then, why not just kill us all? Why not do it a long time ago? I mean..." she shook her head, trying to clear it, "... why are we alive at all? It's like... nothing matters then. It's like..." she sighed again and stopped.

"Now you're just being dense, Madam, not to put too fine a point on it." William smiled, hoping to soften the blow of his words. "Have I not said that this realm of limitations and circumstance is a precious thing? A laboratory for the evolution of consciousness? A font of diversity and novelty to be cherished and nurtured?"

"Yes, but..."

"So the human experiment has gone awry. To the point where it's killing off an entire planet's worth of lifeforms, many of whom are running their *own* experiments in self-awareness. Put an end to that experiment, Madam. Release the miserable human souls from Earth, to find new adventures and walk new paths, whether in the physical bands or elsewhere. Let those who have been chosen continue the physical human experiment elsewhere in the great Mind-at-Large, as they have already begun. Let those who survive Earth's depopulation, if there be some, and if they may, create a new and less-destructive human society on a future Earth we cannot now know. Demonstrate your willingness to self-control, and help the human species as a whole earn its place in the Cosmic Community. Let the struggle end, Madam. Let the Earth rest for a bit."

Linda shook her head. There were tears in her eyes. "But there are so many, many good, wonderful, beautiful people, William. They... how can we..." She stopped and wiped at her face. Her eyes were fierce. "What about all the people who aren't even members of what you call the 'dominant global culture'? Do they have to die because the rest of us went crazy?"

"We and the aliens have been in contact with most of the remnant tribal peoples for some time. They have been *'dying because you went crazy'* for centuries, Madam, and most understand and accept the need for the actions I am proposing. A few are sending representatives with us as we move out to the stars. One people, the Yazidis, chose to be relocated entirely, rather than be completely exterminated by Islamic militants. They're actually all now at Herschel Colony, awaiting their next journey. Most of these groups are choosing to meet their fate on the Earth. Your Inuit friends, for instance. They know death for what it is, and wish to continue their own versions of the human experiment on the land that they love."

"But in the meantime the bad guys get away scot-free? I mean, I know you Element guys are all spiritual adepts and all that, but there's lots of other Family members going too, right? The rich, powerful people? The ones who've done some of the worst, most crazy stuff of all? All us regular folk will be dying down here with your kinder, gentler Ebola virus and you guys will be sipping champagne in your mother ships as the Earth recedes in your rear-view mirrors."

"Would you believe me, Madam, were I to tell you that even *that* has been taken into account?"

"Is that what you're telling me?" asked Linda.

"Yes," said William.

"And I should trust you why?"

William pointed toward the sky. "All of the above, Madam," he said. "Do you think the Cosmic Community wishes to welcome such people to the consensus meta-meta-reality any more than you wish to see justice go unserved?"

"So how would this action *not* be a complete breaking of the Prime Directive, William? Why are you not just letting us continue to choose our way through this? I mean, isn't this interference in our internal affairs?"

"The question has been hotly debated amongst alien groups for millennia, Madam. Humans were born out of interference, and there have been plenty of mistakes made in the time since. I would argue that in these last hours, the rules must change to reflect the situation. The evolution of consciousness is still the highest goal. And I would add that I am not interfering here. I am asking you to."

"So if there's no death, William, then what does it matter if we take every other living creature down with us?"

William smiled patiently. "This too has been hotly debated. From the perspective of the Community, all consciousness is cherished, and planets as full of life as the Earth still is, even now, are thought to be precious indeed, and more rare than many would suppose. In general terms, the Community values life over non-life, and 'higher' levels of consciousness over 'lower' levels."

"Some animals are more equal than others, William?"

"Here's the thing, Madam. Something marvelous happens when a mote of consciousness becomes 'self-reflexive': it gains the ability to hold itself together even through the process of shifting from one band of reality to another. Or, as it is known on Earth: dying. So the vast majority of human consciousnesses, upon dying in the physical, will survive intact, and continue their journeys in one of the ways I've already mentioned. But the matter is much less certain for most of the non- or only partially-self-reflexive lifeforms on Earth. Much more of that consciousness will be lost. And the Community calculates that such a loss would be needless, given how easily a depopulation can be achieved, and how surely humanity is destined to be depopulated in any event."

Linda shook her head. "You've got an answer for everything, don't you William?"

The Fisherman sighed heavily and looked down at his hands. "I have *my* answer for everything, Madam." He looked up at Linda. "But we've reached the point where my answers are no longer important. What matters now is *your* answer. And you already know the question."

"But I don't have an answer, William," said Linda. "Despite your impassioned attempt to convince me, I don't feel any closer to an answer than when we began."

William smiled sadly. "I believe you are, Madam. All you need now is a little incentive."

Linda frowned. "I don't have enough incentive?" she asked. "Are you kidding me?"

"I'm afraid not, Madam," said William with a sigh. "So allow me to lay out the situation for you more clearly." He turned his head and looked off in the distance, in the direction of the 'lobster tank' and Linda's rescued body. Then he turned back to her. "You see, Madam, I regret that, in order to do the work here for which I was chosen, I've had to tell a number of untruths. The first is this: that method for reducing the human population quickly and painlessly? It was dispersed around the planet over the past two decades, and was triggered into activity eleven days ago. It has been breaking out across the globe ever since, and is now causing an exponentially-increasing number of human deaths."

"What?!" said Linda, pushing forward to the edge of her armchair.

"They call it the Quietus, Madam, though it is called by other names by the people of Earth. Some call it the alien flu, as we saw in that virtual video we watched early on. Others call it Greensleeves."

"You bastards!" said Linda.

"Second," continued William, wincing, "there exists a very effective cure for the Quietus. I have placed a small vial of this cure in a cabinet near your *real* body back on Squirrel Island. There is enough there for your scientists to quickly and easily replicate and produce."

"What are you talking about, William? What do you mean by my 'real body back on Squirrel Island'? You told me that *that* body was a copy, a fake." Her eyes were filled with fire.

"Another lie, Madam," he said. He gestured in the direction of the lobster tank. "That body in the glass container over there? Pure theatrics. It's not real, as you might have guessed when you inspected it more closely. The body you found lying on a gurney in the facility underneath your vacation retreat on Squirrel Island is your real body. The problem now is that *that* body is quite dead, and has been for about a day now. I was there and watched them kill you." He glanced cautiously at Linda, who had recoiled in her chair, her face frozen, her eyes wide and hot.

"I can't... believe you'd..." said Linda, seemingly unaware that she was speaking at all.

"And here's perhaps the hardest part, Madam. While your children's bodies are all still alive and well, their conscious selves, which have been roaming about the Astral since you and I began our conversation, are now quite lost in a rather devious Astral-level trap known as a 'Murk.'"

"You lying bastard!" screamed Linda, her voice harsh and sharp. She rose to her feet and took a step forward the Fisherman, as if she meant to attack him.

"Indeed," agreed William. He held her gaze, as if willing now to take the full brunt of her rage. There was a look of wet sadness in his eyes that verged on shame. After a moment he cleared his throat and spoke again in a gentle voice. "And yet I have acted as I must. Moving a mole here. Cutting a power cable there. Making a couple of mysterious phone calls. Letting out some line, then reeling it in. Speaking to the Directorate as was necessary. Somebody had to oversee this project. For better or worse, I was the Element's chosen." He looked around him, out and across Rumi's Field, a wistfulness in his eyes, as if he were seeing it for the last time. Then he looked up at the President. "I have just one last thing to say, Madam." He leaned forward in his chair, making sure he had Linda's attention, looking her eye to eye, almost as if he was pleading. *"Urbem Orsus,"* he said.

And then he was gone.

14.23

Carl looked up to the ceiling. Something had just happened. A flash of light, maybe. A rumble. An earthquake. He couldn't tell. Everything seemed as it had before, as it always had. He looked at Ted. "You feel that?" he asked.

Ted looked up from the game board and glanced around the room. He shrugged. "Something," he said. "Maybe the air conditioning going on?" He flashed a slight smile.

Carl shook his head. "No. Something else. Bigger than that. It hit me in the gut."

Ted looked around the room again, then at Carl. "A great disturbance in the force, maybe?" he said.

Carl shook his head. "I don't know, Ted." He looked at the ceiling again, then at Ted. "I think it was despair."

Chapter Fifteen

15.1

Gabrielle woke in the hairdresser's waiting room to find gray light seeping in through the blinds. The wind outside battered the trailer, howling and coughing and whistling, throwing raindrops at the windows and dropping them on the roof like handfuls of pebbles. Gabrielle pushed herself into a sitting position on the sofa and rubbed the remnants of sleep from her eyes. No dreams. No wild journeys with Zacharael. No zombies at the door. And no one had lit fire to her shelter. Apart from the growing storm, it had been a restful and uneventful night. Which was good. She still had a long walk ahead of her.

In the morning light, Gabrielle could see the trailer's interior for the first time. At both ends of the sofa on which she'd slept were small tables holding stacks of old magazines. At one end of the trailer were two old-style barber chairs and some cabinets, counters, and sinks. Past the sofa on the other side was a partition with an open door, through which she could see a tiny kitchen and more living space. Whomever had had their shop here had also lived here. Gabrielle stood and explored the living spaces, hoping to find something to drink. Her search was quickly rewarded when she opened a little cabinet over a toaster oven and found three large, sealed bottles of sparkling water. She smiled. It was the good stuff. Her favorite, in fact. Whether it was Zacharael who'd left these, or the woman who'd lived here, the water felt like a gift meant just for her. She opened a bottle, drank deeply, and sighed with pleasure.

Stuffing the bottles in her backpack, Gabrielle headed for the door. She wished she'd had a raincoat, as she did not cherish the prospect of getting soaked, but she'd found nothing of the sort in the closet. She'd have to scout one up soon, in one of the many abandoned houses she knew she'd encounter.

She pushed the door open against the wind and her eyes widened. Right in front of her, right at the bottom of the metal steps, was a huge black ball, taller than she was and hovering a few inches above the grass. It was black in the way that crows were black: slightly shiny, with a hint of blue. And it didn't hover really, so much as give off the impression that *it* was the motionless object here, bolted to the girders of time and space, and that it was the Earth that trembled underneath it. The wind couldn't touch it. Neither could the rain. It was right there, and yet it was somewhere else entirely.

Gabrielle stepped out onto the landing and headed down the steps, holding her jacket against the wind and squinting through the rain. She knew this had come from Zacharael. She'd seen a much smaller version of this black ball somewhere before and knew that, should she take the time to access them, she would find flashes of Zacharael's memories of this device in her mind. This was a vehicle of some sort. He'd brought it for her to use.

Reaching the grass, Gabrielle stepped up to the strange ship. She wanted to get out of the storm, but had no idea how the door worked. She reached out to put a hand on the sphere's surface and found herself transported immediately inside. The wind and rain no longer touched her.

From the outside the ball had been black. From the inside it was clear, as if she were inside a giant soap bubble. The strange thing was, she was changed as well. She appeared to be an orb made of pure, white light. And stranger still, her vision now worked in all directions. She was a shining ball of consciousness inside of a huge black ship, seeing spherically and doing so as if it were the most natural thing in the world. It was cool as shit.

Gabrielle closed her eyes, or shut off her visual senses, so as not to be distracted. Zacharael's memories were often fragmentary and disorienting and difficult to understand, but she knew that if she gave it some time, she'd get some useful information. She let the storm rage around her. She let the mysteries be mysterious. She let her excitement beat in her heart, and she let her body and mind be whatever they now seemed to want to be. She let it all go so she could go inside and search through Zacharael's memories.

There must be instructions somewhere for how to fly this darn thing.

15.2

Linda sat in her armchair and fumed. Her howl of rage and despair still rang in her ears, and across the planet called Mars. Her kids were lost in the Astral level? People were already dying from some virus? She herself was dead? And that bastard William just drops these bombs and disappears? Linda wanted to strangle him. But there was something final in his last words. She was pretty sure he wasn't coming back.

The biggest lie was one he hadn't even acknowledged: that he would keep her here until she was convinced of what he said. But he was gone, done, finished, and she was most definitely *not* convinced of anything, beyond the fact that she wanted to find this Fisherman on her own terms and prosecute his ass to the full of extent of *her* laws. How could she be convinced, when he had so cavalierly destroyed any trust she might have had in him at the very end, with his admission of lies? Who could tell the lies from the truths in such a situation? Maybe his admission of lies was itself a lie! It was crazy-making.

Oh, and he probably knew that. Did it on purpose. Loved it. Because he knew it would leave her tangled in uncertainty. Was he a sane person making a reasonable case? Or a madman weaving an elaborate delusion? And how could you know for sure? Triage and evolution and choice and circumstances, the beautiful people and the Little Prince and angels and demons, all woven together to convince her that she was some new creature that had been created to make the most important choice in human history. Yet she couldn't trust it. What was left to trust?

That was the kicker. Perhaps she *was* convinced. Convinced of what, exactly, she wasn't sure. But maybe she already knew what she was going to do. Maybe William already knew. Maybe *they* already knew: the aliens, the Element. Maybe it had already been worked out long ago. Maybe it had already happened. In this crazy new world in which time and space and reality could all be twisted around, maybe anything. In which case, what the hell did they need *her* for? To take on the guilt?

It wasn't fair. What they asked of her should not be asked of anyone. Ever. But there I go again, complaining about my circumstances, as William would say. The circumstances don't care whether I like them or not. Apparently, neither does William. Hadn't he said that he hoped she would love him when they were finished? Linda was not feeling the love.

It occurred to her then that she'd become so accustomed to being trapped in William's shackles that she hadn't even tested the constraints. She pushed herself to her feet and walked around the armchairs. She seemed to be tuned still to the near physical. But the real test was yet to come.

She closed her eyes and zeroed in on the lobster tank and blinked there in an instant. The tank, now an old, cracked, dirty fish tank, had been pushed over onto the Martian sand. The stand it had sat upon, cheap painted plywood, had broken apart at the poorly-stapled corners. And her body was nothing but an old department store mannequin, now splayed out on Rumi's Field like an assault victim, one leg twisted off and a cheap blonde wig lying nearby, partially covered with gravel and dust. Had it always been thus? Had he tricked her with some illusion or glamor? Or had he changed it all around since she'd last seen it, another bit of theatrics meant to teach her something? Was there anything physical here at all, or was it all in her mind? Could she know? Could she tell? Did it matter?

No. What mattered was that her kids were in danger. What mattered was that Cole was caught up in this too, somehow. What mattered was that people were dying of an engineered virus. And what mattered was that, if William could be believed, she was now dead to them all, with no living body to which she might return. Linda looked up to the Martian sky and let out another harsh scream of pain and fury, then bent forward in sobs. She was surprised to find that her habitual body image, or whatever it was called, could produce tears, but this one did, and they streamed down her face, as if mocking her with their physicality.

If William could be believed. That was the key. Linda Travis closed her eyes, keyed in on her naked body lying dead on a gurney beneath her retreat on Squirrel Island, and blinked away, to see whether William could be believed or not.

15.3

The knock on his door was soft but insistent and Cole startled at the sound of it. It was fully light out now, though it was the dark, ominous, bruise-colored light one got when the sun's rays were filtered through a heavy storm. How he'd managed to drift back to sleep Cole didn't know, what with the wind howling as it was, and the rain clawing at the glass. He threw back the covers, pulled on his shirt and jeans, and went to open the door.

"Big day, Stranger," said Annabelle, looking neat and put together, as if she were already two cups into her day.

Cole smiled. "Morning, Annabelle," he said. "Quite a storm."

Annabelle glanced toward the window at the end of the hall, then turned to look up at Cole. "Yes," she said. "We will be." She winked, then turned, gesturing with her head. "Get yourself downstairs soon," she said, starting toward the staircase. "Before those young'uns scarf up all the pancakes." She hurried down the steps.

Cole found his socks and jacket and glanced in the bathroom mirror to check his hair. It would have to do. He pulled on his socks, slipped on his shoes, and followed the older woman downstairs.

At Ken's big dining room table sat Stan and Annabelle, Keith and Eddie. Simon was pouring a new griddle's worth of pancakes and Steve Waymax, the reporter, was washing plates. "Morning, all," said Cole as he took the chair across from Annabelle. The others responded in kind.

"How's Gordon?" asked Cole.

"He's good," said Stan. "Doc's got him resting in bed today, which he's not all that happy about. I guess if a guy's complaining, he's feeling pretty good."

"Everybody else doing okay?" asked Cole.

"Doobie's sleeping one off," said Eddie. "Sten's on the phone with the network. Marionette went into town to check on the boat and get some supplies from Andrew. Seems we're mostly doing well."

"Ken?" asked Cole.

"At the hospital, Stranger," said Annabelle.

Cole knew what that meant. Celia was still battling the alien flu.

"The real question here," said Annabelle, "is how are *you*?" The wind's background roar rose to a howl as she spoke, almost drowning out her voice and adding urgency to the conversation.

Cole looked at Annabelle. There was a note of expectation in her eyes. Or challenge. Part of him wanted to talk about his confusing 'hop.' Or about how he didn't know what to do next. Or about how afraid he was. But that's not what Annabelle wanted or needed. It wasn't what any of them needed. And it wasn't what Cole needed, either. What they needed was courage, and courage wasn't about having no fear. Courage was doing what you needed to do even when you were scared shitless. That's what was in Annabelle's eyes. *Lead us, Stranger,* her eyes said. *Lead us, and let us help. Lead us even though you're terrified. Because we're terrified too.* Cole inhaled deeply and smiled. "I'm ready," he said. He didn't know what it meant, really, but he knew, when he said it, that it was true. Cole was tired of feeling afraid.

Annabelle nodded. Stan sat forward in his chair. "You got an idea for how to proceed, Stra... Cole?" he said.

Cole grinned and nodded. "The plan hasn't changed, Stan. We head out to Squirrel Island and get my wife and your President back."

Cole's words spurred a long discussion about all sorts of things: the weather forecast; whether it made sense to go out onto the water in this storm; whether *The Pokey Joker* was up to that task; whether some other boat would better suit them; whether there was some other way to get there; whether they should wait for the storm to blow out; who should go; how they should proceed once they got there. The discussion was punctuated with crashes of thunder and the slapping rain and the pounding wind. Nerves got frazzled. Tempers flared. Marionette returned just as things were getting heated to report that the boat was fine so far, then threw herself into the debate with gusto. Later, Doobie ambled in and sat listening with a cup of coffee. Stan held down the reasoned, cautious corner of the discussion. Annabelle was quietly insistent that they not lose the day in waiting. Cole asked questions to get as much understanding and information as he could.

In the end, Cole knew it was on him. This was his show. That was his wife over there. He was the Stranger, and this Church was here to serve him. When he'd gathered as much information and opinion as he could, he took a deep breath and spoke. "This is what we do," he said, finishing his last bite of pancake. "Doobie says the *Joker* can manage these waters. The storm may actually be on our side, giving us cover, getting in the way of their surveillance tech. And the last thing they're going to expect is that we'll do *anything* today. If it's true that the electricity is out on the Squirrel, then I say this is our one best chance. No telling exactly where Linda is or how she is or whether she'll be safe when the storm hits. The surge alone might swamp the whole island. I say we go get her."

Annabelle nodded her agreement. Stan shrugged his acceptance. Marionette grinned. Doobie scowled. It was then that Sten came into the room. "Sorry I've been so long on the phone," he said, looking around the table. He saw the President's husband. "Morning, Cole," he said. "Guess what? I don't know what you folks have planned, but I've got us a live video feed for the day. We can broadcast the whole thing!"

15.4

Mary was fourteen, running down the sidewalk as her father chased after her. Mary was thirty-two, sitting knee to knee with Mork in her underground cell, trying to understand the strange being's explanations. Mary was twenty-four, struggling to stay awake during a training exercise. Mary was six, watching as the pretty light came down from the sky and landed beside her sandbox. Mary was nineteen, driving with Danny through a sunlit autumn day to her father's funeral. Mary was.

In the background, it was as though a hard drive were spinning, clicking away, backing up, defragging, upgrading, erasing, rewriting. But the hard drive was not her. Not her mind. Not her past. Not her future. It was the world itself that was resetting. It was space and time and cause and effect that were being re-rendered. Not the whole of space and time, but the sections of it that had shifted in response to the amends she had made. Somewhere in there, Mary could imagine a progress bar, moving slowly from left to right. None of it was under her control. She'd just clicked on the Accept button. It was all automatic from there on out.

All Mary had to do was wait.

15.5

According to Sparks - McAfee couldn't help but think of him as Lieutenant Dan - the cables to the island had been severed. Not simply cut through, but completely separated, with a six-foot length taken out, cut clean as if by a laser. And the break was underwater, halfway between the island and the mainland. Divers had no idea how it could have happened.

McAfee shook his head, sitting at his office desk. He had an idea. He'd seen a wok cut through solid stone like it was fog, leaving nothing but empty space behind, no dust, no rubble. You could cut through a cable the same way, and hadn't there been more than one of those alien contraptions on the island recently, coming and going? Why either DuPont or that William fellow would cut the power he couldn't begin to fathom, but this would not be the first time somebody from The Families had acted in ways that were incomprehensible to him. Perhaps they wished to wipe out all evidence of what they'd done to poor POTUS, with the Colonel and his soldiers and techs just more collateral damage. McAfee sighed. They'd have to deal. He and his peeps. What were they gonna do? Complain? Send a bill?

So far, it appeared that his troops had things under control. They had a minimal but well-armed security detail on the fence line. They had rigged up makeshift food and water systems. And they'd secured the lower levels. The hurricane's center was due to hit them dead on in the afternoon. The ocean surge itself could cover the entire island for a time. McAfee intended that they would all have a safe, underground facility in which to ride out the storm. There was the problem of the President's body, of course. He'd really rather not hole up with the old girl still lying in the next room, stinking up the place. But he'd figured out a solution to that one. People got swept out to sea in storms like this all the time, after all. All she'd need was a little help getting up to ground level.

Really, it all looked pretty good. The only thing that bothered him was that he couldn't find his cat. He hoped the little bastard hadn't been blown away. Perhaps he'd snuck back into the basement. How he'd managed that with the freight elevator down McAfee didn't know, but that cat was a resourceful one. When the Colonel had the time, he'd have to go look.

15.6

That was definitely light below him. Iain could even hold his hand in front of his face and see the silhouette. Real light. And a real hand. It was amazing how good it felt to see his fingers move, even if he could not feel them.

But the light didn't really cheer him up. Not when he studied it more closely. If he had to describe it, he'd say that he was looking at a huge bucket or bowl filled with hot, red, burning embers. The coals were moving around, sliding and tumbling over each other like worms or bugs or something. And all around the bucket was more blackness. All of which would have been bad enough, but it was quite clear now to Iain that he was falling rapidly toward this giant bucket full of burning coals. There seemed to be no way to stop his fall.

There might have been sound. Not a roar, so much as a growl. And it may be that he was actually feeling some heat. He was still so disconnected from his body that he couldn't quite trust his senses. He fell. He fell some more. And it occurred to him, as he got ever closer, that what he was falling into was a mouth. Iain's heart started pounding and he called out once again. "Emily!" he called. "Grace! Dennis! Mihos!"

He fell. A few moments later, he heard something else, a faint voice finding its way through the background growl. He couldn't be sure, but it sounded like Dennis, calling Iain's name.

15.7

Staring down on her naked form, Linda had to accept that, at least in this respect, William had not lied to her: her body was clearly dead. The skin was blue and gray and lifeless, and there was not a bit of movement, not a hint of breath, no subtle sign of pulsing blood. The space was lit with emergency lights now, which was unexpected, and the monitors that showed her vitals were black and blank. An eccentric British voice played in her head as she regarded her body, a snippet of old television about a parrot that was very much dead, just as she was. Unlike the old show, this current moment had no laugh track.

She would have thought the sight of her own dead body would cause her to double over in sobs, but nothing of the sort happened. This was far too surreal for tears. And too much of her heart was devoted to anger right now. Even the thought of Cole sitting with the kids and telling them the news left her with nothing but cold rage. Grief would have to wait. For now, there was too much to do.

But what could she do? How would she spend her rage? She moved over to the cabinet and saw the little brown vial William had mentioned, but she had no hands with which to grab it, and no voice with which to tell somebody about it. She was helpless here.

Sighing, she turned back to her body. No signs of any alien flu, as William had said. Just scam after scam and lie after lie and betrayal after betrayal. And at the end of it, a dead Linda Marie Travis, her body cold and stiff on a stainless steel gurney.

A cat jumped up from the darkness under the gurney and landed on the body's stomach, startling Linda. She stepped back with a tiny yelp as the cat sat down on the body's navel and looked up at her.

"Hello, little kitty," said Linda. "Do you see me?"

The cat stretched his head forward, exposing his neck, as if hoping Linda might pet him.

"Maybe you do," said Linda. She reached out to pet the cat, but her hand passed through it, as she had expected it would.

The cat seemed to shudder at the experience, then stood and turned, placing his front paws on the body's sternum. He glanced back over his shoulder for a moment, looking Linda eye to eye, then returned to his work. He stepped forward, put his nose to the body's nostril and sniffed, then stepped back to massage Linda's chest with his front paws, like he was stretching his claws on a cushion. If Linda hadn't known better, she'd have sworn the cat was trying to administer CPR. Too late for that, kitty cat!

Then it occurred to her: once again she was feeling trapped by circumstances without even testing the constraints. This cat hadn't given up on her, but she had. Didn't she live in a world where magical things could and did happen? Hadn't Cole himself been brought back from a death far worse than this? And hadn't William placed the most important choice of their time directly into her hands? Surely he would not have gone to all that trouble had there not been some way for her to take action? Surely there must be more going on here than she could see.

As if he could hear her thoughts, the cat stopped his massage and sat again on the body's stomach. He looked up at Linda and nodded once. He nodded! As if to say, yes, Madam! Exactly and indeed and quite so and brilliant! Linda inhaled deeply and smiled. Without thinking about it, she reached out again to pet the cat. This time, if only in a faint and shadowy way, her fingers touched fur.

She could act. She had to. Maybe she could get back into her body. Maybe the aliens would help her. Maybe they'd rebuild her as they had Cole. Maybe she'd simply find a way to communicate from this side, a ghost in the works. She didn't know. But the cat had nodded. She was on the right track. She did not have to stay sitting in that damned chair!

First she needed information. She'd explore the cabin. See who was here and who was in charge and what they'd done. Then she'd go find Cole. See if she could find some way to talk to him. She'd just touched fur, after all. She wasn't helpless. She'd find a way. She'd tell Cole and he could get that damned vial.

She didn't know what he'd do with it. She didn't know what she wanted him to do with it. Use it? Hide it? Throw it away? Or get it to somebody so they could make more? That decision could wait. That choice. For now, all she knew was that she wanted it. She wanted that vial in her hands. Or somebody's hands. Until then, there *was* no choice.

"Thanks, little cat," said Linda to the cat. The cat nodded again, then bowed his head forward. Not to be petted, Linda knew. It wasn't that. This cat knew her. Somehow he knew her. And he knew who she was, and the choice before her. This was a bow of respect. Alignment. Encouragement, perhaps. A bow from one realm to another.

The cat looked up at Linda one last time, then leapt softly to the floor and scooted out the door. Linda stopped for a moment to view her body, then thought of where to go next. It was time for her to scoot as well.

15.8

Keeley hovered in sleep, with great waves of joy and acceptance washing over her soul. The Greensleeves virus was neither dying out nor taking her to death, as if it were waiting for events to unfold elsewhere before proceeding. Every few hours a nurse would stop in to check on her, but otherwise she was left alone. It was just her and the television, and the television was still doing all of the talking.

There were reports from the shelters. Reports from the melting Antarctic. Reports from current battlegrounds. There were updates about Greensleeves, the alien flu now responsible for over sixteen thousand deaths, with more falling ill every day. There were reports on Hurricane Alpha, a Category Five storm coming way too early in the season, and now bearing down on coastal Maine, far further north than such a storm should ever be. There were reports on yet another new crop circle, yet another iteration of that strange "circle with an inverted L through the middle" that had now appeared in six different places around the planet, and toward which thousands of people were now being drawn, inexplicably leaving their homes and traveling to, though none of them could explain why. There was a report from the global environmental summit, and on how Linda Travis's participation was being hampered by the storm.

And there was a report from hurricane-blasted Boothbay Harbor, Maine, where ACN's most famous anchorman, and America's current White House Communications Director, Stendahl Banks, was speaking live to members of a small group of intrepid sailors who were going to accompany the U.S. President's husband on a fishing boat out to Squirrel Island, where Linda Travis was being kept in medical isolation. They were going to brave the rough seas of the harbor in order to confront the doctors and military personnel there and insist that Cole Thomas be allowed to speak directly to his wife, and to bring her away to safety from the storm.

Though Keeley was obviously unconscious, one might fairly wonder whether the slight smile on her face was not a commentary on this last report.

15.9

Doobie was going because it was his boat. Stan was going because he was the Director of the goddamned Department of Homeland Security, and because he had a gun and knew how to use it. Marionette was going because she was bright and resourceful and fierce and had been there the last time and knew a little of what to expect. Cole was going because his wife was there and because *he* was the story. Eddie was going to shoot the story. Sten was going to report the story. There would be six of them on *The Pokey Joker*. Six would be enough. It would have to be. As Sten said, "I'm a public figure. So is Cole. What are they going to do, shoot us on live television?"

Cole zipped up his raincoat and tightened the hood, then took Marionette's offered hand and stepped across to the boat, with Eddie shooting the whole thing. The wind beat against Cole's face as he grabbed the railing and made his way into the cabin. The others were already assembled and the boat was fueled and ready to go. Cole gave Doobie, and Eddie's camera, the thumbs up. Their captain gunned the engines. The weather was only going to get worse.

The time to do this was now.

The live feed and the network audience had done wonders for their confidence. The world was watching now. Watching as the President's husband, and his brave crew, ventured out in defiance of the elements to be reunited with his sick and possibly dying wife. Watching as this ragtag bunch stood up to the medical and military establishments and demanded to be included. The live coverage undermined what Cole had thought of as an advantage, that those on the island might not know that they were coming, or where they were in this storm. But Sten had convinced them that, on balance, the live coverage trumped the possibility of surprise. And who knew? Perhaps, with the power out on Squirrel Island, they would not be able to see the news there in any event?

It was good, Cole knew, for his crew to have this new confidence. It might actually prove to be warranted. But he also knew that such things could unravel in an instant. Cameras and microphones and live feeds could fail, especially in conditions such as these. And whomever it was who was really running the show out there likely had other tricks up their sleeve, power outage or not. That was a wok he'd seen last night, after all. They, whoever *they* were, were involved.

Ah well. Cole leaned back against the thrumming metal wall and closed his eyes and breathed deeply. He could not control everything, and there was some relief in just accepting that. And he had another source of comfort and confidence as a backup. He had light in him. Light in his hands. Light that could somehow help them. He didn't know how it would come into play, but he expected that it would. He flexed his fingers and felt the strength in them. It was as he'd said at breakfast. He was ready.

15.10

They were all there now. They'd all checked in. Emily. Grace. Dennis. Mihos. Iain was greatly relieved that they were all okay. He'd been so worried. It seemed that they must be close to each other, as they each reported seeing the same thing, the vast bucket of burning coals into which they all seemed to be falling. But so far none of them could see each other. At least they could talk.

"Feel heat," said Dennis.

"Me too," said Iain. It seemed that the coals beneath them really were burning.

"Does anybody else smell smoke?" asked Emily.

None of the others seemed to smell anything.

"What is it?" asked Grace.

"I think it's like... a mouth, or something," said Iain. "Like it's alive."

"Feels alive to me," said Mihos. "Isn't that just nippy?"

"You ever encounter anything like this before, Mihos?" asked Iain.

The cat took a moment to think. "I've seen some strange critters in this realm, but not one of these," he answered evenly.

"Plan," said Dennis.

"What, Dennis?" said Grace. "You want to plan?"

"Have plan," said Dennis.

"Imagine ourselves all drifting together?" asked Mihos, picking up on the dog's idea.

"Yes," said Dennis. "Then help."

"Right," said Iain. "Good idea. If we're together we can help each other."

The cat, the dog, and the three young humans all imagined themselves drifting closer together.

15.11

Linda Travis made for a terrible ghost. She couldn't get through to Cole, no matter how loudly she shouted, no matter how hard she tried to send him a telepathic message, no matter the effort she put into her attempts to knock things over or write messages on the fogged windows, like she'd seen in movies. Cole just went about his business, meeting with Stan Walsh and Stendahl Banks and people whom Linda had never before seen, talking, eating pancakes, dressing in warm clothes and rain gear and getting onto a boat. Maybe if it had been quiet she'd have been able to be heard. Maybe her voice might sound in Cole's ear, one of those ghostly whispers that sends chills up the spine. Maybe. But there was a huge storm raging now, beating the Maine coast with slabs of hard wind and buckets of rain. That's how it looked, at least. It wasn't like she could feel it.

She'd imagined that her rage would carry her. She'd thought her passion would serve her. She'd hoped her good intentions would open the way. Wasn't that how it worked for ghosts? But so far, she felt as ineffective and lost and powerless as that dead body she'd left beneath her cabin. Being freed from the body and stepping into the so-called "higher layers" might make for a powerful, mystical experience in those other realms, but it didn't seem to mean squat here in the physical. And it was here, in the physical, this realm of things she knew and people she loved, people and things that she could see and hear but not touch, that everything seemed to matter. Linda Travis was not ready to go toward that damned light people talked so much about. And she couldn't believe that that was what William had just spent so much energy preparing her to do. She did not intend to stay dead. She had too much to do to be dead.

She still wasn't sure what she would do if she could do something. Gather her husband and children together in safety, of course. That part was a no-brainer. But there was that damned vial in the cabinet, a vial that purportedly held the cure to the disease that was now set to take out some huge portion of the human population. What would she do with that? She wondered if she should just refuse the choice that had been put on her. She knew that William would argue that no choice was a choice as well, but she wasn't sure she bought that one. But, gods, how could she do such a thing, or allow it to be done? Would it be better to just let this virus do its work? Or would it be far worse? And wasn't she going to feel guilty and despairing either way? Was William right? Or was he really, really wrong? And how the hell would she be able to know?

She needed somebody to talk to about this. She needed Cole. And her advisors and confidants. Smart people who could help her. Who could share this. Linda sighed. In the end, it would probably come down to her heart. Her gut. Something. What a burden to put on one woman's internal organs. And right now, she didn't really have any, did she? Her heart and gut were slowly rotting, leaving her with mind alone. And her mind, it felt like, was exhausted and confused and stuck in a loop she could never escape. Damn them all, for putting this on her.

She stood on the small dock in what she knew to be Boothbay Harbor, a place she'd visited more than once back when she'd been a lowly governor, a small, hilly, seaside resort town of shops and restaurants that was now falling slowly into ruin. She watched as the boat that carried her husband pushed out into the bay, bobbing like a duck on the rough waves and smashing headfirst into the wind and rain. She understood what he was doing now. He was going out to try to save her, bless his heart. All he had to go on was what he'd been told, and the videos he'd seen of the computer-generated, disease-ridden Linda Travis shown on TV. He had no idea where she'd really been and what she'd been doing. And he had no idea what he would find, should he ever make it down to that underground room, to that cold, stainless steel table, and that pitiful husk of a body, that shell that no longer contained her.

He would encounter soldiers on the island. And that Mr. Phelps, now wearing a uniform, whom she remembered from her first fateful meeting with Agent Rice. And who knew what or whom else he'd find? William said that Cole was sorting things out. Something about his own connection with the aliens. She didn't know what that meant, but it gave her a shard of hope. She looked up at the sky, seeing a thick ceiling of swirling dark clouds, knowing that above it was the Grid. The aliens. Spud. She wondered if maybe, in her present condition, she might have more access to them now than she'd ever had in her body. Maybe she'd find out.

It occurred to her then that she could ask for help. Not from Spud, exactly. She wasn't sure she even wanted *his* help, that bastard. But from that Big Whatever that was out there. The Community, as William called it. The gods. The fairies. She wasn't convinced that they could help her, but thought that they probably wouldn't if she never asked. So she asked. *Help Cole. Help my kids. Help me. Help me find a way to do whatever it is I'm supposed to do. Help me to choose. Help us all, we humans here on Earth, we who've made such a mess of things. Help us.*

The boat was almost lost in the wind and rain and distance now. Linda knew she could follow it. Knew she could follow Cole as he did whatever it was he needed to do. But it occurred to her that he might be best left to his own work now. And she was fairly certain that it would be nothing but anguish for her, to be able to see him, but to have no power to help. In a moment the boat was lost to sight. Linda prayed for Cole's safe return.

But now what? She'd already tried to find the "devious trap" in which William had said the kids were trapped. That "Murk." She hadn't seen a thing. She'd also tried to locate William's vibration, his pattern, and go to him in this level, perhaps to find some way to communicate with him. Again, there was nothing to find or follow. She did not know how to reach him.

She considered heading off into the great unknown. With her ability to blink restored, she was free now to explore the Astral plane. Perhaps there was help there. Maybe some of the beings Grace had encountered in her adventures. But she did not think she could bring herself to leave the Earth. The thought of doing so just made her want to cry. That would be like going toward the light, she feared. That would be leaving this world behind. And Cole. And the kids. That would mean accepting, and acting, like she was as dead as that body under her cabin insisted that she was.

And she was not ready for that.

15.12

The tiny wok rose up from the ground, passed through the garage roof as if it were mostly just empty space, and ascended into the sky above the Presidential Home in Augusta, Maine. Around the city, soldiers and nurses and business people and government employees stopped what they were doing and looked to the sky. The wok glowed pearly white against the dark gray clouds, seemingly untouched by the wind and rain.

As though adding an exclamation point to a newly edited paragraph, the wok flared, a single strobe of brilliance, a beacon, a flashbulb. Those who saw it knew its meaning: it was a flash of intention. And they knew who was inside that wok.

Mary was back.

The intention was hers.

15.13

By the time the kids and animals all found each other, the gaping maw of burning coals had grown vast and hot underfoot, and was rushing up hungrily to meet them. After an infinity of blackness, they found themselves back in their astral bodies, reconnected to their senses, finally able to feel and see and hear. But they did not like what they could see and hear.

They fell through the Murk as though it were open sky now, as if they'd all been pushed from an airplane, five small bodies diving without parachutes into a volcano of writhing flames, holding hands to form a ring. There was no magic carpet to save them. There was no blinking away. There was no changing of form. They might as well be in the physical now, in real bodies, with a real volcano beneath them, for all the power they seemed to have.

Mihos glanced frantically around, then called out to the others. "Look at the edge!" he shouted over the Murk's hungry growling. "Is that a ledge?"

The others peered downward. It did seem that the edge of this field of burning coals was some sort of ridge or ledge, with fire on one side and black Murk on the other. It had some width to it. "It might be something we could land on!" said Iain. He leaned his head and angled his arms in a way that seemed to change their direction as they fell. The others followed suit as best they could. Slowly, very slowly, the five of them, a ring of skydivers, steered toward the ledge.

They'd decided that it was not really fire beneath them. The writhing coals and flames and heat were just how it looked. What it was, really, was some fundamental force of life. It wasn't fear. The Murk did not feel afraid. It wasn't hatred or anger or revenge. It was just simple need. Hunger. The will to survive. As if the Murk was just another living organism. One that first rendered its prey insensate, then slowly transported them to its hot, roiling stomach, where it might break them down and consume them. Like one of those Venus flytraps, say. An organism. Feeding. There was nothing at all personal about it. It was just doing what it did.

But none of the five wanted it to do what it was doing to them. Whether personal or not, getting consumed by the Murk felt pretty darned final. So they leaned and angled and shifted together, holding themselves just right so that their movement through this strange sky would take them over to that edge. So close now. So close. And just in time, as the hungry coals - giant, writhing, crawling, living embers the size of pillows - were now yearning, stretching, lunging up to grab at them and pluck them out of the air.

It was Mihos who was able to reach out and seize the ledge. The surface, maybe six feet across, was smooth and slick, but his cat magic allowed him to get a hold and land on his feet. The ledge rose up a few feet from the sea of hot coals, giving Mihos just enough time to reach down and grab the others before they fell into the fire. He swung them up and around and they landed at his feet in a hard tumble of bodies and heads and limbs. Dennis would have slid off the far side into the blackness, his claws clicking and skittering, had Mihos not reached out and grabbed the dog's tail. Grace hit her head on what felt like solid rock and cried out. Emily grabbed her little sister and pulled her close tight. Iain landed on his knees and slid to a stop right next to them.

For a moment they were all stunned. Then Iain started to laugh, and he leaned over and hugged his sisters to his chest. Mihos went over to help Dennis to his feet. Dennis thanked the cat with a tongue to the cat's nose. The five of them sighed and shouted and laughed and hugged. Mihos was given high praise for having grabbed the ledge like he did. Relief washed over them all like cool water.

Dennis walked carefully to the outer rim and peered over the edge. "Look," he said, glancing back toward the others. They did. It wasn't all blackness, as they'd assumed. Far below was a circle of light. Daylight. "Smell ocean," said Dennis, sniffing the air.

They backed away from the edge. "So is that the way out of here?" asked Iain.

"Yes," said Dennis. "Like tunnel. We jump. Slide. Go through hole."

None of them were all that keen on once again jumping into such blackness, but that tiny bit of daylight felt like home. And none of them had any better ideas. They certainly couldn't stay here. The heat was almost too much to bear. They stood in a circle and discussed their options, but the answer was obvious. Once again, they would trust Dennis's sense of smell.

It was then that one of the burning coals reached up over the lip of the ledge, grabbed Iain's ankle, and began to pull. Dennis leapt into action, grabbing the fabric of Iain's blue jeans and pulling in the opposite direction. But the giant ember was too strong, or too heavy, and Dennis could get no traction on the smooth stone surface. Iain, tall and lanky and caught off guard, began to tumble. The burning coal pulled and Iain followed and Dennis hung on and, in a moment that seemed to last forever, all three of them fell into the sea of fire.

Grace screamed.

15.14

McAfee stood in the surveillance tower they'd built just north of the Presidential retreat, scanning the waters of the bay. The storm was howling now, and it sounded for a moment like a young girl screaming in pain. The Colonel smiled. Whoever it was that designed this storm had spared no expense. They were getting really good.

Lt. Danny Sparks pointed out toward the water. "There," he said.

McAfee looked where his second was pointing. Yes. That had to be them. "Amazing," he murmured. "Who'd'a thunk it? Those crazy bastards."

"It's incredible that they're still above water," said the Lieutenant. "Look at those waves."

They watched for a moment as boat pushed its way through the huge breakers.

"Do we let them dock?" asked Sparks.

McAfee shook his head. They'd learned that Cole and his crew were coming from a news broadcast one of the soldiers had picked up on his phone. "Not when they've got Sten Banks and a cameraman on their crew, Lieutenant," said McAfee. "I can see the headline now: 'US soldiers fire on, kill President's husband.' You want that sort of coverage?"

"So what do we do?" asked Sparks.

"We got anything that'll sink that boat without being noticed?" asked McAfee. "I mean, wouldn't sinking be the most obvious thing for that boat to do just about now?"

Lieutenant Sparks smiled. He gestured with his head to the tower further up the slope. "How's about an old 242 Bushmaster with DU armor-piercing rounds, Colonel? Punch a hole in the hull. In this storm nobody will notice, and we can clean up the wreckage before anyone else gets a look at it."

McAfee nodded. "Range?"

"Three thousand meters, Colonel. Our gun's got the SmartTech upgrade. It can't miss."

McAfee turned to his second. "You seem rather eager to take out the President's husband, Lieutenant."

Sparks nodded. "You and I both know who we really work for, Colonel." He looked McAfee in the eye. "And we both know that it no longer really matters."

The Colonel nodded. "Good point," he said. He turned and peered out into the storm. The boat was still coming. Brave bunch of folks, he had to admit. Or stupid. And there was something kind of sweet about Cole Thomas coming to rescue his wife. But he wasn't going to like what he found when he got here, was he? Maybe they'd be doing him a kindness. He turned to his Lieutenant. "Do it," he said. Then he turned back to watch the boat some more.

15.15

Linda was back in the facility, standing next to her dead body, examining it. This was like before, when she and William had hovered in space next to Phobos, when William had said "I'll tell you inside" and then disappeared, leaving her on her own to figure out how to join him. He'd told her where to find her dead body. He'd told her about the vial. He'd told her the virus was already working its way through the global population. Now she had to figure it out on her own. Which meant that she had to find a way to bring her dead body back to life. Nothing else had worked.

But how to achieve such a thing? She'd tried thinking herself into it. Willing herself. Pushing herself. She'd tried just lying on top of it and sinking into it. She'd tried to go inside, like she was a little spark of consciousness exploring a huge cavern. Nothing. There was no pattern she could key in on, like she had with William. No vibration. No whatever it was that allowed her to blink from one place to another. Because living in a body wasn't like being someplace. It wasn't like sitting on a sofa in her chest cavity, or lying in her head and looking out through the eyes, like she had with that wok. Living in a body was *being* the body. Filling it. Melding with it in some way she'd never really ever thought about before. The body had to *want* her. And this body was beyond wanting anything.

Urbem Orsus, William had said, there at the very end. Maybe that was some clue. A magic spell? An instruction? She'd tried saying it, but it hadn't done a thing. Just another bit of mystery to add to the confusion. Linda had even risen up through the storm to the Grid, intending to pound on the gates of Spud's little kingdom and demand his help, but she found herself unable to get near. She must have passed through it on the way here from Mars, but now it would not let her approach, let alone pass through. And no amount of shouting had provoked Spud to show his face. Or Alice.

So she stood, looking down at her body, trying to see what she must have missed, and failing to see it.

15.16

Cole's heart pounded. That last wave had risen up and bashed them like a giant fist, washing over the entire deck and taking over the railing anything that hadn't been firmly secured. Cole worried for a second that they were going to flip over. Then the sound of the engines changed.

The twin diesels were struggling now, and black smoke was pouring into the cabin from below. Doobie bent to check the engine compartment, then slammed the hatch and zipped up his raincoat. "Take this!" he shouted to Marionette over the din of the storm, gesturing toward the wheel. He stumbled through the door and out onto the deck.

Cole watched as Doobie made his way along the starboard rail, leaning over to inspect the hull. Another wave rose and broke and crashed and it was all their pilot could do to maintain his hold against the force of rushing water. Ahead, through the fogged windshield and the storm, Cole could just make out the rough outline of Squirrel Island. The engines beneath them sputtered and coughed. Eddie got it all on his video camera.

Doobie made it to the bow, leaning over the railing as far as he dared as he slowly moved forward. Then he turned and shouted something back to them. They could not hear what he said. Another wave rose and crashed and Doobie slid back toward the stern, gripping the rail but allowing the force of the wave to push him along. At one point he fell to his knees. It looked like he'd lost his grip. Then he grabbed a handhold on the cabin and hauled himself back to his feet. As another wave rose to hit them, he pushed through the door and into the relative safety and quiet of the cabin.

"We've got a problem," he said, stumbling forward to grab the wheel. The engines sputtered and died just as he took control. He turned to Stan. "Big hole in the hull. Multiple bullets, like a shotgun blast. About a foot across."

Stan glanced up toward the island. "Bastards!" he spat. He looked at Doobie. "Did you feel the hits?"

Doobie shook his head. "Not in this storm," he said. "You?"

Stan hadn't felt a thing. None of them had.

"So what do we do now?" asked Cole.

Doobie raised an eyebrow as he looked at Cole. "We sink," he said.

15.17

Another ember had crawled up onto the ledge. And another. More were following. So Emily and Grace and Mihos did the only thing they could think to do: they jumped into the darkness beyond the ledge's outer rim, hoping to fall through that hole of daylight and out of the Murk, as Dennis had said they would. Grace sobbed as she stood at the edge, screaming her grief and rage at the loss of her brother and her dog. Emily, wiping away her tears, reached out and grabbed her little sister's hand and pulled the cat to her chest. "One! Two! Three!" she shouted above the din. They jumped. The three of them fell into blackness. The ledge, and the embers, were soon lost from view.

They fell through the Murk. Sure enough, the circle of daylight below them slowly increased in size and brightness. As they got closer, they could make out a twisting of thick gray clouds, scudding quickly past the hole. A storm.

The circle of daylight soon engulfed them, and once again they found themselves in the strange astral skies over the physical world. Everything was as it had been before, when they'd first left their bodies: they could move about at will, hover, fly, change form, and blink from one place to another. Only it was not like that at all, because Iain and Dennis were no longer with them.

The three of them sank slowly down through the thick clouds. Below they could see the ocean, and directly underneath, an island. They could see how fiercely the wind and rain were battering the real world, and were glad to be a step up from the physical. But they knew where they were, and were afraid of what they might find.

"That's Squirrel Island," said Emily.

"It would make sense that the Murk would be centered in the place where your mother was being kept," murmured Mihos.

"Was?" said Emily, looking at the cat with one eyebrow raised.

Mihos could only shrug. He didn't know what to say.

They floated down to the island, to an open lawn just north of Linda's cabin. On one edge of the lawn stood three tall steel towers. They could see soldiers through the windows in the top level. In the center of the lawn, standing alone as if newly planted there, standing bravely against the harsh winds, was a large plant almost three-feet tall, almost a cactus, with thick, dark, spiky leaves and a single large cone - orange and red and black at the rim - nestled in the center of the plant and pointing downward. They knew, because they could feel the truth of it, that this plant was the Murk, or how the Murk looked in the physical plane. It had been put here. To guard this place. To guard Linda. To guard against anybody ever knowing whatever it was they were doing here.

Emily knelt beside the plant, grabbed the stem near the ground, thinking to pull it out by the roots. Grace reached out to stop her. "We don't know where Iain and Dennis are," she said sadly. "We don't know what that would do to them." Emily nodded, let go of the plant, and stood. She reached out and took her little sister's hand. Both of their faces were still wet with tears.

Mihos cleared his throat. "We should go," he said gently. The three of them turned and started toward the cabin. The girls had only been here once, but they remembered it well. This was the place that Grace had really, really wanted to go. This was where they'd brought Linda. This was where they would find some answers. They moved quickly to the deck and stepped through the back door. They searched the house. There was no one inside.

Emily suggested that they go to the steel towers where the soldiers were, thinking they might find some clue to Linda's whereabouts there. She led them back out onto the deck and started for the towers. "Wait," said Mihos. The girls turned. The cat stood on the deck railing, pointing along the back wall. There was a soldier, walking up a flight of concrete steps that had to lead to a basement the cottage had never had.

"Ah... " said Grace, realizing in an instant what that meant. She stepped back into the cabin. Emily and Mihos followed. Together in the kitchen, the three of them looked at each other, then sank down through the floor.

15.18

All thought of cameras and live feeds and reaching Squirrel Island had been abandoned. There was nothing to do now but grab their flotation vests and jump into the water. *The Pokey Joker* listed at a thirty-degree angle, stern up, and was slipping further into the sea with each crashing wave. Sten and Eddie were already in the water. Cole and Stan were climbing carefully over the railing. Doobie and Marionette were still in the cabin.

"C'mon you guys!" called Cole. He didn't want to jump until he knew they were all away from the boat. He thought maybe Doobie was pulling some sort of "captain going down with the ship" bullshit. But finally the cabin door slammed open and Doobie and Marionette stumbled out, each carrying extra life preservers.

Cole held tight as another wave crashed over them, then watched as the two young people climbed over the rail and jumped into the sea. With a thumbs-up to Stan, who was hanging on beside him, Cole fell backward into the water, pushing away from the boat with his feet. Stan followed. All six of them were now floating in the churning waters of Booth Bay, rising and falling with the waves. The wind and the current conspired to carry them quickly away from the boat. They watched, cold and wet and helpless, as *The Pokey Joker* gave up her fight and slid beneath the surface of the sea.

15.19

The girls found their stepmother standing near her own body in the lowest level. Grace threw herself at Linda at first sight, managing only to speak Iain's and Dennis's names before breaking down in heavy sobs. Emily joined them and the three hugged as was only possible in the Astral realm, their forms and outlines blurring together as love and life passed between them. Through the exchange of words and touches and brief packets of experience, they soon caught up with each other, and the three of them grieved their mutual losses.

Mihos, for his part, stood off to the side and watched respectfully. Nicky, who had been wandering the halls, had returned to the room with Linda's body soon after they'd arrived. He sat beside Mihos in the doorway, watching the children and their mother. Every now and then the two cats would glance at each other across the realms, but neither said a word.

At last Linda pulled away from the girls, holding them at arm's length. "We're going to look for them," she said, meaning Iain and Dennis. "Okay? We'll do everything we can." Emily nodded, trying to match Linda's determination. Grace gulped another sob.

Emily pointed at the dead body. "But what...?" she said. She shook her head in confusion. There was no red rash on her stepmother's face. "We knew it. You weren't sick." She looked up to confirm that Linda's mole was exactly where she remembered it. "It was all a lie. But now you're... " She couldn't bring herself to say it.

Linda hugged the girls close. "Sshhh," she said softly. "There's too much right now. Things none of us know or understand. Things we have to share. And so much to figure out." She wiped the astral tears from her own habitual self-image and kissed the tops of their heads.

"For now, just know that I don't plan on staying dead any more than I plan on losing your brother. I just need to figure out how to get back into my body."

Grace pulled away to look at Linda. "I did that once," she said. "Remember? Alice helped me."

Linda nodded. "We don't seem to have their help this time, sweetie," she said, smiling gently. "I've tried calling for them. For the Life. For Spud. For Alice. But I think we're on our own this time."

From the doorway, Mihos cleared his throat. "Um... excuse me," he said. He gestured toward Nicky with his head. "Cats here. Duh. Masters of the Nine Lives and all of that." He stepped forward and peered up at Linda. "Good morning, Mrs. President Monkey," he said cheerily. "I think we can help you."

15.20

Even as hot as it had been for the past month, the waters of Booth Bay still felt icy cold. Already, Cole could feel his fingers going numb. And the storm seemed to be pushing them farther from the island, back toward Boothbay Harbor, and apart from each other. Whoever it was on the island had shot a hole in their boat, intending to sink them. Intending to kill them all before they even had a chance to set foot on the island, and in a way that avoided any news coverage. The last thing Sten and Eddie had done before they'd jumped into the water was upload a short report to their network, explaining how the military had fired on the boat carrying the President's husband, how they were sinking, how they were going to have to abandon *The Pokey Joker*. They had no idea if the uplink was still working. That it had worked at all in this storm seemed like a miracle. They'd done what they could.

But that wouldn't be enough, even if it got through. Rescue would take too long. And rescue would not get them to Squirrel Island. Where Linda was being held captive. With the full force of the storm yet to hit them.

Enough. Cole had had enough. It was time for him to do what he could do. He kicked with his legs, leaned back into the life vest, and raised his hands up above the water's surface. Instantly they spouted small fountains of pure white light. Working quickly, instinctively, forcefully, Cole pushed the light up and out and away, waving his hands slowly as he kicked himself back, forming the light into sheets and billows, pure white sails of white light that reached into the sky and spread out across the waves.

Glancing around him, he found the others from his crew. Stan was close by, watching him. Doobie was floundering in the trough of a wave. Marionette seemed nowhere in sight until a wave pushed her upward, silhouetting her against the sky for a brief moment. Sten and Eddie were farthest away but together. Collecting them all in his mind, Cole increased the size and span and strength of his light to include them, then brought it all together, above them, beneath them. He painted a tunnel of pure white light on the canvas of the storm, with himself and his crew inside of it, then raised it up until it sat on the sea's surface, a cylinder of light undulating on the waves.

Up out of the water now, he stood on the tunnel floor and pushed, strengthening it, stabilizing it, forcing it to calmness even as the wind and water raged around it. He pushed the tunnel forward, stretching it further and further across the water, toward the distant shore of Squirrel Island. He formed it and pushed it and stretched it and held it as the others found their footing and stood with him, watching in awe as Cole mastered the light that issued forth from his hands. Doobie's eyes were wide with wonder. Stan nodded his respect. Sten and Eddie hurried to catch up. Marionette, her patch now missing and revealing a reddened concavity where her eye should have been, bowed in appreciation. Cole held the tunnel of light, then looked at each of his companions in turn and smiled. "Let's go," he said, with a nod. The six of them started walking to Squirrel Island.

15.21

Mihos had explained it as a matter of resonance. Things had to converge at the vibratory level in order to align and fuse together. So while Nicky lay on Linda's body's chest in the physical realm, Mihos lay on Linda's astral body's chest in the Astral realm. Linda hovered, stretched out over her dead body, then slowly lowered herself down until she and her body occupied the same space in different realms. She shifted and wiggled until, point for point, her astral body matched her physical body. Mihos' also moved until his body matched Nicky's body. The girls stood on either side, offering their love and support and prayers and intentions. Then the cats began to purr.

None of them could tell how long the purring lasted. The vibrations, shared body to body and realm to realm, seemed to take on a life of their own, enveloping them all in a pearly mist of healing sound. The purred pulses aligned, resonated, strengthened, became one. The two Lindas blurred together, one clothed and richly colored, the other naked and gray. The two cats blurred together as well. After a time their eyes became a single set.

The purring and blurring continued. After a while, Mihos called out in a strained voice. "Help us, girlfriends!" he said. Grace reached out and put her hand on the two cats' backs. Emily reached out and put her hand on Grace's hand. They closed their eyes and began to hum, doing their best to match the pulse of the purring. The power of the vibrations increased with their help. Eventually their hands blurred together.

Then the purring softened and slowed and died out. With a sigh, Mihos raised his head and looked around. Nicky stirred and raised his head as well, shaking it from side to side as if scaring off a bug. He sat up, then leapt quietly to the floor. The clothed, habitual image of Linda had disappeared. All that remained was her naked body on the gurney. And that body was now trembling.

"Is she...?" asked Emily, looking at the cats.

Mihos nodded. "I think it worked," he said.

It occurred to Emily then that they'd made no plans for what to do if it *did* work. If Linda *was* now back in her body, they would no longer be able to communicate with her. Apparently this was the first thought on Linda's mind too. She opened her eyes and inhaled sharply, almost a gasp, then raised a hand to shield her eyes. "Emily?" she said. "Grace? I'm okay, girls. We did it. So go home now, okay? Go home and find your bodies and come back into this world. Your father and I will be home very soon. Go home." She pushed herself up onto her elbows, her face still slack and gray. She glanced around the room like a blind person might, as if trying to locate the girls. "I love you," she said. "Go home. I'll be there soon."

Emily and Grace looked at each other, then at Mihos. "Do we go?" asked Emily.

"Would you defy a Presidential command?" asked Mihos, raising an eyebrow.

15.22

McAfee scanned the bay through his binoculars. The boat was gone, as had been their expectation, but what the hell was *that*? It looked like a giant white worm, crawling toward them on the surface of the sea. Whatever it was, the storm didn't even touch it. It was rock steady in a way that seemed impossible.

"It's about to make contact with the north shore, near the Ferry Landing, Colonel," said Sparks.

McAfee sighed. "I suppose we should go see what the hell we're dealing with, Lieutenant Dan," he said.

15.23

Linda pushed herself into a sitting position, her legs dangling over the edge of the stainless steel table. Her head was pounding. She felt like she might vomit. And she was so cold. So cold. She scanned the room but saw nothing she might put on. Not so much as a lab coat on a hook. She rubbed at her eyes, which were dry and still quite blurry, then pushed herself slowly forward until her feet touched the hard tile floor.

The cabinet was right where it should be and she stepped to it and opened the glass doors. Inside, where she'd seen it before, was the little brown vial that William had told her held the cure for the alien flu. She grabbed for it, but her fingers, so cold, so stiff, knocked it over. The vial rolled off the shelf and fell to the floor. With a yelp Linda looked down. The vial was intact. She bent over and picked it up, making sure to grasp it tightly. Then she tried to stand. A wave of nausea and dizziness swept over her. She started to fall, but caught herself on the edge of the gurney and stood, bent over, until it passed. Slowly, she managed to right herself. The vial was in her left hand. Still intact. Good.

How Linda might escape was not at all clear. She knew she was pretty much alone down here, having been left for dead. She knew a huge hurricane was raging above at ground level. And Cole and his crew might have made it to the island by now. So Phelps and his crew might have a great deal on their plate at the moment. Which meant that she had a chance.

The first step was obvious. It made sense to get out of the lowest level of this facility as quickly as she could. They were sure to come back for her at some point. And the storm surge might fill this whole facility with seawater. Perhaps if she just got to the surface, the next step would present itself. Glancing around the room one last time, Linda clutched the vial to her breast and stepped out into the viewing room, and then the hallway beyond.

"Hello, Mrs. President," came a voice to her right. Linda whirled toward the sound. There stood a teenage girl with short red-blonde hair and a backpack. Behind her hovered a large black sphere that blocked the entire corridor.

15.24

Cole walked steadily along the tunnel of light, his companions in front of him. He needed to be able to see them, in order to hold them all together. And he couldn't talk much. But otherwise, the effort of maintaining and extending the tunnel had not surpassed him. He allowed the tunnel behind them, the part through which they had already walked, to fall away into nothingness as they passed. All that mattered was the tunnel ahead, and his friends, and the island shore he could now clearly see. Another fifty yards or so and he'd be on solid ground, though truth be told his tunnel felt more solid now than the ground appeared to be.

He knew they'd encounter soldiers on the island. And a fence. And some strange force field. But the storm had taken out their electricity, so the force field might be down, and the soldiers, thinking they had sunk his boat, might be huddling inside now, afraid of the storm.

Cole breathed steadily. He was not afraid. He knew who he was now. He knew where he'd come from. And he was learning just exactly what it was he could do. Soldiers? Tanks? Guns? Fences? Cole looked at his tunnel of light and smiled. He didn't think he'd have a problem with any of it.

15.25

"Who are you?" asked Linda. It was all she could think to say.

"Gabrielle Legrand," said Gabrielle with a smile. "I visited you in your Oval Office a few years ago. You returned Alley's scarf. You remember?"

"I heard what happened to your sister," said Linda. "I'm so sorry."

Gabrielle shrugged. The image of this moment had not included conversation, so she was uncertain of what to say.

Linda inspected Gabrielle from head to toe. "You've grown up," she said, warily. This was Guy Legrand's daughter. Which made her a member of The Families. MP Legrand had turned Linda over to Agent Rice, who'd then shot and killed Cole right before her eyes. He was not a nice man. "You have interesting friends, I see," said Linda, indicating the black sphere behind Gabrielle with a wave of her hand.

Gabrielle glanced at the sphere, then back at Linda. "It has been an interesting time, Cousin Linda," she said, stressing the distant family connection. "I've learned a great deal in the past few days."

Linda nodded. "Can I ask what you're doing here?"

Gabrielle's eyes went to the vial in Linda's hand, then back to Linda. "I believe you're supposed to give that to me," she said.

Linda clutched the vial tighter. She'd never felt so exposed, here in this hallway, alone, naked, her head and stomach still churning and pounding. She took a long breath, hoping to calm herself. "Supposed by whom?" she asked. She wrinkled her brow. "Do you know?"

An expression of uncertainty flitted across Gabrielle's face. "Do I need to?" she asked. "I mean... I was given this to do." She jutted out her chin. "A vision," she said.

"This is a cure," said Linda, finding a bit of her old power. "Did you know that?"

"A cure for what?" asked Gabrielle.

"A cure for the virus that your father and his people unleashed into the world," said Linda. "A virus meant to kill off most of the human race."

Gabrielle whirled around to look at the huge black sphere. All this time and she never really knew what it was she was supposed to do. She'd seen the moment, but she hadn't understood it. The President's mention of her father threw her off, and the idea that he was responsible for this virus! She thought of Arthur, back in Montreal, and of him dying with some disease her father had been involved with. Those monsters. But Zacharael! He'd shown her! She had to help. She had to help the living planet! How was she-

She thrust out her hand, grabbing for the vial. "Give it to me!" she said harshly.

Linda stepped back, twisting away before Gabrielle could grab the vial from her cold, stiff hands. "No," she said. "No. You didn't come here to stop me. You came here to help me."

"But how can I know?" cried Gabrielle. "How do we know what will help?"

"Ask him," said Linda. She gestured over Gabrielle's shoulders with her head. Gabrielle whirled. The huge black sphere was gone. In its place stood Zacharael. Linda took another step back, struck by how much this being looked like Agent Rice, yet sure that this was not him.

"Tell me what to do!" said Gabrielle to Zacharael. The Angel smiled sadly, looked up toward the sky as if in prayer, and then disappeared. Gabrielle gasped.

"We need to get out of here, Gabrielle," said Linda. "Will you help me?"

Gabrielle turned slowly back to Linda, shaking her head from side to side.

"I don't know what to do either," said Linda. "I don't know what will help. But I do know that we have to get out of here. That storm might flood these underground layers at any moment. And the soldiers will be back."

Gabrielle nodded, still stunned by Zacharael's refusal to help her. "Okay," she said at last. She pulled her backpack off her shoulder, unzipped it, and pulled out a large t-shirt and some underwear. "Here," she said, handing the clothes to Linda.

Linda smiled her thanks and took the clothes.

15.26

McAfee and Sparks took a Hummer down to the Ferry Landing. The wind lifted them up at one point, almost flipped them over, but then they righted themselves and continued on. When they got through the fence, they found other soldiers at their posts, struggling against gusts that threatened to carry them away, and watching as the white worm of light crawled slowly up the island.

The worm seemed impervious to both wind and rain, and cut across the land, through trees, across roads and lawns and right through the fence as if these obstacles were not even there. Inside, McAfee could see vague human shapes, gliding steadily and quickly southward, up the ridge of the island and toward the President's cottage. Already the tip of the tunnel had almost reached their watchtowers.

"You fired on it yet?" asked McAfee of the nearest shoulder. He had to get close and shout to be heard over the storm.

The soldier nodded. "No effect!" he shouted back.

McAfee turned and signaled Sparks. They got back into the Humvee. "This worm must have a mouth," said the Colonel. "Let's drive up to the end and see if there's an opening."

Sparks put the Humvee into gear and they headed back the way they'd come.

15.27

"Grab that cat!" said Linda to Gabrielle as they ran down the hallway. Gabrielle looked up to see a black cat with a white star on its chest sitting in the shadows near the stairwell door. She bent to pick it up, cradled it next to her stomach, and then pushed through the double doors. Linda followed. At the bottom of the stairs, Linda stopped and grabbed the railing, bending over to vomit onto the floor at her feet. Under the dim emergency lights, the vomit looked like an oil slick. "I can't..." said Linda, breathing heavily.

"We can," said Gabrielle, taking Linda's arm. She guided the sick President around the mess on the floor and up the stairs, moving slowly but steadily. The cat started squirming so she let it go and it ran up the steps ahead of them. This gave Gabrielle two hands with which to help the President. They made it to the landing, then the next floor, and then another floor, and another, resting often but never for long. The vial of cure was now safely stowed in Gabrielle's backpack.

At the top of the stairs they found the cat, sitting by the door, waiting for them. Gabrielle pushed the door open against the wind. The cat ran outside. The women followed the cat.

15.28

Walking felt far too slow. Cole raised his hands and pushed. At once he and his companions were lifted from the ground on ripples of light. Cole waved his hands again and sent them all gliding forward, faster and faster, across the island terrain, through the trees and over the rock outcroppings. Linda was here. He could feel her. And she needed his help.

Nothing was going to stop him.

15.29

Linda could barely move in the wind. Without Gabrielle's help, she'd have already been blown out to sea. How the cat stayed on its feet Linda had no idea, but he seemed to manage. Cats had always been good on their feet, it seemed. And maybe the wind didn't blow so hard that close to the ground. The cat led them around the cottage and to a little trail that wound through the shrubs and roses. Gabrielle used her backpack to push away the thorns. The women slowly picked their way along the path.

15.30

Cole and the others were gathered at the mouth of the tunnel of light now. They'd come to a stop at the edge of the lawn. Before them stood two steel watchtowers. Part of him wanted to take the time to bring these towers down. Cole was that angry. But he knew that such actions would have to wait. The first order of business was to find Linda and get her to safety. The storm was surging now. No telling how high these waters would get.

"Cole?" asked Stan, turning to face him. "You okay?"

Cole smiled warmly. "I'm good, Stan," he said. He turned to look at the cottage in time to see a young woman disappear into the bushes by the cottage's back wall. There seemed to be somebody else in front of her. He looked at his companions and gave a nod. "Let's go," he said.

15.31

"You see where they're headed?" said McAfee.

Sparks nodded.

"Swing up through to the landing pad and come down the back drive. We'll sneak up from the other side."

"Okay, Colonel," said Sparks. He hit the accelerator.

15.32

The cat went first, then Linda, with Gabrielle following right behind. The path had taken them over paving stones and then grass and had then plunged into a stand of trees. The leafless branches were flapping in the gale but the trunks felt stable and the wind near the ground was not so bad. They crossed a slight gully and the path got steeper and more rocky. Linda was hardly able to keep going so they rested for a minute. Then Gabrielle took the President's arm and they climbed the slope side by side.

At the top they found a wide, flat plateau, paved with concrete. Some sort of landing pad for helicopters, thought Linda. The cat sat in the center, looking up to the ceiling of clouds. His fur was flattened in the hurricane-force winds, but the cat himself, solid and steady, did not seem perturbed, as if no amount of wind could tear him from the Earth. Linda stumbled forward, falling to her hands and bare knees when a blast of wind caught her. Her t-shirt flapped and pulled. Gabrielle got down on her knees as well and crawled to the President's side. "Why are we following this cat?" shouted the girl into Linda's ear.

Linda turned her head to catch Gabrielle's eyes and smiled grimly. "I have no idea!" she said.

Then the Humvee squealed to a stop at the edge of the pad.

15.33

"You've gotta be shittin' me," said McAfee from the passenger seat as they neared the landing pad. In front of them was his stupid cat, some girl he'd never seen before, and a woman who was supposed to have been dead. Sparks hit the brakes and brought them to a quick stop. He stared through the windshield with one eyebrow raised, but didn't say a word.

McAfee pushed his door open against the wind. A gust caught it and slammed it back, smashing it against his foot. "Goddammit!" he screamed, pushing the door open again. He slid down to the ground, grimacing as he landed on the newly crushed foot, and quickly stepped to the side before the wind could slam his door again. He looked at Linda. "What the hell is going on here?" he shouted. He knew that his question was small and silly in light of the situation in front of him, but he did not have extra RAM with which to compose a more thoughtful demand. He'd stood there and watched the doctor kill this woman. He'd seen her lying there, cold and blue and gray. He'd smelled her rotting flesh. So how the hell could she be up and walking around in this storm? And who the hell was this kid she was with?

He took a step forward, winced at the pain, and took another step. None of it made any sense. Linda Travis alive again? Some new person on the island? His cat sitting unruffled in the same goddamn wind that had just slammed the door on his foot? In the face of such impossible things, Colonel Aidan McAfee did what his training had taught him to do: he unsnapped the leather holster on his belt and drew his revolver.

The President of the United States, now dressed in a black thong and a wet Miley Cyrus t-shirt, rose up on her knees and looked at him. She opened her mouth, shouted something to him, but the wind snatched her words away before they could reach his ears. McAfee took another step forward. The cat was in the middle of the landing pad, glancing now and then at the storm clouds overhead. The women were near the edge. He decided to get his cat first, then deal with the women. The cat made a bit more sense to him, and he really needed something that made sense right now. Holding the revolver aimed vaguely at the President, he limped out to the pad's center and knelt down to pick up his cat. Nicky, for once not resisting, allowed himself to be picked up.

McAfee turned toward the women. His jaw dropped. Coming up the hill behind them was that damned white worm thing, with the First Gentleman himself standing in the mouth of it like something out of a *Dune* novel.

15.34

Cole had known even before he got to the cottage that Linda wasn't inside. That had been her, running through the bushes. He could feel her presence, though how that was possible he did not know. So he followed them. He guided the tunnel of light across the paving stones, across the lawn, into the trees and through them, following the little path as it crossed a small gully and turned sharply upward. He stood at the tunnel's mouth now, eager, full of anticipation and power and confidence. His crew stood around him as the tunnel moved them along.

He stopped at the top. There was Linda, as he'd known she would be. She was dressed in a soaking wet white t-shirt that clung to her back. She was on her knees. And beside her was a young woman with a backpack. Beyond them stood a soldier with a cat in one hand and a revolver in the other. Off to the left was a Humvee, beside which stood another soldier, this one younger. The soldier with the cat was aiming his gun at Linda. The young soldier looked on in confusion. Linda had her back to Cole, and was shouting at the older soldier.

Cole let the tunnel of light fall away around him. He no longer needed it. He stepped forward, catching the eye of the soldier with the gun. "You stop right there!" the soldier shouted. He pointed the gun back and forth, from Cole to Linda and back again. Cole stopped. He did not feel afraid of this man or his gun. He had caught bullets with his bare hands. This man could not harm him.

But he could harm Linda, if he caught Cole off guard. Cole was too far away to catch a bullet aimed at his wife. And if he tried to shoot the man with a bolt of light, the soldier might get a shot off before the light hit him. Cole might be able to stop a bullet with the light from his hands, but he did not want to put that to the test.

The cat in the soldier's arm looked up once again, then clawed its way out of the soldier's hands and leapt to the ground, running toward the women. So quickly it seemed almost instantaneous, a wok dropped out of the sky and landed in the center of the pad. Whether the soldier with the gun was disintegrated or just crushed flat, Cole could not tell.

The young soldier fumbled for his own revolver as he stepped forward. Cole did not hesitate. He lashed out with his left hand, sending a shard of pure white light to knock the gun from the soldier's hand. The soldier stopped, stunned, and examined his hand for damage.

A door melted in the side of the wok.

Out stepped Mary.

15.35

Something had happened, but Mary could not say what it was. She'd crawled into that wok in the garage and had finally made it into the Astral. She'd sensed the kids' patterns, only to then have them disappear from her awareness. Another wok had appeared before her from out of nowhere. Then things got weird.

It felt like she'd fallen asleep. She'd dreamt of the time long ago when Spud had appeared during one of her father's beatings. The time she'd broken out of their paralyzing fog and demanded that she and her brother be allowed to go with them. It was the defining event of her life. It had saved them both. The dream seemed to go on forever, as if it had scrolled through her entire life. Then she'd awakened to find herself back in the physical band. She was back in the wok she'd found in the garage, and hovering over Augusta.

She considered venturing back into the Astral, but decided against it. It had been so difficult, before, and she'd been unable to find anyone. So she found the helmet and put it on and formed a psychic bond with the ship and asked it to take her to Squirrel Island. Keeley was there. Linda was there. The kids might be there. Mary needed to be there as well. She asked the wok to approach the island cautiously, since she did not really know what to expect, or whom she would encounter. The wok complied.

When she descended through the storm clouds enough to see Cole and Stan and Sten and some others being held at gunpoint, her course of action became clear. However it was that Mr. Phelps had ended up on Squirrel Island in a uniform with a gun pointed at her friends, he now had to go. Mary asked the ship to make him go away.

The wok complied again.

15.36

"Mary?" said Lieutenant Danny Sparks. He glanced down at his pistol on the ground, then at Cole and the others at the edge of the pad. He stepped closer to the wok, holding his hat against the wind and rain.

"Danny!" said Mary, smiling. Shielding her face against the gusts and rain with a raised arm, she ran down the ramp and hugged her little brother in his soaked uniform. "I haven't seen you since before the Grid!" she shouted into his ear.

Danny was overwhelmed by questions for which he had no answer and prospects that were quickly changing. Linda Travis was somehow still alive. He'd just seen his CO squashed like a bug by an alien spacecraft. He'd had his weapon magically knocked away by the First Gentleman, who'd arrived with people Danny did not know, in some weird light worm thing. The thing to do right now, he decided, was to just go with it and get your answers later. He pulled away from his sister long enough to look up at the wok, then put his mouth close to Mary's ear. "I've been busy!" he said above the howling wind.

Mary pulled back, her eyes blinking in the rain, to search for information in Danny's field. "I'm looking for Keeley Benedict!" she shouted. "I was told she's here!" Her face grew worried at what she saw in his aura, a jumble of questions and a wall of secrets, but no knowledge regarding her partner.

Danny shook his head. He knew who the Chief of Staff was, and he also knew that the only people left on the island, apart from that group standing on the edge of the landing pad, were a company of soldiers, the three medical people, and some of the VLT techs. "She's not here!" he shouted into her ear. "Unless you've got more surprises for me!" He gestured toward the others standing around the impossibly alive Linda Travis. Mary, whose face had grown dark and troubled at the news that Keeley was not there, followed his gesture. Here eyes grew wide. There, standing amongst Cole and his friends, was her President. Mary shouted with delight.

Cole and Linda might have watched Mary and Danny's reunion with glad hearts, had they not been involved in their own. Linda whirled her head when Cole's shard of light passed by. Cole was already running to her, and he knelt by her side and pulled her into his arms and held her against the wind and rain. Linda sobbed and sobbed. It was only with Cole's strength that she was able to hold herself together at all. Without him, the storm, and the loss of Iain, her long confinement on Mars, and her own death, would have unraveled her completely.

It was too hard to talk. The gale was too fierce and the rain was beating them into the ground. Cole helped Linda to her feet and took her by the shoulders to look at her face. There was that beautiful mole. And there was no sign of a rash on her face. He grinned goofily, then gripped her elbow and escorted her out to the wok. He remembered another rainy night very similar to this, with Pooch buckled dead inside an overturned van and a helicopter waiting for them in the middle of the road, and muttered a curse for those hidden bastards who had forced them to such moments of extremity. With a quick glance back out over the island, he helped is wife into the strange craft.

The rest of his crew followed: Doobie, Marionette, Sten, Eddie. Stan introduced himself to Gabrielle and helped her to walk without falling. Mary dragged Danny along and they followed the others up the ramp. Even the cat joined them, jumping through the door of the big round metal thing. Mary stopped at the edge of the door and looked out over the island one last time. Her face was covered with tears, though nobody would have noticed them in the rain. Keeley was not here. With a cavernous sigh, she turned and entered the wok. The door melted closed.

The wok was much too tiny to hold them all, but of course it did. When the door was sealed, the wok began to glow: red, orange, yellow, white. It rose slowly into the sky above the landing pad, tilted slightly, then flashed bright white and sped away, so quickly that the eye could not follow.

The storm intensified.

15.37

Ted studied the game board for the longest time, his brow deeply furrowed in consternation. Every now and then he'd glance at Carl, but then he'd return his gaze to the board. The board felt like a useful metaphor with which he might review his last life: his journey from space to space, from start to finish, with help and hindrances along the way, with setbacks and lucky breaks, with monsters to trap him and friends to send him on his way, all of it governed not only by the roll of the dice, but by the choices he'd made. At last he looked up at Carl and spoke, his eyes shying away a bit as he did so. "I really was a monster, wasn't I?" he said to Carl. It wasn't a question.

"You did some pretty awful things, Ted," said Carl, nodding, holding the other's gaze.

Ted smiled grimly. "Don't hold back, Bro," he said.

"It wouldn't help you if I held back, would it?"

"I guess it wouldn't," said Ted.

"I made my own share of mistakes," said Carl. "But by and large I think I had an easier game to play than you did. My parents were more whole than yours. They gave me a good start. And I didn't have Spud messing with me as a kid."

Ted sighed. "Yeah," he said. He stared at the board for a while longer, then looked at Carl again. "It's strange," he said softly. "I mean... all in all, I'm glad I had Spud in my life. You know? It was certainly a wild ride. Fascinating as hell. Exciting. Fun."

"But it was too much for you to handle on your own, Ted," said Carl.

Ted sat back as if struck, then inhaled sharply and forced his shoulders to relax. "Yeah," he said. "It was. We were pretty crazy back in the early days. Scared. Afraid we'd lose control. Afraid other countries would beat us to the punch. Afraid of what would happen to us if we let the Life fully into our reality. Afraid that they weren't really what they said they were. And all the time I knew that there were things going on that I hadn't been let in on. Deeper levels. Secret discussions. Fateful decisions." He stopped for a moment to rub his eyes, the continued. "The Families. And it just felt wrong. Because I'd been brought in as a kid. I'd been there from the beginning. And yet I didn't have the goddamned 'need to know.'"

"Yep," said Carl. "Same with me. It was like I was never going to get to the bottom of things from the inside. That's why I left. Went underground. Started working with the Life on my own terms. Still don't think I ever got very far."

"So what did they want from me, Carl? Do you know?" said Ted.

"What did who want from you?"

"The Life," said Ted. "The Angels. The others that I only ever heard about."

Carl smiled and nodded. "All of the Above, I call them," he said.

"Right. Them."

Carl closed his eyes to think for a moment, then looked at his old colleague. "I think they wanted you to grow up, Ted," he said. "To get more fully conscious. To find healing for your triggers and reactions and old wounds. To open up to a new view of reality. To show that you could be a conscious, thoughtful, creative, life-affirming, adult human being who was bigger than his training, his assumptions, his reactions, his wounds, his stories, his beliefs, or his expectations. Somebody they could welcome whole-heartedly into the greater community of sentient beings in the Cosmos." Carl smiled gently, to soften the judgment of his words.

Ted scoffed, shaking his head. He exhaled heavily, then matched Carl's soft, accepting smile. "I guess beating the shit out of Linda Travis probably sealed the deal for me," he said.

Carl nodded. "That probably cost you a few points, my friend," he said.

Chapter Ø Sixteen

16.1

There was Cole's relief, to be reunited with Linda.

There was Linda's pounding head and churning stomach.

There was Mary's fear for Keeley, her love, whom she could not find.

There was Stan's fury at the hidden powers who were pulling the strings.

There was Cole's grief and guilt and fear for Iain, now lost in the Murk.

There was Linda's determination to find their son.

There was Mary's guilt for having been unable to prevent Iain's loss.

There was Marionette's awe, at what she had seen Cole achieve.

There was Linda's fear for her girl's safe return to their bodies.

There was Cole's confusion about the creatures called "the Life."

There was Danny's puzzled surprise, to have found himself rescued from the storm at the last minute.

There was Stendahl's satisfaction at having foiled The Families' plans.

And there was Gabrielle's self-doubt and confusion, to now find herself living *beyond* the moment she had envisioned so clearly, with no idea how it was she was supposed to help or whom she should align with, and to find herself surrounded by people and forces and questions and situations about which she knew so little. The wok

RUMI'S FIELD | 469

was bursting with need and feeling and urgency and potential, yet the ship itself held its own calm quiet. It flew easily through the storm, taking its passengers smoothly and quickly back to Augusta.

But the wok did not comply with Mary's request to return them directly to MaineCentral Hospital. It came to a soft landing in the middle of Interstate 95 just south of the city, not far from the military cordon. The door melted open and the passengers slowly stepped out onto the pavement, puzzled to learn where they were. The skies were dark and the winds, though calmer than on the coast, continued to pester them. The ground was wet but it was not raining at the moment. It looked as though the rain would come again soon. The wall of dark clouds rumbled with hidden lightning. Nicky, the cat, remained on the ramp, unwilling to get his feet wet.

Stan peeled off his raincoat and helped Linda to put it on. Once the coat was around her shoulders, Linda pulled off her soaked t-shirt. Marionette, seemingly unconcerned about her exposed missing eye, gave Linda her rain pants and let Linda hold onto her shoulder as she pulled them up over her bare, wet legs. Cole helped Linda tighten the hood over her head. Then he took his wife in both arms and held her closely and gently. Linda shivered uncontrollably.

Gabrielle surveyed the scene. Just north of them was an exit ramp, with a sign indicating that it would take them up into Augusta. At the top of the ramp was a fence and gate, and standing at post was a detail of soldiers. Gabrielle pointed and called out as the cordon gate slid open. The others turned to watch. Through the gate stepped an old woman, tiny in the distance, with two tall, thin soldiers behind her. The old woman walked steadily down the ramp toward them. Linda and the others stood in a rough half-circle and watched as the old woman approached. "It's Ness," said Mary at last. Linda nodded, watching, waiting. Her face was still quite gray.

The old woman came to a stop a few yards away from them, the two soldiers right behind her. "Hello, Ness dear," said Linda, her voice weak and shaken.

"Hello, Mrs. President," said Ness. "You remember how we first met here?"

"I do, Ness." She gestured toward the cordon gate with her head. "We were on our way back to the hospital but the wok brought us here. And now we find you, like you were expecting us. What's going on?"

The old woman shuddered and her face wavered as a strange, ghostly figure seemed to step out from inside of her, a figure of translucence and light and power. Ness's face went slack and her head fell forward, as though she'd fallen asleep on her feet. The strange figure, now fully material, came closer, stopping right in front of Linda. The two soldiers followed behind her.

The President smiled. "How very good to see you again, Alice," she said.

Cole inhaled sharply. Mary moved forward.

Alice nodded. She was no longer the tiny hybrid girl who had lived for a short time with Linda and Cole and the kids. Alice was now a teenager, as tall as Ness, thin, lithe, sinewy, her exotic face both disturbingly odd and yet strangely beautiful. She was clothed in a pure white tunic with a wide silver belt, and her jet-black hair shone like the moon. With her fierce eyes, she was the very vision of a warrior goddess. It was as if, in the three years that had passed on Earth, a dozen years had passed for Alice, during which time she'd grown in power and confidence and beauty. "It is good to see you as well, Mrs. Linda," said Alice. She looked at Mary. "And it is good to see you, Ms. Mary." She looked at Cole and nodded, slowly, respectfully. The two soldiers, tall and striking themselves, watched the proceedings carefully.

Cole held Linda with his left arm around her shoulders. Marionette stepped forward to stand on Linda's other side. Cole noted how the girl had so quickly formed a bond with his wife, and how protective she looked, standing there, facing off with Alice, a warrior goddess in her own right, her missing eye a proudly worn battle scar. He turned back to the young hybrid. "Can you tell us what's going on here, Alice?" said Cole. "And why your people's wok has brought us to this place? Linda is sick. And our children are in need of us now."

"And Keeley is missing," added Mary.

Alice looked at Mary for a moment, then turned to Cole and attempted a smile. "I have only just now arrived in this material form, Mr. Cole, but I have observed you all for some time," she said, "dividing my consciousness across space and time, between my body and Mrs. Goodness's body. We have guarded the forms of your children while you were away. We saw the need for them to journey into the next level, and encouraged them to follow their hearts." She looked to Mary. "And we are also guarding Ms. Keeley at the Maine-Central. She lives still," she said. She turned her attention back to

Linda. "Your loved ones are intact, and will await the business be-fore us. All is well."

"My daughters tell me that Iain was lost to some monster called the Murk, Alice," said Linda, her voice pointed with warning. "All is *not* well."

Alice took a step back, her eyes widening in surprise. "We did not know this," she said evenly. She glanced up at the sky, as if wonder-ing what her father knew. "Iain is my friend," said Alice, again look-ing at Linda. Her voice was soft and sad.

"We need to get to our children, Alice," said Cole. "And Mary needs to find Keeley." Whether meant as a threat or a plea or a pass-word, he held up his right hand and willed a tiny fountain of white light to spout up from his palm.

Alice gazed at Cole's light. It reflected in her large, almond-shaped, all-black eyes like a tiny firework in the midnight sky. She nodded once, then returned to Linda. "I regret this delay, Mrs. Linda," she said. "But I have been charged with the making of demands, and cannot forswear that duty to satisfy your haste." She looked from face to face of those assembled, as if assessing her enemies, or prof-fering a challenge. For a moment, her father's strange powers shone through her, and Linda was forced to acknowledge that Alice was not a little girl, or even a human being.

"What are these 'demands', Alice?" asked Marionette, her chin thrust forward as though she had a perfect right to enter this con-versation.

Alice jerked her eyes to Marionette and regarded the young woman curiously. From behind her, another young woman stepped forward, this one with short reddish hair and wearing a backpack. Alice studied them both for a long moment, then returned her at-tention to Linda. "We demand a place, Mrs. Linda. We who call our-selves the Middle Children. We who have been given life by a mix-ing of peoples. Life, but no home. Life, but no belonging, meaning, or purpose of our own to ground us in this realm, save for that which we create amongst ourselves. We have seen promises go unfulfilled. We have been patient and helpful. In exchange for that, we demand a home." She glanced over her shoulder back up the ramp toward the cordon gate, then returned her fierce gaze to Linda. "We will start with this place, Mrs. Linda. This Augusta place. In time, we will negotiate further to meet our needs." She raised an eyebrow almost imperceptibly. "Do you agree?"

Linda slumped in Cole's arms. After all she'd been through, to find herself stopped again so close to home felt like a blow to the stomach. It was too much. Too much grief and too much anger and too much she did not know. And to be stopped by Alice, by this odd being she had tried so hard to love, to find her now grown and fierce and demanding. Linda wanted to scream.

It was then that Gabrielle stepped to the front, putting herself between the President and the hybrid girl. "This is too much, Alice," she said firmly. "And your timing is unfair." She glanced at the other travelers behind her as if needing support. Stan nodded his encouragement. Marionette stepped up beside her and took Gabrielle's hand. Nicky leapt down from the wok's ramp and ran to join them. That was enough. She looked again at Alice. "I propose a council," she said. "I hear your needs, and agree with you that they must be addressed. Yet the President is sick, and her children are in great need. Please. Let us find our bearings and take care of our urgent requirements. Then we can meet again and discuss how to help each other, so that all of our needs get met." With that, Gabrielle bowed slightly, hiking up her shoulders as if in embarrassment. She took a step backwards.

Alice's thin, faint eyebrows bent together in a slight frown. Then she closed her eyes and inhaled softly. She stood like that for a long moment, her head cocked to one side as if listening to distant voices. After a time she opened her eyes and looked at Linda.

"We will escort you to your children," she said with a nod.

Out of the sky dropped two more woks.

16.2

Emily and Grace hovered in the astral sky above Augusta. It was time for them to return to their bodies, but that meant saying goodbye to Mihos, which neither of them wanted to do. The trip back from Squirrel Island had taken little time. They'd moved slowly at first, afraid that they would run back into the Murk on the way home. But they saw no signs of the huge, dark cloud they'd seen before. Apparently it only worked as a trap for those approaching the island, as it presented no problems for them in the other direction. When it became clear that the Murk was not going to hinder them, the three blinked back to Augusta.

"We have to go," said Emily. She pictured their bodies lying together in that old MRI machine where they'd left them. Nobody would know where they were, and her mother had said she'd be home very soon. Iain's body would be there as well. But Iain was... Emily could not bear to think about it.

Mihos stepped forward and rubbed his head on Emily's hand. "I'm going back in," he said quietly. He looked up at Emily, then at Grace. "To find your brother. I'm going to look for him. And for Dennis."

"But you can't," said Grace, shaking her head no. "It's too dangerous. You can't go back in."

Mihos wiggled his whiskers. "You kiddin' me?" he said confidently. "With what I know now? Piece of cake." The cat rocked his head and shoulders back and forth in sassy confidence. He smiled. "Really, girlfriends," he said. "I need to do this. And the Great Ones will be with me. I'll be okay."

Grace flickered in dim sadness. "We will miss you," she said.

Mihos wrinkled his nose. "I think you'll find a pleasant surprise back in the physical," he said. "Yer gonna need a litter box."

Emily knelt down and put her hand on the cat's sleek back. Grace knelt beside her. "You need to be really careful, Mihos," said Emily, petting him gently. "And you need to get word to us that you're okay. Will you do that?"

"If I can, I will," said Mihos. He stepped forward and touched each of the girls nose to nose, then sat back on his haunches and began to lick his front paws. "Go," he said to the girls, glancing up only briefly. "Momma's waitin' and this cat's gotta plane to catch."

Emily and Grace said their last farewells and then dove down into their bodies.

16.3

Jay Sinclair sat with his back against the cafeteria wall and poured his tea. There was little to do now but wait. His life as Guy Legrand was finished. His time here on Earth was drawing to a close. Sometime in the next twenty-four hours, he and his wife would be boarding one of the huge colony ships and heading out to the stars.

He sighed sadly. This should be an exciting and happy time for him. It was not. His daughter, Gabrielle, had evaded all of his attempts to find her. Now he had run out of time. He couldn't find her himself, and all the agents he might have trusted with the assignment had been called back to *Urbem Orsus*. Whatever had caused his daughter to run away, whatever it was that was fueling her hatred and distrust of him, and of their people, it was now too late for him to fix or heal or counter. He might find someone who could pinpoint her via the Astral level. He knew there were people who could do such things, and surely many of them were now here in the vast underground city from which the Giant Leap would originate. But for some reason, he hadn't gotten around to trying that. As much as he wanted his daughter to accompany them, as much as he feared for her future should she remain here on Earth, there was a part of him that knew that, in this matter, he had to allow his daughter the freedom to make her own choices. What was difficult for Sinclair was trusting that her choices were truly free.

He sipped hesitantly at his tea, wondering again about the water and the radiation, deciding again to trust The Families' technicians. Approximately five hundred feet overhead stood the ghost town of Pripyat, evacuated in 1986 the day after the disaster at the nearby Chernobyl nuclear power station. Though most of the radiation from that catastrophe was now held in soils and water, the Directorate's experts assured them that the systems in place in *Urbem Orsus* were equal to the task of keeping them safe and healthy. Sinclair knew that his people were unlikely to take unwarranted risks at this late stage of the game. It had taken them centuries to get to this fateful moment. He could not believe that his hesitancy was anything more than his own, personal psychological reactivity.

It was a clever choice, Pripyat. Where better to congregate, if one wished to avoid prying eyes? Construction on the underground city had begun just months after the Exclusion Zone had been put in place. They knew that they'd need a great deal of space in which to finish construction of the colony, scout, and defense ships, to gather the tens of thousands of human souls who would be chosen for this journey, and to gather the supplies and equipment the colonizers would need. They knew there would need to be a great deal of coming and going as the work was finished, and that this would include accelerated use of the woks, which tended to attract attention out amongst the Sleepers. So when the disaster occurred, plans were quickly made to move their operations to Ukraine. Compared to the frozen wastelands of Antarctica, Ukraine would be a relative paradise, radiation or no. And its central local would make everything easier.

Back then, of course, they had been working directly with the Life, so they had more access to alien ships and technologies. Since the Great Defection three years ago, The Families had had to put the finishing touches on things by themselves. While that only delayed the Giant Leap, rather than stopping it entirely, it had caused some great concern and inconvenience. Since human-built woks did not have the full invisibility and shape-shifting capabilities of Life-built woks, they had to be ever more careful about security issues, which made the use of the Chernobyl Exclusion Zone seem an even wiser and more prescient choice than it had already.

It was the Life's installation of the Grid that has proven the greater challenge, as it necessitated a great deal of study and testing, and then a massive effort and allocation of resources to design and build the huge scalar cannon array and antigrav clusters that they would need to punch through the aliens' rather annoying little interdict.

And it had taken finding and coordinating with a rogue element of the Life, someone who was willing to disable the Life's astral qputer system - which coordinated the continual regeneration of the Grid in the physical bands - long enough for The Families to get away. In the end, that strategy had been the most contentious aspect of the whole affair, as they'd never been able to know, for sure, whether the beings responsible for installing the Grid were actually the same beings with whom they'd worked for so long. There were simply too many types of "Gray" aliens, and they were far too enigmatic, for humans to ever trust that they could fully understand them. Though few of the Directorate wished to openly acknowledge it, Jay Sinclair knew that their reliance on this alien mole boiled down, of necessity, to a matter of trust.

In any event, there was, in Sinclair's mind, a delicious irony to the whole affair. *Urbem Orsus*, City of Beginnings, had risen from the ashes of one of the greatest nuclear accidents in history, just as the colony ships would rise from the ashes of a spent, depleted planet. The city didn't rise, actually, since it had been built far below the rapidly decaying ruins of Pripyat, but the metaphor was close enough for Sinclair.

In the end, it didn't matter, these names and metaphors and ironies. What mattered was that he and his people would finally head off to the stars, a project on which The Families had been working much longer than he had been alive. At last the day was upon them, when they could leave behind this depleted planet and the poor, sick, dumbed-down masses who were eating it alive. Sinclair was excited about the future and proud of his role in making it come to pass. The continuation of the human species was now in their hands. He couldn't think of anybody more qualified for that responsibility. Though it broke his heart to leave his daughter behind, he did not regret the course they had chosen.

He finished his tea and glanced at the clock. Almost seven in the evening. The Directorate would be meeting soon, in one of the spacious, comfortable conference rooms on the level just below. William Reynolds was back and would be giving a report not only on the destruction at Squirrel Island, which allowed them to finally put Project Changeling to rest, but also on his recent out-of-body trip to Herschel Colony, where he had spent the last few days overseeing the preparations being made there. Sinclair was looking forward to hearing Reynolds' reports, as he was one of only a few of their travelers who'd proven able to pass through the Grid at the non-physical level. Perhaps, after the meeting, Sinclair would ask him about the feasibility of finding Gabrielle in that manner.

It wouldn't hurt to ask.

16.4

Their reunion was bittersweet. Cole and Linda made it to the kids' hospital room just as Emily, and then Grace, opened their eyes. Their parents were on them with hugs and kisses even before the girls could sit up, kicking Ness's weird construct aside like a silly toy that had been left out on the floor.

"You're so cold," said Emily, reaching up to put a hand on Linda's gray-toned face.

"I'm still here, sweet girl," Linda said, shaking her head to ward off the tears. "Just like I said I would be."

Grace just buried her face in her father's chest and sobbed.

After a while, they turned their attention to Iain's comatose body lying nearby.

16.5

The rest of the Cole's crew gathered in the visitor lounge, to allow the family some private time, to find their own footing after the events of the last few days, to share their stories and learn of each other, and to begin the discussion about what to do next. Gabrielle sat amongst them and listened and thought.

The forces in play now swirled about them like the storm at the coast. Obviously the dark, secret levels of human control were still active in the world, as they'd all known they must be. They'd kidnapped the American President, held her captive, replaced her with a computer simulation, and lied to the world about her condition, all for reasons none of them could quite comprehend. No doubt the hidden elite were involved in the Greensleeves epidemic that was now spreading around the planet. That epidemic had hit many of them personally.

There were still aliens active in the world as well. Not only had Alice returned, but she'd had something to do with the kids, and their fool's errand into the Astral realm. And now she'd confronted them with a city full of hybrids and a list of demands. They'd seen woks coming from and going to the island. And the Grid still shone in the sky. There were aliens involved, but none of them knew whether they could be trusted.

Then there were Cole's new-found powers. There was the Church of the Stranger and its prophecies. There was the Church's warning about Linda Travis, and how Cole had to stop her, though none of them knew from what. There were Sten and Eddie's broadcasts. There was some monster called the Murk. And there was Hurricane Alpha, that huge, blasting storm that, even here in Augusta, assaulted them with wind and rain.

Gabrielle sat in the corner under the silent television, stroking the small black cat that lay in her lap. This cat had led her and the President up to the landing pad, and to their escape. Then he had leapt into the wok to join them. Nobody there knew his name, but Gabrielle was determined to take care of him. She ran her hand gently along his back. Having dried the rainwater from his fur as best he could with his tongue, the cat had fallen asleep, though he purred continuously in response to the girl's loving touch.

Eventually Stan asked Gabrielle about herself. Slowly, in short sentences and vague references, she began to tell them a bit about who she was and what she knew and what she had been through. She told them of her father, and of what she knew of The Families' plans to leave Earth. She told them she'd been in communication with a strange being called Zacharael, who'd been responsible for her appearance on Squirrel Island. She told them what she knew about Zacharael's great concern for the living beings on the planet, and what little she knew about Greensleeves. She told them how she'd found Linda in the facility underneath her cottage, how they'd escaped to the surface, how the cat had led the way.

But she did not tell them about the vial in her backpack. That was not hers to reveal.

16.6

Mary did not participate in this conversation. She'd been relieved to learn that Keeley was still alive, but angered to learn that Keeley was still at the hospital in Augusta, and in the care of the hybrids. She didn't care what these so-called Middle Children were demanding, or whether their demands were fair. It was just wrong to have moved Keeley to another room and then lied about it, telling Mary that they'd taken her partner, her love, her Keeley, sick with the deadly alien flu, to Squirrel Island. Why had they felt the need to do such a thing?

She pushed through the front door, dragging Danny, wet uniform and all, by the hand behind her. Forgetting her usual cramped hesitancy and wary step, she marched right up to the main nurses' station and slapped both palms down on the counter. "I demand that you tell me which room Keeley Benedict is in," she said to the tall, red-haired man who looked up from his computer screen. The fact that he was a hybrid, or that his field was closed to Mary, did not frighten her now. Alice was obviously their leader, and Alice *wanted* something from them. "Well?" she said, raising an eyebrow.

The red-haired man smiled warmly. "She's in the isolation ward, Ms. Hayes. Third floor. Room eleven. You can check in with the nurses up on three." He swiveled his head and looked at Danny, whose tall, strong frame and handsome face were a match for those of the hybrids. "Glad to have you back with us," he said, his eyes crinkling with secret delight.

Mary turned to her brother. Danny raised his shoulders in puzzlement. Neither had any idea what the redheaded hybrid was talking about, and Mary didn't have time to wonder about it. With a curt thank-you, she took Danny's hand and headed for the elevator.

"We do not yet fully understand the etiology of this disease," said a tiny female with huge green eyes and small, flat ears. She was leading Mary and her brother down the third-floor hallway. "We do know that the virus attacks only human beings and has no effect on the Middle Children." She came to a stop at door number eleven.

"When we *do* understand," said Mary, speaking more from intuition than certain knowledge, "we will know that there is no infectious agent as we would normally understand it. Please." Mary nodded toward the door. "I must see her."

The tiny female turned and punched the keypad to open the outer door. There was a faint shimmering in the air as the door slid opened, like someone had tossed a handful of glitter in celebration of their reunion.

"You sure about this, Sis?" asked Danny? "I mean. I got a shot more than a week ago, but you?"

Mary smiled grimly and entered an anteroom, in which stood another of the Middle Children, the first she'd seen that looked old, her face wrinkled and her hair short and straight and gray. The old nurse, clad only in scrubs herself, insisted that Mary don protective garb, not only a mask and gloves and hat and gown but pants and shoe covers as well. Mary complied without question and dressed quickly, glancing through the glass into Keeley's room. When the old woman was satisfied that Mary was as safe as they could make her, she thumbed a button that opened a second door. Mary entered Keeley's room.

Keeled lay on her bed, looking almost exactly as she had when Mary had last seen her. Her hair was flattened and messy but her face, even with its bright red rash, was calm and peaceful. She was asleep on her back, her chest rising and falling almost imperceptibly. The monitors babbled gently in the corner. Mary walked quietly across the room and sat softly on the side of Keeley's bed. She took her love's hand in hers, noting the warmth of Keeley's body. She breathed deeply and waited.

How could two days have passed? Mary couldn't account for the time. The hybrids had shut her out, so she'd tried to find some answers in the Astral realm. And yet that hadn't worked either, and all of a sudden she was back in the physical, in that wok that had appeared in the garage, and she made it to Squirrel Island just in time to help Cole and Linda and their new friends get away from the soldiers and the storm. Had she fallen asleep in that wok? Had she been that exhausted? Or had something else happened? There were vague memories in her mind, leftovers from a now-forgotten dream about her childhood. Surely she could not have slept for that long. Unless the Life had known more about what she'd needed than she did.

Probably it didn't matter, though the mystery continued to nag at her. Her first concern was Keeley, and Mary had a strong sense that if she tried hard enough, she could see into this Greensleeves, and figure out how to cure it. But then there was Iain, who'd gone missing in the Astral. How could she help find him? And there was the complex mystery of her friend Ness. And Alice, whom she had loved so dearly.

And she hadn't even heard Danny's story yet.

16.7

Danny watched as his sister entered Keeley's room, then made his way back past the nurses' station to the elevators, ignoring the hybrids as best he could, knowing they could look inside his soul if they so desired. Next to the elevators was a stairway and he pushed through the door, taking the steps quickly down to the ground level. There he found an exit door that promised an alarm were he to pass through it. Taking a chance that it no longer worked, and not much caring if it did, he pushed the heavy handle and stepped outdoors. If there was an alarm, it did not sound at the door.

The storm continued to churn overhead. The wind still gusted, but the rain had stopped again for a bit, for which he was thankful. Danny stood in the shelter of the doorway and stared out over the river, the name of which he didn't know. The waters were brown and roiled, like Willy Wonka's chocolate river, stirred up by the storm. Beyond he could see a large park, with what he guessed was the State House on the far edge. The current seat of the American government, with abandoned construction scaffolding in place. He wondered if that building had been overtaken by the hybrids, like the hospital and military had clearly been occupied.

Danny pulled a cigarette from a crushed box in his back pocket and lit it with a tiny butane lighter. He pulled on the cigarette and sighed a cloud of smoke into the rushing air, then reached up to loosen the top buttons of his damp uniform shirt. He chuckled to himself. It was crazy. Whatever this was, it was just nuts. He'd been working with some faction of The Families for most of his adult life and never had he seen things so out of control.

He'd served for almost a decade as a security specialist with The People. After their dissolution three years ago, he'd driven a desk at the BlackBay Services office in London, serving as liaison with the security chief at Herschel Colony. Anxious to get back to fieldwork, he'd jumped at the chance to go deep undercover in the U.S. military. He'd been keeping an eye on Project Changeling, and Colonel McAfee, and reporting back to his contact at BlackBay in London for the past four months. It had all seemed rather routine, and utilized his gifts and abilities fully. It had made sense. It had paid well.

And it had stood in stark relief to the childhood he could only vaguely remember. His mother had died when he was born, and he had no memory of ever having even seen a picture of her. His father had been a monster. And upon the old man's death when Danny was just a kid, he and Mary had been given to a nice, middle-aged couple in Washington D.C. who raised them with love and respect. His new father was a Senator. His mother a lawyer. Danny and Mary had gone to private schools and had had every advantage. Compared to life with his old man, his new foster family had been a gift from the gods.

Danny had a natural ability to know when he was being lied to. When he graduated from high school, he told his foster father, the Senator, that he wanted to go work for the CIA. His father had smiled and said, simply, "I've got something even better." The 'something better' had changed his life. Six months of intensive quasi-military training later, during which time he'd studied security systems and technologies he'd never even imagined, Danny set foot for the first time down in The Rock, an underground joint civilian-military research facility situated directly beneath the federal government buildings of the District of Columbia. His work as a contractor, paid by BlackBay Services, consisted of regular interviews with the various scientists, technicians, and soldiers who worked in The Rock. His secret mission, known only to himself and the Chief of Security there, was to look for lies.

He started hearing the stories almost immediately: how there was a second underground facility right next to theirs; how that one had been constructed, and was inhabited, by a group of aliens with whom the government had been in contact for decades. He kept his ears open. The stories had the ring of truth, and they stirred something deep inside of him that he did not understand.

Then one evening, over dinner, he mentioned the stories to his sister, who'd graduated six years ahead of him and now worked as a research assistant for a law firm inside the beltway. Something about what he said put Mary immediately on guard and she tried to change the subject. But Danny had pushed her, and he could sense the lies in her various responses, and he'd called her on them. Finally she'd burst into tears.

"You don't remember, do you?" she asked through her sniffles.

"Remember what?" Danny had asked.

Mary told him what.

Danny hadn't remembered a bit of it. The abductions. The little gray guys who would come in the night and take both of them and their father up into their ship. The terror. The painful marks and bruises. But as Mary spoke, strange feelings arose inside of him, including a fiery rage he did not understand. "So how do you know all of this?" he demanded.

Mary wiped the tears from her face. "Because I work down in The Rock too, Danny," she'd said. "On the other side. Their side." She took a long breath. "You're not the only one that the dear old Senator invited into the family business."

When Danny learned that Mary was working with a group called The People who served as direct liaisons to the Gray aliens in their lodge next door, he knew he would not rest until he knew more. "Take me there, Sis," he said. "Bring me in. Okay? I need to..." he sighed, unsure of what he was asking. "I need to meet them."

Mary brought him in. He would work directly for Agent Rice on joint Rock-Lodge security issues. Which meant entry into the lodge itself. Which meant that he would meet the aliens, face to face.

It was Mary who introduced him to his first real alien. A female, she said, called "Mork" by the humans, since they couldn't understand her real name. She was a distinguished elder, apparently, and they came upon her as she sat on a pad in a bare, rock-walled room no larger than a prison cell. Mary stepped in and waved on the light. Danny followed. There she was, sitting on her mat in the corner, looking up at him with her huge, black, almond-shaped eyes. "HEL-LO AGAIN, DANNY," she said in his mind.

Danny's fury erupted. "You!" he shouted, his voice harsh and raw. His face turned red. His heart pounded. His fists clenched. His breathing stopped. He struck the rock wall beside him with one hand and shook his fist at the old alien with another. "I hate you!"

he said through clench teeth. He took a step forward, as if he might kick her. He stopped. He inhaled noisily, like coming up for air after a deep dive. Without so much as a glance at Mary, he whirled away and stormed out of the room.

He'd gone on to work with The People for many years, and became an invaluable asset to Agent Rice. He never again showed such rage at the aliens, but he kept his distance, and he kept his mouth shut. He wouldn't even speak with Mary about it. Mary understood, and let him alone. She knew about that anger. When President Travis exposed the operation and the Life disappeared, Danny felt deeply relieved. He gladly took the job in London. He climbed up out of the lodge and caught the first flight to Gatwick. He hoped he'd seen the last of those maddening little creatures.

Danny had little first-hand knowledge about his ultimate employers, the secret elite control group known collectively as "The Families." But he didn't know nothing. While Agent Rice had kept his cards close to his vest when it came to the hidden powers-that-be, the rumors filled the air around him, and there was much that Danny could deduce for himself. Clearly The Families had their fingers in a great many pies around the globe, and had been steering the course of human history for a very long time, to the point where it could be fairly said that they were the true rulers of the Earth. He'd seen first-hand how they'd been in secret contact with various species of alien beings, and about the technology they'd received from them, and about how far advanced The Families were technologically, compared to the rest of the human race. He knew about The Families' program to create a number of human colonies elsewhere in the Solar System. He'd worked directly with the Herschel Colony.

But in the past few months, he'd begun to suspect that other plans were afoot. Darker plans. More secret. More sinister. In the beginning, the work on Squirrel Island had involved a simple security upgrade for the Presidential retreat, and the establishment of a small military base there. Danny had been embedded as a corporal and was made the aide and driver for the commander, Colonel McAfee, so that he could more effectively monitor the operation. Such surveillance was pretty much standard procedure for The Families, and since McAfee knew Danny from their days together with The People, the Colonel's guard was down. While construction crews built barracks and towers, Danny's unit concentrated their efforts on establishing and maintaining the island's security systems, from the fencing and gun mounts to the more exotic e-control fields, toroidal shield wall, and mirror pool. A team of specialists had even flown in one weekend and planted and tuned something called a Murk, a device about which Danny had only heard whispered rumors. Coastal Maine was beautiful, and Danny was glad to be there, and glad to be working mostly outdoors, especially as the winter gave way to the freakish spring heat wave. It made sense to him, that they were beefing up security where the President would be spending time.

Eventually he learned that there was a research facility being built directly underneath the President's cottage, a structure that would house something called Project Changeling. It struck Danny as odd that, given his insider status, and his proven track record and security clearance with The People, he had not been briefed regarding the true nature of their work there. But he'd learned long ago that The Families operated on a strict "need to know" basis, and that Danny apparently had much less of that need than he thought he should.

Project Changeling, he eventually discerned, involved the replacement of the American President with a virtual copy. While he wasn't sure he understood the need for that - The Families had managed to continue controlling anything and everything that mattered even with Linda Travis on the loose - he could see how it fit in with their plan for ever greater control of the global government. And such things as fooling the world with a computer-generated Linda Travis, and building a facility right underneath the President's vacation retreat, was exactly the sort of over-the-top display of power The Families loved to make, as the whole world saw when D.C. fell into that sinkhole. And the President's exploits three years earlier had, after all, thrown a wrench in The Families' plans. Perhaps they were taking out an insurance policy against that happening again. Danny kept his mouth shut and performed his duties.

Then a great many new personnel appeared, scientists and doctors and computer geeks. They went down into the facility and rarely emerged into the light of day. Access became highly restricted, and only a small and specially chosen detail of soldiers was allowed underground. Not long after, a package arrived in a human-built wok, a device Danny had not seen since his days with The People. The package was hush-hush, Above Top Secret, and was delivered into the underground facility in the cover of night by the special security team that had arrived along with it. Nobody in Danny's unit had been involved in receiving the package, and only a couple of them had even got a glimpse of it from their posts on the towers.

Reports were that it was a coffin. Not long after that, Danny learned that the President had been stricken by some new "alien flu bug," and had been taken to Squirrel Island. That probably explained the "package." The research facility underfoot had been built, apparently, with a level-four biocontainment ward at the bottom level. All military personnel were given vaccinations the next day and told to keep their mouths shut.

All of which was disconcerting to Danny. Here he'd thought he was an insider, a BlackBay operative working undercover and reporting back with news which, he assumed, would go straight to somebody in The Families. So why had he not been brought in on what was really happening there? How had they known to build an isolation ward under the President's cottage before she even got sick? And how could they already have a vaccine? Danny shook his head, kept his mouth shut and his ears open, and performed his duties.

Then the news started coming fast and thick. People close to the President started dropping like flies, either disappearing or falling ill. Then the President's husband shows up in Boothbay Harbor and tries to get on the island to see his wife, with this Hurricane Alpha heading straight toward them. Some of the news came through the mainstream media. Some came straight through the chain of command. Some was rumor, bouncing around inside his unit like a Superball. Some came from his contact-of-record at BlackBay, or from other BlackBay friends he had back in London. Danny started hearing about "the Quietus" and "the Giant Leap," "the One-Two Punch" and "the Second Wave" and *Urbem Orsus*," the fabled gathering place of The Families. And he started to put together his own assessment of exactly what was going on. He did not much care for his conclusions.

It seemed that the old rumors about The Families' long-term goal of leaving the planet *en masse* had more truth to them than Danny had supposed. And from what he could see, given the activity he'd observed first hand, the timing he noted, and the facts and rumors he'd gathered, The Families had unleashed a deadly viral pandemic on the human population. They were leaving soon, and they were cleaning up their messes before they did so. Perhaps they were even taking some long-desired revenge against their enemies. And the hurricane now bearing down on them would destroy the evidence of their final acts.

Clearly, Danny thought, it was time to find a way off of Planet Earth. If The Families were fleeing the burning ship, he wanted to flee with them. That they hadn't already invited him on their Giant Leap left him feeling unappreciated, but he knew that there wasn't time for him to indulge hurt feelings. Danny knew he was low on the totem pole. And he knew that the person who could have most persuasively argued for his inclusion in the Giant Leap - Agent Theodore Rice - was no longer amongst the living. Danny would have to recommend himself. And the first step toward that end was to get off of Squirrel Island. He knew that there was a rumored "Second Wave," but his gut told him that that was just a fairy story, told to insiders to keep them hopeful that, even should they not be included in the Giant Leap, they'd be included in a subsequent effort. That did not sound like The Families to Danny. That was a lie, meant only to keep people in line while The Families made their preparations. It would be the Giant Leap or nothing.

When the President's husband stormed the island in a giant light worm, when his sister, who'd left the employ of The Families three years earlier, appeared out of nowhere in a wok and crushed his CO, when the President had turned out to be not only alive but also not sick with some deadly alien flu, Danny knew his opportunity had come. He jumped into that wok, getting while the getting was good, as his foster mother liked to say.

He stubbed out his cigarette and tossed the butt to the ground. The rain had started again and was pouring down heavily now. He glanced up at the sky and smiled. Apparently somebody up there still liked him. He turned and headed back inside. He'd follow this situation as long as it made sense to do so. Until he figured out his next steps. The hybrids were making their move now as well, apparently. Trying to establish a place on Earth just as Danny was seeking to leave. They could have it, as far as Danny was concerned. He started up the stairs to the third floor. Surely Mary had had enough time with her lover by now. Maybe she knew things Danny didn't.

16.8

Stendahl Banks came back into the visitor lounge and fell into his chair. The cable was out because of the storm, but he'd managed to get a call through to the networks. "Mick back at ACN says that they're getting completely hammered down there. Not just the winds, which are Category Six now, but the storm surge, which Mick said might be setting a new record. And with the waves on top of that..." Sten paused for a moment to exhale his surfeit of feelings. "And he said a report just came in about a possible earthquake off the south coast of Nova Scotia, so there's a chance of some tidal wave action added to the mix. I'll be surprised if Squirrel Island isn't scoured clean before this is all over."

Doobie and Marionette, sitting side-by-side on one of the sofas, looked at each other and smiled. Marionette had found a black silk tie and had tightened it around her head at an angle, to replace her missing patch. Doobie reached out and took her hand, then turned to Sten. "Any way to get in touch with Ken or Annabelle?" he asked. "Get word to them?"

Sten shook his head. "I don't know, man," he said. "Phone lines are all gone down there. Mick said he'd look into it. Probably not much we can do 'til the storm blows out. But apparently the eye has stalled just offshore, keeping the whole Boothbay area right in the worst of it."

"It's almost like this is a designer storm," said Eddie with a puzzled frown.

"I'm sure it's exactly that," said Stan. "Weather modification and storm generation are no longer fringe fantasies, you know. Who knows what these Family guys are capable of? I mean, look at the timing, the direct hit, the intensity. And now an earthquake?" Stan shook his head in disgust. "Yeah. It's a designer storm, all right. Designed to kill us all. And the President."

"And yet here we are," said Sten, quietly.

Marionette shook her head angrily and stood. "But *they* can help us," she said, gesturing down the hallway with a wave of the hand.

"Who can help us?" asked Doobie.

"Them," said Marionette. "The nurses. The ones with the strange eyes. The hybrids." Her voice was colored with wariness when she named them. "They've got those space ships. And the storm doesn't touch those things. They can take us down there." She looked down at Doobie. "You comin', Captain?" she asked.

"Coming where?" he asked.

"To commandeer one of their ships." Marionette's eyes sparkled.

Doobie laughed and stood to join her.

16.9

Alice pushed through the hospital's front door and marched quickly down the main corridor to the visitor's lounge. She scanned the room until her eyes alighted on Stan. "We will meet now in conference room B, Mr. Stan," she said evenly. "We have already informed Mrs. Linda." Then she turned and continued down the hall.

Stan looked at Sten, Eddie, and Gabrielle. "I guess it's show time," he said, standing. The others stood as well. Doobie and Marionette had not been seen since going off to ask the hybrids, the Middle Children, for help. The remnants of Cole's crew headed toward the conference room. The cat padded along behind them.

In the side hallway that led to the conference room, they caught up with Linda. The President was shuffling slowly down the corridor, her borrowed rain pants and coat swishing as she walked. Her face was still gray and slack. Outside, the rain battered the windows and skylights. Noticing the others, Linda stopped and turned. "I could use some help," she said, her voice husky and exhausted. "Cole insisted on staying with the gir... with the kids."

Stan nodded. "We've got your back, Mrs. President," he said. He stepped forward and pushed the door open and ushered Linda into the room. Gabrielle followed right behind Linda and took her elbow to help her walk. Sten and Eddie came in last, closing the door once the cat had scooted in. There, sitting at the large mahogany table opposite the door, sat Alice.

"It is time for negotiations," said the leader of the Middle Children.

Linda stepped in and pulled out the chair directly opposite Alice. She sat heavily. "So we're negotiating now?" she asked. She held Alice's warrior gaze. Gabrielle took the seat to her right. Stan sat to her left. Sten and Eddie sat together at the table's end. The cat wandered around underneath.

"We both have needs which the other can help fulfill," nodded Alice. "Is negotiation not the correct word?"

Stan cleared his throat. "So you and your people need a place to call your own," he said, hoping to move this along. "Is that all?"

Alice nodded. "It is in Mrs. Linda's power to cede us the territory we require. We wish to make our home here, and share it as equals with human beings. This is the promise that has been held before us for decades. Now the balance of power has shifted. It is time for us to speak for ourselves."

"You know this place is becoming a hell-hole, don't you?" muttered Stan.

Linda put out a hand to cut him off. "And what needs of ours can you help us with, Alice?" she asked.

Alice turned from Stan to Linda. "First, you shall remain hidden from the world at this time, Mrs. Linda. We adjudge that this confers upon you a distinct advantage, and we pledge our continued aid and protection in that regard. We can hide you. Second, two of your company have requested our assistance in a rescue operation. We shall provide that. They are already making preparations. Third, your son has gone missing in the non-material bands. We have experience in these levels, and will assist in the efforts to find him." Alice stopped and looked from Linda to Stan, as if such things should be obvious.

"So we should make a decision that will forever change the course of human history in exchange for your assistance?" asked Linda with a frown.

Alice nodded slightly. "That course is set to change in any event, is it not?"

Linda sat back and sighed. Stan scowled. Sten and Eddie watched with great attention but kept their silence. Gabrielle leaned forward in her chair and cleared her throat. "Will the human race come to regret it, should the President agree to your proposal, Alice?" she asked. Everything inside of her told her that this being would not, could not, lie to her, any more than Zacharael could.

Alice turned her attention to Gabrielle, who sat petting the cat, which had again settled onto her lap. "You are like Emily," she said. A faint smile flashed across her face. "And you are seeking a place as well. Perhaps we shall be friends." Alice regarded the others in the room: Sten. Eddie. Stan. Linda. Then she returned her translucent gaze to Gabrielle. "I give you my word," she said, "and the word of us all, the Middle Children: you shall remain ever glad of our presence." She turned to look Linda in the eye. "If the time ever comes that you regret your decision, you need but say so and we will leave."

16.10

Doobie, Marionette, Sten, and Eddie, with an equal number of hybrid soldiers, departed soon thereafter for Boothbay Harbor in a single, enormous wok. Their plan was to find and evacuate as many people as they could, including Andrew and Macy, Annabelle, and any other Church members they encountered. They had no idea about Ken and Celia, whether she was still alive, and what they should do if she was. A hybrid doctor had told them that they had not yet determined the transmission vector for the Greensleeves virus, but that preliminary studies indicated that direct, human-to-human transmission could not account for the rapidity of its dispersal. Something else must be going on, but they did not know what that was. The rescuers were less than reassured by that news, and decided that they'd leave those decisions to Ken and Annabelle.

Eddie was excited by the prospect of seeing the storm up close. He'd left a backup video camera stowed in the back seat of the old Mercedes parked at the Thieving Seagull. If it was still there, he and Sten could shoot some footage and do a report from inside the storm. They wouldn't have the uplink gear they'd need. That had all gone down with *The Pokey Joker*. But just getting the film in the can would feel like a victory. And who knows? Perhaps they could uplink it when they got back to Augusta.

The thing was, Sten was not sure what he could, or should, say, were he to file a report. The situation was far too chaotic, and things were moving much too quickly, for him to wrap his head around, and he had no idea which information he could share. The hybrids? The woks? The rescue of the President and the truth of what had happened there? The amazing powers Cole had shown? The loss of their son? He would have to hear from Linda and Cole and Stan and the others before he made mention of any of this. There were dark forces at work in the world. How to counter them was a decision way above his pay grade. The more he thought about it, Sten was glad they had no uplink gear, so he would not be tempted to file a story. The first order of business was rescue. Everything else would have to wait.

The hybrid soldiers took them first to Ken's house in Southport, where Stan and Cole had shared that wonderful meal with the Church less than two days before. The woks settled smoothly to the ground and the soldiers took a moment to monitor the outside conditions. One of them turned to his human passengers and shook his head. "Sustained winds of 166 miles per hour," he said, shaking his head. "Gusting to 195. We cannot go outside." He turned and mumbled something to the wok. The walls of the ship turned instantly clear.

Sten, Eddie, Doobie, and Marionette gasped, to see the devastation this storm had already wrought.

16.11

There was one last fire to put out before she could rest. Linda kissed Cole and the girls on their foreheads and left the room, promising to be right back. She walked down the hall and around the corner to the nurses' station for directions to the infectious disease unit, then made her way up to Keeley's third-floor room. She stopped at the nurses' station outside the isolation ward and waited for the nurse to finish a phone call. In a moment the tall, red-haired young man looked up at her and smiled. "You are here to see Ms. Keeley," he said.

Linda nodded and the red-haired man stood and gestured for her to follow him through a set of double doors. Down the hall on the right the man stopped and waited outside room eleven. In a moment the door slid open. For just a second, the air in the doorway was filled with sparkling energy, but it quickly dissipated. Inside was an old woman, who bowed slightly to Linda and then stepped to the side. Linda saw an anteroom of some sort, with a wall of glass on the far side. The curtains were drawn, but she assumed that beyond them she'd find Keeley. The set-up was similar to the viewing room connected to the underground laboratory in which she'd found her naked body on Squirrel Island. She stepped in and the door behind her slid closed.

"We can only allow you this far, Mrs. Linda," the old woman said, echoing Alice's name for her, and adding to Linda's sense that these hybrids were all connected mind-to-mind. The nurse unfolded a metal chair that had been leaning against the wall and placed it before her. Linda smiled and said thank you and sat down, grateful for the attention, and the rest. Linda shook her head at the irony, that the whole world thought it was *she* who was sick, and contained in a room such as this.

The nurse pulled the curtain open. There was Keeley in her bed, sick with this alien flu, just as Cole had said. On the edge of the bed sat someone in full protective gear. "Ms. Mary was insistent that we allow her in," said the nurse. "We agreed to her demand."

Linda watched as Mary, her back to the viewing room, sat facing Keeley, head bowed as if in prayer. She watched for a few minutes, then cleared her throat and started to ask the old nurse if she could talk to them. Mary raised a hand in the air like a stop sign and Linda fell silent, motioning to the nurse to never mind for now. She watched a bit longer as Mary slowly allowed her arm to return to its resting place. Mary sat for a while longer, breathing slowly, head bowed, then roused herself. She inhaled deeply, lifted her head, leaned forward as if saying goodbye, then turned and stood to walk over to the glass. She smiled at Linda through her visor.

"I am glad you are home, Mrs. President," said Mary. Her voice came through a tiny speaker in an intercom box on the sidewall. "We haven't had a chance to catch up."

"Seems I have you to thank for my rescue, Mary," said Linda. She leaned forward and spoke into the intercom the nurse pointed out to her.

Mary winked. "Seems like there were others involved too," she said, pointing toward the sky.

Linda sighed and shook her head, as if she couldn't even think about that right now. She gestured toward Keeley with a wave of her hand`. "How's our girl?"

Mary glanced at Keeley, then back to Linda. "She's treading water, Mrs. President. And she's very tired. But I sense that her sleep is peaceful and full of joy."

"I thought this disease was really fast," said Linda. "When it... you know."

"The Middle Children were able to slow it down," said Mary. "Something to do with the nullspace field they installed around the room. You may have seen the glimmer when you entered. And Keeley had only a little of the virus in her system."

"Do you know what...?"

"I have been communing with Greensleeves, Linda," said Mary. "I see it now. I will tell the doctors what I know when I leave here."

Linda glanced back to make sure the nurse was out of earshot. The old woman had retreated to the far side of the anteroom and stood quietly near the door, her eyes closed. Linda leaned close to the intercom and spoke in a low voice. "I may have something, Mary. Some knowledge. About how to cure it."

Mary raised an eyebrow. Linda's field was tight with secrets and shame. "I would like very much to know about that, Mrs. President," she said.

Behind them, Keeley inhaled sharply and moaned. Her lips trembled and moved, as if she was trying to speak. Mary turned and walked back to her partner's side. Keeley inhaled again, then managed a few words, her voice a mere whisper. "My love," she said. "Alas."

16.12

Ness awakened in her bed. A storm outside shook her windows. "Now how the hell did I end up here?" she muttered. It was well into the day, judging from the light. She never slept in this long. She should be in the kitchen. Ness rubbed at her eyes. She remembered being at the hospital with the kids. She vaguely remembered building some sort of structure, something that would protect them. She remembered dancing, though why she'd been dancing she couldn't say. She remembered going to sleep. And she remembered a dream of Alice, or at least she thought it was Alice. But already the dream was evaporating from her mind. Ness exhaled heavily. How did she go to sleep in the hospital and end up back in bed? And fully dressed? She must be getting old. They were gonna be wiping the drool from her face before she knew it.

Ness sat up and pushed her legs over the edge of the bed. The storm rumbled outside. She got to her feet, walked across her room, and opened the door out into the hallway. "Hello?" she called out. There was no one around. Closing her door quietly behind her, she headed down the corridor, looking for somebody who could tell her what the heck was going on.

16.13

It was only then that they could let it fully sink in. All of their losses. All of their trauma. All their wild stories. The fear. The anger. The deep grief. The intense stress. The need for action. With these forces and many others swirling about and within them, they retreated once again to the hospital room, in which the kids' bodies had been taken and tended and so carefully guarded.

They let the hospital staff, those strange hybrid creatures, form a wall of protection around them. The family gathered together on the little loveseat along the back wall, scrunched together for mutual support and connection. Cole sat on one end and Linda on the other, with the girls between them, and they joined together with hands and arms and legs, with heads all touching, with shared breath and silence and warmth.

Linda's face retained its gray cast, and her skin was still cool to the touch, even in their mutual warmth. It was only when he noticed this that Cole fully realized that Linda had actually been dead. Death clung to her still like a bad scent, and he understood how much of a struggle it must have been for her to keep going for as long as she had.

Then Cole remembered who he was, and he closed his eyes. Slowly, carefully, he drew out his light, letting it flicker to life like tiny bonfires in his hands. He adjusted the color to a warm golden hue and watched in his mind as it grew larger and stronger. He sent it upward like a fountain, then bent it back and around, the light now covering the four of them like a huge umbrella. He drew it downward, through the walls, through the loveseat, through the floor, wherever it needed to go, until it enclosed them on all sides, a sphere of golden light, warm and wonderful. He set it to pulsing, a soft heartbeat of living light, then drew in a column of light from above and brought it down to Linda's head, letting it seep into her cold, gray body, letting it fill her, warm her, soothe her, heal her. He drew the light all through her body and set it softly pulsing, then formed similar columns for Emily and Grace. And finally one for himself.

He let the golden light fill them all, pulsing like breath and blood and life. He drew it through them, let it return to the sphere, and then cycled it around to fill them all again. He listened as Grace's sniffles subsided, as Linda's breathing eased. He felt Emily's tension soften. He felt his own fears slip away. He did not open his eyes. He could see his light in his mind, and knew it was there, and had no doubt that an onlooker would see it as well. It was real. It was his. It was *him*. And he could use it for healing and love and connection as easily as he had used it for protection and containment and defense on Squirrel Island. Cole formed one last intention and a tendril of light reached out from the sphere to Iain, as he lay in his bed. The light formed a second sphere around their lost boy, separate yet connected to his family.

After a time they slept. The light enfolded them in their slumber. The hybrids stood guard in the hallways and rooms all around them as they went about their duties. They could feel Cole's light emanating outward from their room, and nodded their appreciation. One of them actually grinned.

16.14

Ken and Celia's house was gone, a flattened pile of sticks and bricks. The trees around it were gone. The Thieving Seagull was gone. The marina was gone. The house at Pig Cove was gone. The piers and buildings at Cape Harbor were gone. Everywhere they went they found flattened buildings and twisted trees and overturned vehicles and flooded roads. Viewing it from inside a huge, invisible wok that didn't so much as shudder in the wind, the landscape felt more like a movie than a real place, as if they were all seated in one of those IMAX theaters. It was horrifying, what they saw. Amazing. Almost impossible to believe. And the devastation was so complete and so thorough that it felt like intention to them. Like hatred. Like contempt. Like disgust. Somebody somewhere had clearly wanted to wipe the Boothbay Harbor region completely off the face of the Earth. They had nearly succeeded.

The most disturbing sight was Squirrel Island, which had been stripped bare. Houses, roads, buildings, trees and vegetation, the President's cottage, the military towers and fences, all of it must have been swept or pushed or carried into the sea. There was nothing left, save for odd bits of debris. An overturned Jeep here. A uniformed body there. A baby's high chair. A highball glass. A laptop computer. The only recognizable structure remaining was the paved landing pad from which they'd taken off some hours earlier. And where Linda's cabin had stood, the large metal bulkhead door that led to the underground facility. Otherwise it was rock and bare soil and little else.

They viewed it all from above, sometimes flying high for a longer view, other times dipping in for a close up. Marionette watched with a wide, staring eye. Doobie watched with tears streaming down his face. Sten and Eddie watched as news gatherers would watch, focused and intense in their observations. The hybrids watched without reaction, though one of them, an older woman, seemed attentive to the reactions of her human guests. Most of the tiny seaside resort town of Boothbay Harbor was gone, turned into a huge pile of building materials and gift items. Southport was flattened and flooded. They saw a few bodies, but far less than there would have been had much of the population not fled to the shelters a year earlier. They saw a couple of dogs hunkering down in a tipped dumpster. They saw no living human beings. If Annabelle and Ken and Celia and the others had still been here when the full force of the storm had hit, they were likely all dead.

The strangest was this: as they were flying slowly back up along Western Avenue from Southport to Boothbay Harbor, the storm stopped. It didn't die out slowly. It didn't push on up the coast. It didn't reverse its direction and head back out to sea. It stopped. It had been raging overhead, the rain had been falling by the bucketful, and then it stopped, as though some powerful wall of energy had blasted it out of the sky. The rain stopped abruptly, the wind fell to a slight breeze, and the clouds broke apart, fleeing in all directions as if from embarrassment. In five minutes, at the most, the hurricane was done.

Then the sun came back out.

16.15

Mihos was perplexed. And he was glad that there was no one else around, as the last thing a cat ever wants is for somebody to see him when he is perplexed. Nevertheless, that's how he felt. Perplexed. Confused. Befuddled. Bewildered. Cat's don't *do* bewildered, babycakes.

He had had no luck at all keying in on Iain's pattern. This had not surprised him. He knew that the Murk would block such things. So he made his way eastward, following close to the physical as they had before. There in the distance was the same black cloud they'd seen before. The Murk. But as he neared it, the Murk began to flicker and then, well... lean over. And then it just kind of rolled and tumbled away and was gone in a moment.

Mihos stopped to watch, then proceeded slowly, thinking perhaps that it was a trick, worried that the Murk would catch him unawares. But nothing happened. He continued his slow approach to that Squirrel Island place. There was no sign of the Murk anywhere. Tuning to the physical, the reason became clear: there was one whopper of a storm passing through here. The storm must have wiped out the weird plant that was the manifestation of the Murk in the physical bands.

He attempted again to find and key in on Iain's pattern. Still nothing. And then, as he'd hovered over Squirrel Island, the storm itself stopped, just as quickly as the Murk had disappeared. He'd never heard of such a thing. Not in the physical. Storms didn't just stop like that.

The thing was, now he had no idea how to proceed. Iain had been lost in the Murk. Now the Murk was gone. So where should Mihos start his search for the boy? What had happened to Iain when he fell into that vast cauldron of burning ember creatures? Had the Murk actually killed him, or eaten him? Was he totally gone for good? Or had he been taken to some whole other corner of reality, some other layer, some other realm? Was he still imprisoned in the Murk's deadly blackness? And what happened to Dennis? Mihos sighed. The trail had been wiped clean by a hurricane. He didn't know what to do. Iain could be anywhere. Or nowhere. Without the boy's pattern to sense, there would be no finding him.

16.16

Mary sat in a hard plastic chair in an empty examination room with three nurses and one doctor. The entire MaineCentral staff had been replaced by hybrids while she'd been away, so all four were members of what Mary had learned to call the Middle Children. All four were young and tall and beautiful, though one nurse, a dark-haired and swarthy man named Rogert, had an enormous forehead that gave him an exotic, and somewhat freakish, appearance.

"You can communicate with others in the medical establishment around the planet?" asked Mary.

The doctor, whom they all called Mr. Buck, nodded reassuringly. "Most of us were inserted into human positions some time ago," he said. "Either in government, the military, or the medical establishment. Why do you ask?"

Mary looked at Mr. Buck, noting again that none of these hybrids seemed to have any field whatsoever. She could not read them. "I have information regarding Greensleeves," she said. "It will need to be passed along to your colleagues."

Mr. Buck nodded his understanding. "What is your information?"

Mary sighed and closed her eyes, to aid in recall. "I think your preliminary assessment is correct. Greensleeves is not spreading as quickly as it is because it is highly transmissible." She opened her eyes and looked at Mr. Buck. "It's spreading because the genetic material for this virus was designed and produced and inserted into the genome of the global human population years ago, using genetically modified food products. It was then activated globally a couple of weeks ago, probably by some sort of energetic burst, like a precisely modulated EMP. Its virulence and expression is further modulated by the past and current consumption of certain genetically modified high fructose corn syrups and other corn derivatives. Those who have eaten a great deal of this over the years, and those who consume it still, die more quickly than those who have not. It's this, I think, that helps account for why Keeley is still alive. That plus the power of your combined intentions, for which I thank you." Mary stopped and sighed. It was difficult for her, to speak of Greensleeves, and Keeley, in such stark and clinical terms, but she sensed that overt emotionality on her part would only confuse these people.

Mr. Buck nodded, then closed his eyes, cocking his head slightly as he did so. The three nurses did the same. After a few moments, all four of them opened their eyes. "Your assessment aligns with other bits of data we possess, and strikes us as sound. We shall now contact our colleagues in the human medical world. Do you have insights or instructions regarding the possible treatment of this disease?"

Mary thought back to her hurried conversation with the President. She shook her head. "Not yet, Mr. Buck," she said. "But I'll keep working on that. Perhaps this information will help."

Mr. Buck stood and bowed slightly. The three nurses stood, and all four of them filed out of the room. Mary leaned back in her chair and allowed her feelings to rise within her.

16.17

Gabrielle, Stan, and Danny sat in the hospital's visitor's lounge. Cole and Linda and the kids were asleep. Mary was conferring with the doctors. The rest had gone on a rescue mission back to the coast. These three were left, to drink coffee, and wait, and slowly come to know each other. Outside, the rain had stopped, the wind had softened, and the massive swirl of clouds was moving quickly to the west.

One thing these three had in common was a feeling of surprise. Stan was surprised to learn that his President had returned from the dead, and that her husband had strange, alien powers. Gabrielle was surprised to find herself amongst these powerful people, to be trusted with the vial, and to be asked by the President to participate in her meetings. Danny was surprised by the unshakable feeling he had, that somebody was watching over him, that he'd been rescued for a purpose, that he was cherished and wanted. It was a strange feeling, for someone who had been regularly beaten as a boy.

Danny was keeping a particularly close eye on Linda Travis and her odd husband. The thing was, he found he liked this President. She'd taken the time to greet him on the wok, even having just been rescued herself. He'd watched her deal with the hybrid, Alice, whom he'd remembered as a small child, from when he worked down in The Rock. He noted how she treated Cole's new friends and companions, and this Gabrielle girl, with grace and respect. He'd watched her keep going when it was obvious that she was cold and wet and exhausted and grief stricken at the loss of her boy, and that she felt deathly ill. He'd noted her obvious love and respect for his sister. She was not a bad one, this President, and Danny began to understand just why it was that his sister had switched teams.

This was another thing these three had in common: they were all under, or were falling under, the spell of Linda Travis, a woman who possessed intelligence, wisdom, honesty, compassion, and vision in such full measures that she stood far above the crowd. Stan had been with her for years now, and would do anything for her. Gabrielle was clearly smitten, and felt honored to be included in the President's world. And Danny could feel the force of her personality, even as he tried to maintain his observer's objectivity. As they talked of their lives, and of their current situation, it became clear to them all that there was much more going on in the world than they'd known, which was funny, given that they'd all thought they'd known a great deal. They were not natural allies, after all. Gabrielle was a member of The Families. Danny worked for The Families as an analyst and security systems specialist. And Stan considered The Families to be his enemies. And yet chance, circumstance, and fate had thrown them all together, to sit in a hospital visitors' lounge with surprisingly good coffee, to share those parts of their stories they felt free to tell, to wonder together about lost boys and hybrid aliens and an alien flu bug, and to ponder what would come next. As the day brightened and the sun began to peek through the clouds, they found themselves content to just sit and relax for as long as they could.

All except the cat who, having at last had its fill of petting, slid down from Gabrielle's lap and headed out the door.

16.18

Nicky padded silently along the hospital corridor, glancing up at the nurse half-humans and doctor half-humans as he made his way past a long row of closed doors. While he'd experienced a moment of sadness when the big metal circle thing had come out of the sky to squash his man human, he found that, all in all, he liked these new humans more. The young woman human with the pouch on her back had long, slender fingers, and she knew just how to use them, which was no small matter. And the other woman human, the one Nicky had helped step into her second life, had spoken very kindly to him, and treated him with the respect he knew that all cats deserved. He hadn't seen that older woman human for a while now, but he knew her scent, and had seen which way she'd gone. Nicky thought he'd go pay her a visit.

One of the tall, strange, half-humans saw Nicky approach the doorway in which he was standing and nodded a greeting. Nicky stepped up to the man half-human and greeted him in response, rubbing the bottom of his chin against the half-human's leg. The man half-human knelt on one knee and put out his hand for Nicky to sniff. Nicky sniffed. The creature smelled odd, but it was not an unpleasant scent. Nicky noted the tiny differences in how the half-humans' skin looked, and the lack of those small hairs on their arms and legs and faces. He'd already figured out that their faces did not work the same as the humans' faces worked. But he decided that he could get used to them. This one, at least, had the sense not to just reach out and start patting his head, which so many humans, apparently born without brains, seemed to feel the need to do. That earned the half-humans points right there.

The man half-human made his mouth move up on the ends, similar to the way humans smiled. Nicky could tell that it was an intentional imitation, and did not take it personally. The man half-human stood. He quietly turned the humans' ridiculous door-opening device, then pushed the door inward a few inches. He looked down at Nicky and cocked his head, as if to encourage the cat to go through. Since Nicky, by scent alone, already knew that the older woman human he'd been looking for was inside, he did just that.

In the room, he found the older woman human, and that tall man human she often clung to, and two smaller women humans he had not yet seen before. The four of them were sitting together on one of those long chairs, and they seemed to be sleeping. There was a guardian globe that enclosed them, and another globe that surrounded a smaller man human who was sleeping on a bed. Nicky would never intentionally disturb a guardian globe, so he stepped in front of the four sleeping humans and sat down, just outside the globe's edge. He waited. After a time he decided to clean his front paws, which had no doubt gotten filthy during the walk down the corridor. He'd been cleaning himself for some time, his eyes closed in ecstasy, when one of the smaller women humans shouted. Nicky jerked back in surprise.

"Mihos!" the smallest woman human said. Her face had a much better smile on it than that half-human had managed to make. This time, Nicky took it personally.

16.19

It was time to meet. Decisions had to be made. Linda, her skin tones now healthy and robust, her body warm and full of life, put out the call. They'd gather in the hospital's larger Conference Room A in ten minutes: She, Cole, Stan, Mary, Danny, Sten, Gabrielle, and Marionette.

Eddie and Doobie, having returned to Augusta to report on the situation, would head right back to the coast with a contingent of hybrids, to rescue whomever they might now that the storm had passed. Doobie was intent on finding Annabelle. He leaned forward and kissed Marionette shyly before entering the wok. Eddie would shoot some footage. The hybrids had procured some professional-grade ENG gear from the military base. He was ecstatic.

The news from Boothbay Harbor, now filtering in to the networks and bouncing back out to the public, was grim: The U.S. President, Linda Travis, was missing and presumed dead. Helicopter footage of Squirrel Island put the period on the end of that sentence. It was a barren rock. For now, with Linda safely hidden away in Augusta, none of them could say otherwise.

Linda, dressed now in the jeans and sweatshirt one of the nurses had retrieved from the Presidential Home, sat at the table opposite the door, scribbling a few notes while waiting for the others to arrive. The agenda was short, but it felt like it would take forever to get through. There was the question of the vial of cure, and whether to put a stop to this Greensleeves as soon as they could, and whether they should start with Keeley. There was the question of the secret cabal, The Families, William, and what they were up to, and how they should respond, if at all. There was the question of what to make public, and how, and when, and whether it would serve them for Linda to be "dead" for a while longer. There was the question of the Middle Children's presence on Earth. And there was the question of Iain.

A few tears spilled onto the page as Linda wrote. She wiped them away with her sleeve. How could she sit in a meeting when what she wanted to do was scream in fury or hide in her bed and sob? She didn't think she could do it. But she knew she would find a way. People were dying. Other people were getting away with murder. Something had to be done. She was the someone who had to do it. Iain was lost. On his way to try to help *her*. She would find a way.

The time spent on Mars with William haunted her, a surly mob of words and images and feelings imprisoned in her mind, crowding into her awareness, calling out for her attention, muttering and groaning and pacing back and forth. What he'd done, and how he'd done it, still made no sense to her. On the one hand, he'd infuriated her, and left her unable to trust a thing he'd said. On the other hand, he'd sown her mind with doubts, leaving her unable to trust herself. He'd effectively taken the entire matter of how to respond to this species-decimating virus completely out of the realm of rational problem solving, leaving her with naught but her heart, her guts, her instincts, to rely on. And right now, with Iain gone, because she'd been stolen away, because she hadn't been there to save him, because William had kept her captive for so long, because he'd outright lied to her about how safe the kids were, all Linda's heart and gut felt were hatred for the man.

Linda gulped down a sob and took a couple of deep breaths. William's words again popped to mind. Those were the circumstances. Now she had to make her choices. And somewhere out there was a strange little man with seemed to think he already knew what she would choose. That infuriated her, but maybe he did know. The aliens know us intimately, he'd said. It was that which made them qualified to triage us. And she'd somehow been created for this role, this choosing. Maybe they knew her better than she knew herself.

There was no way out of this. She knew that much. No way out of deciding. No way out of making a decision that would trouble her for the rest of her days. No way out of the human race having to go through a great deal of pain, one way or the other. No way out of paying the consequences for the choices they'd made so far. But wasn't there a way that would be better than the rest? A choice she could make that would minimize the suffering and loss and heartbreak? There had to be. It was just a matter of finding it, and then taking that path. That was why Linda had called this meeting: To gather her trusted friends, and a few new stakeholders, and see if, together, they could find or hash out or create a better wisdom than Linda could find on her own. That was her hope.

Linda sighed and put down her pen. A soft knock sounded at the door. The others were arriving. She did not have to do this alone.

16.20

The makeshift infectious disease ward they'd set up in Boothbay Harbor had been flattened and washed out to sea by the storm that the World Meteorological Organization had dubbed "Hurricane Alpha." The Thieving Seagull Cafe had fallen into the harbor, with only one corner of the deck rising at an awkward angle above the surface of the water. The docks and marina were gone, leaving timbers and boats and miles of rope and cable in a jangled, jumbled mess pushed up against the shore. Sten and Eddie's old diesel Mercedes had been lifted up and deposited far down Water Street, where it now lay upside down, its trunk end raised up on the granite steps of what used to be the public library. The back up video gear was nowhere to be found.

They saw no sign of Ken and Celia. No sign of Andrew and Macy. No sign of Simon and Keith. No sign of Gordon, who'd been injured on Squirrel Island. No sign of the reporter, Steve Waymax. Yet against all hope and probability, they found Annabelle. After seeing Cole and his crew off on their last doomed attempt to reach Squirrel Island, she'd hopped into Ken's beat up Caravan and driven north, back through Boothbay Harbor and up the hill to the Country Club, where she'd once been a member. There she hid from the storm in the club's old fallout shelter, which had been converted for food storage years before. It was the highest and most secure spot she could think of in the urgency of the storm, and though trees had been uprooted and buildings flattened right above her, she'd remained safe and warm and unharmed. It was Doobie who thought to check there, remembering the supply run they'd made months before at Annabelle's urging. When he asked the hybrids to take them there, they found the old woman sitting on an overturned pickle bucket, her face to the sun, munching a handful of potato chips. She looked up and waved, as if the arrival of an alien wok was the most normal thing in the world.

"I ain't no fool," Annabelle said when Doobie expressed his joy and surprise at finding her. "Gonna take more than a hurricane to take me out." She eyed the hybrids suspiciously but kept her mouth shut for the time being. The world had grown far too weird for her to be choosey about her saviors. She looked at Doobie and Eddie and held out her bag. "You guys want a chip?" she asked.

16.21

The easy items Linda dispensed with first. She told them of the agreement she'd made with Alice, and asked whether there was anything they needed to discuss or decide immediately in regard to the Middle Children. As Alice seemed content to accept Linda at her word, they agreed to table the matter while they dealt with more pressing issues. They quickly agreed that Linda's rescue should remain a secret, and to let news of her death provide a cover for them. Sten argued that the secret cabal would have no reason to come after, or defend against, somebody they presumed to be dead. Linda noted that they might easily determine otherwise by sending a spy in the Astral realm. Gabrielle reminded them that the Middle Children had promised to shield her from such things.

It was then that Linda shared her story, catching them all up on what had transpired since her abduction from the Presidential Home almost two weeks before. She described waking up in the "lobster tank" on Mars. She told them of her trips around Mars, to Phobos, and out to the Herschel Colony. She summarized, as best she could, her long conversation with the Fisherman. And she told them of the choice he'd put to her, and the lies he had told her, and how the virus had already been released. Then she motioned to Gabrielle, who unzipped her backpack and pulled out a smaller purse, and from that a small brown glass vial, which she placed on the conference table before her.

"According to William," said Linda, "this vial contains an easily re-producible cure for Greensleeves." The gathered participants stared at the vial for a long moment without saying a word. "The question is," she continued at last, "what do we do with it?"

Stan was appalled at the notion that there was any question at all. Of course they should test it, analyze it, reproduce it, and distribute it as quickly as was possible. Anything less than that was beyond their wisdom, he said, his face stern. There was no question.

Cole, too, appeared taken aback. He looked at Marionette, the sole representative of the Church of the Stranger, then down at his hands, as if he hoped some answer could be found in his powers of light. When Linda asked him what he was thinking, he told them all what Annabelle had told him, sharing parts of his journey to the coast and his meetings with the Church of the Stranger, of the prophecies seemingly come true, and of the prediction, in *The Book of the Stranger.* Stumbling on the words, he looked to Marionette, who quoted from the book. "*He comes to stop his greatest love from destroying the human race*," she intoned, looking directly at Linda. Cole sighed deeply, shaking his head.

Linda jerked back as if slapped. Stan snorted his disgust. "What a load of horse shit,"' he said, his voice a deep, warning growl. Gabrielle nodded, as though a piece had fallen into place for her. Linda reached out and took Cole's hand and held it without looking at him, refusing to let this quote, and this entire situation, pull them apart. Cole squeezed her hand in return. It was Gabrielle who broke the silence.

"I, too, was sent to stop you," she said timidly, looking at Linda. "At least I thought so. It was... a vision. I was given a vision. By Zach-arael... the alien being who taught me and helped me. He gave me the vision. I could see it. I was there, in that dark hallway under your cabin on Squirrel Island. Standing before you. Reaching out to take something from you. I thought I was supposed to stop you from do-ing something. And then I didn't know any more. The vision was... incomplete." She looked around the room. "There wasn't enough information. To tell me what exactly I was supposed to do."

"And that's just what we have here," said Stendahl, speaking for the first time. He looked around the room. "I mean. Linda's bring-ing a valid question here, I think." He glanced at Stan, then back to Linda. "What to do with this vial. Whether to stop this virus or let it play out. Which will be better for the Earth? Which will be better for humans? Or... which choice will 'destroy the human race?'" He put his hands palm down on the table. "I say we don't know," he concluded. Stan rolled his eyes.

Linda agreed. "Yes," she said with a weary sigh. "As much as I hate to say it, as much as I just want to agree with Stan, I have to admit the truth of what Stendahl is speaking." She turned to Cole. "But if this *Book* is true, then there's clearly a choice I can make that will be worse, and you're supposed to stop me from making that choice."

"But it's just a goddamned Bible prophecy!" said Stan, noisily sliding his chair back from the table. He scanned the room, his eyes fierce, as if daring somebody to oppose him.

Linda nodded. "I hear you, Stan," she said to her old comrade. "You really want to stop the dying. And you don't want to trust this decision to a prophecy." She smiled warmly. "But we have to be free to consider this from every possible angle, Stan. Okay? And your passion and anger won't serve us here. They'll just shut us down. So I need you to hold onto those things. We know they are there and we won't forget them. But I also need you to make some room for others to bring their wisdom to the table as well. That's why I called them here. That's why I called *you* here. I need to hear from you all." Stan stared at Linda, his face a dark frown. He shrugged his shoulders but didn't say anything more.

Cole looked at Stan and smiled as well. "The coloring book. The bullet I caught. The light from my hands and the tunnel I created to save us from drowning. The cover on *The Book of the Stranger*." He listed the strange things they'd seen in their journey together. "I mean... I was as doubtful as you are, Stan. But you've got to admit that some weird shit has happened. You know? So I'm inclined to think that there's something to this prophecy thing. Even if we don't know what it means."

"And that's just it," said Stendahl. "Prophecy or no, the question of what to do with that vial remains. And we don't even know if it works yet, or what it is. This William guy could have been lying again. Maybe it's poison in there."

"I don't know if what's in that vial is a vaccine or a cure or what, but if it's what they gave us troops," spoke up Danny, "then it didn't kill us, and seemed to be working. None of us on Squirrel Island got sick, anyways."

"It is what William said it is," said Mary, stepping into the conversation for the first time.

Linda smiled her encouragement. "You can see that?" she asked.

Mary nodded. "I can, Mrs. President," she said, using Linda's title as a means of confirming her authority here, and Mary's commitment to serving her. "It has its own field. And I have seen into Greensleeves, and have told the doctors what I have seen." Mary explained to them all what she had learned about the virus, how it had been inserted into the human genome, how it is not particularly contagious, how it might have been triggered into activity, and the factors which affect its expression and virulence. "I'm beginning to think that there is more than one form of Greensleeves out there. Or that there is more than one trigger." She examined her companions. "Or maybe the onset time is just highly variable. Because none of us have gotten sick so far. And the doctors say that as of today only ten to fifteen percent of the population has taken ill." She looked at Cole, then Linda, then Stan, taking a moment to inspect their fields. "But it's in us all, in varying amounts. I can see it. It's in us. Waiting to be triggered."

Linda smiled grimly. "Thank you, Mary," she said. "Of course my first impulse is to give a dose to Keeley. To see it in action. To make sure it works. And to save Keeley." She inhaled deeply. "If you're sure that what's in this vial will work, I think we should do that right now."

Mary struggled to keep her tears at bay. She bowed her head. "Yes... please," she said. "I can see its field. It will work. And Keeley may die otherwise."

"Will that leave enough for the scientists to reproduce?" asked Danny, reaching out to take his sister's hand.

"I think so," said Mary, wiping away her tears. She glanced at the vial, then at Linda. "Can I...?" she asked. Linda nodded. Mary took the vial and, cradling it in her hands, left the room to find the doctors.

"About goddamned time," muttered Stan. Linda looked at Stan and nodded her agreement.

With the vial gone, the tone of the conversation changed. Cole expressed his deep anger with, and deep distrust of, this Fisherman, recalling that first phone call years ago. "I mean... Jesus, sweetie. They kidnap you. Take you away from me and the kids. Hold you captive. Unleash a deadly virus. Almost kill me when I try to rescue you. And Iain..." His face grew more livid as he spoke and he had to stop. It was clear he was holding back both tears and screams of frustration. He sat looking at Linda, his lower lip trembling, his breath harsh and hurried. "I mean... these guys are evil." He looked around the room, then back to his wife. "I say we do whatever we can to stop them. That includes stopping their goddamned virus."

The rest of them sat in silence for a few moments. Then Stendahl cleared his throat. "I find it notable, Mrs. President," he said, "that of the eight people in this meeting, four of us have worked for the people known as 'The Families.' I don't think any of us knew even a fraction of what they were up to. I know that much of what you've told us comes as a complete surprise to me. But I think that all four of us..." He looked at Danny and Gabrielle. "... and correct me if I'm wrong, folks... but all four of us, when we learned more about what they were up to, and when given the chance, decided to switch teams and work with you. Which speaks, I think, to a general sense that The Families' methods and goals are worthy of our opposition."

Danny nodded. "I figured you were sick and were being treated on Squirrel Island, Mrs. President," he said, speaking slowly and deliberately as he sorted out what he felt he could say out loud from what he wanted to keep to himself. "Just like they told us. Though I will admit that there was something weird about the whole thing. But when we found you on that landing pad and you didn't look at all like you had on the TV, and when Mary showed up in that wok and invited me to come along, something about it just felt right." He glanced at Sten. "So, yeah. After hearing what the President has been through, I'm finding myself rather unhappy with my employer's methods." He turned back to Linda. "I'm open to the possibility that they need to be stopped as well."

"But they're not evil," said Gabrielle.

The others turned to look at the girl, who'd been silent for some time.

Gabrielle shrugged. "If you'd asked me a week ago, I'd have told you my father was a horrible monster, and that I hated him." She turned to Linda. "But now I'm not so sure, you know? After hearing your story, and after my experiences with Zacharael, I'm starting to think that maybe there's something to what William said. About the wisdom of reducing the human population as quickly and painlessly as we can. So that the rest of the life on Earth has a better chance." She looked from one person to another, stopping at Stan. "I'm not sure that that's a crazy or evil idea. I'm not." She returned her attention to Linda. "And I'm not going anywhere, Mrs. President. I've chosen to stay on Earth. And I have loved ones here, too." She inhaled deeply and said no more.

Linda sighed. "So it feels like we have to tease apart two different questions," she said. "First, do we put a stop to this virus? And, second, do we try to put a stop to The Families? Recognizing that what we think about The Families and their goals and methods may or may not shape our thinking about the virus and the cure."

"I don't see why we should separate those two things," said Stan.

"Because whether we do or don't like The Families and their goals and methods," said Gabrielle, her voice growing stronger as she found the courage she needed to counter this older, powerful man, "the question remains: will this virus prove to be good for the living Earth or not?"

"Or should Cole stop the President from *not* using the cure, as the *Book* seems to imply," added Marionette, "before she destroys the human race?"

The door opened. Mary stepped in, relief and hope on her face. "We've administered a small dose of the substance in the vial," she said as she took her seat. She opened her hand to show that the rest of the cure was safely in her possession. "Now it's a matter of waiting." She looked around the room. "So what did I miss?" she asked.

16.22

The little black cat with the white star on its chest had fallen asleep on the love seat, nestled between Grace and Emily. Grace lightly stroked the cat's back. Emily laid her hand on the cat's head. Emily had shared with her sister what Mihos had told her in the Murk, about how cats live double lives in two realms, how in the physical realm he was known as Nicky, and how both parts of him had come together in that underground room to give their mother another life. So they knew it was Nicky who lay between them. But they also knew it was Mihos. And it was the latter name that they had decided to call him: Mihos, the Protector of the Innocent.

When the family had regained its footing, the girls had asked about Ness, and only then had Cole and Linda remembered how they'd left their old cook and confidant in the hands of the Middle Children. They'd left the room, 'Iain's room' they called it now, and headed, as a family, down to the main nurses' station, to inquire about Ness's whereabouts. As they neared the desk in the front lobby, they'd found the old woman, walking toward them. When Ness saw who it was, she'd run toward them with a grin.

Now she sat across from the girls, dressed in dry clothes, lost in her thoughts, her small body curled up in the wooden chair near the window. It was not the Ness who had walked around like a zombie while Alice used her body, though the girls had not met that Ness. And it was not the Ness who'd gone into some sort of trance and built a strange construct out of kitchen utensils and wires and bits of trash and then turned it into a glowing protective shield over the kids' sleeping bodies, though the girls had not met that Ness either. This Ness was the Ness they had known for the past three years, the smart, lively, little old woman who cooked tasty meals for them and hugged them when they were scared and played Parcheesi with them at night when their parents were away. This Ness was the Ness they'd ditched in the hospital in order to go off on their adventure. This Ness was the Ness that was one of their fiercest advocates and watchdogs. And this Ness had not met those other Nesses either, and was confused and befuddled and very sad, to learn how much had passed without her knowing, and to hear of lost Iain. But she was glad to find the girls back, and Linda too. "I just can't conceive of it all," this Ness said. The girls knew what she meant.

Ness had been about to tell the girls her story, but didn't know where to begin. If what Alice had said was to be believed, the young hybrid leader, impossibly older than she should be, and existing bodily far away from the Earth, had projected her consciousness, her spirit, into Ness's body. She'd "walked in," as the saying went, but only partially, leaving a good portion of the original Ness personality in place to function in the world, with Alice steering and guiding her from behind the scenes, and taking over completely when she needed to. Ness wasn't quite sure how to feel about that. It wasn't like Alice had asked her permission.

What surprised Ness the most was that her own full memory had now returned. Her childhood. Her family. Her marriages to Robert, and then Dave. Her daughter with Dave, named Roberta, who'd gone to work for the government. Her life in Tacoma. Her job as a teacher and then a school principal. And then the economic upheavals that had put an end to all of that. It must have been right about that time that Alice had begun to possess her, if "possess" was the right word. She and Dave had lost everything, and were living on the street. Dave had begun drinking heavily. Then one day, without a word or hint, he'd killed himself. Jumped off the Tacoma Narrows Bridge, leaving Ness alone and in shock. Then Ness had begun drinking.

Why Alice had chosen her of all people Ness didn't know. It may have been that Ness, as a result of all the losses she'd suffered, was simply wide open. Whatever the reason, when Alice walked in, much of Ness had walked out, or simply gone to sleep, glad for the respite from a life of lonely anguish. Her memories fragmented. Her own will receded. Her thoughts turned strangely eastward. And she began to walk, starting the long, hard journey that brought her, eventually, to that exit ramp in Augusta, Maine.

What it was all *for*, Ness didn't really understand. Just so Alice could keep an eye on Linda and her family? So she could come back and live with the kids, who may be the only "friends" Alice has ever had? So that Alice could coordinate these Middle Children to take over Augusta and make a plea for belonging on the Earth? All of the above? Or something else entirely? Ness shrugged with uncertainty. Maybe one day these questions would be answered. But not right now. If she kept chewing on those bones, they'd drive her to distraction.

What "right now" demanded was that she be present with these kids, with Linda and Cole, with Mary and Keeley, and with the complex situations that swirled around them. And she had to do that while integrating a new set of old memories back into her body. She knew that not far below the surface there pulsed inside a huge and heavy knot of grief over the loss of her husband. At some point, she would have to take that knot out and start untangling it. But that was for later.

Alice was gone now. There wasn't a trace of the girl in Ness's body or soul, from what she could tell. Why should there be? Alice was here in the flesh herself, from what Ness had been told. While on balance she was glad that Alice had left the building, Ness knew that, in a way, Alice's possession had been a kindness. Ness had needed that hiding time, that rest from her consciousness and memories, that opportunity to just back away from the pain and loss and let some time pass while somebody else drove the bus. But the second kindness was this: Alice had brought Ness to Linda and her family, for which the old woman would be forever grateful. While she may have been mostly absent these last years, the bonds of love that had formed between herself and these children and their parents were strong and real. And they were hers, those bonds, not Alice's. In her strange way, Alice had saved ol' Ness. Maybe it was okay that she hadn't asked for permission.

Ness roused herself from her reverie, looked across to Iain's body, and cleared her throat to speak, continuing the story she'd already begun. "I remember they found you in that MRI machine," she said. "Brought you here. And I remember Mary putting me in charge of watching over you." She blinked her eyes in confusion. "But it gets really foggy after that. Like a dream. Something about dancing and carrots and... and... I was building, like, a dome or something." She shook her head in confusion. "And then I woke up in my bed and there was nobody around. And I got a ride from some soldiers." She leaned forward and lowered her voice. "And who are those guys anyways?" she asked, gesturing toward the door with her head. "Alice's people, I guess, right? The hybrids?"

Emily shook her head. She didn't know much either.

Ness insisted that the girls tell her their story, and sat listening with great interest as they described how they'd gotten into the Astral realm, how they met Mihos, and how they'd attempted to get through the Murk to their mother. "It was that thing about the mole," said Emily, describing how it had switched sides on her mother's face, and how they'd known that something was fishy. "That's what started it all."

"And Iain?" Ness asked, glancing furtively at the boy's body, wanting to know and not wanting to know.

Emily told Ness how Iain had fallen into the sea of burning coals. How Dennis had tried to save him. Grace kept her eyes on the cat and let more tears drop silently to her jeans. But she didn't add to the telling, and she didn't look up. She couldn't face them. Going into the Astral had been her idea.

Ness came over and squeezed in beside the youngest of Cole's children and leaned her head against Grace's head and reached out to put a hand on Emily's shoulder. Ness moaned softly and Grace started to shudder and Emily sniffed and the three of them cried together for as long as they needed to cry. Mihos, understanding his role in the matter, stayed right where he was and purred.

16.23

William had been right: He'd opened up a choice for Linda that would not have been available to her otherwise. Before their long conversation, she would not have hesitated to use the contents of that vial to stop the Greensleeves virus. The decision would have been automatic and obvious. Now, the choice was anything but. She watched as her friends and advisors spoke their wisdom into the circle, arguing first one side then another. But she knew that this choice could never rest on arguments and reasons. It would have to come from somewhere else.

In the end, she thanked them all, then told them what she thought they should do. "As much as I hate to say it, I think we should table this decision for now, but go ahead and act as if we're going to use the vial. Get it to some labs. Get its contents analyzed and put the cure into production. Get ready to distribute it. And in the meantime, continue to search our hearts and guts and souls for the best response." She looked around the room. Stan, still scowling, nodded his agreement. Marionette raised her uncovered eyebrow, her face a map of confusion. Gabrielle bowed her head slightly, a sign of respect. Sten and Danny pushed their chairs back from the table, looking for distance. Cole reached out and took Linda's hand. Mary closed her eyes. There was nothing much more to say on the matter. It was a step worth taking. It would buy them some time to process things further. And it created an opening for new information to arrive, should some of the other forces in play have anything to add. It was Sten who pointed out the downside of doing what Linda suggested. "The more people know about that vial," he warned, "the harder it will become to not use it. And should you choose *not* to use it, the greater the chance that the world will know that."

Linda nodded, but stood her ground. "I think I'm going to go down in history as a monster either way, Sten," she said, smiling sadly. But then she glanced at Cole's concerned, loving face, and added. "But. Yes. You're right. Start with one lab. One scientist. Find somebody these Middle Children know and trust. Maybe a hybrid scientist who could do the work, if there is one. Get it analyzed. Find a single place to produce it without them knowing what it is." She looked at Stan. "Will you make that happen for me, Stan?" she asked.

Stan nodded.

Linda inhaled deeply, then turned to Cole. "Now we have to talk about Iain," she said.

They talked about Iain. What the kids had done and how they had done it and what had transpired. They spoke about the Murk.

Danny explained how the Murk had been installed on the island, how the task had been completed by outside contractors. He knew it guarded the island at the Astral level, just as travelers and protectors had been used for decades by The People, to protect important places and individuals. He knew very little about what a Murk was or how it worked, but thought he knew whom he might ask back at BlackBay Services. Mary related how she'd seen it from a distance, an immense black cloud in the Astral, and how it must block the patterns and signals of anybody trapped inside. Stan reminded Linda of how Alice had promised the help of the hybrids.

It was clearly the most painful item on their agenda, and Linda let her tears flow down her cheeks without wiping them away. Cole sat and watched, silent and sullen, his face a reddened mask of anger. When Linda asked if he had anything to add, all he could say was "I don't know what I was thinking, leaving like I did." Then he shook his head. He had nothing else to say. Iain was gone without a trace, lost in a place Cole could barely begin to comprehend. Cole had not been there to stop him.

Mary offered to head up the party that would travel into the Astral to go look for the boy, but Linda vetoed that. "We need you here, Mary," she said. "The girls need you. I need you. Keeley needs you."

"But doesn't Iain need me?" asked Mary.

"We're going to look for him, Mary," said Linda, nodding her assurance. She gestured toward at Stan. "We're going to get the hybrids' help." She squeezed Cole's hand. "And we're going to confront Alice with demands of our own." She looked at Danny. "We've got Danny to help us from the insider perspective. Somebody at BlackBay must know what a Murk is and how it works and how you defeat it." She turned to Gabrielle. "And we're going to see if we can get in touch with this Zacharael character and demand his help as well." She returned her attention to Mary. "We need you here, Mary. Okay? I know you love Iain. And I suspect that you feel guilty about his being lost. And I know you'd give your life for him. For me. For Cole. For the girls. I know that, my dear. But I need you here. Okay? I need you here to watch over and protect the girls." She looked around the room, settling on Cole and smiling gently, then turning her attention back to Mary. "I need you to watch the girls because I have to leave again." She reached out and took Cole's hand. "And I need Cole to come with me."

Stan sat forward in his chair. "What are you talking about, Mrs. President?" he asked.

Linda met Stan's gaze and nodded. "I need you here as well, Stan," she said. "Because somewhere out there is a man named William, and a group of people who think they can just burn the planet down and then leave." She looked at Cole. "We're going to go find him. We're going to find him and stop him and bring him to justice. And we're going to put a stop to their plans to escape." She caught the eye of everyone in the room. "If we're going down, then they're going to go down with us," she said, her voice low and sharp. "They don't get to run away from the consequences of their choices any more than we do."

The others there sat for a while in stunned, surprised silence, nodding their agreement or shaking their heads full of doubt. It was Marionette, her one eye bright and fierce, who broke the silence. "So how will you find him?" she asked.

Linda turned to Marionette and smiled. "He gave me a clue, I think," she said. "I just have to figure out what it means."

"What was the clue?" asked Marionette.

"*Urbem Orsus*," said Linda.

"Oh!" said Danny, raising his hand in excitement. "I think I know what that is."

16.24

Doobie and Eddie pushed through the hospital's front doors, escorting Annabelle between them. They'd rescued three other survivors in Boothbay Harbor: a woman and her two children who'd survived in a storm cellar in one of the houses on the hill overlooking the water. They'd also found a dog, a young beagle pup that they'd found standing on top of a taxi, barking at them. The newcomers were cold and wet and in shock, and the hybrids had taken them around to the emergency entrance, the puppy included.

They found Marionette in the visitors' lounge and Doobie greeted her with a hug and another peck of a kiss, this one a bit longer. Annabelle smiled. "Bout time you guys hooked up," she said with a wink. Eddie went off to find Sten, but the three Church members sat together in the lounge's corner and heard each other's stories. The two youngsters caught Annabelle up on everything that had transpired since they'd last seen each other: the fateful last voyage of *The*

Pokey Joker, Cole's tunnel of light, the confrontation and rescue on Squirrel Island. Marionette shook her head at Doobie's updates on the destruction he'd seen in the Boothbay area, and was surprised to hear how quickly the storm had blown itself out. Together they bowed their heads and said a prayer for their compatriots, those who had not yet been found. Annabelle closed her eyes and found some wise words of farewell and peace and Godspeed. They had no idea whether other survivors would be rescued in the hours and days ahead. Federal troops were already moving in to continue the search and rescue, but the three of them held little hope that any of their colleagues would be found.

Marionette told Doobie and Annabelle of the meeting that had just ended. Doobie listened attentively as Marionette spoke of the decisions they'd made and the ones they'd had to table. Annabelle, relishing the cup of coffee Marionette had brought her, asked for more details. She nodded when she heard of The Families' plans to leave Earth, as if she'd known that already. She expressed her sorrow that Cole's boy had been lost. But she was particularly interested in the discussion about the vial and the cure, and listened intently as Marionette recounted their discussion of the prophecy found in *The Book of the Stranger*, and the difficulty of knowing just how it applied.

The old woman agreed that it was quite a quandary, then added another. "The problem," she said, "is that you were all operating from the assumption that the action the Stranger has to stop his love from taking has to do with that vial." She looked at Doobie, then back and Marionette. "But maybe that's not it at all, my dears," she said. "Maybe he needs to keep her from stopping The Families from leaving."

"But..." said Marionette, shaking her head.

Annabelle raised a hand to stop the younger woman. "I hate to say it, sweetie, but maybe it's their leaving that prevents the complete destruction of the human race."

16.25

Ted picked up a card. His eyes grew wide in disbelief. Once again he had to go down the Rabbit Hole. He looked up at Carl. "So..." he said. "You got any ideas for how we get out of this place?" He gestured with his hands to indicate the room they were in.

Carl shrugged. "Dunno," he said. "I assume we got the rubix technology from the Life. Did they ever tell us where the dang things sent people? Or does a rubix just kill its victims? Did anybody in The People ever know?"

Ted shook his head. "They were just damned useful, dude," he said. "We always figured they were some sort of tamed black hole. Didn't want to look a gift cube in the abyss, if you know what I mean. In the end, I don't think anybody ever cared where the rubix sent people. We just cared that they were gone."

"Well, now that we've gone through one, it looks like we're beginning to care," said Carl.

"Hard to believe the Life would invent a technology that sent people to small rooms with tables and chairs and board games," said Ted.

Carl nodded. "Sure," he said. "That makes sense. So likely what a rubix does is just kill the person, and this is where people go when they die."

"If this is where people go when they die," said Ted, looking around the room, "shouldn't it be more crowded?"

Carl grinned. "Maybe we all get our own personal afterlife, Ted," he said. "Maybe you and I created this place together."

Ted chuckled. "Our own personal hell?" he asked.

"Just a den, maybe. A place to hang out for a while before moving on."

"So you think we'll get to move on?" asked Ted.

"I hope so," said Carl, looking down at the game. "Cuz this is one boring-ass game."

Chapter Ⱦ Seventeen

17.1

Zacharael hovered above the surface of the Earth, monitoring events in the physical bands, the Astral, and beyond. The Interdict, put into place by those whom he knew as the Inter-Life, did not inhibit him in any way. It had never been intended to bind his people, and while most of the Elders had honored the suggestion, Zacharael had not. The Inter-Life had long since demonstrated their capacity for making mistakes, and the stakes now were much too high for Zacharael to remain on the sidelines. The spirit of the Interdict did shape his actions, for he knew the utmost necessity of choice. But Zacharael was not above the occasional push or pull, and trusted his ability to balance influence with freedom. He served the Beloved above all else. He would not abandon her now. Not if he could choose otherwise.

Still, he was not the only player in motion, and there would be decisions made by others that could overwhelm any efforts he might make. For that reason, he'd done his best to mark the potential safe zones his forward viewing had revealed. Already the symbols and signals were doing their work, as thousands slowly made their inexplicable journeys around the globe, in search of something for which they had no words or reasons. The markers selected only for sensitivity and openness, but that would have to suffice. More than that would have overstepped the Primary, and as rebellious as his actions might appear to others, Zacharael was unwilling to go that far. Whether that was wise or cowardly he could not say.

It could yet turn out that none of that would matter. The girl, Gabrielle, still had degrees of freedom open to her, and she continued to surprise him. And the American President might yet make the better choice. The Cogency's restraint had proven wise, in Zacharael's opinion. And he suspected that The Sages would abide by the Cogency's wisdom for the time being. Zacharael might still have room in which to advance his vision. The boulder would not fall until it was pushed over the edge.

As a small black ball, Zacharael began to accelerate around the planet, sensing the progress of the human disease vector, watching the small but significant number of human souls now beginning to move toward the beacon of his latest marker, and focusing in on those few key players chosen by fate, luck, and intention to represent the human species at this time of great choice. In the background, the cries of the suffering and dying continued, a tragic music he might ignore for a time but could never tune out entirely. He wondered if there was something broken inside of him that left him so vulnerable to the Beloved's painful song. His Brothers and Sisters seemed much more immune to the experience than he. He decided that it did not matter. Broken or not, he was glad to be as he was, and could imagine no other way. The pain called him to service. The service gave him meaning. Meaning gave him both connection and novelty. It all added up to Life. Zacharael was glad to be alive. After so very long, he was still grateful for it.

Even with all the pain.

17.2

To be honest, Linda felt relieved by the fact that the Middle Children had refused her request for one of their ships. A wok would have taken them to their destination in an instant, whereas a more conventional travel plan would give her time, and Linda desperately needed some time. She needed to think. She needed to rest. She needed to plan. She needed to rant and sob and scream. And she needed to find her way back into her relationship with Cole. Her husband had been through his own great changes in the time they were apart, his own trauma, his own awakening, and it seemed that he, like Linda, was now something more than he'd been before.

Who were they now? And who were they together? And how could they act as a team, as a partnership, to meet the challenges before them? Linda needed time, and she was glad to have it.

The hybrids' reasoning made sense to her. In their quest for autonomy, and their desire to share the Earth with humans as partners, they were glad to help whenever they could. But in this particular endeavor, in Linda's confrontation with the secret cabal, their loyalties and responsibilities felt muddled and mixed. There was too much crossover between the hidden layers of human control and the goals and motivations of the aliens. Too much history. Too much that the hybrids did not completely understand. And the Life were still deeply involved.

As the Middle Children, they were declaring themselves a third party, a new race, and felt bound to their own understanding of the Prime Directive. Linda's fight with William and The Families felt like a fight between their parents, and they were loath to get more directly involved. Linda sensed that she could plead with Alice, and appeal to the girl's connection with her daughters, and that Alice might grudgingly agree to provide more assistance. But Linda did not wish to do that. There was something exceedingly delicate about this new relationship between humans and hybrids, and her gut told her that there was some vast and glorious potential to be found in that alliance, should they manage to create it. She did not want to jeopardize that. Alice had a ferocity to her that Linda was hesitant to provoke.

And there was no real need to do so. There were other ways to travel. She was still the U.S. President. She had plenty of friends and connections. She had an entire military machine at her disposal, should she decide to access it. The refusal of the Middle Children would not stop her. It would only slow her down. And she needed to be slowed down.

The first priority was Emily, Grace, and Iain. Feeling like he was abandoning his children once again for his wife's needs, Cole would not agree to accompany Linda anywhere until he was absolutely convinced that his kids would be safe and well-cared for. But safety was difficult to guarantee in a world in which secret elite forces acted with impunity, in which enigmatic aliens flitted about the sky, and in which psychic spies could attack and control through levels beyond the physical.

In the end, it was agreed that Emily, Grace, and Iain's body would be taken into hiding while Cole and Linda were away. In an undisclosed location somewhere in Augusta, the hybrids constructed, in a matter of hours, a nullspace apartment large enough for the kids, along with Ness and Mary, to live comfortably for a few days. Using wok technology, the apartment would function as a sort of giant Faraday cage, blocking any and all types of psychic or astral interference, as well as providing complete protection in the physical. Nullspaces, which the Middle Children considered to be as "alive" as their woks, could withstand even direct nuclear detonations without taking any damage, and could dock with any wok that had the proper pattern. This latter feature was important, as Mary was frantic at the thought that she might not be able to check in on Keeley, whose condition, though still critical, had improved slightly.

Even with these measures in place, Cole was unwilling to leave without adding his own finishing touch. Before departing, he would use his newfound powers to create and maintain a protective field of light around the kids. He'd thought to imagine it into existence around the nullspace, but the hybrids were adamant that such a field would only draw attention, and agreed to provide him the patterning he would need to imagine the protective field *inside* the nullspace. That would provide another layer of protection, it would give Cole a sense of connection with his children, and it might serve as an alarm system, should some unforeseen mishap occur.

The search for Iain was also put into motion. Danny would work in the physical bands to see what he could learn about Murks from his employers and colleagues. Alice, certain that the Murk was actually a living creature from a parallel physical reality, would contact something she called the Cogency, to see what else might be learned about them. A contingent of hybrids were organizing an Astral-band search party in jumptime, in order to see if they could get a lead on the boy's whereabouts along the time axis. And then there was Zacharael, whom Gabrielle would attempt to contact, something she had never before initiated. Should these efforts not prove successful, Cole promised that, upon his return, he would find a way to get into the Astral level himself and join the search. Iain would not be left behind, he said flatly. Nobody would argue with him.

With the kids made as safe as they could be, they turned to other matters. Stan would oversee, with great discretion and secrecy, the analysis, formulation, and production of the contents of William's little glass vial. Alice had quickly identified and contacted a high-level hybrid scientist working at the CDC who had the knowledge and equipment necessary for the job, and who could be reassigned without drawing attention. The Middle Children were willing to help with analysis and formulation, but decided that production and distribution, like the loaning of a wok, would involve them too directly in matters they judged to be beyond them. Stan felt confident that he could source the production himself. If all went well, he said, they would have the Greensleeves cure coming off the line before Cole and Linda returned. That was Stan's hope, anyways, and he promised to do everything he could to make it so.

The rest of Stan's attention would go to matters of administration. So many key players had gone missing. And the hybrids had invaded Augusta. It was time to grab the spinning wheel and regain control of the ship of state, especially with Linda Travis declared lost and presumed dead from Hurricane Alpha. Stan Walsh was just the man for that job.

And he would have Stendahl Banks and his trusty sidekick and cameraman, Eddie, to help with that. There were news stories to track and cover stories to create and reports to file. The international environmental summit was in a shambles. The Vice President had gone missing while they'd all converged on Squirrel Island, leaving the very confused Speaker of the House, Fort Simpson, to assume the duties of President from his office in Kenosha, Wisconsin. There were riots in half a dozen Federal shelters around the country. The heat wave continued, exacerbating the long drought and forcing more water rationing. The alien flu continued to spread around the globe, resulting in all manner of reactions: fear, scapegoating, isolation, preparation, and quarantine. And another of those strange crop symbols had appeared, this one just north of Augusta. Clearly, this was a news reporter's dream come true. Sten and Eddie would be busier than ever.

Having put things into motion as much as they could, Cole and Linda turned their attention to the journey before them. What Danny knew about *Urbem Orsus*, the City of Beginnings - based solely on hushed whispers of rumor, he admitted, but widely believed to be true - was that it was a vast, underground structure built beneath the Chernobyl Exclusion Zone in Ukraine. It served, supposedly, as the gathering place and launching pad for what The Families referred to as the "Giant Leap," the secret, breakaway culture's planned attempt to leave the Earth and venture out to the stars. How they might get near the place, let alone down into it, Linda had no idea. How they would find and confront William and his cronies she could not foresee. All she knew was that she must, and that she'd figure it out as she went along.

Stan thought the journey was preposterous, reckless, and unnecessary, and he said so. He advised Cole and Linda to stay the hell home, take care of their damned kids, and let him deal with those bastards. But Linda would not be persuaded. The question of the Greensleeves cure was too intimately connected to the question of these Families. She had to know what was real and true, and could not do that with her rational mind. She had to see The Families on *her* terms. Know them. Experience them. Feel them. She had to confront William in *her* realm. Eye to eye in *her* world. It was the only way. She didn't know why, but she knew that. This had been put on her. This was her burden. She had been made for this. Created. Guided. Trained. Chosen. And she would not be dissuaded.

Linda had not thought beyond the idea that she and Cole would go together. She would not be separated from him again. Her need was too great. But Annabelle quickly disabused her of the notion that they would go alone. When the two women first met, there in the hospital corridor, it became quickly apparent to all who observed them that Linda and Annabelle were a match for each other in terms of stubbornness. And it was clear that Annabelle was suspicious of Linda and protective of Cole. As the Wayfaring Stranger, Cole was, in her eye, the key to this whole affair, and she and her Church were charged to serve and protect him, and would not be prevented from carrying out their responsibilities. Annabelle, Doobie, and Marionette would accompany them on this adventure. Linda would have to physically restrain them if she insisted otherwise. That's all there was to it.

It was then that Gabrielle stepped forward to declare that she, too, would be going, as she was the only one amongst them who had an actual claim to be there. Her father was no doubt already in *Urbem Orsus*. Her presence might be the key to their admittance.

Cole and Linda stood with their backs to the concrete block wall of MaineCentral's front lobby, with Annabelle, Doobie, and Marionette lined up in front of them, and Gabrielle squeezing in from the side. "The Fellowship of the Vial," said Cole with a loud, deep, expansive voice, hoping to diffuse the situation. He held his arms out to his sides in a gesture meant to include them all. He smiled. None of the others smiled back.

It was decided. It would not be some big military operation designed to take out an enemy. It would not be a stealth operation, with them donning disguises and sneaking in through an air vent. It would not happen because a magical wok deposited them neatly in an underground hallway right outside William's office. These six people were just going to travel there with trains, planes, and brains, find a door, and knock on it. Or something. They had Gabrielle, who belonged there. They had Cole's light. They had Annabelle's feisty arrogance and Doobie's quiet confidence and Marionette's fierce intelligence. They had Linda's determination, her mother's vengeance, and her Presidential authority.

They hoped that they would be enough.

17.3

From: sparxxx@bbs.net (encrypted)
To: baster'D@bbss.net (encrypted)
Subject: SI SecSys

G. Needing access and update info re SI Level 5 security systems, especially wrt M31-119aX38 tri-level lifeform known as the "Murk." Current situation? Thnx. D

From: baster'D@bbss.net (encrypted)
To: sparxxx@bbs.net (encrypted)
Subject: re: SI SecSys

Dan-O! Thought you'd gone down with the ship. Changeling completely flooded. Lots of bodies but not yours. Whereabouts? Enquiring bosses want to know. Re Murk, you don't have the clearance, bud. What's up? G

From: sparxxx@bbs.net (encrypted)
To: baster'D@bbss.net (encrypted)
Subject: re: SI SecSys

Last minute intervention, G. Too much to explain. Sitrep: Tiger by the tail. LT alive and in motion. Working her from inside. Murk access necessary to obtain bargaining chip. Can you help out an old altar boy? D

From: baster'D@bbss.net (encrypted)
To: sparxxx@bbs.net (encrypted)
Subject: re: SI SecSys

Jesus, D! Lady Tiger will eat you alive. And you can't game the Masters. Get yer ass in and let the professionals handle it. G

From: sparxxx@bbs.net (encrypted)
To: baster'D@bbss.net (encrypted)
Subject: re: SI SecSys

Need you to trust me on this one, G. Tiger's guard is down and emotions rule the day. I'm already inside. Rich with possibilities. Your spec re Masters is correct: they are bugging out. ASAP. Following plan to hitch a ride. For now, I need to play this angle. Get me inside info on the SI Murk. You owe me, girl. Miami. D

From: baster'D@bbss.net (encrypted)
To: sparxxx@bbs.net (encrypted)
Subject: re: SI SecSys

Were it not for Greensleeves, D, I would turn yer ass in. Clearly the old rules no longer apply. Look for access datapak at ATS drop site. Best of luck. I'll see you in prison. G

Danny, clad now in some dry civvies he'd found in a hospital storage closet, opened his dropfile folder to see the datapak already downloading. He smiled slightly as the progress bar moved quickly to 100%. He dragged the file to a TabDrive, then deleted the original. He peeled away the drive, slid it into a case, and put it in his shirt pocket. Then he switched off the borrowed laptop, rose from his chair, and headed out of the office Stan had given him. A room awaited him back at the Presidential Home and he needed to get there before he could proceed. For some reason he could not understand, the fact that he was Mary's brother had given him more access than he would ever have believed possible. He was going to take advantage of that. For now, that meant trying to get a bead on the President's oldest. Hopefully, whatever was on that Tab would do the trick.

17.4

Cole could scarcely believe it was still the same day. The same day he'd confronted a hurricane and rescued his wife. The same day Linda had been resurrected from the dead. The same day they'd made a deal with the Middle Children. That any of them were still standing felt like a miracle to him. That they seemed to be thinking clearly even more so. And that he was soon going to leave again was almost too much to hold in his mind.

But this was not a matter of mind, was it? Not a situation for rationality and problem solving. Not to say that he was not using his head. Just that he wasn't *following* his head. He was following his gut, his heart, his instinct, his inner knowing. The rational thing to do would be to hole up with the girls in that nullspace and let Stan and his people handle things. But Linda had said "no." And when she'd said it, Cole knew that she was right. Even when that meant that, once again, he would leave his children behind and step out into a dangerous and mysterious world.

Did he have that right? How could one answer such a question? Ever since Linda Travis had smashed into his life with her old, stolen Buick, Cole's life had been a series of unanswerable questions and extreme situations. Life. Death. Good. Evil. Elite human overlords. Alien beings. And all of these forces playing out against the backdrop of an unraveling world that trembled underfoot like an earthquake that would never end. The fact remained that none of his facts remained. The old rules no longer seemed to apply. The mind, at least Cole's mind, could not keep up.

But that wasn't exactly true, was it? One old rule still applied. Cole loved his children. And he wanted to be there for them, to protect them, to help them. That remained. The flesh, and its longings, remained. And Cole was not convinced that he could ever change that, or should. Love amongst human beings felt, to him, like the only glue that would hold them together while everything else fell to pieces. But what to do when love pulled you in two different directions?

He'd done what he could. The nullspace apartment, with Mary and Ness on guard, and a solid army of hybrids around them all, would provide an impregnable barrier between the world and his children. He'd add another layer of protection, once they were all safely inside. The Middle Children were convinced that these measures would keep his children from any possible harm. But that was on their end. From *his* end, it felt like he and Linda were off to battle Goliath with one tiny slingshot and only three small stones: his light; Gabrielle's Family connection, and Linda's office. Were they walking blindly into a trap? Would they simply serve as lightning rods for the cabal's vengeance? There was no way of knowing. These Families had already tried to kill them both. Why would they hesitate to try again? And how could his and Linda's death serve as any sort of love and protection and help for his children?

What Cole knew for certain was that this would be the last time. He'd been pushed around enough. Used by forces too large for him to fully understand. Made a player in a game he did not want to play. Whether he was really an alien himself, come here to fulfill some agreed-upon role, he neither knew nor cared at this point. Any contracts he'd made on the other side he now considered fulfilled. He was a man. A human man. With a human heart. And children who needed him. When he and Linda got back, he would not leave them again. The other players would have to go on fighting each other without him. The Wayfaring Stranger was done wayfaring.

Their bags were packed. Linda had arranged a flight for them through her many contacts. The Fellowship of the Vial would be in London before morning. And then on to Ukraine. There were a few things left to do. Kiss his sleeping son on the forehead. Say goodbye to the girls. Explain to them as best he could why he had to go. And promise to them that he'd never leave them again. They'd be sealed up in the nullspace and Cole would create his protective shield of light. And then Cole and Linda, Gabrielle, Annabelle, Doobie, and Marionette would board a small jet and fly into the night.

Cole was ready. Let's get this done. He wanted to go home.

17.5

Her loves needed her, so Ness made herself available and present to their needs. The girls had packed some clothes, but they were exhausted and sad and afraid for their parents. Mary was feeling scattered and divided, wanting to be there for both the girls and Keeley at the same time. Keeley's health seemed to be improving, but it was a slow process. At least, knowing now that the flu was not contagious in the usual sense, Mary did not have to go through the tiresome process of suiting up. Cole and Linda were ready to go, and dealing with their own guilt and fear and anticipation. Ness was at their sides as much as was possible, providing good food and drink, sharing a steady smile, and giving them all the experience of being loved. Surely she could do that.

Mary and the girls stood beside a small wok that hovered near the garage. Their stuff was loaded. It was time to say goodbye and then go into hiding. Cole and Linda pulled up in a jeep. Their driver, one of the Middle Children soldiers, opened their doors and the President and her husband climbed out onto the paved drive. Ness walked up to the couple and hugged them together, burying her face between their necks and shoulders. Then they walked over to the wok.

Cole opened his mouth to speak but immediately choked up. So he knelt down and drew the girls in and squeezed them tightly. Linda reached out and embraced Mary, then stepped in to hug the girls as soon as Cole loosened his grip. Grace spoke into Linda's ear. "I know you have to go," she said. She glanced at Emily, who nodded through her own tears, then pulled back so she could look both Cole and Linda in the eye. "You both have to go. We know that. Just like we had to go, when we disappeared. So go, and do what you need to do, and then come back." She looked from Linda to her father. "I know you will. You'll come back. And we'll be here waiting for you."

Linda smiled through her tears. What had she done, to deserve such grace? She sniffed loudly and nodded. "We will," she said to Grace. "If I have anything to say about it, we'll be back very soon." She looked to Emily. "You guys take care of each other, okay? Mary. Ness. You girls. Take care of each other. And take care of your brother. Okay?"

Emily nodded. Grace forced a quivering smile. Then the girls, Mary, and Ness crawled into the wok that would take them to the nullspace, the whereabouts of which only the Middle Children knew. The wok rose against the backdrop of the setting sun, the rich oranges and purples of sunset gleaming off its surface. Then it flashed brightly and was gone.

Cole took Linda's hand and they walked back to the Jeep. It was time to meet up with the others and board their plane. "That was hard," said Linda, softly, as they walked.

"Yeah," said Cole. His voice was low and rough.

"You know what makes it the hardest?"

"What?" answered Cole.

"The fact that I'm not even sure why we're going," she said with a sigh.

17.6

Danny watched the wok depart with his sister, the cook, and the President's children inside. He watched the President and her husband get back into the Jeep that had brought them here and then drive away. He let the curtain fall back into position and returned to the little desk on the opposite wall, where his laptop lay open. He touched the pad and sent one last email, then closed the computer and put it in a drawer. He did not expect to be interrupted here, but saw no reason to leave his things out where anybody could see them.

He walked over and sat on the edge of his bed and took off his shoes. Then he reached up and felt the back of his head with his fingers, pushing his hair up and out of the way to examine the magnetic dock that had been installed in his skull. It had been some time since his last major data transfer and he knew that these docks could corrode. His felt shiny and clean and ready to use, so he pulled the tab from his pocket and opened the case. A thin magnetic disc the size of a dime, yet it would carry all the information on Murks that the Bastard had been able to get her hands on, and a recording of the SI Murk's telemetry since its installation.

He examined the disc on both sides. It, too, was shiny and clean. He knew once he touched it to the dock that he'd be out of it for a few minutes. It wasn't like being out of the body, as far as he could tell from what the travelers reported, but it was an intense blast of data and experience, and it would overwhelm his conscious awareness for a time. On the other side of the experience, of course, he'd know as much about Murks as anybody, and he'd have a clear understanding of what had happened to the President's son. Such knowledge would, if he was correct, be invaluable in his quest to get off-planet. How he would use that knowledge he was not yet sure. But that was a moot question, until such time as he had the knowledge, wasn't it?

Danny lay back onto the bed, rolling onto his left side so as not to dislodge the tab accidentally should he move his head. Some moderate amount of jerking and spasm was to be expected during a data transfer, after all, making him look, to an outside observer, as though he were having a mild seizure. He'd hate to interrupt the process. Danny closed his eyes, inhaled deeply, and then reached up to put the tab in place.

The magnets clicked as they touched. The transfer began.

17.7

Jay Sinclair had not had the opportunity to ask William Reynolds about his daughter's whereabouts. The enigmatic Director had decided to deliver his reports via HereNow rather than in person, and had terminated the connection right after he'd completed his presentation. As a junior member of the Directorate, Sinclair could have pushed the issue. Not with Reynolds, perhaps, but he could have certainly called upon the services of a traveler if he'd wished to. But he didn't. He let it go. The door had not opened easily. Jay Sinclair had learned long ago to only pass through the doors that opened easily.

Not that that approach was always the best. He was thankful, for instance, that The Families had pushed through with the designs and installations necessary for the One-Two Punch, the implementation of which would break them through the Grid, a door that had proved anything but easy to open. But in this matter of his daughter and her choices, not pushing felt like the best possible path for him to take. It was a matter of the Prime Directive, after all. A matter of freedom and choice. And he knew, from his experience with his own parents, that lifelong hatreds and resentments could result when such things were ignored or dismissed. He decided that leaving a daughter behind that loved him would be preferable to dragging along a daughter that hated him. He just wished he could communicate with her one last time, to wish her Godspeed and bless her choice, no matter how much it grieved him. Leaving behind a daughter that hated him seemed the worst possible scenario he could imagine.

Sinclair sighed. There were shouts from the hallway outside his door and he wondered if perhaps he should go retrieve Dierdre from the bar and escort her back home. It was after one in the morning, after all. The whole city was now jam-packed, bustling with activity even at this hour, as tens of thousands of the Chosen Few readied for departure. The Directorate awaited one last test result. The Giant Leap could commence as early as tomorrow. The air buzzed with excitement. The City of Beginnings was set to begin.

Sinclair could feel his heart pounding along with the noise and pulse of the crowd. He wondered, as he had before, why he was not doubled over in anguish at the loss of his daughter, and pondered the possibility that he didn't love her, or was not capable of love. But he knew it was more simple than that. She'd been so long out of his life now that the connection had long ago been lost. He hardly knew who she'd become. She was not a part of his daily life. So her absence left no hole. That thought made him sadder than the actual loss. He sighed again.

Then his laptop pinged. Sinclair rose and walked to his desk and touched his keyboard. There was a new email. He read it. He smiled. A door had just opened easily.

17.8

The seatbelt was as tight as she could get it. Gabrielle needed that right now: that feeling of containment, solidity, limits. With this little jet set to carry her back to her family, she felt as though she might be torn apart by opposing feelings. Her more recent anger with her father had not wiped out the fact that, for most of her childhood, she'd felt happy and close to him. Even her mum, in her own strange way. She missed her family. And part of her really wanted to go home, to the people she knew, to a father who had helped her so many times. And yet his secret life had left her confused and appalled. To find herself a member of an elite group that was planning to leave the Earth behind and let the rest of humanity suffer and die had so overturned her sense of self that she'd never fully recovered. Were these people evil? Was her father evil? Was *she* evil, simply as a matter of lineage? She didn't know how to answer such questions.

Having seen how chaotic the real world had become, she was beginning to understand the impulse to simply get away. Maybe these Families made some sense after all. Maybe they were just acting out the species' need and desire to carry on in the face of possible extinction. Weren't there lots of species that sent out seeds or spores when times got really hard? And maybe there was a part of her that had volunteered for this journey with the hope that she might go with them after all.

But having ventured far from the confines of her sheltered life, she had also seen that there were good, noble, beautiful people in what her father had called "the sleeping world." The way President Travis had welcomed her in and listened to her. The love she could feel between Linda and her husband, Cole. The steadfastness of these Church people. The fierce wisdom of the President's advisor, Mary. The quiet, protective confidence of Stan Walsh. These were not the dumbed-down, snack-munching, morons her father seemed to think "the Sleepers" all were. Sure, many, maybe even most, of the people of the world fell far short of their potential these days. The whole culture had gone whack. But to write them all off as already dead? To leave them behind? Gabrielle wasn't sure she could do that. It wasn't just Arthur. She didn't know how she felt about him anymore. It was something else. It was, for lack of a better term, the human spirit. It was still there. Even in the sleeping world.

The jet engines revved up and Gabrielle grabbed the arms of her chair. She closed her eyes and leaned her head back against the headrest. The Church people had boarded shortly after she and were sitting slightly behind her across the aisle. The President and her husband had not yet boarded. She took a couple of deep breaths, then looked out the window, across the darkening tarmac to the sparse lights of Augusta in the distance.

The trees at the airport's edge stood leafless and brittle against the sunset, victims of the blistering spring heat wave that had returned in full force after Hurricane Alpha had burned itself out. In the end, these were the people Gabrielle felt called to serve. The tree people. The fish people. The insect people. The deer people. Something of Zacharael remained inside of her: a deep ache that would not go away. "We're not dead yet," the living beings had cried out to her in that long, wild vision the Angel had given to her. Just as the human spirit was not dead yet. The life of this planet still needed her help. President Travis seemed to need her help as well. And being needed was a powerful call to being, one that Gabrielle could not deny.

Would it be worth the trade off? To stay on Earth and feel needed versus leaping into space with no sense of purpose? Gabrielle couldn't know. The Families seemed to have everything under control. They sure hadn't expressed any particular need for her. Perhaps she'd just be a cog in their machine.

The President and her husband stepped onto the small plane, Cole ducking so as not to hit his head on the ceiling. Linda bent over for a word with the pilots, then turned and stepped into the cabin, making eye contact with the rest of her contingent, smiling, nodding. She stepped up to Gabrielle and reached out to squeeze her hand. "I'm glad you're here," she said. "How's about we rest for a while first, then have a meeting?" Gabrielle smiled in return and nodded her agreement. Linda turned and spoke briefly to the Church people, then she and Cole took some seats near the back.

The jet engines revved even higher. After a moment, the plane began to move forward. Gabrielle inhaled deeply and watched through her window as the world fell away beneath her.

17.9

The Middle Children had done an amazing job with the hideaway, creating uncanny replicas of the kids' bedrooms, Mary and Keeley's suite, and Ness's two rooms, all connecting to a circular common area with a sunken living room in the center that contained a pair of overstuffed sofas, a large flatscreen, a Blu-Ray player, and a box of their favorite movies. That so much time, energy, and scarce materials had gone into a place that none of them planned to be in for more than a couple of days felt wildly extravagant. That they had built this place in less than four hours, complete and self-contained inside a nullspace shell that was impervious to any outside force, was almost impossible to believe. Obviously they had access to technologies far and above what the humans were used to. That they had put their resources to protecting and caring for the President's stepchildren helped a great deal in creating the bonds of love and trust and interdependence that would be needed should their people hope to share this planet.

Ness, Mary, Emily, Grace, and the cat, Mihos, stepped out of the wok, through the docking chamber, and into the large, open common area. Iain's sleeping body had already been brought here and they found him looking cozy and warm in what looked like his own bed, complete with his usual psychedelic sheets and pillowcases. They'd retrieved Dennis's comatose body from the Presidential Home, where they'd found him in his favorite spot on the sofa. The old Whippet was now tucked in beside Iain's legs. They'd even duplicated Iain's David Bowie poster over his desk. The four of them stood in the doorway and watched Iain for a long time, the women standing behind the girls with their arms around them. All of them shed some tears. None of them said anything. Mihos jumped from Grace's arms, crossed the room, and jumped up onto Iain's bed, nestling in beside the boy's stomach. The cat began to purr.

After a while they pulled his door almost closed, and then went to explore the rest of the apartment, noting how accurate the re-creations were, how warm and comfortable it felt, and how natural the lighting was. In the kitchen they found one of the Middle Children cooking a couple of large pizzas. He introduced himself as Isaac and explained that he would love to stay with them to cook and clean, if they were agreeable to that. Ness was a bit miffed at first, but Isaac's eyes, though large and strangely shaped, were full of life and laughter, and when he made a point of asking Ness if she would be so kind as to teach him some of her culinary secrets, she nodded and smiled. When he looked at the girls and added that he was particularly interested in learning to play board games, of which there was a tall stack in the closet, there was little to do but welcome him for the duration. Isaac asked them which toppings they preferred, cocking his head as if storing mental notes about exactly what they said in reply. Then he turned and went back to work.

Mary and the girls wandered back into the common area and began to sort through the movies. Ness decided to stay and help Isaac slice the pepperoni, an ingredient she hadn't seen in years. A soft clink sounded from the docking chamber and in a few moments the doorway melted open. In walked a tall, thin, beautiful young hybrid woman. She stepped into the common room, scanned the space, walked up to the edge of the sunken area, looked down at Mary and the girls, and did her best to form a smile. "Hello, my friends," she said.

Grace's eyes went wide and she stood and started running toward the young woman. It seemed that Alice would be staying with them as well.

17.10

Danny had not actually been inside the Murk. But he felt like he had. The data transfer experience had been much more vivid than he'd expected. His heart was still pounding and he shook his head, hoping to dislodge the experience. How those kids had come out of that thing with anything resembling sanity was beyond his comprehension. Danny would be glad if he never saw another Murk in his life.

Of course not all of the kids *did* come out, which is why he'd examined the telemetry in the first place. And neither had that little old dog, Dennis, who'd proven to be one smart, brave little critter. Danny had seen the highlights of their experience as they poured into his brain. The first capture and the cat's rescue. The second attempt on that fool flying carpet. The third journey following the dog's nose through the Murk's circulatory system. The inevitable capture and the long slide down into the Murk's burning gullet. The last minute save and the last second tragedy as the boy and his dog were pulled into the Murk's hungry maw. The girls' final escape with the cat. It had been quite a show.

In the physical realm, the Murk was a plant-like lifeform with the official designation M31-119aX38, M31 being another name for the Andromeda galaxy. They'd been found on one of the inner moons of a gas giant in the same star system as the planet Lumen, which had been chosen early on as a colony site, then later abandoned after the first wave of engineers and builders all mysteriously died. What caught the explorer's attention was how the Murk existed simultaneously on three different levels of reality, and how it fed, snaring and then drawing any and all living creatures that came near into its central stomach, where it would completely disassemble them, body, soul, and consciousness. What looked like a spiny cactus in the physical looked like a vast, black cloud in the Astral and a sparkling sphere of blue fire in the Causal.

The first human astral traveler to encounter a Murk never returned to her body, though she did transmit what she saw from the outside before she entered the black cloud. Subsequent travelers, using information they'd obtained from the Life, worked in teams and eventually managed to figure out what the Murk was and how it worked. From that point it had been a simple matter, to figure out how to capture one in the physical, transplant it, breed it, reconfigure it, and learn to tune it for their own purposes. At this point, they'd been used for a couple of decades as astral security systems like the one on Squirrel Island. They offered no defense at all in the physical, apart from leaving a sticky, foul-smelling residue on the fingers of anybody who touched one. And they were little more than a beautiful bauble in the causal. But in the Astral, where opposing forces often attempted to attack, they were one of the most effective warding systems around. Which is why they'd used one for Linda Travis.

The bad news, of course, was that, as far as Danny could see, the boy and his dog were goners. There were no known cases in Family files where somebody survived and returned, once they'd fallen into that pit of burning embers. One traveler team in the early days had managed to pull their colleague's astral body out of a Murk's fire seconds after he'd fallen in, but it was already too late. He'd disintegrated completely in less than a minute, right before their eyes. The boy must be long gone by now.

Bad news for the boy. And bad news for Danny, who'd hoped to use information about his whereabouts as a bargaining chip. He hadn't known how he'd use it, exactly. Get the President to negotiate a berth for him on a Family colony ship, perhaps. Or at least give him the resources to survive here on Earth. But now he had nothing to offer in exchange. He didn't have to tell anybody that, of course. Not right off. But he could only play that game for so long, and the ships might leave at any moment. Danny wasn't sure he had that much time.

Which was why he'd anted up for a different game. Rubbing his face, Danny rose from his bed and walked over to check his laptop. He opened the screen and heard the familiar ping of a new email. He touched the screen and smiled at what he read. It was the hoped-for response from the Bastard.

From: baster'D@bbss.net (encrypted)
To: sparxxx@bbs.net (encrypted)
Subject: re: Have You Seen This Child?

D. Remind me to kiss yer ass next time we meet. Or something. Msg forwarded via Price via McNuge via Ape13. Legrand "extremely interested" in discussing missing persons report. Suggests Kiev eatery coordinates below. Time of the essence. You said wok available. Ours or theirs? ETA? If you pull this off, I'm your slave. I'll be dressed. G

Danny bent over, typed a few words, and hit send. He stuffed his laptop into his shoulder bag, checked himself in the mirror to make sure the civvies they'd given him didn't make him look like too much of a dork, then left the room, leaving his wet uniform in the hamper. Now all he had to do was procure a wok.

17.11

Linda sat by the window, staring out into the darkness, seeing nothing but black ocean lit by the Grid overhead. Cole was snoring softly beside her and Linda held his hand as he slept. She shook her head in disbelief. She couldn't get over the similarities. Three years ago she'd boarded another small jet for a night flight from the far North back to D.C. They'd been on their way to confront Agent Rice and his secret cabal. Sina and her Inuit rebels had helped them on their way. Obie, Cole's brother, was at their side. And Cole had just recently been brought back from death. Now they were on another small jet, taking another night flight, this one to London, where they would make their next connection, their final destination being the Chernobyl Exclusion zone, where they hoped to confront the Fisherman and his secret cabal. They had the Church of the Stranger to help them along the way. Gabrielle, the daughter of one of the members of The Families' Directorate, was at their side. And Linda had just recently been brought back from death. It all felt a little too neat for her taste. As though somebody had planned it out ahead of time. Somebody, perhaps, with gray skin and large, black eyes.

It was the differences, however, that made the... well, the difference. Three years ago, she, Cole, and Obie, had been together long enough to have established some trust between them, enough that they could begin to feel like a working unit. This time, there were six of them, and some of them had just met, and there'd been no time to establish trusting relationships at all. Linda barely understood what this Church thing was all about, and though she could sense Annabelle's personal power, she really didn't understand why she and her people had come along. And Gabrielle, her distant relation on her late husband's side: there was something otherworldly about that girl. Sometimes, when she looked Gabrielle in the eye, it felt like she was seeing stars and galaxies inside of her. And she was of The Families. Linda did not know what *her* game was either.

But Linda had learned three years ago that the only way to survive such experiences was to let go of control and accept the help that presented itself. She hadn't known Obie, but she'd followed him out of that lodge. And she hadn't known the Inuit, but she'd let them bathe her and shave her head and dress her and put her to bed. And she'd let them place her new love's living but spiritless body next to a bonfire on the ice while they entered the world of the dead to bring him back. There just wasn't time to establish trust in the usual ways. Not when things were moving so quickly. Not when lives were threatened. Not when the future so plainly depended on what she did. Even if she didn't buy William's line about how "chosen" and "important" she was, or the Inuit's belief in the same thing, for that matter, she was still the President of the goddamned United States of America. She *was* a player. She had shit she had to clean up. And she needed help.

And Linda still had her basic gut sense, her own ability to read people. Gabrielle just felt good to her. Young and a bit confused, but powerful and wild and aligned with the life of the planet. Same with Marionette. When Linda got beyond the eye-patch, which struck her as just plain wrong on such a strikingly beautiful face, what Linda saw was a fierce, smart warrior who would take loyalty to an extreme. Marionette was clearly on Linda's side, and since the young man, Doobie, was so obviously besotted with her, he was *de facto* on Linda's side as well. Annabelle was more difficult to read. Her smiles felt a tad bit too agreeable. Her deference slightly feigned. But people often acted strange around their President. Linda had seen it thousands of times. With nothing else to go on, she saw no reason to think this old woman was anything but what she'd said she was: a local leader of a church that had sprung up in the past few years, a church that was convinced that her husband, Cole, was some sort of alien savior. Annabelle had promised to help and serve Cole. That felt like a good thing to Linda.

Linda turned and watched her sleeping husband for a few moments. In a way, he was more a mystery now than any of these others. Not that she didn't trust him. She did. It was more that she wasn't sure who he was any longer. There had barely been time to talk, let alone synchronize their mental hard drives so that each knew, as fully as possible, what the other had been through in the past two weeks. Cole's "hops"? The light from his hands? An alien in disguise? Jesus! Linda didn't know what to do with any of that. All she knew was that she could no longer assume that she understood what he was up to. Somehow, here with her husband, her love, hand in hand, her gut failed her. She couldn't tell.

The jet engines roared softly as the plane leapt across the North Atlantic. Soon she'd have to rouse Cole. Call them all together. Make some plans. Talk about the day to come. She needed to phone Stan and get an update about the Greensleeves cure. And the girls. And

Iain. But not yet. Not yet. There was time still. And Linda was so very tired. And she wanted to hold Cole's hand a while longer. She wanted to feel him. She wanted to feel her love for him.

Because she was not at all convinced that she would get to do that for much longer.

17.12

Jay Sinclair tucked his drunken wife into bed and turned out the light, leaving her to fill their tiny apartment with her loud, juicy snores. He grabbed his jacket and headed out the door to make his way to the hangar. This sector of the living quarters, reserved for members of the Directorate and their families, was quiet compared to the major corridors, yet there was still more activity than he'd expected, even in these wee hours of the morning. The last push was on. It was almost show time. There were so many last minute details to take care of. Which would make his little trip to Kiev seem all the more strange, should anyone notice.

He entered the elevator and headed up to the hangar deck where his wok would be waiting for him. It was likely that nobody would say anything. He could hear the concern in the Flight Director's voice when he'd called to requisition his ride, but Sinclair was a junior member of the Directorate. He was a Sinclair. Nobody would question him, with the exception, perhaps, of his superiors. And Sinclair intended to be back long before any of them knew. He looked at his watch. It was almost four in the morning. His contact would be seven hours fresher than he. He'd have to get some caffeine.

The fact that this contact had been able to get to him via the Ape was telling. That meant he had some significant level of insider status, and knew enough to discern that Jay Sinclair even existed, and had a missing daughter. If his story turned out to be true, if this person truly had a bead on Gabrielle, that would make him a valuable commodity. He or she would, no doubt, want something in return. Sinclair could easily guess what that might be.

Ah well. Directorate members had as many comp tickets as they wished. If this person was young and smart and motivated, why not give him or her a berth? Sinclair could always use another aide. He stepped out of the elevator and took the short hallway to the left, turning right and pushing through the double doors to the hangar. Usually there were only a few woks to choose from, as most were in service. But so close to the Giant Leap, almost everybody was now in-house. He had a whole hangar full of woks from which to choose. Since he'd trained on a seventeen, he chose one of those.

The tech checked his credentials - a formality of which Sinclair approved - and handed him a flight helmet. Sinclair stepped up to his seventeen, an old favorite he thought of as "Sadie," and put his hand on her side. Though the human-built woks weren't as alive and conscious as their alien exemplars, they had some truncated sentience. He could feel her muted response of recognition, and patted her in appreciation as her doorway melted open. Sinclair glanced back toward the flight office, then stepped up onto the stairway. He'd be at the diner in Kiev in a matter of minutes. He could already smell the coffee.

17.13

"Yes, Ma'am," said Stan into the phone. "Dr. Pintick arrived a few minutes ago and the hybrids - the Middle Children - are outfitting his lab. He should be up and running before dawn." Stan listened for a moment, then spoke again, his voice soft and low. "No word, Mrs. President," he said. "I'll speak with Alice when she returns from the nullspace. I know they're on it, but not much else. I'm sorry." He listened for a moment longer, then said good-bye and clicked off his phone. Stan sighed, leaning back in his office chair. He put his feet up on his old desk and closed his eyes to think.

The world was facing a deadly pandemic, the bad guys were getting away, and Linda's greatest concern was with the whereabouts of her lost son. That was exactly how it should be. And that's why Stan had to take the lead on these other matters. That was his job, was it not? He was the Secretary of Homeland Security. These were strange and stressful times. Death stalked the land. Evil had gained the upper hand. The homeland was not secure. Stan would not just sit on his hands and watch all of their work fall down around his ears. Not while he still had breath in him. That's not who he was.

Stan had been surprised to find how well the engines of government had chugged along without them for the past few days. Even with Linda at the Squirrel and he and Cole gone to find her, things had kept running on their own steam. That made sense, really. Though the President was in Augusta, the government really wasn't.

The Congress, the Supremes, the Joint Chiefs, most of the Exec, Intelligence, they were spread out across the country, or concentrated in other cities, where Linda had sent them after the destruction of D.C. three years previous. Most of the business of government was transacted now via email, chat, phone, Skype, and video conferencing. And until Alpha hit, most in the government assumed that their President, though ill, was still in charge and running things from the infectious disease containment facility on Squirrel Island, with assistance from her VP, Albert Singer, still in Augusta. Things were running smoothly enough, it had seemed, that she could even attend and participate in the global environmental summit, all thanks to those who had abducted her and replaced her with a virtual doppelgänger.

It was not until earlier today, when the President was reported missing and presumed dead, that things had begun to fall apart. Albert Singer, it turned out, had mysteriously vanished in the night. He was already gone before they'd boarded *The Pokey Joker* for her final voyage. His office, his home, his car, he'd left it all behind. He'd even left his laptop on his desk, open to a half-written email. It was as if he'd been beamed up by the aliens.

Perhaps he had. Stan had always assumed that Singer had close ties to members of the secret cabal. It made sense that some members of the cabal were still deeply embedded in the real world, and Albert's loyal deference had always felt a bit off to Stan. Bank's former ties were out in the open, and the man had worked hard to earn their trust and make amends. The General's involvement was also out in the open, and he'd never seemed to care whether they trusted him or not, so Stan just trusted that the General would one day betray them, and he had. But Singer had never been outed as a collaborator. He just felt like one.

In any event, Singer was gone. The order of succession had been sorted out. The Speaker was now presiding from his office in Kenosha. All was well with the world. The military maintained its watch. The wars banged along. The oil wells pumped what was left. The food trucks showed up at the shelters. They would do their best. And their worst. As they always had.

This intense heat, more fierce than ever in the wake of the hurricane, would no doubt spark a few riots in the coming days. There would be brown-outs and black-outs all over the electrical grid. Water would grow ever more precious as the droughts continued.

Speaker Simpson would be under more pressure than he'd imagined was possible. And the real President would do what she did in Ukraine.

Stan couldn't decide what he thought about that: Linda Travis's insistence that she and her husband travel without protection, and with a group of relative strangers, to Chernobyl to confront this mysterious Fisherman. It didn't make much sense to him. There were too many more pressing needs, in Stan's opinion. Where Linda Travis needed to be was right here in Augusta, doing her job. So the bad guys would get away. Let 'em go. This Fisherman and his cronies. The General. Albert Singer. The whole lot of them. Let 'em go and good riddance. There would be no stopping them anyways. Hadn't she already learned that? And maybe when they left they'd take their damned alien buddies along with them, and good riddance to that lot as well.

There was stuff to do here. Linda Travis was not here to do it. But Stan Walsh was. And he was going to do it.

17.14

There were actually two Alices that had come to see them in the nullspace. The first was their friend, the strange, lost little hybrid girl who'd stayed with Cole and Linda and the kids for a few months after the wild events of three years previous; the smart, wise, inquisitive, yet odd little being who had won their hearts with her funny questions, her direct manner, and her awkward but sincere attempts to learn from them about the human side of her lineage. That Alice had disappeared one day out of the blue, leaving behind a short, vague note. She had reappeared three years later, seeming to have aged twelve years or more. She was a young woman now, not tall for a human but thin and well muscled, like a dancer. Her long, black hair fell straight on either side of her beautiful face, almost hiding the outer edges of her huge, almond-shaped black eyes. Her look was elfish, animal, hyper-aware, and yet there was still something girlish about the way she would cock her head, or move across the room, or slump onto the sofa next to the girls.

This Alice had stood stiff and still and allowed first Grace, then Emily, then Mary, to hug her in turn, and had even reached up to put her hand on their backs as they did so. She greeted them by name, expressed her gladness to see them again, asked how they were, and listened intently as Mary and the girls told some more of their story. The girls were keen to understand how it was that Alice was now so much older than they, and nodded as if they knew just what she meant when Alice explained that she'd "skipped between a number of world-lines in the time since last we saw each other."

The other Alice felt very different: imperious, businesslike, stern, even burdened. It was as if her thoughts did not fit into the human world, as if it was all she could do to make words come out of her mouth that the humans would understand. Her air was that of one who'd been away in battle, who had seen things neither Mary nor the girls could begin to comprehend, who had learned the hard truths of loss and leadership and had come back to aid her people - the Middle Children - in another sort of war, this one a war for place and belonging. This Alice had much larger things on her mind than the humble swapping of greetings and stories. Though she may have been fighting for such things as peace and security, home and belonging, rest and comfort and glad gatherings, it felt as though she herself could only hover on the edges of such things, the seasoned warrior uncomfortable with the peace between battles.

This Alice gave a short, clear account of the Middle Children's search efforts regarding Iain. She told them what she'd confirmed about Murks from the packet she'd received from the Cogency, how they were, indeed, a plant-like lifeform that existed simultaneously in three different layers of reality, how they'd been discovered, researched, and eventually weaponized, and how the chances of finding someone who had fallen into the Murk's central flames were almost nil. There were some in the Cogency who believed that consciousness itself was not destroyed in a Murk, and that it was simply thrown into another time. For this reason, a panel of six Middle Children had set up a sweep through jumptime, in an attempt to find some sign of Iain along that axis. A full sweep would take days to months, depending on how tightly they tuned their nets. Even with the tightest weave possible, there would be no guarantees.

When she was finished, Alice rose from the sofa and started toward the door, as though she meant to leave without so much as saying goodbye.

"Alice?" said Grace, her eyes still wet with tears from the news of her brother.

Alice stopped as if Grace's question had been a knife thrown into her back. Slowly she turned to face them. Her face was dark.

"Are you leaving?" asked Grace. She stood and took a few steps toward the young hybrid woman.

Alice nodded but said nothing.

Emily rose and followed her little sister. The two girls stepped closer to Alice. "What happened?" asked Emily.

Alice cocked her head. "I do not understand what you mean," she said.

Emily gestured toward the hybrid girl, whose stance was tight and wired, ready to run or fight, whose arms looked poised for battle, whose face was dark and angry. "What made you so... I don't know... cold?" said Emily.

Alice jerked back as though slapped. She raised a single eyebrow and scowled, first at Emily, then at Grace. "I... cannot..." she finally said, glancing from one to the other

Mary joined them, standing off to the side between the girls and Alice. "What can't you do?" she asked Alice, her voice soft and loving.

Alice glanced at Mary, then back at the girls. She shook her head from side to side and wrinkled her tiny nose. She exhaled heavily. She looked back at Mary. "This is my burden," she said.

Mary reached out and touched Alice's arm. "Friends share their burdens," she said, offering a gentle smile.

Alice flinched but did not step away from Mary's touch. She looked to Grace again. Then Emily. "My mother," she said at last. She looked at Grace. "I could not find *her* either." Without another word, Alice turned and walked into the docking chamber and was gone.

17.15

"I did my best," said Gabrielle to Linda. The six travelers were gathered together in a rough circle facing each other across the aisle. "Whether he can hear me I don't know. And whether he'll respond..." Gabrielle shrugged, flashing her eyebrows in a way strangely similar to the way William had done, as though it were a Family trait.

Linda nodded. If she was right, this Zacharael character who'd been intruding into Gabrielle's life was the same tall, thin, red-haired man who'd shown up repeatedly in her own life, looking for all the world like Agent Rice and causing confusion at every turn.

One of those Angels, or Elders, that Obie had spoken of, he seemed to delight in messing with people without really explaining himself. It was about time he did something useful for a change. And by useful, Linda meant helping to find her lost son.

She reached out and squeezed Gabrielle's hand and smiled. The girl appeared exhausted and drained, not only from the crazy day they'd had, but from lack of sleep, and from the deep relaxing trance state she'd gone into in order to try to contact her alien teacher. Linda glanced at her watch. Still a couple more hours in the air. Time to end this meeting and send everybody off for a nap before they arrived.

"So we won't know until we land whether this Mr. Bluebird has got things set up for us?" asked Annabelle. She studied Linda with a smiling mouth and irritated eyes, as if she could hardly believe their travel plans were not already rock solid, but didn't want to come right out and say so.

Linda nodded, raising an eyebrow. "I believe you insisted on joining my expedition, Annabelle. Not the other way around," she said, not bothering to hide her frustration. Unlike Gabrielle, the old woman looked as fresh as a sunny morning. How she managed to get pulled from the wreckage of Hurricane Alpha and still feel this good less than twenty-four hours later Linda could not imagine. "You're welcome to drop out at any time, if my itinerary doesn't suit you."

Annabelle glanced at Cole, who sat watching them straight-faced, then back to Linda. "I'm not complaining, Mrs. President," she said. "Just trying to get things straight."

Linda sighed. "I think you're going to have to get used to being out of control if you're going to hang around with me, Annabelle," she said. Linda's voice was distant and wistful, as if she knew herself to be capable of wild and horrible acts.

Annabelle raised her eyebrows at Marionette and Doobie, then leaned back in her chair, as if determined to "get used to it" right away. Linda looked around the circle. "Any other concerns?" she asked.

"Do we need to worry about radiation?" asked Doobie, gesturing to Marionette as though he meant just the two of them.

Cole shook his head. "I don't think so," he said. "Not if Mr. Bluebird hooks us up with a licensed guide. They've been doing tours of Chernobyl for years now. Those folks know where to go. And where not to go."

"So it's just... grab the plane to Kiev, take a taxi to Chernobyl, and then we stand there and wait?" asked Marionette. "That's the plan?"

"They must have sensitive and redundant surface surveillance systems in place," said Linda. "Facial recognition software. IR. Motion sensing. The works. I've seen how they operate. And this is the most important place in their world right now, if the rumors Danny heard can be believed. We'll be seen. Gabrielle will be recognized. Somebody will come to meet us."

"And then what?" asked Doobie.

"Then we do whatever comes next," said Linda with a shrug.

Nobody else said anything for a long while. "Let's see if we can get some sleep," said Cole at last. The weary travelers nodded, and settled into their seats.

17.16

Jay Sinclair sipped at his second cup, his back to the wall, his eyes watching the only door in the place. The Cafe So Good, right down the street from a Family-owned SafeHouse Hotel in downtown Kiev, was one of his favorite spots in the city. Simple. Warm. Dark. Coffee and pastries, soup and sandwiches. All of it served in large, hot portions by smiling people who appeared to be glad that he was there. He didn't care for very many places in the sleeping world, but he loved the So Good. He visited whenever he could.

It was also open all day, every day, and it was always fairly busy. Sinclair could get that warm-body effect he so often craved. Whether it was his early training or a hard-wired monkey impulse, Sinclair preferred to have people around him. Unlike so many others, he was actually looking forward to the cramped quarters of the colony ships, and the close working conditions they'd encounter in the colonies themselves.

The front door opened and in walked a young couple. They stopped just inside the door and surveyed the room. But not for a table. For a person. The man was well built, with closely cropped hair and a steady gaze. Military, from the looks of him, though he was dressed in civilian clothing. That might be his connection point. The woman was short and quirky, with black and purple hair, a pierced eyebrow, and a tattoo on her wrist. Her chin jutted slightly forward, giving her a defiant air that Sinclair liked immediately. The woman spotted Sinclair and raised an eyebrow. Sinclair smiled. The woman took the man by the elbow and ushered him back to Sinclair's table. They came to a stop in front of him.

"Coffee?" asked Sinclair, brandishing his cup.

"Please," said the man. He stuck out his hand to shake. "Danny Sparks," he said. He gestured toward the woman with his head. "This is the Bastard."

Sinclair smiled at the name, raising an eyebrow. He gestured toward the chairs. "Please. Sit." He waved down the waitress, held up his cup, and gestured for two more. The waitress went to get the coffees. Sinclair returned his attention to the couple. "So. You know who I am. Tell me how you know that." He smiled slightly.

Danny nodded. "I'm a security operative with BlackBay, Sir," he said. "The Bastard here does network analysis. Same company. London office. She's got... connections. Enough to get a message through to you." The waitress brought two more coffees and placed them soundlessly on the table.

Sinclair turned his attention to the young woman. "Network analysis?" he asked.

"Yes."

"Multi-band?"

The woman nodded. "Yes."

"qputer?"

"Some," she said. "Sims only."

Sinclair nodded. "Why 'the Bastard'?" he asked.

"Gina Devonne Baster," she explained. "Ginny de Bastard. G.D. Bastard. Goddamned Bastard. You get the idea. The name stuck."

Sinclair smiled politely, then turned his attention to Danny. "Contacts wouldn't get you to me specifically unless you knew I existed. I assume your knowledge of me is one piece of evidence to back up your claim?"

Danny nodded. "It is, Sir. This is another." He held up his phone, to show a photo of Gabrielle he'd snapped at the hospital.

Sinclair glanced at the snapshot, then back at Danny. "So where is she now?" he asked.

"On an airplane, Sir," said Danny. "On her way to meet you." He glanced down, unsure how the older man would respond to this news.

Sinclair's eyes widened. "To meet me?" he said. "You mean in Ottawa?"

Danny shook his head. "Pripyat," he said, taking a risk that their analysis was correct. He looked Sinclair in the eye to gage his reaction. "*Urbem Orsus*," he added.

Sinclair's brow furrowed. "But how can she-?"

"I told them, Sir," said Danny.

Sinclair shook his head in disbelief. "You know about *Urbem Orsus*?" he asked.

Danny nodded. "I do, Sir, yes," he said. "A bit. Just rumors. Enough to put things together." He glanced at the Bastard, reaching out to take her hand. "We do."

Sinclair exhaled loudly and shook his head. "I told them it was a mistake to give it a name," he muttered. He sighed again, looked at the Bastard. "You give a place a name, all of a sudden people start putting it on the map." He rolled his eyes, then looked at Danny. "So you told her," he said. It wasn't a question. "How did you meet her?"

"I figured you might be looking for her," said Danny. "And I was there when the President was rescued from Squirrel Island."

Sinclair did a double take. "I'm sorry, my dear man, but you were what?" he said. His face reddened.

Danny shrugged. "I figured you knew, Sir," he said. "She and her husband on are their way to meet you as well."

Sinclair could hardly speak. "Tell me," he managed to say in a choked voice.

Danny glanced at the Bastard, then back to Sinclair. "Just one thing, Sir," he said.

Sinclair frowned. "What?"

"We want in," said Danny.

"You want in where?" said Sinclair with a frown.

"We want in on the Giant Leap," said the Bastard. "And the real deal. Not your phony 'Second Wave.'"

Sinclair opened his mouth and moved his lips like a fish, but no words came out. He looked from the man to the woman and back again. They knew about the Giant Leap? *And* the Second Wave? And Linda Travis was still alive? And she and Gabrielle were coming to him? None of it made sense. But all of it felt like a massive door swinging wide open. He'd deal with these two first. Sure. Let 'em in. She had qputer training. He'd make a good bodyguard. Why the hell not?

Then, he'd need a bit of time to think.

17.17

Ted took another card and moved his piece forward three spaces, close to the Wibble Wobble Duck Pond. He looked at Carl. "I think I was liking the Scrabble better," he said.

"So why did you change it?" asked Carl.

Ted shook his head. "I didn't know I was, at the time. Or that I was changing it to something from my childhood."

"Well, it did spur some memories that broke things open," said Carl.

"Yeah," Ted nodded. "But that's done now. So what game do we need next, to get us out of this joint?"

Carl thought about that or a bit. "Some say that we have to integrate what we learned from our past life here in this in-between place. Others say we make plans for what we want to work on next."

"Did that, yo," said Ted. He counted off on his fingers. "Don't be an evil prick. Check. Don't torture the President. Check. Don't pick screwed up parents. Check." He looked up at Carl and grinned. "Ain't I the quick learner?"

Carl smiled in return. "You may need a bit more sincerity than that if you want the Great Pumpkin to visit, Ted," he said.

Ted scoffed. "Seems like if I was dead and the whole reincarnation thing was true, then I'd also be remembering a bunch of other past lives right now too."

"So maybe that's not what this is. Or maybe that's not how it works," said Carl.

Ted opened his mouth to retort, then thought better of it. He sighed. "So you got any ideas?"

"I'm just thinking about how you picked up the Scrabble game and when you put it back down it was this game," said Carl. "Like, we have some power here, if we can figure out how to use it. Power to create things. Change things."

Ted raised an eyebrow. "Maybe like we can think ourselves a new door out of here or something?" He turned and looked at the old door that had always been there, but which had never opened. "Or maybe a key for that one?" He turned back to Carl.

Carl winked. "Maybe."

Ted swiveled his head and stared at the wall. "Gotta be more fun than this game," he said. He stared for a good long while.

Chapter ⏀ Eighteen

18.1

Zacharael's people had a natural ability to slide around the edges of the present moment and view short distances into both past and future. It was almost second nature for them, like a strange sort of peripheral vision, and Zacharael paid it great attention as he monitored the situation on his Beloved Earth, and made his moves. These views of past and future were fuzzy, at best, given the natures of time and reality, but they were better than nothing, and often helped him make choices that might otherwise stump him.

From where he stood now, he saw no advantage in responding to Gabrielle's request. To do so would reveal to her that she could, indeed, contact him at will, and that he could be influenced by her needs and desires. That would change the nature of their relationship in ways Zacharael was uncertain would be wise. It would also take focus away from what he considered was Gabrielle's primary role, which was to make choices in response to the actions of the President Travis. Zacharael saw that the loss, or rescue, of the boy child might significantly influence the President Travis's actions with regard to both the human Families and the current pandemic, but the Primary Rule, and his own inability to foresee the correct choices, made him loath to involve himself in that matter.

There was a reason the President Travis had been chosen for this role, rather than Zacharael. Were it up to him, Zacharael would have taken the obvious actions necessary to serve the best interests of the Beloved, the humans be damned. But the history of reality had taught him the folly of such intervention. The evolution of consciousness must be served at all costs. Even the highest cost.

Zacharael would act with restraint.

Even if The Sages might not.

18.2

The small private jet, flown by a pair of ex-military American pilots Stan had procured, touched down at the Woodbridge Airfield, the recently-closed remnant of the old RAF Woodbridge military airfield, site of the famous UFO encounter in the nearby woods of Rendlesham Forest. The Woodbridge Airfield had been used for Army Air Corps training until the Christmas Crash put it out of commission, after which time it had sat mostly idle, save for the occasional private flight such as this one, where secrecy was at a premium. The US government contributed a small amount for the maintenance of the airstrips.

Waiting near the runway as the jet came to a stop was a black stretch limousine, which Linda assumed would contain some representative of Mr. Bluebird's, or Mr. Bluebird himself, come to make sure they made their connection. Their second flight would be made in the significantly larger private jet already sitting on the nearby approach strip. It would be a matter of walking fifty yards or so and they'd be on their way. Unless Mr. Bluebird felt it necessary to speak with them. Linda glanced at her watch. It was going on ten in the morning now, local time. The sun was hot and hazy. What she most wanted was a quick shower and some breakfast, and she hoped this new plane would provide her with both. She needed to scrub the exhaustion and sleep from her face.

Cole stood and grabbed their backpacks from the overhead. The others rose slowly and stiffly and grabbed their own gear. After her short nap, Annabelle finally looked as beat and bleary-eyed as the rest of them, and Linda gave her a smile, hoping to ease the old woman's suspicion and establish a note of camaraderie. Marionette had to jiggle Doobie awake.

The pilots, one tall and thin, the other short and dark, crawled out of the cockpit and opened the door and deployed the stairway. Warm, moist air flooded into the cabin from outside as the travelers made their way to the doorway and out into the morning sun. The distant tree line was brown and mostly leafless, as it had been back in Augusta. The grass was dead. The sea, two or three miles to the east, glinted gray and white in the haze.

Linda started down the stairs, Cole right behind her. The Church folk followed, with Gabrielle in the rear. The President stopped at the bottom, hitched her pack up over her shoulder, and covered her eyes to shade them while she stared at the limo. Nobody got out of the long, black-windowed vehicle, so Linda turned to grab Cole's hand and make her way to the other plane. This jet was of Ukraine origin, if Mr. Bluebird was to be believed, and would be piloted by British pilots. Apparently Stan had access to a network of ex-military secret operatives whom he felt he could trust to keep their secrets. Linda was glad she had Stan on her side.

But trustworthy or not, these operatives were unable to prevent, or stop, what happened next. As the group of weary travelers were half-way between the two planes, a small, silver disc, a wok like the one she'd ridden just the morning before, appeared out of nowhere in the sky above them and performed three acts. The first was to fire a sharp beam of white-hot light down onto the plane they were headed towards, igniting an explosion that sent a huge fireball into the sky. The second was to shoot another sharp beam at the plane from which they had just departed, exploding that one as well. The third was to shoot a third beam down toward the travelers themselves. This one was wider. It was blue. And it grabbed Gabrielle and pulled her, screaming and kicking, into the air above their heads, up toward the wok, and inside. It was over in a matter of moments. The blue beam retracted back into the wok. The wok flared bright white against the blue sky and was gone so quickly that the human eye could barely detect its motion as it headed east, out over the water.

18.3

Mary slid out of bed and checked her watch. It was only three in the morning, but she could not sleep any longer. She stood, checked to make sure there was no dizziness waiting to trip her up, then pulled on her sweat pants and t-shirt and slippers and headed down the hallway to the common area, careful to make as little noise as possible, so as not to wake Ness or the kids. She stepped into the kitchen to leave a note on the pad on the counter, then walked to the docking chamber and pushed the call button, as the Middle Children had taught her. In less than a minute she felt the gentle touch of a wok as it melded with the nullspace dock. A few seconds later the chamber door slid open, revealing the wok's interior and an operator, an older woman with strange slanted eyes, perfect skin, and long, straight red hair. Mary stepped into the wok. "I'd like to go to MaineCentral Hospital, please," she said with a smile. The operator nodded and took her to the hospital.

Pushing through the double entrance doors, Mary made her way up to the isolation ward and Keeley's room. She'd visited her partner just before bed, finding her awake and eating and feeling much better. She'd brought Keeley up to date, and told her of any current developments. Keeley, though tired, had seemed to be clearheaded, and had asked good questions that got to the heart of the situations.

Mary was just reaching down for the handle when the door opened inward, revealing a short, female nurse in scrubs. Mary smiled as the nurse stepped out into the hallway, then entered the anteroom. With their new understanding about Greensleeves and how it was triggered from the outside, rather than spread by infection, the containment procedures around Keeley had been greatly relaxed. Mary donned a mask and gloves, but it was more a precaution against the unknown than as a protection against the alien flu. She looked through the glass and smiled. Not only was Keeley awake, but she was watching the television.

Mary stepped into the main room and waved. "Hi, sweetie," she said, walking quickly to the bedside. There were tears of relief streaking Mary's face before she could get there. "You're looking so much better."

Keeley returned Mary's smile and used the remote to mute the TV, then reached up to comb her hair back with her fingers. "Hi," she said, her voice still raspy from the effects of the flu. "You're up early. Or late."

"Couldn't sleep," said Mary, sitting on the bed and reaching to take Keeley's hand. "Thought I'd come sit with you. Didn't realize I'd actually get to talk with you." She sighed deeply. Keeley's illness had terrified her. This was the most normal Keeley had seemed since she first got sick.

"Me either," said Keeley, sipping some water. "Seems like all I've done for the past week is sleep." She gestured toward the TV with a wave of her hand. "And I wanted to catch up a bit."

Mary turned to glance at the TV, seeing some talking head yammering, with photos and video of Linda Travis playing in the background. She turned to Keeley. "Probably a constant string of... memorials and retrospectives," she ventured.

Keeley nodded. "Yep. It's amazing how beloved somebody becomes once they're dead. I've got the nurses recording it all for later. Linda might think it's a hoot." She drank some more. "Any word from our girl?"

Mary shook her head. "Nothing yet. They should be in London about now. Then it's another three or four hours to Kiev. Assuming it all goes as planned, she'll be getting to Chernobyl by breakfast time here."

"I'm sure Stan's got comm systems set up with his pilots and contacts. He'll be monitoring the whole thing," said Keeley.

"Yeah," said Mary.

"Stan doing okay?"

Mary cocked her head. "Seems... to be in his element," she said. "He's getting that new doctor set up to analyze the contents of the vial. And he's holding Fort Simpson's hand when the Speaker deals with the press."

Keeley gestured toward her face, now mostly clear of the rash. "Seems whatever's in that vial works," she said.

Mary sat and tuned in to Keeley's field for a moment, then nodded. "It's mostly gone now," she said. "Your years of... eating hippie food paid off, my dear. You didn't have much of the virus in you to begin with."

Keeley put down her water and took Mary's hand in both of hers. "So how are you doing?" she asked.

Mary inhaled sharply and closed her eyes. "I don't know," she said, shaking her head from side to side. "I'm just... I've been so worried..." She opened her eyes and looked at Keeley. "About you. And Linda. And the girls. All of it. And... and I..." She sighed again and stopped.

"And Iain," prompted Keeley. She sighed gently. "Any word on him?"

Mary shook her head but said nothing. She wiped a tear from her eye with a gloved hand.

Keeley nodded once. "Nothing yet," she said. "We'll have to give them time."

Mary looked down at her lap. "Danny's gone," she said. "I hardly had a chance to speak with him and now he's gone." She looked at Keeley. "Stole a wok, the Middle Children said, though how somebody could steal a wok from under their noses I have no idea. And I don't know what it means."

"You worried he's working against us?" asked Keeley.

"We just... it was all so confusing. There he was, on Squirrel Island, and we just included him, because he's... my brother. Just let him in. No questions asked. It was all... so hurried and confusing and stressful. But he still works for BlackBay. And his field was full of walls and secrets and... And then he disappears?" Mary exhaled loudly. "Yeah, I'm worried."

"You think he can hurt us?" asked Keeley. "You think he would?"

"I don't know, sweetie," said Mary. "I just... we were always so close. Up 'til the time I left to work with Linda and he stayed with them. Now I don't know if I even know him anymore." Mary glanced over her shoulder at the television, then back to Keeley. "He could tell the world that Linda's still alive."

Keeley raised a shoulder as if it wouldn't matter. "My guess is that they already know. I mean, there's no teeling who all saw her escape. And they've still got operatives in the Astral, so they can confirm it that way. Maybe it suits their purposes to just let her stay dead, as far as the public is concerned." Keeley stopped, closed her eyes, and shook her head. "I can't keep it all straight, sweetie," she said. "Too many players, and I don't have a program."

Mary squeezed Keeley's hand. "I should let you sleep," she said. She rose from the bed and Keeley opened her eyes. "Will you go back to be with the girls?" she asked.

"I promised I'd guard them," Mary replied. She smiled down at Keeley. "You do look better," she said.

"I hope that means I get out of here soon," said Keeley. "Will you get some sleep?"

Mary leaned over and kissed Keeley on the forehead through her mask, then turned and walked toward the door. Halfway there she turned back. "I think maybe Linda is walking into a trap," she said.

Keeley nodded. "I know," she said. "I'm worried too."

18.4

Danny and the Bastard could not believe their good fortune. The Families were just hours away from the Giant Leap and the two of them had been invited to join these people on their great adventure. This just after Danny's seemingly miraculous last-minute rescue on Squirrel Island from a fierce storm that had killed the rest of his comrades. Somebody "up there" clearly liked him. Whether that was just Director Sinclair, or somebody else in The Families, or some of the alien beings The Families worked with, didn't matter right now. What mattered was that he and the Bastard, Gina, had been given bunk space in the tech crew section of a huge Colony Wok known informally, as far as they could tell, as the *Kill 'Em All.*

Not that either Danny or Gina felt particularly disgusted with their fellow humans. They'd grown up in what they knew some in The Families referred to as "the sleeping world." They knew that their friends and families were just stuck in a culture that had them behave in unsustainable and self-destructive ways. They'd been stuck in that culture themselves. But they also knew how very screwed up things had become, and how severe the repercussions of the culture's collective behavior were likely to get, and how soon. They were glad to have found good work with corporations that had turned out to be Family-owned and operated, to have worked themselves up into positions of low-level but not insignificant power and influence, and to have been, very slowly, brought into some of what was really going on behind the scenes. They felt lucky. Gina had done deep data-analysis work at BlackBay and had a keen ear for picking up clues to what The Families' long-term plans might be. She'd begun to collect data on something called the Giant Leap a few years ago, and began to hear rumors of a place called *Urbem Orsus*, and she and Danny had speculated as to how things must be.

This is what *Urbem Orsus* was: a vast, underground hangar deck at least ten miles square, in which sat perhaps twenty huge woks, larger than any he'd ever seen in human use, and as large as some of the Overwoks the Life used for deep space exploration. It was hundreds of thousands of people converging on this one spot, to board these colony woks with little more than the clothes they were wearing: Family members, world leaders, captains of industry and commerce and banking, scientists and engineers and technicians, builders and designers. It was everything needed to populate, fuel, and outfit a dozen colonies, already partially or fully constructed, on moons and planets found in distant corners of the Universe. It was hope and need and intention made manifest, plans put into motion over a century ago, people stepping away from the world that had given them birth and setting out to fulfill their destiny. It was seeds being flung out into the spaces between the stars by the winds of great change. And Danny and Gina got to be a part of that. They were elated.

Not that it would be easy, but they had it easier than most. Danny would be leaving his sister behind, but Mary and he hadn't ever been very close, really. And she had no need of him now, what with that Keeley woman she had as a partner. And Gina would be leaving her mother, but that nasty old woman was in a home, her mind lost to dementia. Their biggest hardship was the psychological disorientation of having their entire futures change tracks so completely so quickly. Jobs. Apartments. Debts. Bills. Relationships. Plans. Dreams. All of it had to be tossed out the window and replaced with something they could hardly begin to imagine. And they'd thrown in together now as well, something neither of them had seen coming. Years of low-level flirting. The occasional overnighter when they were both in the same town at the same time. But they'd never seriously considered that they had a relationship in any normal sense of the word. And now here they were, bunkmates, newbies, meeting these changes together and acting, for all intents and purposes, like a couple.

It was weird. It was fun. It was exciting. And it was frightening as hell. Latest word had them leaping in just a few hours. Into space. Leaving the Earth forever. Traveling to far-flung colonies on strange new planets. Making new lives. Starting over. Hand in hand, with the clothes on their backs, the knowledge and skills in their heads and hearts and hands, and the thanks and patronage of Jason Carrington Parker Sinclair, a member of the Directorate.

It was all as cool as shit.

18.5

The meet-up in Kiev, and the rescue of his daughter, had ended up taking him longer than he'd expected, which meant that Jay Sinclair's little last-minute side trip had, indeed, drawn the attention of the Senior Directorate. When he got back to his room to find Dierdre gone again, there was a message on his comm summoning him to the Master's office. It was all cordial curiosity and just-checking-in and is-there-some-way-I-can-help, but Sinclair knew that the Master was more than a little peeved at having one of his inner circle act so capriciously so close to the Giant Leap. Sinclair explained how his trip had resulted in the successful rescue of a Family member, who could now accompany them to the stars. The Master had little choice but to celebrate the occasion.

Back in his room, Sinclair grabbed his briefcase and his regulation travel bag - all that any of them would be allowed. Packed over a week ago, the bags felt surprisingly light in his hands. Sinclair smiled. Weight and storage room were only parts of the equation. By limiting what people could bring with them, they were also creating a clear break in identification from the Earth. From now on, what they had, what they needed, what they used, would all come from the colonies themselves. Soon, Sinclair planned to discard even the few things he brought with him for the trip itself. Even his clothes would go into the incinerator, as colony-made clothing was made available to him. He did not want any ties back to this dying planet.

He checked himself in the mirror, then headed out of the room. He thought about checking in on his two new recruits, but decided against it. He didn't know which wok they were on, and he wanted to see how well they adapted to the situation on their own. So it seemed the thing to do was to go find Dierdre. Since the computers said she'd already checked onto their colony wok - the smaller craft called Leader One which was reserved for members of the Directorate, their immediate families, and their personal assistants - he would no doubt find her in the ship's lounge. That was probably good. Might as well get it over with and board the wok himself.

But first he had to grab one last piece of luggage. This one weighed considerably more than the bags in his hands. It was a shiny, silver, capsule-shaped cylinder about six feet long and two feet across, made from a portion of the hull material from the wok he'd taken to Kiev. It was, in effect, a makeshift nullspace container that the wok had produced at his instructions while he'd made the flight from Kiev to London.

Inside the container was Gabrielle.

18.6

Mr. Bluebird, a tall, thin, pale man with a bald head and bushy eyebrows, spoke on his phone in what Linda assumed was Ukrainian. He sat in the corner of the limousine's spacious interior right behind the driver, with Linda and her fellow travelers arrayed around him in a circle, sipping glasses of the white wine the driver had poured for them. The conversation sounded animated and sometimes angry, and Mr. Bluebird looked at Linda and the others as he spoke, flashing his eyebrows and smiling and winking, as though he wished to include them in the call. After a rather loud and pointed response from whomever was on the other end, Mr. Bluebird said "Da" and clicked off his phone. He lifted his own glass of wine and took a sip.

"They've found a second plane," said Mr. Bluebird. His accent was more British than Ukrainian, as he'd been living in London since he was a teenager. He'd introduced himself as an "art dealer," but Linda understood that he dealt in all sorts of things, some of which she should probably not ask about.

"So how long of a wait does that mean for us?" asked Cole.

Mr. Bluebird smiled at Cole's question. "The plane comes here from Gatwick, Mr. Thomas," he said. "Not Kiev. It should be here very soon."

Cole nodded and sighed.

Linda gestured toward the burning planes in the distance, amazed that they had not yet been surrounded by fire trucks and emergency crews. Mr. Bluebird, his driver, and she and her companions seemed to be the only people in the entire airfield. "What about those planes?" she asked. "And the... the bodies?" Mr. Bluebird's chauffeur had already determined that all four of the pilots were quite dead.

Mr. Bluebird raised his shoulders in indifference. "We have people who will clean this up," he said.

"And the pilots' families will be notified?" asked Linda.

Mr. Bluebird looked Linda in the eye. "We will do what must be done," he said. Something in his voice told Linda not to push it any further. She nodded once, then turned to her companions. Doobie and Marionette looked exhausted and demoralized. The abduction of Gabrielle and the destruction of the planes had destroyed any hope they might have had that this mission would go smoothly and without cost. They could have been in one of those planes. And they could have been beamed into an enemy wok as well. Or they could have all been incinerated right there on the tarmac. Annabelle regarded Linda with her usual, fierce, defiant gaze, which Linda had decided was indicative of deep, protective feelings on her part, though why Annabelle thought Cole needed protecting from her, Linda was unsure.

Cole cleared his throat. "I could have used my light to stop them," he said, his voice tired and raspy. He looked at his companions, then Linda. "Before they took Gabrielle."

Linda nodded. "You could certainly have tried," she said gently. "Why didn't you?"

Cole inhaled sharply. He shook his head from side to side and shrugged. "There wasn't time," he said.

Linda took his hand. "No," she said. "There wasn't." She turned to Mr. Bluebird. "So do we just sit here in this limo?" she asked. "I mean... it's comfy, and we certainly appreciate your hospitality, but I feel a bit exposed." She motioned toward the sky with her hand.

Mr. Bluebird leaned over to glance out the window. "Will they come back, do you think?" he asked. He looked at Linda. "You have made powerful enemies, Madam President," he said. He turned to converse with his driver in Ukrainian, then spoke to Linda and the travelers. "Mr. Fox will take us to a hangar while we wait," he said.

Before the driver could start the limousine, however, the air was filled with the roar of an approaching plane. Mr. Bluebird opened his door to stand beside the limo and watch as another small jet made a quick, sharp landing that brought it to a stop well short of the burning mass of the first plane. Linda and Cole and the others also got out to watch. The new jet, this one smaller than their intended ride, taxied closer to them but stayed on the air strip. Linda reached into the limo to grab her backpack but Mr. Bluebird stopped her with a shake of his head. "Please, Madam President," he said. "Get back inside. We will drive you there."

18.7

Mary returned to the nullspace to find Alice sleeping on one of the sofas in the sunken area of the common room. The young hybrid, apparently the leader of the newly declared race called the Middle Children, sat with her legs crossed, her back straight, and her eyes closed. Mary stepped into the room and studied Alice for a while, noting the delicacy of her slow breathing and the radiant glow of her skin in the soft, dim light of the room. She tried again to view Alice's field, but saw nothing but the faint, light blue haze she'd seen in other hybrids, as if the fierce light that burned inside of them was leaking around the edges of their attempt to hold themselves together. Mary bowed slightly and stepped quietly across the room, to the door to her own bedroom, hoping to get inside without waking the young woman.

"She was your friend, was she not, Ms. Mary?" asked Alice, breaking the silence with her clear, soft voice.

Mary turned. Alice's eyes were open and her head was cocked to one side. She walked to the sofa opposite Alice and sat down. "You mean your mother, don't you Alice?" she asked.

Alice nodded once. "You called her Bob. Her full name was Roberta Olivia Reese. She worked as a Traveler and Assassin for The People under the direction of Agent Theodore Spencer Rice. She'd volunteered for the Breeding Program and was paired with the Inter-Life male known to humans as Spud. Their mating yielded one surviving offspring. Myself. My mother was taken away to a healing place by the Elder Zacharael shortly before the implosion of the Lodge under the American capitol." The Middle Child's rote recitation and even voice did not match the quiver in her lower lip as she spoke.

Mary sat forward on the sofa so she could speak more intimately. "Yes," she said. "Bob was my friend."

Alice cocked her head to the other side. "And yet she had threatened harm to Mrs. Linda and Mr. Cole, whom you now serve," she said. "And her methods had become harsh and unpredictable."

Mary sighed and nodded. "There were things we were all quite confused about then, Alice," she said, searching for words that might explain what had happened. "There were people above us who saw the world in harsh, competitive terms, and whose worldviews had become twisted by their wealth and power and influence. They could only see the relationships between humans and the Life in terms of more wealth and power, in terms of control and dominance and winning at all costs, in terms of technologies and weapons that would give them the edge in ruling the world. Their viewpoint shaped the group that became The People, and it shaped those of us who served with The People, leaving some of us twisted and broken as well. People like Agent Rice. And your mother." Mary closed her eyes and inhaled deeply. "I was lucky that I was able to break away and find a different path."

Alice closed her eyes for a moment, taking it all in. Then she spoke. "I have been unable to locate her," she said. She opened her eyes. "The Elders will not respond to my attempted communications."

"Are you worried about her?" asked Mary.

"I wish to learn whether she has found healing," said Alice evenly.

"And it will help you," said Mary. "To know."

Alice nodded. "I understand neither of my parents," she said, her voice growing quieter. "And so I do not know myself."

"Are you worried about yourself?" asked Mary.

Alice nodded. "Sometimes I think that they are both broken, and so I must be broken as well."

"Do you feel broken, Alice?" asked Mary.

The young hybrid woman scrunched her tiny nose in distaste. "Sometimes I wish for all the humans and the Life to die," she whispered.

18.8

Jay Sinclair found his wife in the ship's lounge. The bar was almost empty, most of those on board busy settling in before the Giant Leap. Dierdre sat alone near a viewscreen, sipping from a highball glass and staring at the real-time video feed of the Grid. As it was almost one in the afternoon, the video had been processed to show the energy lines, which could rarely be seen in the day-lit sky. In less than an hour, if all went as planned, and if Dierdre was still awake and alert, she would see the One-Two Punch blow a hole in that Grid through which The Families would make their escape.

Sinclair signaled the bartender and ordered a sparkling water, then walked across the room to join his wife. She looked up at him with reddened eyes, gave him a tight smile, then returned her attention to the viewscreen. Sinclair sat beside her and took a sip of his water. "I hate them all," muttered Dierdre, still staring at the screen.

"Whom do you hate, dear?" asked Sinclair. "The Sleepers?"

Dierdre shrugged as if it didn't matter. She downed her drink and signaled the bartender for a refill, then returned her attention to the screen. She didn't even bother to look at the server when he put her drink in her hand.

Sinclair sighed. Part of him wanted to tell his wife about his rescue of Gabrielle, now safely stowed away in her nullspace coffin in Leader One's equipment bay. But the other part of him knew that he should just keep his mouth shut for now. The stress of leaving Earth and heading out to their Colony world, Primus, was great enough as it was. The only reason Dierdre was joining him on the Giant Leap was that she couldn't stand the thought of being left behind with all of her friends gone. There was nothing in her that wanted to leave her comfortable life and act like a pioneer. Telling her of Gabrielle would just add to the strain. Dierdre and her daughter had not been close in years, and Sinclair suspected that his wife had been secretly relieved when Gabrielle had cut and run. He hoped that, once they got settled in on Primus, he and Dierdre and Gabrielle might be able to come together again as a family. But that was for the future.

"The Life, too," said Dierdre, her voice quiet and slurred.

Sinclair nodded. She hated the aliens as well. She always had. "We're doing this on our own now," he offered. He'd said it before.

Dierdre shrugged again but said nothing.

"It promises to be quite a show," said Sinclair, hoping he was right. He actually had no idea what the video feed would show. He didn't think anyone did. First they'd target a circle of Grid points with antigrav cluster bombs. They'd follow those with a constant barrage from the scalar cannon array. A section of the Grid should disintegrate at the edges and tear away like a piece of fabric, leaving a hole through which the massive colony woks could fly. Their alien mole had promised to compromise the Life's astral qputers, such that the hole could not self-repair so quickly. What the hole would look like from the ground in the day-lit sky nobody was sure. And since they were leaving, none of them particularly cared. Sinclair's eyes flared with excitement. He hoped they would light up the sky like a fireworks display. Give the Sleepers one last bit of theater before The Families left them to their fate.

"Quite a show," echoed Dierdre. She turned and gave her husband a blank stare, as if trying to remember who he was. "You brought my book?" she asked.

Sinclair nodded. Dierdre had insisted she be allowed to finish the latest Stephen King, which she was about halfway through. "I did," he said.

Dierdre frowned and returned her attention to the viewscreen.

18.9

Linda felt exhausted and dirty and hungry. The replacement plane came with neither a shower nor a meal, and the flight had been rough: the air in the cabin was cold and smelled of jet fuel and the turbulence was low level but almost constant. By the end of their three hours in the air, she felt like she wanted to scream.

But at whom might she scream? Certainly not the pilots, two kind, smiley men who seemed to understand almost no English. And neither were Cole or her other companions responsible for her pain. Whom she really wanted to scream at was a man named William. And that's exactly what she intended to do. But first she had to find him, so first she had to get to where she was sure he was. *Urbem Orsus.* She was now less than twenty miles away.

They were heading north in two black mini-vans, both driven, surprisingly, by young black American women. They'd followed the P02 north along the Kiev reservoir and then west to Ivankov, where they turned east and north on the P56 to head toward the town of Chernobyl itself, which lay well inside the southern boundary of the CEZ. The exclusion zone, once open to guided tours, was now more strictly guarded than ever, explained the drivers. The global financial crash had gutted what remained of the Ukrainian economy, but the government and church had somehow managed to come together and devise a fairly sane and violence free powering down of their culture, largely avoiding the wars, pogroms, cleansings, and mass relocations that had raged around them on all sides. Though the cities had been mostly abandoned, the Ukraine countryside through which they drove appeared to be a fairly prosperous farming region. There were men and women in the fields, and children playing or herding animals, and some of them smiled and waved as the vans drove past. Linda guessed that the scene looked much as it had over a hundred years before.

When asked how the Ukrainians had managed to pull off what amounted to a modern miracle, the driver of Linda's mini-van, an ex-Air Force major named Brenda, laughed a bit. "It's generally understood that the elite rulers of the world now live in Ukraine, and that it's *they* who have fashioned this peaceful situation."

"They know that The Families are here?" asked Linda, her voice incredulous.

Brenda nodded. "Yes, Madam President," she said. She gestured with her head to indicate the area ahead of them. "They watch the trucks go in and out. And sometimes, at night, they see the strange lights in the sky." She turned her head to eye the President. "They don't know much, but they know that they are here, and they're thankful."

Linda shook her head in wonder. They passed a sign. There was a checkpoint station just ahead and Linda winced, remembering another border crossing she'd rather forget, and the tragic loss of a new friend, and the terrible events that followed.

Brenda slowed to a stop before the closed chain-link gate and rolled down her window to speak in fluent Ukrainian to the sentry who came out of the tiny guard hut. The second mini-van, in which rode Annabelle, Doobie, and Marionette, pulled to a stop behind them. The guard spoke to Brenda for a long time in a low-key manner, then glanced up to see Linda sitting in the front passenger seat. His eyes widened and he looked to the driver with fear and questioning in his eyes. Brenda spoke a short phrase and flashed him a second identification card. The man examined the card, then smiled at Brenda, saying something in heavily accented English that took Linda a moment to decipher: "Bluebird." The guard bowed deeply and gestured for the other sentries to open the gate. The chain link rolled open, Brenda put her vehicle in gear, and both vans pulled through.

They were inside the Chernobyl Exclusion Zone.

18.10

The final boarding announcement, a gentle, firm, computer-generated woman's voice that spoke in English with no discernible accent, repeated itself once per minute now. Danny and Gina lay on their bunks, listening, waiting. There was no particular place they had to be at the moment of launch. There was no strapping in. No special seating needed to counteract the g-forces. No way to be "in the way." On a wok, it was usually impossible to even tell when it was in motion. But they stayed in their barracks just the same. They didn't know anybody here. They hadn't spent the last weeks and months and years working side by side with these folks, as many of them apparently had done. So they weren't sure how to fit in. They didn't feel like they belonged.

They'd assumed that Director Sinclair would check in on them before launch. Make sure they were doing okay. Introduce them around, maybe. But they hadn't seen nor heard from him since he checked them in at the security gate in the small hangar where they'd landed their seventeen-footers. Gina felt snubbed, but Danny argued that the Director must be busy with his own affairs at this very tense time and was simply trusting them to make their own way and prove on their own that they belonged there. He hoped he was reading the situation correctly.

It had occurred to them earlier that they didn't even know where the *Kill 'Em All* was headed. Which colony on which planet or asteroid in which star system in which galaxy. Director Sinclair had said that he wanted to take them both on in his employ, so they assumed that they were headed to the same place Sinclair was headed. But they knew how assumptions could prove to be wrong. Their greatest worry was that somebody would spot them, catch them, accuse them, say that they didn't belong, and kick them off before the colony woks had left the Earth. It wasn't like Sinclair had given them special badges or IDs or anything. The guard at the security checkpoint had scanned their iDent chips, something that he hadn't done with Sinclair. So maybe they were in the computer now. They hoped so. Otherwise they had no proof to back up their story, should they be questioned. Another reason to just stay in their bunks.

Gina had wanted to go find a viewscreen somewhere and see if they could watch the event as it happened. Apparently it would all start with something called the "One-Two Punch," which they assumed meant that the colony woks would have to break their way through the alien's Grid. That might be worth watching. But Danny convinced her that they should stay put. They could watch this historical event later, as it would no doubt be recorded for posterity.

For now... just wait. Breathe. Listen. Stay calm. And start to dream a new future together, on some distant world. They'd find out soon enough what it would look like.

18.11

Alice sat on the sofa in the nullspace common room. Her eyes were closed. Her breathing was soft and slow. But her mind was active. It ranged out to commune with the other Middle Children, those still helping with the rescues at the coast, those slogging through jump-time in search of the lost Iain, those maintaining the social, medical, and governmental systems of Augusta, ME, those working to analyze the contents of a small brown vial. She could tell that the dawn had come to Maine, and knew that, were there a window here, she would have seen the sun just peeking over the tree line. And she could sense the peaceful sleep of Grace and Ness, the quiet activity of Isaac getting ready for the day, the near-wakefulness of Emily and the meditating mind of Mary.

Further afield, Alice could feel the Interdict, and the presence of her father and his people as they awaited the crucial moment. She could sense the minds of those few Middle Children who had volunteered to be embedded in the project the human elite called the Giant Leap, as they awaited the crucial moment from their places inside the huge human-built ships. And now and then, she could feel the bare echo of the being she knew as Zacharael as he, like Alice, monitored the globe. He was searching for someone, it felt like. Someone he had lost. And he was angry. Alice could sense nothing more.

There was a flash on Alice's awareness, followed by a steady glow. It had begun. Alice opened her eyes and pushed herself to her feet. It could all move very quickly now. She had to be ready. Just in case.

18.12

Once inside the CEZ, the van drivers pulled into an abandoned service station, where they picked up a man named Raf, who had worked previously as a Chernobyl tour guide. Like Marionette, Raf had one patched eye. Unlike Marionette, Raf had only half a dozen teeth. His face, dark and pitted and stubbled with gray beard, was nevertheless open and happy and likable, and Linda made friends with him right away. He was a Bluebird man, he said in his broken, accented English. Linda had come to trust Mr. Bluebird and his people.

With Raf joining them in the lead van, they made their way further northward into the exclusion zone. Brenda drove slowly, wary of wildlife in the roadway and giving Linda and her colleagues ample time to view the surroundings. They saw vast swaths of previously cultivated land returning to wildness, as forests and marshes and rivers encroached and overran the countryside. They saw deer and bison and boar, ducks and geese and eagles, one lone moose and what might have been a wolf in the distance. They saw rusting farm equipment, collapsing roofs, burned out houses and barns, the remnants of orchards, and fields filled with flowers.

This area was still quite wet, compared with the new, hot, dry climate regime of Augusta, Maine. There were rivers and swamps and estuaries and beaver dams flooding the fields and forests. There were waterfowl and shorebirds in abundance. And everywhere there were orange and yellow signs bearing the radiation warning symbol. And at each village, a large boulder, on which had been painted the village's name and the number of souls who had lived there. Save for the ruins, it all looked quite normal, a beautiful spring day in the countryside. Yet they knew that there was radiation everywhere, waiting to be dug up from the ground and spilled out with the water. It reminded Linda of Keeley's hospital room, where she'd lain sick with the alien flu, in isolation from the world. It had looked so normal. Yet the air, they had thought at the time, had been filled with a deadly presence. Unseen dangers made the world feel surreal.

Right on the edge of the ghost town Chernobyl, after which the nuclear power plant, and the disaster itself, had been named, they saw a bright flash in the distance. Brenda pulled off the road, into a broken, overgrown parking lot in front of a collapsing elementary school, and came to a stop. The other van parked beside them and the two drivers, Linda and Cole and their crew, and the guide, Raf, got out of the car to scan the sky. Rising from a spot to the north and west of their position, from what appeared to be the abandoned city of Pripyat where the power plant was actually located, was a bright blue-white light with a yellow tail, like a rocket launching to the stars. After a moment, a second bright flash and a second rocket. Then a third and a fourth in rapid succession. Then more, all rising together in a cluster, gaining speed as they ascended, blue-white stars on yellow columns of fire, like giant dandelion puffs on stems. In less than a minute, there were too many to count, and they were all headed toward the same spot in the sky, directly overhead.

18.13

Zacharael saw the energy pulses and quickly scanned the near future to see the human-Life weapon systems known as "antigrav clusters" as they burst into the Interdict. He followed the clusters backward in time and space to their origination point. This was the clue he needed. Gabrielle had been taken from him. Hidden from his sight while his attention had been elsewhere. Now he had an idea where to look for her. Where one found power, one found the wielders of power. It had taken such powers to steal his human agent away from him. Perhaps now he could steal her back.

18.14

Following the dandelion puffs came huge, pulsing beams of sparkling purple energy. They coalesced into what seemed to be a vast tube of light and power that stretched straight and true from the ground to the point in the sky, almost directly overhead, where the rockets were heading. The purple tube roared like a waterfall, sending wave after wave of sparkling motes along its outer shell. The rockets, now inside the tube, began to burst in vast explosions of orange and yellow fire as they reached their target at the edge of space. The blasts sounded in the sky like thunderbolts. Whomever was responsible for this attack, they were clearly attempting to break a hole through the Grid.

Linda shielded her eyes from the display, then motioned to Cole and Brenda. "We have no idea whether this can hurt us!" she shouted over the din. "We need to get inside!" She opened her door and crawled into the van, motioning for the others to do the same. Brenda tried to start her van. The engine would not even turn over. Whether the cars would provide any protection was a moot point now. They had nowhere else to go.

18.15

Sinclair smiled lovingly at his wife. Dierdre had fallen asleep, bless her heart. She was missing the show. He glanced up at the lounge's viewscreen. Behind them stood the bartender, the server, and a small group of fellow passengers, including the Master's Right Man, Club, who no doubt felt a bit useless here inside Leader One. From what Sinclair could tell, the One-Two Punch was proceeding exactly as planned. Though all he had to go on was the visual data from the video, it surely seemed to him that the clusters had done their job and taken out the necessary Grid points. As long as the scalar cannon array could hold the hole open - and that would depend in part on their alien mole having done *his* job - they'd have no problem now. They might already be moving, as far as he knew. It was difficult to tell on the viewscreen, as the feed originated from a ground-based camera.

He finished his sparkling water. Time for something a bit more celebratory. He turned to the bartender. "Do you mind if I grab a bottle?" he asked.

The bartender nodded without looking at him. Sinclair chuckled. The show was so enthralling that the bartender could forget himself and allow a Director to serve his own drinks. That was as it should be. This day would live in the collective memory of the new colonies for decades and centuries to come. The beginning of a new era for the human species. The Giant Leap. Armstrong didn't know what the hell he'd been talking about.

18.16

Linda and her companions watched the pulsing purple energy cylinder rising from the town of Pripyat, just to their north and west. At soon as the dandelion rockets had all exploded, a massive disc rose slowly above the tree line, inside the purple tube that angled up to the sky. It was the largest wok Linda had ever seen or imagined. It must have been almost a mile across, and it glowed orange against the blue afternoon sky.

As it rose up inside the tube, another massive wok followed close behind it, and then another, and another. Soon there was a stack of over a dozen of these vast ships, all glowing and pulsing together. Linda shielded her eyes as their glows changed from deep orange to yellow, and then to a bright yellow-white. As one, the stack of ships flashed a white as bright and blinding as a nuclear airburst. Then they were gone, up through the tube, through what Linda assumed was a hole in the Grid, and off into the depths of space. It had transpired without a sound from the woks themselves, though they could still hear the roar of the purple cylinder.

The Families were gone.

18.17

In the storage hold of the vast command wok known as Leader One, a small black ball appeared. It disappeared a few moments later. It took with it a six-foot-long metallic cylinder.

18.18

Danny rose from his bunk at the sound of a woman screaming in the distance. Gina raised her arm, which she'd been holding over her eyes in an attempt to calm herself. "What's that?" she asked.

"I don't know," said Danny. He stepped toward the door and opened it, leaning forward to peek out into the hall. There was no one. Gina rolled out of her bunk and followed. Together they walked down the hall toward the screaming.

A few moments' walk brought them to a common room, where a great many of their colleagues had gathered. In the center of a small group stood an older woman dressed in expensive clothes, sobbing loudly. Danny stepped to the edge of the circle and stopped behind a young man in coveralls. "What happened?" he asked quietly.

The man spoke without turning toward him. "Says her husband just got sucked through the wall," he said.

18.19

As soon as the woks had disappeared through the hole, the purple energy beams fell away to nothing. The rockets had all burst. The woks were gone. The sky looked like a normal sky, with the Grid, looking as whole and impenetrable as ever, just starting to be visible in the fading late-afternoon light. Brenda opened her door and stepped out to get a better look. Linda joined her. Cole got out and stretched his legs and arms and shoulders before scanning the area around them. Raf, the guide, opened his door and leaned out to peer upward, but stayed in his seat. The driver of the second van, a young woman named Muriel, got out, followed by Annabelle, Doobie, and Marionette. The four of them looked around in wonder and confusion. Whatever it was they had just witnessed, it seemed to be over. The quiet had returned to the Chernobyl Exclusion Zone.

"What's that?" asked Marionette, pointing straight up, where the rockets had burst and the woks had disappeared.

The rest of them stared in the direction she was pointing. Nobody said anything for a few moments. Then Cole spoke. "That little black speck?" he asked. "Maybe a vulture?" Vultures seemed like a fitting sight for this place and time.

"There's another one," said Doobie.

"And a third one," said Linda.

The eight of them stood and watched the vultures.

But they weren't vultures. Whatever they were, they were falling toward the Earth.

And there were more than three. There were many more than three. There were dozens of them. Then scores. Then hundreds. Specks. Falling. Falling toward them.

When they realized what they were, the eight of them quickly returned to their vehicles and slammed their doors shut.

18.20

Jay Sinclair was surprised. Surprised that, when the unseen force had picked him up and pushed him across the bar, he hadn't been smashed into a pulp against the wall. Surprised to find himself tumbling through the sky above the Earth. Surprised to see that young, up-and-coming DuPont fellow tumbling nearby. Surprised to feel how cold it was, and surprised at how quickly he'd gone numb to it. Surprised that he could not draw a breath. Surprised at how he seemed to hang there, at how slowly he seemed to be falling. And he was surprised at how beautiful the Earth looked beneath him.

Alas.

But Jay Sinclair was not hanging there. He was not falling slowly. He was falling at the standard terminal velocity for a human body, which was approximately one hundred and twenty miles per hour, having accelerated to that speed at the standard rate of thirty-two feet per second per second, adjusted for air resistance, which had been almost nil at first. He was falling back to the place from which he had been attempting to escape.

Even so, Jason Carrington Parker Sinclair still got his wish. No longer would he have to live with those miserable Sleepers. And neither would he have to live through the complete unraveling of human society, and the death of the natural living systems upon which that society had been built.

As it turned out, when Jay Sinclair spoke of the Giant Leap, he hadn't really known what the hell he'd been talking about.

18.21

One newspaper called it "The Rain of Evil Men." Another called it "The Great Shake-Down." Yet another termed it "The One-Percent Solution," referring to a nickname for the rich and powerful that had come into vogue a decade or so earlier. In the years to come, it would come to be known, simply, as "The Great Fall." As in Humpty Dumpty. As in nobody could put them back together again.

Linda, Cole, and the others lived through the Great Fall as no others had, ducking down in their mini-van seats as human bodies rained down out of the sky all around them. The first one to land near Linda's van provoked a loud yelp and a "Lord have mercy" from Brenda. It wasn't until another body slammed into the hood and flopped over onto the ground that both Linda and Cole called out. There was one. Then two more. Than a handful. And soon they were falling like a heavy rain. When it was over, it looked like a battlefield from the American civil war.

Over six thousand bodies fell from the sky on the day of The Great Fall. More men than women. More light skinned than dark. More older than younger. Mostly well dressed. They were bankers and CEOs and politicians, scientists and academics, businessmen and lobbyists and brokers and traders. They were rich. They were powerful. They were movers and shakers and behind-the-scenes string pullers. They were members of exclusive clubs and secret groups. And a large majority of them came from old and distinguished families.

They were scattered across the exclusion zone, but were concentrated around the town of Chernobyl itself. They fell alone and they fell together. They fell in clumps and piles and lines and strange formations. They smashed into paved roads and parking lots, crashed through roofs, and splashed into ponds and rivers and lakes. They went splat in the mud. One even landed in one of the higher gondolas of the still-standing but long-defunct Ferris wheel at the amusement park in Pripyat. Not a one of them, as far as anyone could tell, survived the fall. Many appeared to have died before they hit the ground.

"Jesus," said Linda, as she watched it rain. Her voice was little more than a whisper.

18.22

"So why do they wipe our memories?" asked Ted.

"I'm sorry?" asked Carl.

Ted raised a shoulder. "You know. When we go back. The reincarnation thing. Why do we have to start from zero again? Why can't we remember our previous lives?"

Carl shook his head. They were sitting side by side, staring at the wall, trying to make a second door appear, since their repeated attempts to get the first one to open had all failed. "I think a few people do remember. At least as kids."

"Yeah, but then most of them forget. But even if there's a few exceptions, why do most people have to start with a blank slate?"

"Not sure they do, Ted. People come into life with all sorts of talents and knacks and fascinations. Some seem way wiser and older from the get go. And maybe we're all informed by our past lives in terms of what we want and how we react and how we feel and things like that, even if we don't remember it."

Ted turned to Carl and frowned. "You keep dodging the question, Bro."

Carl smiled. "So what is your question, exactly?"

"My question is, if we're all in this system where we come to the physical Earth and live many lives, all to grow and learn and mature and evolve and shit, then why don't they have the system set up so that we remember stuff from life to life? I mean, in everything else we do, we learn things and remember what we learned and apply it. You don't go to school every morning with your mind wiped clean. You build on what you learned yesterday. So why do we have to start each life with a clean slate? Doesn't make much sense to me. Seems the evolution process would proceed more quickly if they allowed us to remember from life to life."

Carl cocked his head in thought. "Maybe we start with a clean slate so we can make the same mistakes over and over and really learn from them. So the challenges are greater. So we're totally free to make choices."

Ted shook his head from side to side. "But that just doesn't make any sense, dude," *he said.* "I mean... Christ. What are these guys? Sadists? Like, we need it harder here? Haven't we already found out what the hell happens when we just keep making the same mistakes over and over? And didn't you just speculate that we've got the collective unconscious and all sorts of built-in traits and reactions and shit? So how are we totally free?"

"Maybe it's more a matter of what choices we make when we're not totally free," *said Carl.*

Ted shook his head in disgust. "You sound like you must work for them, Carl," *he said.* "You got an answer for everything." *He returned his attention to the wall and concentrated on imagining a door into existence.*

Carl sat and thought for a while, then cleared his throat. "Maybe the clean slate is so that we don't get stuck in one place," he said. "Cuz we also learn all sorts of things that limit us and shut us down and close us off. We get our minds made up and we fall into ruts. Maybe the clean slate is a blessing. A second chance. A do-over. A release from the accumulated garbage of a previous life, so we can try some new things. Like waking up in the morning and feeling refreshed and clear and clean and ready to go, rather than tired and bogged down and filled with toxins like the evening before."

Ted sighed but didn't look at Carl. "Maybe," he muttered.

"You just don't want to be a baby again, do you Ted," asked Carl, smiling.

Ted shook his head. "I hate them little buggers," he said. "Shit all over everything."

"Perhaps it would be good to have that judgment wiped clean before your next life, then, eh?"

Ted sighed and stared at the wall. Carl joined him.

They stared.

No door appeared.

Chapter ∅ Nineteen

19.1

Zacharael was filled with self-doubt. He understood, now, the reticence of the others of his kind to get involved. It was impossible to know whether he had done the right thing, or whether there even *was* a right thing. This was why the Primary had been formulated and adopted so very long ago.

Hanging in space above the Earth, he looked at the makeshift nullspace he had taken from the colony wok, just before it had departed forever. His observations and deductions had convinced him that the girl, Gabrielle, was inside. But what to do with her? He'd hoped to mold her into an instrument of choice, to create for her possibilities and options she might not otherwise have, and to put her in a place where her actions might have a significant impact on the fate of his Beloved. But he knew that his interference could shut down choices as easily as open them up, and that continuing interference might trigger her reactivity, causing her to rebel against him. To steal her away from this human exodus: she might not thank him for that. With her father having been selected against, and her human mate from her school having been selected for, she might have preferred to have been included.

The anguish of the Beloved roared away in the background of his being like a fusion furnace. He was both surprised and delighted to see that some justice had been exacted, and pleased that the Inter-Life had taken a stand. But he knew that the larger question remained, the more important choice had yet to be made. That choice was not in his hands. But there was one last action he was willing to take, as hopeless as it felt.

Zacharael gave the nullspace container a mental push. It began to move, dropping slowly down toward the Beloved. Zacharael followed, casting out his awareness through both time and space until he found the perfect spot. He guided the container gently to the Earth, following the general path taken by the woks as they made their exodus. He lowered Gabrielle to a field of wild flowers near the old cooling pond of the entombed nuclear power plant. The field was strewn with twisted bodies. More bodies had fallen into the pond and were now being nibbled on by the giant carp that lived there.

Zacharael landed the nullspace container right next to the body of Gabrielle's father. The body had landed feet first on the overgrown gravel roadway that surrounded the pond, shattering both of its legs and pushing the crushed bones up into his rib cage. The Angel touched the control panel at the container's end and waited for the mechanism to work. When he heard the top unlatch, and saw the cover begin to swing upward, Zacharael disappeared.

19.2

It would take many days for the thousands of bodies from the Great Fall to be collected, transported, identified where possible, and either cremated, buried, or sent back to their home countries to be cared for there. Many of the bodies were horribly mangled, either from the fall itself, and from what the body landed on, or from the predators and scavengers that fed upon them. When it was mostly sorted out, it was clear that those who had died in the Great Fall, at least those who could be identified, were invariably rich, powerful people who'd been responsible for vast amounts of human suffering and environmental destruction over the years. Many of them had turned out to have almost no public presence whatsoever, and what little was known about them simply tied them to one of the world's richest families. Many were never identified.

But what mattered now to Linda, who knew none of this yet, was what to do next. It was difficult to tell, from their particular vantage point, exactly what had just happened. It appeared, from what they could see in the sky before they'd retreated to their vehicles, that there had been thousands of bodies falling. And it looked as though those bodies were falling all across the Chernobyl Exclusion Zone. But they saw no sign of the woks themselves. No huge ships plummeting toward the ground. No large pieces from an explosion. It was Linda's guess that the ships themselves had made it through the Grid, and that perhaps many people, perhaps the vast majority, given the size of the ships and how many there were, had made it through, to make their escape from the dying Earth.

And so one of Linda's objectives may have now flown out of her reach: to stop The Families from escaping the planet they had helped to destroy. How could she know? Did those woks hold the entirety of what William had called "The Families?" If so, who were these that had fallen from the skies? They seemed to be predominantly rich, older men of European extraction, if such generalities could be made from skin color, hair, and the quality of their blood-soaked clothing. Were they the worst of the bunch? William had told her that the matter had been accounted for, that those who had done great evil would not get off scot-free. Was that what they had just witnessed? A dramatic sifting out of the most destructive and psychotic of the bunch? A culling of the Family herd?

If so, then who had done the sifting? Who had called the triage? And how had they decided who would make it through, and who would end up lying in the radioactive dust and mud of the CEZ? And where was William, then? And his inner circle he called the Evolutionary Element? Off to the stars? Sipping their champagne and laughing at the poor Sheeple back on Earth? Congratulating each other on their success in breaking through the Grid? And were there aliens sitting at the table across from them?

Perhaps this had all gone just as William had thought it would. Even the timing. Maybe he'd wanted her right here, to watch what happened. And maybe there was still something else.

"So what do we do now?" asked Cole. He'd stepped around the body of an ancient white-haired man and stood beside Linda as she surveyed the carnage that stretched around them as far as they could see.

Linda turned and gave Cole a bitter smile. "I think we keep going," she said. "We're so close now."

Annabelle spoke up from her spot near the second van. "Surely this Fisherman character is either long gone or amongst the dead," she said, waving toward a pile of three bodies not far from her.

Linda nodded, then took Cole's hand and walked him back toward their van, avoiding the bodies as best she could. She stopped near the van and looked at Annabelle. "That may be," she said, "but we keep going in any event. William's last words to me were *'Urbem Orsus.'* I intend to go there, to see the place The Families built, and to see what it was that William wanted me to see."

"How do you know he wanted you to see something?" asked Annabelle.

Linda's eyes tightened. "I told you before, Annabelle. I'm following my nose." She started to say more, then stopped herself. There was no use fighting this old woman and her fears.

Annabelle scrunched her face in distaste but said nothing more. Linda looked at Brenda, who stood near the driver's door of her van, seemingly in shock. "Brenda? Can you still drive us?"

Brenda swiveled her head, snapping to awareness. "Mrs. President?" she said.

Linda pointed in the direction from which the woks had risen. "To Pripyat. To the nuclear plant," she said. "I think we need to see the place where The Families launched their ships."

Brenda glanced up at the road, to determine if it would be passable now, with all the bodies. She looked at Linda and nodded. "I'll do my best."

Linda smiled. "Good." She knelt down to speak to their old Ukrainian guide, who'd remained in the back seat of the van. "Raf?" she said. "Will you still guide us?"

Raf keyed in on Linda's face as though she were the first living person he'd seen in decades. "Da," he said, blinking rapidly. He glanced out his window at the bodies, then back at Linda. He gave her a thumbs up. "We go now," he said, as if he hoped they would be away from the bodies in just a moment, as if he thought the bodies had only fallen in this parking lot. Linda sighed. He'd find out soon enough.

Linda turned to see Muriel already in the driver's seat of the second van. She nodded to Annabelle, who then turned and spoke a few words under her breath to Doobie and Marionette. The three of them got in their van. Linda and Cole got into the first van with Brenda.

The vans' engines started without a moment's hesitation now. Brenda put her van in gear and began to pick a slow, winding path between the bodies. She got to the road and turned left, taking them toward the center of the town of Chernobyl.

19.3

Gabrielle didn't remember much after she was lifted in the blue beam of light. She recalled screaming and struggling, but then it all got hazy and dark, like a half-forgotten nightmare. She had a snippet of memory of being inside the small ship. Her father was coming at her with a needle. She remembered his voice, all slow and wobbly, saying something about this being for her own good. She remembered feeling like she'd been buried alive. And then there was bright sunlight coming in around the edges of some top or covering and she pushed it up and breathed deeply and shielded her eyes against the glare. After a moment, she sat up and blinked, getting her eyes used to the light. She was sitting in a metal coffin on the edge of a small lake. There was a tall round thing, a cooling tower it must be, in the distance, and a shorter one next to it. And all around her, littering the ground, were what appeared to be dead bodies.

She pulled herself up, swung her legs over the side of the coffin, and sat on the edge. It was warm and very humid and there were huge dragonflies skimming the surface of the lake. A light breeze blew from the direction of the late-afternoon sun. There were no human sounds. No traffic. No machinery. The trees and grass and flowers all had the healthy green glow of spring.

She tried to piece together what had happened. Her father had found her. Somehow he'd known to look for her there at the airport. He no doubt meant to force her onto the colony woks, which were soon to depart, and had blown up the President's jets so that Linda could not follow him. From the cooling towers, and the fact that their group's destination had been Chernobyl, Gabrielle guessed that that was where she was. But how had she gotten away from her father? What was this coffin? And where were the rest of them, Linda and Cole and the others?

Something awful had happened to the colony ships. That's what all the bodies must mean. They must have taken off, and then one of them exploded or something. Gabrielle pushed up to a standing position and stretched her arms over her head. She bent to look inside the coffin. Her backpack was not there. Probably gone for good. Which meant she had no drinking water. Gabrielle sighed with frustration.

It didn't make sense. If a ship had exploded, wouldn't there be emergency crews here looking for survivors? The Families wouldn't just abandon their own people, would they? And shouldn't there be pieces of the wok itself here? Crash debris? The colony ships were huge, according to her father. Surely they'd leave wreckage everywhere?

There was too much she didn't understand, and she wasn't going to find answers just standing there. She had no idea which areas here were safe, in terms of radiation, but reasoned that if the cooling towers were in one direction, she should go the other. She stepped around the shattered, bloody remains of a middle-aged man who lay face down in the gravel beside the coffin, and started down the overgrown road, heading southward along the edge of the lake. It looked like there was a town in the distance.

It was then that she noticed the tiny island out in the pond, and the tiny gray building on the island, and the blinking red light on the building's door.

19.4

Stan shook his head as he walked down the hospital hallway. If this Dr. Pintick was a hybrid it was news to him, judging from his interaction just moments ago. Seemed like a regular guy to Stan. Sure did look human. He'd chatted away about Georgia weather and the hurricane and his gold investments while adjusting a piece of equipment. A regular guy. Which meant, of course, that the hybrids could be anywhere now. Hidden. Embedded. Spies. Whatever.

But Pintick was clearly what he said he was, judging from his dealings with the other hybrids, the ones who you could easily tell *were* hybrids from their strange features and odd manner. You could feel it, sometimes, when they were speaking mind to mind. And the looks they exchanged with each other: there was something definitely nonhuman about them. Pintick had arrived in the middle of the night and gone right to work getting his lab set up. It was only eight in the morning and he'd already begun his analysis of the contents of the vial. He seemed optimistic that he'd solve the puzzle quickly. Which meant that Stan had better follow up on yesterday's calls with the production and distribution facilities he'd decided to work with.

But first, a quick visit with Keeley, since he was here. He made his way to her room and popped his head in. She was awake, so he donned a mask and gloves and stepped into her room.

"'Bout time you got your ass back to work, isn't it?" he asked, grinning widely so she'd see he was joking behind his mask.

Keeley scoffed. "'Bout time you got your ass in here to visit me," she said, putting on a fake frown.

Stan stood beside her bed. "Sorry, old girl," he said. "Been a bit busy lately."

Keeley reach out and took Stan's hand. "Mary told me," she said. "You're stuck running the country while our Linda flits off on yet another crazy adventure."

"That's about the size of it," said Stan. "Though, technically, Speaker Simpson is the President now."

"You gonna tell him the truth?" asked Keeley.

"Linda thinks he'll do a better job if he doesn't know," said Stan.

Keeley nodded. "She's probably right."

"So how you feeling?"

Keeley rubbed her eyes. "Pretty good. Weak. Fuzzy headed sometimes. My joints ache. But mostly pretty good. My memory of being sick was that it was a glorious, euphoric experience. Not that I'd want to repeat it."

"I'm glad to hear you're doing better," said Stan. "I know Mary's been really worried. We all were." Stan sat lightly on the edge of Keeley's bed. "So, this serum from that vial Linda brought back from Squirrel Island: it seems to have done the trick."

Keeley nodded. "Seems to have, Stan. One little shot and I turned right around."

Stan motioned toward the door with his head. "They're analyzing it right now. Figure out how it's made. So we can make more. Get it out to the people Stop this thing. Or get ready to."

"Seems you're of the opinion that we should use it," said Keeley.

"I've made no secret of that," Stan said. "Seems to me we have no choice in the matter. Not if we wish to remain who we are." He squeezed Keeley's hand. "How about you?"

Keeley sighed, shook her head. "I'm not sure we can keep it under wraps at this point," she said. "Too many people know about it. News'll get out. It always does. And that'll force the issue." She reached up to run her fingers lightly over her cheeks, as if to reassure herself that the rash was still gone. "I sure wouldn't want Linda's job."

Stan sighed. "Yeah. And I'm not sure she's even capable of thinking clearly about it right now, you know? What with her son missing. And her wild notion that she can go confront that Fisherman bozo."

"You think she's losing it?" asked Keeley, raising an eyebrow.

Stan shrugged his uncertainty. "Not that, really," he said. "I just know how much feelings of revenge can skew your thinking, you know?" He watched Keeley closely, searching for clues as to how she was hearing his words. "So I'm not sure she's clear enough to make this choice on her own."

Keeley nodded, looking away to think for a moment. "Yeah," she said at last. She turned to Stan. "I wish she'd just come back so we could get this sorted out."

"Me too," said Stan.

"Maybe we don't *want* to remain who we are," said Keeley.

19.5

The drive would have been strange in any event. Radiation signs everywhere. Old murals, peeling and flaking. Buildings in ruin. Trees and plants where they should not be. Fields and yards and side streets flooded. Cave-ins and burn-outs and rusted vehicles. All of it bursting with life, despite the radiation, despite the heat. Flowers and forests and marshes were pushing their way through the Zone, covering up the mistakes of the past. And everywhere there were animals: deer and bison and elk, eagles and hawks and waterfowl and songbirds galore. Wolves and foxes and wild boar.

The addition of hundreds of dead human bodies added little to the strangeness, at least for those who hadn't been here before. In a way, the bodies fit right in, adding the final zombie-apocalypse touch to this surreal, movie-like world. Those same bodies, transported to an earlier time, to a bustling city street or suburb, would have stood out like the horror they really were. Here, they looked more like set dressing.

Such were Linda's thoughts as they made their way out of Chernobyl and north to the nuclear plant. It was a four-mile drive, give or take, but it took them at least thirty minutes. Brenda had quickly proven her skills as a driver, winding her way along the body-strewn highway. Only twice did they have to get out and move some bodies, which meant scaring away the wolves and foxes and birds of prey which were already scavenging the corpses. Cole, Brenda, Marionette, and Doobie did most of the heavy lifting, though Linda pitched in when necessary. Muriel was too horrified to touch anything. Annabelle was too old to lift much. Raf wouldn't get out of the van.

At one point, back in the town of Chernobyl, right in the center of an intersection, they saw a pile of bodies in the form of a cone or pyramid. The effect was so spooky - it looked as though they'd been intentionally stacked there - that Brenda turned the corner and sped away as quickly as she could. There was nobody there to stack the bodies like that, as far as they knew. And there hadn't been time. So it had to have happened by chance. But still...

Soon enough, the Chernobyl Nuclear Power Plant rose up before them through the trees. They drove out of the woods and into the more open flats that surrounded the plant. Ahead, to the northwest, were two cooling towers, one tall, the other short and seemingly only partially finished. To their right was the cooling reservoir, home of the famed "giant catfish." They made their way slowly up the road, scanning the area for something out of the ordinary. Linda, knowing of The Families' love for grand gestures, joked that they probably used the cooling tower as an entrance for wok flights. Cole guessed that there had to be ground-based entrances as well, for the delivery of equipment, foodstuffs, and the like. The question was, could they find one? The other question was, was there anybody still around? They'd assumed that all they'd have to do was show up and that The Families' security people would pick them up and bring them in. But maybe now they were on their own.

Brenda pulled her lead van to a stop. Just ahead, off to the right of the road, was what looked like a shiny, metallic capsule, almost like a coffin. It's top had been opened. Beside it was the mangled body of a middle-aged man in a nice suit. The travelers and drivers got out, to check out the coffin and stretch their legs and survey the area.

"Is the radiation bad here, Raf?" asked Linda, ducking her head down to talk to their still-seated guide.

Raf looked around, then shook his head. "Not so bad," he said, trying to smile. "Okay but not for long time."

"Got it," said Linda. "Thanks." Not an immediate problem. She walked over to the body. The legs were smashed and crumpled. He hit feet first and flopped face forward to the ground. There was something strangely familiar about him. Linda pushed at his chest with her foot, turning him enough to see a part of her face. She gasped. Cole joined her and she pointed down at the body. "Guy Legrand," she said in a low voice only Cole could hear. It was Gabrielle's father. Cole inhaled sharply. Three years before, Legrand, whom they'd hoped would help them, had turned them over to Agent Rice, then sat there and watched and laughed as Rice had shot Cole in the chest.

"Good," he said. He stepped away to examine the coffin with Brenda.

Linda pushed the body back down to hide the face, then followed. "Any idea what we're looking at here, Brenda?"

Brenda shook her head. "No idea, Ma'am," she said.

They heard a voice, calling from a distance, and turned in the direction of the sound. Across the cooling reservoir was a small strip of land. An island. On the island was a tiny gray building with a blinking red light. Standing next to the building, jumping up and down and calling their names, was a very happy Gabrielle.

19.6

Alice sat with the girls on the sofas in the common room. Emily and Grace were eating their breakfast, which Isaac had prepared for them. Ness was in the kitchen now, talking to Isaac about the diet requirements and preferences of the Middle Children. "Really?" she kept saying, over and over. "Really?"

The girls had been unhappy to learn that their parents had been put in danger. Mary had spoken with Stan, who'd updated her regarding the travelers and their progress, how the planes had been blown up, how Gabrielle had been abducted. The girls were relieved to know that nobody'd been hurt in the blasts, and that they'd found another plane, but were unhappy for Gabrielle, even though neither of the girls had got to know her at all. Mostly they were afraid for their folks. The fact that spaceships could appear in the sky and blow things up did not set their minds at ease.

Alice felt pulled in two different directions. Ambivalent, the word was. Torn. On the one hand, she wished to help her friends. She could easily send a couple of woks piloted by Middle Children to watch over Mrs. Linda and her people. But on the other hand, her refusal to involve herself and the Middle Children in the affairs of their parents felt like true wisdom. She'd been worried that, during their latest battle, as humans had struggled to break through the Life's Interdict, one or both of those parents would lash out at the Middle Children. Nothing like that had happened, at least so far, so perhaps the fear had been groundless. But Alice found it difficult to tell. The Middle Children's request to share the Earth with the humans might have seemed a provocative move to the Life. But her alignment was not with the twisted humans whom the Life wished to contain. It was with the rest of them, those left behind.

"So will our Mom and Dad be safe now, do you think?" asked Grace of Alice.

Alice went inside herself and thought for a moment, then looked at Grace and Emily. She crafted a smile, knowing that that gesture would help put the girls at ease. "Preliminary reports from reconnaissance woks indicate that those who have wished harm to your parents have either left the planet or are now deceased," she said. "While those who have left might return, and while the full intentions of the Life are closed to me, and while all who live on this planet now face a higher than normal degree of risk, the odds that your parents will return unharmed are now judged to be high."

Grace exhaled deeply. Emily closed her eyes and nodded her head. "That's good," said Grace. She finished her piece of toast and took a bite of her eggs.

"Do you know where they are right now?" asked Emily.

Alice softened her focus and cast out across the network of hybrid minds. Though the humans had refused direct aid, the Middle Children had kept an eye on the situation from a distance. She took in the latest update, then blinked her eyes and looked at Emily. "They continue on to the place known as *Urbem Orsus*," she said.

Emily nodded. They'd been briefed on their parents' plans by Mary just after they went into the nullspace apartment. "But the people that wanted to hurt them are no longer there?" she asked.

Alice cocked her head. "That is what our preliminary analysis tells us," she said.

19.7

A bit of shouting and gesturing convinced Linda's crew that they should go out to meet Gabrielle, rather than the other way around. It appeared that Gabrielle's island was connected to the mainland by a thin strip, and they understood the girl's big, circular arm waves to mean that they needed to go around the cooling pond to reach her. So they piled back into the vans and drove toward the towers.

They soon encountered a canal between themselves and the towers. It had both rail and vehicle bridges over it, but the bridge that the minivans might use looked like it might fall into the canal at any moment. They backed up a bit, parked the vans, and set out on foot across the rail bridge, moving slowly so as not to twist an ankle on the rails and ties.

"You're thinking that gray building with the emergency light on it is an entrance, right?" asked Annabelle, who seemed to be having little difficulty keeping up with the group.

"I am," said Linda as she led them over the bridge and along the railroad bed. The towers rose up on their left as they walked. Nuclear cooling towers had always given Linda a creepy feeling. But now, here in this site of a major nuclear disaster, where she might have expected to feel even more disquiet, the towers reminded her of her old farm, of rusted silos and dilapidated corn cribs. With the land reclaimed by trees and shrubs, with the warmth of the afternoon sun on their heads, with the silencing of civilization and the rising of birdsong, the place felt serene. The crazy energy that had pulsed and hummed here was long gone, or deeply entombed. Were it not for the knowledge of low levels of radiation surrounding them, Linda might have felt more at peace here than she'd felt in a long while.

The railway continued on across a second canal. Beyond that were roads and parking lots at the base of the unfinished tower on the left, and an overgrown gravel road to the right. They headed down the gravel road, grateful for the partial shade. Brenda, fluent in Ukrainian, found a sign that indicated that this was the way to the cooling pond, confirming what they already suspected. Brenda had to act as guide now, as Raf and Muriel had elected to stay with the vans.

"It's just the sort of thing they would do," said Linda, continuing to answer Annabelle's question. She turned and looked at the old woman behind her, and the rest of their crew behind Annabelle, then pushed on ahead. "Like how they and the aliens built their underground Lodges right under our noses in major cities across the planet. Or how they replaced me with a virtual twin and imprisoned me under my old vacation cabin. Or just building their City of Beginnings under one of the worst nuclear disasters of all time. These guys love grand, theatrical gestures, and situations fraught with irony and meaning. So of course they can't put their ground entrance along the side of the road or in a parking lot. They have to put it out at the end of a tiny spit of land surrounded by radioactive water. Or course they do!" Linda got animated as she spoke, her voice rising and her arms and hands waving about.

She stopped, turned to face Annabelle, and took a deep breath and smiled gently. "In a way, Annabelle," she said more evenly, "that's why I'm dragging you guys around the world instead of staying home and taking care of the things I should be taking care of. I know William, you see. The Fisherman. I know he's got one more grand gesture up his sleeve." She looked at Cole and Doobie and Marionette and Brenda, then back to Annabelle. "And I'm trying to match it with a grand gesture of my own." She turned and peered along the gravel roadway, noting the light area at the end. She turned back to her fellow travelers. "So, yeah," she said. "We didn't stop them going. Maybe that was never a possibility. But there's still something here for me. For us. I can feel it. So, if you'll all just indulge me for a little while longer, I think we'll soon find out what it is."

"Just so long as it's not some trap set to snap down and chop our fool heads off," said Annabelle. She smiled at Linda. It may have been the first time.

Linda led them down the road. It curved to the left and brought them out into a clearing in which sat a cluster of two-story brick buildings, overgrown and in disrepair. On the side of one building was a sign that read "Polevaya Radioecology Center." The path continued on through the woods surrounding the buildings, then turned to the right. They passed a pair of rusted out fire trucks and an overturned rowboat and then found themselves on the shore of the cooling reservoir. The causeway was right before them.

They started out. The tiny island was just ahead now, roughly south and east. Their backs were to the cooling towers. The afternoon sun was low in the sky to their right, and the air was beginning to cool. The causeway was no more than fifteen feet wide, and less in some spots, and it looked to stretch for half a mile or more out to the island. It was covered with grasses and wildflowers and the occasional small shrub or sapling, all growing out of what was mostly rock and gravel, put there to create this strange peninsula. Linda stayed in the lead, with Cole now at her side. The rest followed in single file, with Brenda in the rear. On either side of them the reservoir stretched into the distance. The views were beautiful. The light breeze blowing across the water was refreshing and welcome.

As they walked they could see Gabrielle, waiting at the point where the causeway met the island. Soon they were close enough to see her wide grin.

19.8

Mary had returned to the nullspace to be with the girls and was lying on the carpet in the common room, petting the cat the girls had named Mihos. Ness sat on a sofa. Grace and Emily sat in the two armchairs. They were all eating snacks that Isaac had brought them, crackers and cheese and squares of dark chocolate. Where he'd obtained chocolate none of them could guess. They were just glad that he had. Isaac made a half-smile in response to their inquiries, but said nothing.

"So Stan confirms what Alice told you," said Mary to the girls. "Your dad and Linda are safe and sound and at their destination. Apparently he found somebody he could trust in the military. Somebody who can track their iDent chips via satellite."

"I knew them dang things would have a good side," said Ness. She took another piece of the cheese, a homemade cheddar she found delicious.

"Are they coming back soon?" asked Grace.

"I don't know, hon," said Mary. "Stan hasn't spoken with your mother since just before they drove into Chernobyl. Apparently there's no working cell system inside the Exclusion Zone."

Ness shook her head. "All these high-tech alien gizmos around here and the U.S. government is stuck with bad cell phone service."

"So they made it to the place where all the bad guys live, but the bad guys are all gone," said Emily with a frown. "So why don't they just come home?"

Mary pushed up into a sitting position. "I think your folks just want to look around the place first," she said gently. "I don't think they'll be long."

"Any news about Iain?" asked Ness.

Mary flinched, wishing she'd discussed this with Ness privately. She shook her head. "Nothing yet," she said. She glanced toward the door to Iain's bedroom. They all knew that his body lay right there, in his bed, hooked to monitors and catheters and watched over by a hybrid nurse who visited regularly. Mary looked at the girls. "The Middle Children have done a rough scan in jumptime and found nothing. Now they've begun a much more finely tuned scan." She glanced at Ness for support. "He might very well be out there, lost, trying to find his way back, just like you all were when you were inside the Murk. If Alice is right, and he's lost in time, well, that's a much bigger haystack to search through."

"And Mihos is looking for him as well," added Emily, reminding them of their cat's double life.

Grace sighed heavily.

Mary looked at the younger girl. "What's up, Grace?" she said. Grace's field had darkened considerably.

Grace shook her head from side to side. "He's not lost," she muttered.

"He's not lost?" asked Ness.

"No," said Grace, angrily, as if she might use rage to hold back her tears. "He's gone."

19.9

It took them a few minutes to catch up. Gabrielle told them what she knew so far, and of her suspicion that Zacharael had been involved in her rescue. Linda and Cole told of their adventures since Gabrielle's abduction: the new plane, the drive into Chernobyl, the vast light show as The Families' huge woks had taken off, the rain of bodies. Gabrielle knew little more than they did about what it all meant. She did confirm Linda's assumption that the colony woks were meant to transport tens of thousands of passengers. The number who had fallen back to Earth must have represented a tiny portion of the whole.

Gabrielle had already opened the unlocked door on the little gray building and had scoped out what was inside. There was a wide, stone stairway that seemed to go down into the very bowels of the Earth. And there was a working elevator. But she'd been too scared to go very far inside, and then Linda and her group had arrived to save her from making that choice on her own.

They started toward the building. The island itself was long and narrow, maybe a mile in length and a couple of hundred feet across. It was dotted with trees, and the remains of the old gravel path were still clearly visible, running down to the southern end where the causeway continued on, heading further out into the reservoir. About two-thirds of the way down the island sat the small gray structure. It was built from concrete block, with a gray metal roof and a single, gray, metal door facing to the southwest. To the right of the door was a red emergency light. Inside the light was a tiny reflector that rotated once per second, resulting in the flashing effect.

Cole stepped to the door and pulled it open. Inside and to the left was an office chair and a desk with a computer on it. Apparently they had kept a guard stationed here. To the right was the stairwell. In the center was the elevator door. Cole and Linda stepped to the top of the stairwell and leaned over the edge. They counted at least twenty floors before they could no longer be sure. It was all still well lit. Gabrielle stepped up to the elevator and pushed the call button, as she had before they arrived. The door opened instantly. The elevator compartment was clean and well lit, and it looked like it would hold them all.

Linda turned to her companions. "Anybody wanna sit this one out you're free to do so," she said with a smile. She stepped onto the elevator and stood by the back wall. The rest of them followed.

19.10

Danny and Gina stayed put in their little two-bunk cell and listened to the announcements and waited. Every now and then one of them would stick their head out into the hallway, or make their way to the lounge or dining areas, and listen to the scuttlebutt, and maybe ask a question or two. From what they could make out, the colony woks had all made it to Enceladus and were now hovering over the Herschel Colony, circling the wagons while they figured out their next steps. The man whose wife they'd seen crying had turned out to be one of The Families' major contributors for the Scalar Cannon project. And he wasn't the only one to have been swept out of the woks as they passed through the Grid. Some said that there were hundreds now missing. Others said the total was more likely in the thousands. And all of the missing, as far as anyone could tell so far, were either Family members or higher-ups somewhere in their associate organizations. The missing included most of the Directorate, and the Master himself. They were the rich and powerful. They'd been picked up and tossed from the colony woks by an unseen hand. Where they'd been taken was anybody's guess.

But the hand was no longer unseen, was it? As soon as they'd stopped at Enceladus, small, ghostly figures had appeared in dozens of places in every wok in the fleet. They looked like holographic projections, though where they were coming from nobody could tell. It was one of the Grays, the Life. A little old guy in a long, flowing red robe. He appeared out of nowhere and began to speak.

"Greetings, spacemen," said the little alien, "and bon voyage." He had what appeared to be a slight smirk on his face. "I hope you folks know what a favor we've done you, ridding your ships of rats before you head out across the great seas of space." The little alien's eyes wrinkled as though he were grinning. "Look at me," he said, "Mr. Metaphor." He cleared his throat. "So, anyways," he continued. "We the Living Beings, on behalf of the local group of the vast Cogency, just wanted to wish you well on your new adventure. Those of you who have been selected *for* will soon realize that you still have everyone and everything you need to make your new colonies a success, once you get past the loss of most of your leadership, and reorganize yourselves. You will now be left alone for a period of time, during which you can establish your species in the physical realm, and establish *for yourselves* exactly what sort of people you wish to be from here on out. Further contact with the Cogency, including the possibility of gaining provisional membership status, will depend on the choices you make in the coming years. You will not see us, but we will be watching, as we always have. We understand the exigencies that have compelled you to leave your home planet. Please understand that your decision is irrevocable, and that you will not be allowed or welcomed back. We trust that this aligns with your intent." The little man looked back and forth as though he were gazing out over his audience. Then he bowed a slight bow and smirked again. "For now, may you leave with our thanks and blessings, and may you further life and consciousness wherever you go." With that he was gone.

Neither Danny nor Gina saw the original apparitions. But the little alien's short speech had been captured on video and was now being shown repeatedly on the viewscreens. "Do you suppose Director Sinclair was one of those rats?" asked Gina after they'd watched the video.

Danny shrugged. "Maybe," he said, "But I'm not sure it matters now. The whole project is topsy-turvy. People are in an uproar. Nobody's going to question us at this point. And they're going to be looking for smart, competent people." He reached out and pulled her to him and held her close. "All we have to do is show up and do our best. We'll fit right in in no time."

"We'd better," said Gina, quietly. "Cuz we can't go back."

19.11

There were thirty-three floors in the underground city of *Urbem Orsus*, if the buttons in the elevator were an accurate representation of the whole of the place. Given that the city had to hold tens of thousands of people, the systems to keep them alive and fed, the equipment they'd be taking along with them, the weapons they'd needed to punch through the Grid, and the fleet of colony woks itself, they knew that the underground structure had to be far larger than they could ever fully explore themselves. They had no real idea what they were looking for, nor how they might find it. And they didn't know, for sure, that they were actually alone here. So how should they proceed?

"Signs and portents," said Linda, as she pushed the number two on the elevator panel. "We'll go by gut feelings and intuition and signs and portents. So tune in, y'all, and speak up if you have a feeling or an idea." She looked around at her traveling companions. "The Fellowship of the Vial," Cole had jokingly called them. But it fit, in a weird way. The events of their journey had brought them together as fellows. And that vial still remained the central question on Linda's mind. Cole. Annabelle. Doobie and Marionette. Gabrielle. Brenda. They shared the journey now. None of them had opted out. For some reason the universe had seen fit to throw this particular group of people together, to explore the vast city of *Urbem Orsus*, which The Families had recently forsaken. A city that may yet hold a surprise, a grand gesture, and maybe even an answer.

The door opened to level two. They stepped out into a wide corridor that extended in both directions, with double doors at each end, and more passageways beyond the doors. Everything was well lit. The air was fresh and cool and comfortable. The corridor was smooth, like polished stone, and painted a pastel green, rounded at the top corners but with sharp right angles between the floor and walls. The floor was covered in standard institutional carpeting, though a deep burgundy rather than gray. The light came from a continuous strip that glowed soft and warm overhead. It reminded

Linda of the human side of the vast human-alien lodge she'd been in under Washington D.C. It was founded on alien technology, but adapted to human sensibilities.

Committed to following her nose, but still open to input and intuition from any of them, Linda turned to the left, leading them down the corridor and through the double doors. A little further along the next corridor they came to a T-intersection. On the wall before them, mounted behind Lucite, was a diagram of what appeared to be the entire floor, and underneath that, a side-view cutaway showing the thirty-three floors stacked like pancakes. Everything was clearly labeled in English.

"That was lucky," said Cole.

"There are probably maps like this all over the place, at key points," said Linda. "But yeah..."

"Looks like the elevator we took down from the little island runs through the southern end of the city," said Cole, pointing at the map. "That would put most of the city itself directly under the nuclear power plant, and maybe under Pripyat as well."

"And it looks like if we walked to the other end of the city on this level, we'd run into their wok hangars," said Marionette, also pointing.

"I wonder how far down the top level is from the surface," said Brenda.

Gabrielle stepped forward to examine the cutaway. She followed the floors with her fingers until she found the one she'd been looking for. "The members of the Directorate would have been housed here," she said, pointing to a large section of level four. "Right under the hangars." She turned to Linda. "That's where my folks would be," she said. "Or had been." Her face was pinched into a frown but Linda thought she heard a note of hopefulness in the girl's voice. They had not yet told her about her father, thinking that that could wait until they were away from here. Maybe that was a mistake.

Linda nodded. "We need to learn if there's anyone here at all," she said. She studied the map. "Does anybody see where we might find a security or police office?" There had to be something for a city this size, especially one trying to hide from the entire world.

"Here," offered Doobie, pointing. "There's a small space labeled 'Sec' on every level. Looks like maybe most of the levels share a basic floor plan. The main security office is probably on the level labeled "Security and Operations.'" He pointed at the level on the cutaway. It was fairly centrally located, right under a large, open space that seemed to extend across four different levels.

"So I say we go check out security on this level first," said Linda. She looked around at her crew. "Does it make sense that we all stay together?" Everybody nodded. Nobody wanted to split up.

Linda started back down the hall and toward the elevator down which they had ridden. They passed the elevator and continued down another corridor, this one filled with doors on either side that opened up to two-bunk housing units. Working from memory of the map, they took a corridor to the right and then another to the left. They saw nobody at all along the way. And when they came to the security office on the right, it was empty as well. Lights were on. Computers were still on. There were papers strewn about on the desk. It looked as though whoever had been there had just stepped out for a trip to the bathroom. Apparently those who had left the planet did not care what they left behind.

They continued on with no particular destination in mind. The map had shown elevators all over the place. And they'd passed another map on their way to the security office. There seemed little danger of getting lost. And, so far, no danger of running into anybody who didn't want them there. Linda relaxed a bit and kept on.

The next map showed that they were nearing a cafeteria, of which there were apparently six on each level. At the possibility of finding something to drink, Linda began to feel her thirst. "I could use a cold one," muttered Doobie. The others agreed that some food and drink might be just the ticket in this strange ghost town. They headed that way.

Linda stood staring at the map for a while before following them. There was something familiar about the shape of this city. The levels were not all the same size. The top ones were smaller. Gradually they got longer and wider, but then they reduced in size again as they neared the bottom. If one pulled the city of *Urbem Orsus* up out of the ground and looked at it, it might seem to be roughly shaped like a potato, with a definite, conical bulge at the bottom. She might have expected a cylinder or a cube. But a potato? She had not expected that.

Ah well. There was water nearby, hopefully. Maybe even a snack. Linda hurried to catch up with the others.

19.12

Cole pondered their situation as they stood in the huge, stainless steel, restaurant-style kitchen, eating leftovers from the refrigerator and drinking bottled water and good beer and expensive wine. He glanced at the Lucite-framed map of *Urbem Orsus* on the wall by the door. It was all about choices now, and he was not certain that he understood how things should go from here on out. It was clear to him that Linda had dragged them all to *Urbem Orsus* for reasons of which she was not fully aware. There had never been any hope of stopping The Families from leaving the planet, as far as Cole could see. She was here in search of the Fisherman. Because whether she wanted to admit it or not, she had held out some hope that he could, and would, help her choose, despite his insistence that the fate of humanity was on her shoulders alone.

Cole understood Linda's need. How somebody could choose to allow the deliberate reduction of the human population he could not fathom. And yet, given these times, and given what was possible, perhaps even certain, if such a reduction was not made, he understood that the choice was not an easy one. And to have it forced on you, as Linda had. It would change her forever, whatever choice she made. Haunt her. Maybe even destroy her. Cole regarded his wife from across the chef's prep table. Linda could not escape her burden. That secret hope had been dashed. The Fisherman had gone, avoiding the encumbrance Linda had wished to put back on him. So why were they still here?

The pantry and huge walk-in refrigerator were well stocked with quality foods, like the larder of an expensive organic restaurant. Everything was of the highest quality. There was nothing here off the GroCo truck. Cole had pulled out an almost full pan of some chicken dish, crusty baked breasts rolled with cheese and greens and nuts. He hadn't seen food this good in a long time. The chicken was wonderful cold and Cole took two pieces. Linda had a piece of the chicken and had discovered some salad to go with it. The others found things to add to their meal. Doobie and Marionette had laid out a wide choice of beverages, then grabbed some beers and ducked around the corner for a few moments alone. Annabelle had set plates and cutlery on the counter. It all felt spooky and surreal to Cole. Like they were characters in some disaster film, the last people on Earth. Was it only a matter of time before the zombies arrived?

Cole certainly felt like a movie character. This whole thing about the Wayfaring Stranger and the Church and how he was supposed to stop Linda from destroying the human race: none of that felt like the real world. Once again, life had grabbed him by the collar and dragged him along so forcefully that it was all he could do to stay on his feet.

Cole watched Linda, who stood across the table from him, stabbing at a salad and asking Brenda questions about her job and her connection to Mr. Bluebird. He loved his wife. He did not doubt that. But he was not sure who she was anymore. Something had changed her during her confinement on Mars. There was a hardness to her that was new. A coldness, perhaps. A stern determination that had kept her moving since they'd found each other on Squirrel Island. Circumstances alone could certainly explain that. The urgencies of dealing with The Families, and the disposition of that vial of serum, could not be denied. But it was more than that. It felt, to Cole, like Linda was running. He did not know whether she was running away from something, or towards it. It might have been both.

Though he hated the idea, Cole had to admit that he was no longer sure that he could trust his wife. He'd deferred to her judgments for so long that the idea that she had become somehow unsteady or confused or untrustworthy was difficult to sanction. She was the President, after all. She was strong. She was the leader. It was her job to make decisions. But the idea was there, inside of him, whether he wanted it there or not. He found himself questioning the things she said now, the judgments she made, and the decisions. He found himself wondering if maybe she wasn't suffering from some post-traumatic stress, if perhaps her thinking was no longer clear. They were continuing to explore this vast, vacant city rather than return to their children because Linda was convinced that there was some big thing here for her to find. Cole was not convinced.

Was it that book that had put the idea into his mind? *The Book of the Stranger* that Annabelle had shown him? Was it Annabelle's own skepticism and wariness that had infected him? Clearly the old woman was here to keep her fierce, wrinkled, eagle-eyes on Linda, whom Annabelle regarded as a threat to humanity. And Cole could feel how protective Annabelle felt towards him, and how ready she was to help or defend him should he take action to defy his wife in some way. Cole's bullshit detector told him that the whole thing was nonsense. The Book. The Church. His alien self. All of it. But there was no denying the strange coincidences, and the wild powers that had arisen in him. There was something more than bullshit here. And Linda did seem to hold the fate of humanity in her hands.

But which choices spelled destruction for the human race, and which did not? Cole grabbed a handful of roasted almonds from the tin Doobie offered and popped them one by one into his mouth. Would stopping The Families from leaving have somehow saved humanity? Or was it letting them go that was the correct choice? Would giving the serum in the vial to the world community prevent the extinction of humanity? Or should she hold it back and let the disease run its course? Perhaps a population reduction was the very thing that would save the species? And did any of that matter, now that part of "the species" had left the Earth and gone off to start a new life elsewhere? Was there any way to know? Or were they doomed to play their sad, confused roles in this cosmic game of *Let's Make a Deal*, never to know what's behind door number two until they make their choices and Monty opens the door?

It occurred to Cole that he had changed as much as Linda had in their time apart from each other. He'd experienced those hops, the strange trips that had loosened him up from this present life in some way in a way he had yet to fully grasp. It was as though he'd been given glimpses of past and future lives, to convince him that this person he thought he was - this Cole Thomas in this body with this personality and this life - was not really him. That he, the "he" inside that could step back and ponder such things, was much bigger than any of those lives, and much bigger than his current life. And maybe that "he" was very different from what Cole had supposed. Those experiences had opened something up in him, something that could catch bullets and knock guns from people's hands, something that could create tunnels out of light that would save himself and his friends from certain drowning. Clearly there had been more to him than he'd known.

Cole was coming into his power, it seemed. His true self-knowledge. And so of course he was deferring less to Linda, and doubting her ability to know and see and do all. He had powers as well. He saw things as surely as she did. He had knowings and intuitions and rational capacities. Perhaps all that was happening was that he was finally stepping fully into his marriage as a partner. Maybe it was exactly as it should be. Maybe Linda actually needed him to doubt her. Maybe he should be the one to share her burden.

Cole wiped his mouth with a pure white, crisp, cloth napkin and lifted his beer. "A toast," he said, looking around the room at his traveling companions. "To life," he continued. "To love. To those we've lost and those we will meet again. And to all of us, here in this strange place, doing our best to serve ourselves and each other and the world." He looked from one to the other, offering his smile and his attention, weaving them together in connections in the same way he'd crafted a sphere of light. "I don't know why we're here or what we'll find or how it will all turn out. I just know that, right now, I feel honored by the gods to have been chosen for this task." He put his beer bottle to his lips and finished it, then set in with a click on the stainless steel counter and looked at Linda. "You said we should tell you if we have any feelings or intuitions," he said. He pointed at the map. "There's a huge multi-level room in the center of this city. Something tells me we should go there next."

19.13

Stan looked up at the muted television in the corner of his office and sighed. The whole world thought Linda Travis was dead. The remembrances and farewells and speculations ran almost continuously. Sten and Eddie had taken to creating content for the deception, doing interviews, visiting the hurricane-hit wasteland which was Boothbay Harbor, piecing together the story of poor Linda Travis's last days, how she'd been isolated with the terrible alien flu, and how, just when it seemed she might be recovering, she was swept away by one of the largest storms in the history of the planet. Stan was disgusted with the whole thing. Especially now, with The Families having made their escape. The hybrids, watching from far overhead, had reported how the woks had battled their way through the Grid. And they'd confirmed that Linda and her companions had continued on to the nuke plant. If the bastards were gone, why not get her ass back here and get to work? The Families were the ones she was hiding from, where they not? So let 'em go! Her people needed her. She was alive. Get with Sten and stage some damned miraculous recovery and get on with it, Linda! There's a global pandemic to deal with. There's your lost kid.

He shook his head. Stan didn't like being out of contact, not with his President on the ground and unprotected like this. Bluebird's people were good. He'd used them many times. But Linda's present situation was too far out of his control now. Why he'd allowed it he couldn't say. Linda had a habit of getting her way with things. That might have to come to an end.

Stan grabbed the clicker and changed the channel and sighed again. When they weren't talking about their beloved dead President they were talking about Greensleeves. Death tolls continued to rise. A second spate of cases had made it clear that the disease, whatever the hell it was, was not going away quietly. It didn't matter to Stan that this was a kinder, gentler global pandemic. People were still dead at the end, no matter how easy and even pleasant the experience of dying might have been. And dead was dead, as far as Stan was concerned, no matter what his President seemed to need to believe. Stan leaned back in his chair and put his feet up on his desk. He reached out for a sip of his coffee, but it had gone cold. Why he still wanted a hot drink on such a scorching day he did not know. He just knew that cold coffee was not going to do it for him. Better head down to the cafe and get another cup.

But first, one last email, to the head of that facility outside of Reston. Pintick had all but solved the mystery of the vial's contents. Now it was time for step two.

19.14

The huge room in the city's center was labeled with a large "A," Gabrielle saw, which according to the map's legend meant "auditorium." Marionette pointed out that the entrances to the auditorium appeared to be on level eighteen. Getting to level eighteen would be easy enough; there were elevators everywhere. But getting to the city's center might take a little time. *Urbem Orsus* was huge, at least four miles long at its widest point. Which meant they had a bit of a hike ahead of them. Unless the transport system was still working. "And why wouldn't it be?" thought Gabrielle. Everything else was.

They'd entered the city at the extreme southern end and had spent all of their time since in that area. But according to the map, there was a transportation system here. The map showed a rough circle-with-spokes configuration of lines with the label "Tran." It appeared that most levels had the Tran system. All they had to do was find the closest station. The outer circle did not come all the way out to the edge of the city. They would have to walk toward the center to find a terminal.

It was Mr. Thomas' hunch, so the President insisted he take the lead. He consulted the map, found their current position, and plotted a general route. The scale did not allow for the representation of the many side corridors, but only the major routes. So the first thing to do was to find one of those. Mr. Thomas walked in front, with the President at his side. Behind them walked Annabelle and Brenda, then Doobie and Marionette, with Gabrielle following up in the rear.

That suited Gabrielle. Despite their attempts to include her, and their obvious relief and happiness when they'd chanced upon each other on the surface, Gabrielle still felt like an outsider in this group. Part of that was no doubt due to her father, and his past betrayal of the President and her husband, something which the President had told her about on the plane. But it wasn't just the betrayal. It was The Families themselves to whom the President was opposed. Gabrielle was still one of them in her eyes.

But Gabrielle also felt apart from the group because of Zacharael. He'd schooled her these past few days. Changed her in deep and important ways. And he'd filled her up. Possessed her. Left her with memories and knowledge and images and opinions and values and concerns she hadn't had before. He'd made Gabrielle like himself, in a way. And Zacharael was alien. Which left Gabrielle feeling more than a little alien herself. She didn't think there was anyone else here who knew what she knew, and felt what she felt.

Zacharael must have been the one to have saved her. Her father had obviously abducted her with the intention of stealing her away to the colonies against her will. Zacharael had found her and stolen her back, then put her in a metal container for safe keeping and placed her right where he knew she'd run into the President and her group. For some reason, it was very important to Zacharael that she and the President be together right now.

Gabrielle reflected again on that image she'd had, of that moment of confrontation between herself and the President. Gabrielle had thought she was supposed to stop Linda Travis from doing something. That she was supposed to take something from her. Yet when the moment came, it hadn't worked out that way at all. Gabrielle had become the President's helper and supporter, rather than her opponent. They were working on the same team.

But were they really? President Travis seemed focused on The Families, and revenge, and this Fisherman guy. She was focused on that vial of flu serum the Fisherman had given her. And she was worried about her son, who'd gotten eaten up by some cosmic monster. But was she concerned about the Beloved, as she and Zacharael were? If so, Gabrielle was not seeing it. And that worried her.

Perhaps it just came with the job. Linda Travis had been elected to serve her people. There were always going to be so many human problems to solve that there would never be any time to focus much energy on the rest of the life on Earth, except save for where doing so also helped people. Gabrielle wondered if maybe she wasn't more than a little bit like her father as far as humans were concerned. She'd come to not care so much about the billions of people on this planet. She cared much more about how those billions were destroying the Beloved.

Her father was probably free of that now. Gone off to his colony with the lovely Dierdre. Away from the Sleepers they hated so much. Out in the clear, clean, cosmos. Out following their Plan to join the Cosmic Community. Maybe that was okay. Maybe it was good that some humans have started something somewhere else. And maybe it's also good that some humans were staying behind, to stay with the Beloved as she suffers. To love her as best they can. And maybe to help.

Gabrielle realized that she had a rather strong opinion about that damned vial. President Travis might waffle and wonder about the cure for the Greensleeves virus. That was probably her job, to deliberate all the possibilities. But Gabrielle was pretty clear what she would do, were she the President. She'd hide that vial away in a strong safe and throw away the key. Or pour it down the sink. She'd let Greensleeves do its dirty work. She'd let the disease - one that The Families designed and injected into the human population, after all - run its course and, in so doing, ease the suffering of the Beloved. A large percentage of the humans left on Earth were probably going to die soon in any event, if the experts and scientists could be believed. Why take the rest of the planet down with them?

The group finally found what looked like a major travel route. It was a corridor four times as wide as the ones they'd been walking through, with a ceiling half again as high as the regular height. It was decorated with extensive murals of city streets and forests and countryside done in paint and mosaic. There were potted trees and shrubs on each side at regular intervals, each with its own overhead sunlamp. The whole ceiling emitted light here, rather than just a strip, and it looked like a clear, blue afternoon sky. And the corridor floor was divided into lanes for walking, bicycles, and golf carts.

Gabrielle was impressed by the place. The Families had gone to a great deal of trouble and expense to create this underground haven. They'd probably used alien-sourced technology to do it. And they had more than enough wealth to do it up right. Some of them must have lived here for years. Maybe even decades, since they'd first carved it out more than thirty years ago. Her father had always been so proud of The Families' ability to envision and implement projects and plans that ran longer than a human lifespan. This was an example of that. These people had waited a long time for their chance to leave the Earth.

Mr. Thomas spied a pair of large golf carts down along what he called the "highway." The carts both had keys and appeared to be in good working order. They climbed in. Mr. Thomas drove the first one, with the President at his side and Annabelle in the back seat. Brenda drove the second, with Doobie and Marionette holding hands in the back seat. Gabrielle took the front passenger seat, smiling at Brenda as she sat down. In a moment, they were off.

Gabrielle didn't know if she should be happy or sad or angry about her parents. Maybe it was better for them now. Maybe they'd finally get their shit together. Maybe they'd even be happy. But they were lost to her forever, it felt like. That new fact was so big that she couldn't even begin to wrap her brain around it. It was better to just put the whole thing on hold for the time being. She needed to be clear here. Zacharael needed that from her. The Beloved needed it. The grief and anger would have to wait.

The ride to the Tran was shorter than she'd expected. A large yellow sign announced the station. They pulled off to the left and parked, then entered the depot. The Trans themselves turned out to be single subway cars that held a couple of dozen people at a time. They sat there in a line, waiting for whomever needed them, like taxis at the curb. The President and her crew stepped up to one of the cars, pushed a button, and waited as the doors slid open. The Tran car was clearly meant to be user operated, and looked easy enough. Brenda insisted that she be the one to drive. Nobody argued.

They took their seats. Brenda operated the controls. The Tran car moved forward along the tracks and into a well-lit tunnel. Soon enough they'd be at the auditorium.

19.15

"So why the auditorium?" asked Linda of Cole. They were sitting side by side on the Tran bench, with Gabrielle beside them and Annabelle, Doobie, and Marionette across from them. The Tran had just passed through another station. Brenda had reported that the display on the driver's console said they were nearing their destination.

Cole shrugged with uncertainty. "Not sure," he said. "I mean... I noticed it when we saw the first map. Wondered what it would look like, a room that huge, and four stories tall. Something about it reminded me of what you told us, about that room you were in. The one in the Martian moon. Where the Fisherman had you give a speech."

"Phobos," said Linda, nodding. "Yeah. It was huge."

"So, I just thought... we gotta go somewhere, you know?"

Linda took his hand and smiled. "Works for me, sweetie," she said.

"So why do you think this William person has left something here for you?" asked Annabelle. The Tran car was so quiet that she didn't even have to raise her voice.

Linda frowned. "Hmm..." she said. "That's a good question." She thought for a moment, the continued. "I spent a few full days with the man," she said. "I don't think William - or The Families... or the aliens, for that matter - ever do or say a thing that isn't intentional and planned and well thought out. And as I indicated before, I think they have a penchant for myth, metaphor, and theater, and think of themselves as teachers, and use these techniques in their teaching. The last thing William did before he left me alone on Mars to find my way back home was to lean forward and say the words '*Urbem Orsus.*' It was a theatrical moment. It meant something. He was leading me here. Calling me to follow him. Because there was something more he had to say." Linda stopped and sighed, smiling hesitantly. "So, it's just something I know, Annabelle. In my gut. In my heart."

Annabelle nodded, as if she understood. "So we're being guided by your intestines?" she said. Her eyes were playful.

"They're Presidential intestines, Annabelle," said Linda with a grin. "They get their own motorcade."

Cole laughed at that. So did Marionette. Even Annabelle smiled openly.

"Looks like we're here," called back Brenda from the driver's compartment. The Tran car came to a smooth stop at the station. The signs outside the windows read "Auditorium." The doors opened and the crew stepped out onto the platform. The doors closed automatically and the Tran car began to move back in the direction from which it had come. "They must have one hell of a computer control system for those things," said Brenda.

Linda started across the platform and through the double doors. They found themselves in the large room that must serve as the main lobby for the auditorium, as it had many entrance corridors leading into it. The carpeting here was a rich red and the walls were hung with dark indigo curtains, giving it all the feel of an old theater. To the left was a sign and arrow. They turned and started down the corridor.

The auditorium was vast and cavernous, with rows of comfortable looking chairs and two tiers of balcony seating. The seats, the lights, the decor, and the floor coverings all looked rich and expensive, with reds and golds and yellows predominating. It was not large enough to hold the tens or hundreds of thousands of people they assumed had congregated here before the colony woks departed, but it could hold a sizable percentage.

In the front was a small stage, with a wide array of giant viewscreens looming behind it. The stage, with glossy hardwood flooring and black curtains in the back, was scaled for individual speakers or panel discussions. The viewscreens were no doubt tasked with taking whatever was happening on that small stage and presenting it in a way that it would fit the size of the auditorium and its huge audience. They saw no obvious loudspeakers, but assumed that the sound-system here was top quality. It was quite a setup.

Linda walked down the aisle toward the center of the auditorium. Cole and the others followed close behind. When they reached the point where their side aisle intersected with the wide center aisle that ran from front to back, a single spotlight came on, lighting the podium on the stage. The travelers turned to watch as a well-dressed man stepped through the curtain and made his way to the microphone. They were so far back that it was difficult to see the man clearly.

Then the screens flickered to life. Linda gasped. It was William.

"Greetings, Madam," said the Fisherman.

19.16

It was William. But it was not William. Every now and then the image would flicker or fade. He was a holographic projection, which was being simulcast on the viewscreens. The fabled HereNow technology used by The Families. The flicker surprised Linda at first, as from what she'd heard about HereNow it was indistinguishable, at a distance of a few feet or more, from the physical face-to-face. But then she realized that William must be transmitting this from far off planet. Linda drifted into a seat on the aisle while keeping her eyes on the Fisherman. William waited for a few moments, as if he could see her as well, and in real time. Maybe he could. Who knew what was possible with this alien tech?

After a moment William flashed his eyebrows and smiled in greeting, then continued. "I'm glad to see you made it, Madam. You and your companions. I knew that you would. Or, at the very least, I had hoped." He reached up to scratch his nose. "You've had quite a time of it since I last saw you. I pray you can forgive me for whatever part I've played in your many trials. I am especially aggrieved at the loss of your child, and have done what I could from my end to aid in his search and rescue. I know about the loss of a son. And I understand that part of what has compelled you to find me has been the wish to avenge the crime of his loss." William shifted his weight from one foot to the other. It almost looked as though he had tears in his eyes. "I am now unavailable to offer my condolences in person. I wish it were otherwise. I will simply say that the possibility that you will see your son again strikes me as high. Far stranger things have happened in this great Universe than that, as you are already well aware."

Linda reached up and wiped a tear from her own eye. Cole stood watching with his arms crossed. The rest of their crew had taken seats.

"But more than vengeance," the Fisherman continued, "it is hope which has brought you here. The question of the Quietus, what you call Greensleeves, has yet to be answered, and you still carry some hope that I shall be able and willing to help you with that. I told you at the beginning that I am not a human being, and offered that as the reason why I could not help you with this choice, as if I was far too alien in my empathies to be of any service in the matter. That was a lie. While I feel little kinship with Earth's human population, I am as fully feeling as any of you. The lie was designed to goad you along in the process and nothing more. It was meant to help banish such hopes from your mind. And still you have them." William stopped at that point and smiled gently. It felt to Linda as though he was looking right at her.

"But you already know that, Madam. You know it in your heart, no matter how angry you might be with me. What you are having more trouble accepting is that I cannot help you with this choice because the choice has never been mine to make. Nor is it for anyone in The Families to make. You'll understand when I say that this is a matter of the Prime Directive. It is a human choice, and we have left the human experiment, to embark on our own. We no longer feel ourselves to be a part of your species. We have become something else. So this is a choice for humans to make, and for you to make as the representative of your species. You were selected for this role long ago, and you accepted that role freely. It is now time for your big moment on the stage of life."

William's voice grew softer and more intimate. "What I can tell you, Madam... Linda... is that I do not know how you should choose. I know that I argued long and hard for the active reduction of the Earth's human population in our conversation on Rumi's Field, but that was because it was the only way I could see to make the choice available to you, just as allowing the triggering of the Quietus before we left puts the choice to you in a way you cannot avoid. Whether you choose to stop the Quietus or allow it to continue its work, I will understand either way, and will have no judgment of you. You truly get to freely choose, Madam. Linda. That is why you are here."

The Fisherman's eyes flicked up and to the right, as though he were looking at a clock. Then they came back to the camera. "One last illustration, if I may," he said with a slight smile. "You've just reached the top of the mountain. You have disembarked from the gondola and have put your skis back on. You're ready to go, and see that there are two slopes back down to the lodge. In the first scenario, one slope is covered with luscious new powder and looks beautiful and inviting as it glitters in the morning sun, while the other slope is covered with ditches of flaming oil, filled with horrible monsters, and strung back and forth with nearly invisible, razor-sharp wires that will cut you into pieces if you try to pass through them. In the second scenario, both slopes are beautiful and inviting and covered with luscious new powder, though one veers to the left and the other veers to the right. Now, to my thinking, in the first scenario what most people are confronted with is an obvious decision, which I would define as a choice made based on the rational analysis of data. You don't wish to be cut to pieces or eaten by monsters, so you decide to take the slope with the fresh, powdered snow. It's not a free choice. Nobody wants to be eaten by monsters, right? In the second scenario, and again, to my thinking, what you are confronted with is an obvious free choice. Both of your options look wonderful. There's no real data that would help you make a rational decision, as you'd be happy to take either slope. And so you are given the luxury of freely choosing."

"But here's the thing, Madam. Human beings in the physical realm tend to hate free choices. Partly because most of them have been raised in a culture that elevates data and rational reasoning above all other cognitive states (so that it's possible to make a 'wrong' choice), partly out of the experience of scarcity and the fear that choosing will limit one's options (it's the only choice you're ever going to have), and partly because they don't believe that free choices actually exist (because there's no free anything, and there will always be consequences.) This is quite reasonable, you understand; their thinking about choice has been conditioned by their physical experience, here in this realm of circumstances. So even when free choices present themselves, they feel more difficult to make to most people than you might expect they should."

"Now look at a third scenario, in which both slopes are covered with burning oil, monsters, and razor wire. You can't stay up there on the mountain. You'll freeze and die. And besides, it's part of my illustration that you must get back down to the lodge. So here, even though both slopes look horribly dangerous, you are still confronted with a free choice. You see no real data that will help you make a rational decision. It does not matter which slope you take. Your choice is free." William smiled. "But here's the thing about those horrible slopes, Madam. That's only how they appear, because you've been raised in the physical realm of circumstances and consequences, where bad is bad and wrong is wrong and death is death. And yet I say to you, Madam... Linda... it is possible to stand on the mountain and gaze down those horrible, dangerous slopes and see the same beautiful invitation to adventure you see when you look upon freshly fallen powder. It is possible, even in that scenario, to find and feel the free choice available to you. All it takes is that one realize that the physical realm is only one aspect of the whole of reality, and that consciousness is fundamental to everything, and stretches far beyond the shores of this material playground. Inside of that gnosis, not only can you find and feel the free choice available to you when all choices look horrible, you can find and feel the free choice available to you even when one slope is powder and the other is horrible danger, even when the rational decision is obvious. You can stand on that mountain top and choose either powder or horror with equal freedom, in anticipation of a glorious experience made possible for you by virtue of your being in this land of flesh and stone."

The Fisherman stopped for a minute and peered into the camera. It felt like he was seeing directly into Linda's heart. His face had an open, gentle quality to it, like a friend who had just heard of a death in her family. "And this is the place to which I invite you, Madam. Both slopes look horrible to you. I know that. There's no way to make a rational decision. So find and feel the freedom to choose. Find the beautiful invitation to adventure available to you in your time and place and circumstances. And then choose."

William stopped long enough to breathe a long sigh, then continued on. "I must go now, Madam," he said.

"Wait!" shouted Linda, standing.

But William did not wait, or even act as though he'd heard her. "But one thing remains," he continued. Linda stood and watched. "You may not have realized it yet, Madam, but you've been here before. I wonder... do you remember where to go next?"

The HereNow hologram of William the Fisherman vanished from the stage.

19.17

Linda didn't want to talk to anybody. Not even Cole. She wanted to think. She wanted to remember. She wanted to feel. So they traveled in silence, taking another Tran to the next station, where they would find the elevator that went all the way to the bottom of *Urbem Orsus*. That's where they were going next.

It hit Linda, when William asked his last question, though Cole had pointed to the answer earlier. She knew what the shape of the city reminded her of. The huge, potato-shaped city they saw on the side-view cutaway maps closely resembled the Martian moon Phobos. In which case the "auditorium" of *Urbem Orsus* corresponded in placement and size with the cavernous space William had called the "grand hall" or "conclave" on Phobos, just as Cole had said. In which case, by talking about "where to go next," William was directing her down to the bottom of the city, just as on Phobos they had next gone to that strange, spiral room in which the Fortunate buried, or jettisoned, or said goodbye, to their dead. That's where they were going. Linda had declared it. They were going where William pointed them.

That must have been a recording. Must have. William hadn't responded at all when she'd called out. And Linda knew he would have had it been a live transmission. It was a recording. Something left behind. Because William really *was* long gone. And she really *was* on her own with this one. That's how it felt.

And his last words? His parting advice? What the hell did she do with that? Learn to think of the destruction of the planet and the die-off of the human species as beautiful ski slopes on a mountainside? Freely choose? Jesus! How in Jesus' name would she accomplish that? Linda had no idea. Had William gone truly crazy at the end?

But she knew the answer to that. William was right. Her heart knew him. Knew him to be whole and sane and good, even if he saw the world in very different ways than she. He didn't *feel* crazy to her. If it was all about feeling, if feeling was such a wonderful tool for finding the truth, then that was hers. Whatever he was, the Fisherman felt neither evil nor crazy.

The Tran came a stop at the next station and Linda and her crew stepped out into the corridor. A short walk to the left and a quick turn to the right brought them to the elevator they sought. They opened the door and confirmed that they were correct. This elevator had a button number thirty-four. Linda pushed it and the cab began to drop.

A few moments later, they stepped out of the elevator and into another hallway, this one more narrow. The floor was smooth here, but the walls were rough-hewn. Gray stone, blasted or cut rather than vaporized to glossiness by an alien tool. It looked much as Phobos had. The corridor went only to the right. They followed it. Soon it began to veer to the left while also sloping downward. "A spiral," said Cole, his voice full of wariness and wonder.

"Yes," said Linda. It was just as she'd expected.

They continued on. The slope gradually increased to the point where Annabelle had to grab onto Doobie's arm to avoid falling. The spiral got tighter. The walls squeezed inward. Eventually they reached the end of the corridor. A dead end, it would seem, but Linda knew otherwise. She put her hand up to the end wall and stepped forward. Her arm disappeared into the stone. She turned and smiled at her companions, then gestured onward with her head. "C'mon," she said. "It won't hurt you." She turned and disappeared through what appeared to be solid rock, but which turned out to be as insubstantial as light. Eventually the rest of them followed her through the strange doorway.

They passed through a tiny anteroom and entered a large circular chamber. It had a short ceiling, low enough that Cole had to stoop to avoid hitting his head. Marionette gasped. Linda sighed heavily, almost a moan. The floor of the room spiraled down to the center like a funnel, the successive turns forming steps one could take to the bottom. Laid out on those steps, forming a second spiral, were what looked to be a couple of dozen human bodies.

"Jesus," muttered Linda.

Cole started forward but Linda reached out and stopped him. "Don't," she said, putting a hand to her husband's confused face. "Please. This is for me."

Cole frowned but stayed where he was. Linda stepped across the outer ledge and onto the first ring of the spiral, placing her foot in the space between one body's feet and another body's head. She stopped and looked down to examine the corpses. Most were middle-aged or older white men, but there were women here as well, and a few younger souls, and more than one person whose color or ethnicity was decidedly not Caucasian. They were generally well dressed, and they looked like they'd been healthy in life. She saw no apparent cause of death. Were it not for the unmistakable stillness of the deceased, they might have been sleeping.

Linda took another step down. And another. She glanced up at Cole with a face he recognized as the one she wore when terrified. She turned and took another step further down the spiral.

She could see the bottom now. See the blackness at the center. A circle of deep darkness perhaps a yard across. But it was glossy, this circle. Not an opening into deep space, but something solid, like that black cube that had taken Rice and Obie away. It reminded her of one of the huge black eyes of the Gray aliens called the Life. Linda laughed at the joke, that she should see Spud's eye at the bottom of this huge potato. But her laughter quickly fell to silence. There was William.

"Oh," she moaned again, her breath quickening. "No. No." She stepped around the spiral and knelt down between two bodies and lifted the hand of the Fisherman, who lay on the bottom turn of the spiral, near the black hole. There were tears streaming from her eyes now. Her chest heaved and shook and at last a loud sob fell out of her mouth and filled the room. "No," she said again, shaking her head, wiping at her nose. "No."

But it was William, whether she wanted it to be or not. He was dressed in a sport coat and nice slacks, but underneath was a colorful Hawaiian shirt, this one sporting palm trees and hula girls. His white, feathery hair was neatly combed and his face was peaceful. But the skin of his hand was cold to the touch and his joints felt stiff. He'd been dead for a while. He'd been lying here while they'd watched his recording in the auditorium.

"Oh, William," said Linda, her voice shaky and moist. She barely noticed Cole's hand on her shoulder, or the others who'd come to stand nearby. She could only look at this man and cry and know, in that moment, that he'd been right after all: Linda did love him, just as he'd hoped. Somehow, sitting there in Rumi's Field, they'd managed to meet each other, soul to soul. Only now he would never know it. "Oh..." Her voice was a moan and a cry and a fist, shaking at the heavens. Cole and the others stood quietly and let her grieve.

After a few minutes, she decided she'd cried enough. She let go of William's hand and pushed herself up to a standing position. It was then that she noticed the others. Cole put his arms around her from behind. Linda melted into his embrace and sobbed some more.

"I suppose you think this is funny," she said at last, staring down at William's body.

"You expected a grand gesture," offered Cole in a gentle voice.

Linda turned to look at him. She gasped softly and shook her head. "I know," she said.

Doobie pointed at the body. "There's a paper in his shirt pocket," he said, obviously hesitant to say anything at all right then.

Linda turned and looked. He was right. A piece of white paper protruded from the pocket like an umbrella shade for the hula girl directly underneath. She bent down, plucked the paper out, and unfolded it. She read it. More tears began to flow. When she was finished, she handed it to Cole, who read it out loud.

"One last quick note, Madam," Cole said. "Some of us in the Element had to go on ahead, and have chosen to forego the physical for the time being, given our destination and the nature of the work that awaits us. Call us the Fortunate, if you will, in remembrance of our forebears. And remember what I told you. Death is but the doorway to a trip back home. These bodies are simply discarded shells. I'm off to new adventures! So perchance we'll meet again. I may even find your son. Love, William."

"There's a postscript," said Cole, glancing around at the others. He read the rest. "By the way, Madam, isn't it marvelously ironic that those Heaven's Gate bozos got closer to the truth than most manage to do? Don't mistake me, they were a bunch of nutters, but they got some things right! Ta! Wm."

That was the end of William's note.

Linda wiped her face dry and looked around at her traveling companions. "You guys ready to go home?" she asked.

Everybody nodded.

19.18

Ted and Carl stared at the wall. They had yet to create a second door. Or a key for the first one.

"Does it matter what sort of door we imagine, do you think?" asked Ted.

"Doesn't seem like it should," said Carl.

"Do we both have to imagine the same thing?"

"I dunno," said Carl. "What sort of door are you imagining?"

"A thick, steel door with locks and a keypad on it, like we had in the Lodge," said Ted. "You?"

"I'm imagining one of those hollow-core pieces of shit like you'd find in a cheap house," said Carl. "Painted light blue. With a spy hole in it."

"Maybe we should both imagine the same sort of door. Double our power, you know? Get in resonance and shit."

Carl cocked his head. "Sure. Maybe. You wanna imagine my door or should I imagine yours?"

"I'll imagine your little hollow core door, Carl. That sounds easier to break through, in case it comes locked."

"Okay," said Carl. They sat together and imagined a light blue hollow core door with a spy hole in it.

They sat for a long time.

"I wonder if we've got this all wrong," said Carl.

"How's that?" asked Ted.

"Well, we keep thinking it's about our personal power. Like, we have to actively imagine the door. Create it. Manifest it. Make it so." He scratched his nose. "I'm wondering if it might work better to assume that the door's already there, and all we have to do is see it."

Ted grinned. "Nice hypothesizing there, Maestro," he said. "Let's try it."

Carl and Ted sat side-by-side, trying to see the door that was already there.

They sat for a very long time.

"Maybe if we close our eyes?" said Ted.

"Maybe," said Carl. "Let's try it."

They closed their eyes and tried to see the door that was already there. There it was.

"Son of a bitch," muttered Ted.

"I hear ya, Brother," said Carl. He reached out and grabbed Ted by the arm. "You ready?"

"To leave?" said Ted. "Hell yeah!"

"Okay," said Carl. "Keep your eyes closed and follow me."

With closed eyes, Carl and Ted stood, walked across the room, and exited through the door that had always been there.

Chapter Ø Twenty

20.1

Zacharael had watched as the human named William Reynolds and his twenty-six companions popped out of the physical, oriented themselves to the Astral, and then blinked away to an even higher level. He found in himself great resonance with Reynolds' recorded words, which Gabrielle and her companions had just witnessed: Zacharael was not sure which choice was the best either.

But he had done all he could. All he dared. The choicemakers were all in place. Now all they had to do was choose. Zacharael did not envy them their situation. Yet he knew that all self-aware species must face such things as they grew into maturity. There was great possibility in this moment. But also danger. Not all species survived their own choices.

Zacharael hung in space above the Earth, following the slow progress of the choicemakers. The Sages were near. Zacharael had not yet seen them but he could feel their presence. He knew that they, too, were watching and waiting, to see which events transpired. And he knew, or hoped, that he and the Sages shared a common concern for the Beloved. But Zacharael did not know how these bizarre creatures might act or respond to what they perceived. Having spurned the Cogency, and having created their own, private band of reality, the Sages were not bound by the Primary.

They might do anything.

20.2

Linda sat next to the window, staring out across the ocean. Cole sat beside her, asleep. Night was chasing them back home. Soon it would overtake them. She was glad to be traveling in the daylight, if only for a little while. She needed the sun after so long underground.

Mr. Bluebird had outdone himself this time. The return flight was direct from Kiev to Augusta: a large, richly appointed private jet with a shower, comfortable furnishings, and high quality food and drink. And the sky was smooth this time, rather than choppy. How much of that was due to the skills of the flight crew, whom they had not met this time, Linda did not know. She was just thankful to not be jostled around. The turbulence inside was enough.

What had happened back there? Linda's mind was a maelstrom of thoughts and memories and imagined conversations. And her heart was deeply exhausted. The Families were gone. She now knew what William had meant, when he'd told her that the evil ones had been accounted for. Had the aliens been involved with that? Had Spud? Had the Grid served as some sort of sieve that strained out the demons and cast them back upon the face of the Earth? Linda sighed. They might never know. But it felt to her as though, in some way, the Life, with their Grid, had taken a stand. Not to help the humans on Earth, perhaps, but at least to insist that they be left alone to work things out on their own.

She felt some relief at that. It was good to know that the secret cabal was no longer on Earth to threaten her. And it was good to have the aliens step away. Perhaps she and Cole and the children would be safe now. At least as safe as anybody could be on this crazy planet. But beyond the relief, she felt sadness. And anger. Sadness that humanity had become so polarized that some of them no longer felt like a part of the species, so much so that they'd chosen to leave. And anger at their leaving. Because there was judgment in The Families' departure. The "beautiful people" had flown the coop, leaving the poor sleepers to muddle through on their own until the end of the world. William was right. It was very difficult to step out of that reaction.

Much of her sadness was for William. Or for herself, if she was honest. The sight of William's dead body had disturbed her greatly. Her physical self had recoiled. She'd wanted to flee. The reaction was one of bone and blood, something built into the flesh. It did not matter that she knew and understood with her rational mind that William's consciousness continued on somewhere else. He'd gone out just as he'd wanted to, in control of his destiny, working for the things he valued the most. But here, now, in this world, in her body, it was so very difficult to hold onto that understanding, especially in the presence of his body. William was dead. Dead meant gone.

She imagined the scene: William and his fellows all meeting in that strange spiral room. Greeting, perhaps. Hugging. Making plans. Excited that the time had finally come for them to leave the Earth and make their way amongst the stars and galaxies and realities. Had those bombs been bursting overhead as they'd done so? Had the woks already departed? Had they already seen the culling of the evil and twisted members of their people? What then? They lay down on those spiral steps, head to toe. They straightened their clothes, neatened their hair, took a deep, calming breath. And then... what? Some gentle poison? A pill? A drop of liquid? A haze of deadly gas? Whatever it was, it took them quickly and painlessly, if the evidence of the bodies could be believed. And then there they were, freed from their bodies, their husks, their shells, and hovering in the air just above. Did they congratulate each other? Did they cheer? Did they cry? And did they then dive down through that strange, black, glossy alien-eye at the bottom of the room, and onward to their next lives?

Linda shook her head. Was she angry because she hadn't been invited to go along? Or *had* she been invited? And was the invitation still open to her, if only she were brave enough to put that poison to her own lips? Linda reached up and wiped away the tear that was crawling slowly down her cheek. A part of her was ready to do just that. She would welcome the rest.

No. She was angry to be left alone with the mess. Angry to be left to deal with the fact that The Families, in enacting their centuries-long Plan, had actually made things on Earth worse than they would otherwise have been. And angry to be saddled with the burden of having to make a terrible choice. She thought of the old Inuit saying the shaman Utterpok had shared with her out on the ice. "We must entertain the spirits," he had said, his eyes wrinkled with amusement. Linda frowned. "I hope you're enjoying the show," she muttered to herself, glancing at the cabin's ceiling.

William had said that she'd agreed to her choice long ago. Did he mean that the burden came with the Presidency, and that simply by seeking office she'd accepted the burden? Or did he mean something else? There were, stored safely in the back of her mind, memories she'd yet to access and bring to the light of consciousness. Memories of *them*. The Life. Memories of Spud and his cohort, of dark, strange nights and frightening experiences. And she just a young girl. Was it then that she'd accepted the burden of this choice? Or did it go even further back? To before this life? To between the lives, in some other realm? To a time when she had not been Linda Travis? Was it even weirder? Was she, like the Church of the Stranger considered Cole to be, somehow alien herself? When all the rules were broken, when consciousness could live life after physical life in body after body, when spirits could flit about the cosmos and take an infinity of forms, the words "alien" and "human" got very fuzzy around the edges.

The scariest thing to Linda was the possibility that her mind and heart had been captured by William. Enthralled. Changed. Manipulated. She sensed that Cole was worried about her. And she knew that Annabelle trusted neither Linda nor her mission to Chernobyl. Was her love for William, her caring, her sobbing, her wish that he were still here, just a simple case of the Stockholm syndrome, that strong bonding that can form between captive and captor? Or was it a right and natural reaction to a good human being who was trying to do his best for others and the world, according to the values he held and the wisdom he'd garnered during his life? Had the same thing happened with the aliens during those lost, early meetings? Had she been warped? Molded into something they could use? Programmed?

There was no way to tell.

Linda closed her eyes and inhaled deeply.

Maybe she wasn't really alone with this. When she thought of William being gone, she felt alone. It was not wanting to be alone with this that had compelled her to drag these people halfway around the planet. But *was* she alone? Cole was right there. He'd do anything for her. Give her anything. And she sensed that Gabrielle might as well. Perhaps even Marionette. Back home were Stan and Mary and Keeley and Ness. There was Stendahl Banks. There was Alice, newly returned to Earth. There were the Middle Children. She could gather them together. They could sit for hours and hours, looking at the situation from every direction. Examine all of their assumptions and beliefs. Argue their positions. Take votes. Try to convince each other. And these good, well-meaning people who loved her would do their best to help. But in the end, it felt to Linda that it would always be on her. The final word. The decision. The choice. And she'd already wasted enough time on this strange trip to *Urbem Orsus*. The serum had been analyzed and successfully tested. The urgency felt more palpable by the minute.

In the end, Linda was not sure now that she even wanted help making this decision. That thought made her wince, as she'd been taught not to think of herself in such "high and mighty" ways. But Linda was not convinced that any of her friends and advisors were capable of making this choice. Not in the way that she was. She knew then that she believed what William had told her: she *had* agreed to this. She *had* been made ready. It was *her* burden. Perhaps it was even her honor. She wanted this choice. There was no one else she could trust it to.

And that's what William's last grand gesture had been all about. To point to the spot she needed to get to, where she could make the choice she needed to make. The top of the mountain. Where both slopes, no matter how awful they looked at first glance, also felt like invitations to adventure and learning and growth. Something skipped in Linda's heart then. A twinge of excitement. A gasp of cold water on her tired mind. Like a new possibility spied out of the corner of her eye, peeking from behind the edge of a tall, solid wall. Like a step into the field that Rumi had described. She couldn't wrap her mind around it. Couldn't clothe it in thoughts or understanding. When she tried to she lost it. But when she closed her eyes and remembered William's face as he lay there on that spiraling step in his silly Hawaiian shirt, she could begin, just barely, to feel it.

And she knew. And perhaps that was the scariest thing of all.

Linda knew what she was going to choose.

20.3

Keeley waved her hand and sent another email off into the ether. The Families' One-Two Punch had been visible hundreds of miles from Chernobyl. The falling bodies had been seen from outside the Exclusion Zone. So word of the strange aerial phenomena and the departure of a large number of huge UFOs was already racing through the global media. And local Ukrainian and Belorussian emergency response teams were working through the night to recover the dead. Very few knew what to make of it.

Back in Augusta, Stan and Mary and Keeley knew a bit more that most: The Families had fled the scene of the crime. Stan had been in contact with Linda and Cole directly by phone, once they'd left the Exclusion Zone. The connection had been poor, but they'd managed to tell him the gist of it. The danger had passed. Ness and Mary and the kids could come out of their nullspace hiding place. The President was returning to Augusta.

Keeley, though still in the hospital, was back at work. If the President was going to come back from the dead and resume her duties, she was going to need her Chief of Staff. Keeley was finally feeling up to the job, even though she still tired easily.

The first order of business would be Linda's miraculous rescue. It would have to be handled well. After a full day of national, media-led grieving, and that on the heels of two weeks of orchestrated worry about her health, the public might not take well to the idea that they'd kept Linda's rescue, and her subsequent Ukrainian holiday, a secret from them. Better to stage a second rescue. That was Sten's opinion, at least. And while they'd need to wait for Linda to return to sign off on their plan, there was nothing stopping them from working out the details.

Sten was full of ideas. He wanted to stage a brave adventure, with scuba divers descending into the dark, underwater caverns of the flooded medical facility underneath what had once been Linda's vacation cabin. They'd find Linda alone, afraid, but still alive, trapped in an airtight room in which the oxygen was rapidly depleting. It would make for a marvelous show.

The problem was, there were now so many levels of truth, so many events and circumstances that only a few of them knew about, so many questions that were left unanswered, that neither Keeley nor Sten knew what they could or should reveal. All of that would have to be hammered out upon Linda's return. It was going to be a busy time, when their President's plane touched down in Augusta.

But they couldn't just clobber her with questions and demands. Linda and her family had been through the wringer these past weeks. Iain had not yet returned. They would need time to just be together and process it all.

Keeley sighed. She closed her laptop and stared for a bit out the window, watching as the afternoon sun slipped slowly toward the horizon. She was thankful that the hospital's air conditioning worked so well. Mary had told her that the high had topped one hundred and ten degrees just after lunchtime. She hoped that Chapin, whom she'd been assured was being well cared for by one of the Middle Children back at the Presidential Home, was doing okay in this heat.

There was no time. That was the thing of it. Part of Keeley wanted to usher Cole and Linda directly from the plane to home, reunite them with their children, and then put the house under armed guard, deflecting all visitors and phone calls. But she knew that Linda would not go for that. The matters of her reappearance, and of Greensleeves, could not be put off. She would make some time for her kids. Cole would no doubt give them all the time that he could. But the Linda Travis that Keeley knew was going to come home and get back to work as quickly as her own health allowed. There would be no stopping her.

Keeley picked up her laptop and started an email to Sten, who was no doubt back in his office now. She didn't think that Linda would go along with grabbing footage of her being hauled soaking wet out of the Squirrel facility and rushed away on a helicopter. The last thing she'd want to do, probably, was go back to the Squirrel at all. Could they concoct a scenario that had her being pulled from some collapsed building? Or was there was a large pool in which they could recreate that scene right here in Augusta?

Then she wrote another short note to Stan. He'd have the latest ETA. From that, they could schedule a meeting. Get everybody together. Talk through options and scenarios. Get the go-ahead on the Greensleeves cure. Strategize and plan. Maybe tomorrow morning? Give Linda and Cole and the kids the evening together? Keeley hit send, and then closed her eyes. Perhaps a short nap. That would feel really nice.

20.4

Stan monitored things from his office in the State House. For now, the Middle Children were meeting the obligations of their chosen roles in government, medicine, business, and the military, holding down the smooth operation of the city of Augusta, and helping to hold together the federal government. That would no doubt all change at some point, seeing as how Linda had agreed to let them stay here and share the Earth, and that she'd agreed to give them Augusta as a starting place. Where she and her family and the U.S.

government would end up next was anybody's guess. Maybe there would be no next. Maybe Linda would turn the running of the country over to the hybrids altogether. Take Cole and the kids and go hole up somewhere that nobody could ever find her. Stan wouldn't blame her if she did. He wouldn't wish the presidency on anybody at a time like this. In any event, Stan was thankful that most of the executive responsibilities had been transferred over to Speaker Simpson in Kenosha. That would make it easier for Stan to do what he had to do.

The President's jet would be here before too long. Stan wanted to be long gone before she got back. It was a matter of timing. Though Stan had a great poker face, he didn't think that he could win a face-to-face game with Linda Travis. She was just too damned sharp. He sent his reply to Keeley, shut down his laptop, stuffed it into his briefcase, and rose from his desk. His helicopter would be waiting for him. Stan had a little trip he needed to take.

20.5

Ness whistled an old tune from who knows where as she busied about in her kitchen. The girls were up in their rooms, happy to be back home, probably playing with their new cat, and Ness wanted to make them a surprise. She didn't know how they did it, but the Middle Children had refilled her pantry with items she hadn't seen in months or years. The girls were about to get their first bowls of boxed macaroni and cheese dinner in a very long time. An off-brand. Not the good stuff. But still...

Something about that made tears rise to Ness's eyes and she daubed at them with her sleeve. This was a hard old world they lived in, which nobody can deny. Those poor girls had been through some crazy bad stuff, and though they were doing their best to hold it together, Ness could tell that what they most wanted was to just sit in their folks' laps and have a good cry. They'd cried a bit with Ness when they first got back to home, but Ness was not their mom and dad, and she could tell that there was more to come.

They'd put Iain back in his room. His body just lay there, lungs breathing, heart pumping, all that. They had him hooked back up to his monitors and IV, and the hybrid nurses were keeping him fed and bathed and such. They'd placed Dennis lovingly at Iain's feet, and prayed that, wherever the two of them were, they were together. There were living bodies waiting for them, boy and dog, should they ever manage to find their way back. But damn it was a hard sight, to look in on the boy. He'd been right on the edge of adulthood. Just starting to come into himself. And now he was gone. Off to help his mother and this is what he gets for it. Ness had heard about how all the rich people had up and run away. And she'd heard a bit about how many of them had been killed off. And all she could think was, "Good. Serves them right. And good riddance to the rest of you." It was those monsters that had kidnapped Iain's mother in the first place. The blame was on them. Ness had curses for them all.

Ness knew that holding onto curses wouldn't do her much good in the long run. Just make her bitter and sad. So she said her curses out loud as she worked in the kitchen. To get them out of her head and heart, and send them on to whomever they belonged. "Damn you all to hell," she spat as she stirred the pasta into the boiling water. She looked up to the sky and repeated it, to make sure there was no mistake about who she was damning. She didn't have all that good an understanding of what, exactly, had happened. She'd only gotten bits of pieces of the whole story. But she was no dummy. The rich folk had taken off to start a new life somewhere in outer space. The aliens helped them. In Ness's opinion, the humans left on Earth would be better off if they never saw either group again.

But those hybrids were still here, weren't they? The Middle Children, they wanted to be called. Born of some crazy alien-human secret program or something. Did they really want those guys hanging around now? Ness couldn't make up her mind. Though she didn't really trust them yet - maybe she didn't *want* to trust them - she had to admit that they'd been a great help. Built that hidey-hole. Watched over her and the kids and Keeley in the hospital. Helped look for Iain. Isaac was a sweet man, really, even though his limbic system was about as haywire as it could get. And the kids liked him because he was keen to learn how to play games, but was really bad at them. At the kids' request he had joined them at the Presidential Home, to act as an assistant to Ness in the kitchen, and provide other services to the family as needed. Ness was glad of that. She felt kind of old today. Old and tired. And it was so damned hot. She could use the help.

Ness drained the pasta and cut open the packet of peculiar orange powder and dumped it into the pot with some butter and a little milk. The President and her husband would be home soon.

No doubt all hell would break loose again upon their return. Bad guys to punish and a pandemic to stop and kids to take care of and all that. Ness would probably be busy too, as the Presidential Home came fully back online. But for now, it was quiet. The AC was working. They had mac and cheese. Maybe she'd grab Isaac and they'd play a game. Find a bit of normal for a change. Those girls could use a bit of normal. For a while, at least, Ness would have to be the one to provide it.

20.6

Alice walked the streets of Augusta. She'd just left the nullspace apartment, which the Middle Children had decided to leave in place for the time being, and thought she might head to the MaineCentral, not only to check in on Ms. Keeley, but to confer with Dr. Pintick about the human pandemic. The afternoon sun warmed the back of her head as she made her way southward through the downtown area. She didn't mind the high temperature. Most of the Middle Children had been bred for heat tolerance.

To her mind, the Middle Children represented the Life's most active response to the Earth changes now underway. They had long ago recognized the possibility that humans would not survive the consequences of their collective actions. And, in their own way, the Life, or at least the subspecies Alice derived from known as the Inter-Life, had grown to love those over whom they had been tasked to watch. Over the years, some of the humans had seen random bits of evidence for the Middle Children program and speculated that the Life were breeding hybrids in order to save themselves. Given the humans' high capacity for self-deception and projection, this made perfect sense. Never would it occur to them that the hybrids had been created in order to save some portion of the human animal.

She didn't know if it would come to that. Partly because the human colony project held some measure of hope and partly because humans were so surprisingly resilient. The human experiment might continue elsewhere in the physical universe, should the colonists manage to survive the challenges facing them. But it might also continue here on Earth, even should the climate restabilize at a far hotter global mean temperature. The planet was large and varied, and there were humans all over it. It was surely possible that some would survive.

Which is why the Middle Children had disengaged from the Life and declared themselves a distinct and free people. Though they might inherit the Earth entirely, should the humans die out, they knew that they might end up sharing the planet with a remnant population. Were that the case, they wanted to create that sharing on their own terms. They did not like being pawns of the Life. They were tired of their off-planet or underground existences, or of having to hide amongst the humans on Earth. Nor did they wish to become second-rate citizens in the eyes of their human parents, who had a disturbing habit of judging harshly those who are different from themselves. Having been given life, the Middle Children were ready to take their lives and craft the future they wished to have. Which is why Alice, the first known hybrid to live openly amongst them, and with the American President, no less, had been chosen as their representative.

Alice walked past the fast food restaurant that had been so prominently featured in the news the past few days. This was the site where the first case of the Quietus - were one to discount the scam involving the President - had collapsed on the sidewalk. The door was locked and the windows had been covered with thick plywood. Alice passed through the plywood and glass and examined the darkened interior. It appeared that the owners had left in a hurry. Probably out of fear. Possibly due to retaliation from other frightened humans. They were a reactive, confused species, these humans. Most of them, anyways. She was concerned that living openly with them might be more difficult than any of them had supposed. Alice slipped out of the restaurant and continued down the street. There were few places that were open for business now. The humans were all but gone from Augusta already.

Much of this would await the future. The President Linda needed to return first. There were urgencies to tend to. Meetings to have. Decisions to be made. And then, an announcement. Eventually the Augusta city would be formally turned over to the Middle Children. That and enough of the surrounding countryside to meet their needs. Trade agreements would need to be put into place. Diplomatic relationships forged. The Middle Children might wish to create some sort of governing body to interface with the humans. But it would be a facade. Connected mind to mind, the Middle Children needed no such institutions.

Alice looked skyward. Her eyes, sensitive to more of the electromagnetic spectrum than human eyes were, could see the Grid clearly, gleaming at the edge of space. She was not at all sure she understood why it was still there. It had performed one of its functions admirably. Perhaps it had others of which she knew nothing. Her father's mind was closed to her. But sometimes she picked up bits of information that left her wondering whether the Inter-Life had some other concern. Perhaps the Grid was also intended to keep something out. She did not know what that something might be.

She would let her father worry upon that. Her work on Earth was enough to fill her attention. The second report from jumptime had come back negative. That meant that they would now have to send a pair of Middle Children through a finely-tuned scan of the entirety of physical time. The energy and attention that would require would be prodigious, and all of the Middle Children would have to bear some part of the cost. The project would take almost three Earth years. And there would be no guarantees, even then. Alice allowed her heart to pinch inward a bit, a feeling she had come to associate with the human word "sadness." Her friend Iain was lost. Alice had sent the initial impulse that had sent him into the Astral in search of his mother.

She was responsible. She would do what she could to make amends.

Ahead of her was the river. The Kennebec. Across the river was the hospital. Alice strode forward to complete her tasks.

20.7

Gabrielle watched as the President walked back up the aisle and took her window seat next to her husband. Inexplicably, she thought of a watch she'd received as a Christmas gift some years ago, a vintage Casio with one of the first LED readouts ever produced. Her father had given it to her, having searched online for it for months. Her father, who was dead now. The President had just told her how they'd found him, right next to that container Zacharael had put her in. Gabrielle had actually seen him. Seen his crumpled body. She just hadn't realized who it was.

She was having difficulty holding onto thoughts. Her head was buzzing. And her heart seemed to have almost stopped beating. Her father had plummeted to Earth, and to his death, cast from the colony wok like a bag of trash. Judged and found wanting. Unworthy of passing through. Her father was dead. Gone in a way that felt much more real to her than just his going off to the stars.

Their jet was back over land again and Gabrielle glanced out the window at the terrain far below. It looked hot. Brown. Dead. Hazy. Even smoky. It was the world from which her father had been attempting to escape. The world from which he'd tried so hard to save her. The world she was now stuck on. The Beloved was dying, and Gabrielle was alone. Her father was dead. Her mother, who'd never really felt like family anyways, might be found amongst the dead too. And the whole of her people, The Families, were either gone or dead as well, including, no doubt, a great many Sinclairs, her direct kin, whom she'd never even met. Leaving her alone. Alone.

She was supposed to be feeling something, wasn't she? Maybe she was, and it was just obliterated by the buzzing. Maybe she just didn't feel anything. Maybe the buzzing was the feeling. Maybe something else. Something had shifted. That could not be denied. Her parents hadn't been a part of her life for some time now. She'd shut them out. Run away. Denied her family and her heritage and her rightful place in the Giant Leap. But still there was a hole in her life at the news of her father's death. She'd loved him once. Perhaps she still did. And a part of her had been happy, to know that he'd followed his heart and his dream, and would be living the life he chose out in the stars. Even if it wasn't what she had wanted. Even if it meant they had to be apart.

But that dream had been taken from him at the last minute. A cruel trick, it felt like. The aliens and their Grid. It had made her father so angry when the Grid had first gone up. To be betrayed like that. And, in the end, the aliens got the last laugh. Maybe Gabrielle was angry now as well. Maybe that's what the buzzing was.

Gabrielle glanced over at the others. Annabelle and Doobie were asleep. Marionette was reading. The eye-patched young woman looked up as Gabrielle stared at her, as though she could feel Gabrielle's gaze. She smiled. Gabrielle smiled back. Something in her wanted friend all of a sudden. Now that she was alone on the planet, perhaps it was time for her to find some people to call her own. Marionette gestured toward the back of the plane with a nod of her head and a questioning expression, inviting Gabrielle to maybe go back there and talk? Gabrielle glanced to where she was pointing, then looked at Marionette and nodded. Marionette stood and headed back, careful to be quiet so as not to wake the others. Gabrielle rose to join her.

All at once there were tears on her face.

20.8

Had that been another hop? Or just a dream? Cole wasn't sure if there was even a difference. Whatever it was, it was fading quickly. He'd been himself in this dream. Standing outside. Looking up at the sky. The air was filled with rumbling thunder, louder than any he'd ever heard. And above the tree line, a strange glow, as if an airliner had crashed nearby. Had he just witnessed the air disaster that had killed his first wife, Ruth? Or was it something else entirely? The thunder in the air was far more powerful than a crash could explain. And then everything had gone black. Cole opened his eyes, squeezed Linda's hand, and rose to grab their backpacks. The jet was on the ground in Augusta and was slowly taxiing to the gate, where two men waited with a stairway.

The AC had been turned off. Already he could feel the sweltering heat outside. It had topped one hundred ten degrees earlier in the day, one of the pilots had told them over the intercom, with an accent Cole could not place. Over a hundred ten degrees. In March. Great. He lived in New England to get away from such heat. So much for that plan.

He couldn't wait to see the girls. They'd told Stan to have Ness and Mary keep them at home, rather than meet them at the airport. But it sure would have been nice to be able to grab them and hold them and pick them up at the bottom of the stairs. Cole sighed. Any thought of the girls brought the inevitable after-thought of Iain. He did not want to think about his son right now.

The others were waking up and grabbing their gear. Cole looked from one to the next, smiling and nodding. Annabelle arched an eyebrow and Cole had no idea how he might interpret that. Anything from a concerned "how are you doing?" to a more pointed "are you going to stop your wife from destroying humanity?" Right. Like he knew what to do any better than the rest of them.

He glanced down at Linda and smiled gently. She seemed surprisingly awake and alive, given what they'd just been through. But Cole knew that most of that was probably just her habitual, practiced Presidential poise, the product of endless meetings, dinners, and trips around the world. He could tell she was exhausted. She'd hardly spoken during the flight. She had nothing left. "You ready, babe?" he asked. Linda raised her eyebrows and sighed. Cole offered her his hand and she stood to join him.

The Choice, as Cole thought of it, weighed heavily on them both. They planned to just go home, hang with the girls, and get a full night's sleep. But Cole knew that the Choice would haunt them in their dreams. The Fellowship of the Vial had done what they could. If Annabelle had been right, and if stopping Linda from destroying the human race had meant not allowing her to prevent The Families from leaving, then they'd succeeded in that, though their success had come simply from being too late. But if the Church's prophecy had to do with the contents of that damned vial, then success had not yet been won. And Cole was no closer to knowing the right answer to that puzzle than he'd ever been.

Linda would say that it's not a matter of knowing, not a thing for the brain to figure out. She was probably right. Which meant that all he could do was wait until the right moment arose, and then act from his heart, or his gut. He'd run both scenarios through his mind a thousand times and tried to feel his way into his right course of action. That had yielded no clear answer. He had to wait for the moment. He hated waiting. And he hated the idea that, come tomorrow morning, his wife might make a decision that he would have to oppose. This whole thing was tearing her apart. He could see that. What would it do to her, to find, at the most crucial moment, that her husband was not her ally?

Cole sighed as they made their way slowly toward the closed door. The crew was waiting to open it until the stairway was in place. With the plane stopped, the AC was back on. They didn't want the President to stand in the heat any longer than was necessary. Maybe this Church prophecy crap was all just a scam. The clever delusions of a bunch of whacked-out UFO buffs who needed desperately to make sense of their world by concocting prophecies of epic events and grand players, and telling stories of life and death and good and evil and magical powers and salvation.

It would surely be easier to just ignore Annabelle's raised eyebrow and let Linda make her Presidential choices and let them all just get on with their lives. They had a boy to find. Or grieve. They had a government to regain control of. They had a bunch of hybrids to deal with, and a future to figure out. They had girls who needed their parents. Girls who were shaken and grieving as well.

But it wasn't easy. It hadn't been easy since the morning Linda had crashed into him. She was a force at work in the world. She changed everybody who came to know and love her. The forces that swirled about were huge and mysterious and unstoppable. They swept aside all chances of a quiet, normal life. And Linda stood at the center of it all. If there was a single person who needed either to be helped or stopped, it was Linda Travis.

And that put Cole in the unenviable position of being a major player as well, whether he wanted to be or not. Cole with his mysterious past and the light in his hands.

He could not just dismiss the prophecies of the Church of the Stranger.

20.9

Mary had received a call from the airstrip, so she and the girls were waiting outside the front door when Cole and Linda's limo pulled into the circular drive of the Presidential Home. The car came to a stop and the doors pushed open and out crawled the two travelers. A second vehicle, a van, pulled up behind them. Annabelle, Doobie, Marionette, and Gabrielle would be staying there as well. The Home had plenty of guest rooms.

The girls ran up to their parents and hugged them tightly, all four together in a bunch. Then they hurried inside, as though they were surrounded by obnoxious reporters shouting questions. The limo driver grabbed Cole and Linda's backpacks and traveling bags and took them inside. Annabelle and the other travelers grabbed their own gear and followed him in. There would be an aide inside to show them to their rooms.

Mary just stood and watched. Linda and Cole had been so caught up with their girls that they hadn't even noticed that she was there. And she didn't really know the rest of them, these new folks who had gotten pulled into the current of Linda Travis's life. They nodded at her. Smiled. Marionette greeted her by name. But they, too, were focused on being back and getting settled and figuring out what would come next.

She could hardly complain. Mary knew what it was like, to be focused on something to the exclusion of all else. There were times when Keeley had been sick that she'd hardly noticed the world around her. And, in a way, it was better this way. It gave her a chance to observe the President and her companions, to scan their fields, and learn, perhaps, things that only she might learn.

Linda was clearly exhausted and grieving. Things had not gone as she'd planned. Foremost in her aura was an image of an older man in a Hawaiian shirt lying dead on a slab. William, Mary knew. The Fisherman. Great pain swirled around that image. Loss. Anger. All wrapped together with the screams of her son, burning in a sea of hot lava. Mary thought that if one were to reach out and touch Linda's field it would fracture and explode into a thousand sharp, jagged, sizzling pieces. The President was at the edge of breakdown.

And there was a second thing in Linda's field. A gray mist that Mary's mind's eye slipped over and around, like a star caught in the blind spot. It was as if it did not want to be seen. A mystery. A secret. A shard of shame. It was taking Linda every bit of strength she had left to hold that gray mist at her center and keep it under wraps.

Cole's field, too, held a secret, though his was easier to read. His aura danced with images of himself and Linda facing off in anger. He was anticipating a fight. His mind was clouded by uncertainties and second-guessings. And his heart was filled with guilt, that by allowing himself to be swept up in the ongoing extremity of Linda's life, his children had been affected as well. With Iain having now fallen, a victim of the vast forces opposed to his wife, Mary could sense a new resolve in Cole. A new defensiveness. A distancing and wariness. He was not going to allow his children to come to risk and harm again. And he was worried about what that might cost him in his relationship with his wife.

Mary hadn't had as much time to read the others, as so much of her focus had been on Linda and Cole. The old woman, Annabelle, clearly shared Cole's wariness, and was full of protective thoughts and feelings. The young couple, Doobie and Marionette, though clearly in the throes of love, were mostly just tired and dazed. The other girl, Gabrielle, had a heart full of grief and a head full of questions.

Mary turned and gazed out over the treetops at the late-afternoon sun. She felt a swell of relief pass through her body and allowed herself a bit of hope. They were home. The Families were gone. Keeley was well again. And they now had a cure for Greensleeves. Perhaps things might settle down for a bit. Maybe they'd even get easier. Not that there weren't plenty of pains and problems still, in this tired old world. There was suffering and struggle aplenty, enough to keep them all busy until the end of their days. But if they could be left alone to deal with their struggles without having to fight either strange aliens or the hidden elite, that would be all right with Mary.

As for herself, though she'd told no one yet, it was Mary's intention, once things had settled down, to step back into the other levels of reality and go in search of Iain. She knew that Keeley would disapprove, but it was what she had to do. It wasn't that she felt she was to blame, exactly. She'd done what she could with the best of intentions. But she did feel responsible. Able to respond. She had talents in those other realms. Talents she hadn't used for a long time. And with her new ability to see fields in the physical, perhaps her talents were stronger than ever. There were Middle Children out there right now, searching not only the many bands of reality but the whole of time. That was wonderful. She greatly appreciated it. But there was something missing that Mary could provide. Iain needed somebody who loved him to be in on the search. He needed a friend calling out his name as they walked through the levels.

Mary could be that friend.

And while she was searching, she might find out what happened to Danny as well.

20.10

Bedtime had come early for the family. The overwhelm of emotions had left them all spent. And Ness and Isaac's good, hot food had filled them up and calmed them down. Cole had told the girls as much as he could about the journey they'd taken and what they'd seen. Linda added bits and pieces along the way. The girls had shared about the worry they'd felt when they'd heard about the airplanes being blown up. And they talked about life in the nullspace apartment, and their time with Alice and Isaac and Ness. Cole expressed a great deal of relief, just knowing that the secret government that had been Linda's enemy for so long was finally gone. "I think I've been on edge since the Fisherman called on the phone that night almost three years ago," he said, looking at Linda. Linda nodded her understanding.

Mostly, though, they just wanted to sit together and hold hands and not speak very much. Iain's body lay just down the hall in his room. Dennis's body lay at his feet. They were gone but not gone. Dead but not dead. And the uncertainty was almost more than they could bear. Grace sat with Mihos in her lap, stroking his long back and scratching under his chin. She wanted to talk to him. Ask him how he was doing in the Astral world. Ask him if he was still searching for Iain. But she didn't. She wasn't sure she wanted to hear the answers.

Cole fell asleep on the sofa, with the girls sleeping in his arms. Linda dozed in her armchair, then turned down the lights and walked softly to the bedroom. She didn't know if she could sleep, but she knew that she had to try. She felt numb, and her head was flipping and flickering with memories and images and snatches of conversation both real and imagined. William on Mars. A fleet of woks rising up before her. Dead bodies falling from the sky. There was so much to process that she'd just shut down. But shut down did not necessarily mean restful sleep.

She stepped out of her clothes and crawled into their bed and switched off the light. The sheets felt cool to her skin and she sighed with gratitude. She closed her eyes and settled into her pillow.

"Hello, Madam," came a gentle voice. But it wasn't William. Linda opened her eyes and whirled to see who had spoken. She was standing at the edge of a huge inland lake, surrounded by a vast desert plain. Standing before her was the small, red-robed Gray alien she knew as Spud. The alien wrinkled his tiny nose, an expression Linda knew meant that he was glad to see her. "We meet again," he said. His thin lips did not move.

Linda exhaled loudly. She'd been holding her breath. "You," she said.

Spud bowed a slight bow. "The one and only," he said. He pushed back his hood, revealing his gray, pebbled head. Linda was surprised to see a few long hairs sticking out at random angles.

Linda turned to examine the area around them. The last time she'd been here, people had been running and screaming, as fireballs rained down upon them from above. "What is this place?" she asked, turning back to Spud. "And why do we meet here?"

Spud lifted his hands on both sides, bent at the elbows. "This is Rumi's Field," he said. "On the surface of the planet you call Mars."

"I was just there," said Linda. "I don't remember the lake."

"This is a long, long time ago," said Spud.

"Have you come here to help me?" asked Linda. She teared up at her own question. How greatly she longed for help.

"You don't need my help, Madam," said Spud, his voice warm and open. "You've always been adequate to the moment. That is why you were given this task, and that is why you accepted."

Linda frowned. Other people were always telling her how strong she was. She was the only one who knew the doubt and uncertainty that ate away at her from the inside. Spud had no idea the burden she carried. She stuck her chin out a bit. "So why are we here?" she asked.

"Two things," said Spud.

"Okay," said Linda.

"First, I wanted to thank you," said Spud.

"Thank me for what?"

"For showing me that good people remain in your world," he said.

Linda scoffed. "Yeah. Well, we'll see what the history books have to say about that."

Spud stood quietly, just looking at her.

"What's the second thing?" asked Linda.

Spud sighed heavily. The expression was almost human in its weight and meaning. "I just want to say that, no matter how this goes, it has been my honor to be on your side."

Linda's brow furrowed. "You're on my side?" she asked.

Spud nodded once. "I am," he said.

"I don't understand," said Linda, raising an eyebrow. "If you and I are on the same side, then who's on the other side?"

Spud glanced up at the sky for a moment, then back at Linda. "It is my fervent wish that you never have to learn the answer to that, Madam."

Linda opened her eyes. The room was still dark and cool. Cole snored lightly at her side. Linda rolled to her other side and fell quickly into a restful sleep.

20.11

The meeting was held in the small conference room in the Presidential home at seven the next morning. All the key players were there. Linda. Cole. Stan. Mary. Annabelle. Gabrielle. Sten. Doobie. Marionette. Alice. They'd even let Keeley attend, though she was under orders to return to the hospital immediately afterwards.

Linda closed the door when the last of them arrived, then took her seat just inside the door and looked out at those assembled. "Good morning, everyone," she said.

The others returned her greeting. Doobie grabbed a donut from the tray, courtesy of the Middle Children.

"I see two items for our agenda this morning," continued Linda. "Both of which need to be dealt with quickly. The first is the matter of returning me back to both life and Presidential authority in the eyes of the American people, and the world. The second is the matter of the alien flu." She looked from face to face. "Agreed?" she said.

All of them nodded or said yes.

Keeley and Sten launched into their thoughts about how to stage Linda's miraculous rescue, and the various narratives they might use. But Linda raised her hand to stop them, shaking her head. "We're not going to stage anything, people," she said, looking around the room. She smiled at Sten. "We're going to tell the world the truth."

"Including how your real rescue came two days ago but we kept that a secret and let the people think you were dead?" asked Sten, one eyebrow raised.

"Including even that," said Linda. "We tell them everything. My abduction from the Presidential Home. My captivity. The false story of my illness. The computer generated copy of me they used to make it look like I was active in world affairs." She glanced at Cole for support, then back at the others. "We tell them about William. About Mars. About The Families and their escape from the planet. About the Herschel Colony and the long history of the Breakaway Civilization. We tell them how they killed me on Squirrel Island, and how I found my way back to life. We tell them how Cole rescued me, and how he's found some new powers. We tell them about *Urbem Orsus*. We tell them about the thousands of bodies that fell from the sky. We tell them about William and his departure from this realm. We tell them about the Middle Children, and how they are going to live openly on Earth from here on out." She inhaled deeply and continued. "We tell them everything we can think to tell them, folks. If that kills my chances for re-election, then so be it. They need to know the truth. People cannot make real choices if they don't have all of the information."

"You're running for re-election?" asked Cole, reaching out to grab Linda's hand. A quick smile flashed across his face.

Linda cocked her head. "William showed me the announcement the fake Linda Travis made while I was on Mars," she said. "I'm sure the Committee immediately printed up posters. I'd hate to waste them." She grinned. "Besides," she continued, turning to look at the rest of them. "We're on our own here now. The opposition party has withdrawn. Maybe next term we can get something accomplished." The standard political rhetoric brought smiles to the faces around her.

Linda's face went serious. "We tell the truth. All of it. Every one of us. If any of you have any questions about that, come see me."

The group went quiet.

"But there's one truth we will not be telling," continued Linda, inhaling sharply. Her voice was shaking. She closed her eyes for a moment, as if trying to remember something, then opened her eyes and continued. "After hours and days of deliberation and thinking and feeling, and after the events I witnessed in *Urbem Orsus*, I'm going to choose to let the Greensleeves illness run its course. The contents of the vial, and the analysis Stan and his people accomplished, will remain a secret amongst those of us in this room. And may the gods have mercy upon my broken soul."

Gabrielle nodded her approval. Her heart told her that this choice would serve the Beloved.

Annabelle looked at Cole and lifted an eyebrow.

Cole dropped his head.

Mary shook her head in surprise and reached out to grab Keeley's hand.

Keeley exhaled loudly and stared.

Sten started writing on his notepad.

Alice cocked her head and watched the others around her.

Cole cleared his throat and opened his mouth to speak. His head was shaking back and forth in disagreement.

Stan said "No."

Cole looked over in surprise. Annabelle opened her mouth to speak, then stopped. Linda spoke. "What is it, Stan?" she said.

Stan reached into his jacket pocket, pulled out his cell phone, pushed a button, and then spoke into his phone. "Run it," he said. He turned off his phone, slipped it back into his pocket, and looked at his President. "I said, 'no,' Mrs. President."

Linda cocked her head quizzically. "I don't understand, Stan," she said.

Stan grabbed the remote for the television that hung on the conference room wall and pushed another button. The television came on, showing a news report on ACN. After a moment the newsreader was interrupted with a breaking story, to which they cut immediately. There was Stan, sitting in front of the camera in a newsroom with a mic on his lapel. Linda and the others watched as Stan announced to the world the discovery of a safe and effective cure for the virus known as Greensleeves. It was already being mass-produced and distributed around the globe. The Pandemic would soon be brought under control.

They watched in surprised silence. When the clip was finished, Stan turned the television off, placed the remote on the table, stood, and walked toward the door. He stopped next to Linda. "My resignation will be on your desk," he said.

Then he opened the door and left.

The others watched Linda in silence.

"Jesus," muttered the President.

20.12 Epilogue

Four weeks later...

Zacharael hung in the depths of space in the form of a small, black ball, watching the entire operation from a safe distance. He did not wish to draw the attention of the Sages. It had taken a few weeks for these long-absent beings to revive their ancient ship, Deimos, and pilot it free of Mars orbit and out to the edge of the solar system. Now it was here, bearing down on the massive ball of ice and rock he'd shown the girl, Gabrielle, on their nighttime journeys together. The ship's approach was slow and sure. They had, no doubt, calculated precisely the desired change in trajectory. No small feat, even for the Sages, given that the comet was over twice the diameter of Deimos, and was spinning at an oblique angle.

The event itself was not dramatic. A slight nudge. A gentle touch. The contact resulted only in small pieces of broken ice flying away from the point of impact. Yet Zacharael could sense that it would be enough. The Sages intended to correct an ancient mistake. That comet would do the trick nicely.

Deimos pulled slowly away from the comet, then began to spin on its axis. Zacharael did not expect the Sages to stick around. Whether they intended to park the Martian moon back in its usual place he did not know. They might not bother. They would not expect that anyone on Earth would notice. Nor would they care. Probably they would simply leave it drifting across the system and return home the way they had come.

Zacharael watched the departing Sages for a moment, then blinked back to Earth. He had more symbols to create on the planet's surface. He now knew better where to place them. One would go very near the spot where the President and her husband had first met.

***

Six weeks later...

Danny and Gina pulled on their hats and gloves and jackets and made their way to the dining hall. Except for the fact that they were always cold, life in Third Colony was better than they'd expected. The food was plentiful and good, they had their own bathroom, and they'd both found good positions in the newly structured colonial society. The colony's heating system was undersized, given the outside temperatures on Three, but things would slowly get better as the atmosphere shifted and stabilized. Until then, there were extra layers of clothing.

They hadn't seen or heard from Director Sinclair since the Giant Leap. That had not turned out to be a problem. Since Danny and Gina had been on the wok when it left, everybody just assumed they belonged, and the pair quickly made good use of their skills. Still, they wondered. Queries to their local representative indicated that Sinclair was not to be found anywhere in the colonies. The presumption was that he'd been one of those selected against by the Grid. His wife, apparently, could be found at the pub on any given night.

Life on Third was not easy. Danny worked long hours in the security detail. Most of his attention went to maintaining the defense line against the planet's primary indigenous lifeform, a tenacious, lichen-like creature that had an uncanny knack for finding its way into the interiors of the various domes and Quonsets that the advance woks had dropped into place. While these lichens didn't seem to be toxic to humans, they stank horribly, and had a knack for eating through wires, pipes, and ductwork. Gina's back ached from sitting in her chair, programming the colony's secondary networks.

The qputers were amazing, but she was having trouble getting the feel of them. They felt almost alive to her at times. She often stayed late, working on her console long after her shift ended. She was trying to establish a personal relationship with the colony's core qputer. She had a gut feeling that that might be a smart move.

Neither of them thought much about Earth. They were too busy. And memories of Earth were discouraged. They were no longer Earthlings. They were something else. Something new. Thirdlings, perhaps. A new people. One day an entirely new species. They'd been given this one chance to grow and thrive and earn their place in the Cosmic Community, the Cogency. They looked to where they were going. They did not look back to from whence they'd come.

Danny understood. There was survivor guilt there. Old, habitual disdain. And there was the remorse of what they'd had to do to make their break. They'd spent the Earth to fuel their Giant Leap, leaving behind a beat up planet they'd made even worse than it would otherwise have been. Though the nastiest offenders had been swept aside, the rest of them could feel their own complicity, even if they denied it out loud. The guilt would shape them in the years and decades and centuries to come. Perhaps that would be a good thing.

Gina got into line and grabbed a tray. She handed a second tray to Danny. "Meatloaf," she said with a grin. Gina loved the meatloaf here. He reached out and grabbed her gloved hand in his own and squeezed. It wasn't too bad here. Not bad at all.

***

Nine weeks later...

Cole pulled Linda close to him in the warm, early-morning air and kissed her. In a moment she would get on the wok that hovered just behind her, there on the front lawn of the Home. That was one benefit of living amongst the Middle Children: there were no more trips to the airport. Two of their strange new comrades stood waiting on either side of the door, watching them openly as they kissed. Cole winked at them and kissed her a second time.

"I'll only be gone a week, sweetie," said Linda.

"A week here and a week there and pretty soon it adds up to a lifetime," he said.

Linda frowned, pulling back. "You know I have to go," she said.

Cole sighed. "Yeah. I know. I'm sorry. I just... I miss you already."

"We need to get some of that HereNow gear The Families left behind and install a unit in the house," said Linda.

"Still wouldn't be the same," said Cole, running a finger along Linda's face.

Linda inhaled deeply. "I know," she admitted. "But Pastor Clinton's bashing me constantly on the religion issue, dear. I gotta get the debate back onto the issues. Restarting the Global Environmental Summit, face-to-face this time, might just do that. Especially with those new methane bursts in Siberia last week. People are demanding strong leadership."

"And you're just the one to give it," said Cole. He pulled Linda to him. She laid her head on his chest.

"I'm the one who'll at least talk about it in realistic terms," she said.

"Terms which Clinton will just latch onto and use against you," said Cole into Linda's hair.

Linda sighed. Cole sighed as well.

"So you'll be at the Hilton again?" asked Cole.

Linda shook her head. "Bluebird's found me a wonderful apartment right in London," she said. "'Luxurious, and completely secure,' he said. You know I love London."

"Hooking us up with Mr. Bluebird was one good thing Stan did, I guess," said Cole.

Linda pulled back and looked at him. "Stan was a good man, sweetie. He took really good care of us."

Cole sighed and nodded. "You heard from him at all?"

"I don't expect we will," said Linda. "He's disappeared. I just hope he's found a quiet place to live out his life."

"You don't sound very angry at him," said Cole.

Linda shook her head. "He was just doing his best, Cole," she said. "I can't fault him for that. I could have kept the vial way more secret than I did. But I didn't. And Stan acted from his heart. I know he did." She raised her shoulders. "So now we've got new circumstances to deal with. We'll keep slugging it out. And who knows? Maybe it's better this way?"

Cole frowned. "You know I was gonna..." He stopped. All of a sudden he seemed nervous and unsure. His face went dark.

"What?" said Linda.

Cole inhaled sharply, then looked down at the ground. "Nothing," he said.

Linda glanced at her watch. "Okay, sweetie," she said. "I gots to get goin', ya knowin'?"

Cole nodded. "Yeah."

"I'll call you when we get to Bluebird's secret Presidential suite. The girls should be up by then."

"Okay." Cole leaned forward and kissed Linda again. "I love you," he said.

Linda smiled. "That do make it nice," she said. She turned and nodded to her pilots, then gave Cole one last hug. Releasing him, she stepped onto the short walkway that angled up to the wok. She turned and performed a parody of a Presidential wave and salute, as though saying goodbye to a cheering crowd. She grinned. It was only her, Cole, two Secret Service agents, and the two Middle Children. "I'll be back before you know it," she called down to Cole. Then she turned and ducked into the wok. The pilots followed. In mere moments, the walkway retracted back into the wok and the door melted closed.

The wok rose slowly into the air. It leaned forward at an angle, began to glow, and shot off in a flash of bright white light. Linda was off to save the world and get herself re-elected. Cole would stay with the kids and keep their life as stable and normal as he could. Such was their life together.

Cole glanced at the sky. It was going to be another hot one. Really hot. He turned and walked back into the Presidential Home.

***

Only a moment later...

"Okay," said Carl. "One... two... three!" The two of them opened their eyes.

"Oh, my," said Carl at last.

"You have got to be shittin' me," said Ted.

Postscript

Here ends Book Two of the *None So Blind* series. Book Three, *Imbolc*, like the Ghost of Christmas Yet To Come, will arrive in its own good time.

About the Author

Timothy Scott Bennett was born in Michigan in 1958, the same year the U.S. launched the Explorer 1 satellite and the Great Chinese Famine began. Always the polymath, he has studied astrophysics, theology, anthropology, and philosophy; painted watercolors and installed broken tile mosaics; founded and lived in intentional communities; raised children; restored houses; performed stage combat and local theater; learned a bit of Russian, and played in a rock band. He's a dogged questioner of cultures, paradigms, beliefs, and assumptions, and seeks to balance paradox and uncertainty whenever he can. In 2003 he met his second wife, Sally, who was able to fully see who he was. Thus empowered, he wrote, directed, and edited the feature-length "cult classic" documentary, *What a Way to Go: Life at the End of Empire*. He followed that up with the science-fiction adventure novel *All of the Above,* and the sequel, *Rumi's Field*. He lives in North Carolina, where squirrels stare at him through the windows and jabber their unsolicited advice. He 's working on a non-fiction account of his relationship with Sally tentatively titled *Asperger's in Love: A Relationship Across the Spectrum*. He walks the unraveling human world while reaching for the stars, pondering the eternal questions, and wondering whether the squirrels can be trusted.

A Brief Excerpt from *Imbolc*, the Third and Final Book of the *None So Blind* Series

Chapter 1 - The Year 29, 2049 in the Old Calendar - Probably February

1.1

Rabbit took off up the slope. Coinin followed, trying not to slip on the dewy grass. The sky went black for a moment and Coinin almost lost Rabbit as his guide hopped behind a huge, feathery sarsen. The frosted stone face loomed over him in the darkness, glowing in the faint light of the stars. Coinin put his hand out to touch its cold surface. And to steady himself. Rabbit was standing, waiting, just beyond the boulder.

"You coming?"

Coinin nodded, brushing the long, white hair from his face. "You said you had something to show me."

Rabbit laughed and started again up the slope. Coinin willed the sun to rise, then followed once more.

They came to the hill's rocky shoulder and stopped. Below them the land fell away. The sharp, grassy slope they'd just climbed poured into a ripple of low ridges. Beyond the ridges was the wide plain that stretched down to the lake. To the East, the sun rose over the woods, limning the mountains that loomed up from behind them. To the West, a darker forest, still and thick, stretched out for as far as Coinin could see. He turned back to peer upslope, to the North, matching Rabbit's gaze. The hill rose in a series of steps, growing more rocky toward the peak. At the summit stood an impossibly tall stone tower, striped with black and white granite. As they watched, a huge eagle, just a speck against the blue sky, leapt from the peak of the tower's conical slate roof and swept down the hillside toward them. In a moment it was perched on a nearby rock. It cocked its head and caught Coinin and Rabbit in the light of its yellow eye.

"Hey, Eagle," said Coinin, raising his hand in greeting.

"I know you," answered Eagle.

"We need to see," said Rabbit.

Eagle shook her shoulders, fluffing the feathers of her neck. She nodded. "I will take you."

Without hesitation, Rabbit jumped onto Eagle's back and dug his claws into her feathers. Coinin, more clumsily, stepped onto Eagle's wing and pulled himself up like a rodeo clown, slipping and grunting and flailing about before finally remembering where he was. Laughing at himself, he rose into the air and settled himself gently on Eagle's back behind his friend. Rabbit snorted but held his tongue.

Eagle leapt into the air and flapped her great wings. Three times they circled as they gained the summit. The tower's polished blocks flickered in the morning sunlight like mirrored tiles. Still they climbed, until they were far above the hill, halfway up the tower's tremendous height. The morning air ruffled hair and fur and feather. The sun filled them with light. Rabbit shivered in cold excitement.

"You ready?" he called back.

"For what?" asked Coinin.

"For this!" said Rabbit with a laugh. He raised his hind end and struck out with his powerful rear legs, catching Coinin off guard. The old man fell backwards with a yelp, his arms windmilling for a hold they never found. He plummeted Earthward and Rabbit laughed all the louder. "Thank you, Eagle," Rabbit called out as he dove from the bird's back to go after the old man. Eagle veered away and soared off toward the Eastern wood.

Rabbit sped through the air, gaining on the old man. "Coinin, you idiot!" he shouted. "Use your brain!" But Coinin appeared not to hear, and fell like a corpse.

With a sigh, Rabbit put himself underneath Coinin and broke his fall in mid-air. The old man was heavy, so Rabbit grew large enough to hold him in his paw. "Coinin?"

Coinin lay slack and silent in Rabbit's paw. Rabbit drifted slowly downward toward the tower's base. "Coinin?" Still there was no response. Worried, Rabbit touched down gently on the rocky hilltop near the tower's massive foundation. Lifting his paw to his face, he sniffed his friend's body.

"Coinin?"

The body started to jerk and wiggle and Rabbit realized with annoyance that the old man was laughing. He tossed Coinin to the ground in disgust and shrank back to his regular size. "You shit," he said.

Coinin jumped to his feet and brushed the dirt from his robe. "Me?" He danced around the rabbit, rubbing his hands together. "You started it!"

Rabbit crossed his arms. "That was uncalled for."

"And pushing me off Eagle's back wasn't?"

Rabbit rolled his eyes, as if tired of explaining. "Remember where you are, Coinin. Everything has meaning here."

"And what meaning is there, oh wise bunny-wunny, in tossing me off the back of a bird?"

"One thing," said Rabbit, holding up a finger. His moist brown eyes glinted in the sun. "Get used to the unexpected."

"Ooh!" mocked Coinin, dropping to his knees in false adulation. "The Unexpected! I'm so scared!"

Rabbit hopped away from Coinin, stopping at the rusted iron door at the tower's base. "Like I said, Coinin," he said, looking over his shoulder. "You're a shit." Rabbit pulled open the door, entered the tower, and disappeared up the stone stairs.

Coinin stood and scratched his old, veined nose for a bit. He'd seen Rabbit mad before, many times. But this was different. It wasn't even anger, really, so much has sadness. Or disappointment. As if Coinin's shortcomings had finally become more than Rabbit was willing to tolerate. Coinin had screwed up in the past, and Rabbit had always forgiven him. He'd had to, didn't he? He'd had no choice. But now Coinin wondered. His bonds here were tenuous, even after twenty-some very odd years. How would he survive if the gates were closed and locked now? How would they all survive? Resolving to apologize for his behavior, Coinin ducked through the doorway and started to scale the Endless Climb.

"Took you long enough," said Rabbit, staring out over the Northern plateau. The hill on which the tower stood hugged up against a massive cliff wall, base to base, and the view from the tower's top allowed a glimpse over the cliff's sharp edge to the lands beyond. Flat and dry and dusty, without a tree in sight, the Northern Plateau looked like the end of the Earth itself. Coinin had never been this close to it before. He had never been allowed to climb to the tower's highest floor.

"It's a long climb," huffed Coinin, bent over to catch his breath. He felt a bit silly, stating the obvious as he had, yet the moment felt tender and he was afraid of making a misstep.

"What is gravity here?" muttered Rabbit. "Why do you insist on wearing your physical limitations like a heavy cloak? You can be anything."

Coinin stepped forward to the balcony's edge and tried to find what Rabbit was staring at. "I know," he said at last, grabbing the iron railing with both hands. "It's a choice I make sometimes. To remind me of who I am."

Rabbit nodded but did not speak. Coinin wondered if his friend was finally beginning to understand. He hoped so.

"I'm sorry, Rabbit. For what I said. I should not have mocked you."

Rabbit gazed out over the plateau, giving no sign that he had heard Coinin's words. "She's coming," he muttered. In the far distance a drumbeat sounded, just above the edge of hearing.

Coinin tried to follow the rabbit's line of sight. "Who's coming?"

Rabbit turned to face the old man. A tear slipped from his eye, streaking the fur of his face. He shook his head. "I'm not allowed to say."

"But... Rabbit... what is it? Tell me. Who's coming?"

Rabbit looked down at the stone floor. "This is the end," he murmured.

Coinin froze. "What are you talking about?"

Rabbit turned and looked again to the North. The heavens had filled with thunderclouds. Lightning sliced the air like a rapier, leaving a gash in the fabric of the sky through which poured a river of ice. In a moment, the land about them was frozen dead. Rabbit looked at the old man. "There are not enough of you!" he whispered.

The drumbeat quickened. Rabbit tore off down the steps. Coinin flew to keep up. Down the tower stairs, down the stepped hillside, over the ridges and into the dark Western forest, Rabbit ran and ran and ran. Coinin, compelled by the drum, followed as best he could, and finally let him go, calling out one last time as his friend disappeared into the trees. "Who's coming?" he said again, his voice failing with the realization that he would get no answer. Not even the echo replied. With a sigh, Coinin dove into a hollow stump he found at the edge of the woods, slipped up the tunnel, and returned to his bedroom.

He opened his eyes to see Janie standing over him, her small frame drum tucked under her bare arm. She smiled, bent to kiss his forehead, then turned and placed the drum on a shelf by the window. "There's eggs on the stove," she said, stopping to pick up her fur-lined jacket. Coinin watched with a mixture of love and amazement as Janie slipped into her coat, fastened her buttons, and pulled a stocking cap from the pocket to mash down over her fiery hair. Janie winked, blew him a kiss, and started down the hallway. "Don't forget the spirits," she called back to him. Coinin sighed and smiled and listened as Janie left the house. The wind howled its chronic frustration as she closed the door and was gone.

Coinin closed his eyes, taking a moment to re-trace the steps of his journey. Rabbit's words stumbled around his soul like a toddler demanding attention. But they would not be understood. Nothing was ever as it seemed. Myth and symbol were the rulers of the underworld, obfuscation the language of the gods. Yet Rabbit's warning chilled Coinin in ways the cold could only envy. He pulled the covers up to his neck and closed his eyes. "Who's coming?" he whispered to the empty room. There was no answer, but the breath of his words hung for a moment in the icy air above his face.

Just another ghost in this haunted world.

Connect with Timothy Scott Bennett

The best place to find me is on Facebook:
https://www.facebook.com/tswabbit

Sometimes you'll find me on Twitter:
https://twitter.com/TimothySBennett

Sometimes I post blogs at *Everything is Research*:
http://everythingisresearch.com

And I have a new website coming soon where I'll focus on my writing: timothyscottbennett.com

Endnote

Thank you for reading my book. I hope very much that doing so was a valuable experience for you. I've heard it said that the best way to thank an author is to write a review. In my experience, reviews are crucial to the process of an author and his or her readers finding each other. If you enjoyed this book, please, take a moment and post a review at your favorite retailer. And then post it wherever you hang out, on Facebook or Twitter, or even your own blog. I will be eternally grateful. Pax, Tim

www.ingramcontent.com/pod-product-compliance
Lightning Source LLC
Chambersburg PA
CBHW051927020726
47501CB00001B/9